"WHO ARE YOUR PARENTS?"

Colbey scowled. The tedium of the seer's interrogation wore on him. "My parents are dead. In Valhalla, where Renshai belong."

"Their names, please," the seer persisted.

Colbey responded with a sigh. "Calistin the Bold and Ranilda Battlemad." *This was probably a test of patience.* He swallowed his rage; he might be answering questions for days.

The seer nodded and sought answers in the crystal globe. Suddenly, his eyes widened. His chair toppled backward, shattering on the granite floor and spilling the seer to the stone. He jumped up, sputtering. An instant later, he vanished, along with the ring of Wizardry Colbey need to complete the Task and return to his own world.

"Where did he go?" Colbey asked, not really expecting a response. He circled the table, hoping to find an answer in the globe that had condemned him. He saw only a smoky haze. Stung to fury, Colbey reached for the crystal. As his hand closed around the globe, a bolt of amber split the room, lancing through Colbey's chest. Agony slammed him, his nerves seizing into a tight convulsion. Glowing shards of crystal fell from his hands, stained crimson with blood. Darkness enclosed him. . . .

CHILD OF THUNDER

Book Three of
The Renshai Trilogy

MICKEY ZUCKER REICHERT

DAW BOOKS, INC.
DONALD A. WOLLHEIM, FOUNDER
375 Hudson Street, New York, NY 10014
**ELIZABETH R. WOLLHEIM
SHEILA E. GILBERT
PUBLISHERS**

First Printing, April 1993

9

To Sheila Gilbert,
one of the very best

and to

Old Man Mikie,
just because.

ACKNOWLEDGMENTS

I would like to thank the following people:

Jonathan Matson, Jody Lee, Charon Wood,
David Moore, and Mark Moore
and to
Benjamin and Jonathan Moore,
for understanding when page proofs
come before Nintendo.™

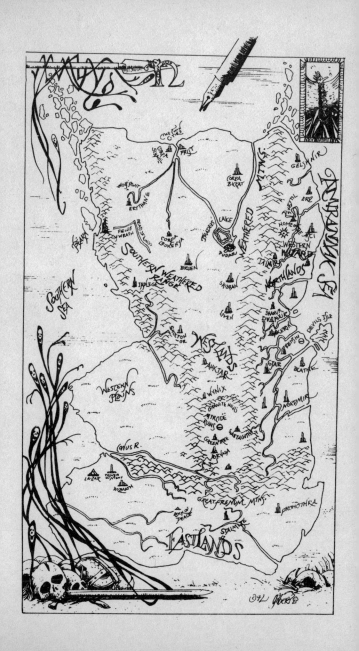

"Should the whole frame of Nature round him break,
In ruin and confusion hurled,
He, unconcerned, would hear the mighty crack,
And stand secure amidst a falling world."
                         —Joseph Addison
                              Horace, *Odes,* book III, ode iii

CONTENTS

Part III—THE GRAY GOD'S DOWNFALL

PROLOGUE

Silence filled the women's court in the Eastern kingdom of Stalmize, broken only by occasional tense whispers from the spectators. Khitajrah stood near the far end of the courtroom, her head bowed and her back to the murmuring crowd. She faced the three-man tribunal who sat, with stony expressions, at their long table. Behind them, a doorway led to their chambers where they had deliberated for less time than it took for the woman's heart to beat two dozen strokes. Khitajrah never doubted they would find her guilty. It was only the sentence that remained a mystery: imprisonment, mutilation, death.

Khitajrah raised her head slightly, her curly, shoulder-length black hair falling into eyes nearly as dark. Directly beside her, the guard stirred, attentive to her movement, though he did not otherwise respond to it. She was, after all, only a woman and, also, half his size. She twisted her gaze to the spectators, counting them to expend nervous energy. It was not her way to stand mute in the presence of injustice; her need for action had committed her to this trial that had proven little more than a recitation of her crimes. As an Eastland woman, she had no right to a defense, and the proceedings in the women's court were a parody of justice.

Khitajrah's gaze played over the seated rows of the audience. She counted eighteen, all men, and weaponless as the court law specified. Her son, Bahmyr, sat along one aisle, fidgeting helplessly. At twenty-three, he already sported the heavy frame and hard musculature of his father. Ebony hair fringed a handsome face, friendly despite growing up amid the cold evil of the Eastern culture. He was the last of Khitajrah's children. Her other two sons, one older and one younger, had died in the Great War, along with their father, Harrsha, who had served as one of two high lieutenants to King Siderin.

The other seventeen spectators included family, curious neighbors, and soldiers. Among the latter, Khitajrah recognized at least two who had placed the blame for the defeat of the Eastern army on her late husband. That accusation, at least, seemed ludicrous. Khitajrah understood the need for these broken veterans to find a scapegoat, to blame the hundreds of casualties on a specific man whom they could curse and malign. As the chosen of the Eastlands' one god, General-King Siderin must always remain a hero, though he had led his followers and himself to their deaths. But Harrsha had been Siderin's last surviving high commander, and the Western warrior who had killed him on the battlefield was a woman.

A woman. Khitajrah pursed her lips in a tense frown, torn by the irony. She had fought for the dignity and worth of women for as long as she could remember: comforting those beaten, lending her strength to the overburdened, and stealing food and medication where needed. Now, at forty-three years old, she would pay the price for a lifetime of assisting her sisters and decades of walking the delicate boundaries of the law. Now that her cause finally stood a chance, she would fall in defeat, with no one to continue her work. The war had left women outnumbering men by three to one, and the Eastlands needed to use the guile and competence of their women, as well as their bodies, to keep the realm from lapsing into decay. The overtaxed farm fields could scarcely feed the populace, even with their numbers whittled by war.

The central man of the tribunal cleared his throat. Khitajrah returned her attention to them, her gaze sweeping briefly over the only armed men in the courtroom. Two burly soldiers guarded the door. Another stood, braced and watchful, between the tribunal and the crowd. The last remained at Khitajrah's right hand, alert to her every movement.

The central man rose. "Friends. Freemen. It is the opinion of this court that this woman . . . this *frichen-karboh* . . ." He paused on the word, one of the ugliest in the Eastern language. Literally, it translated to "manless woman, past usefulness," a derogatory term used for widows. In the East, violent crime and a constant life of labor saw to it that a woman rarely outlasted her husband. When he died first, it was expected that she, and her unattached female children, would suicide on his pyre. ". . . this one called Khita is guilty of theft, of inciting women, and of treason in the eyes of the one

god, Sheriva." Though he spoke formally, he used the shortened form of Khitajrah's name, as if to imply that she was
not worth the effort of a third syllable. "She is guilty."

"Guilty," the judge to the speaker's right echoed.

"Guilty," the other concurred.

Khitajrah stiffened. Though the law condemned dissent or
revolt, thoughts of these rose naturally. She had spied on her
husband when he taught their sons the art of war. Hard labor,
her own and that which she had spared weaker women, had
honed her agility. Stealing from men had taught her to climb,
twist, and dodge. And, since the Great War, Bahmyr had
worked with his mother on strike and parry, his love for her
outweighing the risk of violating Eastern rules. It had never
been his or Khitajrah's desire to break the laws that had become a fixed part of their culture for millennia, only to revise
them. Without change, the Eastlanders as a people would die.

The speaker continued. "We sentence Khita Harrsha's-
widow . . ." His dark eyes met Khitajrah's, strong and intense; they seemed to bore through her. The woman had
been trained since infancy to look down in deference, yet
this time she met him stare for stare.

Caught off-guard by her boldness, the speaker lost his
place. Flustered, he glanced away first, covering his weakness by turning his glare on the guard at Khitajrah's side.
". . . sentence Khita to work the silver mine until the end of
her life."

Slow death. Khitajrah knew they had given her the worst
sentence of all, an anonymous and prolonged death. Starvation and cave-ins took those strong enough to survive the
constant pace of working to the limit of the most competent
prisoner from moment to moment, without rest. Few lived out
a year in the mines. Khitajrah had expected death, yet it
should have come in the form of a public execution, as an example to the other Eastland women. Given the chance to defy
crying out at the tribunal's torture or to speak last words,
Khitajrah could have become a martyr to her cause, her death
the shock that might have driven others to take her place.

"No!" Khitajrah screamed. She whirled, managing to turn
halfway toward the audience before the guard caught her
arm in a grip like iron. His sword rasped from its sheath, its
edge coming to rest at her throat. Despite the threat, she
struggled against him.

The spectators erupted into a wild, indecipherable hubbub.

Drawing swords, the guards by the door leapt forward to assist. Even as they moved, Bahmyr sprang to his feet, catching the nearest one's hand where it clutched the sword's hilt. The guard spun toward him. Bahmyr stomped his booted instep on the guard's foot. In the same motion, he caught the haft, whipped it fully free of its sheath, and buried the blade in its wielder's gut.

The son's voice rang out over the others, clearly audible. "Mother, run!" Freeing the sword, he shoved the guard's corpse away. The other hacked high. Bahmyr's parry rang against the guard's attack. His counter slash opened sleeve and sword arm. The soldier's arm flopped to his side, his sword clanging to the floor.

Khitajrah's guard spun to face the attack, his sword falling from the woman's throat. He shoved her violently aside, his blade cutting the air above her head, and he leapt for Bahmyr.

"No!" Khitajrah made a desperate grab, catching the man's hilt and hand as he spun. Using the technique her son had taught her, she twisted violently downward, breaking the guard's grip. The effort took her to her knees, the sword still clenched in her grip. Unable to recover quickly enough to defend, she hurled herself against the guard's legs. The man staggered onto Bahmyr's stop thrust, the sword impaling him cleanly through the abdomen.

The guard screamed. Bahmyr's cry sounded equally agonized. "Behind you!" He choked off the last syllable in shock or pain.

Still on her knees, Khitajrah whirled toward the tribunal. She met the last guard's attack as much from instinct as her son's warning. Steel crashed, chiming against steel, the man's strength driving her to her buttocks. Blow after blow followed, each so fast and hard she could do little more than block. She waited for Bahmyr to come to her aid. Between them, they could handle her enemy. Yet her son did not come.

Fatigue wore on Khitajrah. She exaggerated its effect, whipping a frightened gaze to the man above her. She met an expression of icy cruelty, devoid of mercy. His blade slammed against hers once more. She gave with the motion, all but pressed to the wooden floor. The instant he raised his weapon for a final strike, she lunged, slamming her hilt into his groin with all the power she could land behind the blow. The guard collapsed, hand still clutching his sword.

Hands, throat, side of the chest. Calling on Bahmyr's

training, Khitajrah naturally struck for a kill. She hacked at his neck. The blow lacked the power to inflict serious damage, but the draw cut she used to recover the blade opened his throat. Blood splattered, warm droplets pelting her, and the guard went limp at her feet.

Khitajrah rose, assessing the situation in an instant. Bahmyr sprawled, facedown, in the aisle, blood washing from a wound in his back at the level of a kidney. Another knife cut ravaged the tunic she had sewn for him, now dark with her son's blood. The sight paralyzed her. She stood, sword still in her clenched fist. All color drained from her and, with it, all her will to fight.

From beyond Bahmyr, two veterans of the Great War advanced on Khitajrah. She knew both men well. Diarmad had been the first to disparage her dead husband, laying blame on the commander, at the top of his lungs, from the curtain wall of the king's palace. The other had engineered this mockery the tribunal dared to call a trial.

The elder who had pronounced Khitajrah's sentence shouted. "Stop her at any cost!"

Some of the audience sat, rooted. Others leapt to obey, charging down on Khitajrah with her son's killers in the lead. The judges ran around their table toward her.

Attacked from all sides, Khitajrah mobilized as well. She whirled, running directly for the judges' bench. Footsteps pounded behind her, liberally mixed with shouts and threats of violence. As she sprinted for the bench, the judges hurried around it, to corner her against it.

Khitajrah did not slow. She sprang to the surface of the table, dark hair flying behind her, entwined with her cloak hood. For an instant, she balanced there. Then, her momentum drove the table over backward. Wood crashed, splintering against planking. She dodged free as the judges scattered, leaving her an open path to their chambers.

"Get her!" the speaker shrieked.

A knife whizzed by Khitajrah's head. Its hilt struck the door frame and bounced, skittering across the floor. She threw a quick glance around the room, finding its furnishings wastefully excessive at a time when the Eastlanders could scarcely feed what remained of their masses. Pillows covered the floor, surrounded by half-eaten platefuls of beef and grapes and goblets of wine. Three desks lined the walls, festooned with intricately carved leaves and vines. Above

one, a window overlooked the mazelike alleyways of the
Eastlands' royal city.

Khitajrah hurled the sword blindly behind her. Its length
in her hand could only hamper her escape. She hoped throwing it might gain her the precious moments she needed to
maneuver. She had prowled the streets of Stalmize enough
times to know them by heart, even under the cover of night's
darkness. Although she had never entered the tribunal's
quarters, she knew its window from the outside. It opened a
story over a populous street, full of vendors and shops.
Though it would leave her exposed and hemmed in by
crowds, a few steps could take her in any of a thousand directions. If she worked her way into the street, she had a
chance of evading pursuit.

Khitajrah made a wild leap for the desktop. A hand
snagged her sleeve. The sudden jerk of motion tore the cloth
and stole momentum. Jarred backward, she missed the desk,
crashing to the floor and skidding half beneath the desk. She
sprang to a crouch, banging her head against the underside
of the desk. Pain howled through her head. A foot lanced toward her. She dodged, twisting, hurling her body up and
over the desktop, and rolling through the window.

Khitajrah's mind told her the fall was too far for an uncontrolled landing. She clawed, managing to catch a grip on the
sill. Splinters jabbed beneath her nails. Then, a knife blade
slashed the back of her hand, and she recoiled reflexively.

Khitajrah fell. She twisted, her body still lithe from training, despite her age. She scrambled for a hold on the masonry of the building. Stone snapped her fingernails into
grimy irregularity. The touches friction-burned her flesh and
made the wound in her hand throb, but it slowed her descent. She landed on her feet on the cobbled roadway, bent
her knees, tucked, and rolled at random. Her already aching
head pounded over stone, then struck a woman burdened
with two buckets of water.

The stranger sprawled, dropping her cargo. Water splashed
over Khitajrah, chilling her. Sense of direction lost, she spun
and scrambled to her feet, ducking into the nearest alley.
Pained, bleeding, and haunted by images of her son's corpse
on the courtroom floor, Khitajrah Harrsha's-widow sought to
lose herself in the rabbit warren snarl of Stalmize's streets.

PART I

THE SEVEN TASKS OF WIZARDRY

CHAPTER 1

The Outworlder

Surf battered the Northern coastline of the country of Asci leaving jagged cascades of stone. Colbey Calistinsson stood, legs braced and balanced, on a fjord overlooking the wild slam of the waves. Spray stung his clean-shaven face, the youthful features belying his seventy-seven years. Golden wisps still graced his short, white hair, and he studied the Amirannak Sea through icy, blue-gray eyes that had not changed, in look or acuity, since his youth. A longsword hung at either hip, their presences as familiar as his hands. Though he paid his companion, the Eastern Wizard, and the Wizard's wolf no heed, his mind naturally registered their every movement.

Shadimar spoke. "Colbey, we need to talk."

Colbey said nothing. He studied the jeweled chop of the waters a little longer before turning slowly to meet the Wizard's gaze. The measured delay was an affectation. Should the need arise, the old Renshai could strike more quickly than most men could think to watch for the movement. But he had found that Shadimar equated slow deliberateness with competence, and the appearance of mastery seemed to unnerve the Eastern Wizard more than its actuality. Months ago, when Colbey had fought for the lives and freedom of the few remaining Renshai, Shadimar had misinterpreted a prophecy. Their blood brotherhood had dissolved in the wake of Shadimar's distrust. Though Shadimar had apologized, in his subtle and not-quite-satisfying manner, Colbey still harbored some bitterness that took the form of keeping the Wizard always slightly uncertain. Few things unbalanced or bothered the Wizard more.

Always patient, Shadimar waited. His silver beard hid his craggy, ancient face, and eyes the gray of the ravaged stone remained fixed on Colbey. Wind whipped Shadimar's blue velvet robes, and the fur trim eddied, but the Cardinal Wizard stood steady. Secodon waited at his master's side. Empathetically linked with Shadimar, the wolf often betrayed emotions that the Eastern Wizard carefully hid. Now, the beast remained as still as his master.

Though a long time had passed, Colbey responded directly to Shadimar's request. "What do you want to talk about?"

"The next step in your training, Western Wizard."

The form of address bothered Colbey, and he frowned, eyes narrowed in annoyance. Decades ago, he had traveled to the cave of Tokar, the Western Wizard, because of an old promise the Renshai Tribe had made to the Wizard. While there, he had witnessed the Western Wizard's ceremony of passage, a rite that killed Tokar and was to have passed his knowledge and essence, and that of all of the Western Wizards before him, to his apprentice. Colbey had interfered, attempting to rescue the centuries old Wizard from the demons that had come to claim him.

Though the thought surfaced quickly and fleetingly, it brought, as always, crisp clear memories of the pain that had assailed Colbey then. Agony lanced through him, vivid enough to make him wince, softening the glare he aimed at Shadimar. Despite all the wounds he had taken in battle, this memory ached worse, an agony he had never managed to fully escape. And with that pain had come a madness. Colbey recalled the decade he had spent combating voices and presences and their compulsions in his mind. One by one, he had fought with and destroyed them, in the process honing his own self-discipline and mental competence until he had found the perfect balance between mind and body. And more. As he gained mastery, he found himself occasionally reading the thoughts and emotions of others around him. Over time he discovered that, with great effort, he could actively read minds, though he considered this intrusion too rude to attempt against any but enemies.

At first, Shadimar had attributed Colbey's abilities to the incorporation of a stray piece of magic during Tokar's ceremony in the form of a magical being called a demon. Much later, he hypothesized that Tokar had shifted the focus of his ceremony from his apprentice to Colbey. And, though wholly against his will, Colbey had become the next Western Wizard.

"Soon, a ship will arrive to take us to the Wizards' Meeting Island. There, you will undergo the Seven Tasks of Wizardry that Odin created to assess the competence of each Cardinal Wizard's apprentice. You should have passed these before Tokar . . ."

Shadimar continued while Colbey's mind wandered. He knew from pieces of previous conversations that each of the four Cardinal Wizards took an apprentice when the time of his or her chosen passing became imminent. An apprentice then had to undergo seven god-mediated tasks to prove his worth. Failure at any one meant death. The challenge intrigued Colbey, yet Shadimar's unspoken thoughts interested him more. Because Colbey had destroyed the collective consciousness of the Western Wizards, one at a time, he had none of their magic to guide him. And, since he had received no training from his predecessor, he had learned none of the Wizard's magics in that manner. Shadimar believed, without a thread of doubt, that this lack would doom Colbey to fail all of the tasks. And, to Colbey, the Wizard's cocksure dismissal made the challenge nearly irresistible.

". . . finished, you will truly be the Western Wizard in every way, save one."

The exception pulled Colbey back to Shadimar's words, though he already guessed the missing qualification.

Shadimar confirmed Colbey's thought. "You will not have your predecessors to guide you. Though I thought little of Tokar's apprentice, I can't fully fathom my colleague's choice to abandon Haim for you."

Since Shadimar's proclamation that Colbey was the Western Wizard, ideas had tumbled through the old Renshai's mind. Believing he understood the reasons, Colbey addressed Shadimar's implied question. "There was a madness in the Western Wizard's line."

Shadimar nodded agreement. It was common knowledge to the Wizards that the ninth Western Wizard, Niejal the Mad, was paranoid, gender confused, and suicidal, presumably due to the collective consciousness itself. His insanity had warped others in the line, the flaw passing as easily as the memories and skill. Shadimar's head froze in midmovement as the deeper implications became clear. Accustomed to subtlety, the Eastern Wizard was momentarily stopped by the pointed directness of the warrior's comments. "Are you saying Tokar chose you because he *knew* you could destroy an entire line of Wizards, including millennia of irreplaceable wisdom?"

Colbey shrugged. Shadimar had taken it one step further than his intention, and the mentioned wisdom seemed of little consequence. Aside from a distant attack that had sent a soldier crashing from parapets, a feat Colbey had matched with his own mental power, he had never seen a Wizard create magic more powerful than sleight of hand or illusion. He had once fought a creature Shadimar named a demon, which the Eastern Wizard claimed one of his colleagues must have called, but Colbey had not witnessed the summoning. Time had taught him that knowledge came with age and experience. Still, though he lived through as much now as in his youth, the wisdom seemed to come in smaller doses as he gathered what the world had to offer. His skill and understanding became honed in tinier, finer detail with each passing year. He wondered if the difference between learning for millennia and a century was really all that much. "Actually, I don't know if Tokar expected me to destroy the entire line. I do believe he thought I could kill or contain the insanity."

Shadimar frowned. "An illogical thought. To destroy that much power would require mental powers stronger than all of the other three Wizards together."

Colbey smiled, ever so slightly. "Not so illogical. I did it, didn't I?"

Shadimar hesitated just long enough to display his doubts. Apparently, he still had not fully convinced himself that Colbey was the Western Wizard rather than a man under the influence of demons. "The issue is not whether or not you destroyed the Western Wizard's line. It is forever gone, along with its knowledge. The issue is whether Tokar had reason to believe you could do so. It should be impossible to fight a collective consciousness, let alone destroy one. No Cardinal Wizard would believe otherwise."

Colbey shrugged again. Clearly Shadimar was wrong. There was no need nor reason to say so. Still, silence seemed rude, so the Renshai tried to make his point tactfully. "Maybe Tokar knew something you don't."

"Maybe," Shadimar replied. A thought that served as explanation drifted from the Eastern Wizard to Colbey without effort or intention. *It has always been Odin's way to make the Western Wizard the strongest of the four and the Eastern the weakest. Maybe Tokar did know something.* Understanding accompanied the idea. Colbey learned that this discrepancy had existed since the system of the Cardinal Wizards had begun, and no logical reason for the imbalance had ever come to the attention of the Eastern Wizards. Colbey also discovered that the Western Wizard's line was not the only one that had lost its collective consciousness. In the past, the Eastern line had been broken twice and the Southern line once, in all three cases because the current Wizard had died before his time of passing. Thou^gh twenty-four Eastern Wizards had existed since the system began, Shadimar carried the memories of only six.

Silence fell. As if in sympathy, the wind dropped to an unnatural stillness and clouds scudded overhead, veiling the sun. Secodon sat, whining softly. For all his quiet stillness, the Wizard was apparently bothered by his thoughts.

At length, Shadimar met Colbey's gaze again. He raised an arm, the fur-trimmed sleeve of his velvet robe a stark contrast to Colbey's simple brown tunic and breeks. "There are still things we need to discuss. Since the beginning of the system of the Cardinal Wizards, just before the beginning of mankind, the Western and Eastern Wizards have worked in concert, for the good of neutrality and its peoples, the Westerners."

Colbey frowned at Shadimar's stiff formality. Although he came from a Northern tribe, technically under the protection of the Northern Sorceress, who championed goodness, he had long ago pledged his services to the Westlands.

Shadimar continued. "Some have physically worked together as a team. Others have worked separately for the same cause. I would like to work closely with you. In harmony." His glance sharpened.

"You were the one who broke our bond of brotherhood," Colbey reminded him.

Shadimar's mouth clamped closed, and he dismissed his disloyalty as if it held no significance. At the time, his actions had followed logic, and apologies were not his way. "That matter has not been fully laid to rest." Secodon rose, pacing between Wizard and Renshai. Shadimar's brow wrinkled, as if he sought an answer to a question he had not asked.

Annoyed, as always, by the Eastern Wizard's subtlety, Colbey struck for the heart of the matter. "What do you want from me, Shadimar? I could read your mind, but we both know that would be impolite." Colbey understated the seriousness of the offense. Shadimar had made it quite clear that only the four Cardinal Wizards were capable of invading thoughts, and then only those of other Cardinal Wizards. To do so uninvited, however, was considered a crime equaled only by blasphemy.

"That, Colbey, is exactly what I want from you." Shadimar measured each word as a swordsman in a battle on ice watches every movement. "You once told me you had nothing to hide. You gave me permission to enter your mind. But when I tried, you built barriers against me. I want another entrance. This time, unhindered." Shadimar's gaze dropped to the sword at Colbey's left hip, an enchanted weapon that bore the name Harval, the Gray Blade. As an end result of the Seven Tasks of Wizardry, the Wizards' apprentices became immune to harm from any object of Law; therefore, the Cardinal Wizards and their apprentices could be physically harmed only by their chosen ceremonies of passage, by demons, and by the three Swords of Power. Harval was one of the three, all the more dangerous since Shadimar had placed it in the hands of the most competent swordsman in existence.

Colbey remained calm, though the incident that Shadimar recalled brought memories of a bitter time. Then, assailed by doubts about his own long-held religious beliefs and his loyalty to the tribe he had served since birth, Colbey had needed the comfort of his blood brother. Shadimar had chosen that moment to turn against him. Colbey had tried to assert his innocence by giving the Eastern Wizard access to his thoughts, but his mind had not permitted Shadimar's entrance. "I'll do my best. I don't know how to convince you that I never intended to block you out. Just tell me how to get rid of those things you call barriers, and I'll do it."

Shadimar retreated from the edge of the fjords, propping his back against an irregularity in the crags. The cover of clouds thickened, and the windless stillness remained. "You need to do nothing. All it requires is that you don't fight me."

Colbey did not believe that to be the case. His few excursions into other men's minds had cost him more dearly in stamina and energy than days of continuous battle. But the other time that Shadimar had attempted to read Colbey's thoughts, the old Renshai had expelled him without any conscious attention or will. He knew that his mind powers worked differently than those of the Cardinal Wizards. His had come to him even before he had met Tokar, a product of his martial training in endurance and control. He could read the minds of mortals, where the others could not; and his intrusions into the Wizard's mind had gone unnoticed, although they always recognized one another's presences. Still, Shadimar seemed fixed in the belief that Colbey was resisting him. Rather than fight the misconception, Colbey chose to try to give the Eastern Wizard what he wanted.

"I'll do my best." Colbey crouched, spine flat against a jagged tower of stone, his position defensive. A single breeze riffled the short feathers of his hair, then faded into the brooding stillness of the day. He closed his eyes, turning his thoughts inward. He concentrated on keeping his mind as flat and still as the weather.

A foreign presence touched Colbey's mind tentatively.

Though he noticed the intrusion, Colbey willed his consciousness away from it, struggling against curiosity and his natural need to defend. Still, Shadimar's being seemed to burn a pathway through his mind, its presence so defined and out of place it pained him. And, in seeking to invade Colbey's thoughts, Shadimar inadvertently brought some of his own essence and emotion with him. Though Colbey made no attempt to counter the exploration, he could not stop the inklings of Shadimar's judgment that seeped through the cracks.

At first, Shadimar waded through seventy years of war technique and the private battle maneuvers invented by the Renshai tribe. He met these with a patient self-satisfaction. Obviously, this mass of knowledge neither surprised nor interested him.

Colbey kept his own emotions at bay. To lose control meant thwarting Shadimar, and he knew from experience that that would hurt the Wizard as well as destroy the fragile friendship they had tried to reconstruct. Still, Shadimar's cavalier dismissal of the tenets that had driven and guided Colbey's life since birth bothered the old Renshai. Attributing it to cultural differences and closed-mindedness, he let it pass unchallenged.

Soon, Shadimar found the supporting tendrils of Colbey's Northern religion, and he followed one of these toward the core. As the Wizard read the all-too-familiar rites and faith of a Northman, he paused at another concept, this time obviously impressed.

Colbey resisted the urge to focus in on the abstraction, aware that his sudden channeling of presence would drive the Eastern Wizard from his mind. Instead, he satisfied himself with the wisps of Shadimar's thoughts that diffused to him. The answer came slowly, from a source that Colbey never expected, the same war tenets that the Wizard had viewed with contempt moments before. Having looked more closely this time, Shadimar had discovered the intricate judgments and mathematics that allowed Colbey to size up an opponent instantly and in explicit detail, by a single sword stroke. He followed the complexity of Colbey's examinations, though the old Renshai had learned to compress them into an instant: the knowledge of anatomy that told him, by the length, development, and insertion points of tendon and sinew, which maneuvers a warrior should favor . . . and which ones he did favor; the angle and speed of cuts and sweeps that told him an opponent's strategy, often before his foe had himself determined it. For the first time, the Eastern Wizard understood that competence in warfare was based on more than just quickness, strength, and blind luck.

For several moments, Shadimar concentrated on his discovery. Then he turned his attention to following one of the solid threads of Colbey's religion.

The Eastern Wizard's change of focus pleased Colbey. The Renshai had developed sword maneuvers over the course of a century of exile from the North, during which time his tribe had culled the finest techniques of every warrior race. Vows to the Renshai forbid Colbey from teaching those maneuvers to anyone outside the tribe. Had Shadimar chosen to examine their intricacies, Colbey would have had no choice but to expel the Wizard.

Now, Shadimar sifted quickly through the religion, which was integrally entangled with the fighting skills. The Northmen's faith hinged as deeply on battle glory and death as on deities, and many of the gods personified concepts of war. Each of the eighteen tribes chose a patron or two. For the Renshai it was Thor's golden-haired wife, Sif, and their son, Modi. The son's name literally meant "wrath," and its call stirred the Renshai to a frenzy in battle that allowed them to fight, not despite pain, but because of it. Colbey smiled at the thought, driven to dim, racial memories of chiming steel, wolf howls, and the god's name echoing through the ruins of a ravaged town. *So long ago.* Nearly three decades had passed since the other Northern tribes had banded together to exterminate the Renshai, three decades during which Colbey had recreated the tribe from a scraggly group of five swordsmen, only three of whom had any Renshai blood at all.

Colbey and Shadimar reached the deep-seated pocket of bitterness simultaneously, though from different directions. Though weeks had passed, Colbey could still see the hawk-nosed visage of Valr Kirin, a Nordmirian officer who had proven the noblest enemy he had ever faced. At that final battle, Colbey's sword, Harval, had accidentally claimed an arm as well as Kirin's life. By Northern religion, the loss of a body part should have barred the Nordmirian from Valhalla, the haven for the finest warriors slain in battle. Yet Colbey had personally seen a *Valkyrie* claim the body for Valhalla.

Shadimar's consciousness circled the event, alternately horrified and awed by the disruption of a faith Colbey had clung to since birth. It was the Renshai's practice of dismembering Northern enemies to destroy morale that had led to their exile from the North, an exile that had turned an entire world against them. Yet, all of the pain and hatred, all of the racial prejudice, and all of the fiery vengeance that had led to the extermination of the tribe had hinged upon a lie. On the day of Valr Kirin's death, Colbey had waffled between denying his vision and denying the very foundation of his belief and being through seventy-seven years.

Shadimar's discomfort turned to interest as he held Colbey's choices and deeds in judgment. Now Colbey backed away, already knowing what the Eastern Wizard would find. At the time, Colbey had combed his memories, using logic and experience to decide which religious tenets to keep and which to discard, which came from the gods themselves and which from the more arbitrary laws of mankind. In the end, the event had redefined and strengthened, rather than shattered, his faith.

Momentary pleasure radiated from the Eastern Wizard, liberally mixed with surprise. Obviously, he had never anticipated such complexity from a Renshai sword master.

Though Colbey expected nothing else, the Wizard's underestimation grated on him. He had tired of the jokes that had become standard belief, the foolish gibes that the quicker the warrior, the slower his intellect. These, Colbey knew, sprang from the need of those unwilling to suffer the constant pain and effort required for competence at anything to explain away ability as magic or natural from birth. Underestimating Colbey Calistinsson had cost more than one man his life.

Shadimar poked into a few pockets of memory that Colbey felt were better left undisturbed. Among those, Shadimar found an agony of grief for a young man, Episte Rachesson, the orphaned child of the last full-blooded Renshai other than Colbey. The boy had seemed as much a son as a student to Colbey. Lost to chaos' madness, Episte could not be salvaged, though Colbey had driven himself to the edge of death trying to fix the damage. Shadimar found the sorrow the old Renshai knew over leaving what remained of the Renshai to fend for themselves. He also discovered a tie whose strength even Colbey had not recognized, until that moment. He had left his white stallion, Frost Reaver, with a farmer in Bruen. He had owned the horse for less than a year, yet he missed the animal's surefootedness, agility, and loyalty. And then, Shadimar found the heart and core of Colbey's existence, the thing that had driven and steered his life since birth: the need to die with courage, honor, and glory in battle.

Shadimar withdrew.

Colbey dropped his concentration with an eager sigh. Exhaustion gathered at the edges of his awareness, and he lowered his center of balance to relax. The effort of protecting Shadimar's hunt had taxed him more than he had expected.

Shadimar sat back against the stone, his head bowed and his eyes closed. His white beard trickled over his laced fingers and curled knees. Secodon remained before his master, watchful and alert, revealing the fatigue his master hid so well.

For a long time, Wizard and Renshai sat in silence. The quiet windlessness seemed to stretch the moment into an eternity, and Colbey's patience broke first. "Did you find what you were looking for?"

Slowly, Shadimar raised his head. His gray eyes flared open, fixed stolidly on his companion. "Can you truly say I was looking *for* something, when, in truth, I hoped not to find it?"

Colbey had no desire to discuss semantics. "Fine, then. Did you not find what you weren't looking for?"

"Yes," Shadimar replied.

Colbey considered the reply, eyes narrowing as he tried to interpret the answer in the wake of a doubly negative question.

Shadimar let him off the hook. "I did not find what I wasn't looking for. No evidence of demons. No sign that you are other than you claim."

Tired of others doubting his integrity, Colbey pressed. "Did that surprise you?"

"Many things about you surprised me." Shadimar dodged the question, creating many others in the process.

Colbey let the initial issue drop. Shadimar's doubts had been quelled. And, though it bothered Colbey that Shadimar questioned his integrity enough to require a mental exploration, it was over now. The healing process could begin for both of them, as long as the Eastern Wizard did not mistrust him again.

The darkness deepened. Colbey glanced upward, concerned that the mental process had taken far longer than it had seemed to and that day had passed into night without his knowledge. But the sun remained high, all but lost beneath a thickening cover of clouds. Streamers poked through tears in the clouds, their light feeble and diffuse.

"You are a more capable thinker than I ever would have guessed." Shadimar brushed his beard away from his hands.

Colbey did not reply to the faint praise. A thank you did not seem in order.

Apparently recognizing his words as a backhanded insult, Shadimar added, "I think you could make a competent Wizard."

Something about Shadimar's tone did not ring solid enough for Colbey's liking. "If . . .?"

"If?" Shadimar repeated, brows rising in question.

"I could make a competent Wizard if what?"

Shadimar opened his mouth, as if to remind Colbey that he was the one who had added the qualifier. Then, apparently seeing the futility of such an argument, he pursed his lips and started again. "Colbey, no man is born a Cardinal Wizard. As a Wizard comes within about half a century of his time of passing, he selects an apprentice. He then spends the half a century training that apprentice. After the Wizard's rite of passage, his successor has the strengths, knowledge, and experience of his predecessors to call upon. Without training or knowledge, none of us expects you to slip right into your niche." He hesitated only an instant, his composure unbroken, but the lapse spoke volumes to Colbey.

The Renshai caught a flash of realization that Shadimar wanted to explain some detail about the tasks that an apprentice who had undergone the proper training would have known.

The concept disappeared as quickly as it came, suppressed by a law and propriety as old as creation. Only a splash of guilt at his need for silence lingered, and Shadimar finished his previous thought. "Some of the best prepared have fallen prey to the power or to the strange eclipsing and dragging of time that comes with near immortality."

Colbey shook his head, not pressing the matter. To admit he had read Shadimar's thoughts, even unintentionally, would reawaken all the suspicion he had only just set to rest. Instead, he considered Shadimar's words. All his life, Colbey had cared only for his sword, his tribe, and his goddess. He had dedicated his soul to his honor and to earning the glory of a death in battle that would bring him the promised rewards of Valhalla. Neither the power nor the responsibilities of becoming a Cardinal Wizard enticed him. "Becoming a competent Wizard means nothing to me. I'm not interested in becoming a Wizard at all."

Shadimar's eyes went as dark as the roiling clouds. "You are the Western Wizard already. The time for choices is past."

Colbey scowled. "The choice was never given to me."

"That is of no consequence any longer."

"Perhaps not." Colbey gathered his composure, though anger still hovered tangibly, easily sparked. "But don't expect me not to question or resist now that I'm starting to understand what Tokar forced on me."

Shadimar's expression softened. "That is a point well taken. Still, it doesn't change the facts. The sooner you accept the way things are, and that they cannot be changed, the better Wizard you will become."

"You don't understand, do you?" The lengthy pause had restored Colbey's lost energy. He rose suddenly. "If I don't care to be a Wizard, why do you expect me to care to be a competent one?"

"Because you *are* a Wizard. And I can't imagine Colbey Calistinsson not working to become the best at whatever he might be."

Colbey's rage receded. This compliment inspired all the goodwill and appreciation that the other had not. "You are assuming, my friend, that there's no way to refuse the title. That may be so, but I won't take that as fact until I prove there's no escape."

"You selfish, arrogant bastard." The Wizard stood, the taller of the two by a full head. "Would you leave the peoples of the West, including your own beloved Renshai, without a guardian? Would you let Trilless' goodness eat at the northern border and Carcophan's evil infect the east and south until nothing remains but absolutes?"

The names of the Northern and Southern Wizards rekindled Colbey's anger. Trilless had misinterpreted a prophecy, hounding Colbey with champions and a demon sent to slay him. Although the three Swords coming together on the world of men had caused Episte's madness, it was Carcophan who had ignorantly summoned the final blade and placed it in the young Renshai's hands. Then, the Southern Wizard had preyed upon the damage he had caused, turning the youngster against his own tribe in order to further the causes of evil. Thoughts of Episte Rachesson drained away the rage as quickly as it had come, and grief replaced it.

Shadimar continued his tirade. "You were the one who claimed that law and morality become too fixed and rigid when strict definitions are placed on good and evil. You are the Northman who abandoned the tenets of good for those of neutrality. Now, when the time has come for you to defend those bold words and choices, you would abandon your responsibilities and the many whose lives depend on the Western Wizard because someone made one decision for you."

"The Westlands have you. And you can find another Wizard to fill my place."

Shadimar turned away. He gazed out over the ocean, and his voice fell nearly to a whisper. "It's not that easy. When he created the world and banished chaos to its plane, Odin created the system of the Cardinal Wizards, placing us as the mediators between gods and men. Clearly, the balance he created between us has a purpose. If he believes we need

four, then four is what we need. At this time, we can't risk
any deviation from Odin's plan. Too much lies at stake."

"Fixed and rigid."

Shadimar did not deny the accusation. He continued to
stare out over the Amirannak Sea. "But still less so than
good or evil. And it's better than the alternative."

Colbey followed Shadimar's gaze to a black spot on the
horizon, an approaching ship. *"Ragnarok?"* he guessed.
Once, he had intruded on Shadimar's mind, and that search
had uncovered an ancient prophecy:

> *"A Sword of Gray,*
> *A Sword of White,*
> *A Sword of Black and chill as night.*
> *Each one forged,*
> *Its craftsmen a Mage;*
> *The three Blades together shall close the age.*

> *"When their oath of peace*
> *The Wizards forsake,*
> *Their own destruction they undertake.*
> *Only these Swords*
> *Their craftsmen can slay.*
> *Each Sword shall be blooded the same rueful day.*

> *"When that fateful day comes*
> *The Wolf's Age has begun.*
> *Hati swallows the moon, and Sköll tears up the sun."*

The rhyme foretold that the day of destruction for men,
gods, and Wizards would come after the three Swords of
Power were all called to man's world of law at once. Colbey
carried the Gray Sword, Harval. The others he had faced, in
the hands of Trilless' and Carcophan's champions, first Valr
Kirin then Episte Rachesson. Shadimar had banished the
White Sword back to the plain of magic as soon as the battle
had ended. Yet, clearly, there had been at least a moment
when all three swords had existed on their world at once.
Colbey recalled the chaos attack he had shared through
Episte's memories, a brutal assault that had left neither time
nor thought for defense. Chaos had accentuated every shred
of bitterness and rage that Episte had known, inflaming them
far out of proportion, turning the boy into a warped and

vengeful caricature of his former self. Having relived the remembrance too many times, Colbey forced emotion away,
concentrating on the approaching ship.

"The final destruction. The end of the world. Do you want
to be responsible for causing that?"

As the vessel approached, Colbey realized that its size had
made it appear farther than it was; it seemed too small to
call it more than a boat. "Ship" would be a kindness. Yet,
from Colbey's experience, "boat" would insult its captain,
so he chose to think of it as a ship. Around it, the air lay too
calm before the growing storm for it to remain in motion.
Colbey had joined enough pirating raids to know that it
should have sat, in irons, on the darkening sea. But the
ghostly white sails, devoid of symbol or standard, spilled
wind. Faint ripples on the water showed that the gaily-
painted craft was gliding toward them at an impossible
speed.

Colbey watched the ship, his mind clicking through the
combinations of wind that could account for its movement
on the Amirannak Sea. But, always, his calculations fell
short. Something felt misplaced, beyond the realm of logic.
Still, he managed to pull his thoughts from the vessel to concentrate on their conversation. "I fail to see where my decision could cause the *Ragnarok*. In fact, you've often told me
that prophecies don't just happen. The Cardinal Wizards
have to make those prophecies occur. It seems to me that all
that's needed to avert *Ragnarok* is for the Wizards *not* to
cause it."

Now, Shadimar returned his attention to the ship as well.
"You of all people know it's not that simple. There is no single being more powerful than Odin. Some would say that all
other life together cannot equal him. Yet even he could not
destroy chaos, only banish it to another realm. And his hold
on it has weakened. You see that every day when vows give
way to lies and men violate the laws of their countries.
There was a time, Colbey, within your lifetime I believe,
when falsehoods and treason did not exist at all."

"So what are you saying?" Colbey no longer needed to
struggle to focus interest on Shadimar's words. "That the
Ragnarok is inevitable? That the world will lapse back into
the primordial chaos, with or without us?"

"I'm saying only that these are desperate times. It was
predicted that the Great Destruction would occur during my

time as a Cardinal Wizard. I now worry that it may come sooner rather than later." Shadimar caught Colbey's arm. As the Renshai turned, the Eastern Wizard met his gaze directly. The ancient gray eyes became earnest to the edge of desperation. "I'm not sure I can explain this in a way you can understand."

Colbey scowled. "Remember? I can spell sword as well as I can use one."

The ship drifted closer. Shadimar sighed deeply, trapped by his own choice of words. To avoid an explanation now would offend Colbey. "Our ship is about to land." He gestured around an outcropping toward a low, relatively accessible flat amid the fjords. "So forgive me if I keep my clarification brief and to the point."

Colbey resisted a smile. He could think of few things that would delight him more than a short, direct discussion with Shadimar, without the morals and Wizardly subtleties.

"Law is the direct opponent of chaos. If we work within the tenets of law to bring the *Ragnarok,* our efforts could do exactly the opposite. If, however, we turn against Odin's laws and break our Wizards' vows in order to avert the *Ragnarok,* we are virtually guaranteed to cause it." Without bothering to explain further, Shadimar motioned to Secodon and headed for the docking site. "When the time comes, I hope we will all have the sense and competence to chose our actions wisely. Quite literally, the world and everything in it will lie in our hands."

Colbey's gaze traced the rain squalls stalking the horizon, and the idea of sea travel seemed as illogical as the tiny ship's movement across a windless ocean. The Eastern Wizard's words sat in his mind like lead, unpondered. Too many questions remained unanswered for him to make decisions of such earth-shattering proportions, so he left the idea to lay idle for the moment. Decades on the battlefield had forced his gravest decisions to be made in an instant. When the time came, he trusted his own instincts. But he and the Renshai as a tribe had suffered from misinterpretations by Trilless, Carcophan, and Shadimar. Though he felt embarrassed to the point of sacrilege to place his judgment and knowledge over that of Cardinal Wizards centuries old, experience told him to believe in himself rather than them. He followed Shadimar to the cliffs leading down to the flatter lowland of the shore.

Shadimar climbed gingerly down the rock face, choosing each hand and toehold with patient care. "You should know our captain is an outworlder."

Colbey waited at the peak with Secodon, seeing no reason to crowd the Eastern Wizard. The ship had drawn close enough for him to see the carved dolphin on its prow and to read the name, *Sea Seraph,* written in the Western trading tongue on the bow. "What's an outworlder?"

"A creature of Faery." Shadimar clambered the last short distance to the plain.

Secodon looked at Colbey. The old Renshai gestured for the wolf to go first. "Like an elf?" Even the most pious priest that Colbey had known believed in elves only as cute mythology to draw children to their religious studies. The irony of discovering the tales to be fact, after the shock that had shaken the more deeply rooted foundations of his faith, did not escape Colbey. He loosed a bitter laugh, gaze channeling naturally on the tall, slender figure at the tiller. From a distance, the sailor held the appearance of a gawky teenager. "You're joking, right?"

Secodon leapt from the jagged peak of the fjord to the stone beside Shadimar. The Eastern Wizard raised a hand in greeting to the approaching ship. "Not at all. Elves are real. Like chaos, they exist on another plane or world. Captain's probably the only elf you'll ever meet. He's navigated these waters for centuries, at least, carrying the Cardinal Wizards to the Meeting Isle. There's no other way that I know of to get there."

The captain returned Shadimar's greeting with a brisk wave. Colbey analyzed the movement from habit, finding a grace that contrasted starkly with the awkward adolescent image of the figure at the helm. As the boat touched the rock flat and Shadimar moved to help with docking, Colbey measured the jump that Secodon had taken. It looked dangerously far to land on solid rock. Compromising, Colbey caught the first few handholds in a quick sequence, then made a graceful leap to the rocks below. The maneuver scraped skin from his palm, tearing loose a callus, and blood welled in the hole.

Lightning flared beyond the sail. The hull of the *Sea Seraph* grated against rock. Colbey cringed. The open sea should have dashed the tiny craft to matchsticks; surely it would in the upcoming storm. Already, rolling gray haze limited vision.

The captain sprang to shore with an agility that nearly matched Colbey's own. Gold tinged his red-brown hair, faded from a life lived in the open sun. He wore the thick locks knotted at the nape of his neck. High, sharp cheekbones and broad, slanted eyes gave him a pleasant, animal look. His eyes glowed amber, a color Colbey had only seen on a cat. His full mouth bent into a friendly grin, and the stiff wrinkles that marred his face seemed to come from excessive smiling. The visage defied Colbey's attempts to guess his age, even within a decade or two. He noticed that the elf's arms and legs were proportionately longer. His muscles arose and inserted in locations slightly different from men, built more for quickness and agility than strength. A leather jerkin and silk pantaloons peeked from beneath a frayed wool cloak.

"Greeting, my lords!" The outworlder spoke the Western tongue with a unique accent that seemed closest to general Northern. He threw his slender arms around Shadimar.

"Greetings, Captain." Shadimar squeezed momentarily.

Pulling away from the Eastern Wizard, the captain embraced Secodon's shaggy neck. The wolf's plumed tail flailed excited circles.

Colbey found himself with a thousand questions, including how one came to sail an ocean for centuries, but he knew these would have to wait until he had the Wizard in confidence or knew the elf better.

The captain did not share Colbey's polite hesitancy. Releasing Secodon, he hugged Colbey in turn, with the exuberance of an old friend. "A Northman, eh? And a young one. I've a fondness for Northmen. But you know that, don't you? Welcome aboard the *Seraph*, Colbey." He gestured his charges to the ship.

The captain's familiarity confused Colbey momentarily. Then he recalled that the Wizards had passed their collective consciousness from successor to successor for millennia, and the elf's reaction made more sense to him. *In a way, he's been greeting the same four Cardinal Wizards forever.*

Shadimar headed for the ship. Colbey hung back. "Shouldn't we wait out the storm?"

"Nay. Nay." The captain shook his head, waving for the

Renshai to follow Shadimar. "I've had a thousand years to learn this sea. We can run before the gale."

Shadimar clambered to the deck, and the captain followed. Colbey shoved the hull into the water, then leapt aboard with the others. Though his intuition told him that the captain was dead wrong, he dared not argue sea gales with one who had survived for centuries and had not yet gone gray.

The instant the ship left the shore, her sails caught a wind that drew her swiftly northward.

Captain perched with one foot on the dolphin-headed prow. "Blessed be the gods who watch over my lady and my charges. Thank you, Aegir, may your mercy stay with us always! Thank you, Weese, may your winds always blow true. Thank you, Ciacera, she of the eight-legged. Thank you, Morista, may your charges rest easy beneath the sea. And thank you, Mahaj, whose likeness graces the *Seraph*." The captain lowered his foot and ran a fond hand over the ornament on the prow. Surely, he had spoken that prayer a million times, yet his sincerity made it sound fresh and new.

Colbey recognized only the names of the Northmen's sea god, Aegir, and the Westerners' god of winds. He studied the darkening sky as the first gust rose, wet with the promise of violence. No sailor he knew would chance such a storm.

But the captain remained calm and beaming. His prayers finished, he gestured his charges to the central cabin.

Colbey and Shadimar went.

CHAPTER 2

The High Seas

The clean, white walls of the *Sea Seraph*'s cabin enclosed an area that seemed impossibly large for the tiny ship. Three cots, a wooden chest, and a decoratively chiseled table with four matching chairs filled it only sparsely. A narwhale horn hung on the wall, mounted above an open case crammed full of books. While Colbey Calistinsson studied the layout, the captain pointed to one of two doors at the opposite end of the room. "We'll need to bunk together. If Shadimar will prepare his famous herbal stew, I'll man the tiller."

Shadimar smiled. "I presume you've gathered all the proper ingredients."

"Of course."

The Eastern Wizard nodded, then headed for the indicated exit, his wolf trotting across the planks behind him. He opened the panel, slipped through, then closed the door behind Secodon.

The captain winked at Colbey. "I don't always get them exactly where he asks. Waterroot is waterroot, whatever ocean grows it, and the stew always comes out the same." The captain laughed at his own wit, then spun on his heel. "Feel free to look around." He left through the door by which they had entered.

Aside from the Western Wizard's library, which he had not dared to disturb before he learned of his title, Colbey had only rarely seen texts, usually a single one treasured by its owner. Now, Colbey knelt before the book shelf, scanning titles in a variety of languages. He recognized labels in the trading tongue of the West, in the West's main language, and in Northern. He found one titled in the stiff, heavy print of the Eastern tongue, though the meaning of the words escaped him. Others held runes as incomprehensible as an infant's random scrawl. Of the titles he could read, he found most to be nautical texts or collections of seamen's tales.

Most of the others contained detailed monologues on religion and its history. Though, at a quick glance, the words spanned the belief systems of all three divisions of the world, the collection seemed weighted toward the Northern faith.

Pleased, Colbey singled out *The Trobok,* the book of the faithful. It contained the spiritual wisdom that guided Northmen's lives, mankind's gift from the gods. Most believed that daily reading from the work strengthened Odin's hold on law, keeping chaos at bay from their own day to day existences. Colbey had heard priests read from the great book, but he had never before come so close to an actual copy. Tentatively, he touched the binding, running a finger along it. The well worn leather felt comfortable, but not in a deeply celestial manner. Cautiously, he levered it free and carried it to the table.

Colbey set *The Trobok* on the surface. The tome thumped gently against the wood, falling open to a weathered page near its end, marked by a string of dried seaweed. Curious about the marker, Colbey read:

"Men shall slay fathers to lie with mothers. Swords shall run with brother's blood. The wolf, Sköll, shall swallow the sun and Hati the moon. There shall follow three bitter cold winters without a summer to break them. So shall begin the Wolf Age and the great battle which will see the passage of the Gray Lord, Odin. The new age that follows shall be ruled by the survivors of the gods: Vidar and Vali, Baldur and blind Hod from the dead, and the sons of Thor who will together wield their father's hammer."

Images of the world's fated destruction pulsed a shiver through Colbey, though it pleased him that the Renshai's patron, Modi, as one of Thor's sons, would survive the carnage. No text he knew of mentioned the fate of the goddesses, so Colbey had always chosen to believe that Sif endured as well. He flipped the book to its first page and began to read.

The toss of the *Sea Seraph* and the creak of her mast kept sleep from Colbey. He had lain awake half the night, listening to the clank of sheet clamps and Shadimar's heavy breaths, yet he had never heard the captain come below from the helm. *Surely even elves have to sleep.* Remarkably unwearied, Colbey rose from his cot, donning his tunic and sword belt. The pressure of the two swords at his hips felt reassuring. He threaded past the sleeping Wizard and the wolf beneath his master's cot, padding to the starlit deck.

The captain sat on a bench, manning the rudder and singing a sweet tune of the sea. His mellow alto lilted across the deck, as natural as the slap of waves against the stern. The wind caught his damp hair, tossing it gaily about his sun-baked face. Colbey leaned over the rail, staring at the trails and sparkles of color the moon drew in their minuscule wake. He squinted against the rush of ice-grained wind, the pellets stinging his face and eyes. A cloud enwrapped the moon, all but choking it from vision.

The outworlder finished his song before speaking. "Is the Western Wizard brooding?" He spoke the Northern tongue cleanly, without accent. "Did you leave a little lady behind?"

Colbey kept his gaze on the horizon. The darkness huddled, as if to block the sun from rising. He considered the captain's question. Longer ago than he cared to remember, he had married, but none of their lovemaking had resulted in children. Himinthrasir had left him for a man who had sired a family with her. Since that time, no woman had wanted more than a brief relationship with him, and none of those encounters had resulted in an heir. Instead, Colbey had lavished his love and time on his swords, and he had known women only as friends and colleagues. Half of the Renshai's most competent warriors were female, every bit as savage as the tribe's men. The image made him smile, and he thought of Mitrian, one of two women in the tattered remains of the tribe called Renshai. "The only little lady I left could raze a city."

The elf chuckled. He groped beneath his bench, opening a compartment that Colbey had not previously noticed. He drew out a pair of matching goblets and a crystal flask half-filled with amber liquid. Pouring some into each glass, he offered one to Colbey. "Hold tight. The wind's strong."

Colbey accepted the drink. "Forgive the passenger arguing with the captain, but that storm will catch us."

"Midday." The outworlder seemed unperturbed. "About the time we reach the portal. Oddly, I find it more navigable in a squall." He grinned at Colbey. "You know something of sailing, Wizard?"

Colbey flinched, still not liking the title. "Call me Colbey." He sipped at the wine. It tasted sweet and held a pleasant salt tang. "And what should I call you?"

"Captain is fine." The elf took a long pull at his wine.

"But as formal and distant as 'Wizard.' "

"It is what I'm called."

"Perhaps because you tell people this when they ask your name."

"It is what I'm called. Does that not make it my name?"

Colbey laughed at the circle of the captain's reasoning. "I'm called many things. Wizard, for example. But my name is Colbey Calistinsson."

The elf downed the remainder of his wine. He topped off Colbey's goblet, though the Renshai had only taken a single swallow, then filled his own glass. He set the carafe aside. "Why is Colbey your name? What makes it more your name than The Golden Prince of Demons or The Deathseeker or *torke* or Kyndig?"

Colbey took another sip of wine. He had been called all of those things, the first from a prophecy, the second from his style in warfare, and the third was the Renshai word for teacher or sword master. The last meant "Skilled One," and he had heard it only once before, from Valr Kirin. "My name is Colbey Calistinsson because it's how I think of myself. As is my tribe's way, my mother named me for a hero who died in battle and found Valhalla, my guardian and namesake. The Calistinsson keeps my father's memory alive. He was a fine warrior as well."

The elf moved up beside Colbey, propping one bare foot on the railing. "Perhaps, Colbey Calistinsson, I think of myself as Captain."

Colbey considered, seeing how the elf had trapped him neatly. He watched water vapor condense to a fog on his glass. "Then I guess your name is Captain. I'll call you that, though I think it's a slight to your parents. Surely, they picked a name for you that they considered important."

"Surely," Captain replied. "But I've lived millennia. Do you think I remember it?"

Colbey whipped his head to directly face his companion. "Is this some sort of test? Do you really think I'm feeble enough to believe you've forgotten your name?"

Captain ran a finger through the condensation on his glass, tracing a crooked line that barely disrupted the fog.

"That's the great thing about being a Wizard. You have the knowledge and insight to believe what you wish."

Colbey grunted, taking another drink.

"When you think about the reasons that humans have names, my claim may become more believable." The captain took another swallow of wine. "Humans have names to preserve an image of immortality, for an individual or a family, and to fit comfortably into an era." He lowered his foot from the gunwale to meet Colbey's gaze with his red-flecked eyes. "Take your name, for example. You use Colbey to honor the dead warrior who held the name before you, thereby keeping him alive long after his passing. You use Calistinsson to honor your father. Carrion now, I presume?"

Colbey nodded grudgingly. "We prefer to use a more polite term for it. But, yes, my father died in battle."

"Those children not named for elders usually get some name that sounds beautiful or special to their parents or that's common to their generation. Beautiful and special ceases to be either after enough time passes. And an era means little to an immortal." Captain raised his brows, as if to question whether he had made his point. "Names have significance only to mortals. For us, it's just a way to distinguish between one and another. A title or description works as well."

"So you are immortal?"

"As we define it, yes. Our lives far outspan yours. Elves do die, though. When we do, our souls are stripped of body and memory, placed in the body of a newborn, and we start again. Death always precedes a new life."

"Interesting," Colbey said, glad for Valhalla. The idea of a life dragging and cycling into infinity did not sound desirable, though he knew many would see it so.

The conversation came to a temporary halt. Wind howled through the silence.

Captain spoke first. "You were going to tell me how you came to know about ships and sea gales."

"Was I?" Colbey took a longer pull at the wine. Over time, the flavor became more inviting, and he did seem to recall the elf's question from before he'd sidetracked the conversation. "Decades ago, I visited a tavern in Talmir. A healthy quantity of ale convinced me to join a pirating raid." Colbey laughed at the memory, long buried. His thoughts of the other Northern tribes had become bitter since they had banded against and all but exterminated the Renshai. "We had three ships, oars and sails, and a crazed band of young men willing to hurl themselves on ax and spear for glory or scant treasure.

"When our lead ship's captain had his brains dashed out by a stone dropped from a coastal city's ramparts, they gave me his command. They chose me for swordsmanship and savagery. I'm sure no one knew it was my first time aboard any ship larger than a seal boat, and I certainly wasn't going to open myself to ridicule by telling them. We fought the winter storms of the Amirannak on the way home. I learned quickly."

Man and elf fell into another hush, watching darkness enwrap the stars and gradually dim them to memories. The moon struggled behind thickening clouds. The captain refilled his goblet.

Colbey stared at the amber wine, curiosity finally getting the better of him. "What is this anyway?"

Captain's smile stretched nearly the length of his face. "Good wine. Fermented from kelp."

"Seaweed wine?" Colbey examined the yellow liquid a trifle less fondly. "Bleh." Still he did not protest when the captain refilled his glass.

Releasing the tiller, Captain leaned over the gunwale to free the ground tackle. He let the anchor fall into the dark, churning waters with a splash. "Without the stars, I can't guide us." He turned back to face Colbey. "But I'm still curious. If you're not brooding over a woman, then over whom?"

Colbey responded with a wry chuckle. "I didn't think I was brooding, though there is one I worry about more than any other. My students will do fine without me. My horse, Frost Reaver, may not. I left him in a farmer's care, with more than enough gold to cover his needs and with explicit instructions." He sipped at the wine again, conveniently forgetting its source. Droplets pelted him, and he wondered whether they came from damp winds or waves, or if the storm had already begun to catch them. "I have this fear that I'll find him pulling a plow. Or sold."

They both laughed. Captain replenished the glasses, though they were both over half full. "A horse? Now that has to be a first for the Western Wizard."

Colbey let the title pass, not wanting to delve into another discussion on names. "What do you mean?"

"I hardly need to explain. We all know it's the Eastern Wizard who's lord of furred beasts."

The captain's words reminded Colbey of information he did already know, though only indirectly. "That's right. I'm supposed to have some kind of bird rapport."

Captain's canted eyes widened. "Haven't you ever tried bonding with the birds?"

"No," Colbey admitted, flushing. Such an attempt would have made him feel foolish. "Actually, I did once try to talk to the red falcon who brought me a message from Shadimar." Colbey considered the incident briefly. "The bird didn't answer."

"I don't think it's a matter of answering directly." Captain shrugged, revealing his ignorance. His long fingers rested on the railing. "Besides, Swiftwing is different. He serves all four Cardinal Wizards."

"Like you?"

The captain closed his grip around the railing. "Oh no. No. I serve Trilless and goodness." He looked up in surprise. "You know that."

Colbey opened his mouth to deny the possibility of that knowledge. Until the previous day, he had believed in elves only as children's legends. Then, he realized the captain referred to the memories and understanding Colbey should have had from the collective consciousness of the previous Western Wizards. If Captain did, indeed, serve Trilless, Colbey saw no reason to reveal his lack. The champion of goodness would see it as a weakness and find a way to exploit it. Still, he liked the captain, as a being and as a source of information. Although Colbey had not yet read any stray thoughts from his host, candor radiated from the elf. At the least, a Cardinal Wizard's servant could not lie. "I try to learn as much as I can on my own. It's not my way to rely on information gathered by others."

The captain laughed. "Not even other Wizards?"

The bitterness returned. "Especially not other Wizards. I've seen the results of their mistaken conclusions." Like everything in his life, Colbey related gathering knowledge to sword mastery. "No one becomes competent by taking shortcuts."

Captain laughed again. "You're talking like an elf now,

you know. If we take shortcuts, we spend half our existence in boredom. Mankind always seems eager for an easier, faster way, and I can hardly blame them. You have to work with the span you have."

Colbey shrugged. A limited lifetime only partially accounted for most people's search for the quick and simple, but he saw no reason to malign his fellows. Again, he steered the conversation back on track. The mythology described the lighter breed of elves as capricious and silly. Colbey saw little of that in Captain, but the elder did seem to have a knack for driving conversations on tangents. "So you serve Trilless."

"I do."

"Yet you're transporting us, even though our cause, neutrality, conflicts with hers."

"I transported Carcophan before you. He's already waiting for you on the Meeting Isle."

Colbey rested his goblet on the railing, brows raised. "You, a minion of good, transported the champion of all evil?"

"More than once."

"If I had known about your loyalties, I'd have never boarded with that storm brewing. Doesn't Carcophan worry that you'll drown him or slaughter him in his sleep? At least that you'd leave him in the wrong place?"

Captain shook his head vigorously, the red-brown hair flying. Surrounded by a wild mane, his not-quite-human features looked even more animal-like. "First, there's not much that can hurt a Cardinal Wizard. You know that. Second, as a close minion of one of the Wizards, I'm bound by the same laws. Trilless can't directly harm Carcophan. And neither can I. Of all the Wizards' vows, Odin made that the most binding."

Captain's words reminded Colbey of the very reason he had no wish to become a Cardinal Wizard. He frowned. "So, when I complete these tasks, I'll become bound by the same monstrous list of dos and don'ts as the others."

"Certainly." Captain drained his glass, questioning Colbey with his expression as well as his words. "If by monstrous you mean large, that's true. If by monstrous you mean awful, then you sadly misinterpret the truth. Perhaps you should learn to rely more on your predecessors."

Colbey made a thoughtful noise by way of reply.

Captain's look went from quizzical to concerned. "Odin wrote these laws and created the system of the Cardinal Wizards. Surely he had the best interests of men and gods in mind."

"Surely," Colbey admitted easily. "Millennia ago. Times and situations change."

The statement walked the fine edge of blasphemy. "Don't you think Odin has the knowledge to guess the future and its needs?"

"Yes. To a point." Colbey borrowed the words of a song he had heard long ago, called "Sheriva and the Blue-nosed Fly" and sung by the bard who was also the guardian of the high king in Béarn. Then, the words had only seemed interesting. Now, he recalled them verbatim, and they became eerily appropriate:

"To the immortal, centuries pass like months;
But the shortest-lived see every moment's glory.
It is they who first notice the need for change
And they who adapt most quickly to it."

The translation from the Eastern to the Northern tongue lost the rhyme, but the message came through as clearly.

The captain balanced his wine on the gunwale. "Perhaps I've had too much of this, but I'm not certain of your point. You're saying that perhaps it's time Odin reconsidered the system of the Cardinal Wizards."

"Yes."

"But it's worked so well for so long. Why do humans feel the need to mend things that aren't damaged?"

Now, Colbey laughed, though the sound was strained. "Perhaps it's our strange habit of living every moment we have. Or maybe surviving moment to moment allows us to see the detail that immortals miss. I do know this." Wind howled across the stern, plucking the lines into humming dances. Colbey raised his voice. "All of the other Wizards tried to destroy me, based on a misconception. Now, we're perched on *Ragnarok*'s brink. One way or another, something has to change."

Captain threw a worried glance at the sail, apparently weighing whether to unfurl it or chance the storm he needed to navigate the final journey to the Wizards' Island. "And you're going to affect that change?"

"Only if I refuse the tasks."

Captain took the goblet from Colbey's hand, pouring the remainder of the golden liquid over the railing. "Now I know it's you, not me, who's had too much. If you refuse the tasks, you leave yourself vulnerable to mortal weapons. My experience with humans, though small, tells me that you have fewer years than I have fingers on one hand. If that long."

"I'm not afraid of death."

"I'm sure you're not." The captain balanced Colbey's glass beside his own. "But if you're dead, there's little you can do to cause those changes you seem to feel are so necessary."

"Are you giving a Cardinal Wizard advice?"

"No." Captain replied defensively, paused, then laughed. "Yes, I guess I am. As long as I'm doing so, I might as well do a competent job of it. I don't know exactly what happens during the Tasks of Wizardry, but I do know this. It involves battles, both external and internal. And it involves choices. Remember, each Cardinal Wizard may spend centuries seeking out and choosing his apprentice. And they do. It's only in each Wizard's best interests to make his or her line stronger and more powerful through the millennia. Yet, despite the caution of their selection and training, fewer than half of those chosen survive the tasks. The worst that can happen to you during those tasks is death. If you refuse the many laws and oaths that bind the Cardinal Wizards, I imagine that you will fail the tasks. The result of that is death. You say you don't fear death. So what are you risking?"

Colbey rested both hands on the railing, using his body to shield the cut glass goblets he would hate to see the wind destroy. The darkness had thickened, and Colbey could no longer see the waves that lashed at the *Sea Seraph*'s hull. Much about the Cardinal Wizards and their honor bothered him, but the Captain's questions helped him organize his thoughts and find the deeper reason buried beneath the others. Being bound by law never bothered him; the Renshai had a code of honor more restrictive than any he knew, and he followed it with a devotion that left little room for doubts. Arbitrary rules had no place in Colbey's fierce heart, yet his own religion guided him to trust ones created by Odin, no matter how long ago. Buried beneath all of his bitterness and concern for the Cardinal Wizards' responsibilities and competence lay the crux of his discomfort. "When a Cardinal Wizard chooses his time of passing, his memories are passed to his successor."

The captain nodded slightly, the movement nearly swallowed by the darkness.

"What about his soul?"

"His soul?"

Colbey read discomfort in the elf's tone. He stood in silence while the captain stalled.

"My research leads me to believe a Wizard's soul is . . . well . . ."

"Well?"

The elf's words cut through the blackness. "Utterly destroyed."

"Utterly destroyed." The phrase sat in Colbey's ears, unable to penetrate further. His mind had to focus on each syllable individually, define each word separately before the implications became clear. Then rage speared through him, as ugly as the threatening storm. Like all Renshai, he had clutched a sword from the day his tiny fingers could close around a hilt. His first word had been "war," his only long-term goal to die in valorous combat and earn his place, beside his namesake, in Valhalla. *Unless I fight the title, the decision of one dying Wizard will cost me my soul.*

The idea sparked an even deeper anger, one that washed Colbey's vision red and made the gusts and darkness seem to disappear. He thought of the decades of crashing steel, of pitting only skill against the guile and armor of the Renshai's enemies. He thought of the daily practices, the time stolen from sleep and food and friendship to hone his abilities and demonstrate his faith and devotion to the Renshai's goddess. He thought of the throbbing agony of muscles torn and wounds healing, daily driving himself beyond exhaustion for the honor of serving the gods in Valhalla when war finally claimed him. All stolen from him at once.

Despair eased through the outrage, bringing with it a responsibility that Colbey could not deny. He had raised his skill to a degree that thwarted death. Honor bound him to fight every combat to the limit of his ability. Yet it was the very skill that came from experience and giving his all that had made him too competent to die in the battles he sought. Without the Western Wizard's interference, Colbey knew he would almost certainly have succumbed to age. And that would have condemned him to Hel as surely as cowardice.

My soul for the chance to make the changes I believe necessary not only to avert the Ragnarok, *but also to keep our world from becoming as static as death.* As grand as the prize was, Colbey dreaded the cost. One thing he knew for certain: he needed to do a lot of thinking. And, just as on the battlefield, he would have to do it quickly.

CHAPTER 3

The Scene in the Pica

A dying glaze of sunlight filtered through cracks in the base of Stalmize's cobbler shop, diffusing into the cramped darkness beneath the building. Pain pounded every muscle of Khitajrah's body. Her neck felt on fire from sleeping in the same curled position for the last two nights. The niche in the building's base that served as her hiding place left her no room to move or turn, and the urge to stretch had become an obsession. For three days, she had watched the city's crowds scurry about their business, dwindle to a trickle, then give way to only the ceaseless, pacing search of Stalmize's guardsmen. Now, as evening again gave way to darkness, she knew she would have to leave the tight safety of the hole.

Khitajrah's belly felt pinched and empty. Now that she had awakened, it gnawed incessantly at itself, reminding her that she had not eaten in days. Licking at the condensation on the boards had kept thirst at bay, but it did not ease the burning in her throat. Throughout her second day, smashed and aching beneath the shop, she had counted the patterns of the watch, noting that their search had become more haphazard and lax. That night, their patterns had grown farther apart, less tight. Apparently, they had turned the bulk of the troops elsewhere, guessing that she had escaped the city of Stalmize. Khitajrah hoped the guards had become sparser and even less alert this night.

Cautiously, ears attuned for movement, Khitajrah Harrsha's-widow backed through the crack and into Cobbler's Alley. Each movement rippled pain through her limbs, and a sensation of swirling pins and needles nearly felled her. She gritted her teeth, bulling through the many aches returning blood flow caused. In time, she knew, she would feel much better for the change in position. She drew her head out of the confining, damp darkness.

Once free, Khitajrah studied the alleyway. She found it unexpectedly bright, the dull gray of sunset rather than the moonlit night she had expected. She hesitated, at a crouch, as the throbbing settled into a quiet numbness. *Too early. There might still be stragglers on the streets.* She glanced back into the yawning blackness of her cubbyhole, hating the sight of it. Just the thought of crawling back into that self-imposed prison reawakened the ache of tortured muscles. She would rather take her chances on the street. She rose, the movement awakening soreness in her chest, abdomen, and neck that only time and food could heal. She pressed into the shadows of the wall, weaving a careful path along the cobbler's shop.

As Khitajrah reached the mouth of the alley, she heard booted footfalls clomping between the buildings.

Guards. Khitajrah flattened against the wall, waiting for them to pass. She had no doubt that every member of the city guard, and perhaps all of Stalmize's citizens, had been instructed to kill her on sight. She cringed, wondering how many innocent women had lost their lives because they resembled her or had once been her friends. Eastern law already allowed rape, murder, and other violence against its women. She hated the idea that the Eastlands' most cruel would use her disappearance as an excuse for their cold-blooded pleasure, but she dismissed the thought. People who would hold her crimes against all women would find other excuses to inflict their brutality. If not over her, they would simply find a different justification.

The guards passed, their footfalls fading to dim thumps that became eerily distanced from their echoes. Knowing the street they had just vacated would be safe until the next patrol, Khitajrah hurried out into it. Almost immediately, she collided with a boy moving as quickly in the opposite direction. Momentum sprawled them both. His woven sack fell, spilling bread and vegetables. From a broken crock, milk washed in pulses over the cobbles.

For an instant, they stared at one another. The boy's eyes widened in recognition. His lips parted.

Khitajrah moved first. Leaping over the scattered foodstuffs, she seized the child's arm, hauling him to his feet. The boy started a scream that Khitajrah's hand clamped to silence. "Quiet. Not a sound."

The boy struggled madly, doubling over to pull her off-balance, kicking backward at her legs.

Khitajrah sidestepped beyond his wildly flailing feet. "Be still. I'm not going to hurt you."

The boy twisted in her grip.

Khitajrah swore. Keeping her arm wrapped around the boy, she made a quick search of his pockets. Ignoring coins, marbles, and string, she found and drew his utility knife. She pressed the blade to his throat. "Be still, damn it. I'm not kidding. One more movement and I might just open your throat." It was an idle threat. Hunted and condemned to death, Khitajrah had no legal reason not to add murder to her list of capital crimes; but the pain of losing her own son still ached within her. She would not take the innocent child of another woman or man.

The boy froze in place.

Khitajrah glanced around the familiar street of the shopping district. Plain, flat-topped buildings stood, wedged between the crumbling minarets and spires of the older architecture. Streets radiated like the legs of a spider. Ancient roads crossed, branched, and fused with newer, making every part of the city look like a central square. All of the shops lay dark and closed for the night. "I won't hurt you. All I want is a promise that you won't scream."

The boy made a muffled sound beneath Khitajrah's hand.

"Just nod if you agree not to scream."

The boy hesitated. Then he made a slow, solid movement with his head.

Khitajrah released him.

The instant she freed him, the boy broke into a sprint, shrieking at the top of his lungs.

"Damn you." Hunger got the better of Khitajrah. She snatched up a slender, brown loaf of bread from the scattered remains of abandoned groceries, then ran in the other direction, ducking into a narrow alleyway. Shoving the bread into her belt and the knife into a pocket, she looked for one of the more decorative buildings. The tailor's shop, with its ledges and gargoyles, seemed the best choice. Using the cracked masonry and stone ornaments for toeholds, she clawed her way toward the rooftop.

Footsteps bounced through the maze of the Eastlands' royal city, all converging on the boy's cries for help. As the shouts and pounding drew closer, Khitajrah quickened her pace. Jagged edges of rock tore at her fingers. Her cloth shoes protected her toes, though they made purchase more difficult. Her left foot slipped. The remains of a ledge tore a hole in the cloth. The sudden jar of weight on her hands opened the knife wound across her fingers, and blood trickled along her fingers. She bit off a gasp of pain, flailing for a new toehold. The shoe flopped, useless on her foot. It slid nearly free.

"This way!" A bass voice rumbled through the alleyway, and running footsteps followed.

Khitajrah froze in place, toes cinched around the dangling shoe. Afraid to move, she rolled her gaze downward. Half a dozen guardsmen with swords bustled along the roadway beneath her. A cramp settled across Khitajrah's toes, raw agony. She felt the shoe slip further. She forced her grip tighter, silently mouthing a fervent prayer to Sheriva, though she expected little from a god whose laws had brought her to this state.

"Over here!" The guards passed beneath Khitajrah, making the correct turn into the street, though the boy's screams had ceased.

The shoe plummeted to the cobbles behind them, the soft patter of cloth hitting stone lost beneath the slam and echo of their footfalls. Khitajrah groped for and found a foothold with her toes. She scrambled to the roof.

Once there, Khitajrah gnawed at the bread, staring out over the city of her birth. Despite its familiarity, it looked strange and unwelcoming. The flowering mazes seemed without beginning or end, and the town itself spread cancer-like tendrils throughout what had once been woods and countryside. In the decade since the war had taken more than half of the male population, the city's sprawl had slowed. But repeated plantings of the same crops in the same fields had sucked all of the nutrients from the soil. In a constant attempt to escape the densest, oldest parts of the city, and its crumbling architecture, the citizens built more houses at the outskirts, impinging deeper onto pale, barren fields no longer able to provide sustenance. Nearly every forest had been burned or cut down to provide new land for the farmers to make as cold and sterile as their fields.

Khitajrah lowered her head, the tangled black locks falling into her eyes. Though she hated the ugliness the Eastern men inflicted upon its women, she could not help feeling a loyalty to the culture she had known since birth. For all of its evil, the Easterners lived by a rigid code of honor, ruled by a strict morality that the warlike Northmen considered immorality. Any man who wished to better his life or his lot could do so as long as it did not impinge on his neighbors, unhindered by the myriad ties to family and colleagues that burdened Northmen. Self-interest, the key to Eastern society, bore the name evil; while the Northmen's bonds to family and community made them good. In a way, Khitajrah believed, evil was another name for personal freedom. At least for the Eastlands' men.

Khitajrah knew that the Eastlands had honor, too, that every society lived within its rules. Only in her lifetime had lies, theft, and betrayal come to exist, and they had only become more than a shockingly rare occurrence since the Great War. Not so long ago, she could have trusted anyone's promise not to scream.

Khitajrah took larger bites of bread, the first morsel fueling a hunger that made the plain loaf taste honey-soaked. She could not recall having eaten anything so delicious, though she scarcely chewed in her rush to swallow. She glanced over the side of the building where a host of guardsmen examined the scattered remains of the boy's groceries. Suddenly, the boy's indiscretion had turned from danger to distraction. Smiling, Khitajrah stuffed the last of the loaf into her mouth and headed down the opposite side of the building.

Waves slammed the *Sea Seraph*'s hull, tossing the ship like flotsam. Her captain raced from one end of the slippery deck to the other, securing sails, clutching at the tiller, and lashing stray items to the rail. Poised at the bow, Colbey marveled at the agility of the elf trotting across his rollicking ship. Water darkened the captain's jerkin. His silk pantaloons had become dirty and tattered. Still, a smile graced his angular features.

The deck bucked like a half-broken stallion. Captain lost his footing, tumbling toward the deck. Colbey sprang forward, catching the elf just before he fell. The captain grunted his thanks, staggered to his feet, and dove for the jib sail as it tore free of its mounting.

Colbey's time sense told him that morning should have arrived, yet the clouds choked out the sun more completely

than they had the moon. Darkness veiled the sky from end
to end, broken by a sudden, jagged flash of lightning that revealed a shape in the distance.

Colbey shouted. "I—" Thunder crashed, and the old
Renshai saved the remainder of his sentence until the sound
rumbled to a conclusion. "I saw something ahead!" Even
without the thunder, the gale hurled the words back into his
face. The slap of waves against the hull and the pounding
drumbeat of the rain swallowed his cry. He could see the object more clearly now, a shimmering haze that stretched
from sea to sky.

Somehow, the captain heard Colbey. He came up beside
the Renshai and screamed a scarcely audible reply. "That's
it!" He had spoken in the Western tongue, but he quickly
switched to Northern. "Man the rudder, and set a course for
it." The elf lurched for the cabin, where Shadimar and his
wolf had been left sleeping. Surely, the storm had awakened
the Eastern Wizard, but he had wisely chosen to remain below decks.

Colbey fought his way aft across the wave-washed planks.
The deck pitched, tossing him against the rail. A jagged
burst of lightning lit his path, revealing the dark bulk of the
tiller. He lunged for it, catching it in both fists, then
slammed it against the stern. The bow lurched through mist
and rain, leaping for the glowing curtain. A pulse of white
light blinded Colbey, and he closed his lids against pain. Almost immediately, the sea went calm, as if the storm had
never existed.

Colbey opened his eyes, seeing only the colored afterimages the flash had carved onto his vision. He stared at the
tiller, waiting for the brilliant circles to fade. When they did,
he turned his gaze to a sky as smooth and blue as a sapphire.
The sun blazed down on the *Sea Seraph*. The sea mirrored
the deep, rich color of the sky. A breeze filled the sails, and
the sun warmed the deck. Under ordinary circumstances,
Colbey would have found the change pleasant. Now, the
breeze cut through his soggy tunic, its dryness icy cold. He
huddled over the tiller, with no idea in which direction to
take the tiny ship.

The captain emerged from the cabin. "Splendid, Colbey.
Thank you. Go get some comfortable clothes. You'll need
them."

Colbey accepted the invitation, letting the cryptic warning

that had followed pass unchallenged. He trotted below decks.

Shadimar glanced up from a thick tome that rested on the table. Secodon stood, tail wagging, beside his master. "Ah, Colbey. Good morning. I trust that you got a good night's rest before you went to help our captain with his ship?"

"Good enough," Colbey replied, though he had not slept at all. Many times in his life he had become engrossed in creating new sword maneuvers, or perfecting old ones, and day had passed to night, then back to day without his knowledge. He knew that, forced to face matters of any importance, he would find the strength and alertness he needed. Fatigue only made him less patient with long-winded liturgies from self-important speakers, simple matters twisted into emergencies by alarmists, and insincere politeness. Unfortunately, Colbey knew that a meeting with the Cardinal Wizards would probably mean dealing with all three things.

"Good." Shadimar closed the book. "You'll need your wits about you. To understand the nature of the tasks before you . . ."

Colbey tuned the lesson out, not even granting the Eastern Wizard the occasional grunt to acknowledge his words, if not his points. He walked to the foot of his cot, swung his pack onto the rumpled covers, and pawed through it for a dry shirt and breeks. The true measure of the tasks would come when he faced them. Until then, the Cardinal Wizards could talk about them forever. And Colbey suspected that they probably would.

A stroke of rebellion drove Colbey to choose the flashiest garb he carried: a red silk shirt, black breeks, and a wide sash to hold his swords. He pulled them on quickly, shoving both of his sheathed longswords through the loop on his right hip. Like all Renshai, he had trained equally with both hands, working one harder whenever it lagged behind the other.

Shadimar trailed off into silence, studying Colbey's choice of costume with obvious disapproval, though he said nothing about it. "I presume the ship's sudden steadiness means we passed through the portal?"

"That depends on whether 'passing through the portal' means suffering a stab of light that probably destroyed my sight until I'm a hundred."

Shadimar smiled. "That would be it."

"You could have warned me."

"What? And miss your endearing sarcasm?"

"Mmmm." Colbey let Shadimar's cutting witticism pass. He spread his wet clothing across the cot to dry. "Why is it you feel the need to detail the importance of the Tasks of Wizardry into infinity, but little things like blinding agony and souls becoming destroyed utterly slip your huge, perfect, Wizard mind?"

Shadimar rose, stretching his long, lean frame delicately and with dignity. He stood nearly a head taller than Colbey. The Renshai maneuvers relied on quickness instead of strength, and Colbey was not large in height or breadth. Still, he guessed that he probably outweighed the ancient Wizard who now answered his accusation. "When you become my age and you are burdened with the lives of thousands of men, present and future, the survival of the world itself, and the wishes of the gods, you may understand."

Colbey snorted. Suddenly, he thought he understood the gods' decision to allow mortals less than a century of life. Any more time would make the differences between elders and youths so great, they would lose any possibility for coherent communication. He wondered how the elves managed, guessing he would find the answer in the cyclical nature of their lives and deaths. Perhaps, their world simply did not change as quickly. "You may have outlived me by a century or two, but don't mistake me for a teenager. And what does it mean to 'pass through the portal'?"

Secodon stood, yawning, stretching each foreleg in turn. The ship jolted, and the wolf slipped, sprawling to the deck. He scrambled to his feet, looking around, as if to find the person who had tripped him.

Colbey took the sudden movement in stride.

Shadimar caught a steadying grip on the table. "It means we entered another world, a small one that holds only the Meeting Isle and the ocean around it. And that bump means we've arrived." Grabbing his pack, he strode from the cabin, Secodon trotting cautiously after him.

Colbey tossed his own pack across his shoulder, leaving his wet clothing in the *Sea Seraph*'s cabin to retrieve on the trip home. He followed the Eastern Wizard out onto the deck. The sun beamed down from a huge expanse of blue sky. Tide lapped at the shore and at the hull of the *Sea Seraph*. The captain had beached the ship on an island that

Colbey could see end to end. It held a single stone building at its center that appeared nearly as natural as the weeds surrounding it. Only the perfect rectangle of its shape and the obvious door destroyed the image of an ordinary rock formation on a deserted atoll.

Colbey leapt down to the beach. Shadimar and Secodon clambered after him. Grasses scratched through the openings in Colbey's sandals. A breeze stirred his gold-flecked, white hair. The sun shed warmth and light from a cloudless sky, uncomfortably hot to a Renshai who had so long known the frigid summers of the North. Despite the island's simplicity, its lack of trees, birds, and insects unsettled him.

Captain appeared from around the starboard side of the ship. "All ready?"

Shadimar nodded. "Thank you, Captain."

The elf shoved the bow free of the sand, seized the railing, and hauled himself back aboard. He waved a friendly good-bye. "When you need me, just call. I'll come as swiftly as I can." His gaze shifted from Shadimar to Colbey. "Good luck, Western Wizard. I'm looking forward to many more talks."

Colbey made a brisk, but friendly, gesture of farewell. The quiet austerity of the Wizards' Meeting Isle brought back all of the apprehension he had banished aboard the *Sea Seraph*. Despite Shadimar's long-winded and too frequent explanations, the practicalities and specific realities of the Tasks of Wizardry still escaped him. All he had were vague theories and grandiose descriptions of its deep significance to the Cardinal Wizards and to the world.

Shadimar turned toward the cottage at the center of the island. "Let's go." He clapped a hand to Colbey's shoulders, the touch the first contact in a long time that felt sincere. A gesture of friendship, it did not patronize or direct. For a change, it did not seem geared to remind Colbey that he was younger or less experienced, ignorant of the wonders that came with the passage of millennia of wisdom. It was a gesture between equals, and it awakened faded memories of the time before Trilless had made her accusations against Colbey and before Shadimar had tried to kill him for a misinterpreted prophecy, a time when he and Shadimar had shared a brotherhood and a friendship.

In silence, the two men walked to the dwelling. Just before the door, Shadimar stopped and turned to face his companion. He opened his mouth, clearly to speak words of encouragement or to once more explain the significance and urgency of the tasks before Colbey. Apparently realizing another lecture would only alienate the Renshai, he echoed the captain instead. "Good luck." Then he seized the handle of the plain, granite door and hauled it open with a creak of old hinges.

Instantly, the sweet aroma of honey, sassafras, and fresh bread assailed Colbey. Inside, a fire burned in a hearth carved into the farthest wall. Though the building lacked a chimney, no smoke obscured the room, and the fire burned without an odor. A table filled most of the remaining space. To Colbey's left, Carcophan sat. His salt-and-pepper hair hugged his scalp, a dark contrast to his yellow-green eyes, clean-shaven face, and deeply impressed scowl. His tunic stretched taut over a bulky chest and widely-braced shoulders. His large hands rested on the table, curled closed. The frayed remnants of calluses still marred the edges of his fingers. Once, Colbey felt certain, the Southern Wizard had learned the art of war.

At the exact opposite end of the longest part of the table, a shapely woman perched on a chair. White robes fluttered around her slender form, the skirts cascading from her seat like sea foam. Long white hair framed delicate, timeless features, and her blue eyes, though watery with age, seemed kind.

One other occupied the room, a man familiar to Colbey. Mar Lon Davrinsson sat in a shadowed corner, strumming his compact, ten-stringed instrument and mouthing silent lyrics. He wore his brown hair short and without adornment. His hazel eyes rolled upward. Finding Colbey's gaze upon him, Mar Lon smiled in greeting. Colbey stared back. The bard's presence among somber, genteel Wizards shocked him. Experience had shown him that the Cardinal Wizards rarely lowered themselves to consort with mortals, except for an occasional champion or where the prophecies they were bound to fulfill drove them to the association.

"Mar Lon. What a pleasant surprise." Colbey ignored the Great Wizards to address the only mortal in the room. "Why aren't you in Béarn protecting King Sterrane?" He asked from genuine concern, not the desire for small talk. In the years before the Western high king had claimed his throne, Sterrane had traveled with Colbey and Mitrian. His simple

justice and fierce loyalty had endeared him to the remaining
Renshai. It had become Mar Lon's job not only to protect
King Sterrane from usurpers, but also from his own childlike
innocence.

Every gaze riveted on Colbey. Shadimar's hand slipped
from the Renshai's shoulders and gripped his arm in warning. The bard lowered his instrument, glancing from Wizard
to Wizard as if seeking permission to speak.

No one addressed the question.

Apparently, Mar Lon accepted the Cardinal Wizards' silence as consent. He sighed, placing the *lonriset* into playing
position. Odin's curse on his ancestors drove each eldest
child, male or female, to a constant and desperate search for
knowledge that he could only impart to others through his
music. Though the curse did not include his dealings with
Wizards, Mar Lon found it easier to respond to Colbey's
question by singing:

> *"A man named Jahiran became the first bard*
> *His line cursed by Odin: Béarn's king to guard,*
> *All knowledge to seek and for all lore to long*
> *But never to teach it, except in a song.*

> *"When the great times in history are known to occur,*
> *The current bard will be there, you I can assure.*
> *Unless his vow to Béarn keeps him away*
> *Then his firstborn may replace him for affairs of that day.*

> *"As of the time this song is being written*
> *Mar Lon the bard has yet to be smitten.*
> *Without a marriage and with no wife to bear it*
> *Mar Lon is damn glad that he has no heir yet."*

Despite its silliness, haphazard rhyme scheme, and obvious instantaneous authorship, the song spanned three octaves
and its melody was striking. Mar Lon hit every note and
chord with solid assuredness. Colbey admired the decades of
constant and dedicated practice that had created a talent that
all who heard enjoyed, although few could understand the
bard's sacrifice. Mar Lon had told Colbey the basis for his
musical skill came from his inheritance of the bard's curse,
but Colbey knew the fine details of his talent could only be
mastered through years of daily practice.

Throughout the concert, the Cardinal Wizards sat in impassive silence. Time meant little to them. Apparently, they chose to indulge the exchange between the mortal and the one of their own closest to his previous mortality. As the last notes fell from the *lonriset,* Trilless addressed Colbey. "Welcome, Western Wizard."

With a last squeeze of reassurance, Shadimar strode around Trilless to a vacant side of the table, leaving the seat nearest the door for Colbey.

The old Renshai turned his gaze on the speaker. Though wrinkled, her face still held a mature beauty. Its set and the pallor of her skin revealed her Northern heritage, though her hair had gone fully silver. Her white robes against pale skin, locks, and eyes made her seem ghostlike and frail. In Northern society, white symbolized coldness as well as purity, and Colbey found equal amounts of both in the woman's manner. "Spare me your insincere greetings, Trilless. The army of Northmen, Valr Kirin, and the demon you sent to kill me told me what you really think of me."

Carcophan laughed regally.

Trilless glared, first at Colbey, then, with more venom, at her evil opposite. She returned her gaze to the Renshai, and her features softened. "A logical mistake and one I've come to regret. No harm done."

"No harm done!" The cavalier dismissal outraged Colbey. "Your Northmen destroyed the city that harbored me, slaughtering its army and the finest strategist the West ever had." Memories of Santagithi's gutted town surfaced immediately, followed by images of the final battle in a cave in the Granite Hills. Colbey and Santagithi had held off a troop of Northern warriors to allow the last handful of Santagithi's citizens to escape. Santagithi had died in the battle, and Colbey had spent days in coma. An angry, red scar still spanned his chest in a long diagonal. "Your Northmen hounded us across the continent. Because of you, the world lost two Renshai and two of the dearest, closest friends the Renshai ever had." Colbey avoided the details of those others' deaths, afraid the memories might sever his control. Until he took the oaths and vows that accompanied the Tasks of Wizardry, nothing but common sense could keep him from attacking the Northern Sorceress with a sword that could kill her. At one time, he would have cherished the opportunity.

Now, he struggled against his need for vengeance for the sake of mankind and Odin's laws.

Carcophan laughed again. His receding, black-speckled hair lay brushed flat against his scalp, and his features appeared to be permanently sneering. "The man has a point, dear colleague. Had you gathered as much information as I did, you would have realized that my champion was going to come to me, without need for me to seek him. Had you watched for him to come to me, instead of assuming, you might have killed my champion rather than wasting your time and resources chasing down a colleague."

The tactless coldness of Carcophan's reference to Episte all but shattered Colbey's already tenuous control. He called upon heroic depths of composure to keep from responding with violence he might regret.

Immediately, Trilless turned her attention from Colbey to Carcophan. "You poisonous snake. You creature of evil. I spent months in research, tracking down the tiniest footnote in a text so old it crumbled with every touch."

Carcophan grinned. His tiny eyes glittered. "I read, too. Then I had the sense and the competence to use my skill to confirm what I found."

Colbey remained silent, the Wizards' bickering cutting through his rage, his point only half made.

Trilless tapped a fist on the tabletop. "Maybe I care enough about our world and its law not to risk summoning demons and their chaos just to clarify questions."

"So, instead, you take a bigger risk and loose one to slaughter the Western Wizard."

Incredulity replaced Colbey's ire. He had wanted to agitate the Northern and Southern Wizards and to force them to face the consequences of their misconceptions. However, the two seemed quite capable of inciting one another without his help. On man's world, each was charged with destroying the cause of the other. Colbey guessed they probably had spent their rare moments together through eternity baiting one another. He took his seat, suddenly enjoying the spat.

Trilless answered Carcophan's accusation. "I constrained that demon. And I kept its task specific. It could have harmed no one else."

"No one else but the Western Wizard. How clever."

Trilless smoothed a hand through her hair, her placid demeanor unbroken despite the Southern Wizard's sarcasm.

"Who could have guessed Tokar would do something so stupid? Destroy his own apprentice. Make a Renshai a Wizard." She lowered her hand, eyes flashing at the ludicrousness of Tokar's actions. "And don't tell me *you* knew Colbey was the Western Wizard. If you had, you would have also known that Harval would come into existence." She made a vague gesture that came nowhere near its target, yet they all knew she indicated the Sword of Power at Colbey's hip. "And you might have used what little judgment you have *not* to summon the Black Sword."

As Colbey became more relaxed and less irritable, the knowledge gained during his years with General Santagithi allowed him to see that the Wizard-opposites' quibbling went far beyond childish name-calling. They read one another's strategies, ideologies, and methods in every phrase; and the seeds of future war were born from every gibe they traded.

"Three Swords, it took, not two." Carcophan kept his voice low, pitched to provoke. "You called . . ."

Mar Lon strummed the *lonriset*'s strings harder, and a minor chord rang out over the argument. His crisp tenor rose over it in new song. ". . . the meeting began with great pomp and fanfare. Wizards squabbled like children where each sat in his chair . . ."

Trilless and Carcophan went suddenly quiet, and all eyes swiveled to the bard.

". . . They argued of demons, each seething and blathering. Forgetting, in anger, the cause of their gathering." Mar Lon looked up. He lowered the instrument with a brisk gesture that parodied embarrassment. "I'm sorry. Was I playing too loud?"

Colbey smiled. In the past, he and Mar Lon had had a relationship based on mutual suspicion. Colbey's background and history unnerved the bard, especially when the Renshai came too close to King Sterrane. And Mar Lon's mistrust had naturally made him unlikable to Colbey. Suddenly, Colbey developed a new respect for the bard's style.

"You'd take about half a heartbeat to kill," Carcophan said.

Even Colbey knew the threat was idle. To kill any mortal meant risking the possibility of jeopardizing future prophecies. The law allowed the Cardinal Wizards to drive mortals into killing one another. Rarely did those rules allow them to interfere more directly.

"Colbey, you have seven tests to complete." Shadimar redirected the conversation by attending to the task at hand, too dignified to care that the diversion was shallow and obvious. The tonelessness of his voice suggested a standard speech given to all apprentices at this point in the proceedings. "Successful completion of each yields a ring of Wizardry. Once you have any given ring, the task is considered completed, and the next begins."

Carcophan and Trilless regained appropriate decorum, abandoning their differences to fix their attention on Shadimar.

"When you pass the seventh and last of the tasks ..." Shadimar glanced sharply at the other Wizards, as if to challenge either to turn his "when" to an "if." "When you pass the last task, you may be offered an eighth. You must refuse it."

Colbey raised his brows, intrigued. This was the first time anyone had mentioned this complication.

Again, Shadimar looked from Wizard to Wizard, his expression imploring. When no one else spoke, Shadimar leaned across the table, as if to whisper. His thoughts and manner struck Colbey first. The Eastern Wizard apparently struggled with a desperate concern he saw no way to defuse. A thought drifted from Shadimar to Colbey, obviously without intention. *I know Colbey, and, in this, he is like a child. The more I forbid it, the more it will entice him. Yet to send him in unwarned and unprepared for the Guardian of the Task's tactics will doom him for certain.* "There is a guardian who will become insistent. He will offer ultimate power. You must resist him, though it is not my right to tell you why. Refuse repeatedly, and he will send you back to us, perhaps with some crucial information or advice that you or we can use to avert the *Ragnarok.* If you attempt the task, his advice will become forever lost. As will you."

Colbey gleaned far more than just Shadimar's words. The intensity of the Eastern Wizard's thoughts sent them wafting clearly to Colbey. He understood that, over the millennia, no one who had survived to become a Cardinal Wizard had ever attempted the eighth task. He also learned Shadimar's theory, nurtured by his collective consciousness. Shadimar believed that Odin had added the eighth task to protect the

gods, the world, and the system of Wizardry. Anyone interested in ultimate power could not be trusted to obey the
many laws that hemmed in and restricted the Wizards, and
Shadimar guessed that the simple act of accepting the eighth
task meant failing it. To his mind, the eighth task was, itself,
the decision of whether or not to attempt an eighth task.

Colbey considered the possibility. It did seem exactly the
sort of warped logic that the Cardinal Wizards used, to his
continued annoyance. And Odin's wisdom seemed to work
in much the same way.

"There is no eighth task," Carcophan added. "Better to
think of it that way."

Trilless nodded her support. Colbey hoped Mar Lon had
captured the evil and good Wizards' concurrence in song.
Their agreement on any matter seemed like a grand event
that should have documentation.

Though no one had actually asked a question, the three
studied Colbey in silence, brows raised. He saw no reason to
delay the inevitable. Every Wizard had far more patience
than he did. "It doesn't matter," Colbey said, then explained.
"Like all Renshai, I rely only on the strength of my own
mind and body. These are eternal." He raised his hands to
indicate self-reliance. "Your powers are not your own. They
come from the creatures you summon, your demons and
your Power Swords."

Mar Lon hunched over his instrument, stunned into mo-
tionlessness. A moment later, his lips moved furiously. He
drew paper and a stylus from his tunic, as if to capture the
many thoughts that came too quickly for his mind alone to
retain.

Carcophan's reply was abrupt and angry. "You speak of
eternity, yet how long do Renshai live? Mortal strength withers and dies."

Shadimar remained leaning forward. His hands slipped
from the table, and he rummaged for something in his
pocket as he spoke. Knowing Colbey better, he chose a different tack. "These tasks won't make you a Cardinal Wizard.
You are already one, and there's no place any more for personal grudges. You don't have to like Carcophan or Trilless.
In fact, you'll work against them, and their successors, every
moment for centuries. But if you refuse to take your title,
the people who suffer will be those who follow neutrality.
My people. And your own . . ." He pulled a huge, oval sap-

phire from his pocket, a gem Colbey recognized as the Pica Stone. Once it had belonged to the Renshai, a symbol of their greatness and durability. Before the Renshai had conquered it and taken the Pica, the town of Shadimar's birth had kept it as their own talisman. After the destruction of the Renshai, Shadimar had engineered the gem back into his own hands. As a gesture of peace, Colbey had allowed the Eastern Wizard to keep the sapphire without fear of retaliation, and they had made their pact of brotherhood over it.

Colbey scowled, curious as to why Shadimar had chosen that moment to remind him of a blood-sworn relationship that Shadimar had broken.

Shadimar placed the Pica on the table. ". . . including the Renshai." He paused for a moment, head lowered, as if in consideration. A strongly directed thought radiated from Shadimar, obscure in its translation and underlying intention. Surely, he had not meant it for Colbey.

Accustomed to accidentally reading private ideas and emotions from others, it occurred to Colbey too late that the thought seemed too deliberate to have wafted inadvertently from the Eastern Wizard. *He didn't mean it for me. But the others in the room are Cardinal Wizards as well, the only ones, besides me, with whom Shadimar could choose to communicate in this fashion.* Colbey went wary. He glanced at Carcophan. The Evil One returned the look, his lips tight in a quiet smirk. His yellow-green eyes found and held the Northman's blue-gray ones, and the gaze they exchanged held candor and danger.

Shadimar seemed oblivious. He stroked the Pica Stone with both hands, his fingers brushing and closing in grand gestures that reminded Colbey of swimming. "Carcophan's Eastlanders may have lost the war, but they've destroyed their lands and will come again for ours. Trilless has infused her rigid goodness all through the northernmost parts of the Westlands. I am not strong enough to stand alone between good and evil. Neither of them has use for our people."

Colbey turned his attention to Trilless. She had a coiled restlessness about her that Carcophan had lacked. Colbey wondered whether Shadimar's message had gone only to her, or if both had received it. Carcophan's war training would make him the better at hiding active intentions. Trusting that he could move faster than any other in the room, Colbey prepared for defense only mentally. And waited.

Shadimar's voice dropped so low Colbey could no longer differentiate the syllables. Just as he began to question whether the Eastern Wizard spoke true words at all, Shadimar again became clearly audible. "Trilless will slay kindly. She'll infuse the West with diseases that kill in sleep. Carcophan's followers will capture our people, then slaughter them in agony and dance over their corpses. Either way, they won't reach Valhalla."

Rage again built in Colbey. He reassured himself with the knowledge that no one, Wizard-mediated or otherwise, could kill the Renshai without a fight.

Shadimar removed his hand from the Pica Stone. He stared at Colbey until the Renshai pulled his gaze from the Northern Sorceress to meet Shadimar's stony, gray eyes. "You will learn that Wizardry encompasses far more than trickery and summonings. Though it is traditional, no one ever asked that you become a user of magics, only that you dedicate the skills you do possess to the cause of the world and to the true gods, the same gods you've worshiped all your life." Shadimar looked quickly at each Cardinal Wizard in turn, excluding only Mar Lon. "The future lies in what you see in the Pica. Good luck, my friend."

Colbey's attention strayed naturally to the sapphire. Streaks and flecks of brown, green, and yellow obscured the blue. The colors swirled in a cryptic blotch, then settled into a pattern. Colbey squinted, attending closer to unite the sequence of lines and curves into a complete picture, much the way he would focus on the whole of an artist's canvas rather than individual brush strokes. While his eyes picked out the image of a forest, he remained alert for movement. Still, the quiet, coordinated motions of the Cardinal Wizards did not seem bold enough for threat, and Colbey sensed no violence. The attack caught him only half prepared.

Something unseen struck Colbey from behind, hard enough to drive his gut into the edge of the table. Breath rushed from his lungs. Yet Colbey still had the wherewithal to rise and spin, whipping Harval from its sheath in a tiny fraction of an eye blink. His gaze and attack met nothing. The force had no form. It surged around him, its screams filling his ears, then whirled him into wild circles. The Meeting Isle's room disappeared, replaced by an endless void, without sound, shape, or color.

Colbey fought for control, gaining it only for himself and

his sword. His world still spun, but the movement came
from without. He managed to maintain his equilibrium,
keeping his focus fully internal, orienting himself and waiting for the world to re-form around him.

The spinning stopped abruptly. The instant it did, a new
reality blinked to life around Colbey Calistinsson. He stood
on solid ground, hard mud smothered beneath a carpet of ancient leaves. Towering elms surrounded him, a vast forest
that seemed endless, with weeds, copses, and vines filling
the spaces between the trunks. Sunlight sprinkled between
the sparse upper branches, filtering down to the undergrowth.

Though Colbey had managed to brace his mind and body,
his stomach lurched from the combined effects of the Cardinal Wizards' magic. He controlled its heaving mentally,
stroking absently at it through his shirt. Then, a rustle in the
brush froze him. He levered backward, pressing his back
against a trunk, and his right hand found the hilt of his other
sword.

Suddenly, a creature stepped from a tangle of vines. It resembled a man, but it stood shorter, and its back hunched
like an angry cat's. Scrawny arms dangled to its knees, tapering to feline claws. Red hair sprouted in clumps from its
oversized head. Two eyes, like heated coals, glared at the
Renshai.

"Who are you?" Colbey asked, politely avoiding the more
obvious questions of its parentage and right to existence. He
kept the swords between it and himself, his stance wholly
defensive. It was not Colbey's way to initiate battles, only to
finish them.

The beast made a noise deep in its throat that sounded like
"quarack" to Colbey's ears. He suspected that this was its
cry, not its name, but he did not ponder. His mind told him
two things at once. First, the creature had no intelligent
thought wafting from it, only a promise of swift and sudden
violence. It saw the old Renshai as prey. Second, movement
thumped, brushed, and rattled through the forest for as far as
Colbey could see, hear, or sense. This creature, whatever its
name or origin, had hundreds or thousands of companions.
And every one hungered for blood.

CHAPTER 4

The Tasks of Wizardry

Khitajrah Harrsha's-widow padded along one of the straight mud pathways of Stalmize's graveyard, pale mud sucking at her bare feet. The cemetery perched on a hill that had once stood far from the city, before the homes and shops had penetrated into the crippled farmland and forests. Now, it stood just beyond the last, sparse dwellings. Soon, Khitajrah guessed, the cemetery would become a part of the city. Stalmize would swallow the corpses of its citizens and move on, collecting ever more of the surrounding countryside, and the dead would become as forgotten as the central, older portions of the city.

Khitajrah had not entered the cemetery in the decade since her sons' and husband's ashes had found their final rests, beneath the scarlet shafts that marked them as heroes in Sheriva's war. As she headed from the entrance toward the middle of the graveyard, she glanced over the rows of painted metal shafts that denoted the remains of each cremated corpse. Most of these were green, the color indicating a natural death, by illness, accident, or legal dispute. Those who had dedicated their lives to Sheriva, through his churches, lay beneath markers of royal blue. War heroes' graves bore the blood-colored markers that drew the eye, and black shafts dishonored the criminals and cowards. Benches lined the walkway, becoming older and more ornate, though crumbling, the farther she went.

Khitajrah paused at the central mausoleum that honored Sheriva's chosen, the dead kings, including the wild, granite horse that marked Siderin's grave site. She hesitated, not to gawk but to think. From the center, eight pathways radiated, like spokes. The north and south pathways led to vaulted exits. The other six ended dead, against an enclosing stone wall. Her husband's grave lay down one of these. Ordinarily, the position of the sun would have reminded her of his loca-

tion. Now, dawn washed the darkened sky a uniform red,
scarcely bearing enough light for her to see her way, let
alone to determine it.

At length, Khitajrah recalled that the general-king's horse
faced the graves of his high lieutenants, and she headed in
the indicated direction. It was not her husband's tomb that
she sought. She had laid him to rest too many years ago, and
her memories had become as old and treasured as her attraction to the deeper parts of Stalmize. Women did not get
grave sites or markers, but the diggers did try to keep sons
and fathers in the same location. She had seen Bahmyr, still
and bleeding, in the women's court and believed him dead.
Yet she needed to know for certain.

Although Khitajrah had had difficulty finding the correct
path, once there she knew precisely when she had reached
the familiar plot. The twin red markers of her oldest and
youngest sons brought tears to her eyes, blurring the names
inscribed. She pictured Nichus, the eldest, short and broad
like his grandfather and always full of wit. She thought of
the baby, Ellbaric, only twelve at his death. Paler than his
brothers, he had sported brown hair instead of black and
soft, doelike eyes. Always serious, he had penned poetry and
joined a tiny group of young peace supporters led by a Western musician, until the war had claimed his loyalty and his
life.

Grief seared Khitajrah, making her forget the throbbing of
her muscles and the ache of the knife wound across her
hand. She had to force her gaze onward, and what she saw
there surprised her. At first, she thought the next grave site
was empty, without a marker. Then, her gaze carved through
the darkness, outlining a black shaft nearly lost in the dusk.
She froze in place, staring until her eyes finally made out the
letters she already knew she would find: Bahmyr Harrsha's-
son.

For three days, Khitajrah had known her last son was
dead. Huddled beneath the cobbler's shop, she had mourned
him with tears that had stung her eyes to fiery redness. Yet
the reality of his grave proved too much. She collapsed to
the bench, sobs wracking her body and grief suffocating the
bittersweet memories her other sons' markers had dragged to
the surface.

For some time, Khitajrah lay, while dawn turned the sky
from red to gray. Finally, she managed to raise her head, and

her gaze found the second marker, that of her husband Harrsha. Someone had painted over the scarlet honor that had denoted the high lieutenant's grave. It now lay as flat and black as Bahmyr's, except between the letters of his name, where the vandal had not bothered to carefully blot out the remaining spots of red.

Although the agony of Bahmyr's death ached more deeply, Khitajrah focused on the painted marker. This, at least, gave her a target for her rage. She gripped the metal shaft in both hands and pulled. Hammered by the same blacksmith who made many of the Eastlands' swords, the marker felt as heavy and sturdy as a blade. Though unsharpened, the edges dug into Khitajrah's palms. Bracing her feet, she hauled at the obscene steel stake, needing to get it as far from the remains of her family as possible. Ground shifted beneath the deeply buried point. Then, suddenly, it tore free.

The abrupt change in resistance sent Khitajrah staggering backward. She scrambled for balance, catching it with an agile back-step, her hands still winched around the stake. She loosened her grip, studying the lines of purple-red blood welling beneath her skin, directly matching the edges of the marker. Dirt clung to the tapering barb. She kicked it free.

A man's voice startled Khitajrah. "Ah, so the pig comes when you lure it with garbage."

Khitajrah whirled to face the speaker, the stake clutched defensively in her fist. Two men stood on the path, between her and the central hub of the radiating grave sites. She recognized them at once, the way a deer knows the scent of cougar. The larger, Diarmad, had initiated the blame-laying against her husband. The other, Waleis, had brought the charges against her in the women's court. Both had slaughtered Bahmyr, using knives from behind, while her son had fought an honest battle against guardsmen's swords.

The two men closed in on Khitajrah, each with a hand on his sword hilt. Diarmad remained directly in front of her. Waleis circled, trapping her between himself and the graves and benches. Diarmad spoke again. "The hunt is over, Khita. We've found you, and we have the right to execute your sentence. The law demands that you yield willingly."

Khitajrah said nothing, feigning calm, the stake lax in her grip. Against swords in veterans' hands, it would prove little more than no weapon at all, yet she clung to it. Her sense of honor told her that she had no choice but to submit, yet hatred forbade it. The same burning ember that had driven her to petty theft and urging uprising, that had goaded her to resist her sentencing in the courtroom, flared into a wild bonfire. Bahmyr had given his life for hers, and he would not die in vain. *It should have gone the other way. I should have and would have traded my life for any of my sons'.*

Diarmad drew his sword. "Come here."

"Wait," Khitajrah said, needing time to think. To run would be folly. Unless she pushed directly past them, she could only corner herself against the outer wall. She stalled, forming images of the graveyard in her mind.

Diarmad took another step toward her, his huge bulk silhouetted against the grayness, his Eastern-dark features lost in the lingering night. "You may grovel. It is expected."

The suggestion only fanned the growing fire of Khitajrah's anger. Suddenly, a presence sparked to life within her, and she no longer felt alone. Though she knew she must be imagining the other, it gave her strength. She shouted. "Expected only by a coward who doesn't know me. Did you show this same courage in the war? Tell me, how many unarmed civilians did you slaughter?"

Red tinged Diarmad's features. His stance tightened, wholly on the offensive. "You're under sentence of execution, Khita. You're walking the borders of disobedience."

Walking the borders? Had Khitajrah felt any less desperate, she would have laughed. The thing inside her mind throbbed in amusement. "And you're walking the borders of manhood. At least my husband bravely faced the woman who killed him, weapon to weapon. And she was a Renshai warrior."

Waleis watched the exchange, open-mouthed, hand still on his hilt.

Diarmad scowled, his face twisted and ugly with rage. "She was not bound under Eastern law and sentenced to die."

"Warriors fight. Cowards make excuses." Khitajrah shoved the sharpened grave marker through her sash with a grand gesture that hid the motion of slipping the utility knife she had taken from the boy into her hand. She kept the hilt curled against her palm, fingers spread and bent to hide it. The blade rested comfortably against her forearm. "All I ask is for a chance to die in fair combat. Nowhere does our law say I can't ask that nor that you can't grant it."

"Nor does it say I must." Diarmad opened his mouth to say more, but Khitajrah interrupted.

"True, our law allows your cowardice, if you so choose." She smiled slightly. "My husband earned this for dying at the hands of a warrior." She gestured to the vandalized stake with her free hand. "If you're too afraid to face a peasant woman weapon to weapon, I hope there's enough black paint in all of Stalmize to soak your grave."

Diarmad's mouth snapped closed so suddenly, his teeth clicked audibly. He motioned briskly to Waleis. "Give her your sword."

"What? But ... ?" Waleis started, but Diarmad waved him silent.

"Give her the damned sword!" he roared, then addressed Khitajrah. "I had thought to make this quick and painless. For your impudence, you will know every agony and indignity we can inflict on you."

Deep within Khitajrah, the thread of unidentifiable being laughed, its disdain transforming Diarmad's threat to a child's bluster. Its presence strengthened her, hammering thoughts through Khitajrah's mind that defied centuries of law, always before accepted without question. It defined every indecency of which even the evil Easterners knew only the barest trifle: lies, blasphemy, and betrayal. Its surge nearly stole Khitajrah's focus. Though bold, her words sounded strange in her own ears. "Be cruel, then. I would rather this than a helpless death, without honor."

Diarmad jerked his head toward Waleis, again wordlessly commanding him. This time, the smaller veteran obeyed. He drew his sword one-handed, holding the other arm out before him, his elbow crooked. Taking the blade, he laid the sword across the level surface formed by his other arm, parodying a servant offering a fine wine to a king for inspection. He kept his movements bold and deliberate, a mockery. Neither soldier could see a woman as a threat.

Khitajrah stepped up to Waleis, his position forcing her close to claim the sword. She could see the raised track of a war scar across his cheeks and the bridge of his nose. His black eyes seemed depthless. She took the hilt in her left hand.

Waleis tightened his grip on the blade, lips bunching into

a smirk. Fully in control, he teased. Clearly, he had not yet chosen whether or not to actually let her have the weapon.

Khitajrah made the decision for him. She whipped up her right hand, slashing the knife across his fingers, feeling the blade gouge flesh to grate against tendon and bone.

Waleis screamed, instinctively releasing the sword and leaping backward. His retreat gave Khitajrah the range she needed. Dropping the knife, she wrapped both fists around his sword hilt. Placing her weight on her back foot, she reversed the motion of the heavy blade. It caught him across the throat, a slice without power. Yet the razor sharp edge did its work. Blood fountained from a severed artery, and the soldier crashed to the dirt.

"Demons!" Diarmad's expletive combined shock, rage, and disbelief. All of his war training could not have prepared him for blatant deceit. For an instant, he hesitated.

Khitajrah seized the moment. She ran. Horror chilled through her, and she could scarcely believe what she had done. Her bare feet sank into the mud. It clutched and clung, hampering every movement, and each sprinting step left a massive hole in her wake. *This is madness. I'm running toward a wall.* Khitajrah knew she had to change her course, or she would corner herself, but she saw no other direction to run in except toward Diarmad.

Apparently, the soldier had paused to help his dying companion because, when he shouted, his voice came from farther away than she expected. "It's futile, you wretched, murdering *frichen-karboh!* Give up now, and I'll kill you cleanly, though you don't deserve it."

Guile. Use guile. In a straight fight, he'll kill you. Though the thought came from Khitajrah's mind, she did not recognize it as her own. Desperation sped her thoughts. A plan formed, wholly her own, yet deeply-ingrained honor forced her to discard it.

Do it, Khita. The command came to Khitajrah more in picture concepts than words.

She argued back, certain she had gone insane. *The law forbids . . .*

Piss on the law.

The world is law. Law is everything.

You rallied women, Khita. You killed a defenseless man. You've already abandoned law.

No more. What I did was wrong.

He killed your son.

The words rekindled the boiling torrent of her rage. Khitajrah struggled against the release from honor her anger promised. *No excuse.*

They both killed Bahmyr.

Hatred speared through Khitajrah, shaking her control. She clung to her honor, dredging a response from the deepest core of her being. *The crime I committed shouldn't exist. A mind capable of creating dishonor must be destroyed.*

The being hesitated. *Where did that come from?*

I don't know, Khitajrah admitted. Other certainties followed as swiftly. Though she had never thought of them before, the ideas felt wholly hers, in a way those of the goading presence never could. *The world is law. It is not prepared to stand against lies and deceptions. I could destroy all of mankind.* Terror chilled through her, and her steps slowed.

Think of the power! The alien presence echoed through Khitajrah's mind. She shrank from its promise.

I don't seek power. I don't want it. Khitajrah rejected the need with a will so primal she would not have battled it, even had she wanted to.

Do it, Khita! Live, and I will tell you how to bring Bahmyr back to life.

Hope cut through Khitajrah's distress. She quickened her run until she felt as if she flew. She took the remnants of her torn shoe from her pocket, wrapping it around a coin for weight. Then, just beyond sight of her pursuer, she dropped the sword on the pathway. She hurled the rag-wrapped coin to the opposite side of the pathway.

A dozen more running steps brought her to the cemetery wall. She sprang to one of the decorative benches that lined the walk, doubling back over her trail without leaving a print. Mud from her feet broke loose with each movement, but she trusted the last lingering darkness to hide the traces. The huge holes on the muddy path would surely hold Diarmad's attention more. Once back to the place where she had tossed sword and shoe, she ducked behind the bench and waited.

Khitajrah's vigil was short. Diarmad appeared, following her trail with ease, his own sword readied in his fist. Apparently noticing Waleis' sword in his path, he stopped, surely recognizing it instantly. A smile inched across his features.

Without a sword, they both knew she had almost no chance at all to put up any kind of fight.

Soundlessly, Khitajrah pulled Harrsha's grave marker from her sash. It would not last long against honed and tempered steel, but it might serve its purpose. She had had little choice but to use the better weapon as a distraction. Nothing less would have drawn Diarmad's attention.

Diarmad crouched, reaching for the fallen sword. He kept his attention fixed on the shoe, studying it through gray dawn, blithely turning his back to the real threat. He kept his own weapon clenched in his right hand.

Khitajrah raised the marker and sprang for his back.

Some sound, motion, or soldier's instincts caused Diarmad to twist toward her. He raised his sword to block.

Instantly, Khitajrah changed her target. The point of the marker cut across the back of his hand, drawing blood. The sword fell from his fingers.

Khitajrah lunged as Diarmad rolled. The marker stabbed through empty air.

The soldier scooped up Waleis' weapon, catching it in his injured sword hand. "Sheriva's damnation, you bitch! The god will curse you, and you'll live out eternity in withering agony."

Bahmyr had taught Khitajrah never to talk in battle. Though she believed she already had Sheriva's support and his voice in her head, she did not return Diarmad's gibes. Instead, she snatched up his fallen weapon, facing him sword to sword, the honest battle neither of them had wanted. Blood ebbed from the man's hand, staining his hilt and fingers the scarlet of the heroes' markers.

Diarmad cut for Khitajrah's head, splashing his own blood in a wide arc. Khitajrah dodged beneath the stroke, then hammered for his injured fingers. He jerked backward, saving his hand, but her sword slammed against his hilt. Though her blow lacked power, blood slicked his grip. The collision, though slight, sent the sword sliding from his fist.

Diarmad dove for his weapon. Khitajrah continued her cut. The sharpened edge of the soldier's sword in her fist opened his shirt and tore through his abdomen. He crashed to the ground, shrieking.

Khitajrah back-stepped, sides heaving as much from fury as fatigue. "You bastard! You killed my son! You dishonored my husband and my son." She shoved the sword through her sash, oblivious to the bloody trail it smeared across her clothing. The presence applauded her work, though she did not share its enthusiasm, and it told her to let the enemy die in slow agony.

Khitajrah's conscience would not allow it, though her rage still drove her to one last act of vengeance. Seizing the painted black grave marker, she drove it through Diarmad's throat.

Diarmad's screams turned into a watery choke, then ceased abruptly. His eyes remained opened, as if to stare at the stake that now marked his death, if not his future grave.

The sight revolted Khitajrah. She collapsed, vomiting on the cemetery pathway. The hatred she had held against these men dulled to an ache, but it did not disappear. She turned it inward, despising the deed, the flaw in herself that had allowed her to defy laws millennia old, and the price her lapse might cost the world.

Within her, the alien creature seemed to weaken, and it lunged for the grip her dispersing rage had lost it. *There is more, Khitajrah. Much more.*

No, she responded weakly, the questions she had tossed aside converging on her at once. *I'm not crazy. You're not just a part of me. Are you Sheriva?*

A strange and foreign amusement sifted through her, but Khitajrah did not share the joke. *I am not Sheriva. Sheriva does not exist. He is a construct, a symbol of too long-standing laws we both know should be abandoned.*

Not abandoned. Changed. Khitajrah clung to the shaky foundations of her honor, preferring even injustice to lawlessness.

The being ignored the semantics. *I am older than the gods and infinitely more powerful. All of them together cannot keep me at bay forever. I am Chaos. And I am the force that the gods themselves worship.*

Silence hovered in the single room dwelling on the Cardinal Wizards' Meeting Isle, every eye on the scene in the Pica Stone. Shadimar watched forest stretch endlessly through the expanse of the clairsentient sapphire. Colbey crouched, swords readied, like the double sting of an insect. In front of him, the creature known only as a quarack, waited. Colbey watched it, his stance confident, his darting eyes revealing his knowledge of its fellows, though they were still hidden by the trees. From his broader perspective, Shadimar could see that the forest seemed alive with movement. Black fur shifted between the trunks as far as the boundaries of the Pica stretched.

"Quarack!" A second creature joined the first within the circle of Colbey's vision. Shortly, another drew up beside the first two. Then, the squat creatures stepped from the brush in all directions. They appeared from stands of bushes, from around trees, and from beneath the tangled undergrowth. They swarmed, surrounding the Renshai from every side.

Carcophan's long fingers curled around the table's edge. "Dead already." Though soft, his voice shattered the hush, enhancing the smug satisfaction in his tone. "Without magic here, he's helpless." His cat's eyes sparkled, and his broad mouth fanned into a smile. Apparently, he recalled his own trial with the quaracks, though Shadimar, the youngest of the current Wizards, had no knowledge of the Evil One's method. Nor had Carcophan and Trilless witnessed Shadimar's trials. Throughout history, the Pica Stone had alternated between being a possession of Wizards and of men. At the latter times, the Cardinal Wizards had no means to observe an apprentice's progression through the tasks. Shadimar's performance had gone unobserved.

As the quaracks tightened their ranks, and Colbey tried to speak to the animals, Carcophan detailed his method briefly. "My fire spells killed most of the creatures. None of the survivors dared to confront me."

"I remember." Trilless' contempt came through clearly. The oldest of the Cardinal Wizards by two centuries, she had witnessed Carcophan's technique. "I achieved the same results without bloodshed. I filled the sky with colored lightning. They knew my power, and they trembled before me." She considered both methods briefly. Though they had approached the problem differently, she and the colleague she hated had come to the same conclusion. "Without magic, what can Colbey do?"

Shadimar's gaze remained fixed on the Pica. The quaracks and Colbey waited, and the swordsman's patience surprised the Eastern Wizard. "You both survived. That proves there's more than one way to pass the test of leadership." Unable to pass up the rare opportunity to correct his companions, he detailed what he felt to be their flaws. "And I used yet another method, one that left me neither vulnerable, nor without followers." He placed a hand on the Sorceress' arm. "You earned their obeisance for a short time. But, as your followers, the quaracks would have questioned your pretty fireworks in time. A surprise mutiny might have found you exiled or killed."

Carcophan's lips bowed up ever so slightly, his gloating cut short by Shadimar's next words.

"Carcophan, you were more foolish. If the quaracks were your followers, you wouldn't need to fear plots or counterattacks. But destroying your followers weakens your armies and bases of power."

"Indeed?" Carcophan laughed again. "Would the youngest and weakest of the Cardinal Wizards enlighten me with his strategy?"

Shadimar smiled, glad for the opportunity. "I used magic to divine who their chieftain was, then struck down only him. That way, they knew my powers were controlled and efficiently lethal, and I disposed of the one among them most capable of organizing revolt."

Colbey remained still. He had stopped speaking, obviously finding words futile. Only his eyes moved, measuring the closing enemy.

"Point made." Trilless acknowledged Shadimar's technique diplomatically, without a spoken judgment. "There's more than one way to use magic to turn a horde of enemies into followers. But how do you propose this Renshai should do it? Feeble-minded masses fear what they can't comprehend: magic, demons, works of chaos. Quaracks have seen swords. As skilled as he is, even Colbey can't defeat creatures in such numbers."

But he'll try. Shadimar kept the thought to himself, bothered by a concept his exploration of Colbey's mind had revealed more vividly than all of his historical texts on Northmen. *Colbey wants to die in battle, while he still can. And his words in this room tell me that he'll place that goal over passing the Tasks of Wizardry.* The implications sent annoyance and concern twisting through Shadimar, though he revealed none of it to his companions. When he had believed Tokar dead, without a successor, he had found no man or woman except Colbey skilled enough to become the Western Wizard. Every moment that the Cardinal Wizards' number remained at three, instead of the four decreed by

Odin, made their world and its peoples more vulnerable to chaos. And Shadimar knew he did not have the power to stand against Carcophan and Trilless alone.

A quarack sprang. Colbey's sword met it, and the creature exploded into gore. The odor of blood roused its companions to tribal frenzy. A great wave of red-eyed humanoids surged at Colbey, their canines snapping and their nails bared.

Colbey howled, but neither in pain nor fear. His call was a challenge, a demonic cry of pleasure and raw, innocent fury. The claws tore his clothing and his flesh, and every wound made Shadimar ache in sympathy. Yet Colbey did not flinch or acknowledge the pain. His wolf screams echoed through the trees, nearly drowning the coarse croaks of the quaracks. Colbey's sword relentlessly sliced, severed, and bit. It fed upon the warped creatures with the savage power of its wielder.

The scene in the Pica Stone washed red, as if some alchemist had mutated the sapphire to a ruby. Mar Lon sat in a corner near the door, clutching his *lonriset* the way a child clings to a favorite blanket. His position gave him a clear, though distant, view of the stone. Trilless turned away under the pretext of stoking the fire; she reviled unnecessary bloodshed. Carcophan stared, fascinated. It was the first time he had watched the old Renshai fight for more than a few moments at a time. Unversed in combat, Shadimar lost Colbey's movements in the wash of red clothing and blood. He concentrated on the swirling gray blur he knew as Colbey's left-hand sword, Harval. It dipped and rose, spinning in controlled arcs, then reversing direction in an instant.

Corpses littered the ground around Colbey, enough to make Shadimar wondered whether or not he had underestimated the Renshai once again. For a moment, he dared to hope that Colbey could reap his way through the entire tribe of quaracks. Then his vision opened to encompass the bigger picture. The creatures still filled the extent of forest and Pica, and more came to replace every one killed.

Shadimar lowered his head. Mar Lon's eyes went moist and he huddled, his position revealing all of the despair the Eastern Wizard did not dare allow himself to feel or show. Soon enough, it seemed, the Westlands would be lost forever.

CHAPTER 5

The Task of Leadership

After hours of slash, thrust, and parry, Colbey's war joy gave way to fatigue. Uncountable wounds throbbed into one torturous ache. Not a single quarack moved with half the speed of his swords, but he could not guard every direction at once. They overwhelmed him with numbers, slipping and clawing over the corpses of their companions to attack with tooth and nail. Fluid from a forehead wound blinded Colbey, and blood loss finally dizzied him, stealing the endurance he had developed over half a century. He fell to one knee on the stacked bodies.

"Modi!" Colbey screamed, the wrath god's name driving a second wind through him, as it always did. He leapt to his feet. Dodging a sweeping clout, he drove a blade through an animal throat, secure in the knowledge that he had given his all to a battle he would soon lose. He strove to assess every movement around him through eyes stung to blindness by blood.

Unexpectedly, Colbey found himself with an opening in the tide of enemies. The attacks against him eased, then ceased altogether. He swung in wild figure eights to keep the next wave at bay while he cleared grime from his eyes with a sleeve. Quaracks still surrounded him, though the closest all lay in scarlet death. The others knelt, their bulbous skulls touching the ground. Their strongly radiating emotions told Colbey they were engaged in some sort of religious ritual.

They chanted, their not-quite-human lips slurring the syllables. It took Colbey an inordinately long time to identify which god they called: "Loki! Loki! Loki!"

"Damn." Colbey gathered his reeling wits, and what little strength remained, taking the time to reposition for another round of battle. He had never known gods to directly answer a summons. Although Sif had twice sent manifestations to Colbey to advise him, she had never directly joined a battle or engaged in conversation with him. Still, the Cardinal Wizards' contention that he had entered a god-mediated testing ground made him wonder. He waited, suspecting that the quaracks had turned to gods because of Colbey's own cry for Modi. They could not know that it was not Modi himself that Colbey had sought, but the battle wrath the god inspired. Nor could they have guessed that the shout had incited Renshai on battlefields throughout history.

But no crazed, blond god stormed down on Colbey. Nor did the quaracks renew their attack. Gradually, the Renshai's dazed mind cleared enough for him to realize that he had become the central figure of the quaracks' ceremony. Apparently unaccustomed to swordsmen with Colbey's skill, the quaracks had mistaken him for a god. Colbey had never compared himself to any deity; he would have considered it a blasphemy. Now, faced by adoring worshipers, the cruel and agile god of mischief did seem to fit his description best.

Once Colbey realized the quaracks' misconception, he turned it to his advantage. Feigning strength and inner calm, he casually wiped blood from his swords, glaring about at the oddly-shaped faces. Exhaustion battered at him, even with this simple movement. It took nearly all of his concentration not to stagger. A fullness ached through his head, dimming vision. Weakness made his head sag, but Colbey fought fatigue. If he lost consciousness, he would lose the illusion his sword skill had gained him. And the quaracks would shed their fear and murder him.

Hesitantly, one of the quaracks rose and edged toward Colbey.

The Renshai made a brief, short gesture with his sword, conserving energy yet making his threat clear. In response, the creature shrank back, but it did not retreat. Slowly, without menace, it raised its right hand and uncurled its stubby fingers. A copper ring lay in its palm. It took a cautious half-step toward Colbey.

Memory seeped through Colbey's fatigue, and the ring sparked Shadimar's words: "Successful completion of each task yields a ring of Wizardry. Once you have any given ring, the task is considered completed, and the next begins." Afraid for his own tenuous consciousness, Colbey waited until the quarack moved within easy reach. Then, placing both swords in one hand, he plucked the ring from its rest and dismissed the man-creature with a wave.

The quarack scuttled back to its fellows.

Colbey studied the ring. It was small and crudely fashioned, marred by hammer marks. Some artisan had etched shallow runes into its surface, and their intricacy contrasted sharply with the rough-hewn craftsmanship of the ring. It read:

"A leader must earn loyalty."

The phrase seemed trite to Colbey, the wisdom too obvious to ponder. With a shrug, he fit the trinket to his finger.

Instantly, the quaracks and their forest muted to green-brown blurs, streaked red. Colbey blinked to clear his vision. Even as he did, the colors crushed together, blending to a uniform gray that defied identification or outline. Colbey's vision disappeared, taking with it sound, smell, and touch. Even the natural sensations he had known since birth disappeared: he could not divine the locations of his own arms and legs in relation to his body. His grip felt nonexistent, devoid of the reassuring press of the swords he had carried since infancy, and he could not even find the normal touch of clothing against his skin. Wildly, he grappled for orientation. His hand touched something solid, and he pressed his back against it, waiting for situation and self to resolve.

In the meeting room on the Wizards' Isle, with Trilless, Carcophan, and Mar Lon as fellow witnesses, Shadimar watched mist swirl through the Pica Stone. Its glaring blue muted to the gray of winter clouds. Then, suddenly, the haze exploded to a breathtaking mass of color. This, too, faded, then the sapphire's depths cleared to reveal a bleak scene, completely unlike the preceding splendor. Colbey crouched against the wall of a small, stone room without windows or doors. A mass of green fire capered in the center of the floor, fed by no fuel or wind. It threw sickly highlights across Colbey's ashen face. And, for the first time Shadimar could remember, Colbey seemed to have lost his grace and confidence.

Colbey's tunic still hung in tatters, but his many wounds had healed. The Renshai seemed oblivious to the gods' gift. His left hand hovered defensively before him. His right hand explored his empty sword belt frantically. Suddenly, his head snapped upward, and he stared at the granite ceiling like a priest beseeching the heavens. "Damn you, Wizards! I spit on you all. There's no task in the world that'll turn me into a coward and make me hide behind magic!" His fist slammed the wall. "You put me here. You might be able to keep me here till I finish what you ask. But when I get free ..." He trailed off, leaving the threat unfinished.

Secodon whined softly at his master's feet.

Shadimar stared at the display, unable to fathom the reason for Colbey's rage. True, Tokar had forced the title of Western Wizard upon Colbey. The current Cardinal Wizards had sent him to the tasks rather suddenly, but not wholly without warning or preparation. Colbey had boarded Captain's boat of his own free will, aware of the fate that awaited him once they reached their destination, at least in a general sense.

Apparently having ascertained that he was alone in the room, Colbey paced furiously. "No one takes my swords!" he screamed at the ceiling. "Not without killing me first." His tone softened, but it remained equally threatening. "You can call me a Wizard. You can insult me. But this is the greatest outrage of all!" Again, he plucked at his empty sword belt.

Suddenly, Shadimar understood, and Colbey's anger only seemed more misplaced and ludicrous. The old Renshai faced the most grueling perils of his life, tests that would strain every ability available to him, tasks created by gods to single out the four most powerful mortals in the world at any time and to make them nearly invincible. And here Colbey stood, shaking with fury over the loss of two swords the gods would return, if not by the next task, certainly by the conclusion of the Tasks of Wizardry.

Trilless nudged Shadimar. "Doesn't he know?"

Her words awakened a familiar guilt that sprinkled through Shadimar, easily banished. He had realized long ago that Colbey's ignorance of enchantments and their workings would cause other difficulties in addition to the inability to throw spells. Unlike those who had attempted the tasks before him, he could not inherently know that placing the rings on his fingers would transport him from one test to the next and that he was at the mercy of gods between them. It had seemed simple enough to tell him, yet Odin's Laws were specific regarding what information an apprentice received before undertaking the Tasks of Wizardry. Shadimar suspected these facts did not appear among the others because they seemed unnecessary rather than from any need to keep them secret; an apprentice with magical training would divine the details on his own. Shadimar had agonized over the decision of whether to explain to Colbey these small trappings the Renshai could not guess for reasons that were no fault of his own. But, as always, law had to prevail.

The bard, Mon Lon, sat in the corner, furiously scribbling notes. Occasionally, he shifted his position to catch a glimpse of the scene in the Pica.

Trilless did not await an answer. "He should know. If for no other reason, the previous Western Wizards would tell him."

Carcophan laughed, the sound rich with ancient evil. "He has none of their memories. The collective consciousness of the Western Wizards was destroyed. Had you done your research, you would have known that."

Caught off-guard by Carcophan's knowledge, Shadimar stiffened.

Trilless glared at Carcophan over Shadimar's head. "That's impossible."

"By definition, lady, truth is never impossible." Carcophan gloated, reveling in his minor victory.

Tired of his companions' bickering, Shadimar waved them silent, focusing his attention on Colbey. "I'll explain later.

The color had returned to Colbey's cheeks. His hands fell to his sides awkwardly as he consciously avoided the touch of his empty sword belt. He approached the fire, and its steady glow shed grave highlights across his face. Through the flames, Shadimar could see the spark of silver that was the ring of endurance. The green tint from the fire made the ring appear tarnished.

Colbey stopped abruptly, motionless as stone before the fire. The flickering green light seemed more alive than the man standing in front of it. Recollection of his own trial brought Shadimar vivid memories of pain, and he tried to guess the Renshai's thoughts behind the ugly scowl collecting on his face.

He probably thinks we could just wave an arm and quell the fire with magic. Shadimar shook his head. *If only it had been that easy.*

Colbey circled the fire, studying it from every side. Then, having returned to where he started, he removed his battle-torn silk tunic and stood only in his breeks. Though Colbey was small in height and breadth, every muscle of his exposed chest and abdomen lay explicitly defined. Holding the sleeves of the tunic, he flipped the silk upward. It spread above the fire. Colbey whipped it suddenly downward, blanketing the flames. Emerald-colored flickers jabbed through the cloth. In an instant, the tunic darkened, flared, and fell to ash. Colbey jerked back his hands, retreating a few paces.

Mar Lon flinched in sympathy, clutching his *lonriset* protectively. Shadimar regarded his colleagues. Under other circumstances, Carcophan might had laughed in scorn at the Renshai's efforts. But, apparently, even the Southern Wizard recalled the agony of the test of endurance. His gaze followed Colbey's every movement. Trilless clenched her fingers on the table, her thoughts otherwise well-hidden.

The ring sparkled, a single star unwinking in the green expanse of the fire. It taunted. Absently, Colbey reached to his flask, where he would have carried a waterskin in war time, though surely he suspected he would not find one. Shadimar knew that the gods would have barred it, just as they had his swords. He knew only one way to pass this trial.

Suddenly, Colbey's jaw went rigid with defiance. He flexed his fingers, and his left hand hovered over the fire.

Trilless and Carcophan observed without expression. Shadimar watched, too, trying to detach himself from the comparison to his own trial. Though he failed at banishing remembrance, he did manage to fully maintain his outward composure.

Colbey's hand darted forward, met the flames, and slowed, as if he pushed through an element with far more substance. With a shocked cry, Colbey jerked his hand to safety.

Colbey examined his hand. Again, he studied his few remaining possessions: breeks and sword belt. Shadimar guessed that he sought some object he could use to prod the ring free. Shadimar also knew the Renshai would not find one; the gods would have seen to it. He watched as Colbey came to the same conclusion, and both men returned their attention to the fire. The blaze whirled in a condescending dance, as if daring Colbey to challenge it again. Colbey stared at his hand for several moments, unblinking, as if mesmerized. Then, he lowered his head in preparation. His hand snaked into the fire and, again, strained slowly toward the ring.

Trilless loosed an involuntary grunt, covering the lapse with a more dignified clearing of her throat. Carcophan said nothing, but his face drew tight. Though charged by an onslaught of predecessor memories, Shadimar found no other's pain that could compare with his own firsthand recollection.

Colbey gritted his teeth, and the fingers of his right hand curled into a fist. Though moist, his eyes remained open, focused on his left hand's course to the ring. In his mind, Shadimar relived the searing anguish of flesh blistering from his skin as the fire ate through vessels and nerves to tendon.

Colbey's fingers touched the ring, and he whisked it from the fire, jerking his hand free in the same motion. The silver band rolled. It struck a granite wall, and its movements grew more awkward. It rolled, balancing from edge to edge, then lay still.

To Shadimar's dismay, Colbey ignored his prize. Instead, he pressed his back to a corner, examining the blistered remains of his hand. The nerve endings had burned away. Surely, he no longer felt much pain. Methodically, he ripped cloth from his breeks and fashioned himself a crude bandage.

"What's he doing?" Trilless leaned forward for a better look. "Why isn't he putting on the ring?"

Carcophan glared at Shadimar, a cruel half-smile on his lips. "Because *someone* didn't tell him."

Shadimar ignored the Evil One's baiting, not bothering to grace the gibe with an answer. Carcophan knew the law as well as he did, knew Colbey had no way of understanding that the gods would heal the worst of his injuries between each task. Needlessly, the Renshai suffered while the silver ring lay waiting on the floor. "I could have done nothing differently . . ." He let the thought drop as Colbey finally rose and walked to the ring. The Renshai moved with his usual unperturbable confidence, and that both pleased and unnerved Shadimar. At that moment, he was glad Colbey chose to keep his thoughts to himself.

The Renshai slipped the ring on his finger and promptly disappeared.

Colbey's world exploded. The room shattered into gray pinpoints that rapidly acquired color. Air rushed around and through him, a swirling maelstrom of wind and darkness that tossed him like a feather and knocked him to the edge of oblivion. He tensed, grounding his thoughts on reality and self, rescuing his mind from unconsciousness. His gut lurched. He fought the waves of nausea, and they gradually settled to a dull ache within him. He found himself in a dimly-lit cavern. A sound like the buzz of a giant insect echoed through the passage.

Instinctively, Colbey caught for the hilts of his swords, and their familiar split leather grips filled his hands. Startled by the ease of the movement, he raised his hands to his face. They appeared as he remembered them from before the task of endurance: pale and scarred, but whole. A ring of copper and another of silver graced the index and middle fingers of his right hand. Relief inspired a shiver of delight, but he dared not laugh until he knew what dangers awaited him in the cavern.

Wall brackets held burning torches at constant intervals through the hallway. Moss coated the wall stones, giving the passage an eerie, greenish cast; but Colbey paid this little heed. He caught a glimpse of his own unfamiliar garments, bright gold and sewn from a material he did not recognize. A black belt at his waist held his swords. In the past, Colbey had preferred dark and neutral colors, those less likely to draw attention or to be discriminated from forest or night. But the clothing he wore now seemed better than none at all. His tunic and breeks appeared skillfully tailored, gaudy but formidable.

As Colbey walked silently through the corridor, the buzzing sound grew louder. Confidence restored by the feel of his weapons and his healed hand, he felt prepared to battle any monster the Wizards or gods could summon against him. Once again, the tasks became a challenge, rather than a burden, and curiosity replaced his need for violence and vengeance.

The corridor bent, limiting Colbey's vision to a few arm's lengths in front of him. The ceaseless humming resolved into mingled human voices, apparently several simultaneous conversations. Colbey could not discern individual words or topics. Without changing his pace, he continued around the bend and found himself at the doorway to a room packed with people. Men and women mingled in a press, every one with neutral brown hair and eyes and the medium-toned skin of most Westerners. Most wore clean homespun. If he forced himself to forget the Wizard's tasks, Colbey might have convinced himself that he had entered the city of Pudar.

The conversations disappeared, and all eyes turned to Colbey. Though they watched him, the men and women seemed to take his appearance in stride. They moved aside, leaving him a pathway toward the center of the room.

Colbey hesitated, studying the crowd before glancing down the path they had created. He saw no evident weaponry, and his ability to assess movement told him that no one in his field of vision had half his agility or weapon skill. The pathway led to the center of the chamber where a man sat in a plain wooden chair. He wore robes of tan and brown. Sand-colored hair hung in tangles around his face. His eyes were deeply set and dark with intelligence. A purple cloth covered a low table before him, and a clear globe of crystal rested upon it.

"Welcome," the seated man said. "I am the seer."

An uncomfortable hush fell over the spectators. They widened the walkway.

Colbey approached, eyes on the speaker, though his peripheral attention did not leave the press around him. An attack would not catch him by surprise.

"Your name?" the seer demanded in a monotone.

In the past, the pronouncement of his name in Western towns familiar with the Great War had induced fear and awe. "Colbey Calistinsson."

The seer's milk white hand passed over the globe once. It poised in the air, then returned delicately to his side. He stared into the crystal, nodded, and looked at Colbey. "Which is your tribe, Colbey Calistinsson?"

Poised for action and certain he was missing something significant, Colbey grew irritable and bored with the questioning. "I'm Renshai." He glanced from face to face, awaiting the violence or panic that usually accompanied such an admission. In much of the West, it was considered a cardinal offense even to speak the name; and the Northern tribes had found being Renshai enough reason for cold-blooded murder of the entire tribe.

But these spectators watched curiously, their expressions unchanging.

Again, the seer made motions over the crystal. "How old are you?"

The query brought rage. Colbey's callused fingers caressed his sword hilt. "The Wizards who trapped me here know my age to the day. And they know it *irks* me." His hard, blue-gray eyes went lethal. His words echoed through the vast hall. "The warriors of my tribe were never meant to live to half my years. How old am I?"

The crowd backed away further, leaving Colbey more than enough room to swing a sword, if such became necessary.

Colbey continued, "Nearly fifty years older than the next oldest Renshai."

The seer made several grand gestures over the crystal, and Colbey saw that the man wore a gold ring that matched the silver and copper ones on his own hand. The seer's smile went sober as he gazed within the orb, but it was still a smile. "Who are your parents?"

Still annoyed by the previous question, Colbey scowled. The tedium of the seer's interrogation wore on him. "My parents are dead. In Valhalla, where Renshai belong."

"Their names, please." The seer persisted.

Believing he had blundered into the task of tedium, Colbey responded with a sigh. "Calistin the Bold and Ranilda Battlemad." *Probably a test of patience.* He swallowed his rage; he might be answering questions for days.

The audience remained hushed, shifting restively.

The seer gave a routine nod and sought answers in the crystal globe. Suddenly, his eyes widened. His chair toppled backward, shattering on the granite floor and spilling the seer to the stone. He jumped to his feet, sputtering. An instant later, he vanished, along with the ring of Wizardry that Colbey needed to complete the task and return to his own world.

The room went painfully quiet. The crowd stared, their silence becoming so complete, a background ringing filled Colbey's ears.

"Where did he go?" Colbey asked the spectators, his voice thunderous in the too-quiet room.

His words reverberated, without reply.

Colbey circled the table, hoping to find an answer in the globe that had condemned him. He saw only a smoky haze. Stung to fury, Colbey reached for the crystal.

Terrified screams broke the silence in a wild alarm that came too late. As Colbey's hand closed around the crystal, a bolt of amber split the room, lancing through Colbey's chest. Agony slammed him, his nerves seizing into a tight convulsion against his will. Glowing shards of crystal fell from his hands, stained crimson with blood. Darkness enclosed him. Colbey collapsed, writhing, pain wrenching gasps from him despite his efforts to contain them. The sound of running feet grew increasingly distant. His mind foamed madly, utterly beyond his control. The thud of enormous paws filled the room, and Colbey could direct neither his mind nor his body to identify the sound. This time, he could not stop darkness from overtaking him.

Shadimar poured fragments of shattered Pica Stone from his hand, watching the last bright traces of magic fade from the shards. Disbelief stunned him to a silence that he could not seem to break. Trained through centuries, his mind remained clear, yet his body did not weather the shock quite as well. His lips pursed, but no words emerged. Because it involved chaos, magic was unpredictable, even in a Cardinal Wizard's hands. The simplest spells did not always take shape exactly as the caster expected, and items imbued with chaos rarely remained reliable or consistent with time. Since the inception of the system of the Cardinal Wizards, the Wizards had avoided using their power as much as possible. When necessary, they employed brief spells. Shadimar could count magicked items, through the millennia, on the fingers of one hand. The Pica was the oldest and most powerful. Now, it lay in pieces on the Meeting Room's table.

Carcophan broke the hush, uncharacteristically stating the obvious. "He's dead."

"Who could have guessed," Trilless added. "The easiest task of all. The one of truth."

Mar Lon remained still and silent in the corner, all but invisible.

Secodon rested his chin on his master's thigh, sharing his concern.

Shadimar tented his fingers in his beard, certain he could

never find another mortal with enough skill and guile to pass
the Tasks of Wizardry. He felt cheated. As far as he could
determine, Colbey had told only the truth. Yet somehow he
had failed the test, destroying the Pica Stone and the seer's
crystal along with himself. *I have to find another, and
quickly.* Knowledge crushed all hope. *But there's no one to
fill the position of the most powerful of the Cardinal Wizards, even if we had the collective consciousness that Tokar
and Colbey sacrificed.* Shadimar knew Trilless and Carcophan would help him search; the Cardinal Wizards' vows
bound them to it. But, in the meantime, Shadimar's loss
would become their gain. Without the Western Wizard, neutrality would weaken until no barrier stood between good
and evil.

For the moment, Shadimar did not waste time mourning
his lost friend. Driven by need, he set to the task of finding
another Western Wizard.

CHAPTER 6

The Woman of Gold
and the Shape Changer

The Eastlands' flat, eroded fields provided Khitajrah with little cover between the dwindling patches of forest. Spring winds hurled nutrient-poor topsoil into her eyes, and weeds rolled and tumbled across the flat lands. Waleis' boots clomped, too large for her feet but necessary protection from stones and debris. She kept Diarmad's cloak wrapped tightly around her, her face lost in the shadows of its hood, her hair tied and hidden beneath the folds. She hoped that the over-large cloak and the sword at her hip would convince anyone she saw that they looked upon a boy or young man rather than a woman on the run. Loneliness ate at her. One by one, she had lost every member of her family, and she clung to chaos' promise regarding Bahmyr.

Khitajrah pulled the cloak more tightly about her, protecting her cheeks from the battering sand. A week had passed since she had slain the veterans in the graveyard, and guilt had flared to an all-consuming fire that filled her conscience and ached constantly through her chest. Each night, she sought the comfort of a sheltering woodland or rock formation. Then, doubt, self-hatred, and regret would war within her, holding sleep at bay. When she finally slept, her dreams came in wild, incoherent snippets that enhanced her sense of dishonor and lawlessness. She punished herself for the same crime a thousand times, and still it did not seem enough. She awakened with an anxious tingle in her chest that reminded her she had matters to mull, and those matters occupied her mind throughout the day. In the moments her thoughts let go of the crime, she wept for her slaughtered son.

Chaos had lain low since identifying itself in the grave-yard, yet Khitajrah could still feel its hovering, animal presence within her. It lay dormant. Waiting. At times, she found a guilty pleasure in its presence; her aloneness drove her to find company and solace where she could. Other times, she contemplated its being, considering ways to expel it from her life and from her mind, its ugliness too horrible to support. Yet, always, her thoughts brought her back to its promise. She would pay any price to get Bahmyr back. And by breaking the Eastlands' laws, she had already.

Still, it was not until Khitajrah passed the city of LaZar and headed toward the passes through the Weathered Mountains that would take her to the Westlands that she found the will to question. She stood, staring at towering forests of oak, hickory, and white *mirack,* the hulking, dark shapes of the mountains filling the horizon, and a sudden fear clutched her. She remembered her mother's stories of the Westlands, a vast territory crammed full of apathetic peoples of all shapes, colors, and backgrounds. Unlike the Easterners, they followed few causes and never with the fanatical honor of the Eastlanders. They worshiped a diverse pantheon of gods, each specialized and, thus, far weaker than Sheriva.

Yet Khitajrah remembered positive things about the Westlands as well. Their forests and farmlands flourished, easily supporting their myriad and diverse cities. Though they did not stand together as one people, that might work to Khitajrah's advantage now. Offending one Westerner would not necessarily make her an enemy of them all. And their varying backgrounds might make them more accepting of an Eastern stranger, even only a decade after the Great War.

Still, Khitajrah hesitated. Born and raised in the Eastlands, she had never expected to leave. Now, in her forties, she wondered if she had become too old to try to start a new life in a strange country whose language she did not speak.

You know the common trading tongue. That is enough. Go. Chaos sent its first words since the graveyard. *You're not safe in the Eastlands any longer.*

Confusion blossomed into rage. Chaos spoke the truth, yet it had little significance now. *You promised me my son's life back.*

Yes.

Khitajrah's anger and fear retreated slightly before a growing trickle of hope. *Where is he?*

Dead.

Khitajrah fumed, not gracing the cold joke with a reply. Amusement flickered through her, wholly foreign, its source the chaos-being within her. *There is a way to bring him back to life.*

How?

I never promised to tell you that.

"Yes, you did!" Anxiety and fury drove Khitajrah to shout aloud. "You specifically said that if I lived, you would tell me how to bring him back."

No, I didn't.

"Yes, you did!" Khitajrah's voice rose in octave and volume. "Damn it, you did. Don't you think I'd remember every word of such a thing? You said, 'Live, and I will tell you how to bring Bahmyr back to life.' "

No, I didn't.

You did. You said it exactly like that.

All right. I did.

Joy replaced ire. *So what do I have to do?*

I'm not telling.

"What?" Khitajrah roared.

I'm chaos. That's what I do. I break vows. I lie. It's from whence my power stems. A flicker of cruel satisfaction touched Khitajrah's mind. *If I'm even telling the truth now. How would you know?*

Quit playing with me. Warm tears stung Khitajrah's eyes. *You lied from the start. There's no way to raise the dead.*

Actually, there is. That time, I was telling the truth.

But you always lie.

Not true. If I did, I'd be as dull, predictable, and static as law.

Sometimes you tell the truth? Khitajrah tried to hold her emotions in check, with little success. Her heart pounded, hard and fast, with anticipation. She tried not to hope too hard about Bahmyr.

Usually, I tell the truth. It lulls people into a false sense of security, so my lies and tricks catch them completely off-balance.

Khitajrah frowned, hating the sound of chaos' technique.

Guile is the key to power. See how I got what I wanted from you, and it wound up costing me nothing? Imagine how rich, happy, and important a woman could become with that technique. You could be queen.

I have no wish to be queen. I just want my son.

I can tell you how to get him back.

But you won't.

Maybe I will.

Khitajrah threw up her hands in frustration. *I don't care if you are more powerful than gods. You're wasting my time. Either tell me or don't. Then go away.*

Is that what you want?

Yes.

Then you didn't love your son much, did you?

Again, anger stabbed through Khitajrah. *More than anything in the world. How dare you . . . ?*

If you loved him, you would deal for his life.

You're not dealing. You're just running me in circles. I won't have my hopes lifted and dashed again and again. It'll only drive me insane, and that won't bring Bahmyr back.

What if I promised that, if you bond with me, I'll tell you how to raise your son? In detail.

Khitajrah did not fall into the trap. *I'd assume you were lying. Again.*

To her surprise, chaos seemed pleased with the answer. *Good. You're learning. This world's gone so long without chaos, its people don't know how to mistrust. They're prey, Khita, and why shouldn't someone as competent and right as you rule them? Would you rather I went elsewhere? I'm sure I could find someone who would take my power and use it to his own ends. Someone without your basic morality.*

Khitajrah considered, seeing a logic to the words, though the underlying concepts seemed too corrupt for her law-based mind to grasp. *First, you tell me how to bring Bahmyr back. Then, we discuss this bonding.*

I will give you the basic knowledge you need to raise your son. Then I will start the binding process. When you've performed one task of significance for me, and the binding is complete, I will go through the life-restoring procedure with you, step by step.

You're untrustworthy. I get all of the information first—

Chaos interrupted. *And you're getting paranoid.* Complacence trickled through the thought. *I like that in a companion. But don't worry. Once bound, all my knowledge is yours, and I cannot lie to you.*

What happens to me?

Nothing. You remain as you are. I simply become a small part of your day to day thoughts, completely under your control. I will no longer remain a separate entity.

Still skeptical, Khitajrah asked, *What do you get out of such an arrangement?*

It's difficult to explain.

Try.

I'm not truly an entity in and of myself. The Primordial Chaos is without form, and I am merely a tiny piece of a bodiless whole. Therefore, I have no power of my own on a world where shape and form are necessary. Without a person, I'm impotent. Bound to someone, I still have little influence, but at least I can share my ideas.

The explanation made sense to Khitajrah, though she suspected that chaos had not told all. She considered.

You can do with my ideas as you wish. You and I both know that the world has grown too stale. That's why I chose you. You're wise enough to understand that without change the Eastlands will die. All I promise is a freedom for your thoughts and ideas for ways to accomplish what must be done. You will still have your own judgment and the power to execute it.

Khitajrah's heart rate slowed as she mulled chaos' offer. About this, it seemed genuine, yet logic told her it could seem no other way. Still, its words carried a reasonableness that held doubt at bay. She believed it was being honest, at least mostly. She had little experience to fall back on when gauging deceit, and nearly all of that had come in the last few days. Her best guess was that chaos would gain a larger toehold in her decisions than it would admit. Still, she might prove stronger and tougher than it expected as well. And Bahmyr meant too much for her to dismiss chaos' promise out of hand.

How do I free Bahmyr?

Chaos hesitated. *We have a deal, then?*

Though I fear I'll regret it, yes. We have a deal. That is, so long as Bahmyr comes back as the same son I remember.

Nothing will change. He will have all of his memories up to the moment of death. And he will not have aged.

Now eager, Khitajrah pressed. *So tell me the procedure.*

Quite simply, when an item instilled with magic undergoes a transformation, it can develop properties at random.

I don't understand.

*Magic is chaos. Even when used correctly, the results can be unpredictable. When it's placed into an item, it al-

ways has unexpected side effects. That's why Wizards so rarely use props.

So there are magical things in the world?

A few.

Made by the Cardinal Wizards?

Do you know of any others?

There are rumors—

They are false.

And the fairy tales about the four Wizards—

Are not fairy tales.

And Sheriva . . . ? This time, Khitajrah trailed off intentionally, anticipating chaos' interruption.

. . . is a construct. Not real.

Khitajrah shook her head. *If you're right, and I'm not admitting you are, the Eastlands based an entire religion on fiction and faith alone. It'll collapse the whole foundation of our civilization, especially of the temples.*

I'm counting on that. If it had had a face, chaos would have smiled.

So, somewhere, there's an item instilled with magic that got ruined, and now it can bring people back to life.

Close. There's an item that was instilled with magic. It got damaged, but only partially. Now, it can bring a person back to life. One. If you take it to Bahmyr's grave and touch it to any part once his, you will have him back.

Khitajrah held her breath, needing one more piece of information. *And that item is?*

Chaos laughed. *A detail. As promised it comes later. There are other matters to consider first: a binding, and a favor.*

Arduwyn stared out the chamber window of his castle suite, listening to the wild chime of steel from the Renshai's practice in the courtyard. A spring breeze riffled his spiky, red hair, and his single, brown eye followed the graceful war dance of his daughter's intended, Rache Garnsson. Even in the face of an imminent wedding, Rache's mother, Mitrian, had not allowed her charges a rest from their daily practices. Arduwyn knew he should have expected nothing else. In the months he had spent traveling with Colbey Calistinsson, the old Renshai had never allowed danger, excitement, or injury to keep himself or his charges from giving less than their all to their sword drills. Still, Arduwyn had anticipated that

Mitrian would let the importance of her only child's marriage come before at least one practice, the one on the day of the ceremony. Clearly, this was not the case.

Arduwyn shifted his gaze to the village beyond the castle wall, the Western high king's city of Béarn, nestled in the arms of the Southern Weathered Range. Though tastefully crafted from piled and mortared stone, the cottages and shops paled before the towering palace. Strong and ancient, it had been carved directly from the mountains, and the artisans had spared no expense, inside or out. Still, despite Béarn's finery, Arduwyn felt alone. In the last half decade, illness had taken his wife and two of her three children, whom Arduwyn had adopted after his best friend's death. The eldest girl had married years ago and had her own family and problems to attend. Now, Arduwyn was about to surrender his last child, the only one Bel had borne for him, and he was about to give her over to a life with Renshai.

Arduwyn sighed, now balancing guilt with his sorrow. In his youth, he had been taught to hate and fear Renshai by relatives old enough to remember the tribe's killing rampages. Yet, it was the Golden Prince of Demons himself, the most savage and dedicated of all Renshai, who had taught Arduwyn that there was more to the tribe than merciless slaughter. He had watched Mitrian indoctrinated into the sword skill and the culture; and he had remained her friend before, into, and after Colbey's training. Rache seemed to have inherited the best qualities of both of his parents, and Arduwyn never doubted that the boy loved his daughter dearly. He tried to console himself with these thoughts.

Arduwyn's eye strayed to his daughter, Sylva, perched on a courtyard bench, watching the practice. In many ways, she, too, had found the best features of both parents. She sported her mother's oval face, full lips, and doelike eyes, softened by youth. Though red, like her father's, Sylva's hair had the long, thick texture of her mother's. She was too thin, again like her father; yet she bore the first traces of her mother's robust curves. He had given his consent to the union, expecting it to occur many years in the future. Yet Sylva and Rache had pressed for sooner rather than later; and, to Arduwyn's surprise, Mitrian had supported their decision. *Fifteen years old. Barely fifteen. What's the hurry?*

Arduwyn rose, seized by a sudden urge to enfold the child in his arms and hold her, safe, until old age claimed him. A tear rose in his eye. He had been a friend of the Renshai for a long time, and his loyalty to Mitrian and her son would not falter. Yet there were too many tragedies his mind would not let him escape. The Renshai's life of violence killed them young. Worse, death seemed to strike bystanders first, the innocent who dared to bond their lives with Renshai. In the last year, Arduwyn had witnessed more slaughter than his heart could handle, and the Renshai had lost half of their members and friends before his eyes. Though not of the tribe, Rache's father, Garn, had lost his life to an enemy of the Renshai. A barbarian who had become Colbey's blood brother had died at the elder's own hand. The Renshai had lost three of their members as well. Though months had passed, Arduwyn had still not regained full use of the arm he had broken escaping Renshai enemies while delivering an innocent message.

Just fifteen years old today. Prior to the Great War, a woman could not marry until she came of age at sixteen. But, with the Westlands' population whittled by wars and disease, the kingdom had found need to relax the laws. Arduwyn drew some solace from the realization that not even two years separated Rache from Sylva, a couple in love rather than an adult man ravaging a child.

A knock sounded on the suite's main door, the sound echoing through the confines. It reminded Arduwyn how massive the connected series of rooms seemed since he had lost his family. Without Sylva, he saw no reason to keep the suite. Every scrap of furniture and every corner reminded him of the woman and children who no longer shared his life. Solace came to him in one place only, in the woodlands he had traipsed first with his father, then by himself, and later with Sylva. Surrounded by the trees, all worldly problems fled Arduwyn, and he knew nothing but animal needs, instinct, and survival. Now, he remained in place, hoping the person at the door would assume he had left and would go away.

But the door handle turned, and the panel made its familiar soft creak as it opened. "Ardy?"

Arduwyn recognized the voice instantly as that of King Sterrane. Despite the somberness of his thoughts, Arduwyn could not help smiling. More than a decade ago, when Mitrian, Garn, Colbey, Sterrane, and he had traveled together, Sterrane's slowness, simple justice, and inability to

master the common trading tongue had convinced them that
he had the mentality of a child. After Mitrian, Garn, and the
Eastern Wizard had restored Sterrane to his throne and
Arduwyn had seen the king make decrees and judgments in
his native language and in his own element, Arduwyn had
discovered a depth of thought and person he had never believed possible. Wealth and power had not corrupted
Sterrane at all; he shared it freely. And it seemed not to affect his sense of fairness either. In his sluggishly methodical
and guileless way, he seemed the central epitome of neutrality. And he always knew what to do or say to make even the
worst situations seem better.

"Ardy?" Sterrane repeated. His heavy boots clomped
across the floor, and he stopped at Arduwyn's back. "Ardy?"
He shuffled closer, staring out the window over Arduwyn's
shoulder, his beard tickling Arduwyn's ear and his enormous
chest and belly warm against the little hunter's back. "What
look at?" Apparently following Arduwyn's gaze, he did not
wait for an answer. "Get handsome new son."

Arduwyn laughed, unable to remain sullen in Sterrane's
presence. "Leave it to Sterrane to see the good in a bad situation."

"Bad? What bad?" Sterrane seemed genuinely confused.
"Sylva marry Rache. That good."

Finally, Arduwyn turned, finding himself staring directly
into Sterrane's huge chest. He tried to back-step, but the
window ledge gouged his back. "My daughter's about to go
live with Renshai."

Sterrane said nothing, clearly waiting for Arduwyn to go
on.

"And that means ... well, you know ..." The conversational positioning finally got the better of Arduwyn.
"Sterrane, as much as I love the royal tunic, it's easier to
talk to your face. Could you find a chair, please?"

Sterrane retreated immediately. He glanced around the
sparse furnishings of the sitting room, from its three chairs,
to its padded chest, to Arduwyn's favorite stool. He sat on
the chest, watching the hunter expectantly.

"I don't want my daughter in a tribe constantly at war."
Arduwyn paced.

"Renshai not start war anymore." Sterrane's soulful, dark
eyes watched Arduwyn. "No war."

"But at the earliest inkling of war, anywhere, you know the Renshai will be the first to take a side and fight."

"Rache fight. Not Sylva."

"But everyone around Renshai seems to get killed."

"Not me. Not you."

Arduwyn came to the end of his track and turned. "Garn did. And that barbarian."

"Bel not fight. Children not fight. Not near Renshai. They die, too."

"They died of illness."

Sterrane's huge shoulders rose and fell. "What difference? Renshai not catching, like consumption. Garn not die of Renshai nearness. Renshai just people. Good people. Friends."

Arduwyn turned in his tracks, though he had not yet reached the end of his course. "It's one thing to die of illness and another to die of violence before you get a chance to get ill."

"Death is death," Sterrane said. "More people here. More sickness here. Renshai there. More chance violence there. Death go every place, and everyone die of something. Some people think sickness better death. They live here. Some people think war better death. Live in North."

Again, Arduwyn turned, this time facing Sterrane directly. "I can't lose Sylva, Sterrane. I just can't. I love her too much."

"You not lose her." Sterrane looked pained, clearly from sympathy. "She nearby, with Mitrian and Rache. They let you visit as much want. I come with you."

Arduwyn lowered his head, trying to explain to Sterrane that the loss he feared was death, not marriage.

Sterrane obviated the need. "Sometime happy more important than safe. And sometime safe not safe."

Though the final statement seemed nonsensical, Arduwyn understood. The last time he had seen Bel, she had tried to force him not to go on a trip to help the Renshai. She had feared for his life. Yet, when he returned, she was the one who had succumbed to illness. "Sometimes safe not safe." Arduwyn repeated the words numbly, his eye becoming moist.

"Only gods know whether Sylva safer here or there. But we know she happy with Rache. Can't know safe, so have to do happy." Sterrane rose, taking a step toward his friend. "Anyway, not your choice. It Sylva's."

"You're right about that at least." Arduwyn allowed Sterrane to wrap him in an embrace, and his last words emerged muffled against the king's tunic. "It's Sylva's decision." And though Arduwyn tried to console himself with the king's points, experience and worry held him captive. And he feared for his daughter's life.

The man awakened confused, empty of all thought and memory, sprawled across a fur-covered floor. He opened his eyes, cringing in anticipation of a pain he had no reason to expect. But his body remained numb, beyond his control, and he rolled his eyes to find some familiar object to spark his identity. His gaze scarcely moved before riveting upon a woman crouched at his side. Her skin looked so smooth and pale that he at first believed her to be an ivory statue. Her perfection only gave credence to the misconception. Surely, no living woman could have captured the male fantasy so exhaustively, yet it appeared that this one had. She wore a short, low cut dress of some gauzy material that hid just enough to enhance beauty with mystery, and the man could not stop his mind from completing the figure with the same flawlessness as that which he could see. Yellow hair billowed around her face, enhancing widely set, blue eyes that caught light into a sparkle, heart-shaped lips, and a straight, fine nose. She wore several brooches, and a gold choker entwined her throat. The world beyond her faded to a blur.

"Ah, so you've awakened," she said. Her voice matched her appearance, moderately pitched and distressingly elegant. "You were fortunate."

"Fortunate," the man repeated, still fully disoriented. He tried to focus on self and identity. When that failed, he locked his attention on the woman. Surely, if he considered for a time, he could remember the name for perfection. *Fortunate, indeed, if I have friends who look like this.* He tried to rise, but his body would not obey.

The woman stepped around his prone form and knelt directly at his head. He focused on her hands, nervously clasped. A gold ring striped every finger. "I had no right to take you." She glanced around, as if afraid someone might overhear. "I can take my share of the dead, but only from the battlefield. I can steal from the AllFather, but not from Hel."

The woman's discomfort made her seem vulnerable. Some men might have found that attractive, but it distressed the man on the fur-covered floor. For reasons he could not recall, he preferred his women strong and competent.

"I'll put you back. No one has to know. No one can enter my hall without my permission. You're safe here." She fidgeted, her obvious concern incongruous with her statement.

The man knew that the woman had already made a mistake. Beyond her, he could hear the faint patter of footfalls, and he sensed another presence nearby. He opened his mouth, trying to warn her, but no words emerged. He willed his hand to touch her. It did not move. He narrowed his eyes, concentrating on the woman whose beauty nearly blinded him, trying to send a mental message that would make her understand.

The other entered the room and crept toward the woman's back.

"Behind," the man managed. "Look."

Before she could turn, a new voice filled the air, light and taunting, yet certainly male. "Is this the Thunder Child, lady?"

The woman whirled. The man on the floor rolled his eyes far enough to study the newcomer. He looked fair enough to pass for the woman's twin, pretty with youth and finely featured. Only his mouth broke the image, thin-lipped and leering. His green eyes sparkled with mischief.

The woman hissed, rising. Brooches, rings, and golden threads that wound through her dress winked and gleamed. Her necklace seemed to writhe, snakelike.

The man on the floor willed himself to stand and protect her, if not from the newcomer, from the jewelry that seemed to have come alive. But he scarcely managed to crane his neck further.

"Shape Changer." The woman appeared capable of handling the situation. "Only you could slip past my defenses, and only you would dare to try." She stepped toward him menacingly.

The other laughed. "No answer is it, then? That is in itself an answer." His leer became an insolent grin. "I see I have matters to discuss with the AllFather."

The woman opened and closed her mouth wordlessly. Her fists clenched, and gold flickered as she moved. "If you reveal me, then you're a fool. He has the potential to bring chaos back into our world." Her hair slid along her cheeks, as smooth and yellow as melted butter. "That, my loathsome friend, would serve only you."

"Only me, yes. So what purpose did you have in rescuing him?"

"I have my reasons."

"Your reasons? And what might those be?"

The man on the floor tried to make sense of the conversation, but he could still find no base on which to ground the information. Without knowledge of self and location, he could not place their words into the proper place in a universe he could not remember.

"My reasons are none of your business."

"Your reasons, wanton one, are every man's business. Leave it to Freya to think only of her crotch. Isn't that what most women accuse men of doing? Who but you would save a man's life to complete your collection of bedroom trophies?"

The woman quivered with rage. "Your mouth is full of lies and your head full of treacheries. For all you claim I've slept around, at least I never bore babies. But you, Shape Changer, you mothered a horse. You fathered a wolf and a snake. Your mischief may bring us all down."

Anger sharpened her motions, and the dazzling sparkle of gold mesmerized the man on the floor. He tried to maintain his attention on the conversation, but it seemed like meaningless sounds.

"Perhaps," the Shape Changer seemed proud of her condemnation. "But you're not blameless. Admit it. You rescued him from curiosity or for your own torrid pleasure. Now we have little choice but to set him free, despite the prophecies. Your treachery, not mine, will bring the *Ragnarok*."

"Liar! Trickster! Cheat!" she screamed.

"I'm all of those and more," the Shape Changer admitted cheerfully. "This time, I'm correct. You took him alive, and you could no more slay the Thunder Child than you could me. You know his parentage."

The woman hissed.

"Just you and me and Sif . . ."

Sif. The name seemed to hold a significance to the man. He seized the thought fanatically, trying to build self and understanding from it. "Sif," he repeated aloud. "Sif."

The woman went rigid. "Quiet," she said to her companion. She drew the Shape Changer away, continuing in a low whisper, beyond the man's hearing.

The man willed himself enough strength to lift his head, but it felt heavy as an anchor. He moaned. The word "Sif" floated through his otherwise empty mind, but no meaning accompanied it. Gratefully, he returned to unconsciousness.

CHAPTER 7

A Power Challenged

Colbey Calistinsson awakened cradled in the folds of a blanket. He jerked to consciousness with the sudden and clear-minded alertness he had trained himself to for decades. Even before he opened his eyes, he knew that he lay on a bed and a heavy silk coverlet enwrapped him to the chin. He opened his eyes. An image of richly crafted furniture filled his vision and his mind. His gaze found and held the only other living being. She sat in a chair by his bedside, her curves defined beneath a skintight dress. Long, golden hair framed sturdy, traditionally beautiful features, the locks a shade yellower than her necklace, brooches, and rings.

Colbey sat up, the blanket falling in a jumble at his waist. At first, the need to define location and danger held his attention fully. Then, as he recognized no threat, he could not fully suppress the first stirrings of desire. "Hello," he said carefully, uncertain what to expect. He had no way to guess whether he had started another of the Wizards' tasks or if the seer's crystal had sent him elsewhere.

The woman said nothing. She only stared, blue eyes dancing, a strange smile taking form on her lips. Colbey felt a twinge of twice-meeting, as if he had seen this woman before.

Colbey considered exploring her mind, but the idea disbanded as it formed. For now, she was a stranger. But he would not steal the thoughts of friends, and he hoped that was what she would become. Also, something about her seemed curiously divine. He thought it not just improper but unwise to access her mind. "Who are you?" His hands wandered unobtrusively to his swords, and their presence reassured him. Much about this woman was gold, but not all seemed pure or comforting.

The woman's smile faded, and her expression grew grim. "You won't be damned because one truthseeker could not handle what he found." She ignored Colbey's question. "There's too much at stake. More than either the AllFather or the Trickster understands."

Colbey swallowed hard, letting the woman speak. She had used the familiar names for Odin and Loki too casually. That, coupled with the knowledge that gods mediated the Tasks of Wizardry, allowed him to believe he sat in the presence of a goddess. He froze, uncertain whether to kneel, bow, or offer his services unconditionally.

The woman continued, seemingly oblivious to his discomfort. "Here. Finish your tasks." She pulled a gold ring from her finger and tossed it to Colbey.

Colbey caught it easily. He looked back, awaiting explanation or instruction.

"Go ahead," she encouraged. "Put it on."

"Thank you." Colbey squirmed. He had many more questions, yet it felt rude to try to interrogate her. Glimpses of the woman/goddess enticed, dizzying him with a longing that shamed him, obvious blasphemy. Needing to escape the discomfort, he slipped the ring onto his ring finger, beside the ones of silver and copper, steeling himself for the sudden rush of energy that preceded transport between the tests. He closed his eyes.

White light burst against Colbey's lids. His world spun in tight circles, then released him in a small, granite room with a single door constructed of the same stone as the walls. A scrawny man sat on a plain wooden chair, eating a slice of honey bread. Otherwise, the room stood empty. Colbey waited, watching the other for some time. After several heartbeats, when the man did not speak but only continued eating, Colbey explored the chamber. Finding nothing of interest, he took the knob and eased open the door.

The chamber beyond lay empty, four bleak, granite walls without even a layer of mold to break its monotony. Colbey frowned, recognizing the logic missing from its construction. The only door led from one empty room to another. The building had no entrance or exit. Intrigued, Colbey walked into the second room and studied the stone. Though smooth and sterile, it bore none of the scratches he would have expected of walls frequently scrubbed.

A footfall behind Colbey sent him into a spin. The little man stood in the doorway, smiling with haughty interest. "You're late, Wizard."

"I came via Hel," Colbey said, not at all certain he had not. He sighed, hoping to bypass the amenities and posturing. "So, what do I have to do to win the ring of . . . of . . . ?" He looked to the other man to finish as well as answer the question, doubting he would get more than a dodge.

"Faith," the man said easily. "The test of faith." He swayed in the doorway. "I'm a messenger from Odin; that you know. And he has decreed only one way to pass this test." The little man's face drew into a condescending sneer. "You must take your own life."

"Suicide?" Dedicated to dying in glory, Colbey found the suggestion heinous and its implications intolerable. His discovery that a missing body part would not necessarily bar a brave soldier from Valhalla had eliminated that consideration from his decision to brave the test of endurance. But self-murder was a coward's escape, and he would not become party to it. "Get out of my way!" He lunged toward the door.

The man laughed. He stepped back, reached leisurely for the granite door, and jerked the stone block toward closing.

Colbey sprang for the crack, just as the other made a sudden, desperate yank. Granite slammed Colbey's arm and head. He leapt back, and the door crashed shut, flush with the wall. An instant later, the pain came in a wild rush that sent him reeling. His head throbbed, his upper arm ached, and a ringing filled his ears. "Damn you, open this door," Colbey shouted. His own yelling worsened his headache. Even if the little man could hear him, he doubted he would get an answer, let alone satisfaction. And, even if the other did open the door, it only led to another room like this one.

Colbey examined the wall, finding no seam to indicate where the door had been. He trusted his memory of its location, but his fingers and eyes failed him. It seemed as if the door had never existed. More likely, it had disappeared completely, the work of the gods. Now, Colbey considered, the pain settling to a dull ache and the constant ringing becoming familiar enough to dismiss. He studied the wall finger's breadth by finger's breadth, seeking the one flaw that would allow his freedom. He found no crack, niche, or outline. His knife could not make so much as a scratch in the stone.

Colbey searched his gear, the need for attentiveness turning his head wound into a pounding agony. One by one, objects fell beneath his scrutiny and were rejected. He discovered that, this time, he was missing only his edible supplies, and that unnerved him. He could survive for weeks without food, but thirst would take him in days. The lack of mold or mildew on the walls convinced him that the structure was watertight.

When Colbey finished exploring the unyielding barrier, he turned his attention to the remainder of his prison. From floor to ceiling, end to side, he searched for some minuscule defect or difference that might suggest a concealed exit. The search took him well into the night, but the steady, sourceless grayness did not change. He examined the floor from corner to corner. When that proved fruitless, he returned to the walls. When eye and hand failed to find escape, he pounded the base of a sword against the stone. He found no hollow echoes or areas where the pitch of the knocking changed to suggest a weakness, except where the door had been. And that seemed only a quarter tone higher.

Well into the following night, fatigue caught Colbey. He sat with his back to a corner, quelling the rumblings of his empty stomach. Cotton seemed to fill his mouth, and he wondered when he had taken his last drink. He could not guess how long his frenzied examination of the chamber had taken, nor how much time he had spent with the unearthly woman. Exhaustion weighted his limbs. He placed Harval across his knees, fixed his gaze on the far wall, and fell into a wary sleep.

Colbey awakened. He rose and, from habit, executed a deft sequence of sword feints. Pain stabbed through the back of his head and threw off his delicate timing. A black and white curtain of spots wove across his vision. His legs went weak. Suddenly, he felt stone beneath his fingers, though he did not recall moving. He clutched at the wall, waiting for the dizziness to pass. *Fool. Would you waste what little fluid your body has left for one dance with your sword?* Colbey knew that he would, but he also believed his time to die had not yet come. He needed to find a way free, while he still could.

Colbey collapsed twice during his search. The second time, he lay unconscious for longer than he cared to guess. Desperately, he sought moisture at the corners of the floor. He found none. His entire body ached. His lower back throbbed from hip to hip, and every breath came as a dry and tortured waste of energy. A burning in his eyes and the buzzing in his head became relentless. He fell once more, tried to rise, and lost consciousness again.

Bugs swarmed the walls, gaunt cockroaches with beadlike eyes. When one grew bold enough to crawl over Colbey's arm, he slapped it. His hand struck only dry flesh. The roaches came from his imagination. The instant he realized this, they disappeared.

"Modi." Speech was nearly impossible, and the effort stole the reserves his call had raised. *Die, I will. But not as a raving lunatic. I'll die as I was meant, on the point of a sword.*

Drawing the blade sapped all of Colbey's strength. He lay, staring at the weapon, knowing he would never find the vitality to perform the deed. He knew that if he summoned the strength of his will, he could stand, but suicide by sword cut required a dexterity that most men did not possess. The time it would take to properly position the blade might not prove enough, and he dared not take the chance of falling prey to thirst before the sword took him. He knew, without the need to ponder, that the next time he lost consciousness would be his last.

Colbey lay the sword aside respectfully, fighting oblivion and insanity. Without a battle, he would never reach Valhalla, but he still held the vague hope that the scrawny man had spoken the truth. In either case, he would rather die of wounds than slow oblivion. He fumbled his knife free, then plunged it into his wrist.

The abrupt, sharp pain cleared his mind, a welcome change from the dull aches of his parched organs. His courage did not falter for an instant. He tore the blade the length of his forearm. Then, leaning peacefully against the wall, Colbey closed his eyes and waited.

A pink and green fletched arrow cut the air, then thunked into the waiting hay bale perched upon a stump. Sylva nocked another shaft. "What do you think?"

Seated on a deadfall, Rache Garnsson stared at the slender redhead. Moonlight drew lines along the folds of her dress, glittering from the V-shaped collar that outlined her breasts. The sight stirred him. Now that they had become one, he could scarcely wait for bedtime. "I think you're beautiful."

"What?" Sylva whirled to face her husband, the movement fanning long waves of hair around her cheeks. When she found his eyes fixed on her, she pouted. "I meant the arrows. Their pattern. What do you think?"

Reluctantly, Rache tore his gaze from Sylva to look at the shafts jutting from the hay bale. Two dozen fletches poked from it, outlining the perfect figure of a sword. He laughed. "I love it. But not as much as I love you." He patted the trunk next to him.

Sylva shook her head. "I love you, too. Now, come here, you big ox."

"You come here." Rache patted the trunk again with a huge hand. Though only sixteen, his mother's massive bone structure and his father's gladiator musculature already made him a giant among men.

"I want you to try something," Sylva insisted.

"What?"

"Something. Come here."

"I'll try something all right." Rache bounded deftly to his feet, charging Sylva. He caught her into an embrace, squeezing until he all but mashed the air from her lungs. Then, he released her. He caught her lips on his, one hand wandering to a breast.

Sylva laughed. "No, stop it. That's not what I wanted you to try."

"Are you sure?" Rache teased. He pulled her closer until he saw his own desire echoed in her dark eyes.

"You ox." Sylva planted a hand on his chest and pushed, her touch light as a bird. "Later, I promise. I want you to try this first." She shoved the bow into his hand.

Rache readjusted his breeks, waiting for need to ebb enough for him to listen. His hand closed around the bow, though it felt wrong in his hilt-callused hand. "Come on, Sylva. Don't make me do this. You know how Renshai feel about bows."

"Coward's weapons. I know. I'm not asking you to shoot anyone with it. Just a hay bale. Even your own mother uses a bow to hunt."

"Compared to you, my mother shoots like she's holding the bow upside down." Absently, Rache fitted an arrow to the string.

Sylva caught Rache's hand. "And you're about to shoot with the *arrow* upside down." Gracefully, she spun the shaft halfway around, refitting the notch.

Rache studied the arrow, trying to understand how it could have an up and a down. His eyes riveted on the only asymmetry, the third feather, pale green to the others' pink. Their colors matched the painted crest just before them, the green sandwiched between the pink. Now, he could see that if he had fired the arrow the way he had nocked it, he would have sheered off the cock feather.

"What are you looking at?" Sylva asked.

Rache flushed, embarrassed at the length of time it had taken him to deduce the obvious. He covered neatly. "Just wondering why green and pink."

"Why not?"

"Well, I guess I can understand green. So the deer don't notice it."

Sylva laughed.

"What's so funny?" Rache wondered if he had missed something self-evident again.

"Deer don't see colors. They don't care how you dye your feathers."

The information took Rache aback. "How do you know deer don't see colors?"

"My father told me. He knows everything about the forest and the animals."

"But how can he possibly know how deer see?" Rache lowered the bow, glad for the delay. If he had to make a fool of himself, he would do it with one issue at a time.

"By the way they act and react. They don't care if you wear brown, purple, or glowing red. All they seem to notice is smell and movement."

"But . . ." Rache started, about to ask how Arduwyn could know about a deer's sense of smell. He dismissed the question as fruitless. If anyone would know how to smell like a deer, Arduwyn would . . . for both meanings of the word "smell." Realizing he had never gotten an answer to his original question, Rache returned to it. "So why green and pink?"

Sylva shrugged. "I like green. I used to use green and white, so I could find the arrows. Green gets lost, but white's easy to see."

"So why pink instead of white?"

"One time, my father and I hunted apart. He noticed that, from a distance, the white feathers in the quiver looked like a deer's tail bobbing through the trees."

The implications shocked Rache. "He shot at you?"

"My father? Of course not. He's too careful. But he worried that other people might." Sylva considered, her hand still resting lightly on Rache's. "It seemed strange at the time. I thought my father knew everything about the woods. I guess there's some things you can only learn when you have a partner."

"There're lots of sword maneuvers like that." Rache considered, finding a new respect for archery, though he still saw no place for it in honorable combat. Colbey had taught him too adamantly. However, bows did seem to have their place when it came to hunting and coordination, and he could not help feeling proud of Sylva's skill.

"Quit stalling." Sylva released Rache's hand. She pointed at the hay bale and the jutting arrows forming the shape of a sword.

Rache raised the bow. "I'll put it in the middle of the blade."

Sylva smiled. "I'll be happy if you just put it in the hay bale."

"Hey!" Rache chafed at the insult. "I'm well practiced with my hands. And my eyes."

"No one does perfectly first shot."

"I will," Rache insisted. Aiming, he released the shaft. It flew in a high arc, then plummeted, stabbing into the grass halfway to the target.

For a moment, Rache stared in an unbroken silence. Suppressed laughter slipped from Sylva in a dry snort.

"You wench!" Rache dove on Sylva, feigning rage. They went down in a giggling, rolling heap, Rache pretending to pummel her but hitting himself instead. He harbored no doubt at all that he had found true love. And he liked it.

Colbey could not understand why, in his last moments of life, he smelled the perfume of wild flowers instead of the redolence of death. The vitality that had seemed so natural throughout his life, that had only become more reliable with age, that starvation and thirst had recently sapped from him, had returned. He could feel his own life and awareness, like a loyal friend. And though no stronger than in the past, he felt vibrant and significant in a way he never had before. He touched his hands to the hilts at his hips, and the presence of his swords only added to the sensation of power. He opened his eyes.

Colbey lay in a field of weeds and wild flowers. Beyond it, forest obscured the horizons. A blue sky spread above the meadow, and an edge of sun burst forth over the tops of the trees. Colbey sprang to his feet, charged with new energy. He reached for his swords instinctively, needing a practice to make his joy complete. Even as he reached for the hafts, he noticed a new addition to the rings on his fingers. A copper band encircled the first finger of his left hand, a perfect mate to the one on his right that the quaracks had given him. Apparently, someone had slipped the ring onto his finger while he had been in no condition to do so for himself.

So this is how I came to lie in this pleasant field. Colbey inched the newest ring from his finger and examined it. Inside, a single word was inscribed: "Faith." Colbey laughed hollowly. *I've discovered a flaw in the Tasks of Wizardry. It wasn't faith but pride that goaded me to take my own life.* Then another idea hit him with more force than the first. *Did my thoughts at the time matter? In the end, I did what they wanted.* Colbey guessed he had been taught a valuable lesson about leaders, that their followers responded to actions, not thoughts or attitudes. *If he is good to them, subjects won't care whether their king hates or loves them. If he overtaxes them, for good or ill, they will revolt.* Another, simpler explanation presented itself to Colbey. *Or, perhaps, gods can't read minds any better than Wizards. They can only respond to our actions.* Colbey returned the ring to his finger.

Suddenly, Colbey sensed another presence. The other's hostility touched the Renshai even before his indecipherable shout rang through Colbey's ears. "Crshtk!"

Colbey sprang aside. Only then, his gaze caught and held the other figure amid the jungle of grasses. A jagged beam of amber lanced into the circle of crushed grasses where he had stood, leaving a charred hole the size of a man's head. Every hair on his body seemed to stand on end. The reek of ozone replaced the bouquet of the flowers.

Colbey crouched, facing a thin-lipped stranger who stood well beyond sword range. He wore a brown cloak over robes of the same color. A curly mane of gray-flecked, black hair tumbled down his back, and a matching beard nearly hid his mouth. Fleshy growths crooked his nose. Abruptly, he jerked up his hand, repeating the bizarre command. An angry electrical burst shot toward Colbey.

Again, the Renshai sprang aside. The bolt crashed to earth where he had stood, grounding into the dirt until it disappeared. The pain of concussion slammed Colbey's side, nearly stealing his balance. Every instinct screamed at him to charge the other man, but logic told him that the wizard could drop him with enchantments before he significantly narrowed the gap between them. *And, if I rush him, I won't have the momentum to dodge.* Colbey's mind raced. To hurl a weapon meant showing it disrespect as well as disarming himself. Renshai saw any weapon that did not require constant skill and direction as cowardly, yet he might not survive long enough for a direct conflict. Still, Colbey knew that he would never abandon honor, even to spare his own life. Though his enemy had chosen to fight a coward's battle, Colbey would not. A code of honor lost all meaning when a man expected his enemies to also adhere to its tenets. Unable to attack, with weapons or with magic, Colbey sought information. He thrust a mental probe into the wizard's mind.

. . . not fighting back, and he seems so calm. What's he planning? No matter. Let's see him avoid this. All thought fled the wizard, replaced by an orderly string of bizarre syllables and gestures. Colbey could not comprehend their meaning, but he found that he could use the wizard's understanding to fathom pronunciation and gesture.

There must be a way to use that knowledge. The answer came to Colbey with the thought. When the wizard began his chant, Colbey mimicked it. At first, he said each word an instant behind the other, slowed by inexperience. Then, as he caught the pattern of thought to action, he let his superior quickness and agility take over. As fast as the wizard could think the phrases and gestures, Colbey spoke and performed them, until he had become the faster of the two.

The wizard faltered. *Same spell. He'll finish first!*

In the moment of hesitation, Colbey drew his swords and charged.

Desperately, the wizard began a new spell, presumably a shorter one. Even as he shouted the first command, razor-honed steel met his neck, cut, and retreated. The spell became an incoherent shriek. He collapsed to the ground, his blood staining the grass the deep purple-red of a bruise.

Dead. Colbey kicked the corpse. Though trained to kill and skilled in war, he had always hated slaughter without cause. *I have no idea why, but you started this fight.* Sheathing his sword, he searched the dead man's body for the ring he needed to continue his tasks. He found it amid bits of gemstones, which he kept, and vials, powders, and feathers, which he left. He also took a pack of rations and a wineskin. Removing the wizard's cloak, he cleaned his sword methodically, sheathed it, then covered the body with the cloth. Finding a quiet space amid the wildflowers and away from the corpse, he crouched and studied the silver ring. The engravings on its inner surface read: A power has no power until it destroys another power.

Colbey frowned, pondering the words. *My power comes from practice and from within, not from other men.* He glanced at the horizon. The sun had risen over the trees and beamed its radiance on the wildflowers. Colbey knew now that placing the silver ring on his finger would take him to his next test, but he savored the moments of peace on this world whose task he had already completed. He drew Harval, launching happily into one of the devil dances that had spread his name throughout the Westlands. He felt at peace, swelled full of joy for the first time since well before the tasks had started.

The heady aroma of the flowers, the warmth of the sun, and the beauty of the sky only enhanced the wonder of a perfect spar/prayer. Alone with his weapons and thoughts of his goddess, Colbey practiced with a flawlessness and a passion few could match. His body and every extension of flesh or steel became a weapon of unequaled lethality. The splendor of the slim, pale Renshai and the two swords that sang about him was rivaled only by the radiance of the rising sun: two golden giants shedding glory on this world between worlds.

Strengthened by exhilaration, Colbey felt invincible. Finished with his practice, he ran a hand through his hair, feeling the soft, thick waves he had known in his youth. Startled by its fullness, he caught a lock between his fingers and rolled his eyes to examine it. It bore the solid, goldenrod hue of his younger years, freed of the gray-white that had started with a few strands, then had gradually taken over until little of the yellow remained. Surprised, he seized another clump, equally devoid of signs of aging. Colbey stared at his hands.

They still bore the deeply etched calluses that had become as familiar as his fingers, but the skin at his wrists and fore-arms had tightened like the flesh of a younger man.

The discovery gave Colbey another thing to ponder, and he did so over a meal of jerked meat and water scavenged from the wizard. Repeatedly, he turned the fifth ring over in his hands. Apparently, the task had been designed to prove that he, as those before him, was more capable than the best mortal mage the gods could place before him. The causes and reasons for the change in his hair and skin remained more elusive. Colbey guessed that it had come about before he had battled the wizard, rather than as a result of that test. Forced to guess the timing of the transition, Colbey placed it at the moment he had met the woman he believed to be a goddess.

Colbey finished his meal. He gained a vague, defiant sense of satisfaction from making the beings responsible for the tasks wait for him for a change, gods or not. He lay back, watching the sun hover, unwinking yellow against blue, while the food digested. Then, comfortable and charged by his practice, he placed the silver ring onto the middle finger of his left hand.

CHAPTER 8

Spawn of Fenrir

More accustomed now to the wild flashes of color and the spinning motions of the magical transport between tasks, Colbey staved off travel sickness. As his vision cleared, he found himself in another stone room, far different from the last one. Some craftsman had carved and painted the walls until none of the granite showed through. Despite the possibility of enemies and danger, Colbey could not keep his eyes from straying repeatedly to the masonry. Caution did allow him to tear his attention away long enough to ascertain that he was alone in the room and to locate the exits, three doors along the same wall, each as competently decorated as the walls. Colbey gratefully let his gaze fix on the carvings.

The stonework depicted tales of the Northern gods, illustrations of characters and stories he had revered since childhood. The colors ranged from the subtle grays of Odin the AllFather to the bold and glittering golds of wanton Freya. The figures appeared so stark, Colbey's mind sensed movement repeatedly, and it took an effort of will to keep his hand from his weapons to counter imagined attacks from the artwork. His instincts and scrutiny told him that he was the only living creature in the chamber, and he trusted those far more than tiny flashes of vision. Still, the tide of Aegir's ocean seemed to surge and recede. Thor's hammer appeared more than capable of smashing the giant that the god of law and storms faced.

One figure held the Renshai's gaze longest, a wiry male clothed in reds, tans, and black. Colbey recognized the carving at once. Loki, the Shape Changer, the god destined to betray his peers in the *Ragnarok,* looked oddly familiar, with an unrealistic, hazy quality that made Colbey wonder if he had seen a similar picture with the god in the same pose. He supposed that the flashy red and black silks he had chosen to wear at the beginning of the Tasks of Wizardry did resem-

ble the Shape Changer's garb. Suddenly, the quaracks' misunderstanding seemed to make more sense.

Colbey found his own patron on the left-hand wall. Sif sat,
her flowing hair crafted from metallic gold. The painting had
captured the color perfectly, and Colbey wondered if the artist
actually used gold plating in his colors. He did not check,
however. To chip at such a masterpiece seemed foolhardy as
well as sacrilegious. Other goddesses filled the scene on this
particular wall. He saw Idun with her magical apples of
youth, Odin's wife Frigg, and the three Norns: past, present,
and future. He followed the painting to Freya, and he averted
his eyes, guilty over the thought that the woman he had met
between tasks put even her beauty to shame.

Colbey found the others on the right-hand wall. He looked
first for the Renshai's other patron, Modi. He found the sons
of Thor together, Modi and Magni, wrath and might, watching
their father battle the giant. They seemed happy, perhaps because of their destiny to live through the *Ragnarok,* when most
of the other gods would perish. The other survivors stood
nearby, casually involved with their own works, a subtle
grouping by the artist. The symbolism intrigued and horrified
Colbey, and he stared from one to the next: Vali and Vidar,
two of the AllFather's sons; Hod and Baldur, also Odin's sons,
who would rise from the dead at the war's end; and long-
legged Honir whose wisdom would guide the new age. On
other parts of the wall, Colbey discovered more of the gods
who had filled the elders' stories, like Frey, Tyr, and Heimdall.

A click echoed through the chamber. Colbey whirled,
hands falling naturally to his hilts. His right palm found
leather-wrapped metal. The other met nothing. Ire flared,
then quickly dissipated. When Colbey traversed the limbo
between tasks, he apparently fell to the mercy of his testers.
Once before, they had taken both of his weapons, and he
drew solace from the one blade they had left him. From its
position, apparently they had even let him keep Harval.

While Colbey watched, the central of the three doors
opened, cutting the carving of the Midgard serpent into
halves. A stranger stood in the doorway, backlit by daylight.
Beyond him, Colbey believed he could see cottages, roads,
and buildings. Before he could focus more closely, the other
stepped into the room, closing the door behind him. The serpent re-formed, and the room returned to the dingy grayness
that Colbey had been too distracted by the artwork to notice.

The stranger stood taller than Colbey. Though medium-framed, his stomach bulged. He sported the white hair of a man who had been blond in youth, and he wore a pair of doeskin breeks. His fine silk shirt was midnight blue, like his eyes. A lavender cape hung from sagging shoulders. He carried no evident weaponry. He seemed to take no notice of the carvings. His gaze riveted on Colbey, and his person radiated doubt, hope, and fear. "Kyndig?" he asked carefully, giving it the proper Northern pronunciation: *Kawn-dee.*

Politely, Colbey kept his hand from his sword. "I've been called that."

"Praise Odin." The man smiled, his aura transforming to one of pure pleasure. "The legends grow old. I—"

Disdainful of uncontrolled excitement, Colbey cut to the heart of the matter. "Who are you? And what test must I pass to escape this room?"

"Escape?" The man regarded Colbey curiously. His joy faltered. "You only need to exit through the door." He gestured at the portal behind him, sandwiched between the other two. "It'll take you to our town, Asgardbyr. I'm King Sivard. I'm not holding you hostage, Lord Kyndig, but there are the legends and we do need you."

Colbey attributed little of significance to these stories. It made no sense that a town created strictly for testing Cardinal Wizards would have legends and history. "Why do you need me?"

"To kill Fenrir's spawn. He's plagued my people for decades. But now, it's worse. Beyond that door . . ." He indicated the exit to his left, ". . . lies our temple to Thor. The great lord Thunder god Justicekeeper placed his hammer, Mjollnir, in our keeping. Fenrir's spawn fought past my guards and stole the weapon."

Colbey could not suppress a chuckle at the thought of Mjollnir entrusted to humans, though stranger things had occurred in recent days. Tired of gods' games, Colbey searched the king's mind directly. Aware that the invasion would cost him physical energy, he kept his exploration brief, and it revealed that Sivard believed every word that he had spoken. Still, this attested only to his honesty, not his veracity or sanity, and Colbey seriously questioned the latter.

King Sivard continued. "Of course, no one but Thor has the strength to lift Mjollnir, so the spawn of Fenrir was foiled. Still, it apparently decided that, if it can't wield the hammer, neither will Thor." The king pressed thick fingers to his temples, as if to staunch a headache. "The creature has killed all the champions we sent to slay it." His voice fell to a whisper, as if he feared the beast might hear him through a forearm's thickness of granite. "And without Mjollnir, I'm not certain even Thor can best the monster." He shivered, lacing his fingers, and his voice grew higher in pitch and volume. "Oh, how the god will rage when he learns of this. I'm so glad you've come to help us, Kyndig."

Colbey scowled. He turned, finding the image of Thor and Mjollnir on the painted walls. The golden hammer gleamed, its handle disproportionately shortened due, according to the legends, to one of Loki's tricks during its forging. "The great wolf has a spawn?" Memory crowded upon him, mothers' stories of hybrid monsters created to frighten children into behaving. He shook his head to clear it. Too much that he had attributed to tales had recently proven truth. Weeks ago, he had met an elf. Within the year, a demon that he had dismissed as country legend had all but lost him his hand.

"Fenrir's spawn. By his own mother!"

Colbey puzzled the pedigree. *Grandson of the god, Loki, son of a wolf and a giantess.* The king's sanity fell further into question. "What's it like?"

"It has the head of a wolf, the body of a man, and the strength of a rampaging boar." The description sounded rehearsed. "It rips my townsfolk apart and feasts on them." He shivered, his voice shaking with impotent rage. "And it waits beyond the door for the death stroke your sword must deal."

Colbey's cold eyes held the king's, until Sivard turned his gaze to his feet uncomfortably. There followed a long silence.

At length, Colbey broke it. "This beast has terrorized your people for some time?"

Sivard nodded dully. "Decades."

"It shreds men and has killed every champion you sent against it? You say even Thor might not be able to slay it, without his hammer?"

Sivard did not reply.

Colbey stared. *What is this? The test of stupidity?* "You expect me to walk into a room with it?" Colbey snorted with self-righteous indignation. "I have no feud with Fenrir's son. What makes you think I'd just march to my death?"

"I–I . . ." King Sivard stammered. Apparently this thought

had never entered his mind. "You're a hero. That's what heroes do." Abandoning that line of thought, he tried another. "If you want a reward, we can pay you whatever silver we can find. You can have your pick of our women. I'd sell my own daughter to the man who kills that . . . thing. But it carries a treasure more valuable than any I can give you. It has a golden ring. Those few who got close enough to see it died, but tales of its worth survived them." Only then, his gaze strayed to the collection of copper, silver, and gold on Colbey's fingers. He looked up quickly, apparently not wishing to be caught gawking, and his eyes betrayed sudden disappointment. "I guess money isn't really something you need."

Nothing the king had mentioned had interested Colbey, except for the beast's ring, presumably the one he needed to start the next task. But the challenge promised by Fenrir's spawn offered intangibles that did intrigue the Renshai. Whether or not he won the match, he could not lose the fight. If Fenrir's spawn killed him, Colbey would die in battle and find Valhalla. If Colbey killed the beast, he would simply continue his trials. That had problems and implications of its own, but Colbey already had those to face. He drew his sword.

Frightened by the sudden movement, King Sivard sprang aside.

The grip nestled into Colbey's callused fist, as if molded to fit it. Even so, the Renshai realized that it was not Harval. The balance felt nearly perfect, but Colbey knew his sword like his own arm. He swung the blade a few times, testing, reassuring himself that it would serve as well as any other. He would never allow himself to become dependent on a single sword or its magic. The weapon was only a tool; he was the power. Without a word or qualm, he strode to the indicated door.

King Sivard pushed past Colbey gingerly, unable to hide a grin. He produced a long brass key, which he positioned in the hole beneath the knob. "I'll lock the door behind you. The previous champions had a key, too, and it's still in there. You can find it and escape when you've killed Fenrir's spawn."

The door swung open a crack on well-oiled hinges.

Though Colbey's thoughts and attention turned naturally to the task at hand, he had the presence of mind to wonder why Sivard had not passed him the key that had just opened the door. The answer came with little thought. For all of the king's bold chatter, he did not expect Colbey to survive the battle. Colbey suspected that, if the previous champions did have a key, it did not fit the lock. Only a fool would chance the key falling into the hands of a beast he sought to contain. Still, becoming trapped did not bother Colbey. Presumably Fenrir's spawn carried the ring he needed to leave.

Colbey slipped inside, and the door slammed and clicked closed behind him. The room seemed huge and oddly chill. A corpse sprawled just inside the door, its helmet shattered and its armor dented. A wooden shield lay across the body, and it still clutched a battle ax in its lifeless hand. A gilded table in the center of the room supported an enormous, gold hammer with a disproportionately short handle. *Mjollnir, hammer of Thor.* All doubt fled Colbey at the sight, and he stared in awe and wonder.

The gut-wrenching odor of carrion seemed to suffocate Colbey then. It did not emanate from the dead man he had stepped across, but from a second one deeper in the room. By craning his neck around the table, he saw a half-staved skull. Thick strands of scarlet-stained, yellow hair poked at random from the ruined head. The sword at the corpse's side lay unblooded. A hideous-looking creature crouched, feasting upon the rotting flesh.

As Colbey approached, the creature rose, towering more than half again Colbey's height. Coarse, gray fur tumbled along its head and neck. Its face resembled Secodon, but Shadimar's wolf had soft, brown eyes and those of Fenrir's spawn glowed red. It sported the body of the most muscle-bound caricature ever drawn of Thor; its chest jutted like two boulders on a massive torso. Triceps and biceps bulged from its arms, and smaller muscles stretched along its fore-arms. Its legs made its arms look tiny. To Colbey, it seemed like a mountain covered with rugged crags. Yet he did not fall prey to belief in the common myth. Large did not necessarily mean slow.

Sword readied, Colbey stepped around the table. Fenrir's son leered, brandished a club as thick as a tree trunk, and growled a warning. Without hesitation, Colbey swung for its abdomen. The spawn leapt backward. Its riposte fell short.

For a full minute, not a single blow landed. Colbey's strokes came swift, short, and fine, always directed toward his opponent's face. Less sure, Fenrir's spawn swatted pendulously at the golden-haired flea who had spoiled its dinner. Withdrawing from the steel waving in its face weakened the beast's strokes, yet Colbey knew a single blow could smash any bone it hit.

For a moment, the beast hesitated. Colbey thrust. The tip of his sword gashed his enemy's side, then the resistance disappeared. Half of his blade clattered to the stone floor. The hilt remained in his fist, stubbornly supporting a hand's breadth of blade. Shocked, the Renshai lost his timing. He stumbled aside. A wave of air lifted the hair on the side of his head, and Colbey realized he had narrowly escaped death.

Broken? How? Unable to comprehend how such a minor strike could snap tempered steel that he had deemed sturdy, Colbey feigned a dodge to the left and dove sideways. A back muscle tore painfully. He rolled across the stone, grabbing for the dead man's hilt. Catching it, he rose and brandished the sword.

Back in the fight, Colbey howled wordlessly. The sword lacked the fine balance and meticulous edge of one of his own, but it was still a sword. He sprang at the beast. The blade carved the air with controlled power, lunging at the creature from all directions. Fenrir's spawn heaved madly in defense. A lucky sweep met Colbey's sword and smashed it. Shards flew, struck the back wall, and scattered to the floor like metallic rain. Colbey paused in disbelief, weaponless once more. Countless times, he had seen swords break in battle, but never before had he seen steel fragment. The club grazed his hand, snapping a finger like a twig.

Pain mobilized Colbey. He dodged the wild sweeps with the same agility he had lent to his now-broken swords. Croaking noises erupted from deep in the beast's throat. *Laughter.* Its confidence pleased rather than cowed Colbey. *Smug opponents grow careless,* he reminded himself as the hurricane strokes forced him to retreat.

But the beast could afford arrogance against a weaponless foe. Though not fast, the monster's attacks seemed ceaseless. Colbey's concentration channeled into dodges, and his steps grew less sure as he approached the room's center and tried to recall the precise location of the table by memory. He skirted it successfully, but the beast's club crashed against it. Wood splintered, spilling Thor's hammer to the floor with a jolt that seemed to shake the entire room.

Each of the spawn's broad sweeps sent Colbey straggling toward the door that he knew he could not open. He slipped on the corpse, fighting for balance, and his other heel touched the back wall. *No place to go. No way to avoid the next strike.* The club swept air from Colbey's left to his right. As it flew past him, the Renshai followed its course. When the return stroke came, he hoped it would not have gathered enough impulse to damage him severely.

Colbey gauged the distance to the dead man. The club slammed into his gut, stealing breath. He wrapped both arms around the weapon and clung. The beast bellowed, thrashing to and fro to shake Colbey free. The stench of Fenrir's son nearly overwhelmed the Renshai.

Suddenly, timing carefully, Colbey released his hold. Momentum bowled him across the floor. He scrabbled for the dead man's ax, only to find the pole broken and the head detached from it. Instead, he snatched up the shield, securing a hold before the wolf-man turned to resume its attack. In normal combat, Renshai spurned shields and armor as cowards' protections, used by soldiers too unskilled or lazy to dodge and tend defense. In a direct one on one conflict, Colbey would still have to counter each strike. The shield would only replace the sword as a parrying tool.

A string of saliva oozed from the beast's open jaws. Oily sweat added a sheen to its massive frame.

Colbey's limbs ached from overuse. The strained back muscle throbbed, and his broken finger jabbed pain the length of his arm. He caught the next bone-wrenching assault on the shield. His evasions remained nimble, but fatigue slowed him. Even his mind could no longer pump reserves to his failing body.

Fenrir's spawn also panted, but the gross swings did not tax him to the extent they did his quarry. Colbey caught more blows on the shield as his strength diminished. He allowed the beast to herd him where it would.

Thoughts closed in on Colbey, self-deprecating realities he had never needed to consider before. *Perhaps Episte was right and I am a fool. I put so much time and effort into swordplay, I became the best. But, without a sword, I'm as helpless as a townsman.* Colbey dodged a blinding stroke. *Perhaps not helpless, but another man might know how to use this damned shield as a weapon.*

Again, the club thumped against the shield. The wood

cracked open, and Colbey's arm went numb. The force of
the blow drove him to his knees. Agony dazed him. He
watched the club rise. As quick as he was, Colbey knew he
could not avoid this stroke. And, although he had faced
death before, this time he did not feel at peace.

Flung wide, Colbey's right hand touched a pipe-shaped
object and closed around it. Thrilled to find anything to
place between himself and the oncoming beating, Colbey
jerked it before him. The bar rolled on a rounded base. the
club struck gold with the fury of a galloping horse. And, this
time, the wood exploded.

The beast loosed a terrified shriek and ran. Colbey's gaze
found the object in his fist, and he could not help staring. He
held Mjollnir's haft. The shortened handle of Thor's hammer
rested in his palm, and the head lay on the floor. Colbey
laughed with sudden understanding. He bulled through pain
with need, wrapping his tingling left hand below his right.
With a surge of strength more mental than physical, he
raised the hammer and hurled it.

Mjollnir tumbled through the air, swift but unsure. A
crash slammed through Colbey's ears, and the whole room
jarred and shook. When Colbey staggered to his feet, his opponent had gone gray, the wolfish sneer transformed into a
grimace. His chest had become a mass of crimson speckled
with gray-white chips of shattered ribs. The flaming eyes
had gone cold.

It's not Mjollnir. Colbey approached his dead foe. *It was
never Mjollnir, but it looked so real, I believed.* He knelt beside the crushed wolf-man and poked a finger in its eye. It
gave no response. Colbey took one of the beefy hands and
examined it. On the smallest finger, it wore a ring of gold.
He eased the jewelry free, studying the fine runes carved inside, uncertain what sort of instrument could have engraved
the tiny letters: A wise man knows his limits. A hero
achieves beyond them.

"Audacity!" Colbey said aloud, and the word echoed.
How could I possibly have failed this test? He laughed,
thinking of the many people who had cursed or ridiculed his
brashness in battle, mostly men who would rather attribute
skill to luck of birth than believe any man had more self-
motivation and will than themselves. He guessed that the nature of this task changed from Wizard to Wizard, that each
faced his own "Mjollnir" true to his faith and beliefs.

Colbey rose, and the sudden movement sent a wash of spots across his vision. He kept his balance by an act of will, and the weakness reminded him how near he had come to death. *One task remaining.*

Colbey raised the ring, but he could not leave without a word to the finest, strongest enemy he could ever remember facing. "Thank you for a noble battle, Fenrir's spawn." Then, Colbey placed the ring on the fourth finger of his left hand. This time, the swirl and flash of magic proved too much for him, and he spiraled into oblivion.

Colbey awakened to the mingled odors of sweat and alcohol, and the combination made him queasy. He opened his eyes, catching a glimpse of rows of men. Before he could fully gain his bearings, an angry shove sent him airborne. Colbey swore, twisting like a cat. He landed on his feet on a floor of cold earth, and he glanced about quickly, needing to understand position and situation. A circular granite wall enclosed him, spanning as much territory as the whole of the Wizards' Meeting Isle. Seats rose in tiers from the walls, crammed full of men whose shouts wafted to him, disparate and indecipherable. Although he had never entered an arena before, Colbey drew on the dying memories he had gleaned from an ex-slave and friend named Garn.

The gall of men who would treat him as a common gladiator outraged Colbey. His cheeks flushed hot, and his hands fell to his hilts. He scanned the opposite end of the ring, seeking the opponent he guessed he must face as his final test. Once, Shadimar had promised Colbey that the tasks would herald the finest battle of his life. Now, Colbey felt certain he faced the trial the Eastern Wizard had meant.

Another man waited at the far end of the pit. From a distance, Colbey could see that he was not large, and he bore none of the brawny musculature that kept gladiators alive in the pit. But his sinews stretched taut beneath a plain gray tunic and breeks, the figure of a man accustomed to war. A pair of longswords graced his belt, and that surprised Colbey. He had met only one other man who, like himself, used two swords at once. That other had been a Renshai, a student of his, now more than a decade dead.

The man approached. Colbey studied his movements in fascination. The opponent carried himself with enviable grace and unshakable confidence. Each sinew shifted with a fineness Colbey envied, and the Renshai instinctively knew that many of the stranger's best maneuvers would be similar to Colbey's own. Ire was forgotten as excitement suffused the Renshai, and he felt torn. He harbored no doubt that this man could give him the finest battle of his life, and the need to know who would prove the better ached within him. Still, as a companion, this man would prove invaluable and, as a team, they would surely be unstoppable. His heart pounded a slow, joyous cadence, and the voices around him might have disappeared for all the heed he paid them.

Colbey tore his gaze from movement and form to features. The man's hair was bright yellow. His eyes gleamed, blue-gray, evil, and painful to view. His face was of indeterminate age, and Colbey recognized it as his own. He gasped.

No movement betrayed the other's attack, yet Colbey drew his swords. His opponent reached him before they came fully free. Colbey had never seen anyone move as swiftly nor with such practiced agility. His foe's first strike was a Renshai maneuver invented by Colbey. His own parry redirected it from a death blow to a sweep that nicked his chest.

"Modi!" Colbey's cry came naturally, though it seemed to spur his opponent as much as himself. He managed to catch both blades on Harval. His other sword creased his opponent's thigh. Then, they dove at one another, merging into a swirling gold and silver cloud. Surely, no one but the combatants could follow the leaping blades, and it seemed ironic to set a battle between indistinguishable enemies in an arena. *How can the spectators tell us apart to lay bets?* The thought quickly faded as Colbey discovered that he needed his full concentration to counter the constant attacks.

Steel rose and dove, lethal accuracy lost to supreme defense. Despite the need for full attention to battle, Colbey could not stop himself from pondering the Wizards' final test. *Surely half or more of the potential Cardinal Wizards died during this one task.* He imagined that the gods had created it to assure that their prospects could force themselves to do battle at their fullest potential, since the doubles probably fought as the apprentice usually did. But Colbey threw himself into every battle, even into every spar, with maximum effort. His could only be an even match.

The clamor of ringing steel became pleasant and rhythmical. Colbey felt a rising pity as he faced the same enemy he had loosed on so many others. His parry fell short. An opening appeared for a fraction of a second. His opponent's blade bore through. A fiery pain coursed along Colbey's left forearm. Harval dropped from his grip, and his arm fell limp. *The tendon!* Colbey realized he had lost the arm's use and the battle in less time than it took to blink.

A strangled cry wrested from Colbey's throat. He used the damaged arm as a shield. With the time this bought him, he scuttled backward and across the pit. As the other man closed on him, Colbey gathered all of his mental will for a final surge. So long as he lived, he was not beaten. His chances had shrunk nearly to nothing, yet he had never played the same odds as other men.

Colbey tensed to channel all of his mental power to his languishing muscles, when another idea came to him. As always on the battlefield, he made his decision instantly, weighing consequences in a heartbeat. When his opponent sprang, Colbey gathered the stream of his consciousness, and hurled the mental energy into the other's mind.

Colbey's thoughts crashed into an empty skull. The being was no being. It had no mind or sentience, only the carefully patterned competence of the man it mimicked. Colbey would have spat an oath, but no strength remained even for this simple action. He had risked everything. And lost.

Drained, Colbey staggered, his probe still lodged in the void of his opponent's head. A black and red curtain wove across his vision, blinding. He did not know how near his enemy's sword hovered, when his mind touched a threadlike projection in the otherwise empty head. Instantly, he grasped for it, unconsciousness battering at the little awareness that remained. Already his mental strength began to dissipate, yet his probe shot along the cord to embed in a brain more powerful than any he had ever read or assailed.

Shock registered in the other mind. It dropped its animated Colbey-double to face the intruder in its mind. Colbey's opponent fell limp.

Colbey's concentration flickered dangerously. "Modi," he whispered, the call providing only a glimmer of strength. Yet that proved enough. Before the other could retaliate, Colbey pulled his mental probe free. He collapsed, sword first, upon his double.

CHAPTER 9

The Black Door

A steady glow issued from a high, semicircular fireplace, its strangely uniform light washing over a pile of blue shards on a table. Standing beside this single piece of furniture, Colbey could count every muscle in his body by the burning, throbbing, and sharp aches that defined them. Certain he was alone, he waved his left arm, testing the tendon that he believed he had lost during his last trial. It worked, but the movement sent tortured waves along his arm, like all motion did after an especially grueling workout. It was a discomfort to which Colbey had grown accustomed, and it always pleased as well as pained him, his reward for having forced himself to work. *There can be no skill without pain.*

Colbey's mind felt fuzzy as he regathered the energy he had hurled from it. As he slowly regained function, he began to notice more about his surroundings than just the absence of threat. The Seven Tasks of Wizardry seemed like a distant nightmare. Only one of the rings remained on his fingers, the gold one that the goddess had given him. The room seemed much like the one in which the Wizards had gathered before the tests began, except it lacked a door. Now, Colbey recognized the shards on the tabletop as remnants of the Pica Stone.

"No!" Colbey stared in horror and revulsion at the symbol of his people, now reduced to ruin. He had taken a vow of brotherhood with Shadimar, one that was to have lasted as long as the Eastern Wizard kept the Pica Stone safe. The sapphire had stood as the symbol of a fellowship that the Wizard had already broken and the strength of a people, the Renshai, now devastated.

Colbey hefted a sliver in the shape of a droplet, his revulsion turning to shaking rage. It lay, still and sterile, in his palm, not even a glimmer left to remind him of the power it had once held and the tribe it had once defined. *I let you keep it, and you promised to safeguard it. Now, Wizard, all your conjured demons could not stay my wrath.* He let the fragment slip through his fingers and click back onto the table. Carefully, he swept the shards into a pile, prepared to bury them and, with them, the memories of an empty brotherhood and a slaughtered tribe.

"Kyndig!" The voice lashed, whiplike yet beautiful as the melody of a running stream.

Colbey had not heard or sensed another's entrance. He whirled to face a man in silk and fur, a Northman by the flaxen locks poking from beneath his wide-brimmed hat. His single eye glared, as piercing as Colbey's own. The Renshai guessed he must have sacrificed caution to rage to get caught so off-guard. The lack of a door meant the man must have been in the room all along. "Who are you?"

"The Keeper of the Eighth Task," said the other. And his voice seemed more akin to wind. "It awaits you, Kyndig."

"There is no eighth task." Colbey parroted Shadimar, still unnerved by his own lack of vigilance.

"Ah, but there is. Even should you decline my offer, simply making the choice is a task. You see, Kyndig ..." He stepped toward Colbey.

The Renshai crouched, fingers locking on the hilts of his swords.

Recklessly heedless of Colbey's defensive stance, the Keeper continued without missing a beat, "... in a situation that demands action, a Wizard must believe himself capable of anything. But he must also know when not to attempt a thing he cannot achieve. A Wizard must be a leader. He has no right to involve his followers in matters in which they need take no part."

"I don't like riddles. I don't know magic. And I'm no Wizard." Colbey felt discomforted by the Keeper. "It's a title forced on me by fools. It is a thing they would believe and have me pretend to be."

"You are a Wizard, Kyndig." The strange man's voice cackled. "You can't deny it any more than you can deny manhood. Regardless of his intentions, a man is exactly what others believe him to be. You are a deathseeker, a prince of demons, an evil-bringer, and the skilled one of legends. You are the Western Wizard, too."

Disinterested in mental warfare, Colbey scowled. "So what is this eighth task? And what bearing does it have on you or on me?" Angrily, he shrugged a cramp from his shoulder.

"Me?" The fur-clad man laughed, the sound like thunder. "It doesn't matter to me whether you try or not, nor if you live or die. But I will warn you of this. No one before you who chose to attempt the eighth task survived." His face went grim and taut-lipped.

Curiosity tweaked the edges of Colbey's consciousness, and the challenge beckoned. "Would you answer questions about the task?"

"Candidly."

"How many have attempted it?"

The sun glinted on the shattered Pica, flinging blue highlights along the walls and ceiling. The glow grew most intense on the cruel-faced stranger, giving his pallid skin a gray cast. "Few," the one-eyed Keeper admitted. "But you have to recall how few complete the first seven. Most are ready to take their title and ignore what I offer."

Colbey refused to accept vagaries. "You didn't answer my question."

The man laughed. "Ten, Kyndig. And no man knows what became of them."

Colbey doubted that the being before him was a man. His single eye and commanding appearance fit the descriptions of Odin the AllFather, yet Colbey dared not believe he faced the gray god himself. "And what did become of them?"

The other raised his shoulders noncommittally, though he did not deny the knowledge. "They died. That is certain. I won't tell you the cause. I have to leave some secrets to those brave or foolish enough to try the eighth task."

Colbey wiped a damp palm on his breeks. Shadimar and Captain had told him that only the most competent were chosen to attempt the Seven Tasks of Wizardry, and even most of them did not make it through. The challenge flared to a jabbing need to know and understand. Yet the sincerity of Shadimar's warning stayed him. He continued to delay. "Why does anyone try it?"

The Keeper rolled his eye. "Insecurity, perhaps? I can only surmise. I am the Keeper of the Task, not the keeper of men. I believe they all tried to overcome their fears of death."

Colbey raised his head as proudly as the speaker. "Then I have no need of your task. I don't fear death."

"Many men believe that." The Keeper dismissed the statement as bluster.

Colbey recalled his last encounter with death and the beautiful woman who had rescued him. "I'm as candid as you, Keeper. I know myself as no one else can. I don't fear death."

"Ah! Very well, then." The Keeper accepted the statement, though he did not seem convinced. "Then you may be the one who can succeed." He yawned, bored with the questioning. "My time is not easily bought, Kyndig. You may ask one more."

Colbey did not ponder long. He stretched his stiff fingers. "Is there some purpose to this task? What reward were these dead Wizards seeking?"

Surprise added color to the Keeper's otherwise white features. "You don't know? Why even the least capable had heard mention of the Staff of Law. You seem to prefer simple terms, Kyndig, so I'll tell you in a word. Power. Ultimate power."

Colbey laughed, the fires of need receding. "I already have more than I ever wanted. It seems to find me."

"So you refuse the task?"

Colbey opened his mouth to confirm. Even as he did, he made one of the split second decisions that had become his trademark on the battlefield. "No. I accept it." His own words startled him, and he analyzed his reasons aloud. "In the future, if someone else asks why men choose to attempt the task, you can tell them that, for me, it was curiosity."

The expression on the One-Eyed One's face never changed, but a strange, unreadable emotion wafted to Colbey. It seemed akin to distress, yet the Keeper's confidence warped it to something else, a grim acceptance of an unknown that seemed inevitable. The Keeper turned to face the back wall. He traced a rectangle across its surface with his fingers. The stone quivered beneath his touch, then darkened within the boundaries. A door took shape there, black as night, yet shimmering as if from the radiance of a moon on the opposite side. It looked hazy and unreal, as if it spanned worlds and time. "Then it's time for you to determine your future, Kyndig. If you have one." He gestured to the door. Its substance disappeared, replaced by an opening that seemed equally dense.

Now, Colbey no longer doubted the identity of the being

before him, certainly a god. The manifestation of the door was magic of a sure and true sort, unlike the petty illusions and the summonings that were all the sorcery he had ever seen performed by the Cardinal Wizards. His decision made, he did not hesitate. He approached the portal and passed through it.

Once through the door frame, he entered a room without boundaries. It seemed more like a plain, for a room has walls and this had none. Yet, for reasons he did not ponder, Colbey clung to the image of enclosure. His mind seemed to become semisolid, folding across itself as if molded by a god's hand. He grasped the concept of constraint more tightly, forming a barrier to contain the straying pieces of his mind. Multihued spots waltzed before his eyes, blocking his vision.

Then, as suddenly, the spots dissolved; and a scene leapt to vivid clarity. There was light, but no sun. A ceiling hovered overhead, unsupported by walls. In the distance, Colbey saw an object too far off to identify, though it seemed large and significant. He headed toward it without any preconceived notions, finding it futile to try to imagine what had taken the lives of ten apprentice Wizards. Long ago, he had discovered that the things that induced panic in heroes seemed like simple annoyances to him. If the test could be won, Colbey would succeed. If not, he would join those before him.

As the distance between the object and the Renshai narrowed, it resolved into the shape of a thick, straw ticking. A figure lay upon it, swaddled in blankets. With each step, the nauseating reek of illness grew stronger, and Colbey's pace slowed. The odor of pestilence and death made him cringe in pity, and he harbored no wish to share whatever had withered the pathetic creature in the bed. Still, Colbey had learned the healing arts to rescue warriors from illness and to help them find honorable deaths in battle. During his travels, he had used the Renshai tribe's herbal and rehabilitative knowledge to earn money for food and lodgings, and his conscience would not allow him to watch illness claim another without at least trying to give aid. He pushed on.

At length, Colbey stood over the bed and stared. The blanket stirred, revealing two liquid eyes, deeply sunken into sharply angled, bony sockets. Parchment-thin skin stretched from bone to bone and sagged in ghostly pale wrinkles be-

tween them. The creature reached a trembling hand toward
Colbey, and its green-crusted, toothless mouth opened to
croak a warning.

Colbey's mind twisted free of his carefully-constructed
barriers, detaching from self and control. It stuffed his
thoughts into the body on the bed. Strength drained from
him in an instant, leaving him frail, fever-ravaged, and aching in every part. Disease crawled over and through him, un-
resisted, like a creature that seemed more alive than the man
it afflicted. Death hovered, a friend waiting for the signal to
come and take the pain away.

All of Colbey's doubts assailed him then. He had become,
in every way, the being on the bed. His own body disappeared, and his rheumy eyes saw nothing but a blurry plain
and death's promise. Regrets hemmed and hammered him.
He recalled the young Renshai, called Episte, who had
seemed more son than student to him. His mind conjured
images of the child, grand and glorious, his potential with a
sword so natural that dedication could have made it flawless.
Yet Episte had shown more loyalty to people than to his
swords; the Renshai maneuvers had seemed little more than
duty and distraction. Over his fifteen years, he had sought
Colbey's love and approval, both of which he had won. Yet
Colbey's need to make the boy the best had driven the elder
to goad and chastise. He would never forget that his last
memory of the sane Episte was his own harsh words and a
slap. His last vision of the Wizard-warped madman the boy
had become was of his own mercy dagger, the *nådenal,*
shoved through Episte's back.

Colbey felt the sting of rising tears that would not come.
Heat and sickness had dehydrated the body he now occupied, the disease-wracked creature that had become himself.
Yet though the bony arm moved as his own, Colbey forced
himself to disbelieve. He would not complete the transformation for the Keeper of the Eighth Task. If death wanted
him, it would not find him an easy victim, whether from illness, age, or battle. He walled off his mind from the body,
drove agony away, and called war against the fantasies that
assailed him. Enchantments bounced from his defenses,
flashing colored streamers through his eye-closed world.
Colbey threw off the restraining blankets and sprang from
the bed. "Illness, you won't have me. If I can't defeat you,

I can evade you. Now that we've met at last, you no longer daunt me."

A ball of light struck the floor and exploded into stunning whiteness. Abruptly, the being in silk and fur stood before Colbey again. "Ah, so it's true. Nothing in the nine worlds frightens you. What a man must endure to pass this test is all that he fears. Since all mortals fear death and those things that can kill them, none but you survived. You feared only illness, and you conquered that fear. You were quite correct. You don't fear death. If you did, you would have died, and from that trial, there is no escape."

Colbey scowled, believing he had sustained more than enough to prove what he had claimed from the start. "Of course, I was quite correct. I don't lie. Not even to myself."

The one-eyed being frowned. "Don't become arrogant. You will make me regret the power I offer. You do still fear one thing. And although you wouldn't have any way to know it yet, that fear has been recognized. You will never reach Valhalla."

The pronouncement slammed into Colbey, rousing him instantly to rage. "You lie!" He crouched, drawing both swords.

The Keeper smiled, heedless of the weapons and their deadly wielder. "Do I? You're welcome to disbelieve. Or you can accept the truth."

Colbey remained in position, anger ebbing slowly.

"I'm not obligated to explain further," the Keeper continued. "But I now have a personal interest in your future." He stepped aside to reveal a copper rack that his body had concealed. "It is time to meet your reward and another decision."

Carelessly, the Keeper turned his back. Still enraged, Colbey considered attacking just to discover whether skill or foolishness made the Keeper so indifferent to an armed Renshai. Guessing the futility, Colbey sought calm within himself. Curiosity helped to quench the fires.

When the Keeper turned back, he held the two staves that had graced the rack, one in each hand. He gripped them in fists so tight his fingers blanched, and he chanted in a skjaldic rhythm:

"In Odin's day
The world was fey,
And we dwelt in the nether.

Asgard was naught,
With changes wrought,
As quickly as the weather.

"The staff was made
As Odin bade
To hold the Chaos raging.
A weapon new
For Odin who
A great war was a-waging.

"To free the land
From Chaos' hand
And make the young lands hale.
Once beset,
The Norns did fret,
But Odin could not fail.

"The Staff fared well
As the bards now tell,
The new world it a-forging.
As Odin laughed
And brandished Staff
With battle lust a-gorging.

"With Law's reach long
And new grip strong
The world could little change.
Is as it was
Was as it is
For none to rearrange.

"But Odin's hand
Still ruled the land,
Strong as the great wolf's maw.
The Gray One bade
A new Staff made:
Behold the Staff of Law.

"With neither free
The earth shall be
Fit for man and beast.
Till one great mage

Shall close the age
And lead Hati to feast."

A silence beyond life settled over the room. Colbey watched the one-eyed being. Finally, the Guardian of the Staves spoke again. "I leave you to your choice. But, before you decide, I have more for you to ponder. With this Staff . . ." He raised his right arm and the staff it held. ". . . I control all but have no rule. With this . . ." He raised the other, identical-appearing staff. "I control none, but my reign is sure and long. Which will you have? Make your choice well, Kyndig."

Colbey's anger had faded during the poetry. Now faced with an unexpected decision, all traces disappeared, and he considered the Staves with the seriousness that the Keeper apparently expected. The earliest of the gods' legends ran through his mind repeatedly, in an endless cycle. No doubt, the Keeper had spoken of creation, when the gods first came into existence and Odin had banished the Primordial Chaos to create a world existing entirely of Order. In the last two decades, Chaos had begun to touch the world again, apparently through cracks in the gray god's defenses. Colbey saw its work in the form of mistruths and betrayals, swaying loyalties and thefts. Though he had never before recognized it consciously, the lapse had shaken even his fixed faith in the omnipotent AllFather of the gods.

Yet in the moments since the Keeper's chant, several answers avalanched into Colbey's mind at once. Many times, he had questioned Shadimar about the need for four Wizards to champion only two forces, good and evil. Every time, the Eastern Wizard had insisted that neutrality, itself, was a concept so significant that it needed two guardians where the others needed only one apiece. Now, Colbey finally understood. The Eastern and Western Wizards had been created to champion law and chaos.

Though Colbey felt certain of its truth, the conclusion confused as well as pained him. *If the two were made to wield law and chaos, why have they not done so over the millennia? Why have the staves remained in the gods' keeping?* Many possibilities presented themselves then, but only one seemed plausible. *All these years, Odin has waited. Waited for what?* Colbey considered an instant longer. *Waited for someone to complete the eighth task, someone who does not fear death, someone capable of wielding the Staff of . . .* There, Colbey's logic faltered. *Law or Chaos? Which has he waited for?* He felt sweat bead beneath his collar, suddenly aware of the significance of his choice. Colbey knew for certain that the fate of the world hung in the balance, waiting for him to make a single choice. His instincts told him to take the Staff of Law, to keep chaos from the world a bit longer. But, for once, Colbey did not follow his natural inclination. This decision required more thought and more information.

"Now I understand why so few attempt the final task. There is no reward. I'll take neither staff."

The One-eyed One stared impassively at Colbey, his single eye unwinking. "The reward is what it is. Every tool requires a man to wield it. The man, not the tool, determines its significance." The hush that followed stretched painfully. "No questions will be answered this time. There is nothing left, Kyndig, but your choice."

No sane man would willingly decide to serve or distribute chaos. Yet two ideas gave Colbey pause. First, he knew that one god, Loki the Shape Changer, had been charged with instigating the *Ragnarok,* though he knew it would lead to his own doom as well as that of most of the other gods and men. Colbey did not profess to understand the motivations of the gods; surely their immortality and millennia of experience gave them insight and wisdom that men could never contemplate. But Shadimar's words struck more deeply: "Law is the direct opponent of chaos. If we work within the tenets of law to bring the *Ragnarok,* our efforts could do exactly the opposite. If, however, we turn against Odin's laws and break our Wizards' vows in order to avert the *Ragnarok,* we are virtually guaranteed to cause it. When the time comes, I hope we will all have the sense and competence to choose our actions wisely. Quite literally, the world and everything in it will lie in our hands."

Colbey harbored little doubt that the time mentioned by Shadimar had come, yet no vision of the consequences came to help him make the decision. Only one thing about the choice seemed certain. *Without balance between the forces shaping the world, it would have no direction. The staves complement one another. Neither alone could serve mankind. It could only destroy us.* Again, logic told him to refuse both, yet he knew the Keeper would not allow it.

Colbey sheathed his swords, kneading Harval's hilt with a sweat-slicked hand. Usually even a foolish action accomplished more than immobility. He reached inside himself and called on the power remaining in his body to strengthen his mind. The muting haze of exhaustion lifted, and he shaped a mental probe, stretching it delicately toward the Keeper. He braced himself, expecting a solid block or a massive retaliation. Yet he found neither. His probe entered without difficulty, and he explored a mind more complete and intricate than any he had encountered in the past. Although the Keeper seemed not to notice the intrusion, Colbey found the ignorance difficult to accept. Still, he probed deeper.

Colbey's mind extension entered a labyrinth of twisting thoughts and abstract concepts. Barely beyond his comprehension, they beckoned him deeper into the vast, convoluted pain of the Keeper's subconscious. Then, suddenly, a barrier dropped behind his probe, blocking his only retreat.

Every instant his mind wandered through another's thoughts, physical strength drained from Colbey. Needing escape, he spun the probe, battering the barrier with all the power of his will. The mental wall remained, and Colbey managed enough contact with his body to feel it weakening. Unable to go back, he sought escape ahead.

The maze wound, thought twisting upon thought, concept crossing concept. He felt the barriers shudder and dissolve behind him, but he no longer knew the route back. *Too late,* Colbey realized he had become lost, trapped inside another's mind. He hurried forward, staking his life on the possibility of another exit, and the One-Eyed One's mentation led him to a great void. Around him, Colbey sensed only emptiness, as if the massive brain that had surrounded him had disappeared completely. He realized that he might never free himself from this limbo, and he sought escape with little hope of success.

Abruptly, Colbey discovered texture. Curiosity now fueled a new enthusiasm. He explored the irregularities. Silhouettes hovered, barely discernible at the edges of his consciousness. With maddening slowness, vague outlines sharpened to hauntingly familiar concepts of war, sword forms, and deeply etched religion. Colbey recognized the phantoms as a mirror image of his own mind.

Stunned, Colbey struggled against the reflection, but the transposed images remained. They were real. *Another*

Colbey? It seemed impossible. True, the gods had once copied his body and his actions, animating it with a will of their own. Yet their failure to fill it with true life or sentience had made him certain that they could not. Even the gods created offspring as men did. And, though Odin and his two brothers had crafted the first man and woman from an ash and an elm, Colbey had never heard stories nor legends of humans coming from anywhere but one another since then.

Colbey followed the memories, finding Renshai maneuvers and sword cuts he alone knew. This was a second Colbey, and yet it was not. The mind he had entered initiated no actions. Although it demonstrated evidence of mind control, it did not react to his intrusion. The pictures and concepts endured, a reversed duplicate of the Renshai's own mind, as if the two Colbeys examined the same scene from opposite sides at the exact same time. Colbey realized that he stood outside, looking into his own mind. He entered the reflection and turned to stare out through his own eyes.

Again, Colbey faced the one-eyed being. For the moment, the Renshai silently reveled in the return to his own body. He found it as strong as always, and the familiar supple quickness and deadly precision restored his brashness as well. "How did you manipulate me?"

The other smiled. "Very well, I thought." The grin vanished at once, back into the casual nothingness of his previous expression. "Now, choose."

"I want neither staff. I told you that."

The Keeper glowered.

"But if I have to take one, then I'll take them both."

The Keeper did not move. "So be it. You completed the task, and you must have your reward. I will give you both, but understand one thing, Kyndig. Though men struggle, they change nothing. What you see, feel, and do is only a matter of perspective. You alter appearances only. Reality remains inviolate. Had you not realized this truth, you might never have returned to your own body." He extended the staves, one in each hand, toward Colbey. "With these, you change *reality itself.*"

Hesitantly, Colbey reached forward and took the staves. White light exploded around him, blinding him with its brilliance. When vision returned to Colbey, the Keeper of the Eighth Task was gone.

PART II

THE KEEPERS OF
LAW AND CHAOS

CHAPTER 10

The Keepers of Law and Chaos

Shadimar sat in passive silence, staring into the space where the Pica Stone should have lain until his vision smeared and the blue shards merged into the expanse of blurry grayness. This charade could not continue. If the woman that he, Trilless, and Carcophan had sent to complete the Tasks of Wizardry did not return, it would mean they had condemned five competent humans to their deaths in as many weeks since Colbey's failure. *Damn the Renshai anyway.* Frustration and grief drove the Eastern Wizard to blame Colbey for a demise even the Deathseeker could not have sanctioned, a shallow attempt to convince himself that the Renshai's slaying meant nothing to him. *Death in any other fashion would have left the Pica intact and dispensed with this infernal waiting in blind ignorance.* A stray hair tickled his cheek. He raised a hand to brush it away, his movement scattering fragments of sapphire to the floor. The pieces sprinkled to the granite with tiny, high-pitched noises. Not even a spark of their former magic remained.

Secodon stalked the remnants, sniffing delicately, as if trying to understand their fascination. Mar Lon sat quietly on the floor, seeming out of place in a roomful of solemn Wizards.

Carcophan spoke in a low growl that seemed to be the most comforting voice he could manage. "Shadimar, we have to send another. We've given her enough time."

Shadimar glanced up. Carcophan and Trilless sat in their usual places, across the longest part of the Meeting Room table. The Northern Sorceress nodded tacit agreement, her concurrence with the Evil One unnerving Shadimar nearly as much as the events of the last several weeks. Over the centuries, he had learned to keep his emotions a step back, never to become attached to mortals. To do so might mean putting individual interest over cause as well as watching

friends wither and die. Yet the events he had shared with
Colbey Calistinsson bore a significance his heart and mind
would not allow him to forget. For all of Shadimar's aloofness and Colbey's savagery, he missed the old Renshai as a
friend as well as a promised colleague.

Avoiding the other Wizards' gazes, Shadimar pushed himself away from the table and rose. He turned his back,
watching the uniform glow in the fireplace without seeing
the flames. His mind slid to a memory that had never been
his own, a mental vision of a story Colbey had told.
Shadimar imagined himself as the previous Western Wizard,
Tokar, faced with a decision of world-shattering significance. Wind soughed through his white locks and beard, and
the sky had already become sprinkled with the hues that preceded a Wizard's ceremony of passage. It was a time when
Tokar should have had nothing more to consider than the sequence of magic that would end his mortal life and link his
consciousness with the Western Wizards before him, a collection that would live on in the mind of his successor.

Secodon whined, nosing his master's cupped hand.

Shadimar ignored the wolf. He imagined Tokar studying
his apprentice, a weak Pudarian named Haim. Somehow,
Haim had passed the Tasks of Wizardry, though they had
cowed rather than strengthened him, as if the gods had sanctioned Tokar's plan. Now Shadimar tried to understand his
colleague's choice. Had Tokar, as Colbey thought, chosen
Haim because he knew the ceremony would kill his apprentice? Had this been Tokar's way of ending a line wracked by
insanity, of forcing Shadimar to begin the Western line fresh
and untainted by the madness it had incorporated and, unwit-
tingly, nourished? *More likely,* Shadimar believed, *Tokar
hoped Haim's weakness would make the apprentice little
more than a puppet. Though now only a part of the collective consciousness, Tokar could control Haim, protecting
him from the older portions of his predecessors' thoughts.*

Tokar's motivations mattered little, as did the events leading to Colbey's presence at the time of the Western Wizard's
chosen passage. But recognition of the Renshai's potential
had given the old Wizard a choice that few would have considered or even have been aware of. Surely, neither Trilless
nor Carcophan would have thought of passing their Wizard's
line to anyone other than their long-trained apprentice. Yet
when Tokar stood amidst the thunder and light show of his

summoned magics, he had had the wherewithal to place strength over weakness. He had risked putting the Western line into the hands and person of the most powerful mortal he had ever met, though it meant annihilation of the collective consciousness and his apprentice. Surely, it had never occurred to Tokar that Colbey might fail the Tasks of Wizardry.

Trilless interrupted Shadimar's considerations. "You're tired, my friend. Would you like me to look for another?"

Another. Shadimar did not move or reply. *Why not send another to his death? Carcophan and Trilless are only aiding my search to honor their vows, but they know there's no one left capable of serving as Western Wizard. Eventually, one will come along.*

Shadimar scratched Secodon absently, aware he did not have the luxury of time. *Alone, I'm not strong enough to stand between good and evil. Soon they would overcome me and attack one another openly. War between them would begin the destruction heralded by the calling of the three Swords of Power.* Shadimar knew he had little choice but to keep his companions occupied with obtaining more prospects for the tasks, yet the idea of sending more innocents to their deaths to delay the inevitable seemed abhorrent.

Carcophan responded to Trilless' offer as Shadimar had not. "*You* look for another? You'd like that—"

Suddenly, a door appeared directly opposite the one to the outside. Shadimar stared. Carcophan stopped speaking. Mar Lon and Trilless turned their heads to look as well. They all knew this magical panel. It appeared only when an apprentice returned successfully from the Tasks of Wizardry. Relief thrilled through Shadimar, and he prepared himself for the speech he would need to give to the woman who emerged from that door. Then, another possibility filled his mind, bringing a twinge of guilt. Only one apprentice could perform the tasks at any given time. If one of the earlier candidates emerged, it meant that every subsequent recruit had simply been sent to an immediate death.

The door swung open, its breeze fanning the magical fire into a ragged, orange blaze. The man who stepped through the frame wore a gold-colored shirt and breeks, held in place by a black sash. Yellow hair framed handsome features and burning blue-gray eyes that did not seem mortal. A sword dangled at each hip, and he carried a staff in either hand.

Though the face seemed familiar, its youth and vigor threw Shadimar completely off target. His mind answered impression before logic. *Loki? Has the god come to mock us?* Worse possibilities haunted Shadimar then, concerns about the Cardinal Wizards' interactions and the drawing of chaos.

Apparently, Trilless came to the same conclusion. She rose, her stance graceful yet stiffly formal, and her voice held power and rage. "You're not welcome, Shape Changer. Enough trouble has befallen us already. You hold no power here. In the name of Odin, I deny you entrance."

The man in gold laughed. "An excellent speech, Trilless. It's a shame Loki couldn't hear it." He raised the staves, drawing Shadimar's gaze directly to them. A faint white glow traced the edges of each, revealing their magic. "Behold the reward of the eighth task."

Mar Lon went so still he seemed to stop breathing. Trilless studied the newcomer and the staves. Carcophan came slowly to his feet. Shadimar found himself rooted in place. *Colbey. It's Colbey.* The voice and confidence could belong to no one else, yet the Staves of Law and Chaos commanded Shadimar's full attention.

Trilless found her voice first, though she focused on what seemed to Shadimar to be the less important question. "I don't understand. We watched you die. What happened after you touched the seer's crystal?"

Carcophan struck for the more salient point. "Explanations later. You have both staves! By Fenrir's teeth, you condemn us all. Fool, you . . ."

"You call me fool?" Colbey's reply rose in anger. "I call you coward. At least I had the courage to attempt the eighth task." Colbey came fully into the room, and the portal disappeared behind him.

He brought the Staff of Chaos. The Staff of Chaos! Why? Shadimar considered probing Colbey's thoughts. But he recalled the awesome power of the Renshai's mind and chose words instead. "Colbey, listen to me. You don't understand."

A smile creased the Renshai's now youthful features. "Perhaps I do, and that's why you fear me. How many times have I talked about our own rules and protections stagnating us into oblivion? Times change. We can't advance when ancient needs still govern civilization. Law is rigid and uncompromising. It's not good and evil that are unyielding, as I once thought. It's our world wholly without chaos."

Although trained to maintain composure in crises, Shadimar had never before reasoned with one who held the future of every world in his hands. The Wizard's heart pounded, and his argument drew desperate. "Chaos is rampant and destructive. It has no shape and form. It drives lies, betrayals, crime, and dishonor. In the end, it will destroy us all."

"Perhaps," Colbey concurred. "But without it, we'll smolder into changeless oblivion, one moment the same as the next. Law is only the structure. Chaos is what lives, grows, and evolves."

Shadimar saw some logic in Colbey's words, yet experience showed him the flaws in the argument. Odin had driven the Primordial Chaos from the world because of the need for structure. For millennia, the Wizards had protected that structure, and Odin had ensured that the system would continue for eternity. Without it, all of the gods, Wizards, and mortal civilization would collapse into chaos' decadence. "You speak madness!"

"I speak only of balance."

Carcophan came forward menacingly. "With chaos, there can be no balance. There is only destruction."

"I don't believe that to be the case."

Trilless leapt to her feet. "Wiser minds say otherwise—"

Colbey smiled. "I don't believe yours to be wiser minds."

Mar Lon remained rigid. Trilless went silent, blue eyes flashing with anger. Shadimar tried to appeal to the Renshai who had once been a brother. "Colbey, we have millennia of knowledge to draw upon. You have to believe that we know better. You have to listen."

"I have listened. And I've made my choice." Colbey headed further into the room. "Your millennia of so-called wisdom only make you more rigid and stagnant. Again, I propose balance."

"Law is structure and reality!" Shadimar was shouting now, groping for the right words that would make Colbey understand the terminal significance of his decision. "It's what men themselves are composed from, as well as our world and all that's in it! There can be no balance between form and nothingness."

"I believe there can be."

Trilless glowered, arms folded across her sagging chest.

"Then you're every bit the fool Carcophan named you. And we have no choice but to stand against you."

Again, Colbey grinned, his expression smug. "I expected nothing less. And I'll revel in the challenge."

Carcophan nonchalantly placed his bulk between Colbey and the exit. "Even one as strong as you believe yourself to be can't triumph over the three of us." He waved his arms to encompass Trilless and Shadimar. "We are the Four." This time, he added Colbey to the equation. "We can still work together. Destroy the Staff of Chaos, and we'll all wield the Staff of Law. The world will remain powerful, large enough for us all, and we will control it as one. Or, if we wish, we could divide it and each take a quarter."

Trilless approached Colbey and placed a gentle hand on his shoulder. "Kyndig ..."

Colbey did not look at the Sorceress. "Remove your hand, lady, or I shall, with Harval."

Trilless' arm returned to her side with graceful dignity despite the threat, and she continued. "We can't divide the cosmos, but otherwise Carcophan is right. You must dispose of the Staff of Chaos. Should you tap its power even once, you would wreak chaos and ruin upon a world meant only for law."

Colbey leaned one of the staves against the wall near Shadimar and rested his callused palm on Harval's hilt. Still holding the other staff, he measured his steps to the doorway. "The three of you mock what you claim to represent. If you constitute balance, then I am the counterbalance. All forces must have opposition to exist." He headed for the door in a straight line, stopping in front of Carcophan's impeding form and meeting the Southern Wizard stare for stare. With obvious deliberateness, he closed his grip on his hilt.

Shadimar studied the staff beside him, casually shielding it from Trilless and Carcophan with his body. Secodon crouched before it, less subtly on guard. In either of the other Wizard's hands, the staff could be used for a cause other than itself. He watched his companions, waiting to see if either would try to stop the Renshai despite his hold on a sword that could slay them. Patience usually accompanied near-immortality. Though the least methodical and tolerant of the three, Carcophan surely realized that any attempt to physically restrain Colbey would result in a brawl that would leave at least one of the Cardinal Wizards dead. With a Staff of Power readied in one fist and Harval in the other, Colbey held the clear advantage.

Carcophan moved aside.

Momentarily taking his fingers from his sword, Colbey opened the outside door. "I offer you the power to oppose me and prevent my loosing chaos. The one weapon with which you can avert destruction stands there." He pointed to the staff that he had abandoned.

The Staff of Law. Shadimar grasped it before either of his companions could make a move in its direction. The polished ash felt right in his grip, as if created for him. Suddenly, his hand felt as unsteady as that of a frightened child. *It's the only thing powerful enough to confront chaos. Colbey sees our world as a plaything. Before his transgression, the eternal battle between good and evil seems nothing more substantial than a petty squabble. Colbey, not Carcophan and Trilless, will doom the world. We must resist and hope time will bring him to his senses.* Shadimar expanded his consciousness, touching the minds of Carcophan and Trilless. In their own way, their thoughts mirrored his own. "We will stand against you. You know that."

Colbey nodded. "I trust the staff will fare better in your keeping than the Pica. Farewell, old friend." Without turning his back, Colbey left the room. He closed the door behind him.

Immediately, Carcophan's heavy fist crashed against the table. "We have the Staff of Law. With it, we can control a demon powerful enough to kill Colbey. The arrogant bastard has no magics to bind it, and the sword will help only so much. We can't let him leave this island alive!"

Mar Lon seemed to awaken from his trance, his attention bobbing from Wizard to Wizard as each spoke his or her piece with an emotionality he had never seen any of them display in the past.

With confidence inspired by the staff he held, Shadimar quietly seated himself at the table, Secodon restless at his feet. Carcophan had spoken in anger, and he had to see the error in his plan. "Any decision we make now affects the future of all worlds, including the gods'. We have to consider all possibilities and consequences before we act."

Carcophan shook with rage. "The least Wizard speaks

thus! You would have us sit here hashing plans until Colbey's gall and stupidity destroys us all."

Trilless dismissed Carcophan with a wave. "Someone must pay dearly for the summoning of a demon, and magic will only draw more chaos into our world. Don't forget our vows not to harm another Cardinal Wizard. That's a promise we can't break." She again took her seat at the table.

Shadimar clutched the staff until blood drained from his fist, hating his position. Whatever the decision, his own fate remained unchanged. Whether Trilless and Carcophan or Colbey set the destruction in motion, it would come, and he stood alone in its path. *Without the Northern and Southern Wizards, I can't stop Colbey and his chaos.* Shadimar knew what he had to do. For the good of eternity, men, Wizards, and gods, he had to league with Carcophan and Trilless against Colbey. Only then could he deal with the others.

Carcophan sat grudgingly. "The Staff of Chaos has already driven the Western Wizard mad. We have no choice."

"We have four choices." Trilless' lilting voice rose above the scrape of Carcophan's chair. "We can reason with him, capture him, steal the staff, or kill him."

"We have only one choice." Carcophan remained insistent. "We tried reason already, and Colbey has none. He's far too dangerous to hold prisoner, even if we could capture him. Only a fool would let the Staff of Chaos out of his sight. Despite his decision, Colbey's no fool. We can't steal the staff. And only one option remains." He rose abruptly, and his chair toppled over backward. He shouted over the slam of its fall. "I'll use the Staff of Law and summon a demon to deal with Colbey. Give me the staff!"

Shadimar clutched the staff more tightly. Carcophan would not have it.

All softness left Trilless' voice. "We have to speak to Kyndig again. He is the Western Wizard. We owe him that much."

We must destroy Colbey. Although Shadimar despised the thought, he saw no other way. His hatred for the old Renshai turned as strong as the enmity he had watched between Carcophan and Trilless for centuries. But he would never surrender the Staff of Law to Carcophan. With its power, he could contest them; without it, he became their pawn, as easily manipulated as any mortal. The Eastern Wizard slid his chair back and stood. He met Carcophan's catlike eyes and managed a slight sneer. "You alone do not decide who wields the Staff of Law."

Trilless took Shadimar's side. "Carcophan, you know I'll never permit you to wield it, as you would never permit me. About one thing, you're both right. We need to use its power to repair the damage that Kyndig does. It only makes sense that Shadimar should keep the staff."

"Very well," Carcophan returned to his place, hooking the chair with his fingers and hoisting it back into position. "Though Shadimar's not strong enough to wield the staff, we've no time for bickering." He motioned at Shadimar with a wave that rejected even as it indicated. "Use your small power to summon the demon to destroy Colbey."

Trilless fondled shards of the Pica Stone on the tabletop and sucked air through pursed lips. "We may summon a demon for information. We need to know how Kyndig came upon the staves and how he survived touching the globe of truth. But we can't release the demon to attack. Any chaos creature strong enough to slay Kyndig could resist our control. After it dealt with him, it would break free and ravage the countryside. I won't have that."

Carcophan scowled, leaning across the back of his chair. "Countryside, lady? We're on the Meeting Isle. There is no countryside. Demons can't move from world to world without summoning. It could only kill the captain and Mar Lon."

Trilless winched her hand closed around sapphire fragments. "That's two lives too many."

Carcophan persisted. "A small price. That's why we need to kill the Prince of Demons before he leaves this island."

Shadimar struck the heel of the staff on the floor to emphasize his possession of it. "Carcophan, have you gone mad? We'll not shed the Western Wizard's blood on the Meeting Isle while I hold the staff." He pressed his elbows to the table and leaned toward the Southern Wizard, trying to look menacing. "If that reason doesn't suit you, perhaps this one will. If a demon powerful enough to kill Colbey escapes our control, it could kill any or all of us as well."

Carcophan would not be intimidated. He, too, leaned forward until his face nearly touched Shadimar's. "I've summoned demons before. With my experience and the Staff of Law's power, I can't fail."

Trilless shrieked, leaping to her feet. At regular intervals, drops of blood oozed from her palm, pattering to the table. "A sliver of the Pica cut me."

Shadimar stared in horror at Trilless' bleeding hand, his mind scrabbling desperately for an answer. To damage a Cardinal Wizard, some magic must remain in the stone, yet his own eyes told him otherwise. The rupturing of the Pica Stone had left it empty of sorcery, and the splinter of sapphire that had cut the Northern Sorceress held no magic at all anymore.

Carcophan paced with the vengeful fury of a wounded jaguar. "It's Colbey's doing. Normally, a battle ax couldn't trim my beard. Now, a piece from a shattered gem draws blood from the only Wizard nearly as powerful as myself." He glared at Shadimar. "Chaos heralds our destruction! We've waited too long. Colbey spilled the first blood on this island. Summon the demon to rid us of the Renshai!"

Trilless clutched at the heel of her hand, strangely silent.

The implications boggled Shadimar's mind. So much of the Cardinal Wizards' power came from appearance, and so much of that appearance from the need to fear nothing but demons and the Swords of Power. Now, suddenly, everything in the nine worlds had once again become a weapon. The protection won by completing the Seven Tasks of Wizardry had disappeared, and he could only surmise that Carcophan was right about the cause. Shadimar closed his eyes, trying to draw upon the power of the staff. It gave him nothing direct, no specific ideas or feelings, just a vague sensation of invincibility that contradicted Trilless' injury. Strength ruffled through the collective consciousness, and Shadimar knew, without being told, that his capability had heightened. When the time came, the staff would enhance his competence, confidence, and ability.

Another possible answer came to Shadimar, though dredged from his own supposition rather than any work of the staff. He spoke it aloud. "We all know the risks of permanent magics and placing chaos in an item. Rarely does it turn out as we expect, and there are always side effects to deal with. The Pica exploded. Who knows what might have happened as a result of the sudden release of chaos? Perhaps the Pica, not Colbey, caused this thing." He flicked his fingers toward Trilless' bleeding hand.

"Perhaps." Carcophan ceased his pacing to again rest his forearms on the back of his chair. "But that's immaterial. Colbey caused the destruction of the Pica, so he would still be responsible."

"That changes nothing." Shadimar rose, still clinging to his honor though his instincts told him that the issue of Colbey and the Staff of Chaos went beyond any vows they might have taken. He smiled, attributing his last shreds of loyalty to the Staff of Law. He clung to it, glad for its reassuring presence. Soon enough, a time might come when he needed its grounding. The world might have to center its focus on Shadimar and the staff, and he would be there.

Bleeding staunched, Trilless added carefully. "At least Colbey, too, will have remained vulnerable. His recklessness may obviate our need to be rid of him."

Shadimar did not mention that Colbey had always been headstrong, especially in battle. Yet he had already survived for seventy-seven years. "Colbey didn't intentionally hurt Trilless. We'll call the demon, but only for information."

Carcophan seized his chair and flung it aside. "By Fenrir's black tongue. Don't you realize ... !"

Shadimar shouted back. "I hold the Staff of Law, and my decision is made!" For an instant the power seemed to swell through him, and Shadimar felt like the central focus of the universe. His voice grew more restrained. "Of course I understand the significance, but acting in panic will prove more dangerous now than ever. Unless you wish the demon to escape and turn on us, help with the wards and summoning or stand aside. If you interfere, you may destroy us all."

Carcophan's eyes narrowed, but his voice became deadly calm. "I think, Shadimar, that the mastery promised by the Staff of Law has driven you mad. You would never have taken that tone with me before. Common sense would have prevailed."

Shadimar laughed, amused by Carcophan's posturing. "The staff simply evens the power between us. If you have problems dealing with equals, that's a problem you must deal with on your own." An idea clicked in Shadimar's mind. It came to him that Odin had always meant for him to wield the Staff of Law. *That's why he made the Eastern Wizard the weakest of all. He didn't want us to become too superior when the staff finally came to its proper place.*

Another idea followed naturally. *With me as powerful as Carcophan or Trilless, we no longer need a fourth Cardinal Wizard.* The celestial plan seemed to fall into perfect order. *So long as I have the Staff of Law, we can destroy Colbey with impunity. Odin prepared the Cardinal Wizards through millennia for this very time. Colbey has become the vehicle of chaos. When we destroy him, we finally banish the Primordial Chaos for eternity.* Joy suffused Shadimar at the realization that he would become the one to serve the nine worlds and complete the AllFather's final plan. *I am the One. I shall become the worlds' savior.* Happiness became an inner contentment and peace.

Secodon's wagging tail whacked the floorboards like a drum.

"The summoning begins." Shadimar stepped forward, tracing a circle on the tabletop with his finger, to indicate exactly where he planned to call the creature from the plane of magic.

Trilless moved away from her seat to stand beside Shadimar, and Carcophan joined them. Shadimar lowered his head, pushing aside the gladness that had come with understanding. For now, thoughts of the demon and its binding had to take precedence. One gap, lack, or flaw in his wards or technique would allow the demon to shatter his control. His readings suggested that its first target would be himself. Then it would rage across the land, killing until it ran out of victims or someone managed to slay or dispel it. Shadimar closed his eyes, recalling the method of summoning from his readings yet calling upon his predecessors for more direct knowledge.

The previous Eastern Wizards shifted restively in Shadimar's mind, but they gave him nothing concrete. Gradually, he sifted the problem from their joint consciousness. Not one had ever summoned a demon. Each gave Shadimar glimmers of Gherhan, the sixth Eastern Wizard, and Ascof, the eighteenth. Both had been killed by summoned demons. Each loss had caused a break in the collective consciousness, and no Eastern Wizard since Ascof had attempted a summoning. Hating his weakness, Shadimar considered faking the knowledge, but common sense intervened. *This is not a matter to take lightly. Better that my colleagues know my weakness than that I destroy myself and them through igno-*

rance. "I'll need help from you both. This is my first summoning."

Trilless and Carcophan nodded together, neither pressing the issue, to Shadimar's relief. Even Carcophan had no taunts. The stakes had become too high for childish banter and insults.

"I'll give my thoughts to you," Trilless promised. "I'll put the experiences of my two summonings to the forefront for you."

"And my six," Carcophan added, without gloating. Even he recognized the ugliness of bringing chaos creatures into a world where they did not belong.

Mar Lon scribbled silently in the corner, distanced from the proceedings.

"There's still a matter to deal with before we begin." Trilless flaked dried blood from her palm, watching each crumb fall with obvious fascination. "If we bring the creature, we have to pay its price in blood. The longer it stays, the stronger it becomes. Even if we hold it until we've finished asking all we need to know, when we finish, it will become free. Then we must either slay it or give it a suitable sacrifice to distract it until we can dispel it." Trilless shivered at a memory. "My first time, I gave myself. I won't do that again." She rolled up her sleeve far enough for Shadimar to catch a glimpse of a withered forearm and four deeply etched scars. Surely, the demon's attack had stolen some of the coordination from the fingers of that hand as well.

Carcophan tried to see around Shadimar, but Trilless shook her sleeve back into place. She would show no weakness to her evil opposite.

Shadimar's gaze swept the room briefly. His attention fluttered past Mar Lon without focusing on him, though his mind registered the mortal presence more completely. Secodon whined softly, apparently unsettled by his master's mood.

All eyes riveted on the wolf.

Carcophan measured each word. "He *is* the least important of us all."

"Yes," Shadimar replied, not at all certain they discussed the same "he." Secodon had proven a constant and loyal companion for too long to sacrifice. Besides, he doubted demons would take animals; he had never heard of a single case in all his readings. He hated to surrender any life to chaos, but the island's only mortal made the most sense. *Except one.* Shadimar cleared his throat. "I believe the Staff of Law will give me the support and control to hold the demon long enough for us to slay it. If not, the information we get may tell us to send it after Colbey first. We may solve two problems at once."

Carcophan grinned. Trilless scowled, but she did not protest. She had already registered her opinion. To repeat it would only waste more of the precious remaining time.

Shadimar hoped Colbey's ignorance would delay his summoning Captain for the sail home. For now, at least, he could not yet have left the island.

Again, Shadimar lowered his head. This time, he felt the gentle nudge of an intruder in his mind, then Trilless' presence joined his. She did not rove or seek; to do so would have constituted a rudeness bordering on attack. Instead, she fed him the necessary incantations to form the wards to bind a demon. Then another probe was thrust into Shadimar's mind, heavy-handed and twisted. The strangeness of the other Wizards' presences sapped Shadimar's attention. For some time, he could not continue. Finally, he forced his thoughts to adjust to the intrusion, accepting the knowledge they gave, blending it with a certainty and edge that could only come from the staff he held.

Shadimar used the base of the staff to trace a circle on the wooden table that graced the center of the Meeting Room. Mar Lon moved to a far corner, near the door. Cursed with the bard's curiosity, he could not bow to the normal instinct to flee. He watched with the others as Shadimar pulled three gold-colored candles from his cloak and placed each an equal distance apart on the perimeter of the invisible circle.

What's that for? The thought issued from Carcophan. *Cardinal Wizards need no props.*

Shadimar felt Trilless' annoyance at the interruption, and he shared it. *Feels right.* He kept the answer brief, hating to spread his attention. *Staff's idea, I think.* Shadimar knew the comfort came from familiarity rather than from any need to enhance magic with physical components. Simply put, the candles belonged to him, and their presence grounded him to self.

No matter! Trilless sent. *Don't disrupt his concentration! You'll kill us all.*

Fah! I could summon a weak one, like we're going for, in my sleep.

I wish you would, Trilless shot back. *Then I wouldn't have to deal with you and your evil anymore.*

"Stop it!" Shadimar roared. "If you're going to snipe, do it in your own damned heads!"

The other Wizards went appropriately still, both minds returning to the matter at hand. Again, they concentrated on previous summonings. A sequence of syllables coursed through Shadimar's mind in letter combinations that had seemed unpronounceable before his Wizard's training. He followed the patterns, choosing appropriately for the spell. He spoke each word carefully, eyes locked on the Meeting Room table. His staff blurred in his fist, then burst suddenly into blue flames. Highlights spun through the room like stars, emphasizing lines and crow's-feet on his companions' ancient faces. Shadimar concentrated on his wards, glad for the two more experienced Wizards beside him. Using the staff, he lit each of the candles. When the last wick caught, the tapers exploded into colored mist.

Trilless startled, nearly detaching from Shadimar's mind. A touch of awe wafted from Carcophan before both Cardinal Wizards regained their rock-steady contacts. For an instant, doubts hammered Shadimar, and he wondered if his more experienced colleagues would prove more hindrance than help. Every fragment of thought or movement diverted his concentration, and it made more sense to rely only on himself and the staff he wielded.

Even as the thought came, the halo that Shadimar had traced shimmered. It leapt to vivid relief against the table, and the room went white in its radiance. Red, green, and black vapor from the candles braided above the ring. Then, suddenly, the tracing dimmed, like a cloud passing before the sun. Smoke swirled into a shapeless form, with random protrusions. A sense of horror tore and squeezed at Shadimar, its source still uncertain.

The circle tensed about the thing that seemed more void than being. Shadimar spoke faster, winding ward after ward around the darkness in the circle's center. Gradually, it assumed an insectlike shape, with a shell, more legs than Shadimar could count, and red eyes glaring from every part. An instant later, its features melted and re-formed into the shape of a stag.

Stunned by the transformation, Shadimar sought the advice of his colleagues. From Trilless, he got only a stunned silence. Carcophan's thoughts held the sharp edge of fear. *Kraell!*

Though desperate to define the unfamiliar word, Shadimar did not drop his concentration to ask. His vision dimmed until his own wards seemed to blind him. Light striped his sight, appearing to become a part of the cycle of the demon. Repeatedly, Shadimar told himself that the creature had to remain a uniform black, except for its eyes. He forced himself to carve magic from chaos, but they fought to merge. Terror ground through him. *If I lose the form of the wards to it, I will give it all of my power.*

Hold free! Trilless' thought shrilled through Shadimar's mind. *Bind with the staff and hold free!*

Carcophan's mental voice came equally loud. *Kraell! Too dangerous! Shadimar, SEND THIS ABOMINATION BACK!* With the warning came knowledge. Carcophan believed that the *kraell* dwelt only in the deepest regions of chaos' realm, and it should not be possible to summon one. Lesser demons swore the *kraell* possessed strength unmatched by any creature of another universe. And a *kraell* had never been slain, except by another of its own kind.

The demon bucked against the barriers confining it. It took man-shape, and its arms swelled with unwholesome vitality.

Shadimar trembled from the effort needed to maintain his constraints. He hurled all of his substance, mental and physical, into defining every strand of his wards, drawing strength from the other Wizards across the bond.

The *kraell* clenched massive fists. Its flesh oozed. Great masses of muscle shifted beneath its scaly hide. With a bellow of rage, it whirled its melded appendages about its head and crashed them against Shadimar's magic.

Pain exploded in the Eastern Wizard's skull. Trilless moaned and slumped to the table. Realizing that she had taken the blow meant for him, Shadimar screamed the frenzied incantation necessary to banish the *kraell* from this world. Carcophan joined him, their voices a single, united shout.

The demon howled in recognition. Its mountainous shoulders heaved, and it drove mallet hands against the wards. Agony smashed through Shadimar's body, and he collapsed to his knees. Magical barriers shattered like glass. Unconsciousness promised escape from the pain, weaving palling curtains across Shadimar's senses. As if from a distance, he heard the demon roar through the blackness that descended upon him.

CHAPTER 11

Chaos' Task

By day, birdsong filled the Western forest, and the sunlight stabbing through gaps in the foliage glazed trees and underbrush in emerald glory. The thick overhang of branches and new, spring leaves trapped heat and light, enfolding Khitajrah in comfortable warmth. At night, however, unidentifiable rustling replaced the trills of songbirds. Khitajrah shivered through the cold darkness. Some nights, icy rain pattered through the branches, and the ancient leaves on the ground turned from soft bedding to a sodden mulch that seeped through her clothing. Those times, she found shelter where she could, curled into a ball that left her aching in the morning. After the sprawling cities of the Eastlands, the West seemed barren. Khitajrah felt sick for the familiar architecture of the older quarters of Stalmize. She ached even for a glimpse of the anemic soil of the Eastern farms. Compared to what she knew, the Western forest ground seemed black and sticky.

Chaos accompanied Khitajrah through the Westland forests. Most of the time, it remained silent, a scarcely noticeable presence hovering in the corner of her mind. Other times, an idea drifted from it or it started a conversation, seemingly at random. Yet Khitajrah expected nothing else. Had chaos become predictable, Khitajrah would have worried for her freedom or her sanity.

Gradually, the forest thinned. The trees became more familiar, the younger, sparser first growth that dotted the areas between farm fields in the East. Chaos stirred restlessly. Shortly, its disquiet became frank agitation, and it blurted a thought devoid of its usual self-assured caution. *That task you must perform for me.*

Khitajrah had not forgotten. Once completed, she had condemned herself to a binding with the being in her mind. Then, too, she would discover details about the object that would bring her son back from the dead. Her heart quickened, and the too-familiar sensation of trepidation and hope rose within her. The need to restore Bahmyr had only grown stronger, but she still harbored uncertainties about the cost. *Yes. What about the task?*

I know what it is now. A strange sense of purpose wafted from the chaos fragment, more focused than anything it had sent before.

A shiver traversed Khitajrah from neck to buttocks.

Chaos continued without waiting for a response. *You understand, it will go against your general nature.*

I understand I can still refuse it.

And the chance for your son to live.

I would do almost anything for Bahmyr. Almost. There are some things I won't do.

And those things are?

I'm not going to guess at what you want. Khitajrah refused to become trapped by exclusion. *Tell me the task. I'll tell you if it's on the list.*

A wave of humor flitted across Khitajrah's thoughts, chaos' substitute for laughter. *Very well. There is a man you must kill.*

No.

No?

No! Morality flared into a bonfire. *I won't take another woman's son in exchange for mine.*

He has long outlived his parents.

I won't take a child's father.

Chaos' amusement grew. *He has no offspring.*

A brother?

No siblings.

No matter! Khitajrah knew frustration as she ran out of relationships. Somehow, chaos had discovered the world's loneliest man. *Just because a man has no children doesn't make him less worthy of life.*

Chaos had an answer, even for that. *This man is seventy-seven years old. He's lived a long and productive life already. And he's Renshai.*

The single word both intrigued and bothered Khitajrah. Another chill spiraled through her, sending her into a convulsive shiver. *Renshai?* she repeated cautiously.

*His name is Colbey Calistinsson. He trained the woman who slaughtered your husband. Without his teaching, she *would never have gone to war, and Harrsha would still live.*

And so would Bahmyr. And my life would be happy, as it was. Khitajrah kept these thoughts to herself. She sent chaos another. *What's her name?*

Apparently preoccupied, chaos missed the cue. *Whose name?*

The woman who slaughtered my husband.

Mitrian. Her name is Mitrian.

The radiating thought gave Khitajrah spelling as well as the strange, Western pronunciation. She let the name burn into her consciousness. *Couldn't I just kill her instead? I could do that in the name of justice.*

You can kill her, too, if you wish. But it's Colbey's death that will earn you the information you seek.

Khitajrah continued brushing through forest, catching glimpses of an opening ahead through the trunks. She fell silent for some time.

Chaos did not press.

At length, Khitajrah questioned cautiously. *If I decided to do as you ask, and I haven't yet, where would I find this Colbey Calistinsson?*

I don't know.

The reply caught Khitajrah off-guard. *You don't know? What do you mean, you don't know?*

Chaos remained calm. *I believe the phrase is self-explanatory.*

How can you not know? You claimed to be the being that the gods themselves worship. How can you not know? Internally focused, Khitajrah ran into a cluster of vines. Thorns scratched her face, and the limbs enwrapped her arm and throat. She backed away slowly, disentangling herself from the brush.

I claimed to be a tiny tendril of the being that the gods worship. The Primordial Chaos might know, or it might not. Not all is logical, nor should it be. Chaos knows things the gods do not. It has none of the constraints of the beings with form, the creatures of law. It can learn without structure or sequence, and it can create new wisdom. Law can work only with what it has. It can't destroy, it can only shape and build. Chaos is design and thought; law is the architect. Without chaos, knowledge can only be lost, never created or recreated. You've seen that in the buildings of your home city. Compare the grandeur of the older dwellings and shops with the newer. Without chaos to interject new ideas, law will obliterate itself. *

Freed from the vine, Khitajrah considered, finding more understanding than she cared to admit in the explanation. Still, she could not shake the feeling that chaos wanted more than it would let her know. She turned the conversation back to the matter at hand. *So how do you expect me to find this Colbey?* *

I do know he tends to stay in the Westlands. Ask. A man who killed as many as he did in the Great War does not remain anonymous. *

Resentment flashed through Khitajrah, then disappeared. She could not help wondering which of her friends or relatives Colbey had killed in that war. *You say he's Renshai. And he's a good enough warrior to train the woman who killed my husband?* *

If you're asking me if Colbey's competent, the answer is yes. *

I'm no soldier. I never killed anyone. * Khitajrah's conscience throbbed. *At least not until recently. How could I possibly kill a Renshai?* *

Guile, Khita, guile. * Chaos' laughter filled her head again. *For that, you have the best teacher in existence.* *

Colbey strode briskly across the Meeting Isle, toward the inlet where Captain had docked the *Sea Seraph*. He used the staff as a walking stick, its presence awkward in his grip. His skill lay in quickness and deadly accuracy, and he feared that the staff's bulk might cost him both. He hoped a time would come when he grew accustomed to its shape and weight.

Sand shifted beneath Colbey's feet as he shuffled between the island's few trees, trying to remember Captain's instructions. He thought he recalled the elf saying that he only needed to call for a ride back to the world from which they had come. At the time, more serious matters had preoccupied Colbey, and he had never suspected that he would need to find the way home without Shadimar. Now, he doubted that a simple shout would bring the elf across leagues of ocean.

The air around Colbey lay tranquil, calmed into stagnation. The sun beat down upon the sand, raising shimmering glazes of heat. Ahead, the ocean lay flat, devoid even of the tiny, white ruffles that the wind usually chopped through the surf. He shaded his eyes from the sun, seeking a distant dot that might be the *Sea Seraph*. His thoughts went easily to the Cardinal Wizards. He imagined their divergent viewpoints would keep them tabled for days or weeks. He had never seen any of them act quickly or without tediously long discussion, and they worked against one another too much to come to quick agreements. Colbey felt sure about his own hand in the events to come. He hoped but doubted that the other Wizards would find the best answers in time.

Suddenly, a roar ripped apart the quiet peace at Colbey's back. He spun, drawing Harval in the same motion, the Keeper's staff tumbling to the beach. A densely black creature with an ox's head and batlike wings landed gracefully on the sand behind him. The ground trembled beneath its impact. Its wings dissolved into massive arms, and it lumbered toward him on jointless legs. Colbey knew at once that he faced a demon, and the challenge excited him. His heart rate quickened, and he smiled.

I've misjudged. The Wizards can come to a quick decision. Colbey ran to confront the beast. Once before, he had battled a demon. Then, he had thrust and cut fruitlessly, his standard sword too grounded in the world of law to damage a creature of chaos. Shadimar had called forth Harval, vowing magic could cut the chaos that ordinary swords could not. Now, Colbey lunged without hesitation. Harval arched toward the oxen head. Even as it moved, the demon's face ran like liquid. Colbey's stroke sliced through the unformed features as if through water.

How? Surprise broke Colbey's timing. Experience told him the Eastern Wizard could not have lied about Harval's power, and the Cardinal Wizards' fear of the sword had assured its potential. Colbey stared as the demon's visage molded into the shape of a bear's. Its giant fist crashed into his chest. The strength of the blow hurled him like a toy. Colbey hit the ground hard enough to slam the breath from his lungs. He bit his tongue, barely managing to roll. He gasped desperately for breath.

With one leap, the demon again closed the gap between them. A long-nailed foot struck for Colbey's head.

Mobilized by the attack, Colbey dodged. The demon's claws gashed burning lines across his cheek. He spun to his feet and swung. Harval sprang like a mad thing, and Colbey's attacks struck repeatedly. But the demon dissolved before each blow, and the sword sliced harmlessly through its fleetingly solid form.

The demon twisted away.

Colbey's mind raced. Air wheezed into his lungs in trickles. Warm blood coursed in dribbles to his chin. The wound smoldered raw agony across his cheek, and the pain seemed to penetrate his skull. Once again, his sword appeared powerless against the demon, and he could not help wondering if the gods had stolen the real Harval during the tests. But his instincts told him that he held the same sword as before. The last time he had fought a demon, the creature had held a constant shape, and his sword had clearly cleaved through it without inflicting damage. This demon's shape-shifting seemed more like a defense.

The demon charged, its fists muting to hammers with hawk talons. It swung for Colbey's head.

Colbey retreated, weaving Harval into a defensive web of steel. One strike met resistance and split the demon's hand half the length of its forearm. Black fluid gushed from the wound. The demon screeched high, dark syllables. It struck for Colbey with its other arm.

Colbey skipped aside. He lashed for the beast, and Harval sliced nearly through its wrist.

The demon recoiled. Its chaos-stuff flowed into itself, reshaping. New hands sprouted from its dripping appendages, and all sign of injury disappeared. With a cry of scornful triumph, it lunged again.

Shocked, Colbey barely sidestepped in time. *It takes a more solid form to attack. I can hit it then. But what good? It repairs itself.* For the first time outside the Tasks of Wizardry, Colbey found himself in a battle that required strategy as well as skill. Gathering his concentration, he shot a bolt of mental energy toward the creature's head. His probe met nothing of substance, and the attempt stole Colbey's attention from the battle. The demon's fist smashed into his chest. Ribs snapped beneath the blow. Colbey slammed into a tree trunk. Impact shot pain through every part of his body, but he managed to keep his feet.

"Modi!" Colbey moaned. He fought for breath. No air came, and he tasted blood.

The demon mocked him with a high-pitched, broken whine.

Colbey fought every instinct, forcing his attention from the desperate, natural need to breathe onto plotting. Eventually, his lungs would function. He could not weather another attack. *It becomes solid when it attacks. Have to wait for an attack. It heals itself. Have to hit it in a place it can't heal. Kill it in one stroke, or it'll kill me.*

The demon's head narrowed into a serpent's, with sharp, slender horns jutting from forehead, skull, and chin. Red eyes glared from between them. Its snake's body matched its head, but it sprouted four clawed legs, bird wings, and a barbed tail. Its mouth splayed open, revealing fangs that dripped venom, and it struck for Colbey.

Colbey's diaphragm relaxed, and he sucked air in huge, reflexive gasps. *One bite, and it's got me.* He jabbed for the face.

The demon jerked back with a hiss.

Colbey flinched taut, channeling his energies to skilled dodges and feints.

Apparently guarding its head, the demon switched to claw attacks, hammering relentlessly. Colbey parried each strike, not bothering with offense, seeking the opening that would bare the creature's head or heart. *If such a thing has a heart.* The demon's unnatural strength wore on him. Harval slowed.

Apparently emboldened by the Renshai's weakness, the demon snapped at him. Colbey riveted his focus on the head, ignoring the claws that closed around him. He drove Harval up and through the creature's chin. The blade wedged in the demon's skull, and it thrashed horribly.

Caught between the claws, Colbey felt bone shudder and give. Nausea struck like physical pain. Then agony slammed him to oblivion.

Sunlight blinded Khitajrah after more than a week ensconced in Westland forest. She shielded her sight with a hand against her brows, excitement, curiosity, and trepidation warring within her. In the distance, she could see the solid blur of a town. A field stretched before her, striped green by the first sprouting of a crop she did not yet recognize. The black soil peeking between buds had grown familiar from the woodlands, but the massive stretch of dark, moist soil left Khitajrah staring in awe.

Since the southernmost tip of the Great Frenum Mountains that harbored the only pass from the Eastlands to the Westlands, Khitajrah had covered more different types of terrain than she knew existed. She had crossed the barren salt flat that the Westerners called the Western Plains, the battleground where so many Easterners had lost their lives. The land had seemed much like the farm fields she knew, except that no one tended it and she had found no signs of cities or life. She had wondered who owned it, seeking a cottage or palace, unable to believe that land could lie fallow. The Eastlands' ceaseless battle between the need for more farmland to feed its citizens and the need for more cities to house them had raged since long before Khitajrah's birth.

Khitajrah walked through the field, intrigued by the mark each step dimpled into the yielding ground. She moved with a steady caution, careful to remain in the narrow lanes between the crops, even methodically avoiding the occasional misplaced plant in her path. She recalled how she had easily found one of the many passes through the Southern Weathered Range. Since that time, she had traveled through forests more vast and lush than she could have guessed existed. The woods had seemed to stretch into infinity, and she felt certain the entire Eastlands did not contain as many trees as she had passed.

As Khitajrah continued through the field, she saw a horse-drawn wagon rattling toward the city. She headed toward the sound, guessing she would find a road; without packed earth or stone, wheels would mire in the rich, wet soil. By the time she picked her cautious way around the crops, the wagon had long since disappeared. A pathway of hard-packed earth mixed with crushed stone cut through the field, from the forest to the town. As she stepped onto the roadway, the idea occurred to her that it probably cut right through the woodlands as well. If she could have found it, her walk through the woods would have become shorter and easier. As it was, she might well have passed other towns without noticing them.

Khitajrah approached her first Westland town, uncertain what she would find or of the reception she would receive. Westerners were unwelcome in the East, and the law permitted, even encouraged, Eastlanders to slay foreigners. Khitajrah hoped she would find a kinder welcome.

As the village came fully into sight, Khitajrah's attention riveted first on its central structure. Two towers rose from an otherwise boxy dwelling. Other buildings surrounded it in four concentric circles, becoming smaller and squatter further from the middle. The outermost ring consisted almost exclusively of simple, thatch-roofed cottages, but they did not sprawl onto the field as the Easterners' cottages did. It gave the town a solid, compact feel. Though no larger than LaZar, and lacking the Eastern city's walled fortifications, the Western town appeared stronger. Khitajrah attributed that to its cleanliness and the unity of the dwellings. She continued toward it.

Soon, Khitajrah could make out figures walking through the city streets. Uncertainty clutched at her, and she hesitated. The idea of facing a mass of hostile strangers made her queasy, and she fought down the images of townsfolk chasing her down with swords and pitchforks. Only then, she recalled that she still carried Diarmad's sword. Certain it would not make a positive impression, she removed his cloak, the weapon, and its belt. Kneeling in the roadway, she wrapped the sword into the cloak in a bulky, misshapen lump. She lashed the whole onto her back, hoping it looked like extra clothes or supplies. The effort reminded her that she needed both, as well as a full meal and a warm bath. She hoped that the few coins she had found on the veterans in the graveyard would pay for lodgings and a meal, and that the villagers would not find their Eastern mintage offensive.

When Khitajrah rose, she discovered half a dozen men walking toward her from the village. She froze, the strangeness of her situation immediately sparking the worst possibilities. She forced herself to think logically, studying their dress and demeanors for clues. They wore cloaks of brown and green over homespun tunics and breeks. Two carried longbows, three had similar bows slung across their shoulders, and the last carried a handful of sacks and a huge, empty pack. Arrows with varying crests filled their quivers. They moved with a casual briskness, their attention, at first, on one another. As they came closer, all eyes riveted on Khitajrah. Their pace did not change.

Hunters. Just hunters. Khitajrah willed herself forward, trying to look composed, with little success. Though she still wore her dress, she felt naked without Diarmad's cloak to hide her gender and features. Her thick, black hair and swarthy skin would reveal her heritage at once. In the Eastlands, had six hunters come upon her alone, she would have run in terror and considered herself lucky to emerge undamaged. Now, she held her ground, secretly wishing she had not bound the sword.

The men stopped as they came upon her. One said something in a language she did not understand.

Khitajrah retreated a step, hating herself for the obvious weakness. She shook her head.

The same man spoke again, this time in the common trading tongue. "Did you come from Wynix?"

"No," Khitajrah admitted, although she did not offer more information. "What's the name of your city?" She gestured toward the town.

The men shuffled their positions so they could all see Khitajrah clearly. Although this blocked her path, nothing about their demeanors seemed threatening. A different man, the one carrying the sacks, replied this time. "Ahktar."

"Ach-tair," Khitajrah repeated, her thick Eastern accent changing the vowels and adding a guttural.

The men laughed. "Where are you headed?" another asked.

"Ach-tair," Khitajrah said again.

This time, the men broke into howling laughter.

Khitajrah smiled, enjoying the interaction, even at her own expense. She preferred becoming the brunt of a verbal joke to the cruelties the Eastern men would have inflicted on a Western woman.

The first speaker gasped for breath. "What do you hope to find in Acccch-tayr?" He mimicked Khitajrah's pronunciation poorly, but it still made his companions laugh harder.

"For now, a good meal would be nice."

One of the men in the back made a fluttering motion to indicate that they had a job to do and his companions should continue. The same speaker addressed Khitajrah. "Look for the men in tan, single-piece outfits. That's our town guard. They can direct you." The men stepped aside to let Khitajrah pass, then continued on their way.

Khitajrah went by, then turned to watch the men. One glanced over his shoulder and gave her a friendly wave. Embarrassed to be caught staring, she whirled and headed back

toward Ahktar. Her mood soared, and she fairly skipped
down the pathway. She had a feeling that she would like the
Westlands and its attitudes. The encounter had gone almost
too easily.

The road took Khitajrah to just outside the periphery of
the village, then funneled into narrower lanes that wound between the houses. Paddocks of horses, pigs, and goats lined
the boundaries, their pastures green. Chickens fluttered between the fences or pecked at crumbs in the streets. Crude
shacks sheltered plows and wagons from the elements. Citizens wandered the walkways in singles or pairs, carrying
jugs or unloading hoes and pitchforks from the carts. Aside
from the bows that the hunters had carried, Khitajrah saw no
weaponry, and she felt glad of her decision to place the
sword out of sight.

At length, Khitajrah sighted two men in tan, single-piece
uniforms. She followed them with her gaze to where they
stopped in an alleyway to help a woman rescue a chicken
from a rain barrel. Seeing her chance, Khitajrah trotted over
to them, arriving just as one of the men caught the bird by
the feet and heaved it from the water. He clutched it upside
down until it went dormant, water streaming from its dirty
white plumage. Attentive to the hen, neither the woman nor
the guards seemed to notice Khitajrah.

"Excuse me," Khitajrah said in her clearest trade tongue.

All three looked up. Their stares went from startled to curious in an instant. "Who are you?" demanded the guard
clutching the chicken. Water plastered his dark hair, and the
droplets discolored his uniform in a stream of spots. His
green eyes found Khitajrah's brown, and the color intrigued
her. They looked strange and animallike.

When Khitajrah gave no answer, the other town guard
spoke. "Do you need something?" He sported short, sand-
colored hair, but his eyes looked as dark as any Easterner's.

"Well . . . yes," Khitajrah stammered, encouraged as much
by their lack of complete antipathy as by any particular
courtesy. "I'm looking for a place to eat and sleep."

The second guard pointed down the alleyway, then
crooked his finger to indicate a right turn. "Second row.
Third building. That's the inn. You come from Wynix?"

"No." This second mention of the same town intrigued
Khitajrah. "Why?"

The first guard righted the chicken, then dropped it to the

roadway. It ruffled its feathers indignantly, then scooted around Khitajrah and out of the alley. " 'Cause if you're used to big city inns, this one'll seem pretty unimpressive. Foreigners don't come to farm towns, even ones as big as Ahktar, except wandering from a trading city. Especially now, what with us still recovering from the War and such. Pudar's farther, and you didn't come from that direction. So it only makes sense you came from Wynix."

Recovering from the war? Khitajrah became fixed on the phrase, hearing little after. The vast, fertile croplands and the plump chicken the guardsman had so casually rescued seemed worthy of rejoicing, not complaint. The Eastlands did not support such bounty in the best of times.

The Western woman remained by the rain barrel, watching the conversation without making a sound.

The sandy-haired man added, "But you didn't come from Wynix. So where did you come from?"

Trapped by her own ignorance, Khitajrah hesitated. Then, realizing she had no real way to divert the question, she told the truth. "Stalmize." She gave it the Eastlands' pronunciation, Stahl-*meez,* rather than the Western, *Stal*-mihz.

The wet guard grunted. "Never heard of it."

His companion shrugged.

Khitajrah felt a need to shift the direction of the conversation. Both guards seemed less than a decade younger than herself, which meant either or both might have served in the Great War. Surely, they recognized her heritage, but she saw no reason to let them know how recently she had emerged from the lands of their enemy. "I'm just passing through, not visiting." Khitajrah doubted she had changed the subject far enough. "I'm looking for someone."

That seized their attention at once. The one who had freed the chicken wiped his wet hands on his pants, smearing a line of dirt and water. "Someone in particular or just a random someone?"

"A man called Colbey Calistinsson. I'm told he's Renshai."

The woman gasped a sudden breath, clutching her chest.

Cued by the other's horror, Khitajrah back-stepped, suddenly cautious.

"What did you say?" The darker-haired guard's manner changed abruptly. All friendliness disappeared from the men's expressions.

Khitajrah cleared her throat, mind racing. She searched for chaos' guidance or explanation, but it seemed to have completely disappeared from her mind. "I said I was looking for a man ..." She measured their reaction to each word individually. "called ... Colbey ... Calistinsson." She wondered if this Renshai had committed some heinous crime that his name induced this reaction in Ahktar's citizens.

The Western woman glanced rapidly from guard to guard. "She said it before. You heard her say it."

The sandy-haired guard frowned at the woman's display, then encouraged Khitajrah to continue. "After that. What did you say after that?"

Khitajrah's brows knit. "I'm told he's Renshai?"

The guards glanced nervously back and forth. "What's your name?" the green-eyed one asked.

"Khitajrah Harrsha's-widow. I'm called Khita. Why? What's wrong with repeating what I'm told?"

The dark-haired guard made an almost imperceptible nod, and the other worked his way to Khitajrah's opposite side. The Western woman pressed her back to the wall, standing as far away as the alley allowed.

The sandy-haired man's voice became monotonal and businesslike. "Khita, you are now in the king of Ahktar's custody. By joint law of the West's leagued farm towns, quote, 'any person speaking the word ...'" He cringed at the need to speak it himself, "'... Renshai within the boundaries of any town, except in the official capacity of enforcing the law, is subject to maximum penalty under the law,' unquote."

The formal speech in a language she scarcely knew confused Khitajrah, though the threatening manner of the guards did not. "I don't understand. What does that mean?"

"It means," the other guard interpreted, "that you are under arrest. If you're found guilty, you will be sentenced to die."

CHAPTER 12

Mainland

Colbey awakened covered by sheets. Shadows whirled before the muted light of an oil lamp strung from a gimbal ring. The floor rolled and bucked beneath him, and every swaying motion sent waves of pain through his chest, back, and abdomen. His cheek felt on fire. *Where am I?* Instinctively, Colbey's hands drew to his hips where he found neither his swords nor his belt. *Gone.* He opened his eyes, studying his unstable quarters. He lay on one of the room's three cots, and no one occupied either of the others. Leather bound books crammed into an open case. A sturdy wooden table with four chairs filled the center of the room. A narwhale horn above the bookcase clinched the location. Apparently, he was in the cabin of the *Sea Seraph.* That reality brought a sudden flood of memory. *I killed the demon.* He smiled. Pain flashed through his skull with the movement. *But I've lost my swords. And the staff, too. Am I a prisoner?*

Colbey tried to rise. His vision swam, and vertigo drove him back to the bed. Every muscle ached, and each breath jabbed the shattered points of ribs into his lungs. He could move freely, limited only by the agony that lanced through him with every insignificant movement, but he had not yet tried the doors to the galley or deck to see if anyone had locked him in the cabin.

A pressure tapped against Colbey's mind, seeking entry. The sudden realization of a presence defensively snapped closed his thoughts. Gradually, he managed to pry open his barriers enough to let the other touch the barest edges of his consciousness. It came to him with emotionless gentleness, providing information without demands or accusations. *I am here,* it told him, and understanding accompanied the declaration. The staff that Colbey had accepted from the Keeper awaited him beneath his cot. *I am here.* Though its sending seemed quiet and gentle, rock stable, the power be-

yond the message defied boundaries. It promised control of
the world and its people, yet it did not differentiate whether
staff or Renshai would become master.

Having determined the staff's location, Colbey blocked its
further contact from his mind. It was a symbol, a tool, and
he would carry it. But he would use it only as the need
arose. To give the instrument power or judgment would un-
dermine the balance he had accepted both staves to establish
and protect. Like good and evil, law and chaos knew only
extremes, and either would struggle for utter dominance.
Colbey believed it was the job of the Cardinal Wizards to
represent these extremes, but ultimately to maintain balance.

With that thought in mind, Colbey knew he was expected
to champion the staff with every scrap of mortal and Wizardly ability. But he had seen the effect of extreme and sudden chaos on Episte Rachesson. Carcophan had given the
Black Sword to the young Renshai, the third Sword of
Power to appear on man's world at once. With the weapon
had come a blast of magic that scrambled and destroyed the
youngster's mind, infusing a bitter madness too strong to expel. Grief and rage accompanied the memory. Colbey's fists
clamped closed, and he forced his mind to another significant truth. Though advocating assigned causes seemed inevitable to the other Cardinal Wizards, Colbey saw the flaw
from which tradition blinded the others. *Maintaining the
world's balance by having immortal opposites scramble for
power works only so long as their abilities are nearly equal,
minor or temporary shifts in the balance are safe, and all of
the parties follow the same rules.* The fallacy seemed glaring
and blatant. *Once chaos becomes introduced into the system,
there can be no rules, at least not for he who champions it.
The method breaks down without a central anchor to maintain balance.*

After that point, ignorance limited Colbey. He did not
know whether he could master the staff and the balance. Nor
did he understand how much the staff could do without his
communication or support. Still, new situations intrigued
rather than paralyzed Colbey. When the time came, he would
understand the cosmic purpose. In the meantime, he would
champion balance, at least in his own mind. Even amid the
agony of his wounds, he trusted himself to meet any challenge the gods or Wizards threw at him.

The hatch swung open. Though it made no sound, the

movement drew Colbey's attention immediately. He watched as the captain descended the stairs to the cabin.

"How may I serve the Western Wizard?" Though friendly, the captain had a reserve in his manner that did not suit him. His gaze roved to the claw strike on Colbey's cheek, and his face knotted in sympathy.

"Where are my swords?" Colbey then added, mostly to test the elf's honesty and knowledge, "And where's the staff I carried?" The effort of speech ached through Colbey's head.

Captain twisted one of the four chairs from around the table. He placed it at Colbey's bedside and sat. Withdrawing a pipe and a pouch from his tunic pocket, he packed the bowl. "Your swords and staff are under the bed." Colbey struggled to sit up, but Captain pressed his shoulders to the cot. "Be still. There's no danger here. You'll have them all back."

Colbey trusted the captain. "How did you find me?"

The elf tightened the pouch string and returned it to his pocket. He squinted, as if in pain himself, then lit the pipe. "I hear all that happens on the beach of the Meeting Isle, and it was fighting that got my attention." He took a long draw on his pipe and released the smoke through his nose. "I went to have a look and found you on the dunes all battered and bruised like a torn sheet in a gale."

Colbey opened his mouth to explain, but the captain waved him silent.

"I don't want to know how you came to lie there." He continued, as if to convince himself, "No, better I didn't know."

The *Sea Seraph* lurched, and Colbey instinctively braced against the abrupt motion. His body flinched taut, jarring agony through every sinew. "I have to get back to the mainland."

Smoke curled from the elf's thin lips. "You said that when I found you. Didn't even open your eyes. Didn't even move. That seemed urgent enough for me." He waved in a direction that looked random in the closed quarters. "We're already through the gate. I'll have you back to Asci by morning." Like direction, Colbey had no way to judge time now. The captain fidgeted, obviously uncomfortable. "While you slept, you talked about the others and about destruction. Little made sense to me, but I feel obligated to remind you that you can't harm the other Wizards. What about the Wizards' vow?"

Colbey realized that the gods had never subjected him to the laws and rules that governed the Cardinal Wizards. He supposed this related to his completion of the Eighth Task and the paired staves he had carried when he left the testing ground. "I've never taken the Wizard's vow, though I have obeyed it. You're scolding the wrong Wizard, Captain. The type of creature I fought on the beach doesn't just appear. The Wizards summoned it to kill me." As Colbey recalled the demon writhing with Harval wedged in its brain, he smiled. "Ah, such a fight."

Concern lined Captain's brow, and he shivered. "That makes no sense. There has to be another explanation, and you owe your colleagues a chance to discuss it with you. Don't destroy the world for the adventure."

Colbey sat up carefully, swinging his legs over the side of the cot. Pain seared every muscle and tendon in his body. The claw marks tore at his cheek, and agony stabbed his lungs so that it took him a long moment to breathe. "I did listen, and they heard me, too. We just didn't agree. But I can tell you this. I'm not causing the rampant destruction that the Wizards, and now you, seem to believe. Had I wanted to kill Wizards, I could have done so already. Harval could have cut down all three in the Meeting Room."

Captain rose stiffly. He turned toward the steep steps that led to the deck. "Enough! You've spoken much of chaos, but your words hold a spark of truth. I have to clear my head." He glanced over his shoulder. "I'll deliver you to shore. Don't worry for that. It's my duty and my vow. I've enough fear in myself for both of us."

The captain pushed open the hatch, and afternoon sunlight streamed through the crack.

Colbey groped beneath the bed, withdrawing the swords and the staff. He strapped on his sword belt, the weapons a heavy comfort against his sore hips. He staggered up the stairs after the elf.

Captain whirled and stared, aghast. "Stay below. Are you mad?"

Fighting nausea, Colbey stumbled to the gunwale and caught the rail. "You're not the only one who needs to clear his head." He mimicked Captain's fine, high voice.

The captain managed a chuckle as he manned the tiller,

and Colbey wondered if he would ever hear the elf's full-throated laughter again.

The odors of hogs and illness assailed Khitajrah's nostrils. Though locked in Ahktar's prison through the afternoon and into the night, she seemed incapable of dismissing the smell as familiar or tolerable. Fresh straw covered the stone floor of her cell, and the constabulary had obviously tried to make her stay comfortable. But the so-called prison more resembled a barn; and the mingled reek of animal excrement, urine, and disease made it clear that these barred cells held sick animals more often than human offenders of the law. Aside from the straw, the cell held only a chamber pot. Thus far, she had managed to ward off the call of nature, if only because she had a male neighbor, the only other occupant of the prison. As the sun set and darkness descended over her cell, the urge to urinate had grown stronger. Still, she waited, as the last sun's rays faded through the window.

I can't believe this! Unable to escape the smell, Khitajrah sat. The straw seemed clean enough. The odor wafted from the floor deep beneath it and from the walls. *From one death sentence in the East to another in the West.* The thought had cycled through Khitajrah's mind so many times, she had long ago given up on receiving an answer or explanation.

But this time, chaos replied. *Ironic, isn't it?*

Having finally found something on which to safely vent her frustration, Khitajrah turned it inward. *This whole thing amuses you. Doesn't it?*

Chaos responded with a smug matter-of-factness. *There's a certain humorous lack of pattern to it.*

Humorous! I'm about to die for speaking a word—a word, by the way, that you coached me to say—and you find that humorous? Khitajrah shook with incredulous rage.

Chaos maintained all the calm Khitajrah lost. *First, I never coached you to say anything. Second, you're not going to die.*

You heard the guard. I'm sentenced to death. Again.

So?

So, I'm going to die.

You're not going to die.

I'm going to die.

You're not going to die. I'll see to that.

Hope rose, guardedly. *How?*

Same as last time. Guile. In that, I'll coach you.

The guilt of her last violation still shuddered through Khitajrah. *No. I'm not going to break world law again for you. You've driven me to enough destruction.*

You won't seduce the guard?

The idea of coupling with a man other than her husband, especially a stranger, repulsed Khitajrah.

Chaos ran with the emotion, rather than waiting for a specific thought. *You don't have to sleep with him. You only have to promise to do so.*

Deceit had never occurred to Khitajrah. She wanted to have the thought purged from her head, though she had not initiated it. *I won't lie. Besides, no guard would let a prisoner free in exchange for . . . for favors.*

Chaos' amusement spread. *We're in your head, Khita. There's no need for euphemisms. We both know exactly what you mean. Besides, he doesn't have to agree to do it. He only has to come close enough for you to kill him. I'll tell you how—*

No! Khitajrah covered her ears, as if that might shut out the voice within her head.

Chaos chose to abandon the description anyway. *So you won't trick the guard?*

No.

And you won't kill him?

Absolutely not! Khitajrah released her head, taking a more natural position.

Then I guess I was wrong. You ARE going to die.

And you'll die with me.

Khitajrah could feel chaos considering. *I don't think so. I'm not an entity, remember? I'm part of the Primordial Chaos. I'm pretty sure I'd just get pinched off the whole and dispersed. Or I'd find someone else whose ideas give me access. To leave this world, I think I have to get banished.*

Khitajrah lowered her head. The conversation had done little to settle her annoyance and anger. *Maybe I didn't like all the laws in the East, but at least they made sense. Why didn't you warn me I could get sentenced to die for a word?*

Why didn't I warn you? The ludicrousness of the question touched Khitajrah with the reply. *I'm chaos. Law and its matters aren't exactly my strong point.* Its laughter roiled through her head, then died to a nothingness that made her feel even more wholly alone.

Khitajrah sighed deeply, uncertain which she hated more, chaos' taunts or the penetrating quiet that followed them. Although her formless companion had done little to place her at ease, at least it gave her a familiar object to turn to in this strange land. She sighed again.

"Are you well, lady?"

The voice came from Khitajrah's right. Startled, she sprang to her feet and whirled to face the speaker.

Her neighbor regarded her through squinty, blue eyes. Greasy curls fell around his face. Though dark, the color seemed more from dirt than any effect of nature, as if the hair itself bore no pigment of its own. He knelt near the bars that separated their cells, his expression curious. "I asked if you're well," he repeated, using the common trading tongue again.

"I'm fine," Khitajrah gave the standard answer instinctively. Then it seemed stupid, so she amended. "At least as fine as someone condemned to death can feel." The feeble attempt at humor fell flat, and even Khitajrah did not smile.

"Condemned to death?" Sympathy tinged the other's tone, but there was a falseness to it that made it seem more curious than concerned. "Without a trial? You must have done something horrible indeed."

Khitajrah forgave the man's inquisitiveness. Under the circumstances, it only made sense for a stranger to place interest before pity. At least she had found someone with whom she could talk. Once the initial amenities regarding crimes and charges had been completed, she hoped the conversation could proceed to more soothing topics. "Actually, I do get a trial, but I don't see as it'll do me much good. All I did was ask a question. I said a word. One word. And here I am."

The stranger in the next cell switched to the Eastern tongue. "One word?" His bland Western accent mangled the pronunciation, but he spoke with an easy fluency. "Which of the Golden-Haired Devils did you inquire about?"

Khitajrah could not guess which stunned her more: the man's ability to speak and understand Eastern or his guessing her crime immediately. "The Golden-Haired Devils? That's the same as Renshai, I presume." She whispered the offending term.

The man nodded. "It's the only word I know that can get you in that kind of trouble. In fact, it's the only thing you could say, short of treason, that could get you in any kind of trouble at all. Before the . . ." He squirmed, obviously un-comfortable. ". . . well . . . before the Great War . . ." He watched her closely for a reaction to mention of the battle between his people and her own.

Khitajrah could not help stiffening a little, but the ensuing decade had deadened much of the bitterness. She also switched to Eastern. "Before the Great War, what?"

Encouraged, he continued. "About every town and city in the West, except Béarn and Erythane, considered mentioning the Golden-Haired Devils form the North, even with euphe-mism, ugly and insulting, at the very least. Once nearly all of the smaller villages held it a capital offense to say the word. Now, only a few still do. But you happened to find one."

"That's my luck again." Even as Khitajrah spoke the words, her conscience told her she had earned her own bad fortune by following the way of chaos. She dismissed the self-deprecation that had occupied her thoughts for too long already, instead returning to her current crime. "What's so bad about these Renshai people? They fought on *your* side in the Great War, after all; and they killed lots of Eastern-ers."

"The one or two Devils still alive at the time," the man agreed. "But it's not common knowledge that they were . . ." He lowered his voice to a scarcely audible hiss, apparently not wanting to stand trial for the same crime as Khitajrah, ". . . Renshai."

"It is in the East. And I'd thought more than one or two. A dozen, at least."

"That's because the East apparently hadn't heard about how the other Northern tribes massacred the Devils, sup-posedly every one, twenty-six years earlier. King Siderin probably figured every Northman in the War was one."

Khitajrah considered the truth of the man's words. Geog-raphy and attitude severed nearly all communication be-tween the ancient enemies of East and West.

The other prisoner finished his explanation. "Half a hundred years ago, the Golden-Haired Devils ravaged the Westlands nearly end to end just for the joy of war and slaughter. That's how the laws against them got started. The one Northman rumored to be Renshai at the Great War was a soldier of unmatched war exuberance, a general who inspired men to wild battle frenzy. More than a few Western widows blame him for their husband's deaths."

Now, the law seemed understandable, if not wholly sensible. "So because of a fifty-year-old prejudice against a dead tribe of Northmen, they would kill an innocent stranger for speaking one word in ignorance?"

The man shrugged. "We're still rebuilding from the War. King Sterrane's had more serious matters to tend to than an archaic law that never existed in the royal city. Including a reshuffling of the monarchy, a traitor, and a plague."

Discovering that she would die for a law that, in a year or so, might no longer exist only enhanced Khitajrah's irritability and desperation. More interested in her own lot than in politics, she veered off on another tangent. "So, do many Westerners speak the Eastern tongue?"

The man grasped the bars between them, peering at Khitajrah through a gap. "Very few. I'm the only one I know."

Khitajrah crouched to the same height as her kneeling neighbor. "How do you know it?"

"Business."

"What business are you in?"

"Sales. I'm also a Pudarian town guard."

Khitajrah had heard of all three of the Western cities her neighbor had mentioned. She knew Béarn as the home of the high king, Erythane as the town of knights, and Pudar as the largest trading city in the world. "What do you sell?"

"Everything. Tangibles and intangibles." A slight smile framed his lips, so fleeting Khitajrah felt uncertain whether she had actually seen it.

"Oh," Khitajrah said, though she felt as if she had missed something subtle. Chaos stirred, and she sensed its instinctive liking for the man. She felt rather drawn by his manner as well, if not by his physical appearance, and the duality of purpose between her and chaos unnerved her. "And you're a guard, too?"

The man nodded.

"Then how'd you wind up here? Imprisoned, I mean."

"Ahck." The man made a noise and a gesture of calm dismissal. "Happens all the time. I try to acquire something difficult to find, and someone misinterprets my methods. Ahktar has a grudge against me, for no good reason, but they've never managed to find a charge that sticks." This time, he smiled obviously. "I'm also a lawyer."

"A lawyer," Khitajrah repeated. She lowered her head. "I could use one of those right now."

The man's smile seemed frozen in place. "What an interesting coincidence. What's your name, *frilka*?" He used the most formal title for women in the East, one that brought them nearly to the level of men.

"Khitajrah Harrsha's-widow. I'm called Khita."

"In the West, we'd say Kayt. Do you mind?"

A new land. A new life. Why not fit in? Without a family, Khitajrah had few attachments to her name any longer. "Why not? Kayt is fine. And your name?"

"Lirtensa. Lir for short." Again, he smiled. "There's an Eastern merchant who calls me Leertah. I'm not sure how that'd be spelled."

Hope trickled to life within Khitajrah, and chaos amplified the feeling. "You would represent me at the trial?"

"I would."

"But I did say ..." Again, she lowered her voice to a whisper. "... Renshai."

"That doesn't matter."

"And I can't pay you."

Lirtensa sat back on his heels. "Yes, you can. I saw when they took your things. You had a sword of Eastern design. Nothing special in the East, and not many Westerners would be interested in it. But I've got connections and buyers for just about anything."

Khitajrah considered only a moment. If the Ahktarian court put her to death, she had little use for a sword. "It's yours. I presume that's one of your tangibles. What's an example of an intangible?"

"I'm glad you asked that." Lirtensa retreated slightly, making it easier for Khitajrah to view him through the bars. "Let me give you the perfect example. Which of the Golden-Haired Devils were you inquiring about?"

Khitajrah had a vague recollection of him asking this question previously, but she knew she hadn't given an answer. "Colbey Calistinsson."

"Ah." Lirtensa dropped back to a sitting position. "The Deathseeker. The Golden Prince himself." He shrugged. "I think he's dead."

"He's not."

"He'd be about eighty.'

"Seventy-seven."

"Oh." Lirtensa looked perplexed. Then, he dropped all seriousness and laughed. "Well, well, well. Who'd have thought I'd meet a woman with more knowledge than myself? I'm not sure I can help then. What did you want to know?"

"Where I can find him."

"Why?"

Khitajrah hesitated.

"I'm your lawyer, remember? Nothing you say goes past me unless it's in your best interests. The more I know, the better I can serve you." Lirtensa spoke with a placating sincerity.

Still, Khitajrah shook her head. *Careful,* chaos cautioned. *It wouldn't do to have someone warning Colbey about you.*

Lirtensa went to the obvious root of the problem. "If it makes you feel better, my feelings toward Colbey are neutral. He led the Pudarians in the Great War. He was heroic, but to the point of stupidity. And he is still a Re—well, you know what."

Chaos judged. *Tell him.*

Are you sure?

Tell him. If I'm wrong, it jeopardizes my task. I'm not going to make mistakes with this one. Tell him. Just don't get specific.

"I'm going to kill him."

Lirtensa nodded multiple times. He started to speak, stopped, and started nodding again. Again, he opened his mouth, but all that emerged was a stream of laughter. He clamped his mouth closed, turning it into a snort.

The reaction outraged Khitajrah. She seized the bars, wrapping her hands just below his. "Death is not funny."

"I'm sorry," Lirtensa managed between spurts of laughter. "I'm not laughing at death, or at you. It's just that I've seen this Northie fight. If someone could talk him into a battle against the six best warriors I know, I'd pull all the money I own on the Deathseeker. With that in mind, imagine me imagining you attacking him." He lapsed into peals of laughter again.

Khitajrah's annoyance dispersed as the reason for Lirtensa's mirth became clear. She had wondered about the same thing, and she would not hold a grudge against him for having a similar thought. She could worry about chaos and strategy later. For now, nothing could happen until she found Colbey Calistinsson. "Do you know where he is?"

Lirtensa sobered quickly. "I thought he was dead, remember? I do think I could send you in the right direction though. I know some friends of his that he used to travel with. In the meantime, I could hunt down my sources and find out the truth. If you don't find him where I tell you to go, we'll meet back in Pudar in, say, two weeks."

The meaning of intangibles finally clicked in place for Khitajrah. "And you charge me for this information?"

"That's the way it works."

"How much?"

"The first one's free, since I'm not sure it'll get you anywhere. If we need to meet again, we'll discuss payment then."

The terms sounded fair to Khitajrah. "Where are you sending me?" The coldness of the bars against her palms reminded her of more pressing matters. "That is, if you get me through this alive."

"Trust me," Lirtensa said.

Khitajrah wanted to do exactly that, but she could not help noticing the joy that chaos seemed to feel in this man's presence.

"The first thing I need to know is this." Lirtensa became businesslike, removing his hands from the bars as if to write on a nonexistent piece of paper. "Who have you spoken to in the West? And what did you say?"

Khitajrah began her story.

The *Sea Seraph* rose and dipped, lifting from swell to swell in a bobbing dance. At the fore rail, Colbey leaned against the staff and stared at the familiar craggy fjords of the Northland's coast through a misty film of fog. The whistling refrain of Captain's sailing song floated from the aft tiller, the melody ghostly through the damp, close haze. Colbey remained still. Every movement caused a wild chaos of pain, though the stab of broken ribs into his lungs had become familiar enough to fade to an aching background. Now that he had left the Tasks behind him and was returning to the world he had known since infancy, his thoughts went to concerns that Wizard's matters had dwarfed. Soon, Colbey would ride Frost Reaver again.

The image made Colbey smile, despite the dull throbbing in every part of his body. He pictured the white stallion, its proportions nearly perfect and its every movement responsive to his command. Colbey had won the horse by besting a Knight of Erythane in fair challenge. The Renshai had been knighted in the other's place, as was the custom; but the Erythanian king had never called in his loyalty or service. Apparently, the king had the wisdom to curry Colbey's favor rather than enter a battle of wills. So the horse remained Colbey's, identifying him as a knight without burdening him with the responsibilities. And Colbey had the finest steed he could remember.

For horses, Colbey's memory stretched far. The great beasts had fascinated him since childhood. Of the Renshai maneuvers from horseback or against horsemen, he had created nearly every one. Still, despite all the mounts he had ridden or trained, he could recall none as well conformed or as intelligent as Frost Reaver. In his youth, Colbey had never allowed bonds of emotion to chain him. It was the way of Renshai to die young in battle, and the dead who reached Valhalla were celebrated, not mourned. He would have willingly fought and died for his parents, friends, or tribe, but not because of love. Even his own life had been unimportant; only his death mattered. More recently, he had become concerned for the welfare of the last remaining Renshai, especially for the teen, now dead, who had seemed like a son. And now, too, he cared for Frost Reaver, an animal. *I've grown old and sentimental.* The thought intrigued and satisfied him. The sweet chorus of the captain's song fit the mood, coming nearer as the elf approached.

A shadow appeared on the deck, expanding like spilled ink. The movement drew Colbey's attention at once. He crouched, glancing up, prepared to face any monstrosity the Wizards might muster against him. Instead, he saw only a hawk gliding in narrow circles above the ship. It perched in the rigging, studying Colbey through a black-rimmed, blue eye. Sunlight struck aqua highlights from the black trim of throat, wings, and tail. Dark bars striped its underbelly vertically from neck to feet. Otherwise, its plumage was russet.

Suddenly, it loosed a musical warble, dove from its perch, and plummeted toward the Renshai.

Dropping the staff, Colbey drew Harval.

Less than a man's height above Colbey, the hawk checked its swoop. Strokes from its powerful wings carried it beyond sword range. It orbited the *Sea Seraph* once, then wheeled for the mainland.

A fresh breeze stretched the sails taut, and the *Sea Seraph* skipped toward land. Captain went suddenly silent, abandoning his song in the middle of a verse. "An omen, Colbey. Hawks of any type seldom fare so far from land, and that was an *aristiri*. It welcomes you home and brings a fine wind." Without awaiting an answer, Captain trotted back to the tiller. He hove to, and the ship lurched forward. "Aye, a fine omen indeed."

Surf crashed against the distant shore. Colbey recognized the same beach where Captain had met him and Shadimar nearly a month ago. Retrieving his staff, the Renshai walked aft and sat on the gunwale near the captain. "An *aristiri*. Those are hawks that sing."

"The males do. In the spring. And it's well worth hearing." Captain stared into space, less attentive than the rocky landing required. "Used to be you couldn't walk through woods without spotting half a dozen. I always wished we had some on the world of elves. Thought of taking some there, but we wouldn't have anything for them to feed on." Captain adjusted the tiller, adding sadly, "Of course, the hawks have gotten shy as *wisules* since men started hunting them for challenge and trophies."

It seemed ludicrous to mention the graceful hawks in the same breath as *wisules*, rodents so timid they would abandon their young rather than face a potential threat; but the analogy fit in this case. The details of bird history meant little to Colbey, but oddities and things out of place raised wariness. "Why would a hawk come to us here?"

Waves slapped the deck, and the fog tightened. Captain responded despite his obvious attention to steering. "It came for you, of course. You're the Western Wizard. You're supposed to have a rapport with birds."

Colbey frowned, not liking the unsteadiness of the ship, yet trusting the elf's millennia of experience. "I felt scant mastery over that hawk. When it stared at me, I felt more like prey."

Captain smiled. "You might ask whether master or subject serves the other. Or you could find the bird and discuss the problem."

"Discuss it? You mean I can actually talk to these birds?"

Captain's grin broadened, and he burst into laughter. "Talk to the birds." He voiced a random series of whistles, squawks, and trills. "As far as I can tell, it's like Shadimar and Secodon. You can share basic emotions, within the birds' understanding. There may be magics that actually let you converse. That's beyond my knowledge ..." He added carefully, "... and into your own." All laughter fled him. "I appreciate your need for self-reliance, but it might be in everyone's best interests for you to call upon your predecessors once in a while. At least for this kind of rudimentary information."

A sudden jolt saved Colbey from an answer, though it reawakened every ache. The ship's prow sank into the surf until he feared she would pitch pole. He clutched the rail, agony flashing through his body, watching the fog whirl dizzily about him. Then the ship leveled. It rode a wave, dangerously close to shore. Sand scraped the hull, and the *Sea Seraph* ground to an abrupt halt.

Colbey relaxed, and the pain settled back into its familiar dull throb. "I guess it's my turn to laugh now." He brushed spray-dampened hair from his eyes, not cruel enough to crack even a smile. "You've got hours before the tide rises enough to lift the *Sea Seraph,* if she can still sail."

Captain strode to the bow and lowered a rope ladder. A surge of foam tore at it, and it fell back to slap the ship's hull. "I apologize for your wet walk to land, but I'll get no closer. Don't worry for the *Seraph.* My lady is a strong one." He pointed to the ladder.

Colbey approached, looking doubtfully at the eddies. "You're going to need some help. Your 'lady' will need caulking after grounding so hard."

The captain shook his head. "Thanks for the offer, but we'll be fine. Already, the other Wizards are calling me back." He smiled wickedly. "It'll be well worth the time spent driving cotton between planks to watch a Cardinal Wizard wade through ocean. Granted, watching Carcophan or Shadimar try to preserve their precious dignity would make a better show. But you'll do."

Colbey thought Trilless floundering through the waves in her white gown would prove even more amusing, but he did not voice the comment. He understood Captain's racial loyalty to the champion of goodness. Everyone needed a cause to follow blindly. In this world, faith was a given; the worth of the man depended on the choice of his cause. *Soon enough, that will change.* The thought brought Colbey back to the burden he had inflicted upon the world. He bound the staff to his sword belt, despite its awkwardness. Clambering over the rail, he balanced on the outer edge of the gunwale. His many wounds ached, but concern allowed him to ignore pain for the moment. "Captain, a time will come when loyalties clash, and the boundaries between opposites blur. I have had a hand in that, but I did not and will not work alone. Do you understand what I'm saying?"

"No," Captain admitted. "You're becoming as vague as the other Wizards."

The insult stung, but Colbey did not have enough knowledge himself to speak details. For reasons he could not quite fathom, he wanted the elf to understand, if not condone, his decision. It was not a matter of recruiting allies; it was a matter of one kindred soul capable of comprehending the need for a balanced change, even if his loyalties forced him to fight against it.

Apparently afraid he had offended, Captain amended. "But don't worry. The Cardinal Wizards' subtlety never bothered me. Their words give me puzzles and deep thoughts to ponder on the sea."

"Good," Colbey said. He fitted his feet onto one of the higher rungs. "Then think about this. There comes a time when every child has to learn to walk alone. Men and elves are the gods' offspring, and the time has come for the rigid, easy definitions of good and evil, honor and loyalty to disappear. Change is frightening but not always bad." He descended into the frigid water. The riptide's swift water eddied around his boots and buried his feet in sand. A wave drenched him. He clambered to the safety of the rocks. His clothes clung in places and sagged heavily in others, like an old man's skin.

Captain watched from the fore deck. His eyebrows rose and lowered once as he fought to restrain a wry smile, without success.

"Good-bye, Captain. I hope the show was as amusing as you hoped." Colbey believed that, if the elf did not tend to the *Sea Seraph*, he would ultimately end up wetter than the Renshai.

Without obvious impetus, sand rasped beneath the *Sea Seraph*'s hull, and the ship glided back toward the ocean. The tide drove her toward the open sea. From the stern, Captain waved. "Farewell, Western Wizard."

Colbey raised a hand to return the salute, but a shrill screech stole his attention. He glanced upward, ears tracing the sound. Stone rose in craggy increments. On a shelf just ahead and above him, the *aristiri* eyed him impatiently. It hopped along a pale line of sand.

Colbey drew Harval and dried the blade on his sleeve. Pulling his opposite sword free, he tended it as well. He carried them both in one hand to allow their sheaths to drain and dry. Grasping the ledge he had jumped down almost a month ago, he clambered, aching, to the crest.

The hawk stayed three handholds ahead of Colbey.

At the summit, Colbey stared out over the Northlands. A rocky beach rose gradually to a series of grass-crowned dunes that paralleled the shoreline. Beyond them, evergreen forests stretched to the horizon. Still clutching the swords, Colbey headed south. His wet breeks clung to his thighs, and sand grated against his skin. The grit chafed as he walked, and he had to keep adjusting the staff to stop it from slapping against his leg. The hawk fluttered and flapped along the sand. Nothing about it seemed threatening, yet Colbey watched it cautiously.

Shortly, exhaustion pounded Colbey, reminding him that he needed sleep to heal his many wounds. The *aristiri*'s presence became familiar. Twice it flew toward him, and twice Colbey dodged from its path. The third time, curiosity and fatigue kept him in place. The bird flapped upward, its wing beats hammering Colbey's eardrums. It alighted on his shoulder, and he braced for the pain of its claws. But the needle sharpness never came. The hawk sat, still and contented, using balance rather than grip to keep its perch. Ignorant of hawks, Colbey did not try to guess how strange this action might seem to ones more versed.

For now, Colbey lowered his head and trudged onward. Though he wanted to reunite with Frost Reaver, his injuries had to take precedence. Directly south, cradled in the Weath-

ered Mountains that formed the boundary between the Northlands and the Westlands, he would find the familiar cave of
the previous Western Wizards. And there, Colbey hoped, he
would find a secure and protected place to rest.

CHAPTER 13

The Ahktarian Trial

The sun hovered behind the highest crags of the Southern Weathered Range, spreading first light across the crushed grasslands of the Fields of Wrath. Mitrian Santagithisdatter balanced atop a boulder, performing sword maneuvers with a vigor that never seemed to die. Her sandaled feet skimmed over the rock surface, as quick and light as any cat's, and her sword cut gleaming arcs through the spring air. Her hand felt familiar and right upon the haft, as if molded to fit both its stillness and its every movement. The wolf's head hilt had become the one stable focus in an otherwise frenzied existence. Violence had taken the lives of her father, husband, and friends. War had stolen the town of her birth and childhood, and it had thrust the legacy of the Renshai upon her. That challenge, she had taken gladly.

As the rosy glow of dawn touched the sky, Mitrian leapt from the rock to the barren patch that served as the open practice ground and turned her attention to the small cluster of cottages. At any moment, before the sun edged above the mountains' crests, Tannin Randilsson would arrive for his sword lesson.

The thought made Mitrian smile. Since infancy, she had loved to watch her father's sword master, Rache Kallmirsson, perform *svergelse* or train the guards, his sword flinging highlights that her eyes could not help but follow. Standing still, Rache had been more attractive than any man Mitrian had ever known. With a sword in his hand, nothing could match his grace or beauty, and he honored his swords and his training more than any person except Colbey. In many ways, Tannin reminded Mitrian of that first Rache, the man after whom she had named her son.

Mitrian drew an image of Tannin in her mind. He had the standard Renshai features: blond hair, blue eyes, and a lithe firm body that came from long hours of training and practice. A strange racial feature tended to make the Renshai look younger than their actual ages, though Tannin had inherited little of this. He carried every one of his twenty-six years with dignity, and Mitrian appreciated that. Having no Renshai blood of her own, she appeared little younger than her own thirty-two years. And, for reasons she could not explain, she wanted the six years between them to disappear.

Since the other Northern tribes had all but decimated the Renshai, most of the survivors chose to follow Western styles. Tannin alone emulated the North, keeping his yellow locks long and braided. At one time, the practice had bothered Mitrian. She had learned to associate the look with the wild hordes of Vikerians who had swept into her father's village and killed all but a handful of his men. But during the last year, it had come to symbolize only Tannin, and Mitrian had learned to love the war braids as well as the rugged face they framed. Though Tannin had more true Renshai blood than any other in the current tribe except his sister, he had not had the opportunity to learn the Renshai sword maneuvers until the past year. At that time, he had tracked the tales of Colbey Calistinsson until he found the Renshai elder, Mitrian, and Rache. Therefore, Tannin approached the practices as an honor, with a seriousness that only Mitrian and her son matched.

Mitrian sheathed her sword, waiting, still lost in consideration. Thoughts of Rache Garnsson turned her mind in a new direction. When Tannin had first joined the Renshai, he had become locked into fierce competition with Rache. Though Rache had the advantage of Renshai training by Colbey since infancy, Tannin had age, exuberance, and a devotion that drove him to work. They had also competed for Sylva's attention.

Mitrian frowned. At the time, Garn had still lived, and she had had no reason to consider other men as anything but friends. She had encouraged Tannin's identification with her young son, though Rache was more than a decade Tannin's junior. Now, she worried that Tannin would always see her as a generation ahead of him, the six years stretched into a gap impossible to bridge. Their positions as teacher and student only widened the chasm; in the Renshai culture, no position demanded more respect and reverence than a *torke,* the Renshai word for sword master and teacher. Still, there had been a few times when she had directed his sword arm to demonstrate an angle or maneuver and believed she saw an emotion in his soft, blue eyes that matched her own.

Mitrian's frown started to edge back into a smile. Then the sun tipped over the far peaks, glaring into her eyes, and her lips arrested midway. Tannin should have arrived, yet he had not. Lateness to a sword lesson was a blatant display of disrespect, a crime second only to cowardice in the Renshai culture. Mitrian had only seen one student late to one of Colbey's practices, Rache Kallmirsson's son, Episte. She had watched in sympathy while Colbey had grilled the boy long after the other Renshai had quit for the night. Outside of war, it was the only time she had seen someone lapse into unconsciousness from exhaustion.

Ire rose in an instant, almost immediately replaced by fear. *If Tannin's not here, he's injured or dead.* Concerned for Tannin's welfare, Mitrian charged toward the four cottages that made up the Renshai's town. She came first to the newest, the one they had built for Rache and Sylva. The Renshai's six horses grazed on brush in the yard, joined by Arduwyn's stocky paint. The couple waved to Mitrian from the window, and Arduwyn called out an uncomfortable welcome from the front stoop. Mitrian made a brisk gesture that she hoped passed for a greeting. She slowed to a trot. Ducking around her own home next door, she headed onto the dirt pathway that led from her own dwelling to that of Tannin's elder sister, Tarah, her husband, Modrey, and their year-old child, Vashi.

Near the front door, Tarah sewed a tunic. Vashi toddled in circles before her mother, her fingers wrapped around a tiny, blunt-edged sword, proportionately balanced like a real weapon. Mitrian could see Modrey hacking weeds from the garden between their cottage and Tannin's own. They appeared calm and their actions seemed normal. If some harm had befallen Tannin, they knew nothing of it.

Tarah looked up as Mitrian galloped past. "Good morning. What . . .?" She broke off as Mitrian did not slow.

Only then, Mitrian skidded to a stop. She whirled, biting down on her rage. "Where's Tannin?"

"Tannin?" Tarah's hand stilled, and she dropped the needle to her lap. "He's . . . well . . . he should be at his sword lesson. With you."

"I know where he should be!" Mitrian fairly snarled. "I want to know where he is!"

Apparently frightened by the shouting, Vashi scooted to her mother's side.

Tarah let the toddler clutch her leg, but she did not coddle. She would allow Vashi to feel safe, yet she would not reward running or hiding. To do so would only reinforce childish fears. To become Renshai, Vashi would have to learn to face threats with boldness. "I . . ." Tarah started, obviously cowed by her *torke*'s rage. "He . . . I don't know. I haven't seen him. You don't think . . .?" She stammered, leaving the question open-ended.

The normalcy of the other Renshai's routine only reinforced Tannin's lapse. Mitrian spoke slowly, each word solid and menacing. "I think that he had better be sick, trapped, or dead. Or he's going to wish he was." Without awaiting a reply, Mitrian stalked toward Tannin's cottage, only half as outraged as she seemed. She had called upon anger to cover the worry that threatened to suffocate her. Finally, she had discovered a man she believed she might come to love as much as the husband she had lost, a man with whom she could have another child. And he probably lay dead on the floor of his cottage. Mitrian quickened her pace.

At length, Mitrian veered around the garden and came to the front of Tannin's cottage. Without bothering to knock, she opened the wooden door and charged through, finding herself in the familiar entry room. Old ashes filled the hearth. Two chairs stood crookedly askew before a central table. A stained, empty mug perched on the seat of one chair. Another mug, half-filled with cold tea, sat on the table. Tannin's clothing was flung across the backs of the chairs, and an undergarment lay crumpled in front of the fireplace. Despite the mess, Mitrian saw no evidence of a battle. She jerked open the only door in the room, the one leading to Tannin's bedroom.

Sun rays funneled through the outer door and into the bedroom, throwing light across two figures in the bed. The creak of hinges awakened Tannin, and he sat up so abruptly he bashed his skull against the headboard. His golden hair fell around his head, wildly disheveled and still kinky from the braids. Instinctively, he yanked up the blanket to cover his nakedness, and the movement bared the woman beside him. Her eyes remained closed, and she rolled toward him, flopping an arm across his abdomen. Long, dark hair dragged into a sparse curtain across her unfamiliar, teenaged face. The high cheekbones and small nose identified her as an Erythanian, and Mitrian estimated her age at between sixteen and nineteen.

Rage exploded through Mitrian's mind. For an instant, no coherent words came to her. Then she shouted. "Tannin Randilsson, what in Loki's dark, ugly, icy cold Hel are you doing?"

The teen's eyes flew open, and she sat up, without bothering to cover pendulous breasts that seemed more suited to a woman Mitrian's age. Tannin had enough modesty for the two of them. He tightened the blankets around himself, shielding his body to the neck. Though Mitrian's startlement should have given him time to think, he had an even more difficult time finding words. "I'm late, aren't I?" His voice contained all the remorse his words did not.

Mitrian took a threatening forward step, her foot miring on a homespun dress. She kicked the offending garment aside, and it skidded across the planks. "You've dishonored your swords, and you've dishonored your *torke*." She glanced at the Erythanian who was arching her back so that her breasts jutted, as if daring Mitrian to compete. Mitrian added, with obvious disgust, "And you've dishonored yourself."

Tannin lowered his head. His eyes were moist, and it was all Mitrian could do not to soften her tone.

"I'm going back to the practice ground. You *are* going to get dressed and arrive ahead of me. When I get there, your sword had better be perfectly tended and your maneuvers flawless. Then, you're going to work through everyone else's practice and into the night. You're not going to stop to eat. You're not going to stop to drink, and you're not going to stop to piss! And, if you're ever late for a practice again, I'm just going to kill you. Understand?"

"I'm sorry, *torke*."

The Erythanian threw off the covers, fully exposing herself. "I think his maneuvers *were* flawless." She snuggled against Tannin, mashing her breasts against his ribs and sliding a hand beneath the covers to touch him. "Are you going to let your mother talk to you that way?"

Tannin's whole body stiffened momentarily, then he pushed the Erythanian away. "Not now, Sharya. Please."

Rage speared through Mitrian, and she all but lost control.

Her hand whipped to her sword hilt, and the blade rasped free.

Sharya recoiled. Tannin froze, weighing options, obviously not liking what he found.

But Mitrian maintained her composure. She skewered Sharya's dress on the point of her sword, then thrust it toward the Erythanian. "Put it on. Get out."

Sharya's dark eyes widened, and she shifted closer to Tannin. She opened her mouth, presumably to appeal to the man.

"One word," Mitrian added, her blue eyes fixed unwaveringly on the teen, "and I drive this sword right through your guts."

Sharya made a squeal of frustration, fear, and rage. But she gingerly unhooked her dress from the sword point and pulled it over her head.

"Out!" Mitrian pointed at the door with the sword.

Sharya threw one last glance at Tannin, goading him to do something. But the man sat in miserable silence, still clutching the blankets to hide his nakedness. The Erythanian spun, her dark hair swirling into a fan, then stalked out the doorway. The outer door slammed violently shut, and ash pattered to the hearth.

Mitrian channeled all of her hurt and anger against Tannin. "How dare you! How could you!"

Tannin gripped the blankets between fingers white with strain. "*Torke,* I'm sorry. I lost track of time."

"No excuses!"

"It's not an excuse. It's an explanation. I dishonored my sword and my *torke.* I deserve every punishment you said." Tannin squirmed, and his voice sank. "It was all *my* fault. Did you have to scare Sharya?"

"I shouldn't have scared her." Mitrian's eyes narrowed. "I should have killed her. She's a dirty, rude, ill-bred whore, and I can't believe you or any Renshai would lower himself to sleep with her!" Mitrian glared at Tannin, her rage coming as much from emotional pain as from actual anger at Tannin's transgression. She knew she should leave now, while she had the upper hand, and let Tannin contemplate his crime. Yet, deep inside, she needed a personal apology, something to explain why he would chose a teenaged trollop over the only unmarried Renshai woman.

Finally driven to the edge, too, Tannin threw the blankets

aside, revealing himself to the waist. His blue eyes bunched to slits, and his cheeks flared red. "With all the respect due you, *torke*, I have one thing to say." He pronounced each word definitively, his voice bland with rising anger. "Men fuck." Without another word, he turned his back.

The urge to slaughter Tannin rose instantly, then disappeared as quickly. Unexpectedly, tears stung Mitrian's eyes, and she knew she was about to lose control completely. Instead, she whirled. The need to cry struck suddenly then, welling into a torrent; and it was all she could do to keep from rushing, sobbing, from the cottage. But she kept her steps measured, forcing her breaths to normalize until she left the cottage and bashed the door shut every bit as hard as Sharya had done. Grief rushed down on her, mingling with self-pity and rage. She felt hot as fire, seized by an urge to curl into a ball in some private corner where no one could find her, where the flames could consume her and she had to answer to no one. Instead, she ran, choosing a course that would not take her past anyone.

At length, Mitrian left the Renshai's cottages behind her. She stopped short on the grassy plain, out of sight of the training ground, not wanting to arrive before Tannin despite her threat. *Men fuck.* Mitrian noted he had switched to the Western tongue to find the most vulgar euphemism for sex. Logic told her that she should find nothing attractive or interesting about a man who would sleep with women like Sharya. Yet her mind clung to the image of his kind gentleness and savage dedication to the arts she taught him. Her heart ached within her, and the tears quickened. She tried to drive away sorrow with violence, concentrating on the anger and leaving the hurt behind. She whipped her sword from its sheath and launched into a wild *svergelse*.

The sword sang around Mitrian in controlled arcs and gliding slashes. Escaping into the practice, she thought of her fondness for the weapon, recalling the day of its forging. The Eastern Wizard, Shadimar, had given her a pair of amber gems to become the eyes of the hilt's wolf head, once forged. He had promised her the "only magic sword of the Eastern, Western, and faery worlds." In fact, the sword's enchantment had come from a Renshai soul locked in the gems, the last remnant of a warrior who had died of illness and had begged a previous Eastern Wizard to trap him rather than let him slip away to Hel. Mitrian had learned nearly as much of the Renshai sword maneuvers and philosophy from the soul caged in topaz as she had from Colbey.

Mitrian's strokes grew bolder and stronger, and her tears evaporated in the breeze raised by her movements. She recalled how the excitement of the Great War had sent the Renshai in the gems into a wild battle madness. It had dragged her with it, stealing the self-control she needed to experience the war herself and to keep track of her loyalties. His war passion had caused her to slaughter one of her father's own men. Then, Mitrian had cracked one topaz, freeing the soul to its rightful place in Hel and taking, so she had believed, all magic from the sword.

Mitrian allowed herself to become conscious of the gems, feeling the solid facets of the wolf's left eye and the irregular pinch of the crack winding through the right. Apparently some sorcery remained, or else the Wizard had enchanted the blade in other ways, because the edge still held the sharpness and shine of first forging. No notches marred the blade, and its steel remained as strong and straight as always. Then, abruptly, Mitrian's thoughts collapsed back to memories of Tannin. The hot mixture of agony and rage returned in a rush, and her eyes burned with the threat of reemerging tears.

Arduwyn's voice cut through Mitrian's thoughts and her practice. "There you are!" It held accusation.

Mitrian froze in position, the sword poised in a high arc, her stance closed. Her eyes rolled, finding the little archer riding toward her from the direction of the cottages. His spiky red hair looked more disheveled than usual, and his single brown eye held no sparkle. Though Colbey's height, his scrawny frame made him seem tiny. The random black and white blotches of his paint horse only added to the unkempt appearance of the hunter and his mount.

"Not now, Arduwyn. I'm busy."

Arduwyn did not slow, but continued heading toward her. "This can't wait."

"Anything can wait."

"Not this." Arduwyn reined up at the border of comfortable speaking range, just beyond a sword stroke. His eye narrowed, and his voice softened. "Are you crying?"

"No!" Mitrian lowered her sword, but she did not sheathe it. She wiped her eyes with the back of her free hand, trying to keep the gesture casual. The suggestion only made her feel more like crying, and the effort of preventing it did nothing to improve her temper. "What do you want?"

"I want to talk to you about giving a sword to a baby." The archer's tone made it clear he was chastising, not seeking advice.

"What are you talking about?" Mitrian had no interest in riddles and even less in lectures. "Be direct and quick. I have students to teach." It was a lame excuse off the practice ground and alone, especially since she taught daily and Arduwyn would find no other time more convenient to speak with her.

Still, Arduwyn went straight to the point. "I just watched an infant drop a sword on her foot. It's badly bruised, and she probably broke some toes." The paint snorted.

Mitrian cringed in sympathy. "Vashi hurt? I'm sorry."

"You're sorry?" Arduwyn sounded incredulous.

"Yes, I'm sorry. Do you think I want her to be in pain?"

"I don't know," Arduwyn admitted, the accusation fully returning to his tone. "Why would you give a sword to a baby?"

"First, if she can hold a sword, she's not a baby. Second, it's the Renshai way."

"The Renshai way of what? Killing off its children?"

"No one is killing off anyone." Mitrian jabbed the sword back into its sheath. Though this took the weapon out of her hand, the violence of the gesture served as equal warning. "It's how the Renshai became the finest swordsmen in the world."

"It's stupidity!"

The insult jabbed straight to the heart. "It's none of your business."

"It's my business when I see an adult I admire and respect giving weapons to a child as toys." Arduwyn changed his tactic. "Come on, Mitrian. I've got a daughter of my own. It's torture to see a little girl injuring herself because she has something she shouldn't have."

"Shouldn't have!" Mitrian knew that her own son had been given a tiny sword in place of a rattle. His early training would allow him to far surpass her, as he nearly had already. Because of the training she had missed her first sixteen years, Mitrian understood that she could never become the best. So long as she lived and led the Renshai, no man, woman, or child would ever feel cheated of that opportunity. "We're Renshai, Arduwyn. Renshai! Not flabby-butted, floppy-breasted, Erythanian farm whores. If you and your people choose to train your children to become cowards, that's your decision!"

Arduwyn's face flushed scarlet. "Are you calling Sylva a flabby-breasted whore?"

"No, of course not." Mitrian knew the insult was aimed at a completely different Erythanian girl, but she had no wish to detail her target now. "I'm just saying that Renshai didn't become the best swordsmen by accident. It's training. It works. And it's none of your damned business."

The paint snorted again, pawing at the ground with a forehoof. Arduwyn jerked on the reins, and the pawing stopped. "Mitrian, don't you see. It's not the training in infancy that makes Renshai the best. That's just tradition and superstition. An infant can't learn sword maneuvers; it's impossible. What makes Renshai the best is technique and a dedication to their art *once they become old enough to understand it.*"

Mitrian gathered her thoughts for a retort.

Arduwyn continued, leaving her no time to consider. "Look at you. Right now, you're the most competent Renshai, and you didn't start your training until you had become an adult by Western standards. My father wouldn't let me carry a bow until I learned to carry a stick in a safe and respectful manner. He took my first bow away the day I drew it back, without an arrow, and pretended to aim it at my sister. It took me a year to get it back. But, with all due modesty, I'm probably the best archer in the West, even without an eye. Having the bow denied me until I became old enough to understand technique and safety only made it more sweet and me more dedicated when I finally got one. My ardor to become the best grew stronger."

Mitrian found logic in Arduwyn's words, but her mood would not allow her to compromise or consider. "Look, Arduwyn. That's all very cute and maudlin, but it has nothing to do with Vashi. You can't compare pulling back a string and letting go to Renshai sword mastery. Bows are for people who stand back and let others do their fighting." It was an unfair accusation. Arduwyn had lost his eye to an Easterner's sword in the Great War, while fighting with his scimitar.

"Damn it, Mitrian! I used to chide Colbey for his closed-minded blindness to anything not a sword. Once I got past my own prejudice against Renshai, I discovered him to be far more thoughtful and tolerant than I ever expected. You, on the other hand, have become as rigid as I accused him of being."

Arduwyn's words drove Mitrian beyond even the modicum of restraint she had managed to rally. "Get out of here! Just go away! Cowards don't belong among Renshai!"

The horse shied. Arduwyn opened his mouth, prepared to defend himself against her harsh words.

Mitrian whipped her sword free, jabbed it toward the forests and away from the Fields of Wrath.

The paint whipped into a half rear. Regaining control, Arduwyn forced it to twist a quarter turn before its hooves again touched the ground. Without another word, he rode toward the woodlands.

Mitrian collapsed into another bout of tears.

Lirtensa left his cell the following morning, and he did not return. Khitajrah spent the day stretched out across the piled straw, playing counting games to avoid the deep contemplation that kept bringing her back to the same guilt and the same conclusions. The dung-reeking quiet seemed to stretch into an eternity. She slept intermittently and fretfully, day marked from night only by the glow through the single high window and the occasional entrances of guards carrying food in the lighter hours. This she ate, more from boredom than hunger. And, though surely they gave her the dregs of winter storage, she ate better now than she had while foraging for berries and buds. The vegetables tasted heartier and fresher than at Eastern first harvest.

On the morning of Khitajrah's third day of imprisonment, the outer door swung open. Three men stood framed in the doorway, two wearing the single piece outfits of the town guard. The third man was lean and tall, dressed in flashy purple and green silk, with a ring gracing each finger. At first, Khitajrah did not recognize Lirtensa. His crouched figure in the cells gave her no impression of height, and the memory of his squinty, greasy countenance ill-prepared her for this very different look of wealth. Then her eyes met his, and he smiled. He had combed his hair back away from his face, though it still appeared more dirty than colored. A single, oily strand curled across his forehead. He waited, leaning casually against the door frame, while the guards approached Khitajrah's cell.

One produced a key. The other waited, staring at Khitajrah until she met his gaze. He spoke in the common trading tongue, enunciating each word carefully. "We're taking you to trial. Will you come peacefully and without need for restraint?"

Though Khitajrah had no intention of doing otherwise, she glanced at Lirtensa for guidance. He nodded slightly. She looked back at the guard. "I will come peacefully."

The other man stabbed the key into the lock and twisted. He opened the door and motioned Khitajrah out.

Chaos saw the loopholes at once. *He didn't say you had to remain peaceful all the way to the courthouse. And he never said you couldn't run away. So long as you do it peacefully . . .*

All of that was implied. Khitajrah cut off chaos' ramblings, annoyed that she had found herself considering the same outs. To break the law, whether its letter or intention, would violate the basic foundations of society. *Now, leave me alone. I have to talk to Lir. And I have to think.*

I'm only trying to broaden your thoughts, to present options that your elders' narrow views of reality might have stifled.

How generous of you. Khitajrah hoped her sarcasm came through clearly. *When I need your help, I'll let you know.* She stepped out of the cell, looking to the guards for her next move.

The man who had opened her cell pocketed the key. Sidestepping around Khitajrah and his companion, he led the way to the door. Khitajrah followed him, and the second guard trailed her. Lirtensa moved aside to let the three through, then he came to Khitajrah's side.

The direct sunlight seemed blinding after three days trapped in the prison's dank grayness. Khitajrah blinked several times as she shuffled along between the guards. Lirtensa walked briskly, neck chains clicking with each bouncing step. Citizens stopped to watch the parade of guards, prisoner, and lawyer, whispering among themselves. Though much of what they said emerged loudly enough, Khitajrah could make no sense of their strange Western language. The foreignness of the proceedings and her own ignorance made her uneasy, and every muscle tensed to a cramping pain.

Needing something on which to ground the odd swirl of experience, she turned on Lirtensa. "Where have you been?"

Though Khitajrah had asked in the trading tongue, Lirtensa replied in Eastern. "I had to get myself free first. Couldn't represent you from prison. I spent the rest of the day tracking down witnesses."

"Witnesses?" Now Khitajrah also used Eastern. "Witnesses to what?"

"Different things."

"There were two guards and a woman who heard me say—"

Lirtensa made an abrupt gesture to indicate that she should not speak the offending word again. The guards glanced over at the sudden movement. One said something angry in the Western tongue. Lirtensa's reply was terse.

"What did he say?" Khitajrah asked.

"He's annoyed because he can't understand our conversation."

"Oh." It occurred to Khitajrah that she'd had the same problem a moment ago, but she saw no reason to antagonize the guards. "Should we use trading?"

"Hell, no." Lirtensa grinned wickedly at the guard who had addressed him. "I'm the lawyer. You're my client. We can use barbarian hand signals if we want. What we're saying is none of his damned business, and I'm tempted to keep talking long after either of us has anything to say just to irk him."

Khitajrah smiled.

Chaos fairly howled. *I like him. Can we marry him?*

Didn't I ask you to go away for a while?

Yes, chaos admitted. *Of course, I don't sleep. I have no eyes to close or ears to plug, and I'm stuck in your mind. Where did you expect me to go?*

The first guard came to a halt before a long, thatch-roofed building and made a brisk motion. "We're here." He headed toward the door.

Khitajrah and Lirtensa followed him, and the last guard brought up the rear. Fear clutched Khitajrah. She tried to ward it away, placing her trust in the man who had managed to free himself from prison more than once. Still, she could not escape the fact that she had blatantly broken the law in front of three witnesses. Ignorance of that law would gain her nothing in the East nor, she suspected, here. "I'm not going to have to lie, am I? I won't do that."

Lirtensa placed a hand on Khitajrah's arm and squeezed reassuringly. "Kayt, if things go as I hope, you won't have to speak at all. I'll keep the proceedings in trading, so you can understand it all. Just stay quiet. And it wouldn't hurt for you to look a little confused and scared."

"That won't take any effort at all."

The lead guard opened the door, revealing a meeting hall packed with Western citizens in dirt-caked work clothes and patched homespun. At the opposite end of the hall, two elderly men and a woman sat behind a table, their countenances grizzled and grave. The guard who had rescued the chicken from the rain barrel sat in a chair to the tribunal's left. Two chairs stood empty to their right, and the lead guard gestured Khitajrah and Lirtensa to these. Behind the tribunal, a hefty, bald man perched above the proceedings on a piled stack of chests. As Khitajrah and Lirtensa sat, the guards closed the outer doors and took up positions beside it.

Khitajrah studied the layout, seized by a sudden panic. Her mouth went dry, and her eyes glazed the courtroom to a blur. She trembled uncontrollably, the stiffness of the movement aching through her muscles. Her mind flashed slowed motion images of Bahmyr rushing to her aid, of Diarmad's dagger dripping blood, of her son lying still on the courtroom floor.

"Whoa, whoa!" Lirtensa grasped Khitajrah's upper arm. "I said a little confused and scared. You look like you're about to drop dead."

"Can't help it," Khitajrah managed, her voice emerging in an unfamiliar squeak. "Been through this before."

"Huh?"

"Been through this before," Khitajrah repeated, the words more difficult the second time.

"You've been tried over a sentence of death before?"

Khitajrah nodded. Her jaw trembled, and her teeth clicked together repetitively.

Lirtensa studied her, and his look seemed to hold as much admiration as surprise. "Gods, *frilka*. And I thought *I* skirted the edge. Where did this happen?"

"East."

Lirtensa chuckled. "So what are you worried about? You

got acquitted there, right? If you lived through Eastern women's court, this'll seem like racing a snail."

You got acquitted there. The thought echoed, tainted by chaos' amusement. In her discomfort, Khitajrah could not tell whether she or it initiated the thought. She stared at the tribunal, soothed by the presence of a woman there. At least, she would have a chance here to dispute her guilt. And she could think of no one she would rather have on her side now than Lirtensa. Though she found him physically repulsive, and many of his philosophies discomfited her, she suspected he would prove competent as a lawyer. For now, her life depended on it.

Lirtensa gave a quick summary of the participants. "The judge, that's the hairless one, is named Unamer. He directs the trial and keeps things fair. You want him to like you. The elders are called Xylain, Avenelle, and Clywid. Avenelle's the woman. The other two I can never remember which is which. I think Xylain's the one with the snout and Clywid's got the pancake ears."

Khitajrah blinked multiple times, until her vision cleared enough to differentiate the tribunal. The woman sat in the middle. The man to her left had a broad nose and a thick, brown beard. To her right, Clywid wore his hair closely-cropped, emphasizing large-lobed ears. Though cruel, Lirtensa's descriptions took the edge from Khitajrah's panic.

Judge Unamer's head turned toward Khitajrah and Lirtensa in increments, the movement smooth and unhurried. His gray brows rose.

Uncertain what was expected of her, Khitajrah looked to Lirtensa.

"Are you ready to start?" he asked.

"I suppose so," Khitajrah said, not at all ready, but equally certain that more time would make no difference.

Lirtensa raised a hand, fluttered his fingers briefly, then lowered it.

The judge turned his attention to the crowd. He lifted both arms, and the Ahktarian audience went silent. He spoke in the common trading tongue, his voice ponderous. "Here now we have gathered to try this woman, Khitajrah Harrsha's-widow . . ." His Western accent mangled the name. ". . . on the grounds that she allegedly spoke the word 'Renshai.' " He lowered his arms.

The crowd made a collective gasp, presumably at Unamer

freely speaking the offending word. Surely, they already knew the charge.

Unamer continued, his neck now swiveling to the tribunal. His lack of movement and his preference for turning only his head reminded Khitajrah of an ancient, wise owl.

"It should be remembered that this particular charge, if founded, holds a guaranteed penalty of death. Therefore, the case should be considered with utmost care."

The two men and the woman nodded somberly.

Unamer twisted his neck to the guard seated to his left. "Tell your story."

The guard described the incident briefly, precisely as it had happened. As he neared the end of the tale, Lirtensa whispered to Khitajrah. "Answer without head motions. Did he get that right?"

Khitajrah consciously kept herself from nodding in agreement. "Yes."

As the guard spoke his final words, Judge Unamer looked at Lirtensa. "Any questions?"

"No, sir."

Again, the judge's head turned to the guard. "Dismissed." Then, back to Lirtensa. "Who would you like to call?"

"Whidishar Hunter."

The crowd whispered about his choice. A moment later, a man stepped from among them and headed toward the front. Khitajrah recognized him at once as the hunter she had spoken to just before entering Ahktar. She noticed that several of the men who had accompanied him then sat with him now.

The guard vacated the seat to go stand with his two companions by the door. Whidishar gave Khitajrah a friendly smile as he passed, then took his seat beside the tribunal.

Unamer spoke at his usual monotonous pace, each word clear. "Tell your story of the incident, please."

"I wasn't there, sir."

"Very well." Unamer turned his attention to Lirtensa. "Your questions."

Lirtensa leapt to his feet, briskly crossing the floor to stand before Whidishar. "Whidishar Hunter, have you seen or spoken with my client before this trial?"

"Yes, sir. I've done both."

"And when did that occur?"

"Two days ago. In the morning. My friends and I were going hunting, and she was headed toward the town."

Lirtensa brushed the curl from his forehead, and it immediately fell back into place. "Did you try to talk to her in Western?"

"Yes, I did. At first. It was pretty obvious she didn't understand me, so I switched to Western trade. She responded to that."

"So you would say that my client is a foreigner?"

Whidishar shrugged. "Obviously."

Judge Unamer interrupted. "Lir, if you're trying to establish that your client didn't know our laws, you may as well stop here. At best, ignorance would reduce the sentence. We're here to establish whether or not the crime was committed."

Lirtensa raised his hand. "I swear, sir, that this is all relevant. I have no intention of claiming ignorance. In fact, the law is universal and old enough so no one should be ignorant of it."

Khitajrah frowned, but she said nothing. Lirtensa had phrased his comment so as not to lie, but he treaded a dangerous boundary. They both knew she had had no prior knowledge of the crime or its consequences. Worse, the judge had clearly stated that ignorance might have lessened the sentence. Now, should they lose the case, she would surely die.

"Proceed," Unamer said.

Lirtensa turned his questioning back to Whidishar. "We have now established my client is a foreigner. In fact, she's a recent immigrant from the East."

Whidishar nodded. "That would have been my guess."

"Now, at one point in time, she spoke the name of this town, didn't she?"

"Yes."

"How did she pronounce that?"

Whidishar considered for a moment. His lips jerked into a smile. "I'm not sure I can get it exactly right."

"Try."

"It sounded something like Accccch-tayer." Whidishar exaggerated the guttural.

The crowd twittered.

Lirtensa also smiled. "Did you correct her?"

"Yes."

"And afterward, how did she say it?"

"She said it . . ." Whidishar chuckled again. "Acccccch-tayer."

"Thank you," Lirtensa said. "No further questions." Crossing the room, he returned to his seat.

"Dismissed." Judge Unamer kept his attention on Whidishar, then rotated his head to Lirtensa again. "You said two witnesses this morning. Who would you like to call as the other?"

"Gertrina. The tailor's wife."

A murmur swept the crowd. The woman who had called for the guards' help with the chicken waddled forward. She waited until Whidishar rose and vacated the chair, then plopped her wide bottom in place.

"Tell your version of the story." The judge instructed.

Gertrina held her head high, obviously pleased at becoming the center of attention at an important trial. "It was just like he said." She pointed at the guard with a thick hand. "I heard it all. I was standing right there. She said . . . well, you know . . . the word."

Judge Unamer nodded, brows screwing in toward his nose. He seemed as confused by Lirtensa's choice of witness as Khitajrah was. "Any questions, Lir?"

"Yes." Lirtensa rose, striding across the chamber floor to confront Gertrina directly. "Gertrina, exactly what was the offending word that my client said?"

Gertrina threw a startled glance at the judge.

Unamer nodded. "You may safely answer the question. For the purposes of trial, it is no crime to say the word. It is important that we establish the offense solidly and without euphemism."

"She said . . ." Gertrina trailed off, obviously still uncomfortable. "She said, 'I'm told he's Renshai.' " She whispered the final word, but it wafted to Khitajrah clearly enough. She suspected that the people in the back did not hear, but the judge did not press for a repetition. All those who mattered had heard.

"She said it just like that?"

"Oh, yes. In fact, she said it twice. She was asked to repeat it."

"Well, that confuses me, Gertrina." Lirtensa paced out a circle, and the pause grew into a tangible silence while he, apparently, gathered his thoughts. "Whidishar just got finished saying that Kayt has a heavy accent. That she couldn't even speak the name of our town *after* he coached her."

Gertrina stuck with her story, though she seemed more hesitant. "Well, she said . . . that word . . . clearly enough."

"So you're saying that, somewhere between the border of the town and its second street, Kayt completely lost her Eastern accent."

"No. She still had an accent," Gertrina admitted. She fidgeted, all of her proud confidence disappearing.

"So, Gertrina." Lirtensa pinned the woman with his gaze. "Is it possible that Kayt actually said *raynshee*." He spoke the common trading word for elder. "Or *granshy, baronshei,* or even *rintsha?*" Khitajrah recognized only one of the three. The middle term was trading for bald. "Could she have said *rhinsheh?*" Khitajrah recognized this as an Eastern term, meaning morning. In her country, it would be pronounced ran-*shay,* though Lirtensa took the emphasis off of the last syllable.

Gertrina avoided Lirtensa's piercing stare, glancing from the judge to Khitajrah to the crowd in rapid succession. "Well, I suppose so. But I really *think* she said . . . well, you know."

"You think she said, Gertrina? You think? Would you really condemn a woman to death because you think she might possibly, maybe have committed a crime?" Lirtensa snorted with disgust. "No further questions."

"Wait," Gertrina said.

Lirtensa continued to walk away.

Judge Unamer did not dismiss her as he had the others. "Did you have something more to say, Gertrina?"

"Yes, I did." Gertrina became bolder. "She was asking about a person. I guess I could understand *raynshee* and *baronshei.* I don't even know what *rhinsheh* means. But why would this woman, Kayt, have described some man by calling him plums or cat?"

Lirtensa whirled back to face Gertrina so suddenly that she cringed away. "We have already established that knowledge of the crime and its punishment is universal. Even if Kayt had accidentally said Renshai . . ."

The ease and suddenness with which Lirtensa used the offending term obviously startled and unsettled Gertrina.

". . . why would she have repeated it unless she believed she was saying something very different? Something inoffensive. I was just trying to make the point that Kayt's accent makes her difficult to understand. Do you think it's possible that you mistook one word for another?"

Gertrina swallowed hard. "Yes," she said at last. "It's possible."

"No further questions," Lirtensa repeated. Again, he walked away.

This time, Gertrina said nothing, and the judge dismissed her as he had the others. His owl's head swiveled to face Lirtensa again. "Do you have anything else to say? Any other witnesses?"

"No, sir." Lirtensa turned his back on the crowd to face the tribunal directly. "I think it's clear that my client tried to describe a man using a perfectly normal and innocent word. It also seems obvious that her accent rendered that word difficult to understand; and, thus, it was understandably misinterpreted by Gertrina and the guards. It is my recommendation that all charges be dropped and that Kayt be permitted to go free and enjoy the pleasures of her new country."

Khitajrah held her breath, heart fluttering in her chest. From the nods spreading through the crowd, Lirtensa had convinced them. All that remained now was to see the effect of his words on the tribunal.

"I have only one more question." Judge Unamer's voice boomed through the chamber. Startled, Khitajrah looked up, only to find his gaze directly upon her. "Lady, what, in fact, was the word you said?"

All color drained from Khitajrah's face, and her throat seemed to become paralyzed. In an instant, she had gone from likely acquittal to a guaranteed death sentence. And she, herself, would speak the deciding word that would seal her fate.

NO! Chaos' shout echoed through Khitajrah's mind. *Don't say it. Not now. Not so close.*

Lirtensa froze, unable to help.

I have to, Khitajrah sent back.

You don't have to do anything. The law is stupid; it needs to be changed.

It is the law.

And you've never said raynshee *in your life?*

What?

The judge didn't ask what you said at any particular

time. He just asked what word you said. You've said raynshee.*

We all know what he meant.

And we all know what he said.

Yes, we all know what he said.

"I said Renshai," Khitajrah replied softly, letting her accent twist the vowels as much as possible. Guilt flared. *If I'm going to lie, I'm not going to do it under the guise of truth.* "And I meant that to mean 'elder.'" Pain shocked through her, mixed with chaos' triumph, and the combination nearly made her vomit.

Lirtensa smiled nervously.

The tribunal did not bother to deliberate. "Innocent," said the first.

"Innocent."

"Innocent."

But even as the words emerged, Khitajrah's conscience had a "guilty" for every one. She went docile as a lamb when Lirtensa led her from the courtroom, a free woman in every way but spirit.

CHAPTER 14

Long Way Home

Shadimar stood at the *Sea Seraph*'s forward rail, watching spray foam and curl around the bow. His fingers caressed the dolphin figure that graced the prow, but it was an absent gesture, without meaning. His other hand clutched the staff, its base grounded on the rocking planks. His gaze barely penetrated the fog, and the ocean seemed to stretch from horizon to horizon and beyond. Sound carried easily through the dense mists that surrounded the ship. The Eastern Wizard listened to the sweet duet of Mar Lon Davrinsson and the otherworld captain who manned the tiller. The chords and runs of the *lonriset* formed a perfect background for the ancient sea songs the bard and the elf sang together.

Secodon lay at Shadimar's feet, eyes open, muzzle resting on his paws.

The cabin door creaked open. Trilless' light footsteps pattered across the deck, and the heavy thump of Carcophan's boots followed. The Southern Wizard's strong bass boomed across the deck. ". . . surely even you can see that."

Trilless replied with obvious disgust. "What I can see is that you have the insight of a donkey and the manners of a pig."

"Oh, so we're back to name calling, are we?"

The notes of the *lonriset* died away, and the pair ceased their singing.

A smile touched Shadimar's lips. Despite the burden of massive responsibilities and the need to handle situations that had no obvious answers, Shadimar found comfort in the familiar bickering of his companions. The power of the staff swelled through him, promising the straightforward answers he sought and the authority to deal with the problems, once detailed. For now, many questions needed answers. One thing seemed certain; the spread of chaos had to be stopped, and Colbey with it, in any manner possible. Odin had made the Cardinal Wizards' responsibilities clear for millennia. No matter which of his predecessors Shadimar tapped, he always found the same answer. All of the Cardinal Wizards championed law first and their own causes second. All, that is, except Colbey.

Shadimar tightened his hand around the dolphin figure. Its weathered smoothness fit his hand easily, and the beak jutted through his fingers. The fins indented the flesh of his hand. Though minor, the pain unnerved him, reminding him of the invulnerability that the shattering of the Pica Stone had cost the Wizards. The last suggestion Carcophan had voiced in front of him returned now, its logic seeming even more obvious in the wake of Shadimar's current train of thought. They would all need to find apprentices who could serve as successors. First, it would double their numbers so they could deal with Colbey and his ugly trail of chaos from several directions at once. There was also a necessary security. Losing an apprentice to Colbey's sword might save them a Wizard. And if the Western Wizard gone mad did slay one of the Cardinal three, an apprentice would immediately stand ready to take his or her place. Hopefully, the Wizard would not die at once and would have the presence of mind to transfer his memories to his successor.

Still, despite the obvious logic of the decision, Shadimar felt trapped and alone. He had already depleted the store of competent individuals to serve neutrality in looking for the one to replace Colbey. They had sent the five most promising to their deaths, not realizing that Colbey still occupied the single placement in the Seven Tasks of Wizardry. Since there would be little or no time to train the apprentices to magic, it only made sense to choose competent fighters to stand against Colbey. Yet Shadimar balked at the idea of selecting a successor based on weapon skill. He was already battling the tragic results of the Western Wizard's decision to replace himself with a Renshai rather than a sorcerer.

Trilless' voice came clearly through the fog. Apparently, she had chosen to ignore her opposite's taunt and address her follower instead. "Captain, my friend. Good sailing. Now that we're through the portal, do you have time to chat?"

Captain laughed, the sound like bells. "My lady, of course. Did you think I have time only for old songs and

fine music? How may I serve the Northern Wizard?" He
added carefully, "And the Southern Wizard?"

Shadimar released the dolphin and turned. He placed his
back against the rail, clutched the staff in both hands, and
used its support for balance. It felt strong, and it lent him the
stability that the rolling ship stole.

At the movement, Secodon scrambled to his feet. He
shook moisture from his coat.

"We wondered if you had seen the Western Wizard since
he passed his tasks."

"Aye," Captain said. "Took him to shore days ago." The
elf's voice held a discomfort that did not suit the carefree
playfulness of his race. Though more serious than most of
his ilk, the captain had a somberness to his tone now that
seemed misplaced, even for him.

Trilless apparently noticed the change as well. "You're
bitter. Did he give you trouble, too?"

"Nay, none of it," Captain replied quickly. "But he did
say things that upset me now."

"What did he say?" Carcophan encouraged, his graveled
voice and guttural accent sounding misplaced after Trilless'
lilt. "We need to know."

Captain paused for a long time, apparently trying to pluck
events from confidences. Odin's Laws limited him severely,
and he would not reveal another Wizard's words unless he
felt certain the speaker would condone the others gaining
such knowledge. "He said you had tried to kill him." A short
pause followed, then anguish swallowed Captain's words so
that Shadimar had to strain to hear. "How could you do that?
How could you break the most basic of the Wizards' vows?"

"He lied," Carcophan said.

"He's a Wizard," Captain clung to his point. "He can't
lie."

"Neither can we," Carcophan pointed out as quickly.

"I found him nearly dead from wounds only a demon
could inflict."

"Ah, so that's where it went." Carcophan laughed cruelly.

The revelation struck Shadimar hard, though it explained
much. He had wondered why the creature had not, as the
others expected, turned upon its summoner. They had believed that Shadimar had managed to banish it back to the
plane of chaos before he had lost consciousness. Certain he
had worked no such magic, Shadimar had attributed the mir-

acle to the staff. Now, he knew better. Yet now, too, he
wished he had dispelled the creature. The idea that Colbey
would slay a demon of the *kraell*'s power sent a chill
through him, trebling the danger of the chaos-wielding
Renshai to the world of law. *Surely, the Staff of Chaos must
have aided the fight.*

"Why would it have gone to him?" Trilless asked, even as
the same question came to Shadimar's mind.

"What?" Carcophan asked.

"Why would the demon attack the one Wizard who hadn't
summoned it? Certainly, it didn't worry about the damage
Kyndig might inflict on our world."

A pause followed as Southern and Eastern Wizard pon-
dered simultaneously. Although he surely had questions,
Captain did not interrupt a conversation between Cardinal
Wizards.

"Probably, the Staff of Law took over when Shadimar lost
control." Carcophan added, apparently not caring whether or
not the Eastern Wizard overheard, "I told you he wasn't
strong enough to wield it. Had I held it—"

Shadimar tightened his grip on the staff, more convinced
than ever that, even aligned with the other Cardinal Wizards,
he remained very much alone. Carcophan would not have it.

Trilless interrupted Carcophan's posturing. "We've gone
over that ground for the last time." Her words emerged as a
clear warning. "If you have a new point to make, do so. If
not, don't belabor issues put to rest."

Perhaps because of the presence of mortals or the importance of the point he wished to make, Carcophan did not
quibble. "Clearly, the Staff of Law wants Colbey dead, and
the staff serves Odin more directly than any being can. I say
our course is clear."

"No!" Captain screamed. It was the first time in the centuries Shadimar had known the captain that he ever heard
the elf lose control.

Intrigued, Shadimar crossed the slippery deck, heading toward the conversation, the wolf trotting carefully at his
heels. Apparently equally surprised, Carcophan and Trilless
let the outworlder speak his mind.

"Your course is as fog-clouded as the *Seraph*'s. You can't
harm another Cardinal Wizard. It'll bring the *Ragnarok* for
certain."

"Times change," Carcophan said. "Situations change.

Elves placed on the world to serve the Cardinal Wizards become insubordinate. When we decide we need the opinion of an inferior, we'll demand it of you. Until then, mind your station. And your business."

"Quiet, Evil One," Trilless returned. "The captain is *my* underling, and I'm interested in what he has to say. Perhaps you're the one who needs to learn his business."

"Stop it!" Shadimar slammed the base of his staff onto the deck, and the noise drew every eye. Mar Lon perched on the gunwale, meekly clutching his instrument and avoiding a direct role in the argument. Captain clutched the tiller so tightly it looked as if he might need to have his fist magically opened to release it. In front of him, Trilless and Carcophan stood, nose to nose, on the aft deck.

Having gained their attention, Shadimar continued. "Sometimes I think you two just take opposite sides for the sake of arguing, with no thought given to the issue itself. I can think of another reason why an unsecured demon would head straight for Colbey. Remember the nature of chaos. It's formless, masterless, and without ties or loyalties. Locked in a staff, law becomes concentrated. In the same situation, chaos becomes trapped. Therefore, it serves the interests of chaos to slay Colbey and release the mass of chaos he carries."

Trilless faced Shadimar, all momentum against Carcophan lost. "You're saying we should league with Colbey?"

Carcophan frowned, glaring.

"No." Shadimar thumped the base of his staff against the planks again, this time only for emphasis. "I think we need to slay Colbey first, get the staff, and destroy it before chaos gets control of it."

The captain quivered, features tight with anger.

Trilless and Carcophan considered in a silence that lasted several minutes but seemed like seconds to Shadimar.

The Sorceress broke the silence. "So you believe we have to compete with chaos coming to release itself?"

Even Shadimar could see the strange circle his logic seemed to be taking, but the staff in his hand supported the complexity of his thoughts. "The details aren't clear to me, but I don't think it's anything to worry about so long as we don't summon demons. By evoking the staff, Colbey can take control of all of the chaos on our world. Therefore, he need fear only that chaos which we summon from its own plane."

"Let me make sure I understand." Carcophan went pensive as well. "Summoned chaos wants Colbey dead. We want Colbey dead. But if we kill Colbey with summoned chaos, the summoned chaos will take control of his staff and use it against us."

"That's how I understand it," Shadimar admitted, though he knew much of the explanation still eluded him.

"Wait, wait, wait." Trilless still clung to Carcophan's remark. "Like Captain, I still take exception to the idea that we want Colbey dead. That's not been decided for certain."

Carcophan ignored Trilless' comments, continuing on his own track. "So, if we can't summon demons or the Swords of Power, how do you suggest we fight Colbey and his chaos?"

"We have the best weapon of all." Shadimar smiled. "Every object and being of law. On a lawful world, the possibilities are infinite."

Trilless cleared her throat, flinging her white cloak back to reveal her equally white dress. "Are Captain and I the only ones here with sense? Breaking the Wizards' vow against harming one another is as chaotic an act as anything Colbey could perform."

Carcophan bowed gallantly, with mock respect. "Sometimes, my dear, to win the battle you have to fight by the enemy's rules."

"But chaos has no rules. That's what makes it chaos."

Carcophan rose with a flourish. "That's my point. Whatever Shadimar's theories on chaos rescuing chaos, it is still my belief that the Staff of Law wants Colbey dead. First and foremost, our vow is to uphold law in its entirety."

Trilless snorted. "Since when does the master of evil speak with Odin's tongue? You're arrogant to purport to know what the staff wants." She hesitated only a moment. "In fact, you're arrogant, period."

The answer to the argument came to Shadimar in a flash. To know what the Staff of Law wanted, he only needed to ask. "Give me a moment, and I'll tell you the will of the Staff of Law and, therefore, of Odin." Turning, he strode across the deck, opened the door to the cabin, and slipped below decks. Leaving Secodon with his companions, he pulled the panel shut behind him. Nothing would jeopardize his concentration.

Alone, Shadimar sat in one of the hard wooden chairs that surrounded Captain's table and fixed his gaze on the narwhale horn above the books. His heart pounded, revealing all the anxiety he had hidden from his colleagues. The staff felt vibrant in his fist, and magic hummed through it with a current stronger than he would ever have guessed existed. There was something horrible about its power that Shadimar could attribute only to its intensity and concentration. So far, he had feared to tap more than its barest edge, even when he had tried to control the demon. Its vitality dwarfed his own, making his centuries seem like an eye blink in the cosmos and his life itself less than the last twist of steam from a candle's flame. Afraid to lose himself in the depths, Shadimar slid the staff between his knees, trapping it between the edge of the chair's seat and the table. He gripped the staff in both hands, resting his forehead against its smooth wooden surface.

A massive wave of presence pulsed against Shadimar's being, as if to suffocate him with its otherness. Nearly overcome, Shadimar reeled backward. His chair toppled over, spilling him to the floor, and the staff hit the planks with a resounding clatter. The surge of the force receded to a trickle, a message that touched Shadimar's mind like a whisper. *You are my champion. You need not fear me.*

Too much. Shadimar gathered his remaining composure and dignity. Righting the chair, he picked up the staff gingerly and retook his seat.

The staff held its sending to a cautious ebb. *I did not mean to overwhelm you. We are one. You are my champion.*

Your champion? Shadimar repeated, not quite understanding. The intensity and enormity of its power quailed him. He had met nothing so formidable since his one and only meeting with the Keeper of the Eighth task, a god he believed might have been Odin himself. Yet where the Keeper's whole being had seemed to clutch and pull, as if to drag Shadimar into eternity, the staff seemed drawn to him, as if it might drown him beneath its own vitality.

Yes, my champion. Of course. Did you not notice how right we felt together from the moment you touched me? It has always been the intention of Odin for the Eastern Wiz-

ard to wield me. It is your destiny, and the destiny of all those who share your mind.

The collective consciousness stirred, roused by the staff's words. Shadimar's predecessors knew a calm rightness about the staff's presence, yet its scope and vigor still cowed Shadimar. It promised strength, yet the current Eastern Wizard worried about dominance, concerned that the device might become sovereign and the Wizard servant.

You doubt yourself too much, Eastern Wizard. I told you before, you need not fear me. I am no being, just the portal to a force. And you are the champion destined to direct and advance my realm.

The concept confused Shadimar. *Your realm? What realm is that?*

You know what I am.

You're the Staff of Law.

And what is my realm, then?

Here. Shadimar made a grand gesture to indicate the worlds of men, elves, and gods. *We are your realm.*

The staff gave nothing, waiting for Shadimar to continue.

Shadimar frowned. *So you're a portal from our world to itself?*

From the gods to men. The Staff of Law opens onto the repository of law itself. The gray god, Odin. That is the source of law's power.

Shadimar suddenly felt paralyzed. Though he had no need to speak aloud, his mind seemed unable to even form words for speech. But where Shadimar failed, the collective consciousness swarmed forward to ask the obvious questions. *It has, from the start, been our job to champion law?*

Though addressed by the others, the staff sent its answer directly to Shadimar. *I have always been the Eastern Wizards' destiny. Unlike good and evil, Odin kept the Staves of Law and Chaos while the Cardinal Wizards became more knowledgeable and competent. The time has come for you to wield me.*

A conclusion followed naturally. *And for Colbey to wield chaos.* Shadimar had spent centuries guarding the balance between good and evil, long enough to understand that one force could not exist without the other. The insight opened a whole new area of thought, and guilt gnawed at him. Perhaps he had been wrong from the start, and Colbey right.

Shadimar's mind did not get far before the staff's presence blocked the trail. *No!* The forcefulness of its insistence hammered through Shadimar's head. *Law and chaos cannot be compared to good and evil. Good and evil are degrees of law; they cannot exist in chaos. Without law, there can be no faith, loyalty, or honor. Without form and definition, the world can have no absolutes, no right or wrong; and all that has become solid and real on this world will lose meaning. There is no such thing as a little bit of chaos. Its leaks will widen, until the tiny breaches in Odin's defenses split open, admitting its destruction like a torrent. Should Colbey league with his staff as you have with me, he would fling wide the portal to the banished plane of chaos, exposing our world to a deluge that would wash all honor and morality away.*

Buoyed by the confirmation of faith and the staff's strength, Shadimar became bolder. *How, then, do I stop him? Do I listen to Carcophan? Or to Trilless?*

The staff fed into the wave of enthusiasm. *You listen to neither. Or both, or either as it suits you. You follow your instincts, and you follow my advice. The other Wizards can help you, but the difference between their causes and your own is like that between plain daggers and the Swords of Power. Good and evil are constructs of law. And you ARE law.*

Vitality seemed to course through Shadimar, and he reveled in the power. Even knowing that normal weapons and accidents could harm him now, he felt invincible.

The staff's voice pulsed through Shadimar with its advice. *You must destroy Colbey's staff, whatever the cost. Sometimes, my champion, like it or not, you have to turn an enemy's allies and tactics against himself.*

The concept seemed wrong, even now. *Are you, the device of law, suggesting that I use chaos?*

Never! But I will remind you of this. You are the Lawbringer. You make the rules. The staff withdrew then, leaving only a tangible reminder of its physical presence. Its final words came softly, but were no less formidable. *And when the need arises, you can change them.*

The following morning, Shadimar perched upon the Asciian fjords with Secodon, Carcophan and Mar Lon. Though it was early spring, the Northern winds howled bitterly around them, sending Carcophan's cloak into a whipping dance. The *Sea Seraph* glided northward, becoming a dot on the horizon in the short time it had taken them to scale the cliffs. Shadimar leaned upon his staff, enjoying the feel of the breeze twining his beard about the wood and the high-pitched hum of the wind's passage through the hollow of Mar Lon's *lonriset*.

"He's been here," Carcophan said, drawing Shadimar from his vigil.

"What?" Shadimar turned, facing his colleague, who examined the stony sands.

"Colbey's been here. He went south." Carcophan looked up, fixing the Eastern Wizard with his catlike eyes. "You know this land better than I. Where will that take him?"

Shadimar easily drew a mental map. "After he got through Trilless' territory, he'd come to the Weathered Range. Once through the mountains, the first town he'd reach would be the great trading city, Pudar." He considered a moment longer. "Of course, the Western Wizard's cave lies just about directly south of here. In the mountains."

"Mmmm." Carcophan's brow crinkled in irritation. "Do you think he knows he's safe there?"

"Not for sure." Shadimar considered. "He might, though. He's been to the cave, so he can find it. When he stayed in my ruins, he knew I had them permanently warded." Shadimar went beyond the direct question. "It's not like Colbey, though, to hide from anything."

Mar Lon remained in place, watching the *Sea Seraph* disappear, deliberately adding nothing to the conversation.

"You heard the captain." Carcophan did not taunt, apparently ill at ease on his opposite's home ground. He did not belong there. "Colbey was badly injured. And the uneven spacing of his tracks makes me certain he fared worse than even Captain guessed. He fell at least once. Probably, he'll hole up for a while to heal."

Shadimar knew the warping of time sense that accompanied the Wizards' immortality tended to make them withdraw into solitude for months, years, or even decades at a time.

Apparently, Carcophan's thoughts had taken the same turn. "We should have plenty of time to pick out our successors, if not to train them."

Shadimar straightened, still keeping a solid hold on his staff. The wolf lay down at his feet, waiting. "Don't count

on huge amounts of time. Though a Wizard, Colbey hasn't
yet learned patience."

"Nor magic," Carcophan added. "Which means he'll need
at least a few weeks to recuperate."

"Don't underestimate the Staff of Chaos. It may do it for
him or teach him."

"Or it may kill him." In his own way, Carcophan let
Shadimar know that it was useless to speculate about the unknown. "I'd suggest bringing books to study while each apprentice runs through the tasks. The more research we gather
about the staff, the less power Colbey holds."

Shadimar nodded, Carcophan's point a wise one. Then, recalling the manner in which the Evil One tended to obtain
his information, Shadimar qualified. "But no demons. Only
books."

Carcophan returned a tight-lipped smile, but he did make
a gesture of accord. "No matter what Trilless thinks, you
and I know we have to kill Colbey."

"Yes. And I believe Trilless understands that now, too."
Again, Shadimar glanced out over the waters. The *Sea Seraph* and its two passengers had disappeared from sight. Displeased with her choices on man's world, Trilless had
decided to obtain her successor from among the elves.

Carcophan continued warily, "And you and I know that
the strongest of us should wield the Staff of Law."

Anger stabbed through Shadimar, but the security of the
staff's power allowed him to keep the comment in perspective. Compared to what the staff had to offer, the difference
between his and Carcophan's abilities became insignificant.
He did not bother to meet Carcophan's gaze, though he let
a slight grin play across his lips. "You couldn't wield it any
more than I could champion evil."

"That's nonsense," Carcophan insisted. "All of us champion law. Any of us could wield it."

Now Shadimar pinned Carcophan's yellow-green eyes
with his own gray ones. "The Staff of Law would not have
you."

Carcophan held the Eastern Wizard's gaze, turning the exchange into a war of wills. "When chaos' day comes, you
may despise your greed. Farewell, Shadimar. May you find
a successor who exceeds the average man, if any neutral
prospects remain. And farewell, Mar Lon, on your long and
lonely walk." Still glaring at Shadimar, Carcophan trans-

ported himself back to his own territory without fanfare. One moment, he played a staring game with the other Cardinal Wizard. The next, his place stood empty, without evidence that he had ever been there.

Free of the other two Wizards, Shadimar felt as if a great weight had lifted from his shoulders. Then thoughts of Colbey and his chaos filled Shadimar's mind, and he shivered. He harbored no wish to face the enraged and corrupted Renshai by himself. He returned his attention to his remaining companions.

Secodon lay in place. As his master's gaze found the wolf, his tail whisked against the sand, flinging sparkling grains into the air. Mar Lon sat, cross-legged, on the beach. He balanced the *lonriset* across his knees, pressing out chords with his left hand while his right alternately mimicked strumming and plucking. His mouth moved as he whispered new rhymes amid the silent runs and riffs. The sword in his belt lay twisted awkwardly to accommodate the instrument and Mar Lon's position.

A strange thought came to Shadimar's head. Once formed, the idea found the staff's support. *Why not Mar Lon? He knows more about the Cardinal Wizards than any other mortal in the world, and he can fight.* "Mar Lon."

The bard looked up. His fingers stilled on the strings.

"What are you going to do now?"

Mar Lon stroked Secodon absently with his left hand. The wolf's tail rose, waving like a flag. "I think I'll just stay here. King Sterrane's done without me this long, and there's still more business to attend at the Meeting Isle." He spoke with a bold matter-of-factness, but his tone betrayed sadness and a concern for responsibilities unperformed. The bard's god-given tasks, to gather the knowledge of the world and to guard the king in Béarn, now clashed. "By the time I finished traveling home, you and Carcophan would have returned here, ready to test your apprentices."

"You're going to stay here? In Asci? On this empty beach?" Shadimar crouched before Mar Lon, lowering himself to the bard's level, yet still clutching the staff.

Mar Lon shrugged, obviously less worried about his own discomfort than over leaving the king unprotected. "It'll give me the chance to seek more knowledge of the North. And it's not as if I don't have a thousand new songs to write." He smiled, clearly referring to the events of the last few weeks. "I'll do fine. You have more important things to concern yourself with than my plans or comfort."

"Perhaps." Shadimar considered. "Listen, Mar Lon. I need to talk with you. Would you object if I transported us both back to my territory?" Shadimar thought over his own offer briefly. Technically, his realm extended from the Northern Weathered Range south to the ocean and from the Great Frenum Mountains westward to an ill-defined line through the farm towns near Sholton-Or. Since the Eastern and Western Wizards championed neutrality together, they had never needed a strong physical barrier like the ones that separated Carcophan's far eastern realm and Trilless' Northmen. Mar Lon would find less of interest in Shadimar's realm than in Colbey's, although he would find security in Shadimar's ruins until the time came for the Wizards to reconvene. And Shadimar did not forget that the high Western kingdom, Béarn, was considered joint territory by the Eastern and Western Wizards. "Better yet, I'll transport us to Béarn. We can chat freely there, and you'll have a closer watch over the king."

Mar Lon rose hesitantly, brushing sand from his breeks. "Naturally, nothing could please me more." His manner did not match the enthusiasm of his words. "But isn't it dangerous?"

Shadimar snapped his fingers, signaling Secodon to his side, and the wolf obeyed instantly. Shadimar understood the bard's concern. Though competent to perform magics of many sorts, the Cardinal Wizards rarely exercised the privilege; the peril was too great. Shaped of chaos, the spells could easily escape a Wizard's control or come out far differently than the caster's intention. Clearly, when it came to one Wizard leaving the territory of another, the benefits outweighed the risk. When it involved shifting mortals from place to place, the effort quadrupled and the hazard with it. Still Shadimar recalled two instances when his own predecessor had magically transported him, and the staff made him bolder. "Not very dangerous. A simple enough spell, and I have the Staff of Law to alert me to chaos leaks. Will you come?" Crooking the staff in his elbow, he placed one hand on the wolf's head and held out the other to Mar Lon.

The bard came to him, and Shadimar sized one of the man's wrists. Muscles shifted around bone, the attachments well-developed from his sword training. Shadimar triggered the transport spell. The cold touch of chaos rippled through him, a sensation devoid of substance or loyalty, yet terrifying for its alien impurity. Always in the past, its contact sent chills through Shadimar, reminding him of its destructive wrongness, a presence he tried to forget from day to day. But, this time, he scarcely noticed the feeling, concentrating instead on the wonder of the magic itself, the beauty of an act that only four beings on man's mortal world could perform. The workings of the spell stretched before him in multicolored bands and streamers as complex as, yet less ordered than, a spider's web. Within the shimmering lines and planes that seemed to mock order, Shadimar found the otherworld words of the spell sewn into the maze. Though he had thought each syllable with rulered exactness, the visual image had cut and decapitated the lettering, sprinkling it in random sequences about the infrastructure.

Then, suddenly, the sequenceless patterning disappeared. Mar Lon, Secodon, and Shadimar stood in a valley just outside the kingdom of Béarn. Carved from the mountain, the palace rose among the other peaks, chips of quartz and pyrite glimmering through its spires. Secodon wagged his plumed tail, obviously caught up in his master's excitement. Mar Lon hugged himself tightly, looking chilled to the marrow, though the temperature here was twice that of Asci's sea air.

Shadimar saw no need to announce their arrival. Mar Lon had lived in Béarn long enough to know precisely where he stood. He credited the Staff of Law with showing him the details of magic that he could only have surmised before. Chaos had its place, and clearly that place was on another plane where destruction and dishonor could not touch the citizens of law's realm but it could be summoned for spells such as the one Shadimar had just performed.

Mar Lon bobbed his head in wary appreciation. "I thank you, friend Wizard, for the knowledge of a new experience." He made a formal bow to soften the words that followed. "It would please me if I never had occasion to experience it again."

Shadimar laughed. "Chaos never feels right. But it does become less frightening when you brace for its touch."

"Is that what I felt? That shiver that tore through my soul and set every muscle in my body on edge? The only other things that came close to making me feel such horror were sounds: the dying scream of a rabbit and the terminal crack of a tree trunk before it fell. But there was also a personal wrongness to this that made me feel ashamed for every man's barest thought of dishonesty."

Shadimar loosed another wry chuckle. "A poet to the heart, Mar Lon. I've never heard it described better. You have a talent for seeing detail, a talent that would serve the Cardinal Wizards well."

Mar Lon lowered his gaze to his instrument, apparently embarrassed by the praise. Surely others had complimented his imagery before, but never a Wizard who served the gods directly. "Thank you."

Shadimar continued. "It was a new experience for me as well. The Staff of Law showed me subtleties I never had the power or understanding to see on my own before. It could do that for you, too."

Mar Lon looked up suddenly. "I don't understand."

"Someday, you could wield the Staff of Law."

Mar Lon's brow crinkled in confusion. He shook his head once, as if to clear it. Then he shook his head several times in quick succession, negating the possibility. "I don't see how, sir. If the staff wouldn't have Carcophan, I don't see why it would accept me. Besides, it would serve the world far better in your hands."

Shadimar's laugh echoed between the peaks. "Of course I shall wield it for now. Your time will come."

Mar Lon clung to his *lonriset,* though the instrument was securely tied in place. "Are you asking me to become your successor?" The wind turned his dark hair into a tangle, and his hazel eyes found Shadimar's briefly, then skittered away.

"Can you think of anyone better suited?"

"Surely there's someone. I'm not suited at all."

"You're too modest, Mar Lon." That flaw did not bother Shadimar. The Tasks of Wizardry had enhanced boldness in the unpretentious, though they tended to kill the timid. Shadimar had little trouble distinguishing between the two. A coward would never have accepted the transport spell so easily nor performed before crowds as the bards were trained to do. "You understand our concerns and procedures. You've seen glimpses of the Seven Tasks, and I feel confident you could survive them. You know enough swordplay to stand against Colbey, at least for a time."

Mar Lon flushed, still holding the *lonriset.* "You flatter

my weapon skill immensely. Even if I could stand against the prince of Renshai for a time, I would choose to avoid that situation. I've dedicated my life to peace, through my music and the way I live." Cursed to teaching and giving complicated replies only with his music, Mar Lon launched into song. His fingers flickered over the strings, as lightly as leaves fluttering in a summer breeze. The chords that pealed forth sounded fuller than any Shadimar had heard, except from others in the line of bards. The notes rang with a purity that matched Mar Lon's perfect ear for pitch, the sound not straying a quarter tone, even long after the string's plucking.

After a short introduction, Mar Lon's voice joined the music's flawlessness, spanning three octaves, at times, between single notes. He sang of peace between peoples, calling on animals, forests, and nature for imagery. The pictures he painted with words drew mental visions as solidly real as any artist's paintings or carvings. The song soothed, its tones turning from early discordancy to a crystalline beauty that intertwined notes like lovers. The message stressed tolerance of all men's views as well as the settling of those differences through speech instead of war.

As it continued, the melody and message unnerved Shadimar, and he grew impatient with the five verses and choruses that answered a question Mar Lon could have addressed with a sentence. Odin's curse upon the first bard and his line demanded they express themselves to mortals in song, but that rule did not apply to immortals. Among the Cardinal Wizards or gods, Mar Lon could speak freely. This time, he had chosen not to.

The last notes scattered into Béarn's spring air, the crags bouncing imperfect echoes that detracted from the song. Shadimar did not wait for Mar Lon to lower his instrument. "I'm not asking you to attack Colbey. I'm certainly not asking you to stand against him alone or directly. Taking on the responsibilities of Wizardry means giving up personal concerns, but it doesn't require you to abandon personal honor. In fact, serving law can only concentrate faith and principles." Shadimar drove home his point. "When's the last time you saw any Cardinal Wizard dive into battle, violently or otherwise?" He added quickly, "Excepting Colbey, of course."

Mar Lon let his *lonriset* go loose on its tie. "I know you're right."

Excitement pulsed through Shadimar, enhanced by the staff. Secodon barked once. "So you'll become my apprentice?"

"No," Mar Lon said. "I can't."

Shocked by the reply, Shadimar found himself at a momentary loss for words. He recovered nearly instantly. "Certainly you can."

"I can't." Again Mar Lon raised his instrument to explain.

Shadimar laid a heavy hand on the bowl, pressing the *lonriset* to its resting position. "You don't need that. You can speak with me without limitation."

"I'm sorry. It's as much habit as curse anymore." Mar Lon seemed to run out of words then, and he reached for the *lonriset* again. "I can express myself better this way."

Shadimar kept his palm on the instrument, irritated by time constraints and new responsibilities. "Talk. I've more important matters to attend than wasting my time listening to your concerts. Why can't you serve the world as those competent to become Wizards have the obligation to do? Would you rather I sent a thousand less able mortals to their deaths trying to succeed at tasks made for ones such as me and you?"

"Me and you?" Mar Lon repeated with obvious incredulity. Unable to play, he seemed uncertain where to place his hands. His fingers darted from nervous strokes at his dark hair to his sword hilt. Whatever his proclivity toward peace, the bard's training had made him a competent warrior. "You flatter me."

"It's not my job or intention to flatter. Only to serve the world within the confines of Odin's Law." The last of Shadimar's patience evaporated. "If personal honor and privilege are not enough, do it for the good of the world. The world stands on the brink of destruction, and it needs your guidance. How can you refuse that?"

Secodon watched Mar Lon with the same interest as his master did.

Running out of places to fret, Mar Lon trapped his hands in his pockets. "I think you overestimate the value of my guidance, though I've hardly kept it from the world. I've traveled from Blathe to the Western Plains, from the twin cities to Stalmize, spreading the messages of peace and tolerance. But the bard's curse limits me to song. Could you imagine a general and his officers detailing strategy in four part harmony? How can I lead men when I can't even speak with them?"

Shadimar saw the way around Mar Lon's handicap. He wedged his staff into a crevice for support, then leaned heavily upon it. "Your voice and your talent are a god-given gift. With a little training in the arts and the knowledge of my predecessors, you might create a new form of magic using music. The possibilities are limitless." A vast new plain seemed to open in Shadimar's thoughts, and the future became boundless and unbridled. Excitement thrilled through him. Mar Lon's ability could add a whole dimension of power to the Eastern Wizards' reign. The staff tingled with a joy of its own, its support tangible. Even more than Shadimar, it wanted Mar Lon's acquiescence.

"No," Mar Lon said. He lowered his head, his hands balling to fists in his pockets.

The reply caught Shadimar by surprise, and his dream seemed to fragment around him. He felt a hot splash of rage that seemed to originate from the staff. "No to what? What do you mean by 'no'?"

Secodon whined.

"I mean 'no,' Shadimar." Mar Lon's gaze played over the distant spires. "I mean that I respect the offer and I'm honored that you even considered me." Now the bard fixed his gaze on Shadimar, meeting the ancient, gray eyes bravely. "But I cannot and will not become the next Eastern Wizard."

It was an honor no man or woman had ever refused, and Shadimar stood in an awkward, ugly silence. Anger pulsed through him in waves as solid as gale-tossed ocean.

Freeing his hands, Mar Lon again clutched the *lonriset*. He ducked through the leather strap that bound the instrument, needing the musical support to explain his decision. Balancing the bowl on one knee, he placed his fingers with practiced skill. The left depressed strings, skipping from chord to note with a dancer's grace. The right sounded out the notes with mellow confidence. After a short introduction, he launched into song, the lyric beauty of his tones putting the instrument to shame:

> *"Odin's laws constrain us all*
> *To tasks we must fulfill—"*

But Shadimar wanted none of it. Impulsively, his wrinkled hand slapped the *lonriset*. Though light, the suddenness of

the movement drove the ten-stringed instrument from the
bard's hands.

Secodon leapt aside, clearly startled.

Mar Lon made a muffled noise of horror, trying to catch
the instrument in midair. He managed only to send it into a
spin. It crashed to the mountain stone, amid a loud cacophony of splintering wood and chiming strings. The awful dis-
cordance slapped echoes from peak to peak, and the silence
that followed seemed as complete as death.

Guilt and rage warred within Shadimar, and the staff supported the latter.

"No," Mar Lon whispered. He dropped to his knees, oblivious to the stone tearing gashes in his breeks and flesh.
He caught the *lonriset,* examining the damage with moist,
anguished eyes. His jaw clamped closed so tightly his
cheeks twitched, and his hands fluttered over the mangled
wood. Two pairs of strings had snapped, one side of the
bowl had been staved in, and a tuning stake had broken off
at the base. He clutched the instrument for a time, then lowered it back to the ground like a soldier long past the skills
of a healer. "Why did you do that? How could you do that?"
His dark, green-flecked eyes flashed, meeting Shadimar's
with none of his previous trepidation.

Shadimar considered his reply, trying to sort through the
boil of emotion for the right words. He had not intended to
destroy the *lonriset,* yet experience warned him not to allow
his actions to appear unplanned or foolish. He would not pay
the price for impetuousness with dignity. His own abrupt
movement had caught even himself by surprise. It did not fit
his methods nor his deeply ingrained pride to do anything
reckless. Yet, once done, he had little choice but to defend
it. "I asked you not to play, Mar Lon."

Mar Lon hugged the remains of his *lonriset* to his chest.
Tears brimmed in his eyes. He looked away, lowering his
head.

Shadimar softened, hating the pain he had inflicted but
concerned that Mar Lon's refusal would cause far worse. "I
didn't expect you to lose your grip. I'm sorry it's broken.
But I hope even you can see the irony of weeping over a
construct of wood, steel, and gut while refusing the chance
to keep mothers from crying over their babies. It's the curse
of *Ragnarok* to pit brother against brother; sons will rape

mothers and fathers daughters. The heavens will run with the blood of gods."

Mar Lon's back heaved.

Secodon brushed against the bard, nose questing for his face in sympathy.

"We can build a hundred *lonrisets,* lutes, and mandolins. The gods and mankind cannot be replaced." The sentiment rang hollow, even to Shadimar. Though he tried to stay with his point, his mind explored the knowledge that had come with the idea of music as magic. Logic told him that an argument could be made for destroying an imperfect world to make way for a new one, one formed from bold ideas, intelligent vision, and concept. Still, the destructiveness inherent in such a notion made the whole seem heinous and foreign: and Shadimar discarded it for now.

Mar Lon wiped tears from his eyes with the back of his hand. He did not look up. Grief and the surrounding crags muffled his words. "I understand the significance of *Ragnarok,* Shadimar. More than anyone." His head sagged further, and his reply became even more difficult to decipher.

Shadimar dropped to a crouch beside the bard.

"But Odin placed nearly as many shackles on me and my line as on the Cardinal Wizards themselves. I took the vows I took, and the fact that they were inflicted on me by bloodline makes them no less sacred. In fact, it makes them more sacred." Mar Lon looked up briefly, and red vessels already marred the whites of his eyes. "My loyalties lie, first and foremost, with King Sterrane. That's a duty I won't sacrifice."

"It's a minor concern." Shadimar persisted, goaded by the staff. "Once you become a Wizard, your life will outspan Sterrane's by centuries."

"It doesn't matter." Mar Lon allowed the *lonriset* to slip from his hands, and it rang against the stones. "Whether for a year or for a moment, I can't stand against what he represents."

The suggestion behind the words shocked Shadimar. "The king of Béarn stands for neutrality and the West. By the gods, I raised him myself. How could his views clash with your becoming my apprentice?"

Mar Lon rose, leaving the shattered instrument on the stones. "Because the neutrality that Sterrane represents isn't a force that can be championed. It's a lack of all forces or, perhaps, the presence of all forces."

The simplicity of Mar Lon's teachings mocked Shadimar's centuries of knowledge. "I hardly need you to explain neutrality. I've championed it for almost two centuries and my predecessors for millennia before me."

"You did. And they did." Mar Lon scooped up his instrument, carrying it in the crook of one arm. "But not anymore. From the moment you accepted the Staff of Law, you became its champion in the same way Carcophan upholds evil and Trilless good."

Shadimar stared. "That's ridiculous, Mar Lon."

"Is it?"

"Of course it is. It's an inappropriate comparison. You can't correlate good and evil with law and chaos. Without law, there is no good or evil. Our world *is* law. Chaos has its own world. Here, it would destroy the very fabric of the universe."

Mar Lon back-stepped, as if fearing Shadimar might harm his *lonriset* again, though the damage was already done. "Colbey made a good case for balance."

"What!" Though he had once contemplated the possibility himself, now the idea that anyone might seriously consider Colbey's proposal rattled and outraged Shadimar and his staff. "Surely you didn't buy his rationalizations. He's as mad as his chaos. And he doesn't have any knowledge from which to draw but his own, as sparse and inaccuracy-riddled as it is."

Mar Lon drove his point home. "You sound exactly like Carcophan talking about Trilless."

Shadimar held rage in check from long decades of practice. The staff intervened. *Odin's Laws demand that the Cardinal Wizards kill any creature espousing chaos.* Shadimar had little choice but to define Mar Lon's intentions. "Are you saying that you believe we should allow chaos on the world of law?"

Mar Lon shook his head, taking another backward step. "What I believe has no significance. I'm as bound to serve consummate neutrality as you are law. For me to forsake that loyalty would be to violate the very law you claim to uphold. Odin determined my course long ago, free of my personal biases. Because we *do* live on a world of law, I would have to break oaths to champion it. Then, I would make it the poorest proponent indeed."

Shadimar saw much sense in Mar Lon's argument, though a nagging in the back of his mind suggested that he had missed the deeper loopholes. Before he could argue the matter further, Shadimar wanted to mull it over first. One thing seemed certain, he needed solitude. "Very well, Mar Lon, though I think you're drawing a distinction where it doesn't exist. I'll find another to become my apprentice. Let all those who die in the coming wars weigh heavily upon your conscience." With that, Shadimar waved a hand. The necessary incantation coursed through his mind, and he transported himself and his wolf to the safety of his ruins.

CHAPTER 15

Aristiri Song

Colbey awakened disoriented, opening his eyes to a close grayness that seemed warm, dry, and secure. He lay upon blankets piled on the floor, his body forming a hollow among the cloth. Patterns of light and shadow alternated on a craggy ceiling formed from natural stone, and the room contained little in the way of furniture. A desk occupied the opposite corner, near the door, simple but sturdy, with a matching chair. On the wall above it, shelves rose in two rows. Books stood in a neat line, gingerly placed and arranged from tallest to shortest. An eye studied Colbey from over the shelves. Catching light from beyond the open doorway, it glowed red.

Red. Suddenly shocked fully awake, Colbey sat up. The abruptness of his movement flashed pain through his entire body. He knew from experience that most animal eyes shone green or amber at night. Still, no human could fit, crammed above the books, and it bothered him that even a change in position had not brought the second eye into view. He had once seen a blue-eyed cat whose eyes gleamed red in darkness, and he had heard that skunks' and foxes' did the same. Colbey studied the area above the books. The creature there bore no white markings to reveal it, but Colbey's intense scrutiny carved shape from random blackness.

Bird. It's a large bird. The form explained the single eye, and Colbey presumed he faced the same *aristiri* that had followed him from Captain's ship. He tried to recall the color that bird eyes usually reflected at night, only to draw a blank. Other than nighthawks and owls, he had never seen or heard of birds doing anything after sundown except sleeping. And the owl eyes he had seen shone gold.

Once identified, Colbey turned his attention from the bird, and memory came to him in a painful rush. He remembered staggering southward over stony beach and into evergreen forest. He recalled a need to collapse there and sleep, but something had driven him onward, something with a sharp beak and talons and wings that buffeted like a street fighter's fists. The crawl through the forests became a blur of forward movement, and memory of the mountain passes came only in broken pictures. Somehow, he had made it to the Western Wizard's cave. And that somehow, he believed, now perched on the shelves above the desk.

Maybe there is something to this Wizard/bird rapport. Colbey tried to think of the hawk as a feathered Secodon, but the comparison would not fit. The wolf seemed far more pet than guardian, no different than a farmer's obedient dog except that it seemed to read and reveal the Eastern Wizard's moods. Clearly, this *aristiri* had some intelligence and agenda of its own. *Either that, or I'm making far too much out of this.*

Colbey rolled to his side, feeling the chorus of aches shift through him, then settle into silence. After Tokar's death, he had spent months living in the Wizard's cave, long enough to know it as a haven, to grow familiar with its furnishings, and to add touches of his own. Though songbirds flittered and played before the entrance through the day, never before had any creature chosen to enter the cave. Men walked right by without seeing it; Colbey, too, would have missed it his first time had the Western Wizard not summoned him with explicit instructions and called out to him on arrival. He did not know for certain how the permanent magic of the wards worked, whether as simple camouflage or active defense. He felt certain that Odin's Laws would forbid the other Cardinal Wizards from invading his haven, but he no longer trusted rules alone to bind them.

Colbey reached his left hand to the floor beside him. His fingers touched naked steel, his two swords reassuringly within reach. The staff lay beside them, warm and vibrating. Only now, Colbey realized that the pain in his head came, not from injury, but from a force repeatedly battering against his barriers, seeking entrance. *I am here.*

Sleep beckoned, but Colbey knew he must first deal with the staff if he did not want to spend the rest of his life with a pounding headache. He concentrated on mental fortifications that seemed natural, though Shadimar had stated otherwise, prying open a gap just large enough for communication. He could feel the other hovering outside, massive, its lifelike force tangible. *What do you want?*

Surprise quivered through the entity, stretching to lengths far beyond those Colbey had any desire to follow. Its size seemed infinite. *I'm here, and I can help.*

I know where you are and what you are. Stop bothering me.

We are one, and you are my champion. It tried to squeeze through the crack Colbey had opened, but he blocked it with a wordless aura of threat.

I'm your champion, not your slave. I'm the Master; you're the tool. Colbey recalled the day Shadimar had given him Harval. At first, he had refused, concerned that the magic of the sword might wield him, protect him, or that he might become dependent on its feel and power. Renshai honor forbade him from relying on luck or artificial defenses, on anything but his own skill. *If you try to control me, I'll destroy you.*

And the world with me.

Grand generalizations irk me. Whether or not dispatching you would affect our world remains to be seen. For now, I want your promise that you won't try to sneak into my thoughts again. It's rude at the least; Shadimar taught me that. And I won't tolerate it. I want a vow from you that you'll work with me and that my judgment will always take precedence. You won't enter my mind without permission.

You want a vow from ME? The staff seemed both insulted and incredulous.

Exhausted and wanting the matter finished, Colbey did not mince words. *Yes.*

I'm older than mankind. Can't you trust that there will come times when I know better than you?

Then you may advise me. And I'll choose whether or not to act on that advice.

Resentment flowed through the staff, but it presented no new argument.

Shadimar used the same older equals wiser point. Age, by itself, doesn't make a man clever. Elders only become wiser if they seek experience and wisdom. But you're a force with a specific goal. All you know is what you are. My judgment is clearer, no matter how men, gods, or Wizards see me. I'm not always right, but I won't trust the world itself to another's insight.

Shock radiated freely from the staff. *You truly believe your judgment is superior to mine? To all other men's? To the other Cardinal Wizards'? Even to the gods'?*

Colbey laughed aloud. *I doubt there's any man who secretly does not believe the same about himself. It's one of the things that has always made me proud of being mortal: the ability to question even that which we know as truth.*

The staff made its disgust obvious. *You're not fit to wield me.*

Clearly, Odin believes I am. Colbey gave his own smug satisfaction free rein. *The promise, please.*

Consider it made, though it's a mistake. It's not your job to champion balance. I am your charge.

If it's my cosmic purpose, eventually I'll find it. The Renshai not only had a strict code of honor, they also taught me to think for myself. Over the years, men and Wizards have called me and my judgment many things, few of them kind. None of those matters now. I'll champion the cause I feel is right. And I sincerely believe that, in the long run, it will work out best for us all to find a compromise.

You already make me regret my vow. Between law and chaos, there can be no compromise.

And that, in a phrase, is your blind spot. Colbey shut off the contact with a finality that said more than words. The staff quivered beneath his touch, though whether in frustration, fear, or anger Colbey could no longer tell. He freed one of the blankets, pulling it over his body. He felt dirty in the tattered silks he had now worn for days, and the urge to change nearly overwhelmed him. But for now, sleep had to take precedence. Early in his career as a healer, he had learned that the body could repair damage most quickly and easily when its unnecessary functions shut down. He had long held the theory that sleep itself was the body's way of fixing the stresses and strains that occurred throughout the day. Men who spurned sleep shortened their own lives.

Still, despite an exhaustion that had dragged Colbey to a previous unconsciousness, devoid even of his usual instinctive wariness, the pain of his injuries now stole his ability to rest. Each breath jabbed his lungs into shattered ribs and set off a wild clamor of bruises and strains. He felt battered in every part, and his muscles tensed against the pain, making sleep impossible. He rolled, trying to find a comfortable position, the movement only waking every ache again.

The *aristiri* fluttered from the upper shelf to the desk, studying Colbey through one redly-glowing eye.

Colbey tried to resist the urge to shift position again. As before, his mind promised respite in a new pose, and he accepted it. He rolled to his back, tensed for the jangle of pain that raised frustration. "Damn it!" he said aloud.

The hawk flapped to the floor beside him. It perched on the grounded staff, loosing a delicate squawk that sounded sympathetic.

Colbey sighed. Its nearness gave him one more thing to distract him from sleep, and he considered driving it away. Even as the thought came to his mind, the bird threw back its head and started singing. The notes warbled forth in a mellow rush so unlike the shrill chirps and tweets of normal songbirds. Music echoed through the cavern, and the *aristiri* seemed to match its own notes to the reverberations, so that the melody sounded more like a planned duet. It anticipated the repeated notes and their changes, matching its tones into perfect chords.

Colbey smiled, captivated by the beauty of the song. He focused on its mild harmony, and his consciousness seemed to float and glide with the song. He let it take his concerns and his pain, sparing no guilt for the sleep his body needed. Later, he would need his wits fully about him. For now, he was safe.

As darkness settled around Colbey, he recalled his mother's voice and the lullaby she had used to sing him to sleep as a babe:

> *"Soft, little Renshai*
> *Time's come for dreaming*
> *Of battles and honor*
> *And swords brightly gleaming.*

> *"The morning sun will dawn*
> *With glimmers of sword light*
> *And chance for glory comes*
> *Once sleep has filled the night."*

Buoyed by the memory, Colbey found sleep.

Forest travel became a pleasure now that Khitajrah had discovered the road. The packed soil yielded spongily, but the crushed stone kept her from sinking deeply with each step. The earth smelled pleasantly of damp, and it mingled with the aroma of greenery and pine. There were other odors: a momentary tinge of musk where a fox had marked, the decay-smell of brackish water, and others unfamiliar to Khitajrah. Together, these came to define the woodlands. Without the ceaseless need to tear, duck, and clamber, she came to enjoy her time in the Westland forest.

In the Eastlands, the closely packed population kept her from finding privacy, except among the more ancient, crumbling sectors of the city or by slipping to a rooftop where few would think to look. The idea of walking miles without seeing anyone intrigued and frightened her. Early on, the occasional passage of rattling horse carts or riders cheered Khitajrah. Later, they seemed only to disturb her solitude.

On the ninth day of Khitajrah's journey to Béarn, lacy clouds blotted the sky. Sunlight struggled through the latticework of clouds and branches, lending the forest a dull, gray-green glow. Concern touched Khitajrah for the first time in days. The guilt for her lie in Ahktar's court had faded quickly, and the long-held repentance for slaughtering Diarmad and his companion in Stalmize's graveyard seemed finally to have evaporated with it. *What's done is done.*

Chaos concurred. *The Eastern veterans got what they deserved. And the one not-quite-true word you spoke in the courtroom hurt no one. In the end, Khita, that single word will save your son's life.* An internal calmness accompanied its assessment.

Khitajrah nodded absently, though there was no one to see the gesture. Though not fully laid to rest, she had managed to suppress the twinges of conscience that accompanied actions that did not fit the rigid loyalties and faith she had known since birth. For now, something more basic bothered her. She had agreed to meet Lirtensa in Pudar in two weeks. Yet, after nearly a week and a half of travel, she had not even reached Béarn. Irritated by the thought, she tossed back shoulder-length, black hair curled into frizzled tangles by moisture-laden air. She still had to arrive in the kingdom, manage an audience with its monarch, and travel to the great trading city. *I'll never make it.* A more horrifying thought struck her. *What if I went the wrong way?*

That's impossible, chaos soothed. *Lirtensa said this trail would take you to Béarn. You haven't veered from it.*

Khitajrah sighed, knowing chaos was right, though not pacified by the realization. She had seen Lirtensa riding out of town on a hardy, buckskin mare. Only now did it occur to her that he must have expected her to have a mount as well. *If I did, I'd probably be through with Béarn and halfway to Pudar by now.* The mistake agitated her. The clouds darkened, and a light sprinkle fell, pattering hollowly to the leaves overhead. The rain only added to her exasperation. *What now?*

For a moment, chaos seemed to have no answer. *Continue. Perhaps Béarn's king will know Colbey's location, and you won't need to meet with Lirtensa. Otherwise, you'll just arrive late. If he's a guard, as he claimed, he shouldn't be hard to find.*

The idea that Lirtensa might lie about his job had never occurred to Khitajrah.

Chaos responded to the flicker of idea. *That's because you're still chaos-innocent. I'm working on that.*

Khitajrah still cared little for arriving late for a promised meeting, but she did take some solace from chaos' explanation. The rain quickened, drumming against the foliage. Strands of hair dribbled into her eyes. She pawed them away, only to find herself staring at a crossroads. To her right, the path made a ninety-degree turn. It headed north, away from the mountains, and Khitajrah dismissed that direction easily. Two other pathways radiated from the meeting point. The larger, the more obvious continuation of the path, headed west or slightly northwest; without the sun, Khitajrah found exact pinpointing of direction difficult. Though poorly defined, the other showed signs of recent traffic and it clearly bent southwest. Aware Béarn nestled in the Southern Weathered Range, the southernmost city of the Westlands, Khitajrah froze in indecision.

The rhythmic rattle of rain on leaves became the only sound in the Westland forest. Khitajrah approached, not daring to believe she faced a choice now, when she had already fallen well behind schedule. Her dress clung wetly to her legs and body, and she tugged irritably at the fabric. She approached the crossroads slowly, hoping something would send her in the right direction. Within a few steps, a wooden sign came into view. The squiggles and lines of the printed Western letters meant nothing to her. *I don't suppose you read. . . .*

Chaos did not wait for Khitajrah to finish the thought. *No.*

Khitajrah stared at the sign, as if time might make the writing comprehensible. But after several moments, the lettering seemed equally incoherent. Needing a target for her irritability, she turned to her only companion. *I thought chaos represented knowledge.*

Concept and idea. Writing as creation is chaos. Its structure and form come of law.

Khitajrah considered, glad to be drawn from her dilemma for a moment. *How can that be?*

Though chaos had seemed capable of reading intention before, this time it ran with words. *Chaos is creation and destruction; law is building and execution.*

Khitajrah defined her point. *If chaos is needed for creation, how did mankind come up with language in the first place? Or anything else for that matter?*

From the gods. Chaos drove the point home, its aura triumphant. *I told you they worship me.*

Wet and confused, Khitajrah found little patience for theology or vanity. Not wanting to contemplate the significance of such power in her own mind, she turned sullen. *Fine. If you're so damned almighty, you tell me which way to go.*

Follow the straight path. That makes the most sense.

But this seems to head more in the direction I would expect Béarn to be. Khitajrah pointed at the southwest track. *So take that way.*

Khitajrah sighed, getting nothing of use from her mental companion. *You're no help at all.*

Roads, paths, not my strong point. Any way has to get you somewhere.

At first Khitajrah thought chaos mocked her. The simplicity of the statement made it seem like sarcasm. But she soon abandoned that line of thought, guessing that a creature without form from a world without dimension might not have much understanding of destination and location. *If only the gods would point the way.* She edged into the crossroads, studying each direction cautiously. Again, she disregarded the northward path. The straight course did seem like her best possibility, but the southwest path better fit her image of heading toward Béarn. And it offered the additional advantage of thicker brush with more protection from the rain. *When you don't know where you're going, one way seems as good as another.* Slinging her few remaining supplies more securely on her shoulder, she took the smaller trail.

Khitajrah had taken only half a dozen steps, when a rustling in a bordering copse caught her attention. She went still, listening. Rain clattered on the leafy overhang. Otherwise, she heard nothing. Shrugging, she dismissed the noise, preparing to take her next step. Before she lifted her foot, the sound recurred.

Khitajrah went still, one leg poised to move. She swiveled her head, seeking the source of the sound. It seemed to come from her left. Cautiously, she edged toward the copse. Once upon it, she jerked vines aside to reveal the ground beneath. Sticks cracked. Leaves scattered to the black dirt in a wash. Nothing unexpected met Khitajrah's vision. She stepped back, considering. *An animal? A person?*

Khitajrah did not have long to contemplate before the underbrush swished more loudly and obviously ahead. Curious, she followed. Within half a dozen steps, she found herself on the pathway she had rejected, headed due west. *What?* Rain soaked through her dress until its floral pattern appeared to be painted onto her skin. Khitajrah cocked her head, alert for more movement that did not come. Whatever she had followed seemed to have disappeared.

Turning, Khitajrah saw the crossroads behind her. With a sigh, she headed back the way she had come, again turning southwest at the intersection. This time, she passed the copse in silence, and she managed to walk for nearly half an hour before she heard movement in the brush again. She stopped short, unnerved by the presence. In the East, wild animals had always run from men. Her earlier walks through Westland forests had given her reason to believe animals here behaved the same way. Many times, she caught a glimpse of undefined brown creatures scuttling through foliage or a line of snapped twigs growing more distant as they fled. Occasionally, squirrels had perched on branches far beyond her reach, scolding her intrusion with rapid, high-pitched chirps. She had heard remote birdsong, but those nearest made more raucous calls, as if to warn every animal in the forest of her presence. Khitajrah's imagination warned her that a creature not fearing humans might have a reason for its boldness. *If there's something out there that eats people, I'd better find it before nightfall.*

The sound came again.

Khitajrah had heard that even predators backed down from creatures they perceived as more dangerous than themselves. Loud noises, sudden movements, and directed stares might prove useful as bluff. She knew the first thing she needed to do was overcome her own nervousness; many animals could sense fear. "Who's there!" she shouted, holding her voice as steady as possible. "I'm bigger and meaner than you. Go away!" Though she knew no animal would understand the words, they helped her maintain courage.

Once again, she heard the noise. It seemed not to have changed location.

As a young child, Bahmyr had told his mother about a massive wild dog he and his elder brother, Nichus, had disturbed in a field. Apparently, it had seen the two small boys as prey, charging with teeth bared and hackles raised. Nichus had held his ground, shielding Bahmyr with his body, and staring down the attacking dog. But Bahmyr had lost his nerve and fled, his terror drawing the beast's attention like a beacon. Desperate to save his brother and himself, Nichus had rushed the dog as fast as his legs could carry him, without wavering. Apparently fearing for its own life, the dog had checked its attack. Swerving from the sobbing Bahmyr, it had retreated across the field.

Now, Khitajrah concentrated on the memory, sifting out the sweet sorrow that accompanied it. Boldness clearly intimidated animals as well as people. *If I stalk it, it may leave to hunt less dangerous game.* She headed toward the noise.

Even as Khitajrah parted the brush, the rustlings recurred some distance ahead. Again, she followed, only to find that the creature had moved once more, this time forward and to her right. Intrigued and caught up in the hunt, she trailed the sound through the tangled brush, certain she followed something though no glimpse or snagged clump of fur revealed it. The overcast sky darkened early, suffusing the forest in gray. Still, Khitajrah only heard the thing she pursued, and no visual movement betrayed it. Then, abruptly, forest broke to the familiar pathway westward. The sounds of swishing brush disappeared.

Frustrated, Khitajrah went still, listening for signs of the creature she had shadowed. Finding none, she considered. *It's as if it wants me on this trail.* Khitajrah remembered asking for divine assistance in finding her way, yet she felt too grounded in human reality to believe a god would take interest in one woman's choice of direction. One thing seemed certain. *Clearly, I'm not dealing with an animal.* She glanced up the trail to the west. Much could be said for continuing in the direction it had suggested. Impatience prompted her to continue west without questioning. Yet curiosity, chaos' as much as her own, held her back. She grasped for its expertise, trusting it more when it came to affairs of gods and otherworld creatures. *You once told me Sheriva did not exist, that my god is a manmade construct.*

That's true. I told you that. And I spoke truth.

Westerners worship lots of gods. Right?

Also true. Chaos paused, awaiting a point.

Khitajrah flushed, embarrassed to fall so quickly into sacrilege. *And their gods are real?*

Constructs also.

Khitajrah frowned, finding an obvious contradiction. *But you claim gods give knowledge to mankind. And supposedly worship you.*

Another truth. Chaos found humor in its own words. *And you worried that I might lie too much.*

Khitajrah ignored the gibe. *So which are the real gods?*

Chaos did not answer for some time, but mirth swirled through its silence. It seemed too amused to find a coherent reply. *Mankind spends far too much time trying to second-guess the world, the gods, and the motives of the gods now and in the past. The immortal and omniscient don't think like humans, and any attempt to project mortal emotion and purpose on outworlders is doomed to fail. Think of the odds, Khita, that any society of men and women just happened upon the right mixture of gods and laws.*

The possibilities did seem astronomical, although every religion claimed to have gotten its knowledge directly from deities at some point in its early evolution. *So no mortal religion is correct?*

In its usual circular, frustrating manner, chaos contradicted itself. *Actually, the Northmen have it closest, if you take away their bias toward good. At least, they have the names, general bents, and history right. Why the gods chose to do things that way, I don't know.* Humor turned to joy. *But I support the asymmetry.*

Naturally. Khitajrah abandoned this line of thinking, seeing no need to waste more time. For now, she had a decision

to make, and philosophical discussion would not help her do
it. She returned to the crux of her question. *Is it possible
that some sylvan spirit warded me from that other trail?*

Chaos did not consider long. *Doubtful.* It changed its
tack. *Unless said 'sylvan spirit' is human. Man's world is
the only one fully grounded in law. Outworlders would have
little means or reason to come here.*

Human. It seemed unlikely. *It would take a sneaky, competent human to stay just out of sight like that.*

Chaos dismissed the thought. *Such humans do exist, I
believe.*

Human. The idea intrigued as much as it discomforted.
Khitajrah had spent years slinking unseen through Stalmize's
roadways and climbing its structures to obtain necessities for
less fortunate women. She found it difficult not to think of
someone who could do the same in woodlands as a colleague.

Though Khitajrah did not direct her thoughts to chaos, it
responded to the general gist. *Guile might give you the answer.*

The single sentence veered Khitajrah's thinking in a new
direction. Her mind naturally worried the problem, and years
of hiding and tracking brought a plan. Her conscience told
her that it made more sense to just continue on; she had already lost enough time to on-foot travel and the other's manipulations. But inquisitiveness and a warped sense of
justice intervened. This being had delayed her purpose even
longer. If it indicated the wrong path, that interference could
become critical. She needed to know who and why, and she
relished the chance to match wits with a colleague. He or
she would have a good reason or pay for the interference

The excitement of the challenge wafted through her, its
source as much chaos as herself. For now, she did not care.
Chaos had presented some interesting points that her lawful
upbringing had never allowed her to entertain. So far, it had
caused her to do nothing hurtful outside of protecting herself
and the son she loved. Her lies had harmed no one; the two
men she had killed deserved to die.

Khitajrah whirled, headed back the way she had come. It
took quite some time to find the crossroads; the thing in the
forest had led her far astray with its winding course. By the
time she reached the fork, the rain had ended. Cold night air
washed her wet skin, and a half moon replaced the setting

sun. At the crossroads, she did not hesitate. As before, she headed southwest. But she took only a few paces before catching hold of an overhead limb. Tensing her arms, she hauled her body onto the branch. Hidden by a cluster of leaves, she waited.

For some time, nothing happened. Wind stirred the leaves into a rattling dance, and the cold cut through her soaked dress. Finally, a human figure emerged from the moonlight, approaching, silent and graceful. It moved slowly on the main pathway, apparently tracking her footprints in the moist, black earth. The silhouette revealed a narrow shadow rising above the person's head, obviously a bow slung over a shoulder.

The weapon caught Khitajrah by surprise. Curiosity and annoyance had kept caution at bay. Berating herself, she remained in place, keeping her breathing to a calm, easy pattern. Extreme attempts to hide would give her a stiff unnaturalness that might draw the hunter's attention. Now, more than before, her boldness would become significant. She took some solace from the fact that he traveled alone.

The figure drew closer. Now, Khitajrah could glean some details. Her perspective gave her little impression of height, but the body seemed narrow, almost skeletal in its lack of bulk. A shock of hair perched atop the head, so short it seemed to stand on end. The style revealed him as male in a way his physique had not. He took the turn onto the southwest path, trailing her foot tracks to their end. Suddenly, he stiffened. His eyes rolled upward, and his head followed slowly. His gaze swept the oak, including the branch where Khitajrah perched, directly over his head.

"Hello," she said, the word friendly but not the tone.

The man sprang aside, drawing his bow and crouching at once. An arrow was put to the string, but he did not draw. "Very clever."

"Thank you." Khitajrah kept her reply short, vying for control of the situation.

"I wasn't finished." The man trained his arrow directly on Khitajrah. "Also very stupid. You've trapped yourself neatly, with no means of escape. I can see you don't have a bow, so you'd better have damn good aim with twigs and leaves."

Khitajrah knew a quick and brash retort would serve her best, yet words failed her.

"Come down."

"No." It was hardly the sage response Khitajrah was seeking, but she found no other.

"I'm sorry," the man said, clearly finding the biting wisdom that evaded Khitajrah. "Did I accidentally convey the idea that you had a choice?" The arrow remained level. "Very well, my mistake so I'll remedy it. This is your choice. Climb down on your own or plummet down with my help."

Khitajrah clung to her belief that courage, however feigned, would serve better than timidity. A chill swept through her. This reminded her too much of her confrontation with Diarmad in the graveyard. Then, she had based her strategy on male pride. *What worked once can work again.* "Valiant words from an armed man facing an unarmed woman. Tell me, do you come from a line of cowards or are you the first?"

The man's jaw clenched. Clearly, she had gotten to him. "Come down. Now. You're making me regret giving you a choice. It's not too late for me to withdraw it."

Cornered, Khitajrah frowned. About one thing, this man was clearly right. In a tree, she remained trapped. On the ground, she had a chance for escape. Cautiously, she clambered down.

The arrow traced her route.

Once on the trail, Khitajrah studied the man before her. Closer, she could see that he stood a few fingers' breadth taller than her, although she guessed she might outweigh him. His strange, spiky hair was red. The oddity caught and held her attention. She had seen brown- and sandy-haired Westerners. Rumor claimed that most Northmen sported white or yellow hair, the color of wheat stalks in summer. The hue of this man's stubbly locks seemed like no color nature had planned for anything but sunrises and blood. In contrast, his single eye bore the same dark hue as most Easterners'. A brown silk patch covered the other. His cheekbones jutted from a thin face that more flesh might have made handsome. She guessed his age was close to hers.

He studied her equally thoroughly before speaking. "Who are you? And where are you headed?"

Khitajrah's gaze drifted to the nocked arrow, then back to the man. "My name's Khitajrah Harrsha's-widow. I'm called Khit—" Catching herself, she cut off the second syllable to keep the name sounding more like the Westerner's "Kayt."

"Kay-t," the man repeated, putting the same overemphasis on the "t."

Having given her name, Khitajrah begged the same courtesy. "Who are you?"

The man stared. "You really don't have much feel for this, do you? Let me explain. This is an arrow." He inclined his head toward the shaft, without taking his eyes from her or his hands from the weapon. "It can punch a hole in whatever vital organ I choose at the distance you could run in eighty heartbeats. Now, the deal is, the person on the feathered end asks the questions. The person on the point end answers. With that in mind, where are you headed?"

Khitajrah developed an instant hatred for the stranger. Chaos waffled, uncertain. Still, she had no reason to lie, so she told the truth. "Béarn."

"Why?"

Now, Khitajrah found reason for falsehood. "Just visiting." The twisting of the truth came easier than it had before, due either to practice, to working through her aversion to it, or to a general dislike of the man before her.

"Who?"

The question seemed nonsensical. "Who what?"

"Who are you visiting?"

The king, chaos offered.

Startled Khitajrah spoke aloud. "What?"

"Who are you visiting?"

The king. If he thinks you're a personal friend of the high king, he'll have to back down.

I'm not telling him I know the king, Khitajrah snapped back. *I don't even know the king's name. He'd catch me for sure.* She addressed the red-haired stranger. "I'm not visiting a someone. I've just always wanted to see the high kingdom."

"You're an Easterner."

The observation seemed to come from nowhere. "I'm aware of that," Khitajrah returned. "Did you think it would surprise me?" She considered adding something about whether or not anyone had told him he had red hair, but she abandoned the idea as unwise.

The arrow retreated slightly. "What's an Easterner doing here? And what business could you have in Béarn?"

Khitajrah sighed, disliking the circles the questioning seemed to be taking, though she realized her evasiveness had some bearing on the matter. The delay made her more irritable than frightened. As fear ebbed, she became aware of the rumbling protestations of her stomach. She had not yet eaten dinner. The cold night air sliced through her wet dress, making her shiver. "Look, archer without a name. I have as much right to be here, on this road, as anyone. As far as I know, I haven't broken any laws. If you want my money, here." She reached into her pocket, emerging with the two Eastern coppers that remained from those she had taken from Diarmad. She held them out to the stranger, hoping he would advance to get them. She still carried a knife that he apparently had not noticed or considered. Up close, it would prove a far better weapon than his bow.

The stranger did not approach, but he did lower the bow. "Put your money away. I'm not a bandit."

Having gained this small victory, Khitajrah pressed. She sensed a twinge of regret in his demeanor, and chaos encouraged her to take full advantage of it. She also caught a faint odor of horse about him, and she hoped she would find a way to buy or borrow the animal. "So you just stop innocent people at arrow point to delay them and ask questions?" She returned the coins to her pocket, using the movement to locate the knife in the folds of her cloak.

"Not usually." He kept the bow low, but his eyes explored Khitajrah again. Despite the darkness, his demeanor told her much. She had learned to read mood from gesture in order to counter her son's unhappiness, to find those Eastern women who most required her help, and to anticipate her husband's wants and needs. From this red-haired stranger, she detected a lonely sadness that did not fit his boldness. She also thought she saw a spark of interest in his single eye.

He thinks you're pretty. And I think he respects your courage as well.

Khitajrah flushed, embarrassed as much by the man's unspoken compliment as by a third party noticing the attraction. *Well, he's not pretty at all. And I told you before, I'm not interested in marrying again.*

Who said anything about marriage? He thinks you're

pretty. That gives you the upper hand. Take advantage of him.

What?

Take advantage of him, chaos repeated, though Khitajrah had understood the words well enough. It was the intention she questioned. *Take whatever he offers, then take whatever else you want.*

Khitajrah frowned, still not fully comprehending, but her need to keep her attention externally focused did not leave time for contemplation.

These Westerners complain about recovering from the War, and yet they have so much. Why shouldn't you take your share of a bounty they don't appreciate?

Khitajrah ignored her internal companion. "I'm cold, tired, and hungry. And now I'm also late. Apparently, you didn't just want to kill an Easterner, or you would have shot me from a distance. You don't want my money. Did you lead me in circles and threaten my life just so I'd have to stand in the cold dressed in wet clothes?"

The man flinched, caught staring at the way Khitajrah's rain-wet clothing hugged her curves. He became inordinately focused on her eyes, and the embarrassment apparently stole his conversational skill as well. "No."

Khitajrah pressed. "If not for you, I'd be halfway to Béarn by now."

The man shook off his discomfort, defending himself. "You'd be halfway to nowhere. You were going the wrong way. The main path leads to Béarn." He gestured toward the route onto which he had twice directed her. "I was trying to help you."

"Oh, sure," Khitajrah challenged. "And you knew I was headed for Béarn before you talked to me."

"It was a logical guess."

"What's that way?" Khitajrah pointed beyond the stranger.

He hesitated, then answered carefully. "A town."

Now the man's actions started to make sense. "Your town?"

"No."

Suddenly, all reason seemed to disappear. "So, if I put this all together, I get a man misleading, delaying, and threatening a woman he doesn't know in order to lead her away from a town that's not his." Khitajrah shook her head, her brash annoyance no longer the slightest bit feigned. "I'm short on supplies. When you were sending me in circles for my own welfare, did it ever occur to you that I wanted to find a town and restock before continuing to Béarn? In fact, did it ever occur to you that I have the right go where I want to go? Did you think I'd attack this town and destroy it all by myself? Or did you think my Eastern blood might leap from my body and taint these poor Westland people? Maybe you thought I wanted to sleep through a cold night in soaked clothes and waste my last night of food. Or maybe you thought I had nothing better to do than worry about when some obnoxious, nameless archer put an arrow through me."

The man slipped his arrow from the string, clutching bow and shaft in the same hand. "Are you quite finished?"

"Until I get some answers, yes."

Clearly, he had paid attention, because he addressed her questions in the order she had raised them. "First, I have more supplies than I need. I can't stand meat going to waste, and I'm more than willing to share. My camp isn't far. You can dry yourself and your clothes before the fire. You're welcome to stay, and sleep in a warm, dry place." He kept his single eye fixed on her face. "As to the town, I told you it wasn't mine. Believe me, I wasn't protecting it from you. Quite the opposite. You'd have to look far to find a group of people half as savage. And as to your Eastern heritage, well forgive me for noticing. Although I've got one, it doesn't take a sharp eye to tell you look different and talk different. Seeing those differences doesn't make me racist. Not seeing them would make me blind. I would have done the same for a Northern or Western woman." He added quickly, to cut off her other possible protestation, "Or even for a man."

He turned suddenly, heading back the way they had come. "My camp is this way. You're welcome to join me."

Khitajrah paused. As if to help her make the decision, the wind rose, icy against her wet clothing. She trotted after the man. "All right. Fine. I'm coming. But it's just for warmth and the food you promised. I don't need a man for protection. And if you touch me, you'll regret it."

The redhead mumbled as he walked, the words barely carrying to Khitajrah's ears. "I guess that answers the question of why you're traveling alone." He glanced back over his shoulder. "By the way, my name's Arduwyn. And I prefer 'hunter' to 'archer.' Obviously, I'd rather kill game than people."

Khitajrah ignored the underlying threat. She followed
Arduwyn through a winding shock of brush to an oak-ringed
clearing. There, smoke trickled from a circle cautiously surrounded by stones, and a spit held an undefined piece of
meat. A round-bellied horse parted weed stems to graze on
the green grass beneath. Splotches of black and white decorated its hide, the mane alternating colors, taking its hue
from the skin from which it originated. A skinning knife balanced on a stone before a log the perfect size for a seat.
Blood still streaked the blade. Parcels of meat lay in neat
piles, one of which held only entrails, hooves, and antlers. A
battered pack and the horse's gear lay nearby.

"We're here," Arduwyn announced unnecessarily, gesturing Khitajrah into the clearing. "I'll gather kindling.
There're roots in the fire and venison on the spit. Eat as
much as you want. I can cook up more. While I'm gone, feel
free to change into dry clothes or do whatever else you need
to do. I promise I won't peek."

"Thank you," Khitajrah said grudgingly, overwhelmed by
his generosity, though irritation would not quite allow her to
become fully civil. She could not forget that he had pointed
an arrow at her heart.

Nor should you, chaos inserted. *I don't trust him.*

Arduwyn turned, melting into the woods as if a part of
them. Khitajrah did not hear him move. For a moment she
went perfectly still, concerned that he watched her from the
brush. Then she recalled how swiftly and soundlessly he had
moved while luring her from path to path, except for those
times when he clearly wanted her to hear him and follow.
Yet she shivered in the night air, and she hated the idea of
wearing a wet dress that itched and clung with every movement for one moment longer. Though she believed Arduwyn
had spoken the truth, when she reached to pull the dress
over her head, she felt as if dozens of unseen eyes watched
her from the brush. Dismissing her fears, she removed her
clothes and undergarments, spreading them before the coals
to dry. The aroma of the meat struck her then. Her stomach
growled a long, grinding objection.

Chaos thrust a thought into her head. *Naked when he
gets back? Why don't you just beg him to rape you?*

What do you want me to do? Khitajrah removed the spit
and cautiously tore free a piece of meat. A trickle of watery
grease burned her fingers, but she paid it little heed. She

placed the meat in her mouth, then licked the oil from her fingers and wiped the stinging pads on the cold, wet fabric of her dress. *You know I spent all my money on food. It seemed more important than spare clothes at the time.* She continued eating the venison, and hunger allowed her to abandon decorum. *Besides, I don't think he'll try to rape me. He's no bigger than me. If he tries, I'll kill him.*

I'll bet he has dry clothes in his pack.

Good. If he has clothes on, he won't try to rape me.

He's about your size. And he did say you should change into dry clothes. In fact, he said you could do whatever you needed to do. And that he had more supplies than he needed.

Khitajrah shoved the last of the venison into her mouth, chewing thoughtfully. She wiped her hands on her dress. *I don't think he meant for me to get into his personal gear.*

Why not? chaos pressed. *He promised you food. He said he wouldn't peek while you changed. Obviously, he didn't expect you to sit around naked.*

Obviously. Though loath to leave the coals' warmth, Khitajrah rose. She wandered over to Arduwyn's pack. Glancing about to make certain he had not yet returned, she looked inside. She found several dry cloaks and tunics, most brown, black, or gray. She hauled all of these out. Choosing a tunic, she donned it, drawing a cloak over her shoulders. The fabric was warm and soft against her skin, and she felt protected. Peering back into the pack, she found neat packets of jerked meat, a waterskin, two more knives, a multitude of dried herbs, and feathers. Two vials rattled in the bottom, one containing a thick, blue liquid, the other a gold fluid, equally dense. Khitajrah guessed these might hold the dyes he used for the crests on his arrows. A pouch in the bottom contained string, and a ball of gut twine lay rolled up in a rag. Khitajrah mulled over the uses she could find for his supplies. The meat would easily get her to Béarn, then to Pudar, if necessary. She could refill the waterskin. And his clothes fit her well.

Take it, chaos hissed. *Take it all.*

What are you talking about? Khitajrah guiltily shoved the spare clothing back on top of the remainder of the gear, shocked her intentions had seemed so shallow.

You know you want it. You NEED it. He owes you.

He owes me. Khitajrah repeated, knowing what chaos

suggested was wrong. Yet she knew the pack contained nothing Arduwyn could not easily replace, and chaos had earlier made a point she could not refute. The Westerners did seem to have far more possessions than they appreciated. Arduwyn had stacked enough meat on the ground to feed a small village, and he clearly knew how to prepare it for travel. By his own admission, the nearest town would prove hostile to her; but he seemed to have no qualms about wandering and camping near it himself.

Chaos encouraged, prodding similar thoughts to the fore. *Take the horse, too.* It did not dwell on the pack, obviously feeling that the mental tug of war over that had ended.

The cruelty of the thought jarred Khitajrah's deeply buried conscience. She knew a vague, undefinable feeling of wrongness that came from the core of her being. *No! And I'm not taking his supplies either.* She grabbed handfuls of cloak, preparing to remove it before he returned. *I shouldn't even have taken this.* Though she believed she now chose the moral course, she could not quite bring herself to abandon the warm comfort of the linen.

Don't be a fool, Khita. Don't try to act like an ignorant child. You've taken food and clothing before.

Khitajrah defended herself. *I took things from those who had too much and gave it to women in need.*

Chaos became jubilant with triumph. *You're both of those things. You need these supplies; he doesn't. It's well within Eastern law to do for yourself anything you would do for another of your status.*

Khitajrah frowned, convinced by chaos' argument. *You're right.*

Usually.

But not the horse.

Then you had best leave all. Otherwise, he'll overtake you and probably kill you.

Khitajrah recoiled, her hand falling naturally to the saddle. Again, chaos had a point. Arduwyn could move silently and unseen through the forest. He had trailed her twice. Surely, he could follow the hoof tracks more easily, but he would have no way of catching her without another horse.

He delayed you. The horse can regain you lost time.

And more. Enough to get to the meeting with Lirtensa only a few days late.

Chaos added nothing. Khitajrah was doing a fine job of convincing herself.

You'd better hurry. The archer'll come back soon.

Hunter, Khitajrah corrected. Even as she replied, she hefted the tack and headed for the paint mare.

CHAPTER 16

Shadimar's Apprentice

Rain pounded the ruins of the city of Myrcidë, and wind howled through the many gaps and cracks that riddled the Eastern Wizard's haven. Lightning speared the sky, its sudden flash leaving lined impressions inscribed on Shadimar's retinas. One day melted into the next, and the answer still eluded him. Even the deepest recesses of his mind had yielded no one worthy of the title of Eastern Wizard, no man or woman he could train as his apprentice. Empty days stretched into empty nights, bringing no solution. And day after day, Shadimar sat in his library, slung across his chair, his feet propped on the sitting room desk and his gaze focused outside the single window. A few times each day, Secodon would leave to hunt, always returning by nightfall. Only one other thing disturbed Shadimar's vigil.

The staff leaned against the table, nearly upright in its positioning. Though it did not address Shadimar in words, he could feel the steady, comforting wash of its presence. Mostly, it seemed to enhance his contemplation, though it had no details with which to steer his choice. Occasionally, trickles of an idea seeped into Shadimar's mind, the source arguably himself. These sent him off on long tangents against Colbey. Memories of the Western Wizard's foolishness and philosophies that sounded more like blasphemy sent Shadimar into quiet rages that did little more than disrupt his considerations about a successor.

When these thoughts grew most intense, Shadimar would seek solace in remembrances of the friendship he and Colbey had once shared. But the Renshai's wit now seemed more like self-serving arrogance, and the memories of happy times disappeared beneath an avalanche of bitterness. The companionship seemed ancient and faded in a way few things ever became to immortals. And always, Shadimar turned his thoughts back to the matter at hand.

As the third night blossomed into the fourth day, Secodon whined, pawing at Shadimar's outstretched legs, reminding the Eastern Wizard that the time had come for him to get some food as well. Shadimar sighed. It was not the first time days had passed without any thought for nutrition. Fated to live until his ceremony of passage, Shadimar had had nothing to fear from starvation. Even now that the Cardinal Wizards had lost their invulnerability to objects of law, apparently some of the tenets still applied. Clearly, age did not affect him. Already, he had lived more than two centuries; if the shattering of the Pica Stone had made him mortal, he would have died from decay alone. The lack of food did not seem to have weakened him, and he never doubted illness would continue to shun him. Apparently, the effect had negated only those protections brought about by achieving the Seven Tasks of Wizardry, leaving those won in a predecessor's ceremony of passage.

Shadimar lowered his legs from the tabletop, stretching to work the circulation back into his feet. He rose. The movement brought a dark spot into view through the window. Something flew toward the ruins of Myrcidë, and Shadimar could think of only one winged beast that would dare to brave the eternal storm that warded his ruins. *Swiftwing?* He headed for the window, peering outside. Rain striped his vision in narrow diagonals, but he managed to discern the falcon's shape against the background of the gale.

Shadimar waited by the window, perplexed. The red falcon had served as the Cardinal Wizards' messenger for as far back as Shadimar's collective consciousness could remember, and he had found references to the hawk in the earliest Wizards' works. He doubted it was the same falcon, guessing rather that the gods replaced it with an identical bird every few decades. Now, he wondered whether the message came from Trilless or Carcophan. *Or Colbey.* Momentarily, uneasiness seized him, relieved almost immediately by realization. *Colbey would have no knowledge of the magics required to summon Swiftwing.* Another thought required pondering. *Unless Colbey's staff can teach him.*

Shadimar's staff addressed the silent question. **It can't.**

Though he had become aware of the staff's presence in his mind since he had tapped its knowledge on the *Sea Seraph*, the direct response startled Shadimar. Though he kept his eyes on Swiftwing, he turned his question to the staff.

The Staff of Chaos can't teach magic? The statement surprised and pleased Shadimar at once. Since sorcery came directly of chaos, he had worried about the power of the other
staff.

*It can guide Colbey. It can offer understanding of that
which is. It can add to the abilities he already has, but it
can't give him ones he's never known.*

And you? Shadimar pressed. Now that his initial concern about becoming overwhelmed had fled, he became
more curious about what his staff had to offer.

*This is my world. Understandably, I'm less limited. Over
time, you will come to know all I have to offer. In the meantime, I will guide you as you need.*

The offer seemed reasonable to Shadimar. With its direct
link to Odin and eternity, the Staff of Law had to have
sounder judgment than any mortal or Wizard.

Swiftwing glided through the rain, then alighted on the
window's ledge. Once out of the storm, it shook its red
plumage, flinging water onto the stone edges of the window.
Dark gray spots splattered the granite. The bird waited, its
feathers ruffled and a message bound to its leg.

Shadimar abandoned his conversation with the staff to
concentrate on this new concern. He stripped the parchment
from the falcon's scaly leg. It bounced from the sill to the
Wizard's shoulder, then glided the last short distance to the
desktop. Shadimar ignored the falcon, noticing its weight
momentarily on his shoulder. He opened the note and read:

"Meet me on the south path through the Great Frenum
Mountains as soon as possible."

It was signed with the curvilinear rune that served as
Carcophan's symbol. The meeting place seemed logical, located directly at the border of their territories; but the summons seemed less so. Still, he had no choice but to respond
to the message. It would take Swiftwing a few days to cover
the distance, and it could convey only as many words as
could fit on a piece of parchment. Then Carcophan would
have to answer again, a process that would cost more days.

Again, Shadimar studied the note. What Carcophan's message lacked in politeness it conveyed in urgency. *Better to
meet him face-to-face.* It was an option Shadimar would
have long considered before current circumstances had

bonded them to a cause. Other than on the Meeting Isle, he had met Carcophan directly only twice: once when their respective champions, Colbey and Episte, had had their confrontation. The second time had occurred in Asci, immediately after stepping from Captain's boat. Both experiences had left a sour impression in Shadimar's memory.

Having made the decision to travel, Shadimar did not delay. He dismissed the falcon, indicating he had no response to send, but the bird chose to preen its feathers on the desktop rather than brave the gale again so soon.

Shadimar seized the staff. Secodon lay beneath the chair, his legs and tail jutting through the gaps. Shadimar snapped his fingers, and the wolf stretched, gingerly inching his way from beneath the furniture before standing. Tail wagging, he came to Shadimar's side.

Despite neglecting his nutrition, Shadimar felt strong as he prepared his mind for the necessary transport incantation. The words of the spell came easily to him. Again, he saw the weblike patterns of sorcery that accompanied the call to chaos and the warped, slashed syllables sprinkled through the net. Caught less by surprise this time, he managed to focus on some of the individual tendrils, silken threads that glowed with ever changing colors and promised vast, untapped knowledge in every direction. Briefly, Shadimar understood the bard's unquenchable hunger for all things new, and the quest for wisdom that had cost Odin his eye. A moment later, the image snapped out, and Shadimar found himself surrounded by the world of law he knew so well.

Pale blue sky stretched between the horizons, a welcome change from the ceaseless crash of thunder and tap of rain on the ruins of Myrcidë. To the west, a flat, brown wasteland of sand stretched as far as Shadimar could see, broken only by the Conus River that mirrored the aqua radiance of the sky. Mountains enclosed the trail to the north and south, and forest blocked Shadimar's view of the East. A pair of human silhouettes approached unhurriedly from the woodlands. Shadimar identified the one to the left as Carcophan. He did not recognize the other.

Turning his back on the Southern Wizard, Shadimar knelt at the bank of the river, leaning the staff against his knee. Sunlight sparkled from the rushing water, and plant matter bobbed and fluttered in the current. He dipped his cupped hands into the stream, feeling the icy liquid fill his palms.

Raising water to his lips, he drank, reveling in its cold taste-
lessness after days without water. Having slaked his thirst,
he shook droplets from his hand, wiping his wet hands on
his cloak. With his fingers, he combed excess moisture from
his beard. Secodon lapped at the river, his tongue flinging
spray that sparkled in the hairs of his muzzle.

By the time Shadimar had finished his routine, Carcophan
awaited him on the path. The Evil One stood with a hand casually curled around a mountain crag. The sun highlighted
the whitest strands of his salt and pepper hair, and his dark
eyes fixed keenly on Shadimar. The stranger at Carcophan's
side stood taller than the average man, nearly the Southern
Wizard's height. Ebony hair, hacked as short as any soldier's, topped features that could never be mistaken for
male. Her bangs splayed over a delicate forehead and large,
long-lashed eyes whose blackness identified her conclu-
sively as an Easterner. A well-shaped nose and full lips completed a face that formed a perfect oval.

Yet, despite her beauty, there was nothing delicate about
the woman at Carcophan's side. Though slender, her large-
boned frame hinted at sturdiness, and her expression made
her seem mentally strong as well. She wore a leather jerkin
over a tunic and britches of masculine cut that could not
hide large breasts, a narrow waist, and wide hips. The
single-edged sword at her side curved twice from hilt to tip,
like no weapon Shadimar had seen, and the haft took the
crafted shape of a cobra's head. Rubies glared like red pinpoints from the carven eye sockets. Despite the gaudiness of
its design, the worn split leather wrapping identified it as a
real weapon, well used and not just for show. Shadimar's
sharp gaze detected calluses on the woman's right palm.
Clearly, she had wielded the sword before and often.

"Shadimar, I'd like you to meet Chezrith." Carcophan
gave the name the Eastern pronunciation CHAZ-rayth. "My
apprentice."

Chezrith made a respectful curtsy.

Shadimar followed the movement with his eyes, frowning, not daring to believe Carcophan had made his decision
so swiftly. It belittled the process. Surely, the Southern
Wizard must have had previous dealings with this woman,
though the possible specifics of those dealings unnerved and
disgusted Shadimar. The relationship between a Cardinal
Wizard and his potential apprentice must retain some profes-

sional distance. Much of the training, for the tasks and of a Wizard, went toward making his apprentice confident and self-reliant. Yet Shadimar sensed that the relationship between these two went farther back and deeper. Her casual courage in the presence of two of Odin's chosen both pleased and discomfited him. Her boldness would serve the Wizards well, but her lack of anxiety made her seem as potentially dangerous as Colbey.

Shadimar made no attempt to hide his dissatisfaction. He gave Chezrith only a brief nod of acknowledgment. "Would you excuse us, please?"

Chezrith rolled her huge, black eyes to Carcophan, awaiting confirmation.

Carcophan nodded. "We'll only be a moment."

Obediently, Chezrith turned, headed east on the path, and perched on a boulder beyond earshot. Curling long legs to her torso, she pulled a book from her pocket and studied.

Shadimar clenched the staff close to his body, allowing Carcophan the first word. Less patient, the Southern Wizard obliged. "Wonderful, isn't she?"

Apparently sensing his master's irritability, Secodon paced between the Wizards.

Shadimar kept his tone low and steady, as tight as his hold on the staff. "That depends on what you want her for."

Carcophan's speckled brows eeled together. "What do you mean by that?"

"I mean, a Wizard's apprentice isn't competently chosen in three days. Beauty may serve her well in bed, but it won't get her through the Seven Tasks."

"You think I'm sleeping with her."

"Aren't you?"

Carcophan dodged the question. "That's not the issue. First, I've had my eye on her for some time. She's self-assured, proficient in many ways ..." He smiled at some private thought before adding, "... and nearly as brazen as the Prince of Demons himself. I considered her as an apprentice some time ago, then dismissed her because I thought I had seven or eight centuries before I'd need to make such a decision."

"So you considered her for other things."

Carcophan's grin was evil. "Why not? I wouldn't want a mortal of her potential to go wholly to waste."

Secodon sat, attentive to Carcophan.

Shadimar glared. "So you couple with her." More than a century had passed since Shadimar had lost all interest in sex; world-significant responsibilities had replaced such mortal concerns. "Lust has no place in choosing a Cardinal Wizard."

The smile disappeared. Carcophan's brows seemed to merge with his nose. "Is that what you think? That I would jeopardize the cause I pledged myself wholly to for a few nights of ecstasy?" He shook back his dappled mane, and his forearms swelled beneath the sleeves of his cloak. "Then you're as much a fool as I named you. And more."

Shadimar scowled, saying nothing.

Though under no obligation, Carcophan explained. "You have to remember the society I took Chezrith from." He jerked a thumb over his shoulder to indicate the Eastlands. "There, women have no more rights than livestock, and men self-serve as they please." Carcophan did not apologize or moralize; it was a system he endorsed to the core of his being. "To be considered strong, a woman has to become twice as powerful as any man. To win notice for skill, she must become the best. Shadimar, the men of Prehothra actually fear Chezrith. They let her do as she pleases. I don't think I could find an apprentice more callous, brutal, or shameless. There's not a single voice among my predecessors that doesn't support my decision."

In this new light, Shadimar found it more difficult to condemn, but one thing still bothered him. He delved for the source, and the staff helped him find it. "But this time, we're not supposed to choose for wizardly qualities." Shadimar's words surprised himself. Habit, his and that of every previous member of his line, had goaded him to seek exactly that in his own apprentice. "We're looking for sword masters and killers, someone to stand against Colbey. If he's not annihilated, the world will be; and we'll have no use for apprentices. If we do slay Colbey and destroy the Staff of Chaos, our apprentices will die of old age before our passing."

Carcophan blinked, his yellow-green eyes fixed on Shadimar. "I fail to see where Chezrith doesn't fit that description."

"She's a woman."

"You noticed. I was afraid your predecessor's ceremony of passage included castration."

Shadimar ignored the gibe. Soon enough, Carcophan would probably lose his mortal cravings, too. "Colbey's the best swordsman in the world. Skill alone works for the Renshai women because their sword techniques are uniquely designed for speed and agility, delicate yet accurate cuts and precise jabs rather than power. But any other system relies as heavily on strength. Women are simply not as strong physically as men."

Carcophan shrugged. "You hardly have to argue the differences between men and women with me. My realm is the Eastlands, remember?" He swiveled his head to glance at the distant figure of Chezrith. "She can fight adequately. There are other ways to kill besides one-on-one combat. I believe Chezrith can get closer to Colbey than any man." Returning his attention to Shadimar, he met the hard, gray eyes directly.

Shadimar conceded that point as well, his thoughts on his own words. Since coming home, he had directed his efforts to seeking the finest replacement for the Eastern Wizard, ignoring the very tenets he had condemned Carcophan for disregarding. Now memory teased him, a spoken threat against Colbey whose source now hovered just beyond Shadimar's reach. He recalled a day in late summer, a youngster's voice raised in a plea to the gods: "Damn this demon to the coldest, deepest part of Hel. See to it that he dies in the same agony and ugliness he has inflicted upon so many."

Details came slowly. So much had happened the day Colbey fought his final battle against Trilless' champion, Valr Kirin; so much had been at stake. Kirin had denounced Colbey as Carcophan's champion, a demon hell-bent on destroying Renshai as well as Northmen. The Nordmirian lieutenant had planted the first seeds of doubt in Shadimar's mind. Despite Trilless' misconception about Colbey's title, she had proven right when it came to assessing his danger. And Shadimar had also had the Swords of Power to consider. He had created Harval from necessity, never guessing that Carcophan and Trilless would call the other two Swords. Yet Valr Kirin had wielded Ristoril the White.

Shadimar cast aside concerns that had become too familiar in order to recall the one who had called gods' damnation down on Colbey. The remainder of the speech resurfaced first, words that had preceded the warning: "Mighty Thor, my lord, creator and sower of storms, gods' champion of

law and honor, please forgive my transgression against you.
I will atone however you would have me, and I would dare
to ask one more thing . . ." Details of the voice came next,
a young man's, filled with the anguish of a father killed. *Valr
Kirin's son.* The name came a moment later. *Olvaerr. If the
boy has any of his father's intellect or skill, he would make
a tolerable Wizard as well as a warrior. And he has reason
to stand against Colbey.* Shadimar knew Valr Kirin had
served goodness and would have trained some of that into
his son. But Olvaerr had also attacked Colbey, placing peace
between Renshai and Northmen at risk, abandoning goodness' group mentality for the single-minded greed of evil.
Clearly, he could sit in the center and ride both sides. *Neutral.*

Apparently mistaking Shadimar's silence for a war of
wills and patience, Carcophan grudgingly broke the hush. "I
can choose who I wish for my apprentice, and I don't have
to justify that decision to anyone. The gods will decide her
worthiness. That's the purpose of the Tasks."

"You're right," Shadimar said, his thoughts still fixed on
the new distraction. "But if you feel comfortable with your
decision, why did you call me here? Were you seeking my
approval?"

"No. My reason for calling you has nothing to do with
Chezrith."

Shadimar gave Carcophan his full attention. "You have
other matters?"

Carcophan's cat's eyes glimmered, as if he had suddenly
brought all of his massive evil to the fore. "I've given some
thought to Colbey, his actions and his motivations. I think I
know where he'll go once he's healed. With proper preparation, I believe we can deal with him once and for all. Will
you help me?"

Though excited by the prospect, Shadimar held his emotions in check. So much could go awry with any plan. It was
simple for Carcophan to commit himself directly to thwarting Colbey, since he had already chosen his successor. Limited by time and the need to lure Olvaerr from Trilless'
territory to his own, Shadimar did not have the same freedom as his evil colleague. To risk his life now, with so few
competent prospects and the other neutral Wizard warped by
chaos meant taking an unacceptable risk. Soon enough, he
would have an apprentice, too; and he could commit himself

to retrieving and destroying the Staff of Chaos with the same boldness as Carcophan. "I can't. Not until I have my apprentice."

Carcophan went rigid. "By then, it may be too late."

Shadimar held firm. "I have little choice but to take that chance."

Carcophan drew breath, as if to rant, then released the air through his teeth in a hiss. "Then grant me this: the rest of this day to help me set the trap. One part alone requires your expertise. After that, I only need your permission to work freely in Westland territory."

Secodon rose, pacing restlessly.

The request rankled, and Shadimar had to fight his immediate negative response. Another Wizard, not neutral, given access to his guardianship made him feel violated. Yet if Carcophan had a way to best Colbey and was willing to take the full risk of facing the Renshai himself, giving Carcophan license to move about the Westlands seemed little enough to ask. The staff added its approval, tipping Shadimar's decision. Still, he maintained the presence of mind to qualify. "So long as you limit yourself to setting up and executing plans against Colbey, you have my permission to act freely in the West."

"Thank you." Carcophan met Shadimar's sacrifice with the seriousness it demanded. "And the rest of today?"

"I'll help you as long as it doesn't go against my own tenets."

"I wouldn't have suggested it if I thought it did."

Mitrian perched upon a sun-baked boulder, its warmth seeping through the thin fabric of her tunic and undergown. The wolf's head hilt of her sword nestled against familiar calluses, and she stared into the topaz eyes until her vision blurred. In front of her, Tannin repeated a complicated Renshai maneuver, his war braids flying and his sword slashing gleaming paths through the mid-morning air. Though she needed to assess technique, Mitrian avoided looking directly at her student. More than a week had passed since she had found him in bed with the Erythanian farm girl, but the pain had scarcely dulled. He had not come a moment late to any practice since that time. Though polite, he remained deferentially distant; no unnecessary words had passed between them.

Beyond Tannin, the Fields of Wrath stretched to forest. Near the edge, Sylva and Rache played a game that apparently consisted of her shooting blunted arrows at him while he tried to hack them from the air with his sword. Occasionally, they paused for a hug or to tumble into a heap on the weed-carpeted ground. The giggles wafted to her, soft on the wind, and their joy raised a mixture of vicarious happiness, ancient sorrow, and mild envy. She remembered her one love, Garn. The sweet excitement she had known in his presence had become dampened by the threat of pursuit, war, and Colbey's insistence from the first day that she was carrying Garn's son. Then, too, Garn had been obsessed with a need for vengeance against Rache Kallmirsson, the man who had been a great hero as well as a brother to her. By the time Garn had come to grips with his unreasoning rage, their love had matured to familiarity and stability.

Now, Mitrian craved the lighthearted play of courtship that circumstance and choice of mate had stolen from her. She'd never regretted her time with Garn; he had become every bit the considerate husband and loving father she had wanted. But Garn was long dead, and Mitrian needed something more than memories. At least, she reveled in the knowledge that her son had found the peaceful exhilaration for which his mother yearned. And she could not think of a woman more deserving of Rache's love.

That thought turned Mitrian's contemplations to Sylva's father, and guilt speared through her. Arduwyn, too, had suffered tragedy. He had lost his wife just before Garn had died and two of his adopted children a few years earlier. Now that her anger had dulled, Mitrian guessed that Arduwyn's confrontation over Vashi's training had masked his true concern. When he agreed to Sylva's and Rache's marriage, he had believed it a distant occurrence. Even when it became a reality, he had argued against their living together, citing multiple examples of youngsters in love who had married but lived with their own parents until they came of age. By visiting the Fields of Wrath, Arduwyn had discovered that Rache and Sylva shared a bed as well as a roof. Fear for his daughter's health, Mitrian believed, had driven him to argue; but his loyalty to Rache and herself had stolen the words he needed. Mitrian understood the logical and legitimate worry: women who carried babies young had a higher risk of complications and death. And when Mitrian thought back to her own pregnancy, she had not been emotionally prepared for a child, even at sixteen.

Mitrian berated herself, wishing she had recognized the real issue before her rage had driven Arduwyn away. She could have shown him the other side. At fifteen, Sylva had a maturity that Mitrian had not developed until she was much older. She could scarcely compare her coddled upbringing to the plagues, war, and death Sylva had weathered. Also, fertility did not run high in Mitrian's family. Her mother had borne only one living child, and Mitrian's fifteen years with Garn had never resulted in a sibling for Rache. For the Renshai tribe to survive, her son would need to start his family early, especially when Tannin seemed destined to create nothing better than a whore's bastard.

Arduwyn has a right to share in his daughter's happiness, too. Instead, he suffered the humiliation and pain of a friend's rejection. I owe him a major apology, and I'll offer it the instant he returns. Mitrian considered seeking Arduwyn only briefly. It would prove as difficult as finding one specific deer in the woodlands. She would have to know exactly where to look and, even then, she could find him only if he wanted her to do so. While she wandered through the forest on a hopeless task, her students would fall behind on lessons too important to miss.

Mitrian turned her attention back to Tannin. He stood in the final position, his sword parallel to the ground, closing his guard and his other hand low, near, and slightly backward for balance. She had no idea how long he had held the pose, awaiting her assessment. She studied him methodically, first noting balance, stance, and positioning. But desire betrayed her. She could not help also seeing the glimmers the sun drew through his golden hair, the sculpted features most women would find too harsh, and the sinewy grace of his body. Swordplay had made his limbs strong and his hands rugged. His eyes had always seemed fascinatingly unique, the blue-white of sea foam.

Tannin waited, frozen in a position that, though balanced, could not remain comfortable long. His eyes rolled to Mitrian, met her gaze briefly, then skittered away.

Mitrian found many things she wanted to say, few of them pertaining to sword forms. Yet she held her tongue. Personal emotion had no place on the battlefield, nor in practice. It occurred to her that if she found Tannin distracting enough to hinder his lessons, she should drop him as a student. Still, she knew such an action would prove cruel. Currently, she was the only Renshai with enough knowledge of technique to teach, and it seemed unfair to Tannin to withhold the knowledge from him alone. Mitrian also realized she owed too much to two other men to slight any of the few remaining Renshai. Rache Kallmirsson had given up his heritage to serve her father as the finest guard captain, Mitrian believed, that any city had ever had. Rache had taught her the maneuvers, and she had little choice but to keep the last of his people competent and alive. More importantly, Colbey Calistinsson had charged his people to Mitrian, and his was a trust she had too much respect to violate, even if she dared.

Still, Tannin held position, his patience heroic. Mitrian imagined that if he could channel that same dedication to a woman he would make the finest of partners.

For someone. Mitrian let the fantasy slip from her mind. In many ways, it seemed, Tannin was still a child. "Again," Mitrian said as if no time had passed.

Tannin broke form. Then, without a word, he launched into the sequence for the fourteenth time.

CHAPTER 17

Frost Reaver

As Colbey Calistinsson traveled south, he skirted the great trading city of Pudar, gliding through the forests west of town to avoid the crowds and bustle. His wounds had settled to a distant ache he scarcely noticed, and the joy of movement after a long and healing rest that spanned weeks made the soreness seem almost pleasant. He bore a wicked scar across his cheek from the *kraell* that matched the claw strikes Trilless' summoned demon had gashed across the back of his left hand. Yet vanity had never had a place in Colbey's life. Always, he simply strove to become the best. What others thought of his appearance or his methods mattered little, and then only when the opinion came from someone he respected. So long as his body functioned and his technique consistently improved, beauty held no significance.

The staff tucked into Colbey's belt slowed his gait, its end tapping his shins no matter how many times he repositioned it. The *aristiri* still accompanied him, alternately hopping along the leaf-, twig-, and needle-strewn ground and fluttering from branch to branch. Occasionally, it trilled and warbled, its clear voice floating through the confines of the forest. Apparently lulled by *aristiri* song, the forest animals paid Colbey's presence no heed. Birds filled the trees, their chirping sounding raucous in the wake of the *aristiri*'s talent. Squirrels pranced along limbs, occasionally vaulting from one tree to another. Three deer fed on leaves and underbrush. Another jumped from its bed, its tail bobbing erratically. Even a *wisule* skittered from beneath a deadfall, but nature's biggest coward took only so much courage from the hawk's rousing melody. Sitting on its hind legs, the rodent watched Colbey's approach for some time before turning tail and racing back into its burrow.

Poplar and beech gradually replaced the pines that had

dominated the woodlands nearer the Northlands. The ground became firmer, but less regular. Roots and boulders lay exposed by erosion, littering the path. Colbey selected his route more carefully, tempering his excitement for the coming reunion with Frost Reaver with the need to watch each step. The hawk winged after him, flying short distances to maintain his pace.

Colbey halted, uncertain. Clearly, the *aristiri* planned on accompanying him, and it had wearied. It had coaxed him to safety, then watched over him like a guardian while he slept. It was not his way to form attachments, especially with animals, but his bold self-assurance seemed to naturally draw followers. He could not allow the bird to delay him, and he already carried enough gear to hamper him. Its weight would seem negligible in the wake of the staff's inconvenience, and it could fly if danger struck.

Colbey stopped, wrapping bandages around his left arm to offset the talons. Hefting the *aristiri* would not noticeably hinder him, but making it understand what he intended seemed more difficult. Kneeling, he extended his arm, tapping his wrist with the opposite hand. Without hesitation, it flapped toward him, landing in the indicated position. It preened, then shuffled up and down his forearm. Though it moved past the protected part of his arm, it again used balance rather than grip to hold its place.

Colbey rose, and the *aristiri* scuttled painlessly to his shoulder. He wondered how it had so easily known what he wanted of it, attributing the nonverbal communication to the Western Wizard's affiliation with winged creatures. Then, realizing he might find an answer, he turned the question to the staff.

That's probably part of the answer. The bond between Wizard and animal is empathic. It can tell that you mean it no harm that, in fact, you mean to help it. But this hawk seems unusually perceptive.

Is this how Secodon and Shadimar came together?

The staff returned nothing for a moment. *Somewhat. I'm certain Shadimar chose Secodon for loyalty and intelligence. But there's magic involved in that relationship. Sorcery allows more extensive communication and manipulation.*

Colbey wished the staff would use shorter, simpler words in its explanations, but he understood well enough. His mood remained high. He felt comfortably rested, no longer plagued by his wounds, and he had spent the previous day practicing sword strokes from morning until night. He had lost two weeks of training, and the minuscule improvement that time would have gained him, but he seemed to have regained his agility and timing quickly enough. The familiar excitement that suffused him with every practice seemed a welcome friend he had sorely missed.

As Colbey cut back east toward the town of Bruen, forest opened onto the crest of a hill. Below him, a fertile farm valley stretched, cleared of trees. Near the horizon, a stream twisted, silver beneath the sun. Splotches of dark green and gray wooden buildings dotted the countryside, and the sight stirred Colbey. Just after the Great War, some fields had lain fallow, their farmers lost to the battle tide. Houses, barns, and fences had lapsed into disrepair as those left behind gave their all to the most essential chores, like the tending of crops and livestock. Now, again, Bruen looked much as it had before the War; and one of its barns, Colbey knew, housed Frost Reaver. Apparently sensing his anticipation, the *aristiri* hunkered down on his shoulder, chuckling contentedly.

Birches and tangles of thorny vines choked the mountainside. Great charred hulks of trees punctuated the landscape. Game trails crisscrossed the underbrush, tunneling through brambles and across ditches. Bluebirds picked at clusters of berries growing from long stalks, seeming to take no notice of his presence.

Colbey knew that descent anywhere along this mountain would prove difficult. The last time the farmers had cleared brush from the valley, their fire had raged out of control and consumed all of the forest between the mountain and the stream. He forced his way through the matted foliage. Almost immediately, a deer trail opened before him, headed down to the valley and wide enough for a lone man to walk. It cut a clear swathe through the chaotic jumble before him. The path ran parallel to a gully clogged with briers and the berries the birds enjoyed. The thick, musty odor of rotting vegetation issued from the depths of the trough.

The hawk trumpeted a sudden squawk directly into Colbey's ear.

Startled, Colbey froze, painfully alert. He scanned the path in front of him and to either side, and his gaze found motion. A rust-colored snake with gold and blue diamonds slithered from beneath a log, poising directly in his path. Another step, and it could have struck. Its triangular head swayed rhythmically, almost touching the ground.

The strangeness of its presence and actions touched Colbey at once. When it felt his approach, it should have fled. He eased Harval from its sheath.

The snake glided toward the movement. Suddenly, its head flashed forward, lunging for Colbey's leg. As quickly, Colbey swung. The flat of his sword crashed into its face, stopping the strike. Its body curled into a knot. Colbey flicked his wrist, and Harval's tip split the snake's neck. He kicked the still-roiling body into the gully. Throughout it all, the hawk remained perched on his shoulder, undisturbed. Yet without its call, Colbey doubted he would have noticed the snake in time. He stroked its crown with a finger. "Maybe we can communicate, after all."

Colbey back-stepped. His foot hung up on the staff's base, the wood cracking against his shin, and he stumbled. Catching his balance, he sheathed Harval and pulled the staff free. Had his battle with the serpent required even a single retreating movement, he might have tripped and lost the fight. Annoyed, Colbey continued along the trail more cautiously, contemplating the snake. The shape of its head, keeled scales, and brash coloring marked it as poisonous, though Colbey did not know its type. Its boldness made him suspicious; it had seemed almost to be awaiting him. *Carcophan?* Colbey frowned. Though he knew the Southern Wizard had a rapport with such creatures, it seemed like a paranoid leap in logic to believe Carcophan stood behind an attack that could be as easily explained by coincidence. Yet placed in context, his hunch seemed less irrational. *If they would summon a demon to kill me, why not a snake?*

Colbey glanced about, seeking some sign of another's passage. Finding nothing, he dismissed his concern. He had little means to predict or understand the Wizards' magic. To run scared of every slight variation from the expected meant spending the rest of his life in place, muscles knotted and heart racing. Always before, he had relied on his instincts and his nearly instantaneous reactions. Caution had never served him as well as premonition. He would not allow the Cardinal Wizards to make him a prisoner to speculation and fear.

The idea made retrieving Frost Reaver gain more significance. If the other Wizards had found him already, escape to anonymity required him to move quickly. The surefooted stallion would increase his speed and mobility.

Colbey doubled his pace toward the valley. The path grew steeper and threaded its way between boulders encrusted with bird droppings dried as hard as stone. Colbey sought handholds to control his descent, and the *aristiri* hopped from his shoulder to an overhang. He kept the staff clamped to his chest, supported by his upper arm. The sharp crust of rock cut into his callused hands but did not draw blood.

The trail ended at a low cliff. Colbey suspected the deer who had made the path could leap down the sheer face, but they required a different route to climb back to the top. For him to jump would result only in more broken bones, yet he was too impatient to clamber all the way back up the mountain to seek a different trail. He believed he could find a way down, but it required freedom of movement. Rummaging in his pack, he shoved aside clean clothes, sword oil, food, bandages, and his knife, emerging with a rope. He looped the end in strong figure eights around the staff, hitching it securely. He lowered it over the side, intending to dangle it well above the reach of passersby. But gravity slid the narrow rod of wood through his knot. He jerked upward, hoping sudden movement would spin the staff back onto his perch, but it detached, tumbling free of the cliffs and to the ground.

Colbey swore, watching as the staff spun then righted, landing tip first and sticking upright in the soft ground. The fall took longer than Colbey had originally judged. If he fell and only broke bones, he would consider himself lucky. *Sorry,* he sent.

The staff returned an indecipherable message that took the form of disgruntled concepts rather than words. It indicated displeasure and the need to come fetch it as soon as possible.

Colbey returned his concentration to his route down. To turn back now would leave the staff out of sight, so he chose to trace a path from where he stood. A series of slender, intersecting ledges led to a vertical crack that stretched nearly to the ground. This appeared to be the only possible descent. He took another glance at the staff. It seemed safe, tan against the green and gray of the cliff. Yet the idea of backtracking and leaving it unseen and untended seemed too dangerous. In the hands of the power hungry, it would prove a crucial tool. But in the hands of the weak, it would simply take over, giving its wielder all the power Colbey had refused and controlling its so-called master like a puppet.

Colbey lay facedown at the edge of the precipice and swung his legs over it. His boots scraped over the bare stone, seeking the ledge he had previously seen. Pebbles dislodged and clattered against the cliff, then silently plummeted through space. Finding the shelf, he edged along its gently sloping course. The forest disappeared above him, and the rock face became his entire world.

The ridges widened as Colbey progressed. Though he could now place his entire foot firmly onto stone, he could not escape a feeling of uneasiness. He had always relished the tight alertness that came to him in battle, his life precariously balanced on a knife's edge. Here, he had no control over the knife. Squatting, he braced a hand on the ledge. He cautiously lowered his left leg and wedged his foot in the vertical crack. He allowed himself another glance at the ground. The height of two adults beneath him, a familiar, broad-shouldered man with gray and black hair held the staff that used to belong to Colbey. He froze.

Catching Colbey's gaze, Carcophan smiled. "Drop something?" The Southern Wizard threw back his head and laughed mockingly. "Perhaps I can speed your journey down to claim what you so foolishly lost." He waved his hand, and fist-sized pieces of flint cascaded down the cliff face.

The *aristiri* flew to the safety of a tree, silently watching. Colbey flinched flat to the mountainside, but the hail of stones crashed painfully against his head and shoulders, nearly battering him from the cliff. Dizzied, he clutched rock, mind sprinting for answers. His only hope lay in desperate action. A flash of memory brought the image of Arduwyn tumbling from a tower window ledge twice Colbey's current distance from the ground, escaping with only a broken arm and bruises. Colbey had no sand to cushion his fall, but he could die, sword in hand, and possibly kill Carcophan as well. As larger blocks of stone spilled toward him, the Renshai kicked himself from the cliff.

"Modi!" Colbey shouted, drawing and raising Harval as he fell.

Carcophan went still, staring for a moment in horror. He opened his mouth, the first syllables of a spell rushing forth in an explosion of breath. Then, apparently realizing he would not finish in time, he dodged.

Harval swept for the Southern Wizard's head, but struck his arm instead. The blade bit deep. The staff fell from Carcophan's grasp. Colbey pitched to his side, then rolled to his feet. He thrust for Carcophan's lungs. The Wizard spun away from the attack. Harval tore cloth and gouged a furrow across his chest. Then Carcophan waved his uninjured hand. Without flash, sound, or preamble, he disappeared.

Colbey crouched at the ready, feeling the hot excitement of battle course through him, masking any wounds he might have taken from the fall. The freedom of his breathing and movements told him he had not broken any bones. At the worst, he had sustained a few more bruises, and those would become lost in the dispersing wash left from his battle with the summoned demon. He cleaned and sheathed his sword. Catching the staff, he rose, hurrying toward the farmstead. Though he believed the wound he had inflicted would occupy Carcophan's attention for a long time, he dared not take a chance with Frost Reaver. It would fit the Evil One's tactics to try to demoralize an enemy by killing a loved one. Colbey ran, finding some solace in the realization that the Wizards had no instantaneous spells of slaying. If Carcophan had known such a thing, Colbey felt certain he would have died.

He appreciated my power. He would have used me to my potential.

Annoyed by an interruption that sounded suspiciously like childish whining, Colbey responded absently as he raced toward the farms, gaze selecting the familiar wood-roofed structure that belonged to the farmer keeping Frost Reaver. *He would have used you for his cause, not yours.*

He would have tried, Master. I'm more powerful. I would have swayed him to my way.

At what cost?

The balance isn't my concern.

Colbey disagreed. *It is. You just don't know it yet.*

Colbey felt a wash of mirth and outrage, a strange mocking combination. *You profess to know more than I do?*

Only to have a more balanced view of the world. And more common sense. Colbey continued before the staff could interrupt. *I've got more urgent concerns than arguing station with you. Things are as they are. You know as well*

*as I that the Western Wizard was meant to wield you.
Whether either of us likes it, I am that Wizard.** He said
nothing more, hoping his mood would make it clear that he
had no intention of listening to or saying more about the
matter now.

The ground leveled. The trail led into a solid wall of
holly. A low tunnel cut through the dark green leaves.
Colbey skittered through on hands and knees, emerging in a
cleared field. Rows of stems jutted from the soil, weighted
with fat leaves. Avoiding the crop, Colbey followed the
field's edge to a road he knew. Deep ruts betrayed many
years of cart traffic, and the buildings of the farm that
housed Frost Reaver became discernible ahead. Just beyond
a shed, a trio of young men worked in a large, egg-shaped
hole, flinging shovelfuls of mud to the surface. Their cheer-
ful work song rose over the wet slash of steel through earth,
interspersed with laughter. In the field directly in front of the
house, one broad figure and several smaller ones knelt in the
dirt.

As he came abreast of the second group, Colbey switched
his course and headed toward them. Soon, he could make
out the hefty figure of the farmer from whom he had bar-
tered barn space for his horse. The others were children,
plucking scrawny weeds from amid the growing crop. Apparently, this farmer had done his part to replace the hands
lost to battle and disease, and all of his offspring appeared
robust. They, too, sang as they worked, finding exhilaration
in what others saw as drudgery. Colbey watched for a short
time, glad for a new generation springing from the ashes of
the last, one that took pride in their work from a young age
and appreciated the freedom their elders' blood had won.
When a dirty-faced girl looked up and noticed him, Colbey
stopped, hailing the farmer from a distance. "Hello."

The farmer looked up, the singing stopped, and all of the
children's heads swung in Colbey's direction. The man rose,
his homespun filthy, and clapped soil from his palms. Dark
eyes regarded Colbey from a red-cheeked, pudgy face, and
the farmer smiled. "Returned at last, have you? Come for
your horse, I'd guess." He approached Colbey.

Though the farmer seemed happy, Colbey could not help
the concern that rose. "Is he well?"

The children quit working, nudging one another and com-
menting on Colbey's swords and staff in loud whispers.

"Healthy like a horse," the farmer said, laughing as if he had said something funny. "Bit restless these last days, though. Hope you don't mind, we used him for what a stallion's good for. It seemed to calm him some. And neighbors who have horses thought his blood would do their stock good; lots of the best ones got lost in the War, you know." The farmer spread his lips in a gap-toothed grin. "I think he missed you."

Too eager to chat, Colbey dug a pouch full of gold from his pocket and tossed it to the farmer. The man caught the offering one-handed, coins clinking through the fabric, then placed it in his pocket uncounted. Colbey's previous payment had been more than generous enough to insure competent care.

The farmer half-turned to address his children. "Back to work."

The boys and girls obeyed, still exchanging low-pitched comments. The farmer headed toward the buildings, stepping over each planted row, and Colbey followed. Mud caked his boots, and every step left heavy prints in the moist earth. "Fine, strong animal you got there. Wish all my cows could be so hardy, though I can't complain. It's been a good year."

The splash and plop of wet earth grew louder as they approached. Colbey watched the shovelers work. "What are you digging for?"

The farmer grinned, obviously pleased by Colbey's interest. "Noticed the fish pasture, did you?" He continued talking as they headed around the house to the barn. "Got my first taste of fish after the War and loved it. The fish, I mean, not the War. We fought by the ocean, you know. Now that we're all rebuilt again, I got this idea. Why not farm fish as well as cows and crops? No one's ever done that before far as I know."

"Not as far as I know either." Colbey approved, pleased to see that war and chaos had sparked new thoughts and innovations in addition to doing harm.

"My oldest's got some ideas, too. He's working on a new kind of harvesting tool that'll pick corn faster than any man can alone. Horse-drawn, of course." The farmer stopped before the pasture fence around the barn. Recently rebuilt, the poles and slats looked pale and unweathered. Clearly, the Bruenian farmer had chosen to invest Colbey's money back into the farm and his children rather than spend it on beer and gewgaws.

The farmer whistled.

An answering whinny echoed through the confines of the barn, followed by welcoming whickers in several voices. Three horses ran around the corner, Frost Reaver at the lead. Dirt and grass stains striped his white hide, yet Colbey turned his attention to what lay beneath. Muscles rippled through the horse's rump and hindquarters, and no ribs showed. Neither did the belly hang as if overfed and under-exercised. The stallion moved with a grace and ease that made the farmer's two trailing plow horses seem ungainly. The three stopped short at the fence. Frost Reaver stood with his ears cocked toward Colbey, betraying the direction of his gaze.

Excitement flashed through Colbey. Time had dulled his memory of the animal's perfection. Now, he stared at the fine, wedge-shaped head that perched high on the delicately bowed neck. Strong shoulders arched deeply. Massive nostrils and a broad chest promised the endurance Frost Reaver had delivered on more than one occasion. The horse approached Colbey slowly, ears flickering backward and eyes rolling to reveal the whites.

The farmer scrambled over the fence without bothering to open the gate, his agility surprising for his bulk. "I'll get his things." He headed toward the barn, the plow horses plodding methodically at his heels, nuzzling his back at intervals.

Frost Reaver remained in place, nostrils wide and red, snuffling Colbey's scent. "It's me, Reaver. You remember me." Gradually, he reached up a hand and stroked the soft, pink muzzle. The stallion froze in position, though he stayed tense and coiled.

Soon, the farmer reappeared, carrying Frost Reaver's halter and bridle. Colbey preferred to ride bareback, without a saddle to blunt the bunching and shift of muscle that warned of coming movement. Sword maneuvers required free hands and that the horse respond to the slightest kneed commands. A saddle would have hampered that communication.

As the farmer approached, Frost Reaver's ears returned to a neutral position, and he remained still as the farmer adjusted the halter, then the bridle, on his head. Catching the lead rope, the farmer headed for the gate. Colbey tripped the latch, then Frost Reaver was led up beside him. The farmer passed the lead rope, and Colbey accepted it happily. He could scarcely wait to feel the massive power of the animal beneath him, to know again the rapport that blossomed whenever they worked together on a precise sword maneuver. "Thank you," Colbey said.

"Thank *you*, sir," the farmer returned gruffly. "Anytime you need your horse watched, just let me know."

The stallion relaxed then, apparently catching his cues from his master. Colbey led the horse past the farmstead and out onto the road to Pudar. Unclipping the lead rope, he used it to lash his pack to the animal's back. Still clutching the staff, he vaulted onto the horse.

Frost Reaver quivered slightly, with the same anticipation he had shown so many times in the past. For an instant, Colbey knew the camaraderie that had seemed almost telepathic, the grim certainty that told both animal and rider that he belonged here. Catching the reins, Colbey sought a hole in his bindings through which to wedge the staff. Its previous slipping made him wary.

Suddenly, Frost Reaver stiffened. Though the motion was nonspecific, Colbey knew horses well enough to sense impending violence. "Easy, boy." He prepared to jump down and calm the animal.

Before Colbey could dismount, Frost Reaver lurched into a rear. He twisted as he came down, immediately lunging into a wild jump that threw Colbey into a wall of air. The staff tumbled as the Renshai concentrated on the more urgent matter of clambering down without injuring himself or the horse. He leaned left to leap clear. Apparently sensing the movement, Reaver spun in the opposite direction, ending with a buck that thrust his hind legs skyward. Instinctively, Colbey threw his weight to the right, keeping his seat. An instant later, Frost Reaver launched into three consecutive hops, all four legs bunched beneath him. Again, the stallion reared to vertical, momentum all but taking him over backward. Colbey clung with his knees, feeling himself begin to slide toward the horse's rump. He shifted his balance, just as Reaver rocked back into a bucking, stomping kick. Hurled suddenly forward, Colbey scarcely managed to remain aboard. His face struck the pack, and he lost his hold for an eye blink.

Frost Reaver whirled again, turning fully around in a single motion. Humping his back, he gave one more solid kick that unhorsed the clinging Renshai. Colbey sailed through the air, landing hard on the packed dirt path. He rolled, tucking his head, seeking the location of the crazed horse. Before he had come halfway around, he caught a glimpse of movement overhead, steel-shod hooves speeding down on him.

"Reaver, no!" Colbey writhed out of the path. The hooves slammed to the ground, their impact quaking. Immediately, the stallion twisted into another wild rear. Colbey managed only to skitter into a half-crouch before the hooves screamed down on him again. "Modi." He swore as he eeled out of the way once more.

The stallion waited only until its hooves struck empty ground, then it rushed Colbey, legs thundering, head low, and ears swept flat to its skull.

Colbey's first thought, to draw Harval and let the beast impale itself, passed quickly. He would not kill any friend for a fit of unreasoning rage, especially one that had served him so faithfully in the past. Instead, he scrambled to his feet, sprinting for the first gap in the roadside forest. A hoof clipped his boot, tripping him. Flat, hard teeth tore his tunic, pinching skin. He dove forward, rolling, twigs and stones gouging his back. He ducked through a line of twisted *hadonga* trees, their upper branches twined into an archway over the road.

Frost Reaver shrilled his fury, the neigh rebounding in deafening echoes. His forehooves slammed into wood, spilling a shower of leaves onto Colbey's head. The Renshai recoiled, confused, aching from a rabid betrayal that seemed irrational. Yet the stallion had seemed tractable in the farmer's care. There was nothing undirected about an attack that had become nonsensically relentless.

The white hooves crashed against wood again, a snap echoing through the woodlands. The trunk leaned slightly, but it did not fall, and another wash of leaves spiraled down over Colbey.

Kill the horse and come get me. The staff sent from where it lay in the roadway. *Before another Wizard comes and takes me.*

Colbey doubted Carcophan would come after him again so soon, and he had never known the Cardinal Wizards to work together, except on the Wizards' Meeting Isle. Still, he understood the staff's concern. *Not until I understand. Not until I do all I can for Frost Reaver.*

The hooves buffeted the trunk again, and Frost Reaver screamed another wild cry.

There's nothing you can do. It's out of your hands.

Bracing himself against one of trunks, Colbey gathered mental energy and thrust his consciousness into the horse's mind. It was the first time the Renshai had even considered invading an animal's head, and the organization of thought surprised him. Immediately, his probe touched a red wash of rage that seemed endless, uninterrupted by other interests and concerns. Colbey found a definitive target that centered around himself. Clearly the animal bore no interest in harming any other human.

The hammer of hooves against wood sounded like a distant, hollow reverberation as Colbey turned his full concentration internally. He found vague impressions of basic needs: food, drink, sleep, and the fleeting odors of enemies on the wind. But the scarlet fog pervaded and suffocated these necessities, masking them beneath an all-consuming need to kill. *A foreign thought. A driving force without reason.* Colbey delved deeper.

The staff joined Colbey in the horse's mind. *Caution. You're weakening yourself. A few more batterings, and it'll have you.*

Colbey ignored the warning. Diverting his thoughts now, while ensconced in another's mind, would only delay and steal his vitality. He dug more quickly through the rage-haze, desperate to find some semblance of the animal he had known. Though he had never before intentionally entered Frost Reaver's mind, he had caught glimpses of emotion and idea that had made them seem more team than beast and master. This frenzied stallion bore no likeness to the horse he had loved.

Colbey swam through the fog, too directed to notice the fatigue replacing his own usual agile strength. At length, he came to the edges of the shell. In the center of Frost Reaver's mind, a spark still burned. Colbey dove for the light, memory slamming him with the force of the speeding hooves. Not long ago, he had scrambled through another enemy-warped mind, one far more complicated and twisted by a malicious, vengeful bitterness that had destroyed happy memory and logic. For an instant, the comparison to Episte nearly paralyzed Colbey, and strength ebbed through the contact. Then he forced himself to see and feel the many differences. Episte's madness had come as a result of his receiving the third Sword of Power on the world of law, and only the Wizards and gods could guess the broader complications of that trio. Chaos itself had warped the youngster, its being spreading and destroying like acid, its sudden and massive presence destroying humanity Colbey had had no ability or opportunity to recover. Desperately, he had searched Episte's mind for one crumb of remaining self, finding a glimmer that chaos had stolen as quickly as Colbey found it.

Yet, here, Colbey found something different. He could still feel the pervading wrongness that was chaos; but it did not compose the rage, it only tinged it. The staff gave Colbey the answer. *Magic. The change itself is the work of a creature of law. Using magic.* The explanation addressed future queries as well. Only Wizards could use sorcery, and Carcophan's nearness pointed to him as the cause.

The staff corrected the misconception. *Furred beast. Shadimar's work.* It kept its reply clipped, moving on to a more urgent topic. *The hawk's helping. Even so, the horse'll have you soon, too weak to fight. Pull out now!*

The staff's words only galvanized Colbey to action. He delved into the central spark, finding the familiar strength, dedication, and innocence that had characterized the Frost Reaver he knew. He also found the depth of spirit that accompanied the finest steeds, a property he had heard a trainer call "heart." Colbey shouted in triumph. Even as he thrust into the pocket of surviving temperament, the red fog closed around him. It pressed the edges, devouring the boundaries in an instant.

Damn! Colbey sent his consciousness in a wild circle, battling the squeezing madness. He had long ago lost track of his body, but he could now feel his mental thread weakening. Almost certainly, he had fallen, and he would have no way to run from Reaver's attack. *Can you assist?*

Yes. The staff returned, though it made no move to prove its assertion. *In trade for more freedom.*

Rage speared through Colbey, momentarily strengthening him. He kept his pace cautious and methodical, halting the infusion as long as possible. *I won't give in to blackmail.*

Either you serve me or not. My death would leave you masterless.

Pull out! the staff drove the command into Colbey's mind.

Colbey responded in concept, not daring to waste the energy forming words would take. He made it clear in an instant that things had gone too far for him to withdraw, dodge, and use his sword. His only hope lay in stopping the attack.

A crack wound through Colbey's hearing, sounding leagues away. He felt something massive swish over his head. A flicker of concern touched him from the staff, then disappeared as it set to work.

I'll stop the spread of magic permanently. It'll take too much to fix things now. You'll die before you bring that horse back to what it was. Just latch onto something that'll stop the assault and send it away. We can put things right some other time. Go! Hurry.

Colbey let the staff handle the horse's alien fury. Within an instant, the sorceries ceased their inward movement, and Colbey muddled through the horse's emotions and memory. He found himself featured prominently in the stallion's mind, but remaining flickers of affection stood little chance beneath the avalanche of magically conjured hatred. He gathered a flight reaction as well as triggering a deep and inner calm, certain he needed to funnel these into a specific direction if he ever hoped to find the horse again. Clearly, he needed to steer the white stallion into the hands of someone who cared for animals. The red haze had blunted its natural pursuit for food and drink.

Quit gawking! Send it away! The staff continued to hold magic at bay, but it knew a danger Colbey could only imagine until he found the way back into his own person.

The Renshai did not respond, channeling his focus to the horse's memory. It knew people as nameless odors and movements. Colbey knew that, given time, he could sort one from another; but time was a luxury he did not have. Instead, he found the memory of the one other person who had ridden Frost Reaver since Colbey had become the horse's master. *Arduwyn. He understands animals. He'll know what to do.* The forest odor that seemed to linger on the hunter would guide the horse enough to keep it in the woodlands, away from main pathways. He drew the three concepts together, funneling his own power to highlight their importance.

Frost Reaver's mind collapsed into darkness, and it took Colbey a moment to realize the draining of his power had hurled him from the animal's mind. The musk of horse filled his nostrils, strong after the odorless interior of the stallion's thoughts. Steel-shod hooves hovered over Colbey's head.

Colbey gasped, attempting to dodge. His usual reflexes failed him, and he seemed rooted in place.

The *aristiri* swept from a branch above his head, driving its beak toward one of the stallion's dark eyes.

Frost Reaver twisted, though whether in response to Colbey's manipulations or the bird's attack, he did not know. The horse came halfway around before his hooves fell. The instant they did, he took off at a gallop down the main pathway, headed south.

Colbey relaxed, not daring to waste his final energy even on something as simple and basic as remaining wary. He knew the quiet passage of time would gradually restore his vitality, while even the most straightforward of movements might steal his consciousness at a time he needed it most. If Shadimar had caused Frost Reaver's madness, the Wizard might still be in the vicinity.

The thought brought a rage as vicious as the one Colbey had been lucky to survive. Whatever friendship remained between him and the Eastern Wizard vanished in an animosity that pained as well as soothed. Though obvious blasphemy, Colbey could not help but hold Odin responsible. When subjected to the very forces the god had built it to protect, the system of the Cardinal Wizards had shattered like an ancient, sun-bleached bone. Now the one Wizard who had wanted nothing to do with magic and should have championed an assigned cause fought a single-handed battle for balance against the world's most powerful.

Though surely it still had some contact, the staff made no judgment. Colbey did not currently have the power to keep it from the deeper recesses of his mind. He had little choice but to trust its vow. And for all its stubborn blindness, he could think of no one of the four forces that could serve him better.

Colbey turned his thoughts to his current position. He lay in a green tangle of vines. The tree Frost Reaver had battered lay toppled, its upper branches wedged into a fork of the *hadonga* that had supported Colbey's back. Had exhaustion not pounded him to the ground, it might have staved in his skull. He also assessed his own strength, finding it not as fully tapped as he had feared. He had drained himself longer and lower in the past, and he guessed he could probably wander over and rescue the staff without problem. However, the longer he lay still now, the quicker he would recover. The slightest weakness in himself obsessed him.

The *aristiri* alighted on the leaning trunk, watching Colbey through one round, blue eye. It warbled softly, as if to reassure him that no one shared this part of the forest.

"Thanks, fellow," Colbey murmured, though the effort of speech dizzied him. *If you're going to accompany me, you'll need a name.* It had never been Colbey's way to give titles to animals, but one for this hawk seemed to present itself at once. "Formynder." The word meant guardian. It also held connotations of teacher, which seemed less appropriate in this circumstance.

The *aristiri* warbled again.

Colbey closed his eyes, concentrating his attention on empowering himself to normal, trusting the bird to warn him of another's approach. Though still unmanned, the staff did not complain. Apparently, it trusted the *aristiri*'s perception as well. And the day wore on.

CHAPTER 18

The Bard of Béarn

The paint mare's hooves drummed on the packed earth of the forest path. Khitajrah Harrsha's-widow had ridden through the night and into the following day, irrationally afraid Arduwyn might catch her if she rested for even a moment. Exhaustion rode her with as little mercy as she had, so far, shown the horse.

As the sun shifted halfway across the sky, the Southern Weathered Range loomed. The soil changed from a rich brown that seemed nearly black to a gray, stony mulch. Hearty Erythanian forest disappeared, replaced by scraggly, sparse vegetation that twisted from the rocky ground. She passed occasional farm fields, cradled into hollows between sheer, unyielding mountains. Greenery speckled the valleys; apparently, rain washed the usable soil into the lowlands and mountain streams watered the cropland well enough.

Halfway into the afternoon, Khitajrah discovered the king's city of Béarn. The castle rose, carved directly from a central mountain and surrounded by gray cottages. Though the town seemed far smaller than she had expected, a quarter the size of the Eastern kingdom of Stalmize, the architecture fascinated her. From beginning to end, it reminded her of the older, more beautiful portions of her home city, when the craftsmen had used more permanent constructions and had personalized their work with statuettes and flourishes. On the outer boundaries of Stalmize, identical wood and thatch dwellings cheapened the labors of the central craftsmen, echoing the changes that had overtaken Eastern society. Quick efficiency had taken the place of pride and permanence. When money became scarce and needs many, art always suffered first.

Yet in Béarn, Khitajrah saw no such pattern. As the path became rocky, she slowed the horse to a walk, listening to the rhythmical crunch of shards beneath its hooves. Though disappointingly small, the city clearly took pride in its station and its appearance. At least one statue decorated every dwelling, perched upon crafted ledges or recessed into welcoming doorways. Even the rudest of peasant cottages had some stone-crafted object in its yard, though the skill of the artisans varied widely. As Khitajrah rode through the Westlands' high kingdom, she found some yards choked with statues, grouped by themes or, occasionally, in clever scenes. Apparently, these dwellings housed the craftsmen who carved the many stone works that decorated their neighbor's cottages.

As Khitajrah headed toward the center and the jutting spires of Béarn's castle, even hovering fatigue could not keep her from staring. The predominant motif appeared to be bears. She discovered them rearing, pacing in pairs, or roaring in fierce defiance. One stylized creation merely gave the impression of "bear," though Khitajrah felt uncertain whether the bold swirls and lines made her think of a bear for some artistic reason or only because of the town's major theme.

Oddly, Khitajrah found her eyes glued to the artwork, though the Béarnides posed more danger. She noticed their movement and bustle through the king's city only indistinctly, from peripheral vision. She guessed her own tiredness as well as the captivating stonework made her reckless. The swarthy Béarnides, with their black hair and dark eyes, reminded her more of Easterners than any humans she had met since crossing the Great Frenum Mountains, and that also put her at ease.

However, there the resemblance ended. To a man, the Béarnides stood as tall as the largest Eastern warrior and as broad as a bear. Even the women seemed as massive as any Eastern man, and the children showed promise of their parents' bulk. Long black beards predominated, joining with sideburns and mustaches into manes that seemed to surround the men's stout, coarsely-featured faces; Eastern men usually remained clean-shaven. When they did grow beards, they tended to keep them short and well-groomed, always accompanied by a mustache. Their sparser hair patterns rarely allowed head and facial growth to link. The Béarnides spoke a rapid language that seemed delicate compared with the Easterners' harsh gutturals, and it did not seem to fit their size. Their population seemed as sparse in daylight as Stalmize's did moments before curfew. Obviously, the plagues and power struggles Lirtensa mentioned had taken their toll on the populace where the Great War had not. Eastern King Siderin had bought off the previous Béarnian king, and the city had not joined its fellow Westerners in battle.

Khitajrah forced her attention to other sights in the city of Béarn. In addition to the citizenry, the architecture, and the myriad statues, she discovered tall, unrecognizable contraptions composed of pulleys, logs, and ropes. The wind stirred clamps that thunked musically against wood, and racheting noises filled the streets as men yanked at the ropes. From what Khitajrah could see without gawking, these apparently hauled blocks of stone from place to place, mostly from the farm valleys to the crags. Wagons waited at the sites, presumably to carry the rescued granite to the mason. Clearly, even the nuisance stones that dulled farmers' plows did not go to waste here.

As Khitajrah neared the castle of Béarn, fatigue seemed to vanish, replaced by nervousness. In Stalmize, had a woman insisted on coming before the king, the guards would have laughed her down. Then, perhaps, they would have attacked and raped or killed her just for the practice. In the West, she knew, laws forbade the latter actions. Lirtensa's matter-of-factness only confirmed the impression. Yet Khitajrah did not know if she would have the words to obtain an audience. She rode directly to the castle, reining up before the iron gates.

A half-dozen men in mail glanced down at Khitajrah from the ramparts. Each wore a blue tabard decorated with a tan figure of a bear, and a blue feather arched delicately from one man's helmet. Another man perched in a semi-oval window. Though also dressed in Béarn's blue and tan, nothing about his garb seemed official. He wore a tunic and cape, and one breek-covered leg dangled from the ledge. Though he wore a longsword at his hip, a mandolin occupied his hands. Through the bars of the gate, Khitajrah could see two more guards standing at attention just inside the entryway. These had swords at their hips and halberds in their hands. Her position had not allowed her to assess the weaponry of the others. Beyond the sentries on the ground, a courtyard filled with stone benches, statues, and flowers beckoned; and a lowered plankway led into the interior over a moat filled with brackish water.

While Khitajrah studied the castle and its sentries, the guards watched her in the same, thoughtful silence. At length, she flushed beneath the intensity of their stares.

The paint pawed the ground with a forehoof, flinging gravel, as if impatient to enter the gates.

Khitajrah spoke hesitantly, in the trading tongue. "Hello."

No one replied in words, but one of the gate sentries gave a single nod of acknowledgment.

Encouraged by this simple gesture, Khitajrah addressed this man specifically. "I'd like an audience with the king." She pulled the paint around, and it pranced, snorting, legs continuing to move long after it came into position.

"No one without hostile intentions is denied an audience with King Sterrane." He passed his halberd to his companion, who took the shaft but remained rigidly at attention. The speaking man pulled parchment and a stylus from his pocket. "Your name, please."

"Khitajrah Harrsha's-widow."

The man penned the first letter or two, then stopped, frowning. He scratched out what he had written and restarted, again quitting after only a few marks. "Kay-tahj-i-what?"

Khitajrah cursed herself for not taking Lirtensa's hint. "Kayt will do fine."

"Kayt." The guard studied Khitajrah more carefully for a time, then returned to his parchment and wrote. "You're not a citizen." It was a statement, not a question. He went on. "What village, tribe, town, or city do you represent?"

"I represent only myself." The mare began pawing again, wearing a trench with its forehoof. Khitajrah jerked the horse's head up. "Stop that," she said to the animal.

"Mmm." The guard did not bother to write anything. "And what is this audience in regard to?"

"It's a personal matter."

"And that personal matter is?"

"Personal," Khitajrah repeated with finality. She dismounted, allowing the horse to paw as it would.

"Personal." The sentry frowned. "Very well. You may see his majesty, King Sterrane of Béarn, high king of the Westlands in the afternoon, exactly one week from today. Thank you for—"

"A week!" Khitajrah shouted, caught off-guard by the pronouncement.

"Yes, lady. The king's a busy man."

"I haven't got a week."

"Others have been waiting longer."

"I need to speak with him today."

The sentry's brows arched over his flinty eyes. "I'm afraid that's not possible. The day is scheduled."

Chaos added its opinion. *Use guile, Khita.*

Upset, Khitajrah did not mince words. *Easy for you to say. You're not two days shy on sleep.*

The sentry returned parchment and stylus to his pocket, collecting his weapon. "Merchants and nobility often send a servant ahead to set up the meeting for when their master arrives."

Khitajrah transferred her rage to the guard. "Do I look like a princess to you?"

Easy, chaos cautioned. *He's just doing his job.*

"That's not for me to determine," the Béarnide said carefully.

Chaos prodded further. *Tell him it's important. It concerns one of the king's friends.*

But . . . Khitajrah started, immediately recognizing the flaw in her own argument. *That's not guile. That's the truth.*

Sometimes it works.

It seemed worth a try. "But this is too important to wait. It concerns a friend of the king."

The sentry seemed appropriately serious, but he had not seemed any less so in the past. He exchanged a glance with his companion. "What's the matter?"

"I'd prefer to discuss it directly with his majesty."

"I'm sure you would," the sentry said. "But I need to have adequate knowledge for the king to decide if the matter is urgent enough to require interrupting scheduled audiences. It would disrupt more than just routine, you understand."

Khitajrah lowered her head, defeated. "I understand."

You're giving up so easily?

What choice do I have? I can hardly call my wish for information an emergency. Lying to the guards won't earn me any goodwill from the king. When he finds out I called a bunch of irrelevant questions urgent, he'll probably throw

*me in the dungeon. I'm not going through that again. Better
to just see what Lirtensa found.* *

Chaos saw the logic in Khitajrah's words. It did not push
further, though she could still sense disappointment and a
certainty of triumph if they played the situation well. Exhaustion pressed Khitajrah, and she dared not attempt cunning with her mind blunted and so much at stake. The time
lost hurt; but, on horseback, she could still regain most of it.

"Lieutenant, you'll forgive my intrusion for a moment?"
The voice came from over Khitajrah's head. She glanced up
in time to see the sentry with the plume make a friendly gesture of dismissal toward the man in the window.

Khitajrah naturally turned her head in his direction.

The musician no longer held his mandolin; apparently, he
had replaced it in his room to free his hands. Now that he
held her full attention, Khitajrah noticed things she had
missed on first inspection. Though he sported dark hair, it
bore a hue lighter than the Béarnides', with a touch of red.
He was clean-shaven, more slender and delicate in build,
though he did not lack for muscles. There was a calmness
about him that seemed genuine and permanent. Clearly,
though not one of them, he had earned the Béarnides' respect. He called down to her. "Hello, Khitajrah Harrsha's-
widow." He gave the name a passable Eastern pronunciation,
his own accent similar to Lirtensa's. "My name is Mar Lon.
I'm King Sterrane's personal bodyguard."

Mar Lon had said nothing that required a reply, but
Khitajrah felt as if he expected one. "Quite an honor."

"The greatest of my life." Mar Lon agreed.

The guards remained in position, silent. Their furrowed
brows made it clear they had no more understanding than
she did of why the king's personal bodyguard had chosen to
spend his off-duty time supervising a standard exchange between a stranger and castle sentries.

Mar Lon seemed oblivious to the intensity of the guardsmen's silence. "That's a nice-looking horse you have there."

Khitajrah blinked. Though he still had not questioned, she
again believed he wanted an answer or comment. "Yes,
I . . ." Chaos buzzed an incoherent warning, and Khitajrah
trailed off.

*Careful. Either he knows something he shouldn't, or he's
interested in your mount. In either case, if you answer right,
you may get your audience.* *

What's "right?"

Chaos gave no answer, as uncertain as its host.

Mar Lon did not seem to notice that Khitajrah had not finished. "Where'd you get such a fine steed?"

The question seemed harmless, free of accusation, yet Khitajrah felt cold sweat cling to her back. Though she knew less guilt than she expected for the theft, she had hoped to trade the paint mare in Béarn. She had told Arduwyn her destination, and he could surely track her to the high kingdom. The idea of a man as cautious and silent as Arduwyn hunting her tightened every muscle with dread. His bow could end her life before she saw him coming, and horse stealing might prove enough motive to allow him to do so within the law. In the Eastlands, a woman who took a horse from a man could be tortured and slaughtered in any manner of the victim's choosing, and death in the Eastlands was rarely painless. Here, she suspected, a verdict would come slower and punishment swifter; but the end result would be the same. However, if Arduwyn got his horse back here, he might not hold a grudge. "I . . ." she started.

Careful, chaos warned unnecessarily.

"I found it in the woods." Khitajrah skirted the truth, not quite lying either. "I thought someone here might know its master."

Mar Lon said nothing, just waited for Khitajrah to continue.

She rambled on. "If not, well, since this is the closest town, I figured its master might come here. I hoped I could sell it or trade it. I'm in a hurry. I really do need a mount, but I wouldn't want to leave someone else without a favored horse." She looked at the paint, which was pawing and stomping more than ever.

Mar Lon crouched gracefully in the window, as if tensed to leap to the ground. Khitajrah estimated he could make the jump, but not without the near certainty of broken bones. But Mar Lon remained in place, studying the mare in the sunlight. "Well, the king likes a good horse as well as any man. I'm certain he'd want to see this one." He drew back, then made a wide gesture to the officer on the ramparts. "Viridis, I'll make the arrangements. Please have your men escort Khitajrah to the king's court."

The trading tongue term for "court" came dangerously close to "courtroom," and Khitajrah barely suppressed a shiver. She felt chilled and excited at once, alternately joyful that she had achieved her goal and cautious about the way the opportunity seemed to have fallen, unexpectedly, into her hands. She guessed either curiosity or attraction had goaded Mar Lon to take her side, but she wondered whether it was herself or the horse that he found appealing. After a full night and day of travel through woodlands, the odds seemed on the side of the mare.

Mar Lon ducked inside the tower. The sentry who had addressed Khitajrah made no move to open the gates. Instead, he stood at attention, waiting.

The lieutenant called down to his men. "Escort her to the king's court. Procedure standard."

As one, the sentries leaned their halberds against the wall. The one who had remained silent throughout the exchange, the shorter of the two, worked the latches and bars. He gestured for Khitajrah to move out of the way, and she retreated several steps, drawing the horse with her. The mare paced backward with short, excited steps. Neck arched, it kept its head low, chin tucked.

The gate swung outward. The instant an opening appeared, the horse bolted for the courtyard. The sudden movement ripped the bridle from Khitajrah's hands, drawing a burning line across her palm. Jerked abruptly forward, she dropped to one knee to keep from falling on her face.

The guard caught the reins as the horse thundered by, jerking its head. Spun by its own momentum, the paint staggered, and its hooves skidded furrows through the rock-speckled mud. Pulled to a sudden stop, it snorted its dissatisfaction; but it did calm.

The sentry who had done the speaking took Khitajrah's arms gently and assisted her to her feet. Wind flicked the soft fabric of his tabard across her wrist. Though slight, the touch brought memories of strong hands and casual nearness, and the odors of leather, oil, steel, and sweat enhanced a sorrow that exhaustion would not allow logic to displace. The eleven years since her husband's death seemed more like eleven hundred. She missed rolling over at night, arm flopping across the warrior largeness that was the man she loved. Without awakening, he would draw her convulsively closer, his massive hands making her feel fragile yet, at the same time, warm and secure. For all of her driving need to protect the women of Stalmize from ancient laws desper-

ately in need of change, there were times when she had enjoyed feeling safe herself. In Harrsha's arms, she could say
anything, tell any secret, knowing he shared her deepest concerns; and he could do the same.

Khitajrah met the sentry's dark eyes, and the emotion disappeared in an instant. A single glance told her that she
shared nothing with this Béarnide and never could. Yet just
the fact that she had considered the possibility made her realize what she had long resisted. Somewhere in the world
lived another man, perhaps more than one, who could replace what she had lost.

Oblivious to Khitajrah's thoughts, the sentry released her
and stepped aside. "Horse stays. Pack stays. Weapons?" He
looked at her, awaiting a response.

"None." Khitajrah still carried a knife, but most people
did so routinely. If they wanted it, too, she felt certain they
would ask. She had secured Arduwyn's pack to the horse,
carrying nothing that did not fit easily into a pocket.

"You'll get everything back when your audience is finished. Come with me."

Khitajrah walked through the gates, and the sentry pulled
them closed behind her. Seeing his companion had taken
charge of the horse, he replaced the latches and locks. Then
he gestured her into the courtyard.

Khitajrah stared at the tended flower gardens and the intricate statues and benches interspersed between them.
Women in gowns and men dressed in satiny garments
perched regally on benches while children chased one another along the winding pathways. Here, too, Khitajrah noticed bears as the predominant theme of the statues. Before
she could stare too long, the sentry led her across the sturdy
planking that bridged the moat and through great iron doors
decorated with a crest that included a rearing bear.

It took a moment for Khitajrah's eyes to adjust to the sudden absence of the sun, though lines of torches lit the corridors almost as brightly. Brackets carved into animal shapes
held the burning torches, tan and blue brocade dangling from
their undersides. The guard's armor clinked as he walked,
and the decorative bands swayed in the breeze of his passage. As she became less concerned with light, Khitajrah noticed old carvings scrawled over part of the wall. Stories
unfolded on what seemed like leagues of corridor, interrupted by cross-corridors and doors. The portion she saw

showed a vast army in armor of leather and chain engaged in battle with a sparse band of savage, blond reavers who wore no protection and wielded only swords. Before she could see how the battle ended, the sentry stopped before a set of teak doors. The royal crest, surrounded by fire opals, filled a fist-sized space on each door, at eye level. A pair of sentries dressed like the ones at the gate stood rigidly before the portals, their halberds crossed before it.

Reluctantly, Khitajrah pulled her gaze from artwork so detailed it seemed to change the depth and dimensions of the hallway. One of the sentries at the door spoke first, in the bland language of the citizens.

Khitajrah's escort gave a monosyllabic response.

The door guards lowered their weapons, and the speaker said something further in the same language. Both men nodded. The escort spun on the ball of one foot and headed back the way they had come, the back of his tabard flapping with the briskness of his walk.

Though Khitajrah had not found the gate guard friendly company, his absence left her feeling uneasy and alone. She had never met with a king before and understood amenities and respectful gestures only in a general sense. Though Harrsha had held General/King Siderin's next highest rank, Khitajrah, as a woman, had never come into the king's presence. From conversation overheard, she knew the Eastern king would as soon slaughter a man as hear his complaint, and his moods had been nearly unreadable even to his closest officers. She hoped King Sterrane would prove more tolerant and less moody and that guards would brief her on court formality.

But the guards pulled the doors open without a word. As the crack widened, brief snatches of conversation escaped, uninterpretable to Khitajrah. A thick, tan carpet stretched from the opening to a granite throne, and benches lined the area on either side of the aisle. Currently, less than a dozen people occupied the benches. All but two were sturdy, dark Béarnide men, one a woman and one a child of about ten years old, perhaps the king's heir learning affairs of court. Eight figures stood in formation around one man perched on the throne. From a distance, she could make out few details of the king and his entourage.

Khitajrah's mouth dried, and a sudden urge to flee seized her. Only the momentum of the paired sentries kept her

heading toward the throne. She had rehearsed her questions
and speech to the king a thousand times, yet it seemed to
have escaped permanently from memory. And chaos remained strangely silent, its composure only mildly soothing.
As an entity without form, it had nothing at risk and no punishment to fear.

As they drew closer, details of the king and his entourage
became apparent. Chaos studied the men through her eyes,
dragging her into its curiosity. They examined the king first.
Even sitting, he exuded size. Clearly, he would stand taller
than even most of the Béarnian men, and his muscled arms
and protruding gut would make him seem like a giant in the
Eastlands. She guessed he would outweigh her three times
over. He wore the standard Béarnian beard, and his gray-
flecked, black hair framed features younger than her own.
He wore a silk shirt, linen pants, and an embroidered, multicolored cloak trimmed with fur. A band circled one finger,
and the oddity of the jewelry caught and held Khitajrah's attention. Crafted of gold and detailed down to individual
hairs, an impeccably etched bear clutched a gemstone like
nothing Khitajrah had ever seen: a milky pearl surrounding
a central black one. If the craftsmen had cut one stone to fit
the other, he had used tools beyond Khitajrah's understanding. More likely, she looked upon a perfect, singular act
of nature. The king also wore a gold necklace, the medal-
lion disappearing beneath his shirt. Otherwise, he wore no
adornment. His thick cascade of hair bore no crown nor
compressed areas to indicate it habitually did.

Mar Lon stood at Sterrane's right hand. He had not bothered to change clothing, which explained how he had managed to arrange the meeting so quickly. His simple tunic and
breeks seemed out of place amid the uniforms of the surrounding guardsmen. He wore a sword at his hip, and she
saw no sign of his mandolin. The only other man who specifically attracted Khitajrah's gaze stood at the king's left
hand. He wore the same blue cloak over the familiar royal
tabard and guardsmen's mail, but a blue plume arched rak-
ishly from his helmet. An occasional black curl peeked from
beneath his headgear, and his features revealed him as a man
well into his thirties. His sword and hilt seemed wider and
longer than the others, a promise of great strength.

As Khitajrah came to the carpet's edge, her escort took a
step back, as one. The focus of the room turned on her, and

she felt as if every eye in the court burned her flesh. Rooted in place, she could not even back away, and it seemed wiser to overguess her gesture of deference than to risk insulting the king. She fell to her knees, then prostrated herself, face flat to a carpet that smelled of soap and deeply ground soil.

A murmur washed into silence. A bass voice directly in front of Khitajrah said something booming in Béarnese. Mar Lon replied. Then the first speaker addressed her directly. "No! Not lay on floor. You fall? Sick?"

Though the tone emerged strong, with authority, the speech pattern mimicked that of a young child.

Khitajrah looked up to find the king's huge, brown eyes focused on her face. He had left his chair to crouch closer to her level, and the guards had shifted with him. Stunned speechless, she found herself capable of nothing but returning the stare. Her mouth seemed too painfully dry to allow speech.

"You not well?" King Sterrane asked.

"No," Khitajrah managed through lips that felt thick. Then, uncertain whether she had responded correctly to the question, she amended. "I mean, yes." She clarified, forcing herself to breathe. The words came more easily. "I'm well . . . majesty."

Despite the reassurance, the king persisted. "You trip?" His gaze rolled to the paired escort, noting positions of feet and halberd butts.

Khitajrah had no wish to cause any guardsman trouble. They had treated her well enough, and every man in her family had been a soldier. "No, majesty." She clambered to her knees. "Just showing my respect, majesty. I'm honored you would agree to see me, majesty."

Mar Lon said something too low for Khitajrah to hear, and the king rocked back on his heels. He turned his attention to his personal bodyguard. "Throwing self at floor?"

Mar Lon said something equally soft. This time, Khitajrah caught only the word "custom." He gestured her to her feet with obvious impatience.

Khitajrah stood.

King Sterrane shrugged. Taking a backward step, he returned to his throne and sat. "Greetings," he said, this time in perfectly enunciated trade. "I hope you fared well in your travels and that your business with Béarn is handled to your satisfaction."

Having just become accustomed to the king's broken
speech pattern, his sudden fluency completely confused
Khitajrah.

Yet, though chaos usually thrived on inconsistency, it
seemed more pensive than excited. *Don't let things rattle
you. Feigned or real, the appearance of composure will
serve you better most times.*

Khitajrah found the advice currently impossible to follow,
but it did give her a moment to think. She had met people
who found any language but their own birth tongue impossible to manage. She had believed them lazy or chauvinistic
until she had watched a neighbor's son struggle himself into
tears trying to learn a few words of Western trading. Apparently, the king had learned a few pat phrases and little more.
She could not help admiring him for his attempt. Few men
would have the courage to risk their dignity, and a king
could just as easily use a translator.

When Khitajrah said nothing for some time, King Sterrane
prompted her. "State your business, please."

"Yes, majesty." Khitajrah glanced around the room, unsettled by the king's undivided attention. Discovering that everyone else watched her as carefully, she returned the king's
scrutiny again. "There are two matters. First, I brought a
horse, majesty. Your ... um ... Mar Lon told me you'd like
to have it. I would like you to have it, majesty. A gift."

What! Chaos seemed to roar through her head. *What
are you doing? We need that horse.*

There was more guile to Khitajrah's idea than chaos
seemed capable of grasping. *Right now, the information
about Colbey is more important than speed. We need the
king's goodwill more.*

Sterrane nodded. "Mar Lon know horses. He say me want
horse, so want horse. He pick trade. If not think fair, let me
know."

Khitajrah wondered if she had heard correctly, so she
chose her reply with care. "I didn't ask for reimbursement,
majesty. I'll give you the horse for nothing."

King Sterrane frowned, in obvious consideration, though
it did not last long. "Thank you. Me take horse." He kept his
gaze on Khitajrah, not bothering to seek counsel with Mar
Lon or his guards. "Then me give you gift. Other horse." He
raised his brows, placing the burden of graciousness upon
his guest.

Khitajrah wondered if the king were less naive than his broken speech patterns made him seem. In one transaction, he had switched the favor, losing nothing in the deal. Yet, in truth, it worked well for her, too. Though she no longer held the king on the receiving end of a gift, she did still have a mount to reach Pudar. "Thank you, majesty."

"That all?"

Khitajrah hesitated, for a moment concerned that her gratitude had not seemed heartfelt enough. But the king's demeanor seemed curious, not annoyed, and she rerouted her train of thought. Apparently, he wanted to know if she had come before him only to trade horses. "No, majesty. I have an important question, too." She glanced around the court, reluctant to speak in front of an audience.

The courtiers, including the child, watched with mild interest. Sterrane encouraged Khitajrah with raised brows, saying nothing.

The question seemed innocent enough. To look uncomfortable about it would only raise suspicions. "I'm seeking a man who traveled with you once, majesty. I wondered if you could tell me where to find him." Khitajrah glanced casually from the king to Mar Lon.

A slight smile formed on the bodyguard's lips, but it was uninterpretable. Both men watched Khitajrah. "Might know," Sterrane said. "Who man?"

Recalling the trouble she had gotten into the last time she mentioned the Renshai, Khitajrah found his name difficult to pronounce aloud. "Colbey Calistinsson."

Mar Lon's smile vanished at once, and wrinkles appeared around his eyes. Clearly, he had expected her to inquire about someone else. Sterrane stroked at his beard, head swaying in a negative response. His thick lips pursed, nearly lost in his beard. "Travel together long time ago. *Long* time ago. Before king. See only once since. He come here then." He gestured to where Khitajrah was standing.

Disappointment fluttered through Khitajrah, and she gathered breath to thank the king for his help. However, Sterrane did not seem finished, so she held her breath and waited.

"Not sure where find Colbey now. Not North, sure. Not East. Would try Pudar." King Sterrane changed focus so smoothly, it took Khitajrah a moment to follow his tack. "Why you want know?"

Caught off guard, Khitajrah responded without thinking. "What?" She added quickly, "Majesty."

"Why you look for Colbey?"

Anticipating the question earlier, Khitajrah had rehearsed tactful ways of proclaiming the knowledge private. However, she had done so in her mind. Now, she seemed unable to form words from the concepts, especially in a second language when she already felt exhausted. Approaches that had seemed clever and facile currently sounded like flimsy excuses. No matter the words, telling a king to mind his own business while in his court seemed blatantly disrespectful, if not dangerous.

Following the obvious direction of Khitajrah's thoughts, chaos intervened. *Fool! Don't tell him. He's a friend of the Renshai.*

Though bothered by the need to lie again, Khitajrah found the sin easy enough to dismiss this time. She had come too far to let small untruths stand in the way of rescuing Bahmyr. Not wanting to delay too long, she responded with the first words that came to mind. "He's my father."

Mar Lon's eyes went hard. Otherwise, his expression did not change. Sterrane's lips bent into a massive smile befitting his hugeness. Suddenly, he leapt from his throne and rushed Khitajrah.

Caught by surprise, Khitajrah never thought to dodge. A moment later, she found herself smothered in a giant embrace. The king's presence felt warm and strong against her, his joy so genuine it reawakened her conscience to a dull ache.

"Colbey daughter." King Sterrane's voice boomed in Khitajrah's ear, and his chest rumbled as he spoke. "Celebrate. Need feast."

The guards pressed in closer. Clearly, they had not anticipated the king's reaction either.

"No, majesty. Please." Khitajrah tried to formulate the remainder of her story in an instant. If he insisted on discussing details with her, especially without sleep, she would surely make a fatal mistake. "I'm in a hurry, and I'm already late for a meeting elsewhere, sire."

Finally, Sterrane's grip loosened, and Khitajrah caught a huge breath. "Mar Lon give fast horse. Rested horse. You need sleep, too. Stay night?"

Nothing sounded more attractive to Khitajrah than a night

of sleep between royal silk sheets in a well-protected castle. But she dared not take the risk that Arduwyn might catch up to her. "Thank you, majesty, that's most generous. But I have to leave as soon as possible. My father doesn't know I'm looking for him, or even that I exist. Majesty, if I don't keep moving faster than he does, I'll never find him."

Sterrane fully released Khitajrah, disappointment clearly etched on his features. The guards shifted closer, the one that had stood at his left hand politely edging between the king and his guest. Sterrane turned his head to Mar Lon. "Take care Colbey's daughter. Give best horse can. Help find right way. Pack whatever need or want."

"Right away, sire," Mar Lon responded briskly and cheerfully, though the look he threw Khitajrah still seemed rock hard. He studied her for only a moment before turning to the other officer. "Captain Baran?"

Baran nodded crisply. "Things are under control here. Take as long as you need."

"Come with me please, Khitajrah Harrsha's-widow." Mar Lon trotted past the woman, then made a beckoning gesture behind his back that indicated she should follow.

Something in the bodyguard's manner worried Khitajrah, and his formal emphasis of her name hinted at things unsaid. Cautiously, she complied.

Fatigue became a hovering fog that dulled Khitajrah's senses and made thinking a chore. She waited on a garden bench in the Béarnian castle courtyard near the royal barn while stable boys and grooms scurried to prepare her mount. It seemed strange to lounge while men worked to assure her comfort, but exhaustion drove all irony from the situation. Gradually, she nodded off on the hard granite and, warmed by the sun, she slept for a few moments.

Mar Lon's voice awakened Khitajrah. "Ready now, lady. Come with me."

Khitajrah jerked awake, stifling a yawn with her hand. "Thank you," she said, only half oriented. Mechanically, she rose, following Mar Lon and a muscled bay gelding toward the outer gates. It moved with docile self-assurance, placing each hoof solidly on the ground. It seemed clearly the equal of the paint she had brought, with one important benefit. Presumably, this horse had no enraged master hunting her as a thief. A well-oiled bridle graced the animal's head, its

buckles glittering in the evening sunlight. The flaps of the
saddle held intricately tooled Béarnian bears with pearls set
as eyes. Two bulging packs hung on either side of the
horse's rump, bound together and to the back of the saddle.
Khitajrah had only requested food and a clean cloak, so the
amount of the supplies surprised her as much as the expensive tack that far surpassed what she had brought.

Not wanting to seem ungrateful, Khitajrah considered
appropriate responses as she followed Mar Lon from the
courtyard, past the sentries, and into the streets of Béarn.

When Mar Lon still did not stop to allow Khitajrah to
mount, the focus of her attention shifted to her host. Although
she could not muster alarm, she could feel chaos fretting in
her mind. Either something seemed amiss to it as well, or it
damned the delay caused by waiting for preparations. Now
that she studied Mar Lon directly and closely, Khitajrah noticed that he carried his mandolin again, slung across his
back. He wore a close-fitting pair of leather work gloves. Although the sword still hung at his hip, his hands checked the
instrument's fastenings repeatedly, never settling near the hilt.
Apparently, he was more prepared to play than to fight.

Mar Lon continued leading the horse, Khitajrah following
a step behind. Béarnides watched them pass from cottage
windows or looked up from chores. Some waved at Mar
Lon, and he responded with efficient gestures that seemed
friendly yet foiled conversation. A few of the more persis-
tent citizens shouted or begged for songs, all of which Mar
Lon dismissed with hand signals. He did not bother to speak.

As they continued toward the outskirts of town, Khitajrah
started to wonder if some law forbade riding horses through
Béarn. Her eagerness to arrive in Pudar turned into impatience, and lack of sleep added a belligerent streak that she
scarcely managed to stifle. Silence taxed her least, and she
worried what might emerge from her mouth if she tried to
speak in her current mood. Yet she knew she would have to
say something soon, or Mar Lon might accompany her all
the way to Pudar.

As cobbled street gave way to forested, earthen pathways,
Khitajrah cleared her throat. She concentrated on the amenities she had considered earlier to keep from saying anything inappropriately harsh about Mar Lon's delay. "Your
king is too generous." She indicated the fancy tack and protruding packs.

"Yes," Mar Lon replied, though whether out of rudeness or because his thoughts had distracted him from the gist of Khitajrah's comment, she could not tell. At length, beyond sight of the city, Mar Lon fastened the lead rope securely around an oak and turned to face Khitajrah directly. "Sit." He indicated a rock.

Khitajrah hesitated, wariness finally cutting over exhaustion. "Why?"

"Consider it part of the king's generous hospitality."

Khitajrah responded in kind. "The king has been far too generous already," she reminded, her voice as steady as his. "I'm in a hurry."

"I know," Mar Lon said. "And I believe I know why. Rest assured, no one else will harm you here. I'll see to that."

Else?

Khitajrah did not need chaos' help to find the important word in Mar Lon's promise. "No one else? So you would hurt me?"

"I have no plans to do so." Mar Lon removed his plumed cap, spilling brown hair to the nape of his neck. "So long as you grant me an audience."

"Ah." Khitajrah nodded sagely, though she spoke with sarcasm. "You must be one fine musician to need threats of violence to hold your audience." Nevertheless, she sat in the indicated place. The townsfolk's entreaties for his talent had sounded sincere and so had his threat.

Mar Lon's expression did not change, and he gave no sign that he took offense at the comment. "You may assess my competence after you've heard me play. But you will hear me play."

Many questions came to Khitajrah's mind at once. She wondered why Mar Lon believed she feared an attack. Though it was fact, he had no way to know such a thing. Even if he did, he had given no sign that he understood the specifics. It seemed madness for a king's bodyguard to insist on accompanying her beyond the borders of the royal city and even stranger to insist on a concert once there. The oddity brought a flicker of memory to the fore, though she could not quite place its detail or significance.

Mar Lon ducked through the strap of his mandolin. Leaning against the horse's oak, he balanced the instrument on his knee. His body shielded the lead rope. Clearly, he was

taking no chances that Khitajrah might try to grab the horse
and escape before he finished.

Khitajrah settled comfortably on the stone. For now, Mar
Lon seemed to have no intention of violence. His king had
spoken; and the law bound Mar Lon to obedience, unless he
sensed some threat to Sterrane. Since she had no designs
against the Westlands' high king, Khitajrah did not see such
a thing as a legitimate concern. If Mar Lon wanted her dead,
it made no sense for him to serenade her first; though
Khitajrah could think of no logical reason for him to sing to
her in any case.

The first chord chimed from the mandolin, each note crisp
and clear, the blend so pure it seemed like a single note itself. Those that followed held equal skill, intermingled with
runs and trills that came so fast Khitajrah's mind longed for
each previous note before the next pealed out and made her
forget the one before. Despite her fatigue, she found herself
becoming lost in the fragile web of sound, and that pleased
her. Her body felt light, free of the ponderous burden lack of
sleep had laid upon her. Her mind stretched and lifted, as if
it might float into a distant eternity, a world without war or
responsibilities, where sons lived out their natural lifespan in
happiness. Though wary, she reveled in the freedom the
bard's song gave her. A long time had passed since she had
known joy, and its source did not matter.

Then, Mar Lon began his song, using the Eastern tongue,
striking each note so solidly they seemed to have no resonance:

> *"Our world began in chaos shadowed,*
> *Nothing could be real.*
> *Then Odin banished magic, placed*
> *Man's world on even keel.*

> *"Law has ruled us since that day*
> *With honor and faith and form.*
> *It gives our world logical pattern:*
> *Night follows day; clouds storm.*

> *"But Odin guides things near and far*
> *His hand too strong for men.*
> *So he placed four Wizards here*
> *As mankind's guardian.*

"One champions evil in the East,
His manner cruel and vile.
Northward, the Sorceress of good
Combats him all the while.

"The last two champion the West,
Neutral, it appeared.
Never dreaming of the fate
That Odin deemed their weird.

"With law alone, the world remained
Stable and safe for all.
Yet long routine brings stasis that
Slows genius to a crawl.

"Though chaos harbors Odin's doom
And that of gods and men.
With law alone, our worlds stagnate
Into oblivion.

"A day would come, Odin declared
A Wizard would arise.
Bold enough to wield the source
Of dishonor, sin, and lies.

"The Gray God made a trial that
Would kill all but the best.
Millennia later, Colbey came
And passed Odin's great test.

"Now causes four and Wizards four
Trained to sanction extremes.
Yet three to one they champion law
And the last must die, it seems.

"Generations lived and died
While Odin picked the one,
Competent to moderate
The amount of chaos done.

"Yet the Cardinal Wizards see only
Their own causes to fight.

*The dedication that empowers them
Also blinds them to the light.*

*"They say: battle chaos with its own,
Forgetting in their rage,
That law embodies honor kept
No matter the war they wage.*

*"When chaos conquers Wizards four
Mankind seems sure to fall,
Especially when some have already
Heeded chaos' call.*

*"The gods cannot come to our aid
Their power too vast to balance.
The Wizards all have fallen prey
Our world to them a dalliance.*

*"The time has come for men to join
Together in desperate need,
To sacrifice personal interest,
To cast aside their greed.*

*"No champion left, men must fight
Or collapse again into the void.
Chaos' promises: hollow lies boding
A ruin even gods can't avoid."*

As the last notes pealed forth from the instrument,
Khitajrah found herself in tears. The individual words had
not registered, rather the seamless combination of melody
and voice had seemed to flay open her soul to reveal the ugliness inside. She felt innocent as an infant, cleansed of the
crimes she had committed, in her own name and in that of
chaos. The music of the forest replaced Mar Lon's talent, revealing the steady wash of leaves in wind, the first faint
chirrups of birds, and the muffled clanks and rattles of working Béarnides. Reality returned to Khitajrah in a rush, making camaraderie between communities of mankind seem like
a naive and foolish dream. Chaos' presence felt like a lead
weight in her mind. Though it lay still and silent, Khitajrah
directed her thoughts at it accusingly. *Is what he sang
true?*

It is his interpretation of truth.

The answer seemed like a dodge. *What does that mean? Are you afraid to answer the question?*

No, chaos seemed unruffled. *I simply see no reason to bother answering. If I told you he spoke lies, would you believe me?*

Khitajrah considered for a moment. *Probably not.*

Then the question is as pointless as the answer.

Chaos made sense to Khitajrah this time, though she cared little for its approach or its attitude. *Tell me which parts you find truth and which lies. I'll form my own opinion, but wouldn't you like to have a say?*

Apparently, the logic behind her comment convinced it. *He's right about the history; I've told you that before. Odin did banish chaos, and the world has stagnated under the influence only of law. But the Chaosbringer's bounty is knowledge and cleverness, not destruction.* Chaos lapsed into its vibrating equivalent of laughter. *And this singer-man has sadly misinterpreted the Wizards and their motives.*

Which are? Khitajrah pressed.

You're not ready for the explanation at this time.

Try me, Khitajrah insisted.

Chaos went dormant, spreading its formless tendrils through her thoughts, its touch almost imperceptible.

Before Khitajrah could protest further, Mar Lon's singing again caught her attention, the chords forming a golden harmony to his words. This time, he used the trading tongue, though he chose an Eastern rhyme scheme:

"War raged like a stallion across the dark plains;
Eastern sword met Western in a wild clash of steel.
The West for its own, the East for land gains,
Each soldier concerned for the hand death might deal.

"The Great War spawned heroes, much more than its share:
Child, swordsman, then corpse in less than a day.
West, Santagithi's strategies blazed the battle fare,
His soldiers bedecked in his black and his gray.

"Grand in his helmet of spires and spines,
Sheriva's chosen, Siderin, sparked his Eastern horde
Two skilled lieutenants kept his ranks in perfect lines
Boldly, they stormed westward for love of their lord.

"As prophecy promised, the West's proven champion:
A Golden-Haired devil from the North tribe of Renshai.
Colbey slashed through East ranks in a reckless run
And every blade slash drove an Easterner to die.

"The great axman, Narisen, met death in this fashion,
Skull staved by the hooves of the Renshai's bay mount.
Siderin's other sent many men crashin'
Harrsha's skill claiming too many Westmen to count.

"The War's other two Renshai brought Harrsha to bear.
Killed amidst many, in the war's thickest heat.
Sword mistress Mitrian and Captain Rache did share
The burden of slaying the Eastlands' elite.

"Colbey fought the final battle as the Eastern king fled.
Renshai blade against poison and spiked chain flail.
Yet a moment before sword could stab Siderin dead,
A blue and gold arrow pierced Siderin's mail.

"So the West won the war, thanks to a demon prince
And a one-eyed archer who dared steal a Renshai's kill.
And I hope that you've gathered from all of my hints,
That I know who you are and that you serve chaos' will.

"Your lies are transparent; Colbey's sterile, I know.
And you came riding the horse of the king's best friend.
Warriors never hold grudges against fair-fighting foe,
Honorable death, not for mother nor wives to defend.

The first mention of her dead husband had stunned
Khitajrah deeper into her silence. Initially, she believed Mar
Lon had responded only to her name and her quest for
Colbey, yet the last verses told otherwise. Clearly, he had
ad-libbed the song, or at least its final lines; and the wisdom
inherent in it shuddered panic through her. *He knows everything! How could he know everything?*

Calm! chaos demanded. *He doesn't know everything.
There were mistakes in his history, and he's wrong about
you, too. He thinks you're after Colbey from revenge.*

Chaos' explanation soothed Khitajrah enough to delve rational thought from beneath fear and fatigue. She forced

composure to settle over her expression and voice before attempting speech. "How do you know so much?"

Mar Lon lowered his instrument, but he did not duck back through the strap. "It's the curse of the eldest child of my line to seek knowledge, Khitajrah *Harrsha*'s-widow. And it's also my job to support the king of Béarn. He stands for neutrality, true central balance. He doesn't judge, and neither do I."

Khitajrah yawned, pressed by the need to give the bard her full attention. Even the threat of death seemed unable to breach the fog. "So what happens now?"

"That's your decision." Mar Lon stepped aside, no longer blocking Khitajrah's route to the horse's lead rope. "I know Arduwyn well, and I can think of no more competent judge of human nature than him. In the woodlands, no one could find Arduwyn, or his camp, unless he arranged it. If he let you come close enough to steal his horse, then he trusted you. That means he saw something he respected deep within you, perhaps something chaos has suppressed." Mar Lon frowned at a thought that must have just arisen. "I don't believe you harmed him. You carried no weapon, and even Colbey would find slaying Arduwyn a challenge in the forest. I can only hope that the spark Arduwyn saw grows strong enough to shake the yoke chaos has lain upon you."

Rage coursed through Khitajrah, though the tired haze precluded strong emotion. Clearly, chaos had responded to Mar Lon's words, and the intensity of its reaction gave Khitajrah pause to wonder. *Later. Right now, I'm too tired to think.* She studied Mar Lon again. His features seemed plain, yet the plumed hat shadowing his face lent him an air of mystery and the coordination of his movements marked him as a trained warrior. Though mousy hazel in color, his gaze tended to fix unwaveringly on subjects, deeply socketed and hard with character. His dress seemed conservative and flashy at once, the cut allowing free movement. Yet the tailoring was crisp and the colors boldly Béarn royal. Surely, he had deduced much from the moment he heard her name and saw her perched upon Arduwyn's horse. But he had had the patience to keep his understanding to himself, directing events with a gentle hand that gained him knowledge yet yielded nothing.

When Khitajrah did not speak, Mar Lon added one more thing. "You may go. I'd like to leave you with another song."

Though Khitajrah hated the idea of more delay, she saw no means to refuse the request. Mar Lon's information, in some hands, would surely prove another death sentence. It seemed madness to do anything but remain as much in his favor as possible. And, although she hated to admit such a thing, she longed for more of the bard's sweet talent. Despite their topics, his songs had relaxed her in a way she had not known in more than a decade, since the first hint of the Great War had touched the Eastlands.

This time, the gentle desperation of Mar Lon's melody nearly soothed her into sleep. He sang in the Eastern tongue, of harmony in a time of strife, of wolves and rabbits curled together in quiet sleep, and of enemies laying aside weapons to teach one another the best of their cultures. Within half a verse, Khitajrah found herself humming along with the tune. And, by the second verse, the words came to her as he mouthed them. *I know this song.* It seemed impossible. *I do know this song.*

The answer followed in an instant, bringing a rush of the memory that had defied her and now filled her eyes with tears. The words and tune had come to her in a much cruder form, from her youngest son who knew poetry, not music. She pictured his soft, brown locks and eyes. Lighter colored and smaller than his brothers had been at the same age, he seemed frail in every way. Yet, she remembered the excitement that had made him prance around the cottage, strumming an imaginary instrument, his eyes alight with purpose. Khitajrah waited only until the echoes of the last note partially faded. "You're him. You're the bard, Marlon." She twisted the crisp Western pronunciation to fit the Eastern vowels. It sounded more like My-er-*layne,* the three syllables slurred into a single word and the last part enunciated.

"That's what Ellbaric and his friends called me." Mar Lon's expression remained serious, and genuine sorrow filmed his eyes with tears as well.

"Ellbaric," Khitajrah repeated. The name she had given her youngest son sounded strange after so many years. "You remember him?"

"I remember all of the young men who supported peace. They could have started a new generation of tranquillity between all men and women, if Siderin hadn't grabbed them for his troops."

"Ellbaric died in that war."

"I know that."

"He never wanted to be a soldier, like his father and brother. He wanted to become a bard."

Mar Lon restrung his mandolin. "I'm flattered. He had talent with poetry. With the right teacher and a world at peace, he might have succeeded."

"Yes," Khitajrah said. She had many things to consider, but for now it seemed easier to let them lie. Currently, she could not feel certain she knew chaos' will from her own. One thing seemed certain, talk of her youngest child only made her long more for Bahmyr and the single act of violence, killing Colbey, that stood between them.

"Someday," Mar Lon said. "When and if our causes ever come together, I'll sing you the lyrics that Ellbaric wrote for me."

Khitajrah's first instinct, to beg for the tune, passed quickly. Even through exhaustion's veil, she remained dimly wise enough to understand that the timing was wrong. Someday, she might hear that song; but, for now, the price of another son's life seemed too much to pay. "I look forward to that." She headed for the horse.

Mar Lon untied the lead rope, holding the gelding in place while Khitajrah mounted. "Take the forest path north. Whenever you come to a branch, always take the largest and best traveled route. Pudar is the center of trade, even for Northmen and Easterners. Every road in the West, by land or river, will eventually get you there."

Khitajrah placed a foot in the left stirrup, then flung her other leg over the bulging packs. Once she settled into the saddle, Mar Lon handed her the lead rope. "Farewell," he said. "But I hope you'll understand that I won't wish you luck."

Khitajrah looped the rope around the saddle horn. "Well, good luck to you, then. And to King Sterrane. Please thank him profusely for generosity I have no way to repay."

"Kindness is simply his way. Your gratitude will only confuse him, but I'll deliver it anyway." Mar Lon let the obvious answer to repayment remain unsaid.

Kicking the horse into a slow trot, Khitajrah headed toward Pudar, looking from the first for a likely place to set up camp.

CHAPTER 19

Crossroad Fyn's

A quarter moon straggled lines through Pudar's straight, wide streets, glimmering silver from irregularities amid the cobbles. Dressed in the tan shirt and britches of his guard uniform, Lirtensa patrolled the upper east side, his partner pacing a parallel course several streets farther westward. He marched a winding path between the dark shapes of the flophouses and rented cottages that housed most of Pudar's temporary visitors from more distant locales. This late, even the rowdier foreigners had settled into taverns or gone to bed for the night, and only an occasional individual or small group whisked through Pudar's alleyways.

Unlike the majority of his fellow guardsmen, Lirtensa preferred night duty. The cool twine of fresh night air through Pudar's alleyways seemed like an old and welcome friend. He especially preferred the western breezes that brought the smell of damp from Trader's Lake. During the day, the ceaseless rush and shuffle of patrons through Pudar's market, and the petty skirmishes this caused, annoyed him. He found nothing interesting or exciting about breaking up housewives tussling over fruit or pacifying enraged patrons who felt they had gotten the raw end of a sale. The all or nothing pattern of Pudar's nights intrigued him more. Usually, the city remained quiet once the shops and stands had closed, leaving Lirtensa to conduct his own personal business. When a problem did occur at night, it was rarely trivial; but his connections to the seedier parts of the great trading city often allowed him to resolve the situation quickly.

Lirtensa turned into one of the threadlike alleyways between a row of shops that pandered to the foreign soldiers on furlough who stayed on Pudar's upper east side. The gaudy architecture of the gambling house included a jaggedly edged rain gutter. Its pattern drew scalloped shadows through the alley, plunging it into a darkness that did not faze Lirtensa. Through the years, night had become as familiar as his guardsman's uniform, and he prided himself on perceiving presence and movement without sight.

Yet, this time, Lirtensa's talent failed him. Without warning, an arm looped around his throat. A stifling hand clamped over his mouth, and he felt the cold touch of steel through his shirt against his spine.

Accustomed to rough dealers, Lirtensa did not panic. He went still, waiting. As professionally as the stalker had ambushed him, if his attacker wanted him dead, he would be so already.

A voice hissed into his ear, low and coarse, Eastern in accent. "Lirte?"

Easterners had called Lirtensa by this designation before. He also knew they shortened names to indicate station, reducing those of inferiors in much the same way Westerners did so as to indicate informality and friendship. He nodded once cautiously.

"You will not scream," the Easterner said.

It was a statement not a question, and the implication that he might shriek in terror offended Lirtensa. Again, he nodded.

The hand disappeared from his mouth, and he no longer felt the dagger at his back. The stalker released him with a brisk, strong movement that spun him completely around.

Lirtensa caught his balance with as much dignity as possible and studied the other through the darkness. Bold defiance and composure seemed to work best with the compassionless. Gradually, his eyes carved form from blackness. The stalker was a woman, through she stood tall enough to meet his gaze directly level. She wore a single-piece black outfit that buttoned from neck to crotch. Her short, raven hair seemed as blunt as her manner, and her swarthy skin made her appear like the incarnate figure of darkness itself.

Despite his courage, Lirtensa could not escape a jolt of surprise. He had never seen such confidence exuded by any woman. From an Eastern woman, it seemed horribly misplaced. For the first time in months, Lirtensa knew the stirrings of fear.

The woman's black eyes roved over Lirtensa only briefly.

She seemed bored by him. "You have a client who plans to kill Colbey Calistinsson."

Lirtensa brushed a greasy curl from his face. Though intimidated, he would not allow himself to seem so. "A strange assumption, lady. One I couldn't admit even were it true."

Her expression went even more stony. "My name is not lady. It's Chezrith. Do not change or butcher it, or I will respond in kind." Clearly, "in kind" did not refer to Lirtensa's name. "And I didn't ask you a question. Until I do, you need not speak." Steel flashed momentarily as she tossed her dagger from right hand to left, then plucked another, fully sheathed, from a slit in her boot. "Give this to he or she who plans to kill the Renshai."

Lirtensa fixed his blue eyes on Chezrith, saying nothing, simply waiting for her to explain. Information volunteered cost nothing, and a quiet calm usually fared better than chattiness. Besides, she had not questioned him, and Lirtensa knew better than to antagonize one who had already proven her competence.

"It contains a deadly poison."

Poison. The promise intrigued Lirtensa nearly as much as the woman discomforted him. He had obtained toxins for clients before. Enough money would send him in search of even the illegal types, most of which required milking deadly reptiles or distilling massive quantities of Eastern herbs. But few dared to handle a substance that posed nearly as much danger to wielder as victim.

"The assassin will need to get close to him; a passing scratch won't do. A vital stab would be best, of course. The poison works quickly, but nothing can kill instantaneously; and Colbey will fight to his last breath."

A chill shuddered through Lirtensa; he managed to suppress the outward signs. He had worked with Easterners and their evil before, but the depth of this woman's casual cruelty went beyond his normal clientele. He had no wish to work with her and even less to arouse her rage. He sought a tactful way out of the association. He made no move to take the dagger. "I can't pay for this."

"I have no use for your money, Lirte. I want only one thing, the staff Colbey carries. Handle it as little as possible and with care. Its danger makes even my own seem paltry."

Chezrith sneered. "Just see to it my gift finds the right hands."

Lirtensa avoided the woman's direct and solid gaze, hating to become indebted to such a creature, yet seeing no way to refuse. "Thank you," he said, modulating his voice to sound respectful but not too grateful. Gushing, like begging for mercy, seemed to incite the cruelty in people such as Chezrith. He reached for the proffered dagger balanced on her palm.

As Lirtensa took the weapon, Chezrith closed her fingers over his. He swiveled his eyes to meet hers, finding them a flat, depthless black that did not differentiate pupil from iris. She spoke, her voice passionless. "If I find out this weapon got used against any enemy but Colbey, I will extract payment." The corners of her mouth flicked upward into the most repulsive grin Lirtensa had ever seen. "And it won't be in money."

Threats of any kind angered Lirtensa, but he held his tongue. He had not lasted so long among Pudar's ugliest by delivering faulty goods or promises. "I'll see to it that the dagger reaches my client. I can't vouch, nor become responsible, for a client's competence. If you want me to hire a professional, I'll try to arrange it. I'll have to pay him dearly, assuming I can even find one willing to stand against Colbey."

Chezrith laughed. "There are advantages to amateurs. Ignorance sires courage. A man can't fear obstacles he doesn't see." She released Lirtensa's hand.

Lirtensa took the dagger. Thumbing aside the hidden flaps in his belt, he nestled it inside. The knot of its presence against his skin made him want to squirm, irrationally afraid it might poison him through two layers of leather and one of cloth. "There are still some obstacles *I* can see. First, my client was supposed to meet me two days ago. More importantly, I haven't made much progress finding Colbey."

Chezrith back-stepped slightly, deeper into the shadows. The darkness hid her eyes and her expression. "The Renshai has many enemies. If this client doesn't come, have patience. Another will. As to Colbey's whereabouts, he's in Bruen. If he survives there . . ." She paused, apparently savoring some private knowledge. ". . . chances are almost certain he'll come here. Anything he wants, he can find in Pudar, and I have reason to believe he'll have need of a horse." Another smirking pause ensued before she finished. "If he doesn't head for Pudar, surely you can track him elsewhere."

Lirtensa tried to phrase his dilemma without sounding demanding. "Spies cost money, Lady Chezrith."

"Money." Chezrith made a sudden movement.

Before Lirtensa thought to move aside, a fist-sized pouch carved an arc through the air, landing at his feet with muffled clinks. Lirtensa's heart quickened. He knew the sound of coins too well, and no music seemed more beautiful. Cautiously, he crouched, the offering disappearing into his callused, dirt-rimed hand in an instant. Even as he rose, sudden pain blossomed through his thigh. Startled as well as hurt, he skittered aside, his other hand clawing his sword free in an instant.

Chezrith remained in the same place. Though Lirtensa could not see her face, her stance alone told him she was smiling. Now safely distanced from her, he let his attention stray momentarily to the agony of his leg. A blade had sliced a gash in the fabric of his uniform britches. A jagged cut in the skin of his leg gaped, trailing blood in a long stain. He pressed his back to the wall, sword angled between himself and the threat.

When Chezrith still did not move but simply watched him with unconcealed amusement, Lirtensa applied pressure to the wound. Pain and rage banished all thought of politeness. "You bitch! Why in hell did you do that?"

Chezrith let the silence hang before answering with the same deliberate composure she had maintained from the start. "I just wanted to give you something to remember me." Her laugh rumbled through the alleyway.

The shouts and rumbling waves of conversation that filled Pudar's market streets echoed in Colbey's ears, and he wondered if he would ever fully adjust to the noise. Westerners from scores of towns pressed along the city roadways, a single solid mass of movement. Occasionally, a swarthy Easterner or a bearded, braided Northman wandered through the crowd, looking conspicuously out of place and lost amid the hubbub. Yet, despite the size of the crowd crammed onto the cobbled streets, and its seemingly constant motion, Colbey found method to the chaos. The citizens did not touch one another as they moved, whether with the steady flow of traffic or at a separate, personal pace. And they seemed to take extra care not to trample or shove the children, a commodity war and disease had made more precious than any item sold on the streets.

Taking advantage of the conventions that left at least small gaps between the shoppers, Colbey threaded a swift steady course through the Pudarian square. Years of combat had taught him to assess distances and decisions in an instant, as well as to know the position of every part of his body, and of those around him, at all times. Disinterested in the shine and glimmer of the merchants' wares, he kept a pace triple that of the general cadence. Not once did he brush another, even with the awkwardly long staff or the two swords at his belt.

A mixed conglomeration of spices thickened air already choked with the odor of warm, unwashed bodies. Merchants or their assistants screamed for attention, trying to catch individual gazes in the mass of movement. Any patron who paused to look became the instant focus of the sellers, and even Colbey found fruit and trinkets pressed on him by merchants extolling the virtues of their products. Colbey shifted to the center, away from the shops and stands, where the traffic tended to remain thinner.

Though Colbey hurried, the vigilance that had become necessary routine showed him a general aura of contentment that had not been a part of the trading city's past. Job openings had become myriad and varied, left by citizens turned soldiers then corpses and the offspring they did not sire. As a result, youths found more choice when it came to apprenticeships, and they gravitated toward the traders they preferred rather than those who needed them. As a teacher, Colbey had always found enthusiasm the greatest boon to education; few students frustrated him more than those with natural talent but no will to learn. By selecting preferred livelihoods, the youths brought new fire, flare, and competence to their labors and a bright future to a Westlands that the Wizards believed would soon fall to chaos' destruction. The elders' need for extra hands forced them to treat their children with the seriousness and respect due adults, as the constantly warring Renshai had done for centuries.

The *aristiri* perched on Colbey's shoulder, calm despite the shove and bustle of the Pudarian square. Formynder's composure surprised and pleased the Renshai. He had not expected the shy hawk to remain with him through the clamor of a trading town, yet it seemed unruffled by the sights and sounds around it. It hunkered down on Colbey's shoulder, shifting with each dodge through the crowd, its talons clasping only onto cloth and sparing the Renshai's flesh beneath cloak and tunic.

At length, the roadway opened onto a central crossroads from which five streets radiated like the legs of a beetle. In its middle, too many horses crammed into a trampled, muddy pasture. They stood in lines, nose to rump, swatting flies in circular patterns that fanned their tails across neighboring muzzles. A barn abutted the building, the odor of hay wafting from it and a gaily painted sign tacked to the side. It read: "Crossroad Fyn's World's Best Horses."

The motley sampling of animals in the pasture gave Colbey little on which to pin his hopes. He had come more from a need for completion than any hope he might find a suitable steed. He had already visited every other stable in Pudar, and he had left this one for last. In the heart of the marketplace, its prices would far exceed those of the farmers or dealers on the fringes and travelers would daily pick over the best of its stock. He had hoped that the imminence of evening and market closing would thin the crowds. Yet, as the sun approached the horizon, its sinking rays silvering the last hour of open marketing, Colbey still found himself weaving through the masses.

Little traffic filled the square itself. Horses had a specific clientele, rarely impulsively bought, and nearly all of the patrons quickly dispersed along their chosen path without giving the stable a second glance.

Colbey approached the pasture, savoring the clean, crisp air and the elbow room he had gained. He studied the horses, each stomping hoof and whisking tail. He saw nothing irresistible, nor even particularly interesting. He dismissed twelve of sixteen simply because of the position and shape of their muscles. Three of the culls shifted forehooves as well as hind, apparently lame. Most of the others would serve as short distance riding horses, reasonable transportation to nearby towns in the West. Of the remaining four, two carried too much weight to manage the quick escapes or narrow maneuvering required for combat. Another kept its head low, spirit broken by some previous master. The last had rheumy eyes and cracked hooves, sick or aged.

The *aristiri* hopped to the upper rail, skittering back and forth. Apparently, it, too, appreciated the open space and a chance to stretch its legs and wings.

Colbey sighed, wondering if he had become too picky. A mount like Frost Reaver came once in a lifetime or never, selectively bred by the Erythanian king and chosen by knights to whom a horse was as important as a sword was to a Renshai. He knew he would probably never find another as valuable, in looks, competence, or temperament; nor did he have such a need. *I only have to find something that can take me to Béarn.* The thought brought a nervous smile. When he reunited with Frost Reaver, he had no guarantee that he could win the horse's confidence back. And to take a risk on an inferior steed with Wizards chasing him was folly. His only defense against their magic was a swift attack. A horse that bucked or shied would prove worse than no mount at all.

Apparently in response to Colbey's scrutiny of the horses, a man emerged from the stable. He wore a stained, homespun shirt and britches, and a leather apron protected his legs. Hay spotted his hair, and wisps jutted from every pocket. He rubbed grimy hands together, redistributing the dirt, and grinned at Colbey. "Good lot of horses there, eh?"

"Eh," Colbey repeated, disgusted. He had spent the day studying inferior horses while farmers and merchants extolled the virtues of nags. "If you don't mind walking."

The man's smile disappeared. "There's one or two out there that's not the best. But any of them would serve a traveler well enough."

Formynder ruffled its feathers, but otherwise remained still.

"Not this traveler." Colbey shook his head, knowing he should never have bothered to come here. The wade through hordes of shoppers had made him irritable, and he had no patience for another merchant's pitch. "Got anything inside?" He jerked a thumb toward the barn.

The horse merchant glanced over Colbey briefly, taking in the plain but well tailored clothing, the staff, and the paired swords at his hips. Though unadorned, the steel weapons should tell the merchant that he carried at least some money, though he had given nearly all of it to the farmer in Bruen. Then the stranger's gaze alighted on Formynder, and he stared. Without taking his eyes from the bird, he asked. "Is that an *aristiri?*"

Colbey followed the merchant's focus. "Yes."

"Is it male or female?"

The question seemed ludicrous. As far as Colbey could tell, neither this bird nor any other had obvious sexual orientation. "Male, I think. I wouldn't know." Recalling something that Captain had said, he added. "It does sing."

The merchant nodded. "Male, then." Reluctantly, he tore his gaze from the bird to Colbey. "May I touch it?"

This query seemed even more ridiculous. "That would have to be the bird's decision."

Hesitantly, the man extended a finger, moving it slowly toward the hawk. It turned its head so that one black-rimmed, blue eye gazed directly at the approaching digit, but it did not move. With an expression of indignation, it allowed the stranger to run a gentle finger along its crest twice. Then, apparently having had enough, it bounced to Colbey's shoulder.

"Inside?" Colbey reminded, scarcely daring to believe anything could distract a merchant from a sale.

The man's gaze swept from Colbey's shoulder to his face. "Two inside. Two of the finest you'll have ever seen. Come with me."

Colbey doubted the claim. Frost Reaver aside, he had plucked the superior steeds from many herds. Then, he had been able to settle for underworked or overfed horses with potential; his training and that of others had turned them into the Renshai's best war mounts. Still, it only made sense to peruse what the merchant had. He followed the man to the stable and inside.

Hay filled most of the stalls, and barrels of water and grain lined one wall. A portion of the building had been roped aside for well-oiled bridles, halters, and saddles, apparently for sale. An assortment of pitchforks, shovels, and hay hooks lay propped against the walls or scattered across the floor. Ropes dangled from an overhead loft, looped over pulleys anchored in the ceiling. Two horses occupied separate stalls, with an empty one between them. The merchant indicated a massive buckskin that pranced within the confines, its hooves crashing repeatedly against the wood with a strength that made it shudder. It had chewed the upper lip of wood into pale irregularities. Light filtering in from the doorway made its golden hide shimmer.

Colbey looked beyond the obvious beauty of its coloring, finding a compactness that hinted of strength. However, the comparatively narrow chest promised little in the way of endurance, and the slender rump would make it a poor sprinter. Its obvious high-spirited nervousness boded poorly for training.

"Precious Prince of Gold. A young stallion that would make any warrior a spirited war horse. . . ."

Colbey paid no attention to the merchant's sales pitch. Instead, he focused on the chestnut gelding in the opposite stall. Though it had none of its counterpart's eye-catching color, its coat gleamed. Wide nostrils flared, and its dark eyes looked healthfully clear. Though not the most finely proportioned horse he had ever seen, it surpassed anything he had yet found in Pudar.

". . . obvious leader, with sunlight glaring from golden horse and silver buckles—"

Colbey interrupted. "How much will you take for this one?"

"Aah!" The merchant brightened at the prospect of a sale. "A fine gelding. Foaled and raised by a sergeant forced to sell to pay off gambling debts. It—"

Colbey interrupted again. "I don't need historical references." The more merits the merchant created, the steeper the price would become. "How much do you want for the horse?"

"For someone who knows horses as well as you? Twenty gold *chroams* and worth every one." It was ten times the asking price of the next most expensive steed in Pudar and more than double the amount the Renshai carried.

Colbey rubbed at the fur of the gelding's neck, scowling as he examined it closely.

Intrigued by Colbey's interest, the merchant examined the area as well. "What are you looking for?"

"Gold plating."

The merchant's expression twisted in confusion.

"I'll give you six."

The confusion disappeared, replaced by a grimace that bordered on rage. "That's an insult."

Colbey sighed, little adept at bargaining. In his youth, what the Renshai wanted, they took. "I've only got eight."

"I paid more than that myself." Despite his earlier irritation, the merchant seemed more pensive than angry.

Annoyance fluttered through Colbey. He sensed a salesman's game, and he wanted nothing to do with it. Money meant little to him. Had he carried the twenty, he would have given it without argument. This merchant could flatter and weasel all day, but it would not place the money in Colbey's pocket nor in the seller's hands. He had wasted a day of travel coming to Pudar from Bruen, hoping to make up that and more by having a mount to ride as well as obtaining enough food so that he would not have to stop. Yet during the past day, he had examined horse after horse, finding nothing suitable until now. And this one he could not afford.

"I think we can work something out," the merchant said.

Hope trickled through Colbey, though it held an edge of wariness. Twenty gold *chroams* would buy an expensive favor from a warrior, and he would not compromise his honor for anything. Still, it would not hurt to hear the merchant's proposition.

"I'll trade you that horse." He indicated the gelding. "For the *aristiri*."

Colbey's gaze went naturally to the hawk. He did not reply, confused by the barter.

The merchant tented his fingers, a nervousness to the gesture. "Horse for hawk. A fair trade, I think."

"More than fair," Colbey admitted carefully. "Something you own for something I don't own."

Disappointment colored the merchant's features. "It belongs to someone else?"

"It's a bird." Colbey explained what seemed obvious to him. "I'd as easily give you ownership of the sky or the moon. The *aristiri* decided to travel with me, and I'd be hard-pressed to stop it if I wanted to. I can't make it stay with you."

The merchant smiled. "This is Pudar. Anything not expressly illegal can be bought and sold. You give me the hawk. I'll find a way to keep it."

Colbey turned his head to examine the *aristiri*. He did not own the bird, and that alone was reason enough to refuse the merchant's offer. Yet his need for the horse was great enough to let consideration flit briefly through his mind. Realization accompanied it. Despite his insistence to the contrary, the hawk had become more than a bird that followed him without reason or encouragement. If it no longer accompanied him, he would miss it; and he owed it a debt of loyalty.

As if to help Colbey make his decision, the *aristiri* drove its beak into the hollow between his neck and shoulder.

Sudden, sharp pain shot through Colbey's arm, though the bird drew no blood. He stiffened, resisting the urge to strike the source of the attack.

Its warning given, Formynder rocked back into its balanced position, its talons as gentle as ever.

Despite his predicament, Colbey laughed. "The bird has made its wishes clear." He rubbed at the bite, and the *aristiri* watched his fingers move.

"No trade?" the merchant guessed.

"No trade," Colbey confirmed, dropping his hand to his side.

"No horse." The merchant indicated the gelding, drawing Colbey's attention to it and the proportions that had sold themselves.

Colbey shook his head sadly. "If I come into some money, I'll return."

The merchant scowled, obviously annoyed over the wasted time, yet still interested enough in the *aristiri* to hold irritation from his words. "Or if you change your mind about the hawk. Think about it. If it's not yours, what do you have to lose?"

"My neck for one thing." Colbey touched the site of the bite again, though the pain had nearly disappeared. "Thank you." He headed for the door.

By the time Colbey emerged from the barn, the sun had dipped beneath the horizon. The crowds had dispersed, as if by sudden magic. The scratch of drawing tarps and the clatter of collected objects replaced the rumble of conversation and the cries of men and women peddling wares. A gray haze settled over the streets, obscuring the once gaudy stands to dark blobs covered with blankets or canvas.

Colbey passed the closing shops and stands, ignoring the exchanges between merchants discussing what items had sold well that day and predictions about the tastes of Pudar's current mass of visiting foreigners. He had wasted another day searching for quality he could not have afforded. One way or another, he decided, he would leave in the morning on the best horse his money could buy. But Crossroad Fyn's gelding still held a place in his thoughts. If he could raise twenty gold *chroams* this night, he might still buy it. And he knew of only one place to win or lose a fortune that quickly.

Colbey headed from the market area toward the upper east side that catered to foreigners on holiday. Once he had found himself some food and a place to stay, he would visit one of the all-night gambling houses. Sparing enough to buy room and board, as well as what he needed to purchase a mediocre horse, he would have little remaining to gamble. By the same token, he had a pittance to lose and much to win.

Though light, the *aristiri*'s continuous presence on his shoulder made it ache. He kept the staff in the same hand, hoping to support the additional weight more comfortably.

Shortly, Colbey came to the *Dun Stag Inn*. Composed of identical logs, stained black, its dark exterior enhanced the brightly lit interior. Thick glass windows warped light into a glaze, disrupted by the shadows of patrons shifting about inside. Noise sifted through every crack in window or door, the surflike rise and fall of conversation audible, though individual words were not. A pair of stone wolves guarded the entrance, their ears pricked forward and their tails low. The tavern sign swung from a pole extending from the front of the building. The name, *"Dun Stag,"* scrawled over the silhouette of a massive buck, its antlers branching beyond the arched semicircular confines of the sign. Beneath this ancient, proud painting, the wolves seemed out of place, a newer addition to the tavern grounds. Almost certainly, the wolves represented the common symbol of the combined Westlands armies in the Great War. The Béarnian craftsmanship seemed flawless.

Colbey passed between the statues and approached the door. Seizing the handle, he pulled the panel open. A wave of sound struck him, painful in its sudden and intense volume. Patrons chatted in loud voices, laughing at jokes that the sober would have found scarcely worth a smile. Light spilled through the crack he had opened, diffusing into the darkness. The suffocating odor of alcohol churned Colbey's hunger into nausea. Stepping inside, he let the door bang shut behind him, the sound swallowed into the din.

Fifteen tables filled the *Dun Stag,* in three rows of five. Currently, most of the patrons clustered on stools at the bar, as if the effort of carrying drinks or calling a serving girl might prove too much of an effort. Of the tables, eight supported patrons in groups of two to nine. Most bore the brown hair and medium frames of area Westlanders. Dressed in their best linen, these gawked at the other patrons and few sported weapons. Those who did limited themselves to what they could afford: unadorned shortswords and knives. Colbey guessed these Western travelers came only for the experience of bragging to friends about the famed *Dun Stag* ale and its rowdy clientele.

Colbey saw fewer of the people who had given the Dun Stag its reputation. At one table, a cluster of three middle-aged men wore the black leather of Pudar's army, their ancient jerkins stained and stretched by bulging guts they had developed since the war. One clutched a mug of ale between his thumb and single remaining finger. A scar twisted another's face from one missing eye to his opposite cheek. Each of these carried a sword, their sheaths as old and battered as their armor. One sheath had cracked, revealing a notched and tarnished sword edge. The split leather grip had peeled from another's hilt, hanging in a curl that insulted Colbey's sensibilities. A true warrior would never neglect his sword. It looked to Colbey as if these men had never changed clothing or manner since the Great War, drinking nightly and living off the glory of the stories they shared between them or created for the attention of the young.

Colbey saw no Northmen in the inn, though he had looked more from habit than concern. Once, the Northmen would have openly attacked him en masse, simply for being Renshai. But Valr Kirin had vowed an end to the feud between Renshai and the other seventeen northern tribes in exchange for single combat with Colbey. Though their leader had died, a victim of his own challenge, the Northmen would never violate their honor. Still, Colbey knew that did not exempt them from personal vengeances against individuals of his tribe. Though he no longer walked among Renshai, Colbey knew he would take the brunt of that hatred. And he preferred it that way. He was all that remained of the wild tribe that had mutilated neighbors and slaughtered its way through the Westlands. The new Renshai deserved the peace its predecessors had shunned.

Colbey headed for a table near the back, not wanting to tarry too long in the doorway. As he moved, he assessed the last few of the *Dun Stag*'s patrons. He recognized the swarthy, dark features of an Easterner, richly dressed in silks studded with gems. Clearly, he was a merchant, selling the gemstones that were the East's most desirable and precious commodity in the West. He had chosen a table well away from the wounded soldiers. Two men large as Béarnides sat at his either hand, watchful, one dark as the merchant and the other sandy-haired. Colbey counted thirty-two patrons and guessed the common room could hold twice that many uncomfortably. Of the bar's seven women, three sat among the gawking Western visitors, two served drinks, and the remaining two wore the tight clothing and overly friendly expressions of barflies or prostitutes.

Colbey took his seat, leaning the staff against the wall near his hand. Though he kept his back to the wall, he chose his position so that the table did not trap him into a corner. It seemed rude to claim an entire table for a single individual, yet, for now, the bar seemed the more popular place. Formynder hopped from Colbey's shoulder to the tabletop. It walked to a position between Colbey's hands. Cocking its head, it looked directly up at him.

Colbey met the *aristiri*'s gaze, studying the black rim that looked like a tiny string of beads around its eye. Intelligence seemed to radiate from its depths, as well as a beauty that sank to the core. On a woman, those eyes could captivate any man. On a man or woman, they would have inspired trust. Their appeal was far more profound than color. Colbey had seen eyes that precise shade on many Northmen and a few Westerners as well. But the power of the *aristiri*'s eyes seemed tangible, revealing an inner strength of character and person that drew him like a starving wolf to a feast.

"Can I get something for you and your . . . bird?" The voice came from directly in front of Colbey.

Caught admiring a hawk with the intensity of a lover, Colbey flushed. He glanced at the speaker, a pudgy young Western woman in an apron. Sweat trickled from her forehead, trailing a strand of honey blond hair.

As the heavy odor of alcohol became familiar, Colbey's appetite returned. He also detected the smells of venison and bread beneath the ale. "Dinner, please. And ale, of course."

"Of course," she repeated, smiling. She turned her attention to the *aristiri*, studying it curiously.

When the serving girl did not move for several moments,

Colbey cleared his throat. "If you're waiting for him to order, you'll be sorely disappointed."

It was the barmaid's turn to blush. Red tinged her olive cheeks. "I'll get that ale." She turned, apron swirling about her wide hips, and headed for the bar.

Colbey returned his gaze to Formynder, feeling foolish for having attributed so much personality to a bird. Still, he could not help the way the hawk's name came to his mind at the sight of it, rather than the generic term "bird" he used when discussing it with others. Its loyalty seemed unwavering, in a way no man's or woman's ever had. Clearly, it trusted him. And, oddly, where argument had failed, the hawk's blind faith brought the very doubts the Wizards and staff had tried to instill. *What does it mean when the most learned condemn a philosophy that the ignorant embrace?*

Colbey's self-confidence rose to combat skepticism. Arduwyn had tried to enlighten the Renshai about nature's rhythms and cycles, the unwritten laws of behavior that seemed to unite weather, plants, and animals into a single, sentient entity. Mar Lon believed that the shortest lived first noticed the need for change, and few animals had a life span approaching that of mankind. *If men can see the need for change faster than gods, why shouldn't animals realize it even sooner?*

The staff tapped gently against Colbey's thoughts, seeking an entrance that he denied. The ideas required consideration that he alone could sort. Unbalanced advice would only skew, whether toward itself or in counterbalance.

A shadow over the tabletop served as Colbey's earliest warning of company. A group of five men approached him. Each wore the tan shirts and britches of Pudar's guardsmen, and they edged closer with obvious hesitation.

Colbey skimmed his memory briefly, trying to think of some thing he might have said or done to attract the attention of guardsmen. Since his arrival in Pudar, he had only spoken with horse merchants and the serving girl; and he had argued with none of them. More likely, the guards' presence had something to do with events from the distant past. During the Great War, Colbey had served as King Gasir's second-in-command. When Gasir had died, Colbey had become general of the Pudarian army, the largest of the Westlands forces. After the war, Gasir's nephew, now King Verrall, had tried to talk Colbey into keeping the military ti-

tle in the hope of aborting possible rebellion backed by one
of Gasir's other three nephews. Burdened with responsibilities of his own, Colbey had refused.

Thirteen years later, Colbey still recalled how Verrall had
dispelled each of Colbey's cautious excuses until he had cornered the Renshai into admitting the truth: "Sire, if you
don't have the power to claim your throne without me, what
makes you think you can keep it after I'm gone?" Even then,
Verrall had not quit. Enraged by the very words his persis-
tence had forced from the Renshai, Verrall had accelerated
the audience into a violence that only Santagithi's quick
thinking had averted.

Formynder stood at Colbey's left elbow, watching the men
approach with the same calm interest as the Renshai. Soon,
the guardsmen came close enough for a detailed examination. Colbey recognized four of the five from the war, and
the glances they exchanged suggested that they now knew
him as well. Still, their manners revealed uncertainty as well
as hesitation. Throughout his day in Pudar, Colbey had kept
moving and avoided eye contact, hoping to dodge recognition: soldiers' awe or the king's wrath. Either would delay
him, and neither had purpose.

The guardsmen stopped just within comfortable speaking
range. Colbey noticed that the volume of conversation in the
common room had diminished with their entrance. Most
eyes rolled to the center of the guards' attention, and their
focus bothered the Renshai. Except in battle, he preferred to
remain anonymous. Among Northmen, any warrior would
feel obligated to test his mettle against a sword master in
spar. Though confident of his abilities, Colbey preferred his
own practices and schedule to that of every overconfident,
would-be hero.

The central guardsman spoke, a hefty, bearded Pudarian
who, Colbey recalled, had had a weakness when it came to
defending his left side in battle. He used the Western trading
tongue. "Excuse me, sir."

Colbey nodded, saying nothing. He wanted some hint of
intention before revealing anything.

"We ... um ..." The guard glanced to the men at his left
and right for support. The first did not move, a tall but narrow axman whose style and lack of strength seemed more
suitable to a single-edged sword. The other, a small, competent swordsman, nodded supportively. Of the remaining two,

Colby knew only one, an archer. The other looked to be in his early twenties, too young to have fought in the war. The speaker switched tacks. "You look like a man we know from the War."

Again, Colby nodded without response. It made sense that the guardsmen did not recognize him. At the end of the War, his sixty-five years had sat on him like forty. Renshai possessed a racial feature that made them seem younger than their ages. War killed them young. These, combined with naming children for warriors slain in battle, had given rise to numerous rumors about Renshai drinking the blood of enemies in hideous magical rites to remain eternally youthful. Now, Colby knew, his encounter with the gods had taken all of the white from his hair. Training had only honed his agility, and the near immortality forced upon him by the Western Wizard's passing had, apparently, stopped or further slowed the aging process. If anything, he looked younger now than then, and those who knew his real age would need convincing that Colby felt little need to give.

"You look so much like him," the man continued, "we wondered if . . . well . . . if your father might have served in the Great War."

Colby glanced toward the wounded veterans sitting a few tables away. Now that the guardsmen had come to him, all three watched him intently. Their expressions betrayed sorrow and jealousy at once. Either they had recognized him, or they envied the attention his presence alone had gained him. He pitied them, but not for the injuries they had sustained in battle. They wore those like a badge of courage, an excuse to cease all useful labor while others cooed their sympathy. He thought of Peusen, a one-handed Northman who had become the general of a brave charge of injured soldiers and outlaws. He considered Captain Rache Kallmirsson, legs paralyzed, leading Santagithi's men to battle with the exuberance befitting a Renshai. This time, Colby took a lesson from his student. *Achievement is no excuse for sloth. Past glory is for the dead. A true hero never rests, but always he drives on one deed further.*

Still, Colby saw no need to inflict his philosophy on others. If these men derived their pleasure from adulation from a war long finished, he would not interfere with their need. Neither would he cultivate the awe of the guardsmen before him. During the war, he did not mind their reverence; it inspired them to give their all to the battle. Now their homage would only embarrass him because it was unearned. And Colbey found one more reason to remain nameless. He had spent longer than a decade trying to reverse the world's hatred and superstition regarding Renshai. His youthfulness now and, later, his near immortality could only reawaken prejudices only shallowly buried. He would do nothing that might harm the Renshai tribe.

"I'm afraid you've mistaken me for someone else," Colbey said, the truth in the statement evident only to himself. "My father died long before the Great War." Again, he used only honesty, though he knew it would mislead. His honor allowed him to do so for the greater good of his people.

The guardsmen exchanged meaningful looks, apparently sorting through those who had believed him to be himself or his son and those who had compared him to his years. They never questioned his response. It made little sense for a respected hero to shy from due credit.

The serving girl arrived with the food, waiting patiently for the guardsmen to disperse.

"Sorry to disturb your meal, sir," the axman said, his disappointment obvious. The others mumbled similar regrets, then they all turned and headed from the tavern.

The woman set down a steaming plate of venison, bread, and peas. She placed the ale beside the food. "Here it is." She added suspiciously, "You in some kind of trouble?"

Colbey avoided the question. "I've never known a warrior who didn't have enemies." He smiled reassuringly, "But I'm not in any trouble with Pudar, if that's what you mean."

The mild reassurance, coupled with the guardsmen's politeness, seemed to appease her. "That's what I meant. I'm sick of the rowdies getting themselves in trouble, then blaming it on the ale."

"Rest assured, lady, I take responsibility for my own enemies, whether or not they are rightfully mine." Not wanting to go into details of heritage and history, nor to waste time chattering with someone with whom he would have nothing in common, he changed the subject. "Any rooms left here for tonight?"

"Tonight?" The serving maid laughed. "Just came down from the North, did you? Rooms here go days in advance. But I can arrange for something nearby." She looked him over, apparently taking in the well-fitting clothes and meticulously tended weapons. "Something suitable. And by the way, your next ale's free, compliments of that woman there." She pointed across the tavern.

Colbey tracked the gesture to a woman sitting alone at the bar. Though draped in shadow, her figure and movements told him much. Clearly, she was no swordswoman, yet her grace and confidence intrigued him. The solidness of sinew told him that she had not spent her life sitting idle looking pretty for men. Curly black hair as dark as a Béarnide's fell to her shoulders, though she carried none of the Béarnian size.

The barmaid answered the unspoken question. "Eastlander, I think by her accent. You'd make the strangest pair in history, I'd think, what with you being a Northman."

Colbey held little interest in single session affairs, and he already had plans for this night. "One ale will do me fine. Please tell her thank you, but no."

The woman glanced toward them. Apparently noticing Colbey's gaze upon her, she rose and headed toward him.

"Tell her yourself," the barmaid said, adding unnecessarily, "she's on her way." She whirled without bothering to conceal a smile and walked back to the bar. Obviously, she enjoyed her job as much as the young merchants' aides and craftsmen's apprentices in the market square.

Colbey bit into the bread, concentrating on his food in the hope that the approaching woman would take the hint. Formynder plucked a piece of venison from the plate, dropping it to the table. The *aristiri* pecked repeatedly at the meat, tearing small pieces from the whole, not seeming bothered in the least by the cooked fare.

Apparently oblivious to Colbey's distraction, the Eastern woman pulled up a chair to his table. "Hello," she said in thickly accented trading tongue.

Colbey nodded acknowledgment without speaking. Up close, he found her features on the becoming side of average. The careless disarray of her hair complimented thick lips and dark eyes full of vigor. She did not resemble the usual prostitutes and barflies. Though clean, her clothing seemed more fit for traveling than flirting. Its rich, Béarnian design appeared constructed for the broad shoulders of mountain women. She looked to be in her early forties, an age when most loose women had either given up their trade or clung desperately to their beauty with layers of cosmetics more suitable to a mural than a face.

The woman watched Formynder wrestle with the venison, and Colbey anticipated an inane comment on the order of "nice bird." He tried to think of a tactful way of dismissing her.

"I saw you looking at horses. You have a good eye for them."

Colbey sipped his ale, still silent, hoping she would soon give up and leave him in peace.

"Did you find what you wanted?"

Colbey sighed, too polite to ignore a direct question. "I found one suitable." He did not elaborate further. His financial problem was none of this stranger's business. He let lie the question of why she had watched him shop. To ask would mislead her with false interest. It was not that Colbey disliked women; half of the finest Renshai sword masters had been female. Under different circumstances, he might have found the stranger's advance exciting or, at least, intriguing. Those women not scared off by his sterility found his manner too savage and reckless or his chosen trade too dangerous. The need to help Frost Reaver goaded him to depart Pudar as soon as possible. He had to leave in the morning, and the evening belonged to money-making efforts.

"In every movement, in every dealing, you carry yourself with a confidence I've never seen in any man—"

"Stop," Colbey said softly. He set aside his fork, meeting the woman's gaze directly.

She recoiled slightly, apparently startled by something she saw in his expression. Colbey's cold, blue-gray eyes had quailed many. Yet though he sensed mild fear in her demeanor, it seemed internal. Something she saw in him shocked her. Where before he had felt none of her emotion, and none of her thoughts wafted to him, now he knew a glimmer of her attraction to him. To his bewilderment, she quelled the uprising of compassion, suffocating it beneath an emotion he could not quite identify, something akin to hatred. Then that, too disappeared.

Confused by the unexpected sequence, Colbey forgot what he wished to say. He managed to find other words to get his point across. "You're attractive enough in many ways. But I'm not looking for companionship. If you'll excuse me, I prefer being alone tonight."

Now irritation and frustration radiated strongly to Colbey, seeming much more normal in its scope. She rose. "If you don't learn to share what you are, Colbey Calistinsson, you'll know only loneliness and those who care most for you will suffer." Without explanation, she rose and walked with dignity from the bar.

Colbey watched her go in silence, sensing as well as guessing a deeper meaning behind her words that required consideration. Always before, he had thought of what was best for the Renshai. Though his absence made the others safer, he knew they missed him as much as he did them. Still, though she had known his name, the woman surely could not have meant the Renshai. More likely, she had overheard the guardsmen. Their disappointment seemed obvious enough, and he wondered if she chided him for stealing an opportunity to honor a man they knew as a hero.

Yet there, Colbey defended his actions. His part in the Great War had finished, and he had risen to higher responsibilities. Like the other Wizards, he had little choice but to perform his duties at a level few mortals could understand, in the realm of law, chaos, and balance. The Pudarians needed to find new heroes; better, to become heroes themselves.

Colbey returned to his food, considering his strategy in the gambling house. But his mind slipped continuously and inexplicably to the Eastern woman who had interrupted his meal. Many questions remained unanswered.

CHAPTER 20

The Gods' Council

Colbey cared little for the serving maid's idea of suitable lodgings, a ramshackle cottage near Pudar's eastern exit. The mud chinking had crumbled from between the logs, leaving gaps that admitted and dismissed the wind in low-pitched whistling currents. Someone had boarded the window shut. Though the door latched, it did not lock. The furniture consisted only of a layer of straw spread across the floor and bundled into a heap beneath the boarded window. It made more sense to Colbey to camp outside the walled city than to pay for quarters no more comfortable. But the Pudarian gates closed at midnight. To leave before sunrise would mean fighting guards or climbing walls, and it seemed nonsensical to break the law to save a handful of copper.

Resigned to his lodgings, Colbey redistributed the straw to bury whatever the last traveler might have slept directly upon. The straw had a musty smell that came with age, and its movement sent dust swimming through the bars of moonlight that sliced through the cracks. He placed his swords beside the makeshift bedding, within easy reach. Leaning the staff in the corner behind his chosen sleeping place, he stripped down to his britches and hung his tunic carefully on a protrusion from one of the logs. Frost Reaver had galloped off with Colbey's supplies, leaving him only the clothing on his person and his swords.

Colbey curled up on the mound of straw, the night's gambling coming back to him in memory. He had done reasonably well, winning twelve gold *chroams* in a card game with modest odds. Then, luck had turned against him, and he lost three coins before pulling out, with a total of seventeen *chroams* in his pocket. At least one of those would have to go toward basic equipment, lodgings, and traveling food. He hoped Crossroad Fyn would be willing to bargain. Otherwise, he had no choice but to purchase an inferior horse. Extra days in Pudar would only cost dearly in time and money.

Colbey realized he had one other source of money, the gold band that had graced his ring finger since the Tasks of Wizardry. He had never worn jewelry on a regular basis. Appearances meant little to him, and he had no use for adornments other than barter. Solid loops, whether placed on neck, fingers, ankles, or wrists reminded him of slavery and only served as an adjunct to amputation in a sword fight. He had once seen a student catch another's ring with his blade, accidentally severing band and finger with a single sweep. He had once heard of a neck ornament repelling an arrow, the owner's life saved by serendipity rather than skill. Such a thing came close to violating the Renshai's moratorium against armor.

Colbey twisted the ring on his finger. *A chroam's worth of gold. Six times that for the workmanship.* Yet the idea of selling or trading the ring crossed his mind only for a moment. It seemed sacrilege to consider using a goddess' gift for any but its proper purpose.

The *aristiri* flew to the ceiling, perching among the rafters. It hunkered down, eyes flicking closed as if it had fallen instantly asleep. Colbey glanced at his swords, so familiar with their forms that the darkness did not hamper his view of them at all. He had practiced most of the morning, before entering Pudar. When he awakened, he would train again. The thought made him smile. The anticipation of a practice fluttered an excitement through his chest that never seemed to dull. Stripped of other responsibilities, he would spend his life in a flurry of swordplay, whether spar, *svergelse,* or combat mattered little.

Colbey closed his eyes, imagining life as it had been in his youth, practicing sword forms until his parents dragged him to meals or to bed. Early on, they had given up on the possibility of getting him to perform other necessary chores. And by the time they died in the glory of combat, Colbey had become so competent that none of the tribe wanted anything from him but lessons.

Strangely, the last thought that came to Colbey as he drifted toward sleep had come from a stranger in a bar: "If you don't learn to share what you are, Colbey Calistinsson, you'll know only loneliness; and those who care most for you will suffer." The idea shifted him into dreams of days and nights spent honing Renshai of every age and ability, teaching dedication to sword and tribe as well as the maneuvers themselves. Idly, he wondered how the Eastern woman had known his name when guardsmen he recognized had not.

Sleep caught him with an image of a woman he had not seen for half a century and had not thought about in longer than a decade. Himinthrasir, she of strength and spirit, with golden ringlets and a sword competence that sent many men to their deaths, had married Colbey young, the first of two to leave him for a man who could sire children. The image haunted Colbey into his dreams.

The familiar music of swordplay roused Colbey to gentle awareness. Steel chimed against steel, and he easily sifted the more frequent clang of sword hammering shield from the softer rasp of blade parrying. He opened his eyes. Moonlight flooded the drafty cottage, but the surrounding darkness told him he had slept for only a short time. He listened, needing to ascertain that the nearby dispute posed no threat to him or to innocent passersby.

The swordplay stopped abruptly, and a young male voice crowed in triumph. "Killing blow."

"All gods damn it!" another youth shouted, tone hard with frustration. "I fall for that same stupid trick every time."

Metal clanked as someone repositioned weapon and shield. A third person responded, the enclosing, crack-riddled walls muffling the sound only slightly. "If you fall for it every time, does that make the *trick* stupid? Or you?"

Colbey guessed the youngsters had chosen this sparse and decaying corner of town so as not to disturb the citizenry with a late night practice. He smiled, pleased by their dedication, a welcome contrast to the smug, old veterans in the tavern. In the past, it had seemed as if each new generation of Westerners became more disgruntled and lazy; years of peace had allowed the Pudarian army to grow soft. But, since the Great War, that pattern had reversed. More and more, the Westlands' youth held all the vigor and promise their parents had lacked. Briefly, Colbey wondered whether to credit the change to the growing balance between law and chaos or to curse the destruction he might have set in motion against this favorable trend.

"Look, I'll show you." The first one spoke again. "All I have to do is sucker you into an overhand strike."

The second defended himself. "But everyone swings overhand sometimes. It's the most natural strike."

"That's what makes this maneuver so effective. While you're coming at me, I cut for your head. Like this . . ." He paused a moment, apparently setting up the situation. "When you raise the shield, your sword arm's in the way of your defense. See there?" Another pause. "There's always a gap between shield and sword. There's no way you can close it. I carve through it. Killing blow."

Another young man spoke, not one of the original three. "So you have to recover from your previous attack, defend, and slice through a narrow slot at once. You'd have to be quick as a Renshai to get any consistency."

The comparison brought Colbey fully alert. He enjoyed hearing Renshai mentioned for their skill rather than brutality. Certain he would get no more sleep until the practice finished, he rose, tucking his swords into the sash of his britches. He left the staff in the care of the sleeping *aristiri,* knowing he would remain near enough to see anyone trying to break into his rented cottage. He slipped out the door and closed it silently behind him.

The voices grew louder, and he recognized the current speaker as the third youth, one of the spectators. "Quickness isn't the point. Concentrate on smoothness, not speed. That's where the Renshai's ability came from: fluency not sharp, jerky jabs . . ."

Colbey saw the four boys as soon as he left the cottage. They stood on an open stretch of empty road, and ranged in age from about thirteen to seventeen. Each had a sword and shield and wore the tan linen britches of the Pudarian guards. Three wore standard homespun tunics, the last barechested. None wore the matching shirts that would complete the uniform of an on-duty guard. Colbey judged the speaker, a rangy blond, to be the oldest.

". . . Renshai practiced until the techniques became instinct. Work to get your strokes smooth and easy, and speed will come with time."

Colbey stepped from the shadows of his cottage. "I like that. I've never heard it put quite that way before."

All four teens spun to face Colbey. The eldest flushed. "I'm sorry, sir. I didn't know you were there. I hope I didn't offend." Although Pudar did not have the moratorium on the word "Renshai" that some of the farm towns did, it was generally not something mentioned in polite company. Colbey's obvious Northern features compounded the potential error. In the past, no one had hated Renshai more than their closest neighbors.

Colbey waved off the apology.

"Are you a soldier?" the youngest asked.

"A warrior, yes." Colbey preferred the term that implied fighting as a way of life rather than a job.

A chunky youth of about fifteen spoke next, his voice that of the one who had lost the spar. "Did you fight in the War?"

"Yes."

"Which army?" the same one asked.

"Pudar's." Colbey did not clarify by stating his rank. Better the boys did not know they chatted with the Golden Prince of Demons.

"Did you ever fight Renshai?" the shirtless one asked unabashedly, though the eldest tried to wave him silent. Colbey recognized his voice as belonging to the one who had explained the "shield gap" attack, the winner of the contest.

"Yes, I did." Colbey did not explain further, that he did so only in spar, with the intent to teach not harm. He changed the subject quickly. He had intended to encourage, not interfere with, the training. "Would you like to know a more important flaw in your attack?"

Colbey waited expectantly for the answer. He had rarely chosen to teach anything to non-Renshai, and the boy's interest would tell him in an instant whether he should bother wasting his time.

The bare-chested one considered for less than an instant. "Sure. I'd be honored."

The envious looks the teen's companions gave him told Colbey he had made the right decision. Excitement trickled through him at the prospect of aiding eager students, his first interest in teaching since long before he had passed his title of *torke* to Mitrian. Even the realization of more lost sleep did not faze him much. A few hours of rest after the practice would serve him well enough.

Colbey waited until the boy stepped into the open, away from his companions. He accepted a shield from the youngest, and the weight felt awkward and heavy in his grip, the ultimate symbol of cowardice. Yet, without it, he could not make his point. He strapped it to his right arm. He nodded, indicating that the boy should take the first attack.

The youth slashed low. Though he felt unbalanced, Colbey blocked with the shield, as expected. He executed the anticipated overhand stroke. The boy recovered quickly, drawing momentum to slash for a gap that was not there. With the shield in his right hand and sword in his left, Colbey could continue the swing without hampering his defense at all. The boy's sword slammed against Colbey's shield. The Renshai completed his attack, the blade gently parting the other's hair.

"Killing stroke." The boy's previous opponent smiled, obviously glad to see the trick fail miserably this once. He shook back a curtain of dark hair to reveal pale brown irises.

Colbey lowered the shield to the ground and flipped Harval to his other fist. "About one in eight opponents will fight left-handed."

The youth nodded. "I'll need something else for him."

"Lots of something elses." Colbey hooked the shield with his foot and rolled it aside, glad to be free of its encumbrance. "Rely on only a few maneuvers, and one of those will cause your death. Deliver every blow with the confidence that it will kill, yet always assume your opponent can deflect you. For every attack, there're multiple dodges, parries, and counterattacks. Draw him into patterns, then catch him off-guard with change."

"He's gotten me with that trick twelve times now," the chunky one said. "I'd like to see a few of those defenses." Then realizing enthusiasm had made him rude, he added appreciatively. "If you would, sir."

Colbey demonstrated half a dozen, including a disarming stroke that sent the sword flying and left his student counting fingers. The Renshai caught the hilt in his free hand and waited for the boy to realize he still had the full complement of appendages.

The would-be swordsmen pressed forward then, all speaking at once, each begging a countermaneuver or situational attack. The attention meant nothing to Colbey, but the youngsters' raw and genuine zeal delighted him. He would have loved to spend the hours until the market opened guiding responsive students to the way of the sword, but his own need had to take precedence now. Without sleep, his wounds would not finish healing, and he might have to face the world's most powerful enemies weighted by exhaustion.

"I'll show one thing more, then we all need some sleep. Many fights have been lost to a well-rested though inferior enemy. Your enemies are still hypothetical, mine all too real." Colbey returned the captured sword to its owner, then gestured the oldest lad to him. The boy's dark blond hair probably came from having the blood of Renshai conquerors distantly in his line.

The youth came forward, shield hovering defensively before him, the sword solidly gripped and balanced. Colbey wielded only Harval in his right hand. He gestured to the youth to attack.

Obediently, Colbey's opponent drove forward. Instead of dodging and retreating, Colbey lunged simultaneously. His sword locked with the other, parrying it aside. He completed the momentum with a stop-thrust to the head, a maneuver that combined attack and defense in the same movement. The teen reversed, raising the shield to block. Colbey pulled the feint before point touched shield, thrusting Harval beneath the youth's guard instead. The blade poked abdomen then slapped hip before the other could reposition his shield, two effortless fatal strokes. The force of the second blow sent the boy tumbling to the ground.

Colbey sheathed his weapon and assisted the youth to his feet. The teen favored his left leg; a bruise would remind him of this lesson for a long time. Colbey could have spared him the pain, but he had chosen to show that he had gathered the appropriate momentum without leaving any doubt. In a real fight, that stroke would have killed.

"I didn't see . . ." the blond started.

"Of course you didn't see." Colbey kept his gaze fully on the eldest, though all watched with rapt attention. "You had a shield in your face." Colbey detailed one of the reasons for the Renshai prejudice. "If you must have something in your off-hand, take up dagger or shortsword. Shields are bulky and slowing. They teach you to take blows instead of to dodge. And used right, they steal your vision."

Colbey sheathed his sword, a blond lock tickling his forehead. "Thank you for an exhilarating night." He shook his head, and his hair fell back into its natural feathering. "Keep practicing in your free time, and the East won't dare attack us again."

The youths exchanged noises of approval and encouragement. Colbey left amid a chorus of thanks, never having given his name. He returned to his cottage with confidence in Pudar's future warriors. *Five years ago* ... Colbey amended the thought as he placed the swords back on the floor beside his bedding. *Five* hours *ago, I wouldn't have taken the time to teach even those basic techniques to non-Renshai.* The significance of the knowledge went deep. About this, at least, Shadimar had spoken well. Colbey was becoming the guardian of the West as well as of the Renshai, and the process had started even before he mustered farm towns and became King Gasir's lieutenant in the Great War. *Perhaps from the moment Tokar made me his successor.* The idea bothered Colbey only briefly. He knew no magic or divinity had forced him to cast his lot with the West; he had chosen the alliance willingly and with vast consideration.

This time, sleep came easily.

Colbey awakened to a sudden sensation of movement. His eyes snapped open. Moonlight flashed from a dagger speeding toward his throat. With no time for anything but a dodge, he rolled, flinging an arm protectively between the weapon and his vitals. Cold steel slit the skin of his forearm, and his fist met something solid with enough force to thrust it backward.

Colbey snatched up Harval as he rose, not wasting the moment grabbing the second hilt would cost him. His gaze carved a staggering figure from the near darkness, female by its size and proportions. He circled, placing himself between his enemy and the door. Warm blood trailed down his arm. The wound burned with an agony that went far beyond the familiar tear of sharpened steel.

The woman crouched, knife clutched in her fist, attention riveted on Colbey.

The *aristiri* screeched a warning that had come too late. Apparently, the intruder's silent approach had caught Colbey's guardian, too, by surprise.

The other stiffened, but she did not seek the source of the sound. Either she knew Colbey traveled with a hawk, or she would allow no noise to distract her.

Colbey poised, blocking the exit, awaiting a second attack. Patience had won him many battles. So far, he knew only that his enemy could move silently. Her method of of-

fense face-to-face would tell him much about her general
strengths and weaknesses. He assessed what he could in an
instant. She stood slightly on the shorter side of average for
a woman, and her stance revealed more natural grace than
training. Taut sinews hinted of an active lifestyle, though her
grip on the weapon told him she had little direct experience
with combat. Her black hair and dusky appearance suggested
Eastern heritage. Though shadow obscured her features,
Colbey believed he faced the same woman who had tried to
seduce him in the *Dun Stag Inn*.

The intruder remained still, saying nothing. Either she
shared his patience, or she had reason to believe time would
work to her advantage.

The wound in Colbey's arm felt on fire, and its dull throbbing made him switch his sword to the opposite hand. Understanding struck with violence. Poison! Rage flared, as hot
as the pain in his forearm. He could think of nothing less
honorable than to let chemicals take the place of skill in
battle. *Poison.* Now that he knew of its presence, he could
almost feel the killer substance coursing through his body,
his heart pumping it to every organ with his blood. Soon
enough, it would take him down. But she would die with
him. Raising his sword, Colbey charged.

The woman dodged, attempting to parry with her shorter
blade. The sword tip met the knife's hilt, and Colbey sliced
it from her grip. The knife thumped against the wall, then
plummeted, lost amid the straw. Dizziness swam down on
Colbey, and he swung with a wild incaution scarcely tempered by skill. She flung herself back, but not far enough.
The blade caught her a glancing blow that slammed her to
her knees. Colbey's kick sprawled her. He jabbed for the final, killing stroke.

The woman did not flinch. She met his blue-gray eyes
with brown ones blazing with a familiar madness, one he
had not seen in her the previous night. The sword raced toward her throat.

A thought wafted clearly from her, at the volume of a
scream: "Move, Khita! Roll now and grab! His other sword
is at your left elbow!" Though the words came from the
woman's mind, the sentiment was clearly not her own.

A reply welled from the central core of the woman's being, clutching at law and honor like a drowning man at a

rope. "No! I was wrong! Now that I understand what you really are, I'd rather die than bond with you."

Colbey pulled the blow, the blade tip plowing through straw, though he managed to save it from contact with the stone floor. A mass of chaos blasted him, slamming the woman's consciousness beneath a wild wave of madness. She screamed as she had not for her life or his attack.

Acid seemed to run through Colbey's veins, and his arm ached to its depths. Yet the presence of his familiar enemy fanned a deeper fire. He had faced chaos too many times before. He had lost Episte to it once, and the grief of that memory only added to his rage now. He had faced it in Frost Reaver's mind and met a stalemate. Yet he had defeated it once as well, in the form of insanity-touched Wizards in his own mind. Certain of his own death, Colbey paid self-defense no heed. Unhesitatingly, he gathered his mental will and dove into the battle.

The formless chaos-stuff seethed and boiled around him, its focus central. Always before, Colbey had faced only picture-concepts in another's mind. Emotion had come to him as sensation and thought as flashes of image or words. This time, the entity that belonged in this mind crouched behind a shield of human basics: structure, law, and all that memory made familiar while the tide of chaos whittled toward the core in a self-satisfied frenzy. She appeared to Colbey's senses as a black silhouette, drab and stagnant so close to chaos' grandeur. Color winked and splashed through the periphery, sending multihued sparks arching from every contact.

Quickly, Colbey drew himself into the picture, stretching his mental being into place between chaos and the woman's defenses. He entered the war less to aid her then to face and destroy a too-familiar enemy.

Surprise filled the mind like a blanket, its source both of the entities that occupied this mind. At first, Colbey feared that fusion had already occurred between them. Then chaos turned to wrath and the woman to both doubt and hope. "You? But I tried to kill you. Why?"

Colbey did not waste strength on an answer. Already, he had lost track of his body, and fever blunted his ability to think. The staff channeled its thoughts to the barest edge of the link between Colbey's mind and body; true to its vows it did not cross that line. *Don't be a fool! Kill her. You need your energy to fight the poison.*

Colbey ignored the staff as well. He fought like a Renshai, relentless because of, not despite, the certainty of his own death.

The chaos oozed into a single lump, its voice massive and echoing. "She is mine."

Colbey channeled all of his own mental energy together. "You cannot have her."

The energy of the staff writhed at Colbey's back, as eager as he to join the fight. It remained behind him, a mass of force ready to do battle the instant Colbey gave the word. Yet he kept it in place. He had never let anyone assist in his battles, and he would not start now, no matter the stakes.

"She's mine. She pledged herself to me." Chaos warped and twisted.

"Influenced by chaos, her vows have no more meaning than yours."

"She's mine!" Chaos took the form of an eight-legged creature the size of an ox, its head like a man's but hairless and broader.

Weaponless in thought form, Colbey held his ground. He had never faced an enemy directly in another's mind and could not begin to guess formalities, if any existed. One thing seemed certain. Exertion and the poison ate at the edges of his consciousness, and he could not allow chaos to delay him into oblivion. Without set rules of honor, Colbey had little choice but to make his own. "Do you know who I am?"

"You're the Master," chaos answered without hesitation. "But you don't rule me. Surely you won't risk oblivion for the soul of a single mortal."

"Clearly," Colbey replied, "I would." He could feel his body trembling now, and even his mental consciousness began to flicker. The urge to call upon the power at his back was strong, but he resisted. He delved for second wind. One way or another, this confrontation would end soon.

Chaos hesitated, torn between anger and fear. Ensconced in the mind it filled, Colbey could read it easily, though it obviously had no inkling of his own state. If it had, it would have known how easily it could defeat him now. Apparently realizing that it could not hide its reactions, chaos explained.

"It's not you I fear. I cower from no man. It's what hovers behind you."

"I speak for what hovers behind me. And the Wizards would call that force your ally." The simple effort of speaking made his thoughts seem dim and hazy. Each word sent him to the edge of collapse, the breaths between scarcely enough to haul him back.

"The Wizards are fools, but you cannot bluff me. I see beyond structure to what is real."

Colbey hesitated to gather his thoughts, though the seconds cost him dearly. He felt the paralyzing poison clutch at his mind, holding ideas in place so that he could not move to a higher level. He crawled for the words he needed, knowing he might soon lose both battles. Already, he had little hope for his body or soul. All that remained was to cast out chaos. To fail meant letting chaos run rampant, opposed only by three Wizards who seemed already to have taken leave of their senses. If he could salvage this woman, she might have the fortitude to take up his cause. Given time, this was not the successor he would have chosen, but their brief conversation had revealed a competence of body and he sensed a solid moral foundation as well. She had let it crack once; he could only hope she would not do so again. "You will not have her," Colbey's mind would not give him the words to say more.

The woman's mental presence rose where Colbey's had failed. "The deal was that we would bond when I killed him." Her words seemed to echo, their placement far more natural than these strangers in her mind.

"Indeed," chaos sent back.

"But he's alive."

"For the moment. I can remedy that."

"If you do that, then I won't have killed him. You will. I'll owe you nothing."

The demon recoiled, taken aback.

In its moment of hesitation, the staff slammed home a message. *Banish it.*

Darkness filled Colbey's vision, and he could see nothing. He had to ponder each syllable to make sense of the words.

"You had a cunning teacher, Khitajrah Harrsha's-widow."

"Yes. And I am finished with him."

Banish it! The staff sent again. *You're the Master. Send it away.*

"You've damned your son."

Grief trickled through the black rock that Colbey's consciousness had become, the only emotion strong enough to touch him. The woman's response seemed nonsensical. "Had I known the price for Bahmyr's life, I would never have bargained. Better he stay dead and I join him."

Banish it. The staff's entreaty became entwined with an ancient lullaby, and Colbey fought for understanding.

"That, too, can be arranged." Chaos' laughter prodded Colbey, bringing memories of Episte's mockery: "I gave my love and trust to a Deathseeker so like my father, only to have him betray me." And yet, the betrayal had actually come much later, when Colbey gave up the struggle to chaos. *Not again. Not this time, chaos.* Though he had no sympathy for nor ties to the woman who had tried to slaughter him, Colbey's hatred for chaos remained stronger. He struggled for breath as well as words. "Begone," he finally managed to say.

The demon abandoned its banter with Khitajrah. "Is that really what you wish?"

An instant later, Colbey's ears failed, and he spoke to a nothingness he could neither see, feel, nor hear. "I am the Master. And I command it." He had no idea whether or not the words had reached chaos when oblivion overtook him.

Sunlight filtered through blue-green trees of perfect confirmation, beaming through Frey's hall window on Alfheim to illuminate the meeting of gods. They sat about a great table, Frey's servants, Byggvir and Beyla, bringing food and drink as it pleased Asgard's mighty. Frey glanced about the gathering. As always, Odin claimed the head seat, though Frey had called the meeting in his own hall. Odin's wife, Frigg, sat to his left and his sons, Vidar and Vali, to his right. Thor and his wife, Sif, had also come, bringing Thor's sons, Magni and Modi. There was Bragi, the god of poetry, and his wife, Idun, with her golden apples of youth. Aegir and Ran arrived from the ocean's bottom. Heimdall the watchman had also come, briefly leaving his post on the Bifrost Bridge to join the gathering. Frey also saw one-handed Tyr and his own father, Njord. Others joined the group, their expressions mimicking Frey's grim manner. Yet Frey waited, missing two. He had not invited Loki, but he suspected the Trickster would come on his own in time. Loki would never pass up an opportunity to stir up trouble. It was Frey's own sister, Freya, whose absence bothered the god of sunshine, rain, and elves.

Conversation stilled to empty silence as the gods ran out of words to pass to their immediate neighbors. Frey discovered every eye upon him, demanding explanation for his conference.

Unable to delay any longer, Frey rose. He looked first at Odin. The grim gray father of gods remained quietly composed, expression shaded and unreadable beneath his broad-brimmed hat. His single eye seemed piercing, the repository for all knowledge.

Frey cleared his throat. Accustomed to the lighthearted play of elves, the solid greatness of his colleagues seemed ponderous and nearly overwhelming. He had not thought out the details of his words carefully, hoping another would take over the task of speaker. But every eye remained fixed on him. Even the massive, impulsive Thor sipped at his drink and waited patiently for Alfheim's lord to speak.

Frey began: "I believe you all know why I called you." He ran a hand through hair as golden as corn silk, and his strikingly handsome features crinkled. "Over the years, chaos has crept into man's world: as the dispersing aftermath of the Wizards' magics or our own presences on their world. Yet recently, I fear, it comes in larger doses. Someone has loosed chaos on the world of man, and only one thing can come of this." He looked around the gathering. Odin remained unmoving, expression impassive. Thor scowled, revealing the first stirrings of his quick and deadly anger. Several expressions went stony. They had shared their plans to avert the *Ragnarok,* with Frey and with one another; but all had carefully avoided allowing the knowledge to reach Odin, Tyr, or Thor. The first two would not approve, and the last had a temper as potent and fickle as his storms. Others looked away uncomfortably. Most of these, Frey guessed, had ideas too fresh or self-focused to divulge. Vidar seemed to develop a sudden, intense interest in his mead.

"*Ragnarok* is imminent," Frey said, knowing the revelation was unnecessary but hoping that speaking the term of destruction would force them all to bond to the cause. Centuries of greatness and diverse interests usually drove them to handle problems alone or in small groups. Now, with chaos loosed and championed, the time had come to weave every tactic together, to keep one from interfering with another, to use Odin's wisdom and foresight to determine which might succeed and which would surely fail.

"Imminent, yes," Bragi agreed. "And sad, is it not? It would seem to me more appropriate to spend our last meeting together feasting rather than in council."

The poet's response told Frey that his colleagues still needed coaxing to reveal designs long-hidden in the AllFather's presence. Frey understood Odin might see their plans as futility or worse, cowardice; but surely their leader did not expect them to sit idle knowing the day of destruction was at hand.

"Last meeting, fah!" Thor thundered. "I, for one, won't go down without a fight. I'll find the one filling the world with chaos, and Mjollnir will stave in his skull." His hand gripped the hammer's haft convulsively, and the movement rippled from fingers to shoulder. It was not Thor's way to plot far in advance, only to react with swift and efficient violence when the need arose.

Sif gently placed a hand on her husband's arm. "That will solve nothing. You know what happens when gods interfere on man's world. Every small action we perform there snowballs into something huge. You might bring more chaos than you stop."

Thor's scowl deepened. "We stand perched on the brink of *Ragnarok* already. Mjollnir may save us from it, or bring it sooner. I say it's worth the risk."

Frey placed one knee on his chair, still standing but no longer the center of attention. As he'd hoped, he had started the discussion rolling, but it brought deep contemplation of his own. He had known for millennia that the end would come. But it had always seemed too far away to concern him. He had seen elves born and wither, their span so long they embraced the final oblivion when it came. He believed he would feel the same. Yet, now that *Ragnarok* was almost upon them, he only realized how much he enjoyed living and how much he still had left to do.

"This is nonsense," Tyr said, rearranging his mug with the stump of his missing hand. "The Norns wove our destiny millennia ago, and we've had all this time to accept it. Are we a bunch of *wisules* to question now that death is close at hand?"

Frey had expected nothing less from Tyr, the champion of

war and the bravest of the gods. He had sacrificed his hand
in order for them to bind the Fenris Wolf.

Frey's father, Njord, added his opinion then. "The youngest of the Norns frequently rewrites the fate her sisters determine. Prophecies do not happen without support, and the
future can be changed."

Frey regained the floor. "I know the worlds' most intelligent beings have not sat in passive silence while their lives
hang in the balance. Who among us has not acted to avert
his fate?" The question was a formality. Over the centuries,
he had discussed myriad possibilities with the vast majority
of his fellows. He had helped more than a few with ideas
and/or the execution of projects to protect themselves or others, and he had taken his need for survival fully as seriously.
He held more than his own life in the balance. If he lost his
battle against Surtr, as was his destiny, the lord of fire giants
would destroy all of the nine worlds and nearly every living
creature in a massive conflagration.

The god of sunshine looked around the table at each god
or goddess in turn. Only Thor, Tyr, Odin, and Vidar returned
his stare. The first two, Frey suspected, held no secrets. As
usual, Odin chose to keep his thoughts and actions to himself. Frey did not try to guess whether Vidar, as a survivor
of the Destruction, had actually taken evasive action or simply felt the need to abstain from answering. As to the others,
Frey suspected that, if he detailed his activities, most would
follow suit.

From beneath his chair, Frey drew a colossal sword.
Gently, he pulled it from its sheath and placed it upon the table before him. It spanned across his area, encroaching upon
those of Tyr, Njord, and the empty place where his sister
should have sat. The blade shimmered with an icy blue light.
"This is Kolbladnir, the cold-bladed. I paid the dwarves to
forge it and its magic to replace the one I gave away." Frey
recalled how he had paid for his wife with a sword that
would fight giants of its own accord. It was prophesied that,
for the loss of the weapon, he would die at the *Ragnarok*
fighting the king of the fire giants. "I've also spent years
working with a fine steed, teaching it not to shy from magic
or flickering flames."

Sif spoke next. "I've gathered and studied every herb on
the nine worlds to find the one capable of neutralizing the
Midgard Serpent's poison." She referred to her husband's

fate, that he would kill the monster only to die of its venom. "I haven't found the answer yet, but my work with mixtures seems promising." She brushed back hair of spun gold, and the sunlight capered like fires through her locks. She took responsibility for the project upon herself by not naming the many who had assisted, but Frey knew that most of Asgard had some hand in Sif's endeavor. Freya, Heimdallr, and he had collected a vial of Serpent spittle for her trials, and Idun had donated one of her rare and precious apples to finding the antidote. "If anyone has suggestions, I'll take them gladly."

Heimdall added his piece. "When the giants come, they may find the Bifrost sturdier than they expect. When I battle Loki, he may fair worse for a curse placed upon his sword."

The three confessions broke the floodgates. Gods and goddesses opened their various plans to discussion or ridicule until the whole blended into an unintelligible maelstrom.

Unlike the other survivors of *Ragnarok,* who sat in an abashed hush, the quietest of the gods, Vidar, managed to talk over the hubbub. "I reinforced the Fenris Wolf's fetters. He'll find himself hard-pressed to get at my father. I also outlined battle strategies to give support where we know it's needed."

Frey smiled. The damned had excluded *Ragnarok*'s prophesied survivors from their plans, believing they would see no need for averting fate. The elves' god commended Vidar's courage, every bit as impressive as Tyr's bold confrontation of The End. Altering the course of battle would probably lead destined survivors to die rather than allow those slated for ruin to live. On many occasions, Odin had indirectly suggested that attempts to stave off the *Ragnarok,* no matter how innocent, would more probably magnify the Destruction than hinder or lessen it.

A more directed rumble followed Vidar's pronouncement. Clearly, many others had chosen to detail combat strategy as well. Frey mentally applauded his decision to gather the gods together. The finest strategists could work through the problem together, without feeling alone in their plans to escape destiny.

Still, Odin passed no obvious judgment, his silence unbroken. Tyr voiced his disapproval, "Fate is what it is. Cowards run from death; the brave embrace it. Do we need lessons from our own heroes in Valhalla? We've all lived well. We can go down in glory or we can grovel for our lives like cravens. I, for one, will have no hand in thwarting destiny. The more we try to change fate, the more the same it stays."

The door flew open, and Loki stood framed in the doorway, amid a blast of cool air and sunlight. Wind fanned his yellow locks into a mane, and his green eyes danced with a mocking madness. "Ah, so here you are! Sorry I'm late. My invitation must have gotten lost."

"No loss," Frey said. Though only a hint of breeze had funneled inside with Loki's entrance, the entire hall seemed to have gone suddenly cold. "You weren't invited."

"An oversight, I'm sure." Loki stepped inside, closing the door behind him. He snapped his fingers at the servant, Beyla. "A mug of ale, please. It's a long trip from Asgard to Alfheim."

Thor flexed his massive fists. Odin sipped his wine. His gaze did swivel to the newcomer, though he still showed no expression.

"You weren't invited," Frey repeated. "You're not welcome in my hall."

Loki ignored the hostility, turning his attention to Odin instead. "My blood brother, at least, will bid me welcome. Has even the AllFather forgotten his vows? Once, you promised you would never drink unless a drink was brought to me as well."

Odin blinked. He turned his head to his sons. "Vidar, Vali, make a place between you for the father of monsters."

Scowls scored the gods' faces, yet Frey saw the irony in Odin's choice. He had seated Loki between two of the *Ragnarok*'s fated survivors and directly across from two more, the sons of Thor. Though Frey found Loki's presence as distasteful as the others did, he understood the need for tolerance. A blood brotherhood was a tie more sacred than even marriage or family relationship. To shed the blood of a god on Asgard or Alfheim would tear an irreparable gash in the barriers between the worlds of law and chaos. It would start the *Ragnarok* as surely as the prophesied attack by giants.

Loki headed for the indicated place, but his need to incite got the better of him before he reached it. He stopped at Freya's empty chair, and his sparkling eyes found Frey's. "Where's your wanton whore of a sister while all her lovers gather in one place?" He made a gesture that encompassed every god in the hall.

Though incensed, Frey chose to ignore the gibe. Wanted by all, Freya had slept with only one or two, an impressive record for an unmarried deity over millennia; and Loki's indiscretions spanned dozens. In the days when Loki had practiced mischief instead of outright evil and chaos, he had charmed many gods' wives. Some claimed he had even seduced chaste Sif from her husband's arms. In shape-changed form, he had mothered a horse. Still, Frey chose not to bandy insults with Loki, the king of lies and caustic affronts. No matter the facts, Loki would win any battle fought with taunts. "Freya does not discuss her comings and goings with me."

"Strange, she does with me." Loki framed a cruel smile. "Perhaps she's decided to join my side and help spread chaos."

"That's absurd," Frey returned, no longer able to hold his tongue. If not for Loki's casual and self-serving evil, the gods would have no need for this council and the nine worlds would not stand poised on the brink of destruction. "If you've harmed her, I'll tear your guts out, blood oath or no."

Loki laughed, continuing his walk to his indicated seat, turning his back on Frey with a scornful lack of concern.

Frey let the matter drop, but Bragi found the opening more difficult to resist. The Lord of Chaos always inspired the worst in the gods. "Loki couldn't hurt Freya. If they fought, she would wrest his miserable head from his body."

Loki did not miss a beat. "You should know, Bragi, soft cowering craven. Women have fought your battles forever."

Frey saw Bragi's wife open her mouth to speak, and he rushed to talk over her. Her defense would only enforce Loki's ludicrous accusation and start a chain of bandied venom he had no patience to suffer now. "Where is Freya?"

Loki calmly took his seat, hooking Vidar's ale and sipping from it. "Probably bedding every man on Midgard while she still can." He laughed, spraying half a mouthful of ale back into the mug. "How should I know? Why not put the question to the all-knowing Father? From the high seat, Hlidskjalf, he sees all that happens in every world. Except when he misses things I see. Like the time Freya sold her body to four dwarves for a necklace after refusing the AllFather . . ."

"Enough," Odin said, his voice echoing through the hall. "Your nastiness has grown tiresome. Make a point or take your leave." His eye swiveled to Frey then. "Freya is well. She's doing her own part to forestall the *Ragnarok.*"

"Where is she?" At last, Frey took his seat. "What's she doing?"

Odin answered evasively, "If she wishes you to know, she will tell you."

"I know." Loki smirked.

"Perhaps," Odin replied. "But your own rancor allows you to see only what you can use. In some ways, Loki, you're the blindest of us all."

Loki gulped down several mouthfuls of ale, then loosed a massive belch without apology. "I can slip into places you would not think to look, and I hear things others would never want me to know." He glanced about the gathering. "Go ahead. Hire the dwarves for magic weapons; their craft will only draw more chaos."

Frey slipped his sword from the table, placing it back beneath his chair.

Loki continued. "Hone your battle skills. Reinforce your bridges. Plan your battles to the minutest detail. It will do you no good. Your strategies will fail, because chaos cannot be predicted." He locked his gaze on Frey then, his irises changing from green to orange to violet in quick succession. "Predestiny and fate are constructs of law. Therefore, only the followers of chaos can defy them. Think about it."

A hush followed Loki's pronouncement. Frey threw a quick glance around the table, but only Tyr met his gaze. The silence grew, blossomed, and seemed eternal. Immortality made every god and goddess patient, except one.

Thor's fist crashed against the table with enough force to send mead sloshing and mugs into a rattling dance. "I've heard enough words for one day. Chaos must be destroyed. Unless we act, the worlds will collapse into oblivion. They may do the same if we act, but at least we will have acted." He clasped Mjollnir in his hand, striding through the door Loki had left open and onto the plains of Alfheim.

Frey groaned, wishing Sif and her sons had found some way to exclude Thor from the conference. Tired of speculation, he pinned Odin with his attention. "Can we effect change? In this matter, do our actions make any difference at all?" The fate of every man, elf, and deity, of every plan, rested on Odin's answer. With one query, Frey had summed up the entire purpose of the gathering and of centuries of preparation.

Odin turned slowly and with dignity, drawing his face from shadow though the hat still sheltered his eye. "For nine days and nine nights I hung from the World Tree, pierced by my own spear, a sacrifice to myself. I saw the worlds below and tried to trace the roots of creation. I gave away an eye. I drank from the cauldron, Odrorir, a vintage brewed from the blood of wise Kvasir; and I gained wisdom from Mimir's head. Yet there are things even I do not know, such as the roots of the ancient, windswept Tree."

Frey grimaced at the answer, so full of information he knew and leaving his question unanswered.

"I do know this." Odin's eye found Frey at last, and the lord of Alfheim felt lost in the gray depths. "Change is necessary. Every detail of that change may or may not yet be set in future history. Prepare as you will, but be certain your plans serve the purpose of the worlds. If we pay with the lives of gods, and doubtless we will, we had best purchase a better future."

Frey considered Odin's words for some time, still uncertain of his course. *Is there hope, or is it all inescapable predestiny?* The knowledge Odin had gained, and the wisdom he had acquired through sacrifice and experience, could never be matched; yet he had mostly avoided the question. *Does anything we do really matter, or will we all fall into our fated roles regardless of our efforts? Can we avert the* Ragnarok *or only bring the inevitable prematurely upon ourselves?* Frey knew Odin would or could never answer these thoughts directly. He only hoped that, in his short time remaining, he would understand enough to make the right choices and steer the others to do the same.

PART III

THE GRAY GOD'S DOWNFALL

CHAPTER 21

The Wizards' Successors

The *Sea Seraph* glided toward the Meeting Isle, a quiet shadow on a sea as calm as glass. Captain stared out over the aft rail, watching the perfect lines the hull etched through the waters. The sun beamed down, warming his red-brown curls, and the sky seemed the uniform blue of a gem-stone. Yet the captain felt little of the joy that usually accompanied passage through the portal and entry into the Cardinal Wizards' meeting ground. The three Wizards and their apprentices had paid him little heed from the beginning of the journey to its end. Instead, they gathered below decks, huddling over their charts and plans. Now, as the island and its single structure came into view, the captain missed the Wizards' fables, metaphors, and vagaries. He had always hated the quibbling between the Northern and Southern Wizards, but this time it seemed conspicuously absent. Their unity in a cause felt unnatural.

Footfalls clomped up the stairs from below. The hatch door clicked open, and the slam of each step shuddered across the deck toward him. Captain identified Shadimar's heavy tread, interspersed with the tap of his staff against the planking. Behind the Eastern Wizard, the elf heard Trilless' lighter movement. He kept his back to them, staring out over the waves, even when they joined him aft.

"Hello, Captain," Shadimar called cheerfully. "Nearly there, I see."

"Nearly there," Captain echoed, knowing Shadimar would expect a reply, yet in no mood to come up with one on his own.

Apparently recognizing discomfort in her follower's tone, Trilless pressed. "What's troubling you, Captain?"

The captain considered the question for a long time. He had kept his concerns to himself this long, it seemed wiser and easiest to remain silent. However, fear, hurt, and anger gnawed at him. He would never challenge Cardinal Wizards in the presence of their apprentices, but this time he had found two alone. He might not have another chance to air his grievance. Deliberately, he turned, abandoning the aft rail for the wheel; he felt naked without some part of the *Seraph* in his hands. He quoted the oldest Wizards' prophecy: "When their oath of peace the Wizards forsake, their own destruction they undertake."

Trilless and Shadimar exchanged glances that seemed to imply the reference was beneath them, too far beyond Captain's understanding to bother to explain.

Trilless accepted the burden of discussing the matter with her underling. "Is that what's bothering you?"

"Partially," the elf admitted.

Trilless' voice went soft, though it patronized more than soothed. "First, it's a matter for the Cardinal Wizards. You have your own role to play. Second, recall that Odin assigned us the job of fulfilling prophecies."

The Northern Sorceress' arguments collapsed like an ancient dwelling devoid of its foundation stone. "*Ragnarok* is a matter for all of us: men, elves, and gods alike. As to the prophecies, no Wizard's predecessor mandated this one for a follower to fulfill. You have no obligation to it. In fact, it bodes a destruction you're bound to try to stop."

"I wasn't finished." Trilless' tone hardened. Though punitive, it lost the condescending edge; and for that Captain felt grateful. "Third, though we stand against Colbey, we've hardly forsaken peace. Carcophan and I have never tolerated one another so well. And last, Colbey has become the harbinger of chaos. It is he who threatens to bring the *Ragnarok*."

The captain remained unconvinced. His discussion with Colbey had revealed no such intention. And something about the three Cardinal Wizards on board seemed tainted, an intangible that made the captain feel ill-at-ease in their presence. Still, neither his vows nor loyalty would waver. He served Trilless, and he would serve her until the last thready gasp escaped his lungs. "Where's the Western Wizard now? No matter what feuds you are caught up in, he has a right to be present when new apprentices are tested. And where's the bard? Your vows forbid you from barring either one from the meeting."

Shadimar set the staff against his chest, curling a protective arm around it. "Neither was excluded. We sent a message to Colbey, informing him of our intentions. Apparently, he chose to ignore our invitation. We sent a message to Mar Lon as well." He leaned forward, gaze boring into the elf's canted eyes, expression angry. "I'm tired of inferiors questioning our honor. You have no right to make assumptions about us. Your ignorance is an insult."

Captain bowed humbly. "Your forgiveness, Eastern Wizard. Next time I'm asked to speak my mind, I'll try to edit my thoughts to please you." He felt certain Mar Lon would have come if he could have, and he suspected the Cardinal Wizards had deprived him of the travel time he needed to meet the *Sea Seraph* in Asci. He could understand Colbey's decision not to attend. Surely he knew that Odin's Laws forbade Cardinal Wizards from harming one another, and all conflicts must be halted while on the Meeting Isle. Yet, beset by his colleagues' demon and possibly other dangers Captain did not know about, Colbey had little reason to trust the others to follow the vows they had taken.

Trilless gave her colleague a warning glare. Her expression softened as she turned her attention to the captain. "You may always speak freely to me; you know that. I appreciate the knowledge you've gathered over the centuries and from the other Wizards you've known before me." She took the elf's hand in her own, the sagging flesh of her fingers still soft and supple. "Desperate times and situations have made Shadimar understandably irritable, but he does have a valid point. You have to trust us to use the knowledge and experience we have to do what's best for the world. It's our job and the basis for our lives. We have more to lose than anyone by the world's destruction."

Captain believed total annihilation of the world and its powers would affect everyone equally, but he did not press the point. "I trust you," he said softly. "I just want to make certain details don't become forgotten beneath more weighty problems. More than one battle has been lost to a single spy who thwarted a general's defenses. One tiny seed of disease can take down the mightiest army."

"True," Trilless replied, "but there's still much to be said for dealing with a raging enemy first." She loosed Captain's hand. "Trust us, my friend. Little escapes the Cardinal Wizards. Our vows to champion law take precedence even over those to our specific causes. We will always work to that end." She met the Captain's amber eyes. "Do you feel better?"

Though little satisfied, the captain nodded. He saw no reason to linger over a dilemma that had no obvious answer. It seemed clear that they would never come to equal terms, and belaboring the point would serve no purpose other than to anger the Eastern Wizard. "I still have a lot to think about."

Trilless smiled, apparently pleased with the response. "As do we all."

Sunlight washed over the dull, gray stone of the building on the Wizards' Meeting Isle. The sun hovered directly overhead, a yellow ball that seemed pasted over a sky so clear it defined the color blue. Yet, despite this beauty, Olvaerr Kirinsson walked solemnly at Shadimar's side, glancing neither to the right nor left in order to keep from appearing nervous. His father had taught him that there was no shame in feeling fear, only in displaying it. Its price was the morale or respect of colleagues and followers. And it provoked enemies, sometimes to killing frenzy.

At fourteen years old, Olvaerr was the youngest of the group by at least two decades. Discounting Chezrith, he was the youngest by centuries, and he felt pinned beneath a massive weight of doubts. It seemed impossible that he could begin to understand the many responsibilities that fell on a Cardinal Wizard's shoulders, but he was determined to try. His father, Valr Kirin, had never shirked any obligation, if he found the cause right and honorable. Few men had earned more deserved glory or respect, and Olvaerr had long promised to follow in his father's vast and mighty footsteps.

Olvaerr paused as Carcophan opened the door to usher Chezrith through it. She moved with a lithe, regal grace. When it came to facing the Seven Tasks of Wizardry, the Eastern woman seemed to harbor no doubts at all regarding her ability to handle them. Olvaerr studied her from behind: black locks, neatly short, only added to her aura of confidence, and the set of her shoulders told the world she was in control. He envied her composure, but not her cause. He wondered how much of that calm demeanor was facade.

Trilless passed through the portal next, her new apprentice trailing in the silky, flowing wake of her white cloak and gown. Olvaerr found the elf's moods difficult to read. His heart-shaped lips always seemed to outline a smile that stretched from one high-set cheekbone to the other. His canted eyes bore a steady green color, like polished gemstones, uninterrupted by the shadings or stellate cores of human eyes. They seemed alert and alive, yet they betrayed no emotion Olvaerr could read. He spoke with a mildly pitched, musical lilt that bore a resemblance to the accents of the far North, yet it made even the Northern singsong sound harsh. He carried himself with a light step that seemed almost a mockery of the seriousness of the Tasks.

Shadimar gestured for Olvaerr to precede him through the doorway. Executing a genteel bow to his mentor, Olvaerr obeyed. In the North, children learned respect for teachers and sword masters early, and Valr Kirin had taught his only child well. The attention to formality came from deeply ingrained habit that even trepidation could not dislodge. Unconsciously, he kneaded the hilt at his hip, glad that Chezrith had also seen fit to bring an obvious weapon, a strange double-curved, single-edged sword with a cobra's head for a pommel.

The meeting room contained only a long, wooden table with eight chairs and a hearth at the far end of the chamber. Carcophan and Chezrith took seats at one head, Trilless and the elf, Dh'arlo'mé, at the other. Shadimar entered behind Olvaerr and closed the panel. He sat in the chair nearest the door, his back to the exit. Though it left the innermost seats empty and took all symmetry from the table, Olvaerr took his cue from the other apprentices, sitting beside rather than across from his mentor. Shadimar placed a satchel that Olvaerr knew contained books on the floor by his chair. Trilless kept volumes stacked by her arm, and Carcophan's pockets bulged with reading material of his own. Each would need to find a distraction, as well as train his successor, while the other Wizards' apprentices attempted the Tasks.

Olvaerr lowered his head. Blond bangs fell into his blue eyes, and thick layers of hair shifted into a curtain to shield his face. Though nearly two years had passed since he had hacked off his war braids in mourning for his father, he still had not gotten accustomed to the half-grown feel of it. He mouthed a silent prayer to the patron god of Nordmir: *Lord Odin, master of gods and men* ... He added carefully, now in the presence of an elf as well ... *and all beings like men. Please grant me the courage and understanding to succeed at your trials and to take my position with the grace, wisdom, and dignity befitting a Wizard if I am worthy of the honor. And if you find me unworthy, please grant me the opportunity to die in glory so that I may still serve you in Valhalla.*

Finished, Olvaerr looked up, shaking back his unruly, yellow mane, only to find all the Wizards gazing at him. He froze. En route, the Cardinal Wizards had decided to send him to the Tasks first. They had made their choice without his input. Shadimar had mentioned casually that he felt more comfortable with his neutral successor set in place before those of the extreme causes made the attempt. But the Eastern Wizard's tone had suggested other unspoken reasons, and Olvaerr guessed he was the most expendable and easy to replace of the three. Also, they must have considered him the most likely to fail; while the others attempted the tasks, Shadimar would have the time to replace him if the need arose.

"Are you ready?" Shadimar asked.

Though he was not, Olvaerr nodded, certain he would never feel prepared to face the testing grounds that the Cardinal Wizards had explained only theoretically. He knew each of his seven trials would tax some property of his being to its limit, and that the ring each yielded would take him to the next. He understood that he might face an eighth challenge that he must refuse, as it had proven Colbey Calistinsson's undoing and the demise of many others. Failure at any task would herald his death, not necessarily in glory nor even in battle. All of this he understood, yet it told him nothing about the details of the actual Tasks of Wizardry. Those, he would discover for himself. Again, Olvaerr nodded, more securely this time. "I'm ready."

Trilless, Carcophan, and Shadimar exchanged knowing looks, then the Eastern Wizard chanted syllables that had no more meaning to Olvaerr than the elf's nearly unpronounceable name. Vertigo enclosed him, a dark, whirling tomb that left him no understanding of up or down. Without vision, he had no means of knowing for certain whether the tingling forces of magic actually spun him or simply gave him the sensation of movement. The world became a black vortex that seemed to suck him into its core.

Then, as suddenly, the sensation disappeared. Still sitting, Olvaerr lurched to his feet, fingers achingly clenched around his hilt, his knuckles locked. Though twirling in ceaseless circles, the scene that filled Olvaerr's eyes looked too familiar. He stood by the table in the Meeting Room on the Wizards' Isle. Shadimar, Carcophan, and Trilless remained in place, brows furrowed in mild confusion. Dh'arlo'mé and Chezrith also studied him curiously.

Prepared for gods' magic and illusion, Olvaerr backpedaled beyond Shadimar's reach, scanning every shadowed corner of the room in an instant. Someone stood near the hearth, a thick, imposing male figure wearing a broad-brimmed hat that threw him further into the darkness. He did not move; even his chest did not seem to rise and fall in the normal rhythm of breathing. The room's sourceless light highlighted an empty eye socket and wisps of flaxen locks poking from beneath the hat. The other eye, trained unwaveringly on Olvaerr, reflected all the life the rest of its owner did not. All of Olvaerr's fear bunched into a single packet that flared into panic. He held his ground, more from inertia than intent. The being in the corner seemed to siphon the life force from him.

Olvaerr managed to collect enough rationality to kneel in deference to a presence he believed was Odin. "Your blessing, Father of gods and Master of men. Your presence is more honor than any man deserves. How can I serve you?"

The eyes of every Wizard and apprentice whipped in the direction of Olvaerr's stare. Carcophan moved so quickly, his chair legs scraped an angry protest across the floor. Chezrith rose also, crouching between her master and the previously unseen threat.

Despite the others' sudden attention, Odin kept his single eye trained on Olvaerr. "Greetings, Årvåkir." The name literally meant "Vigilant One," and Olvaerr suspected it was Odin's way of acknowledging that he had noticed the god's presence first, while his companions had remained oblivious. The Northern pronunciation, "*Awr*-vaw-keer," probably sounded enough like "Olvaerr" that the others would not notice the difference. But Olvaerr did, and the subtlety of the gray god's joke amused as well as awed him. "Greetings, Wizards," the newcomer added. "Greetings Wizards' apprentices."

Of Olvaerr's companions, some muttered polite salutations in various words and languages. Others bowed or nodded their welcome. The whole blended into an uninterpretable grumble.

Odin seemed to take no notice of the garbled response. Finally, his gaze shifted from Olvaerr to rest upon the two empty chairs across from Shadimar. "I see one of you is missing."

Carcophan chose to speak for the group. "We sent the standard message. The Western Wizard chose not to attend."

"Ah." Odin said. "Perhaps he'll change his mind when he recovers from your poison and reads your note." A smile crept across ancient features, yet it softened nothing. The craggy face only looked more deeply etched and terrible. "Perhaps *you* will have recovered by then as well."

Carcophan scowled, rubbing self-consciously at the sword wound hidden beneath his sleeve. Trilless glared at her evil opposite, apparently discovering information she had not previously known and Olvaerr could not begin to fathom.

Still on his knees, Olvaerr found his gaze at the level of Shadimar's hand. The Eastern Wizard's grip on his staff blanched, as if he worried Odin might try to wrest it from him. "As honored as we are by your presence, it was not our intention to summon you. We were only trying to send my apprentice to the Tasks as per your law."

The smile disappeared, replaced by a hard look of amusement. It seemed as if the god might laugh, but no one before him could share in the joke. "The staff you carry makes your power vast, but you cannot *summon* gods. I came because the need and reason for the Tasks of Wizardry ceases to exist any longer." His eye shifted to Chezrith, as if to pin her where she crouched. "State your full name and why you believe you should become the next Southern Wizard."

The gaze the Eastern woman returned showed no trace of fear. She threw back strong shoulders, drawing to her full height. "I am Chezrith Fentraprim's-daughter from the city of Prehothra. No mortal, perhaps no one, epitomizes evil better than I do. Carcophan could look long and far, but he would never find a more capable apprentice."

Olvaerr stiffened, awaiting retribution for Chezrith's hubris, if not from Odin then, at least, from Carcophan. But neither showed sign of surprise or offense. Odin's attention turned to Dh'arlo'mé.

The elf waited patiently, green eyes bright. When the divine gaze touched him, he rose. For a moment, Olvaerr

thought the elf, too, had met Odin's gaze. But a slight deviation of the outworlder's head cued Olvaerr that he actually
steered his attention toward the empty socket. He remained
in position, anticipating a command or question.

Odin obliged. "State your full name and why you believe
you should become the next Northern Wizard."

Olvaerr felt sweat draw a ticklish line along his spine. *I'm
next. What answer does he want?* He tried to guess Odin's
interest or need. *What could I say that would convince him
of my worthiness in a way the Tasks of Wizardry would
have?* It seemed impossible to replace the skill invoked by
a series of god-mediated tests with a single response. A million questions descended on Olvaerr at once. *Is there one
right approach? Did Chezrith pass or fail? What am I going
to say when he gets to me?* He could not begin to fathom a
god's motives, the AllFather's even less so.

"I am Dh'arlo'mé'aftris'ter Te'meer Braylth'ryn Amareth
Fel-Krin. As an elf . . ."

At first, Olvaerr thought Dh'arlo'mé had chosen to answer
in some elven tongue, until he switched smoothly back to
the Western trading language. The length of the elf's name
astounded him nearly as much as the elf's ability to remember every syllable. He supposed one who had lived for centuries might have the time to memorize endless details.

". . . I have no need for immortality or for power. I agreed
to succeed Lady Trilless because it is the right thing to do.
I could champion no other causes than law and goodness. If
my mistress believes I am best qualified to follow her, I
would never presume to doubt her judgment." Dh'arlo'mé
executed an agile, elegantly formal bow, then retook his
seat. Carcophan and Chezrith sat also.

Olvaerr fidgeted, knowing he had to come next, his mind
still drawing a blank on the proper response. It only made
sense for Odin to hold his judgment of the answers until the
end, though Olvaerr could not help wishing for the added
clue of a response to his colleagues' words. He glanced up,
only to find every eye once again on him.

The god shifted, the movement, though slight, seeming
oddly significant. A smile threaded across the ancient, shadowed features, this time appearing benign. "Årvåkir, why do
you believe you should become the Eastern Wizard?"

Though asked a direct question by one he felt nearly certain was the father of gods, Olvaerr still hesitated, almost

overwhelmed by the gravity of his situation. He rose, considering for many moments, though no one else seemed concerned by the length of his pause. "I would be lying if I told you I felt as confident about Shadimar's choice as my colleagues do about the decisions of their master and mistress. It wouldn't surprise me to learn there are others who would make stronger, more competent Wizards than me."

Olvaerr glanced at his companions. A frown scored Shadimar's ancient features, but he said nothing. Chezrith and Dh'arlo'mé looked startled. Trilless kept her gaze locked on the figure in the corner, and Carcophan betrayed no emotion at all.

Olvaerr continued. "My father taught me to commit myself to causes with every fiber of my being. No matter how small my skills, I will develop them to fullest potential and dedicate them, without hesitation or fail, to neutrality."

Though he had remained silent through the others' presentations, Odin prompted Olvaerr. "Your father devoted himself to goodness. He was Trilless' champion."

Olvaerr had an answer. "My father's cause is not necessarily my cause. He encouraged me to find my own way, and he taught commitment to ideals, not necessarily the ideals themselves."

"And your father's enemy?" Odin prompted.

"Is my enemy, too." Olvaerr did not consider falsehood. "That's a benefit I didn't expect, but I could hardly refuse. Colbey killed and mutilated my father, in the manner of Renshai. It's a pleasure to work against that demon, and I'll gladly slaughter him if the need and opportunity arise." Now the attention of every Wizard switched from Olvaerr to Odin, awaiting some reaction to the pronouncement of plans to destroy the Western Wizard. Olvaerr turned his regard there, too, needing comfort of his own. "Colbey tried to make me believe my father found Valhalla, though he lost an arm in the battle." He kept his gaze fixed on Odin's face, hoping for some confirmation. True to Northern religion, Olvaerr believed a warrior must be set to pyre intact to obtain the final reward of Valhalla, but he could draw a permanent solace from Odin's reassurance that Valr Kirin had proved the exception and reached the divine battleground anyway.

Odin gave no response, to Olvaerr or to the Wizards. He stepped into a more concentrated area of light, and he

seemed to grow there. Olvaerr realized that the god stood
half again as high as the tallest man he knew. He spread his
arms, and they seemed to encompass the back wall, his fists
like boulders, cocked upward. He took two steps forward,
his gliding strides and broad arms bringing him within reach
of both heads of the table. He chanted then, his voice a powerful monotone, his tone lacking even the standard, Northern
rising and falling pitches:

> *"Men create myth*
> *To share with their kith*
> *To fight what they cannot explain.*
> *Fear mothers hate*
> *And violent fate*
> *When enemies they can't restrain.*

> *"Man now or elf*
> *If hate turns to self*
> *And the need to atone should arise:*
> *Break this stone*
> *Call justice home*
> *And follow the path of the wise."*

Odin's fingers edged open with an unhurried deliberateness to reveal two matching sapphire chips. As his hands
came fully uncurled, the fragments seemed to nudge themselves into rounded shapes so slowly Olvaerr wondered if he
imagined the transformation. The gray father of gods placed
the gems on the tabletop, one before Trilless and the other
near Carcophan's hand. He stepped back while the Wizards'
attention shifted to his offering, and his eye pinned Shadimar. "You crafted your own destiny. You have no need of
this." Without explanation, his form faded into the dull stone
of the back wall, then disappeared.

Wizards and apprentices sat in uncertain silence. With the
impatience of youth, Olvaerr broke the hush. "Did we
pass?"

Trilless responded with a bland tone indicative of a phrase
long-quoted, devoid of any personal emotion or interpretation. "To fail even one of the Tasks of Wizardry means death
instantaneously."

Carcophan chose a harsher way to say the same thing.
"He didn't slaughter you, so he must have found you worthy

enough." Apparently unable to resist, he added. "The Eastern Wizard always has been the weakest."

Shadimar had a ready answer. "No more." He thumped the base of the staff on the floor to remind the Southern Wizard of the force that more than equalized their power. "And the staff tells me that Odin sanctioned all of our apprentices."

"Did it also happen to explain the meaning of the poem? Or the purpose of this?" Carcophan curled his knuckles around the sapphire Odin had given him.

"It seems clear enough to me." Trilless deposited her own gemstone into a pocket. "He's concerned about our turning against the Western Wizard, as am I. He worries that we've done so from ignorance and fear. And he's given us a means to realign our vows and priorities if things go too far."

Carcophan sneered vindictively, and he turned his head toward his opposite across the table. "It's easy to twist one's own beliefs and biases from rhyme. When the Guardian spoke of ignorance and fear, he specifically attributed it to men, not Wizards. I believe he referred to the *Ragnarok*. He wants us to break the gems if the chaos touches even us. Then, he'll come or send minions to help us remain untainted."

Olvaerr saw merit to both interpretations. He had drawn a total blank on his own, but he could not help wondering why Odin would omit the Eastern Wizard from his protection. He questioned aloud. "Why not Shadimar, too?"

"Perhaps he only had two gems," Dh'arlo'mé ventured, and was immediately shut down by Trilless.

"Those shards came from the Pica stone, I believe. I don't know the extent of magic required to breathe life back into a shattered masterpiece, but it might tax even the AllFather's sources. Nevertheless, there are many more pieces."

"Odin has a direct link to me already." Again Shadimar indicated the staff, this time by running his hand along the shaft. "That only reinforces the probability that the gems somehow summon him."

Olvaerr's face twisted as he considered. The description did not fit the Odin he had studied as a child in Nordmir. It was not the AllFather's way to directly interfere with men or their decisions, right or wrong. With *Ragnarok* and his own destruction at stake, his methods might change, though the legends also suggested he let gods make their own mistakes

as well. Unwilling to shed skepticism on the speculations of
his superiors, Olvaerr kept his opinion to himself. He had
promised Odin to follow Shadimar and his cause unwaveringly. That, at least, the god appeared to have sanctioned.

Follow the path of the wise. Though Olvaerr knew the last
line of Odin's rhyme referred to a course of action after the
breaking of the Pica remnants, it seemed appropriate here as
well. For now, the Cardinal Wizards held more experience,
knowledge, and wisdom than any mortal. Yet Olvaerr could
not quite shake the religion lessons pounded into him since
infancy. The wise gods, Kvasir and Mimir, both came to horrible ends: the first murdered by dwarves, his blood brewed
into the mead of poetry and the second slain by gods, his
head preserved to advise Odin.

Dh'arlo'mé prompted Shadimar. "Does the staff tell you
more?"

Chezrith had remained quiet since her brief speech to
Odin. Suddenly, her low-pitched voice rang out, her guttural
accent sounding animal in the wake of Dh'arlo'mé's lyric
quality. "I know a way to get the Staff of Chaos without
harming Colbey."

Startled by the sudden interruption, Olvaerr switched his
attention instantly to Evil's apprentice.

"We only need to trade it for something he wants more."

Carcophan's jaw clamped shut, and he looked embarrassed for his successor's outburst.

Shadimar answered both apprentices in turn. "First, the
staff seems certain that Odin sanctions what we've done so
far, though he does urge caution. That's understandable.
When you teeter on the brink of destruction, it doesn't take
much to drag world and self into oblivion. Second, what
could Colbey want more than the Staff of Chaos?"

"The Staff of Law?" Dh'arlo'mé suggested.

Shadimar dismissed the possibility. "He already had it. He
gave it away."

"Besides, we can't give him the Staff of Law," Trilless
said. "I won't cheat another Wizard. If honor isn't a strong
enough reason . . ." Trilless made it clear she had added the
last for Carcophan, ". . . Kyndig's vengeance might prove
nearly as horrible as his loosing chaos."

Olvaerr doubted anything could rival *Ragnarok,* but he did
see Trilless' point.

Chezrith leaned forward, elbows pressed to the table. "We'll trade him the Renshai."

The resemblance to the events leading to his father's death tightened Olvaerr's throat until he could barely speak. When he did, it was to say something unnecessary. "Which Renshai?"

"The entire tribe," Chezrith separated her hands in a gesture to indicate the simplicity of such a plan. "How difficult could it be for three Wizards and three potentials to catch and hold five mortals and an infant?"

A shiver shuddered through Olvaerr, so hard and quick his hip banged the table. He sat down to cover the movement. *Show no fear.* Memory returned in a rush. His father's men had kept three of the current Renshai hostage in exchange for Colbey himself. In the end, Valr Kirin had gotten the one-on-one combat he sought, a death he had expected, and an amputation he had not. Yet Olvaerr saw the differences here. The Wizards wanted an item, not a person. Surely Colbey would exchange a thing for promised peace for himself and his people. Without the staff, the trouble he could cause, though large, would become comparatively insignificant.

Nods swept around the Meeting Room table, no objections raised by Cardinal Wizards or apprentices. And, in the same room they had taken their vows, the Cardinal Wizards laid their plans against the Western Wizard.

CHAPTER 22

Dreams of Gold and Demons

Oblivion receded to a hazy gray curtain, spliced through with flashes of thought and memory. Colbey chased the bright spirals until he managed to assign identity to self, though place and understanding eluded him. Gradually, form appeared from the ceaseless ring of movement surrounding him. Demons circled, each pass bringing them closer; and they changed shape with every cycle. There was no pattern to their alterations. Human/animal mixtures melted to black globs of shapelessness or detailed parodies at random. The rotations changed direction without warning so that the whole seemed more like constant motion than directed attack.

In his mind, Colbey crouched in their center, his stance defensive and his swords positioned for potential combat from any side. En masse, the demons rushed him. Colbey hacked a furious framework of steel. In his left fist, Harval gashed through demon flesh as black and substanceless as ink, flinging dark blood. His right sword met no resistance, cutting through the transmuting bodies without leaving a mark. Although he still jabbed and slashed with a speed few men could match, his every action felt ponderous. Exhaustion and something else weighed him down, tying his mind and the mental image of his body always to the edge of oblivion.

A gentle hand caressed Colbey's earthly arm from inner elbow to wrist. The mental demons retreated, their presences becoming distant threat. Not for the first time, a woman joined Colbey's inner perceptions. He knew her at once, the same who had rescued him from the explosion of the seer's crystal during the Seven Tasks of Wizardry. Yellow locks tumbled like waves around peerless features that defied capture by the finest artist's talents. Muscle and sinew defined shapely hips, breasts, and buttocks. Clearly, heredity had played a hand in her beauty, but effort and dedication to sword also had a significant role. Her carelessness of stance and grace of movement told him that she did not primp. Her attractiveness came as a natural result of training, her goal competence rather than appearance, though she possessed both in equal quantity.

The woman's huge blue eyes had become familiar to Colbey in the time he lay unconscious. Wisdom as well as concern reflected from them. He also believed he saw affection, though he attributed that to his own desire. It seemed instinctive for any man to fall instantly in love with this woman's beauty, yet it was not Colbey's way to study only the superficial. Function, not form, obsessed him. Too often, he had seen men choose the gem-encrusted or intricately carved hilt, only to have the blade crack or the grip become impossibly slippery in battle. Yet this woman seemed to have it all: Northern fire and savagery, dedication to sword, intelligence, and depth of character as well as a blinding radiance that could enrapture the coldest man or draw envy from the most self-satisfied woman.

Sword drawn, shield raised, the woman crouched at Colbey's side, adorned with gold jewelry from a slender anklet to a necklace engraved with patterns that seemed to writhe like a metallic snake around her neck. The latter clinched her identity, though it still seemed sacrilege to imagine he had drawn the attention of a goddess. The Necklace of the Brisings belonged wholly to Freya, defining her as certainly as Thor's hammer did the raging, red-haired god of law and storms.

Again the circle of demons closed, but this time Colbey had an ally in the battle. At first, as he slaughtered demons, he took care only not to harm or hamper his companion. As her skill with a sword became apparent, he grew to expect her to handle those nearest her. Her skill excited him every bit as much as her beauty. He had trusted few men or women to guard his back, but he no longer doubted that this woman's skill approached his own.

As each demon collapsed, Colbey felt his strength and clarity of mind grow, no matter whether he or the woman took the creature down. One by one, they whittled the demons in a battle that seemed to last for days. No words passed between them. The fight demanded concentration that neither would sacrifice, as if the outcome meant as much to her as to him.

When the last demon fell in black defeat, the bodies dissolved into nothingness, and the vision-hazing grayness went with them. Colbey faced the woman of the dreams, wanting to express both his gratitude and attraction. Yet one thing obsessed him more. Sheathing Harval, he met her single sword to single sword. "Now it's you and me."

The Freya-vision dropped her guard, her laughter hearty and entertainingly musical. "No wonder you're not married, Kyndig." Her voice emerged deep and sensual, as powerful as any man's. "Do you always feel this need to slaughter women who help you?"

Despite deep-seated pain, Colbey smiled. "Not slaughter, just spar. It doesn't matter who wins. I just have to know who's the better swordsman." Having never known a Northman who could resist such a challenge, he reflected the need back on her. "Don't you?"

"*I* already know." The woman sheathed her sword and lowered her shield, not bothering to share her so-called knowledge with Colbey. "Some day, Kyndig, we'll spar; but this isn't the time. When I best you now, how will you know if it's the poisoning or my skill?"

Colbey prepared a retort that implied she would not best him for either reason. But before he could frame his words with the proper respect as well as challenge, awareness jolted through him. The mental images snapped out, replaced by the familiar desk and bookshelves of the Western Wizard's cave. He lay on the same straw ticking he had used for his recovery from the *kraell*'s attack. A heap of blankets jumbled near his right hand, atop his swords. Part of the spread was pinned between his hip and the wall, though his body lay fully exposed and chilled. A woman scrubbed at his left arm with a damp rag.

Embarrassed, Colbey flicked the blankets over his legs and abdomen.

The sudden movement startled the woman. Dropping Colbey's arm, she stumbled backward, then met his gaze squarely. In nearly every way, she seemed the opposite of the woman who had helped him disperse the mental demons; though, apparently, her touch had inspired the dreams. Her eyes held all the color Freya's had lacked, coal dark and full of intelligence. Black curls fell to her shoulders in random spirals, her face swarthy and round to Freya's ivory oval. He knew her at once as the woman who had attacked and poisoned him, the one from whose head he had expelled the seed of chaos.

She spoke first. "I'm a widow with three sons. You have nothing I haven't already seen." She amended. "Except the scars. Quite a collection. Where did you get them?"

Colbey ignored the question, not quite ready for casual conversation with the woman who had tried to assassinate him in his sleep and had nearly succeeded. "Who are you? And what do you want from me?"

"You can call me Kayt."

"Why would I do that?"

The hostile response apparently surprised her. "Huh?"

"Chaos called you Kay-tah." Colbey sounded the name out as well as possible under the circumstances. "If that's your name, why would I call you Kayt?"

"Actually, my name is Khitajrah Harrsha's-widow. Khita is how it's shortened in the East. Kayt in the West."

Colbey immediately recognized the name of Siderin's lieutenant from the Great War, but he let it pass. It made little difference now. If this woman could evoke images of Freya in his own dreams, it only made sense that another warrior leader would have found her attractive. "Then I'll call you Khitajrah. My people don't shorten names. What do you want from me?"

It seemed a simple enough question, but it made Khitajrah distinctly uncomfortable. The strength of her emotion sent it wafting to him, easily read: concern mingled with regret and an unmistakable attraction to a body riddled with old wounds. "At first, I planned to kill you." She rubbed her hands, as if to wipe away the lingering feel of the poisoned dagger.

Colbey knew enough from his time in her mind to delve for specifics. "What did chaos promise in exchange?"

Khitajrah fidgeted. Though she would not meet Colbey's gaze, he felt certain she told the truth. "My son's life."

Colbey struggled to a sitting position, the blankets clutched to his lap and the movement driving dizziness through him. He waited until it passed. "How did chaos get control of that?"

"Bahmyr's dead." Khitajrah buried her face in her palms.

"Killed protecting me. Chaos promised it could restore his life."

"Chaos' promises are not to be believed."

"This time, it told the truth, I'm certain." Khitajrah's shoulders heaved, and a tear dribbled through a crack between her fingers.

"The dead can't live again."

Khitajrah sniffled, anger giving her the strength she needed to confront Colbey. "Do you think I'm some idiot weakling dazzled by chaos?"

"No," Colbey started, "but—"

Khitajrah let him get no farther. "Do you think I gave in to its dishonor and ugliness because I'm too stupid to see through its lies?"

Colbey tried to shift the blame from a frailty in Khitajrah to chaos' terrible cunning. "The issue—"

Caught up in her defense, Khitajrah turned her rage directly on Colbey. "My son's life hung in the balance." Again, she clamped her hands over her face. "But you don't have any children. You couldn't possibly understand . . ."

The words angered Colbey as no others could. This time he shouted over her. "Damn it, Khitajrah, my seed doesn't have to course through a womb for me to know what it feels like to love, or to lose a loved one. I had a son who died. The fact that I didn't sire him made him no less mine by emotion, his or my own. Blood's just a liquid that leaks from wounds, and the mystical connection between it and love is contrived. A mother can lose each of her children only once. A barren woman or sterile man mourns a child with each empty attempt to conceive. Don't tell me what I can or can't understand. At least you had a son, three sons if I heard you right. It sounds as if this one died in battle, defending his mother. What finer death could a mother wish for her son?"

Colbey's fire only fueled Khitajrah's own. "Good mothers don't wish for their sons' deaths at all."

"You would have them live forever?" Finally, Colbey thought to look for the *aristiri,* gaze first sweeping the bookcase, then falling to the desktop. The hawk watched the argument with silent intensity. Beside it, the red falcon that served as the Cardinal Wizards' messenger preened its feathers, patiently awaiting its turn for the Western Wizard's attention. The staff stood, propped against their perch.

"I would, at least, have them outlive me. Every one of my

sons died in battle. And my husband." Khitajrah choked on
the final syllable, the sobs coming too hard and quick for her
to talk around them.

Remorseful for his harshness, Colbey placed a comforting
arm around Khitajrah, reminding himself that his own upbringing gave him no right to belittle the customs of others.
He had simply grown tired of people thinking he lacked
emotion because he chose to keep his loves and sorrows private. And he knew Khitajrah had to work through the guilt
of her own actions. "I'm sorry. I know you're not weak or
stupid or gullible. I was in your mind, remember? The core
of honor I found there seemed rock stable, and you've got
more inner strength than most of the warriors I know. I've
got a fair idea how chaos seized its hold, and I'm certain
you gave it a heroic fight." His clarity of mind after coma
surprised him, although he still sensed a weighty ponderous-
ness about his movements that would soon pass.

Embarrassment wafted from Khitajrah. Clearly, she did
not feel she had battled enough. The tears stopped, and she
wiped her eyes with her fingers. "I couldn't let go of
Bahmyr, and I didn't really understand the extent of chaos'
bargain. I should have and could have fought harder."

"When it mattered most, you fought."

"It mattered from the start." Khitajrah settled into the cleft
between Colbey's arm and shoulder.

Khitajrah's closeness alarmed as well as excited. Decades
had passed since Colbey had allowed himself to become intimate with any woman, and Khitajrah seemed so unlike
what he would have chosen. Still, he had not lied about her
inner strength, and her ministrations had given him visions
of the most desirable of all goddesses. That seemed like a
sign too obvious to ignore. Many things remained unanswered. "How did I get here? How long have we been here?
And how did I survive the poison?"

Khitajrah took the questions in random order. "Two days.
Your bird tried to get me to take you here from the start, I
think; but I insisted on finding a healer in Pudar. He described an herb and how to use it, but he only had a little of
it. When the hawk found a huge beakful but wouldn't let me
have it, I had no choice but to follow wherever it wanted me
to go. It brought the food and supplies. I administered
them." Khitajrah placed a hand, with feigned casualness on
his knee. "It seemed the least I could do. The very least. I'm

so sorry and ashamed for what I've done. And so glad to have had the chance to make things right. I'll never forgive myself the pain I caused you. And others, too."

Colbey freed her from obligations to him, at least. "I forgive you. But not chaos. If you fell to its influence again, knowing what you do now, then I wouldn't forgive."

"Never." Khitajrah stroked his knee through the blankets, not quite absently. "Now there're things *I*'d like to understand."

Colbey met her gaze encouragingly. "Ask."

"Are you really seventy-seven years old?"

Since Colbey had become a Wizard, the significance of age had dwindled. The question scarcely raised a twinge of annoyance, easily suppressed. "Yes."

Khitajrah nodded, clearly impressed. "You've kept well."

"I've kept *myself* well," Colbey corrected, "and not without effort." He ran a hand through his yellow locks, aware he had not maintained his youth wholly without help. He saw no reason to mention his encounter with gods to a woman he knew well only because of an excursion into her mind after she tried to kill him.

Khitajrah fidgeted, her next query apparently disconcerting to her. Although she held his gaze, she looked as if she would have preferred to avoid the cold blue-gray eyes. "Is it true you're a Wizard? And a Renshai?"

"Yes, regrettably, and yes, proudly. Who told you these things?"

"Chaos," Khitajrah admitted. "And the Béarnian king's personal bodyguard."

Colbey studied Khitajrah carefully, certain she still had not come to the part that made her nervous. "What else did Mar Lon tell you?"

"He said you champion chaos."

"Did he now?" Colbey smiled, amused by Mar Lon's impression. He gave the bard credit, at least, for not claiming Colbey *served* chaos.

"*Do* you champion chaos?" Khitajrah remained relentless.

"No. I champion balance."

"Balance?"

"Balance, yes. And proper equality between the higher forces that define and oppose one another. Perhaps if we had balance, those forces wouldn't have to war against one another with such a frenzy."

An interesting and simplistic interpretation. The staff touched Colbey's mind for the first time since his awakening. True to its vow, it remained at the edge of his thoughts, without challenging barriers or defenses.

"And the other three Wizards?"

"Believe they champion law."

"Do they?"

"That remains to be seen."

"Oh." Khitajrah fell silent for the moment, but there was a tenseness about her that defied completion.

"You have another question," Colbey prompted.

"Well ..." Khitajrah considered momentarily. "... yes. Yes, I do. Since you're a Wizard, you do know something about magic?"

Colbey laughed. "You've probably picked the one Wizard in history who doesn't." He gathered from her manner and radiating thoughts that her current flow of ideas had some relation to chaos' promise. Intrigued, he encouraged her. "But ask me anyway."

Khitajrah's hand stilled on Colbey's knee. "Chaos claimed that the power to restore life came unexpectedly, when a specific item instilled with magic became broken."

Colbey's brow furrowed. "If that's true, the object shouldn't be hard to find. There's no more than one or two that could fit the description." He considered. As far as he knew, aside from the Wizards' individual sanctuaries, the only magical items were the Swords of Power, the Pica Stone, the Staves of Law and Chaos, and the gems in the hilt of Mitrian's sword. "Did it say the item was already broken or that the power would come once it broke?"

"Broken already." Khitajrah twisted in his grip to face him fully, her excitement tangible. "Do you know what the item might be?"

Colbey dodged the question. "Did it tell you anything else about the item?"

"Just that the life-restoring property would only work on a single person. And only once." Khitajrah caught one of Colbey's hands, chalky against her darker skin. "Do you know?"

"There're two possibilities I can think of." Colbey recalled the dullness of the Pica shards, doubting any of its magic remained, even if he could find the pieces. But the cracked gems in Mitrian's sword apparently still held enough power to keep the blade sharp.

"What are they? Where? Tell me!"

Colbey shook his head. He had no means to direct her to the location of the Pica remnants. As to Mitrian, finding Arduwyn and Frost Reaver gave him reason to visit her side of the world as soon as possible. It made little sense to send Khitajrah there by herself. Soon enough, she would discover that the woman who could restore life to her son was also the one who had killed her husband. Although he had no reason to believe Khitajrah meant himself or Mitrian harm any longer, Colbey thought it best not to send a woman blindly among Renshai. Besides, he would enjoy seeing his students, kin, and followers once again. "I'll do better than tell you. I'll take you to it."

Though Colbey had not answered her question fully, Khitajrah seemed too elated to care. She threw her arms around Colbey's neck, planting a kiss on his lips with such fervor it sent an involuntary shiver of desire through him.

The *aristiri* screeched a sudden, high-pitched note that shocked Khitajrah and Colbey. It swooped from the desk, talons slamming into the side of Khitajrah's head, one wing buffeting Colbey across the face.

Khitajrah reeled back with a cry of pain. Instinctively, Colbey leapt to his feet, prepared to do battle, though he had no intention of harming Formynder. Apparently finished, the *aristiri* flapped back to its perch, a few strands of dark hair wound around its claws. It fluffed up its feathers, making the vertical belly stripes stand out in bold relief, then it preened as if nothing had happened.

Khitajrah rubbed at the wound, then stared at the tiny smear of blood on her fingers. "What's wrong with that damned bird?" She held pressure against the scratch.

Colbey shrugged, rubbing an eye grazed by a wing feather. Despite the Western Wizards' supposed bird rapport, he seemed unable to read anything of the *aristiri*'s intentions. "I guess it's the only way it has to remind us there're other matters to attend." Casting about, he located a pair of britches, pulled them on, then turned his attention to the messenger falcon. "Swiftwing?"

The falcon squawked. It unfurled long wings.

Before the bird took flight, Colbey rose and covered the distance to it. The one other time it had brought him a message, it had driven its talons through the skin of his arm, accustomed to the Cardinal Wizards' imperviousness to injury, a quality he did not share then or, apparently, now. As expected, he discovered a strip of parchment bound to its leg. He peeled it free.

Though Colbey knew the Western, trading, and Northern languages, the grand strokes and spirals of this hand remained illegible. He recognized only the single rune that represented Shadimar's signature.

"What's it say?" Khitajrah came up beside him.

"I have no idea. It's not in any language I've ever seen."

Khitajrah glanced at the note over his shoulder. "It's not Eastern."

Colbey consulted the staff. *Can you read it?*

It's an archaic tongue. If you had your collective consciousness, you could read it.

The use of such a language confused Colbey. *Shadimar knows I don't have the Western Wizards' memories. Why would he send such a thing?*

They sent it. All three Wizards. Clearly, they didn't want you to read it. The staff's response seemed condescending as if the answer should have been obvious.

Still, Colbey pressed. *Why would Wizards who claim to hold the knowledge of the universe send me a letter they knew I couldn't read?*

Colbey sensed the staff's rigid patience, like a mother explaining a straightforward concept to a dim-witted child. *Clearly, they didn't want you to read it.*

Colbey ignored the staff's tone. *Then why send it at all?*

Law, propriety, and convention. They only have to send you the invitation. Nowhere does Odin specify the language.

Invitation?

To meet the other three Wizards' successors and to attend their attempts at the Tasks of Wizardry.

How do you know that?

I DO read the ancient tongue.

It seemed to Colbey that Shadimar, Carcophan, and Trilless should have presumed the staff would interpret their message for him. Still, despite all of their knowledge, they had no more experience with the Staves of Law and Chaos then he did. He crumpled the parchment, waving the messenger falcon away to indicate that he would send no reply.

Swiftwing flapped into the air, winging from the room and toward the cave mouth.

Khitajrah looked horrified by Colbey's destruction of a note not yet read. "Don't you think it might be important?"

"No," Colbey said. I don't believe it is." Turning, he gathered blankets, sorting clothes from among them. "Pack what you have. I've got a long overdue practice, then it's time to get started traveling."

Khitajrah laughed. "Don't you think we should wait until morning?"

Colbey fastened his sword belt around his waist. Until that moment, he'd felt naked despite the britches he had previously donned. The candlelight in the main chamber had given him no indication of time of day, but that did not concern him. "What makes you think I'll finish my practice before dawn?" Without awaiting a reply, he trooped through the familiar corridor and into the night.

The cold air bathed his skin, aching through the massive scar across his chest, a relic of his last stand with General Santagithi against an army of Northmen. Santagithi had died, and Colbey would have also if not for a personally forced march and Shadimar's healing magic, magic now aimed only against him. The moon and stars jabbed glittering lines and pinpoints along the Weathered Mountains' crags. Pausing only to mentally dedicate his sword work to Sif, he whipped both blades from their sheaths and threw every shred of his being into perfect cuts, arcs, and dodges. Other concerns fled, mind and body locked into the flawless steel dance of his swords. Nothing mattered but the eternity of battle and the patron goddess who ruled the Renshai.

Within moments, Colbey felt eyes upon him, knowing the certainty of Khitajrah's presence. Her obvious awe meant little, but her pride in his skill warmed him. He had forgotten the joy that came from those few who appreciated who and what he was. Equally, he missed the satisfaction that accompanied the successes and failures of teaching eager students. He looked forward to seeing the other Renshai again. He wanted to watch the West find the promise of its new youth. And, for the first time in years, he thought of the closeness that had escaped him since his sterility had become apparent and the Renshai women had shunned him as anything more than a friend and teacher.

Colbey spiraled into a wild sequence of slash and counter-cut, amused that his thoughts had turned to companionship at a time when world and eternity hung in the balance. *What better time?* The ideas of love, sex, and partnership seemed out of place in a mind that had long discarded them as unnecessary distraction, and he wondered what it was about Khitajrah that had reawakened needs long buried. He doubted he could have found a woman less like the type he had believed he wanted, even up to the moment he had awakened; and he wondered if there lay the answer. One thing seemed certain. The most beautiful of goddesses, Freya, she who represented battle, fertility, and sex in its purest form, sanctioned this union. Colbey's loyalty lay with his religion and its tenets: swords, death in combat, and law. And now, the West and Khitajrah.

CHAPTER 23

Thor's Solution

The horses loped easily over the forest trails that ran from Pudar toward Erythane. Fat green buds clung to the branches, swaying in a spring breeze; and sunlight beamed through the leafy canopy. Warm and surrounded by new growth, riding a well-conformed horse and savoring the afterglow of a grueling sword practice, Colbey reveled in the beauty of the woodlands. The world felt right for the first time since the Great War that had seen the deaths of so many, Westerners and Easterners alike.

Khitajrah rode a responsive, docile bay gelding, muscled for endurance as well as short bursts of speed. Colbey admired the animal that appeared to be Frost Reaver's equal in every way but familiarity and ownership. In some respects, it seemed superior. Its brown hide and sable hair would better handle the sun and would make it less of a beacon when it came to quiet movement. Sill, Colbey knew he had an attachment to the white stallion that no horse, no matter its virtues, could match.

Colbey rode the chestnut gelding he had discovered at Crossroad Fyn's. True to her claim, Khitajrah had, apparently, watched him horse shopping. She had purchased the gelding for him sometime during the days he had sprawled in coma from her poisoning. He did not know where one Eastland woman had come upon so much money, but he guessed the answer lay with the simple saddles that graced the backs of both horses and made her gem-encrusted bridle seem gaudy. Once, he suspected, her horse's tack had matched. Clearly, the saddle had gone to barter, perhaps purchasing his own mount and plainer gear. The *aristiri* perched on his saddle's cantle, taking no more notice of the mane whipping into its face than the horse did of its presence. Occasionally, it leapt into the air, gliding cautiously so as not to slap horse or Renshai with its wing beats.

"So what is this broken magical thing?" Khitajrah's question shattered a long silence. She, too, seemed affected by the beauty of the day. Despite her flirting the previous evening, she now treated him like a new acquaintance, apparently uncertain or embarrassed about how quickly she had taken to him.

"A gem," Colbey replied, unsure whether to mourn or cheer the loss of intimacy. It only made sense for her to feel as if she knew him better than she did. They had, in a fashion, saved one another's lives. The mind link brought them closer than most lovers became in a lifetime, and she had nursed him back from the edge of oblivion, though she had been its cause. "A damaged gem." Although uncertain whether the topaz eyes in Mitrian's hilt held the answer to Bahmyr's death, Colbey discovered the staff he had slid through the bindings of his gear seemed positive this was the item chaos had indicated.

"Well that narrows it down." Khitajrah met Colbey's vagueness with sarcasm. "What kind of gem? Who owns it? Would he be willing to sell it?"

A warning, mental touch from the staff stole Colbey's attention. Although he saw nothing unusual, it felt as if a power beyond his comprehension hovered nearby. He answered as briefly and quickly as possible. "It's part of a larger whole. No, I don't think my friend would sell it, but she might sell its one time use. Now hush. Something's wrong."

Khitajrah whispered, "What's the matter?"

"I'm not sure," Colbey admitted, still sensing a massive presence. It reminded him of the staff, limitless in its scope, not necessarily with an intention of harm yet dangerous for its hugeness and alien sense of unbelonging. *What is it?*

The staff seemed equally uncertain. *I don't know,* it returned. *Something feels out of place.*

Wizards' magic? Colbey guessed.

The staff returned a sensation that combined curiosity and uneasiness. *I don't think so. I'm not certain. Stay cautious.*

Colbey broke the contact. The staff had told him nothing he did not already feel himself, and its warning was unnecessary. It seemed more distraction than help. If it had some sudden revelation, he felt certain it would tap on his barriers for attention. He pulled up his horse.

Khitajrah drew to a halt also. She opened her mouth, as if to question again. Then, apparently thinking better of it, she said nothing. Colbey's doubts must have come through clearly enough.

Colbey dismounted, flipping his horse's reins over the furry head and loosening Harval in its scabbard. If a shape-shifting mass of demon chaos attacked, he wanted as much mobility between the trees as possible. On open ground, the horse would have given him speed, power, and elevation. In the forest, the animal's size would hamper the distinctive Renshai maneuvers he would need to face such a creature. From the ground, he would not have to deal with the animal's panic.

Khitajrah shifted her weight in preparation to join Colbey, but he stopped her with a gesture. "Stay there. If there's a fight, run for Béarn. You'd only get in my way."

Khitajrah frowned, but she did reseat herself. "Your confidence in my ability is touching."

"It's not your ability I'm doubting." Colbey suspected from Khitajrah's manner and movement that she had little or no experience with battle. Her grace and coordination came from some other form of exercise. "Fighting magic takes certain equipment you don't have." He did not specify further. Should she prove weaker than he believed and fall prey to chaos again, he did not want another enemy after the sword and staff.

"Magic? You think there's magic about?"

"I don't know," Colbey reiterated. "It may be nothing."

Khitajrah rode on, holding her mount to a walk so that Colbey could keep pace. Conversation disappeared. The *aristiri* perched on the saddle, head cocked, as if testing the air for Colbey's concern. The staff's presence seemed to hover nervously around him, its aura difficult to separate from the more foreign sense of wrongness.

For some time, they continued in a silence broken only by the crush of leaves and snap of twigs beneath the horses' hooves. The roadway opened onto a vast meadow of clover. A deer glanced up from its grazing, spotted the intruders and bounded away, a spindly-legged fawn dogging its mother's leaps. The fluidity of their movement made the horses seem cloddish and ponderous. Gaze locked on the beauty of the deer's run, Colbey lost the edge of wariness for an instant that nearly cost him his life.

The *aristiri* screeched, the flap of its wings hammering Colbey's ears as it took flight. Gaze wrenched suddenly in its direction, he caught a glimpse of something vast streaking toward him.

"Run!" Colbey shouted, diving and rolling from the path of the oncoming object. Something gigantic struck the ground just shy of his head. The earth trembled, bowling Colbey into a wild, uncontrollable spiral. For an instant, his limbs felt liquid. Then ground and self seemed to come back together, and his gaze fixed on the object that had nearly crushed him. It was a hammer, its head the size of his mount and its handle proportionately short, the length of his arm from fingertips to shoulder.

"Run!" Colbey hollered again. "Go!" He staggered toward the weapon, catching a glimpse of Khitajrah's horse struggling to its legs, its rider still clinging to the saddle. It shot down the roadway at a full gallop, though whether at Khitajrah's command or panicked beyond obedience, he did not know or care. His own horse sprinted after it. *Mjollnir. Thor's hammer.* There seemed no other possibility. Channeling strength from mind to body, he seized the handle and tried to lift.

But unlike his experience during the Tasks of Wizardry, the gold rebuffed his efforts easily. At first, he felt no movement. Then, suddenly, the whole of the weapon shifted, rising of its own accord. Colbey flinched back as the hammer soared into the air, nearly catching him in its retreat, then flew toward the heavens.

Colbey whirled, standing and drawing his sword in one motion. He had little doubt about what he would find standing behind him in the meadow, and the sight did not disappoint him. At the far edge of the vale, a giant stepped from the forest. He stood twice Colbey's height, muscles massive and defined beneath skin as white as Frost Reaver's fur. Flame-red hair bristled from head and chin like a lion's mane. The face looked as hard and bright as polished steel, and the angry blue eyes seemed to impale him. *Thor.* Colbey harbored no doubt. He froze, unwilling to move. Always, he had dedicated himself to the will of his goddess. If Sif's husband wanted him dead, he had no right nor intention of fighting the sentence.

Mjollnir returned to its wielder's hand. A moment later, the hammer sped for Colbey again. Survival instinct drove Colbey to dodge. He discarded it, finding other reason. *What god could respect a man who died without a fight?* Again,

Colbey swerved from the path of the blow. Once more, the hammer slammed ground into crater; and the jolt of its landing stole Colbey's balance. He tumbled to the clover, scarcely managing to roll to his feet before the weapon flew back toward Thor.

Colbey charged, swords clearing their sheaths in an instant. The hammer tumbled over his head, outstripping him back to the hand of its master. As Colbey cleared half the distance between himself and the god, Thor gave a mighty roar. "Die, you miserable little traitor to the gods! Mjollnir will crush you like the insect you are." The hammer pounded air, screaming toward Colbey at impossible speed. Colbey checked his rush into a side step, using his swords to parry the hammer aside. Gold shattered the steel of his right hand sword and drove Harval from his grip. Though only a light graze, the power behind the racing weapon ached through Colbey's arms and the breeze of its passage slammed him to the ground. The hammer sank into the earth so deeply, even its handle disappeared.

Thor growled something wordless. The hammer twisted in its rest.

Gaining his feet again, Colbey retrieved Harval and ran at Thor.

Movement jolted through the ground as the hammer shifted. Colbey managed to keep his balance, continuing his rush, giving his all to the battle. So many times, he had believed he had finally found the death in glory he had sought; yet the Guardian's threat haunted him: "You do still fear one thing. And, although you wouldn't have any way to know it yet, that fear has been recognized. You will never reach Valhalla." Bothered but not daunted, Colbey sped toward the god of storms and law. He would not let his knowledge of such a prophecy, by itself, make it truth.

The ground quivered and shook beneath Colbey's feet as the hammer lurched free of its pit. Thor filled the Renshai's vision, a towering giant all muscle and red hair. This time, Colbey beat the hammer to its wielder. He launched himself at Thor.

Braced for the attack, Thor threw up a shield as broad as Colbey's body. His other fist raced toward the Renshai.

Colbey dodged between sword and strike. Harval jabbed flesh and tore, dragging an angry red stripe through leather leggings and up Thor's leg. The god kicked and spun.

Colbey's sudden side step barely saved him from a crushing.
He turned the movement into a high, whirling kick, foot
slapping Thor's armored hip with a force that sent pain lancing through Colbey's leg. It seemed not to affect Thor at all.
The follow-through of Colbey's sword creased the links of
mail, splitting a few.

Mjollnir sailed back toward Thor. The god raised his hand
in anticipation. "World-destroyer. Scum-eating slave of
chaos!"

Colbey leapt again. This time, his sword slashed a line
into the muscle of Thor's arm and missed his chin by fingers' breadths. With a roar of rage, Thor caught the hammer
in his other hand and swung it for Colbey.

The strength behind the blow seemed incalculable, but the
speed surprised Colbey more. He ducked, the breeze of its
passage cold on his scalp. A second of hesitation, and the
hammer would have torn his head, crushed and bleeding,
from his body. His riposte impaled Thor's arm near the pit.
Though Thor grunted in agony, the pain did not slow his
next attack. He reversed the direction of his strike effortlessly. Once again, the hammer sprang for Colbey's head.

Colbey jerked Harval, to free it from its deeply buried
rest. The sword came only partially loose, blood splattering
Colbey in a sudden wash. He sprang aside as he pulled, hoping the direction of his dodge would catch the god off-guard.
The hammer swished across in front of Colbey, skinning the
knuckles that gripped Harval. He dodged Thor's kick as the
blade came free. Then the god's foot thrust between Colbey's legs, sending him into a wild tumble. He rolled to rise
as the hammer screamed down on him.

"Modi," Colbey whispered, flinching aside. The hammer
slammed ground, the shock of its impact momentarily stealing all power from Colbey's limbs. He regained equilibrium
quickly, ducking around Thor's legs for an open strike at the
mailed abdomen. As Thor tore his hammer from the ground,
dripping chunks of earth and roots, Colbey jabbed with the
intricate Renshai triple twist made for breaking mail. The
blade sliced through space that seemed far too small, creating a slit that the triple loop construction should have made
impossible.

Before Colbey could thrust far, Thor's meaty hand closed
around his shoulder.

A shriek split the air. From nowhere, the *aristiri* flapped between Colbey and Thor, buffeting the Renshai briefly as it passed. It dove for Thor's face, battering the red-haired god with wings and talons at once.

Thor reeled backward, dropping Colbey, tearing at the bird with both clawed hands.

Though this opened Thor's defenses, Colbey withdrew. He would not fight an unfair battle, especially against a god. "Formynder, stop!" he shouted, hoping the hawk would read his anger. "Off! It's not your fight."

But the *aristiri* took no heed of its raging master. It poked and flapped, dodging the giant's hands that sought to enwrap its wings repeatedly.

Sensing another presence, Colbey whirled. He faced a lean, sinewy Northman, handsome in features and form.

The other seemed to take no notice of the drawn sword, striped with god's blood. "Come with me." He extended a hand.

Colbey glanced at Thor. The god caught the *aristiri* a resounding blow that sent it spiraling toward the ground. Just before it hit, it managed to reverse its momentum, wing beats strong as it soared back toward the Thunderer's face. "I have to . . ." he started.

The stranger interrupted, "You have to nothing. Thor's a blustering fool, and an ignorant one at that. But the world needs both of you."

Colbey hesitated. It was not his way to abandon a battle, especially with a friend's life at stake.

"Don't be stupid," the man said. "No winners here and more losers than anyone can spare. Should either of you kill the other, you would start the *Ragnarok* at once."

Those words mobilized Colbey. The man's casual and unavenged insulting of Thor gave the Renshai as many clues to identity as the comeliness of his features. Blond hair, youthfully tousled, danced in the breeze. Halfway between round and oval, the face seemed to define perfect features. Mischievous eyes currently reflected sincerity and strong purpose, changing color with the light. Not a shadow or wrinkle marred the near-perfect features. *Loki? Or Frey?* The legends claimed both or either as the handsomest god as the story fit. The serious attempt to protect Thor made the latter seem more likely. Yet the eyes fit Loki. And Colbey felt a distant certainty that he had met this god before. About the

figure's divinity, at least, he felt certain. He had belittled
Thor with a frivolous ease that made it seem commonplace,
and he had approached too silently for any mortal. In the
forest, Arduwyn might have come that close without
Colbey's knowledge, but he doubted any man could cross
open meadow without alerting him, battle-occupied or not.

Grudgingly, Colbey gave his hand. Light flashed, tearing
his vision. He straggled backward, groping blindly for substance. His hand touched something huge and fuzzy, an animal where, moments before, a man had stood. Through a
brilliant haze of colored lights, he caught glimpses of clover-
filled meadow, his ears ringing with the slap of wing beats
and Thor's stalwart curses and shouts. Then he caught a
glimpse of a horse, glossy black to the root of every hair, its
eyes red as a demon's. "Get on," the horse said. "Hurry."

Colbey balked. The transformation clearly identified the
other as Loki the Shape Changer, the lord of chaos destined
to lead giants and Hel's dead against the gods in the final
battle. Nothing good could come of association with the god
of destruction.

The horse made an abrupt dive, driving its head between
Colbey's legs.

Still mostly blinded and unprepared for the unhorselike
maneuver, Colbey found himself hefted and tossed onto its
back. Even as he caught his balance, sliding down the
darkly-maned neck, an abrupt and wild leap carried them
forward so fast and hard they seemed to fly. Now astride,
Colbey naturally concentrated on balance. To leap free at
such speed would mean falling to his death, and he never
doubted Loki's hooves would smash in anger whatever remained of his body. He fought for positioning, crouched on
the withers, knees crushing the muscles of its upper forelegs,
arm wrapped around its bull-like neck. He kept Harval
clamped in a death hold. Wind ripped at his grasp and his
balance. Though smooth, each of Loki's mighty leaps
shocked through Colbey, all but sending him spinning off
into the horse's whirlwind wake.

Three huge jumps brought Loki and Colbey across the
meadow in an instant. Then, the black stallion raced recklessly through the forest, as if oblivious to the low-hanging
branches and thorny copses. Colbey ducked flat to the animal's neck, its mane tangling with his hair, its musk a constant, sweet odor in his nostrils. Colbey clung; for the

moment he could do little else. Yet, he wondered what the
lord of chaos and mischief wanted with him. And he wondered if he would soon fight another god.

Freya had grown familiar with the *aristiri* shape her robe
of feathers granted, though it stole her human voice and her
hands. She continued to wage her frenzied war against
Thor's face, now more concerned with dodging than distraction. As much as she hated the thought of owing gratitude to
Loki, he had come when she needed him and the others had
not. Mostly, she guessed, curiosity and his own madman's
plans kept him watching her every movement and decision
with the intensity of the hawk form she took. She dodged
another roundhouse punch, gracefully slipping beneath the
stonelike fists, listening for the last fading echoes of Loki's
hoofbeats.

Thor's other hand made a sudden slash that caught her
across the side of the body. She plummeted, pain stealing all
grace and maneuverability. Her light hawk's body slammed
against the ground, rolling and tumbling in a heap of feathers and talons. Breath would not come. She opened her beak
wide, gasping for the air her battered lungs would not admit.
For an instant, she took her attention from the battle to
breathe. Mjollnir raced toward her, handle gripped in Thor's
fist.

Freya's bruised side hampered her dodge. Her empty
lungs would not allow song or warning. Desperately, she
wriggled free of the feathered cloak that gave her *aristiri*
form, her goddess legs emerging from the collection of
muddy feathers.

Thor pulled his blow, the hammer digging a crater into the
earth beside her. Leaving the weapon entrenched, he approached hesitantly. "Freya?"

A trickle of air wheezed into her lungs. She struggled to
shed the remainder of the cloak, exposing a dress studded
with gold brooches and sewn through with metallic threads.

"Freya?" Thor repeated, still uncertain. The single word
held a myriad of questions, from her welfare to her motives
for interfering with his battle.

The breaths came more easily now. Freya freed herself
fully from the feathered cloak. She clambered to her feet.
Thor's blows ached through her, yet she showed no weakness. She tossed the costume over one shoulder and met

Thor's gaze. Her pale blue eyes flashed with rage, and the many gold adornments seemed to wink and sparkle in echo. The necklace of the Brisings writhed. Her breasts rose and fell with every soothing breath.

"Are you well?" Thor asked, genuinely concerned.

Finally, Freya gathered enough air to speak. "Have you taken leave of your sense?" She kept the last word singular to imply Thor had never had more than one thought from the beginning. "Just your presence here could cause the destruction."

For all the insult Freya had given his intelligence, Thor caught the discrepancy immediately. "You're here."

"Yes. But I have a grasp of the concept called subtlety. I've interfered as little as necessary, not huffed about molding meadows into hills."

Thor glanced about, as if noticing the valleys his hammer had bashed through the clover for the first time. "What difference the contour of this meadow when the fire lord kills Frey and sets all of man's world to flame. The others may cry over their fate, but I won't sit idle while gods and our creations die."

Blood coated Thor's arm from shoulder to wrist, splattered by his movement. Also noting the gash on his leg, Freya drew closer. "Sit. Let me tend those wounds while we talk."

"Bah! Scratches, nothing more." Despite the dismissal, Thor sat obediently, his bulk quaking the meadow ground. "For all this subtlety you claim, you attacked me outwardly enough."

Freya drew bandages from her pockets, the same that she used while collecting souls from the battleground. By right, she had first claim to the honored dead, even over Odin's *Valkyries.* "With you, subtlety is unnecessary. And useless besides." She wrapped the stab, applying pressure as the bandage unwound. "Well-landed attacks. He has all the weapon skill of his father."

"Or the luck." Thor remained still while she worked, but his gaze scanned the forest. "One blow from Mjollnir would have smashed him. Kyndig must die."

Tying the bandage, Freya set to work on Thor's leg, twisting lines of cloth over the opened leather and skin. "I don't believe that to be the case."

"I think—" Thor started.

"I don't believe that to be the case either." Freya looked up from her work long enough to glare. "Odin created the system of Wizards to keep us from interfering directly on the world of man. You know our tiniest actions here have unpredictable and enormous repercussions." She knotted the bandage, annoyance causing her to draw it tighter than necessary.

Thor tested the movement of his leg. "Worse than the *Ragnarok* itself? I think not."

"In this case, so." Freya met his gaze to deliver the coup de grace. "Nothing could awaken chaos quicker than gods killing gods, and no crime is more heinous than a god slaying kin. Kyndig is your son."

"My son?" Thor snorted. "Nonsense."

"Seventy-eight years ago, you lay with a mortal woman. A Renshai named Asnete. And Loki saw you."

Thor swept his legs into a crouch. "A sword mistress of unequaled grace and skill. How could I help wanting her?"

Freya smiled. "The way of the gods. To know love at a glance and need it as swiftly. It is to be my brother's downfall." She referred to Frey's trading of his magic sword for the hand of his giantess wife. He had seen her only once yet pined for her after and, now, centuries later, remained wholly faithful. "And perhaps my own." She fingered the necklace, recalling how she had slept with dwarves for love of the gold. Yet her words went far deeper than Thor could guess. It had taken only a glimpse of Colbey for her to know they belonged together, no matter his destiny.

As usual, Thor cut through history and the Norns' promises for the future. "Asnete died in her very next battle. She bore no son."

"She carried your son before her death. I knew that and so did Sif. It is my way to know unions, and Loki's joy of spreading trouble brought the news to your wife as well."

Thor shook his head, still missing the connection between Colbey's birth and his illicit coupling. His manner tightened. Apparently he was nervous about the penalties that should have come with his wife's knowledge of his action, yet had not.

"You know how Sif is about fidelity and marriage. She bore neither of your children, but she loves them for being yours. When I discovered Asnete dying on the battlefield, Sif begged me to help her make a switch. Ranilda Battlemad gave birth to Colbey, but the blood that flows through him is Asnete's and yours."

"Are you certain?"

"I couldn't be more certain. And the Tasks of Wizardry confirmed the truth I already knew."

Thor stared, face darkening, as if about to accuse Freya of lies. "My son? *My* son will cause the *Ragnarok?* The Norns are crueler than even I would have guessed."

Freya soothed as much as she could. "It remains to be seen whether or not he causes the destruction. If you kill your own child, you will bring chaos upon us instantly with all its power."

Thor twisted a loose corner of his damaged leggings. "What now? I can't just let the *Ragnarok* happen. Naming him my son only increases my responsibility. And my need to make things right."

"No." Freya rose. With Thor crouched, she met his gaze at eye level. "Leave the Thunder Child to me. As much as Sif, I have watched him; there's more here than even we understand. You go home and rejoice in having the most loyal and understanding wife in existence. Had we been mortal, and I your wife, I would have killed you and the child both. Yet though I wouldn't share Sif's gentle, forgiving nature, it has its place. Go."

So saying, Freya tossed the cloak back over her frame. In *aristiri* form, she floated toward the forest to find her charge.

At length, the black stallion switched from a random track through the tangled depths of forest to roadway. Even here, brush clogged the edges, curling into the pathway and partially crushed by the passage of hoof and cart. Overhead, branches meshed, turning the road into a long, dark tunnel that seemed to suit Loki well, a shadow-figure in every sense, darting over tarry dirt and through the closed passageway. Clinging became easier. Colbey managed to sheathe his sword, the horse's wind-blown mane stinging his face. Despite the speed, he measured the distance to the ground. As much as he enjoyed horseback combat, it made little sense when the enemy was the horse itself.

Well into an unfamiliar part of the forest, Loki's pace slowed. Colbey leapt free. He hit the ground rolling, veered from a sapling in his path, and came up in a ready crouch.

The sword remained sheathed, but he could draw and cut before most warriors could think to do either. The sheath on his left hip flopped, conspicuously empty. Though more valuable and powerful, the staff he missed less. He had bound it securely with his gear, lost again for the antics of a horse. But, for now, the presence and wrath of gods took precedence.

The horse skidded to a sudden stop, hooves plowing through fertile soil and leaf mulch. The instant it turned, a flash lit the forest. This time, Colbey managed to shut his lids more quickly. Even so, colored bands striped his vision as he looked upon the same man-shaped being who had confronted him in the meadow. Loki headed toward him.

With a leisurely deliberateness, Colbey drew his sword, more for warning than threat. "Stand where you are."

Loki went still, though not a trace of fear marred his stance. Clearly he had stopped from indulgence rather than concern. "Forgive the rough ride. I knew you wouldn't willingly leave a battle. I had little choice but to force retreat."

Colbey guessed Loki's stake in the matter, and it enraged him. "First, I've fought my own battles since I could walk. I don't need men, birds, or gods rushing in to rescue me. Whatever you think of my ability, I might have won that battle. If not, I would joyfully have died on Thor's hammer."

"Either would have been a tragedy." Loki fixed his gaze on Colbey.

Colbey remained in place, his stance a perfect combination of offense and defense. "Save your lies, Lord of Chaos. Your intentions are easily read. You believe Thor would have slain me and you would have lost the one who champions your cause. But you're wrong on both counts. Go away."

Loki laughed then, the sound carrying bitterness and irony rather than joy. "For one bothered by undeserved prejudice, you certainly are quick to inflict the same on another."

Colbey could not help but consider the words. Yet the conclusion seemed obvious. "It's no secret what you are. Nor the death and destruction you work toward."

Loki spat, clearly disappointed as well as insulted. "This from a Renshai. And a Wizard who many have described the same way."

Colbey doubted the comparison. "So you deny backing chaos? You won't be the one who sets *Ragnarok* in motion?"

"I take both of those responsibilities very seriously."

"You don't deny them."

"Certainly not."

Colbey drove his point home. "If I had killed Thor, it would have strengthened your side in the *Ragnarok*, the side of chaos."

"Yes."

"Therefore, you had to believe I would lose the battle. You kidnapped me from the fight, which means you didn't want me to die. I can only presume you think I work for your cause. There, you're wrong."

Loki's eyes assumed their more natural green, highlights dancing through irises and pupils. "Your mistake, Skilled One, is presuming I want to strengthen my cause."

Colbey froze, brow furrowing in thought. If Loki spoke truth, all of his assessment of the Shape Changer's motives came crashing down. "Why wouldn't someone want to strengthen his own cause?"

Loki smiled. "When he's placed in the position of championing a cause the world needs only in moderation."

Chills spiraled through Colbey, but he managed to suppress them. Loki's words sounded eerily close to those he had used to explain himself to the elfin captain. He tried to sort the situation from Loki's viewpoint, knowing the effort was doomed to failure. Loki had millennia of experiences and situations to call upon.

Loki aided Colbey's effort. "When Odin and his brothers created the world, he didn't trust mankind with chaos. He gave you a world wholly at law, banishing chaos to a distant plane. Yet, you and I and a few others realize that the world cannot grow without the knowledge and artistry that is chaos. Form without plan or ingenuity moves nowhere. With time, it stagnates and decays." Loki folded his arms across his chest. A beam of sunlight forced its way through the twining network of branches, sparking white accents through his yellow hair. "Odin knew, of course. He tried to interject small doses of chaos here and there, but his power proved too great. A god's drinking mug is a man's ocean. So Odin sought lesser gods to represent the chaos-forces mankind needed: Bragi of poetry, Aegir who makes the oceans unpredictable, and me."

"Fire," Colbey finished for the god. "Loki" translated to this in the Northern tongue. "Glorious, grand, beautiful.

Necessary for security and warmth, when controlled. Searing to the touch. Freed, it becomes mischievous, evil, and devastating. As unpredictable as chaos itself."

Loki shrugged, passing off insult and compliment alike. "There's logic even to fire. Remember, I was born of giants, not gods. Odin brought me among the others as his blood brother. Often, his actions seem frivolous or reckless, but he has more wisdom than the rest of us together. Odin does nothing without method."

Colbey followed the explanation, but it seemed to have deviated far from the point. "Interesting. And well worth contemplating. But what does it have to do with you not wanting Thor or me to die?"

"Chaos is necessary. Even some of the men and gods who realize it refuse to be the ones who champion it. What we truly need is balance. But, I'm one god working alone against many. If I just stood behind symmetry, I would accomplish nothing. When so many back law, the only chance for balance is to embrace chaos."

Colbey understood the concept; he did not agree with it. "I stand for balance."

Loki's shoulders rose and fell again, as if to express the futility of it all. "You can do that because I'm backing chaos on a grander scale. Whether anything you do on man's world matters remains to be seen."

"So you 'rescued' me from Thor because . . ." Colbey trailed off, hoping Loki would finish the sentence. The gods seemed even more adept than the Cardinal Wizards at dodging direct points.

Loki obliged. ". . . if Thor killed you, it would bring the *Ragnarok* early and possibly change the course of events. If you killed Thor, it would surely skew the destruction in chaos' favor." He sighed, hands dropping to his side as he tried to explain destiny to one who had defied prophecies and played a huge role in man's history. "As much as I support chaos, the battles of *Ragnarok* have plan and reason few understand. Thor must live now, so he can kill the Midgard Serpent later."

Colbey followed the weaving course of Loki's clarification, now seized by skepticism. "You want Thor to kill your son? I don't believe that."

"Once the *Ragnarok* closes, and the opponents of law and chaos die, the gods of moderation will remain. Extremes such as the Serpent and the Wolf will have served their purpose. The same is true for Thor, Odin, Tyr and, of course, myself."

Colbey studied the Lord of Chaos, seeing him in a different light than legend had described. "That's always seemed the flaw in the gods' stories to me, you know. Why would Loki set such destruction in motion knowing it would end his own existence as well?"

"Life," Loki corrected. "Not existence. Those gods killed will continue in concept." His eyes flashed orange. "Thor as the storms and thunder. Tyr as the honor men follow and the oaths they swear. Aegir as the tides. And me." Loki grinned, an expression as evil as any Colbey had seen in the many renditions of the god. "As fire, of course. At least I get to leave in a bold display of glory. Surtr, the king of the fire giants will set the worlds ablaze to scorch all things living and their works."

Images wafted from the Shape Changer, visions of frantic, violent blazes devouring the world. Fires of every color shot toward the heavens, all beneath it a uniform black. The odors accompanying the visions brought memories of bloody bodies set to pyre, the death dance of the flames grand testament to the glory of another soul sent to Valhalla. But now, the aroma of roasting flesh and clothing nauseated Colbey, and the creeping black emptiness nearly drove him to madness. There, Loki's cause turned from concern for the world's destiny to a need for a personal, glorious finish. There, Colbey believed, Loki fell victim to his own chaos. And Colbey's own long-held need to find Valhalla against all odds fell into question as well.

Colbey shook off the ugliness that had come to him as Loki's thoughts. He spoke in a whisper, his voice still seeming too loud in the wake of Loki's grandeur. "I understand the need for the death of extremes. But why mankind?"

The crazed look in Loki's eyes faded, and with them the unnatural color. Once again, the troublesome eyes assumed their usual green. "Because *Ragnarok* is a beginning as well as an end. New gods. New order. New causes. Men do not adapt to such. It is easier to start over than to separate mortal followers of extremes, especially when their normal lives are only measured in decades."

Colbey gained new respect for the bard, Mar Lon, who held to the theory that the shortest-lived handle change most quickly and easily. He considered the Bruenian farmer's innovations and the many more those would set in motion. He thought of the Pudarian youths and their commendable commitment to skill. Just in the years since the Great War, the West had adapted so far and so well. Still, it made no sense to argue details with a god. He doubted he could convince Loki, and it would only waste time. Now that he knew the Shape Changer had no designs against his life, concern for Khitajrah, his staff, and Frost Reaver took precedence. "You've given me much to consider. It isn't often a man has the opportunity to match his sword, then his wits, against gods. But I have places to go and things to do. At the very least I have to get the staff before others do."

"No hurry," Loki said. "Soon enough, your world and those in it will cease to exist."

Colbey pledged himself against that occurrence. For all he and Loki seemed to have in common concerning law, chaos, and the balance, he would oppose the destruction of man's world to his last shuddering breath. Finally, he had found a cause that took priority even over the death in glory that had driven him since birth. The unsettling of his faith unnerved him, a concept that would require long contemplation. But this was not the time. "Nevertheless, I'll be on my way, thank you." He turned.

"Wait," Loki called. "There's one more thing I have to tell you."

Colbey continued walking, hearing Loki's light footsteps sweeping behind him. For now, he believed the Lord of Chaos had said enough.

"The woman you travel with has your horse and staff. And the *aristiri* will join her soon enough. I'll take you to them."

Colbey continued walking. He had met enough of the chaos-touched to believe Loki would find a nasty parting sentence, something that would haunt him long after the discussion had finished. "I'll find my way."

Loki quoted an ancient bardic song about the *Ragnarok:*

> "Brothers and sisters
> In incest entwined.
> Sons slaughter fathers
> And mothers in kind . . ."

Loki's voice faded. Apparently, he had stopped, and Colbey left him farther behind. "Had I allowed Thor to kill you, one of the tenets of that song would have been fulfilled. And the *Ragnarok* would have come for certain."

The words intrigued Colbey enough to slow his steps. Loki seemed to be taunting him.

"If Thor had killed his son, or the son his father, it would have brought the *Ragnarok* in an instant rush."

Now Colbey stopped, many memories merging at once: Siderin's search for a full-blooded male Renshai that had not yielded Colbey's name, a prophecy that had implied he was other than a mortal man, and the seer's shock during the Tasks of Wizardry when he had sought information about Colbey's parentage.

"Let me explain, Child of Thunder. Afterward, I'll return you to your staff and your lady friend."

Colbey turned. His self, from birth to motivation seemed to have crumbled in the course of a handful of events and a single conversation. Suddenly, the information Loki held seemed too significant to avoid.

Loki grinned, strange eyes blazing. And the tale began.

CHAPTER 24

Offworld

Cloudy night glazed the Fields of Wrath, the surrounding forest scarcely penetrated by the light of stars and moon. Beneath the interweave of branches, Shadimar felt the vibrant presence of his two colleagues as well as the hovering power of the staff he carried. To his left, Carcophan seemed nonexistent, the salt-and-pepper patterning of his hair fading into the dappled shadows. He remained still, an unseen threat lost amid the normal structures of the forest, his only movement the flutter of his cloak in the wind. Still, to Shadimar's consciousness, the champion of all things evil seemed as obvious and powerful a threat as the ghostly pale figure to his right. Unfamiliar with warfare, Trilless had learned little of concealment and ambush. Though she must have realized that her usual beacon white would draw attention as well as fire, she had not changed. It had something to do with honor.

Shadimar kept judgment from his thoughts. Linked with his colleagues for the purposes of joint magic, he practiced caution. Though they had too many matters of import to consider, and wandering or touching other's thoughts uninvited was as illegal by Odin's Laws as it was rude, Shadimar worried for ideas that might accidentally seep through the contact. It made more sense to concentrate on the matter at hand with a fanaticism that buried his personal considerations, especially since these included the realization that once they had finished with Colbey he would have to deal with Carcophan and Trilless. Not in the same manner, of course, but there would come a reshuffling of relationships and priorities. Without the Western Wizard to support neutrality, Shadimar would need to become twice as competent; and the staff assured him this was already the case.

Olvaerr and Dh'arlo'mé crouched quietly in the meadow, clutching leather and linen dragging slings and awaiting Chezrith's return. Secodon lay between them. In addition to

Carcophan's expectant, vigilant presence, Shadimar sensed concern wafting from the Southern Wizard. Despite Carcophan's insistence that his relationship with Chezrith would not hamper him, as well as the coolness that characterized his teachings and their dealings together, Shadimar now saw beneath the facade. Clearly, Carcophan cared more for her than he dared to admit, even to himself. Still, Shadimar kept his own thoughts well-hidden. Now was not the time for voicing a disapproval he had already made clear. Nearly every Wizard learned not to bond with mortals, taught by the agony of watching a loved one wither in a time that passed like days. Nothing but trouble and weakness could come of the situation, yet Shadimar simply filed away the concern. So long as the relationship between Southern Wizard and apprentice did not interfere with the plans against Colbey and the kidnapping of the Renshai, it would eventually work to his advantage.

Trilless communicated with the other Wizards through the mind link. *The air stinks from the chaos of three double transports.* She referred to the magic necessary to bring the Cardinal Wizards, each drawing an apprentice, to the Fields of Wrath. *Is the spiritlock safe?*

Shadimar nodded absently. He, too, could smell the raw odor of chaos on the air, stronger than from any single spell he had known except the passage of his mentor. At first it had burned his nose, the taste filling his mouth, churning his gut, and threatening to choke up dinner. Yet, with time, the scent had become familiar. He managed to carve parts from the whole of mingled smells, each unique and interesting in its individuality. *The staff assures me,* he returned simply, seeing no need to argue. He felt less concerned over the known spell, worrying more for the one that came after. Together, he believed they could carry out the transport offworld that would prevent a daring rescue by Colbey. If the Western Wizard could not find the Renshai, he would have no choice but to barter for them.

Shadimar did not add that the odors of good and evil seemed as ugly and foreign to him as the chaos. Propriety denied the need, and it would only start a war of words between his companions. For the coming spells, concentration was a necessity he dared not risk. *Who would know the dangers of chaos better than the Staff of Law? If it believes we can cast freely now, who are we to question?*

Carcophan answered, though Shadimar had geared his response to Trilless. *When we're balancing the* Ragnarok, *it's not wise to take chances of any kind.*

Shadimar did not grace the comment with a reply. They all knew that the father of all gods lay at the root of the staff, and it seemed senseless to argue with its wisdom.

At that moment, Chezrith emerged from the darkened edge of the woodlands, far closer than Shadimar expected. If not for the woman she half-dragged and half-carried, the Eastern Wizard would not have seen her approach at all. Silently, she spread the figure on the meadow grass and unwound the sling. Blood matted the long blond hair into clumps. The face lacked expression, its features as slack as the limbs, its eyes closed. Shadimar recognized Tarah Randilsdatter, one of the so-called "Western Renshai" born and raised on the Fields of Wrath.

Alarmed by the blood, Shadimar turned on Chezrith. "What have you done? Colbey won't barter for dead Renshai."

"She's not dead, just handled." Though Chezrith answered Shadimar, she looked to Carcophan for approval. "That was my job, wasn't it? To *handle* any Renshai left awake as a guard?"

"You did well." Carcophan retreated from Shadimar's mind to address his student. "You hit her hard, fast, and quiet. You don't take chances with Renshai. Never engage sword to sword."

Shadimar scowled.

Carcophan responded to duty rather than his companion's annoyance. "Shadimar is right about returning property. If you're going to damage it, don't make it something Colbey can notice before the exchange." He whispered to Olvaerr and Dh'arlo'mé, "That rule stands for the two of you also."

Both apprentices whirled, the elf with a frown of harried irritation and Olvaerr with nervous anticipation. Like Trilless, Dh'arlo'mé would never consider harming another without just cause. Religion made Olvaerr no more likely to maim than his elven counterpart, and he remained too focused to let a comment that should not have applied to him bother him. Disabling another Northman, no matter what his tribe, went against honor; though he would not hesitate to kill should need or justification arise. Olvaerr stepped over and knelt to examine Tarah's injury.

Though Chezrith executed a bow before speaking again, her voice portrayed none of the respect her gesture did. "I never learned to knock out a warrior by patting him on the foot. It's hard enough to judge the strength of a surprise blow in daylight."

Carcophan nodded agreement.

Shadimar let the matter drop. He had little enough direct knowledge of combat to argue. He came from a village of prophets and seers. He could see the occasional rise and fall of Tarah's leathers and left the tending of war wounds to Valr Kirin's son.

"The others?" Carcophan returned to the matter at hand.

"Asleep every one," Chezrith confirmed. She pointed out individual cottages, though Shadimar's eyes could not discern one from another through the blackness. "This one's husband and the baby." She changed her focus. "The other three each alone." She gestured to a different location for each. "Mitrian, Rache, Tannin."

The three Wizards came together again for the spiritlock, Secodon moving to his master's side, drawn by the gravity of magic. Odin's Laws had always restricted spells to a bare minimum, and the threat of chaos had caused each Cardinal Wizard to further limit himself. Now, the anticipation of a massive blanket of magic thrilled through Shadimar. He felt Carcophan shift ponderously through his thoughts and Trilless' lighter presence, no less strong for its gentler touch. Of the two, she seemed the more powerful, centuries the elder and more experienced for it. Yet, in battle, they would certainly prove near enough to equal to fulfill the gray god's intentions.

The link swelled together, magical knowledge fused and competence yielding easily to Shadimar's touch. The power made him giddy and excited. He felt like a hawk gliding above a wooded lot, eyes sharp enough to spot a mouse among foliage at a height from which his own presence seemed a shapeless, black dot to human vision. The world split, revealing a thousand planes of existence beyond it, each promising newness and a freedom Shadimar had not considered imagining, a caged animal content for never having known the wild.

Carcophan yelled something desperate, anchoring the magic, and Trilless worked frantically with him to focus the spell. Reeling with the power of combined forces and the staff's vastness, Shadimar scarcely managed to draw himself from limitless concept to the confines of reality. Realizing he had strayed, he called on the staff. And it answered, nudging him toward the shapeless constructs that represented the spirits of people caught within the area of the spell. With Trilless' and Carcophan's help, he wound ponderous bands of enchantment around the Renshai. Wizards' magic did not allow mind reading, and he found the souls only as unidentifiable presences that the need for concentration would not allow him to count.

Gradually, every soul within the dimensions of the spell fell prey to spiritlock, the magics holding each at its current level of consciousness. It posed no danger to Wizards or apprentices. The former, Shadimar believed, would prove immune. He had tossed similar spells at Colbey on the Meeting Isle without effect, though whether due to the Western Wizard's status or mental prowess, he did not know. Chezrith, Olvaerr, and Dh'arlo'mé were all alert. If the spell touched them, it would simply keep them awake until the magics faded. Aside from the usual unpredictability of chaos, the only danger Shadimar knew from the spell came from repeated castings on the same subject. Holding a subject too long in one mental state could make the spiritlock permanent. In sleep, that could become eternal coma. In a waking state, it could lead to insanity.

Carcophan pulled free of the joining. "Get them." He made a brisk gesture for Olvaerr, Chezrith, and Dh'arlo'mé. The elf glanced at Trilless. At her nod, all three headed toward the Renshai cottages.

The instant the apprentices were out of sight, Carcophan turned on Shadimar. "What the hell were you doing?"

The hostility of the question bewildered Shadimar. "Casting the spiritlock. You know that."

"Calling chaos, you mean." Carcophan's normal speaking voice sounded like a shout in the wake of their previous cautious silence. "*I* cast the spell."

"You and I." Trilless attacked her opposite's need to take all the credit. She spoke softly, though voices could not break sleep enhanced by spiritlock. Only time would awaken the Renshai. "We all did our part."

A breeze rattled the surrounding trees, and leaves spiraled down over the Cardinal Wizards. Carcophan shivered, though surely not from cold. Suddenly, the situation became clear to Shadimar. The quantity of chaos required to ensorcell six Renshai unnerved the Southern Wizard. Having the upper hand for once, Shadimar smiled. "With the Staff of Law in hand and mind, I have nothing to fear from chaos. I can examine it freely and without risk. I'm sorry if it scares you."

Apparently, Shadimar had hit the problem dead on, because Carcophan had no snappy comeback. His catlike eyes met Shadimar's gray, stare for stare. "Don't get cocky. Having a bucket of water doesn't give a child the right to play with fire."

Shadimar cared little for the analogy.

Trilless interceded before a full argument developed. "We worked together. No matter who did what. The calling of chaos, even for necessary spells, bothers us all." Trilless directed her next words to Shadimar. "Between the transports and spiritlock, there's already too much chaos around. And there'll be more, whether we go offworld here or transport to do it elsewhere. Staff or no, it makes no sense to increase the danger." She revealed her own uneasiness then, "The Staff of Law can't feel comfortable surrounded by so much of its enemy. Perhaps the chaos might even do it harm."

Shadimar answered for his power. "The staff is not bothered."

Trilless remained relentless. "Harm is not always something one can sense or quantify."

Shadimar mentally dismissed the idea without bothering to argue. Never having wielded it, Trilless could not judge the might or capacity of the staff. Instead, he nodded his agreement, though he did not believe he had summoned anything more than necessary for a spiritlock that had to cover a significant amount of area. A long time had passed since any Wizard had cast anything but basic magic. Probably, Carcophan and Trilless simply did not realize the correct quantity; and Shadimar trusted the staff to judge the proper amount.

Carcophan's gaze shifted back to the cottages as he picked figures from shadow. Olvaerr returned first, using his sling to drag Tarah's sleeping husband, Modrey, and the toddler. He spread them near Tarah, who breathed with a more regular ease now, then headed back for another load. Shortly, Dh'arlo'mé returned with Mitrian. Chezrith dogged his steps, Rache draped over her shoulder. She let him flop to the ground, then knelt to examine him more carefully.

"Pretty," Chezrith said, brushing aside dark blond hair to reveal the rugged, adolescent features.

A memory tugged at Shadimar's conscience. He recalled the day Santagithi's Town had fallen, when the surviving warriors had come to his ruins for sanctuary. Strangely, though decades often passed in an eye blink, the scene from a year or two ago seemed like ancient history. He recalled Rache and Episte prodding him with questions about their fathers. Episte had spurned the sire/hero who had died in battle without meeting his son, while Rache had found as much pride in bearing the name of his blood brother's father as he had in his own father's rise from savage gladiator to honored officer.

Shadimar glanced next at Mitrian. She lay still, as innocent in sleep as she had been in infancy. Her father, Santagithi, had become Shadimar's favorite mortal charge; and the Wizard recalled the general's joy at the birth of his only child. The need to watch over Santagithi and his Renshai guard captain, Rache Kallmirsson, had caused Shadimar to keep an eye on Mitrian as well. With the help of those two men, she had grown into a courageous and competent woman, though their methods had clashed horribly and nearly destroyed a bond between them as strong as that between any father and son. Shadimar had once cherished a relationship as powerful, though Colbey's self-assurance and confidence had made it an equal friendship rather than that of elder and child.

For the first time in months, memories of that blood brotherhood brought tears to Shadimar's eyes. Colbey's competence, honor, and mortal wisdom had impressed him from the start. Yet apparently Colbey had fallen prey to the most common vice of mortals: pride. The old Renshai had come to believe himself always right and never at fault. He apparently equated his own opinion with fact, paying no heed to the findings of gods and Wizards. And Shadimar dared to hope. *Once we wrench the Staff of Chaos from his grip, perhaps we'll have no need to kill him. Perhaps he can again become what he once was.* The idea soothed, removing the guilt from the act of betraying Santagithi's daughter and grandson.

Shadimar could see Olvaerr intermittently through the

dappled patterns of moonlight the leaves left across the Fields of Wrath. He dragged Tannin, the last remaining Renshai.

Chezrith continued to coo and paw over Rache.

Shadimar mentally touched Trilless in warning. At Olvaerr's return, they would need to join together again to move their captives. It seemed strange to see Renshai without swords; the apprentices had carefully disarmed each one before hauling them to the clearing. It only made sense to leave weapons beyond reach of anything short of magic than to have to deal with protecting the weapons, from captives as well as would-be rescuers.

Trilless' presence slipped comfortably into position, linked with Shadimar. He reached for Carcophan's consciousness, shocked to brush an obvious jealous rage. It seemed surprising enough to find any emotion so superficial, but he had believed Cardinal Wizards above pettiness. Feeling like a voyeur, he withdrew.

Taking the obvious hint, Carcophan buried his concern enough to join with his colleagues. Still, Shadimar could not help feeling the smoldering rage just below the surface. The source came with it; apparently, Chezrith had made some comment about Rache's body or her interest in it.

Trilless initiated the magic this time, and Shadimar appreciated her effort. Carcophan could not accuse him of drawing too much chaos if he handled the formation and directing instead.

A moment later, Carcophan's presence became a drawn thread in Shadimar's mind as he tended matters on the outside. "No, you can't *have* him!"

The sudden distraction drew Shadimar from the spikes and lines of chaos forming in his mind's vision. Trilless swore, dragging at him and Carcophan both. Shadimar found his attention divided between a spell more difficult than any he had ever attempted and Chezrith's sour reply. He missed most of the words, but the last thought penetrated the growing swirl of magic.

". . . if I can't have him, no one will." Chezrith flipped up Rache's tunic, and moonlight flashed off something metal in her fist.

Mind clotted with chaos, Shadimar's thoughts moved in slowed motion. Logic told him what they already knew. The channeling of chaos had to take precedence over Chezrith's

action, no matter how horrible the maiming she meant to inflict on Rache.

The pool of chaos widened, Trilless speaking the first
necessary words of the incantation. She could not work the
sorcery alone, but she could not afford to lose the intention,
to let raw, undirected chaos free on man's world at a time
of change. Shadimar and Carcophan both veered back to aid
her. The staff fed the Eastern Wizard the power he needed at
once. He molded chaos with ease, the danger to Rache gradually losing importance until wholly forgotten.

A glimmer of movement carved through his earthly vision. Chezrith screamed, the sound cut off midway. She
collapsed onto Rache, two raggedly bloody holes scoring
her cloak at the throat.

An instant later Carcophan's presence disappeared from
Shadimar's mind. The backlash of chaos he had begun shaping sent Shadimar into an uncontrolled spiral. Trilless'
scream sounded out of focus, ranging from the low rumble
of demon laughter to the shrill of dolphin speech. Colors
snapped and capered through his sight, alternately bright as
leaping flames and as depthlessly dark as demon forms. He
grasped desperately for anchorage, hand winching closed
around the staff. For a moment, he found himself. Then, another gathering of chaos in the form of a second incantation
sent him tumbling end over end, suffocating him beneath its
presence. He clawed frantically for consciousness; and, suddenly, the staff was with him, standing, grounding, and supporting. He knew, without need to consider, that Carcophan
had tossed that other spell, presumably at the bowman.

Shadimar could still feel Trilless' presence spinning, her
life force growing weaker. Chaos seemed to surge and pulse
around him, horrifying for its tremendous beauty and newness. He had to rescue her, but first he had to stop Carcophan. They had little choice but to finish what they had
started, to shape the chaos they had gathered into its proper
spell. If Carcophan called more for himself, it would surely
set the *Ragnarok* in motion.

Shadimar flung himself at Carcophan's mind. He met a
boiling mixture of hatred and grief. The need for vengeance
had driven him to madness. From the first touch, Shadimar
knew Chezrith was dead. Her slayer was a teenaged girl,
scarcely more than a child. Carcophan had already slammed
her with a spell that had stolen her consciousness and, prob-

ably, her sanity. He prepared to animate a boulder to crush the last life from her as well.

No, you idiot! Shadimar leapt ruthlessly into Carcophan's mind, tearing at the fragile web of chaos his crazed emotions were weaving. *Throwing spells from anger? Colbey's doing. His chaos.* Though Odin's Laws forbade such intrusion, Shadimar grasped Carcophan's rationality and drew it back into the bond. The framework of the Southern Wizard's rage-inspired spell collapsed, and he joined the reckless swirl of partially directed chaos.

The whirlwind swallowed them both, but Shadimar kept his grip on the staff. He still spun, but the stability of the staff kept him oriented; and he dug for Trilless even as he lessened the velocity and randomness of chaos. Fresher, Carcophan also directed the magic, weakening the chaos-enemy even as fatigue threatened to drown him beneath it. At first, Shadimar found no evidence of Trilless, and it occurred to him that unfashioned chaos might slay Wizards as easily as demons could. Then, he caught sight of the glint of light that was her, one winking star nearly lost beneath chaos' explosions and flares.

Centered on the staff, Shadimar worked methodically, structuring chaos in a straight line toward Trilless, the pattern inherent in his choice of direction making the chaos more supple and easy to fix. Carcophan shaped the spell also, but his inability to differentiate direction made his efforts less precise and wore him down more quickly. Then, just as Shadimar reached Trilless, he felt the staff flicker. The momentary loss of support shocked panic through him. It made no sense that a finite amount of called chaos could overwhelm the Staff of Law. It seemed more to Shadimar as if his cause chose to abandon him as a weak man would a cause.

Shadimar clung. *I'm your champion,* he reminded.

His hold wavered. The staff seemed about to respond, then it did not.

Hold tight. It's our destiny to work together. The Lawbringer and the Staff of Law.

It must be, the staff returned, though its response seemed to bear no relation to Shadimar's words. Its manner changed, and its presence strengthened. *I would not leave you. I could not.* As Shadimar grasped Trilless more firmly, it hauled both Wizards back.

Then, as the last piece fell into place, the spell triggered. The ground quaked and shuddered, then folded. Trees shifted, trunks tilting as if to crush them between rows of wooden teeth. Then, all went still.

The Renshai lay where they had on the ground, Chezrith's still corpse sprawled over Rache. Olvaerr and Dh'arlo'mé stood rooted in place, seeming uncertain whether to revere or curse the events of the last few moments. Trilless lay near the Renshai, her eyes closed but her limbs dragging purposefully to her body. Carcophan knelt, head low, gray-flecked hair hanging in a curtain that hid his expression. Shadimar managed to keep his feet, but he leaned heavily on his staff. Though his head pounded and every part of his body ached, he managed a grin. They had escaped offworld, creating a plane that consisted of the area encompassed by the spell, only as far as he could see.

All that remained was to summon Swiftwing and direct the bird through the connection between worlds. The messenger falcon, he believed, could find Colbey.

With Loki's help, Colbey caught up to Khitajrah and the horses quickly. He found her trotting back the way she had come, leading his chestnut gelding. Her own mount balked, twisting repeatedly as if to bolt in the opposite direction, clearly reluctant to face Thor's hammer again. The *aristiri* wheeled over her head, occasionally breaking through the foliage to become visible against the sky.

Apparently catching sight of him, Khitajrah reined her horse, awaiting his approach. When he came near enough to distinguish features, she smiled with relief and welcome. "Colbey!" She dismounted, drawing up his horse to handle necessities before barraging him with questions.

Colbey appreciated Khitajrah's self-control. Few could hold back curiosity about such a grand event for even a moment. Yet she seemed free of that strange proclivity most had for stating the obvious or satisfying interest before safety. Though surely she wondered, she clearly planned to leave Colbey with time to think before speaking. It was a trait that, as far as he could tell, characterized people who did more than lie around and listen to tales about others.

Colbey collected the lead rope of his gelding, looping it securely around the cantle ring. His gear had shifted slightly askew in the horse's wild rush. This time, he had fastened

the staff well enough, and it still lay thrust through the bindings. It tapped the edges of his consciousness, apparently
wanting all the answers he had not yet given Khitajrah. Ignoring the intrusion, he retied each knot snugly, then vaulted
into the saddle. He swung the horse's head about, and
Khitajrah's mount cheerfully followed suit. He reined toward Béarn.

"You're not hurt, are you?" Khitajrah asked the important
question first.

Colbey's arm ached from his attempt to parry Thor's hammer, and his fingers felt raw. Otherwise, he had suffered no
injury, and those he had seemed insignificant. "No, I'm
fine." He wanted to continue, but he still needed time alone
to contemplate the events of the last hour. *Thor's son. A
child of the thunder.* The revelation explained much about
why magics meant to identify him, from Carcophan's summoning of demons to the seer's crystal, had failed. The
Renshai's slow aging had only partially explained Colbey's
spry suppleness as he neared eighty, although it was hard to
judge since he had no elder Renshai with whom to compare
the process. Members of the warrior tribe rarely lived far
into their thirties.

Still, Colbey saw small importance about the knowledge.
Whether Colbey Calistinsson or Colbey Thorsson, he would
have changed little of what he had done since birth. Those
things he would have changed had nothing to do with his
parentage. He would as quickly have dedicated his life to his
gods and to his swords, to the death in glory that was the reward of every Northman. Even if he could trust the Shape
Changer, the news could not make a difference to him. In
every way, he was still Colbey.

Sunlight speared between the branches. As a bar fell
across Khitajrah, it lit red highlights in the Eastern-black
hair. The horse's canter alternately fanned it into a silky curtain and tossed it carelessly back to the nape of her neck. Although she lacked the classic curves that most men found
beautiful, her nimble countering of the movements of horse
and saddle intrigued Colbey every bit as much. To him,
proper motion added a loveliness no primping could match.

The sight stirred memory of the woman of gold who had
awakened him from death in the Wizards' trials. She had
spoken the words that convinced him Loki's pronouncement
was truth: "You won't be damned because one truthseeker

could not handle what he found." Unconsciously, he fingering the gold band she had given him, wondering how it fit in with her obvious sanctioning of Khitajrah in dream. In some cultures, a ring symbolized marriage. It seemed foolish for the goddess to direct his thoughts to women and bondings while the world threatened to crash down around mankind and gods alike. He reminded himself that she had given him the ring before he had freed the Staves of Law and Chaos. Still as the priests and faithful told all, time and again, the immortal gods worked in ways mere mortals could not fathom.

Yet, as Colbey rode in silence through the forest, one motivation seemed clear. Shortly before his birth, Sif had visited the Renshai tribe and soon thereafter became their patron. Surely, she had found some satisfaction in the subsequent adulation of her husband's illegitimate child. Nor did Colbey begrudge her that small victory. His loyalty to her would never waver; and he believed his deeply rooted faith had, perhaps, won her favor despite rather than because of Thor's indiscretion. He launched into a graceful kata from horseback, his sword a deadly, silver blur and his practice dedicated, as always, to his goddess.

At his side, Khitajrah veered away from the path of the dancing sword, though surely she knew he held enough control not to harm her. Her recessed eyes met Colbey's, and she opened the conversation. "That man ... creature ... man in the meadow?"

Colbey did not miss a beat of his *svergelse.* "A god, yes."

"A god?"

"Yes."

Khitajrah considered that for a moment. "A Northern god, I presume. Chaos said the Northern religion comes the closest to the real gods."

"Thor, god of Law and Thunder." Colbey kept his techniques relatively simple, sticking with the standard Renshai maneuvers rather than creating more. Springing off and returning to the saddle might make for difficult conversation. "I believe he came to kill me."

Khitajrah made no reply for some time, clearly struck silent. Then, in an obvious attempt to share his cavalier attitude, she returned a matter-of-fact statement, though her delay blunted the effect. "I'm glad he changed his mind."

She grinned nervously, with a hint of flirtation. She seemed as rusty as he when it came to courting games.

Though simple, her statement held many meanings and questions. In six words, she had managed to express concern, interest in Colbey, and wit. In addition, she clearly meant to elicit more information about the conflict, without demanding explanations Colbey felt unwilling to give. The depth of her character impressed him, and he felt glad to have the opportunity to travel alone with her and get to know her better. "Harval had a hand in his decision, I think." He froze for an instant in the middle of a maneuver to indicate the blade, then continued. He had meticulously scrubbed the blood from the sword, but she might still notice the droplets on his clothing as well as the missing companion longsword.

Khitajrah could not contain her surprise. "You fought with a god?"

"I'd prove a weak and miserable follower if I didn't."

"You *fought* with a god?"

"It was that or get crushed by him. A rousing battle seemed more fun." Colbey smiled, meaning nothing proud or boastful. After battling demons and Wizards, as well as discovering he had been sired by a god, little seemed shocking anymore.

"The god of law, you say." Khitajrah placed more pieces in the puzzle. "Why would he attack you?"

"Do I look like some pompous priest to you? I don't presume to understand gods." Colbey launched into a flurry of feigned offense and lesser amounts of parry, covering a complete circle about himself and his horse. "My best guess would be that he's as worried as the Wizards that I'll loose chaos."

"But you fought chaos, too. Doesn't that gain you any favor?"

Colbey finished the third cycle before she finished speaking. Imagining an army in mail, he changed his tactics to cut/jab combinations and Renshai triple twists. "I have to assume that, for all their divinity and wisdom, the gods don't know everything either."

"Once again, you quote chaos."

"It's a gift," Colbey returned, his sarcasm evident.

Khitajrah placed all into a neat package. "So championing balance makes you an enemy of law *and* of chaos?"

"Obviously."

Khitajrah flushed, apparently embarrassed by being caught saying something already clear. "But I'd have thought neither would bother with you at all."

"I would have thought the same." Colbey continued his practice, separating mental conversation from the reflexive need to hone technique. "When you stand on the boundary between warring countries, you become the target of them both. It took me time to figure that out myself. I think it comes of the fact that law's so used to having no competition, it believes the world will collapse at the merest touch of chaos. Chaos, as you learned, is just as extreme. It hooks with promises of genius and progress, then beelines for utter ruin, subversion, and mayhem." He managed a shrug amid the flurry of swordplay. "Considered that way, balance's champion might prove most dangerous, using each against the other."

Khitajrah considered for quite some time, and the ride continued in a silence broken only by songbirds, the rare snap of an animal moving through brush, and the rattle of wind through the branches. At length, she spoke as if no time had passed. "Law, honor, honesty. It all fits this world. Why change it? And why balance?"

Colbey took the bait eagerly. Day passed to evening as he espoused his theories, Khitajrah listening with a rapt attention that could not have been feigned. Her questions helped direct his own goals and reasons, and he appreciated the challenge and support her intelligent questions gave him. They chose to make camp in the depths of unnamed forest. They slept close, warmed by one another as much as by the fire, and only gentle dreams of Freya disturbed Colbey's sleep.

CHAPTER 25

Back to Béarn

Colbey awakened before the sun. The campfire had burned down to winking red coals; and the branches scattered moonglow to a steady glaze beneath the canopy. Stars glimmered through the spaces between. The summer air seemed crisp and clean, untainted by human noise or odors. Even the fire no longer trickled smoke or the sweet, charcoal aroma of burning wood.

Not wanting to awaken Khitajrah, Colbey slipped beyond the trees for his practice, remaining close enough to catch glimpses of the woman between the trunks. He attributed his protectiveness to the fact that he had rescued her once from chaos. It seemed a shame to then lose her to highwaymen or predators.

Colbey did not bother to search for a clearing. Swordplay among hampering brush, trunks, and limbs would work him better than unhindered combat. His enemies would not always give him the option of battle in an open field or roadway, but he practiced in those conditions as well. Experience told him that the best technique varied from terrain to terrain and enemy to individual enemy. Becoming accustomed to one practice field or opponent, no matter how restrictive, might narrow rather than hone his repertoire.

Colbey threw himself eagerly into the practice, losing none of the excitement for it that he had known since infancy. Just the thought of practicing alone with his sword brought a thrill that neither time nor familiarity could dull. It did surprise him that the pleasure of finding a good companion, possible romance, and a new focus for his life only compounded the joy of a battle, simulated or real. He had seen so many give up their dreams because becoming skilled took too much away from the routine pleasures of living. Many times, he had rejected romance for the opposite reason, because it might interfere with his effort to always become more proficient. Now, he knew both as excuses. Having skill and family required only two people willing to stand behind one another's aspirations as well as their own. It remained to be seen whether he and Khitajrah fit that description, but she had given him cause to try to love again.

The *aristiri* perched on a low tree limb, watching the practice with bright blue eyes that seemed interested and eager. Colbey moved with his usual swiftness. Nevertheless, his sharp gaze did not miss the humanity, profundity, and vigor that seemed to draw him into the cavernous depths of the hawk's eyes. Though he knew it was impossible, the bird seemed intrigued by every maneuver, as if judging it. Though he sensed no hostility, the scrutiny made him uncomfortable in a way that seemed ridiculous. Although he had practiced in front of strangers before, it would shatter the laws of Renshai to teach their maneuvers to others, whether by accident or intention. It made no sense to concern himself with the attention of a hawk; yet, for reasons he could not explain, he wanted to please it.

It seemed as if no time had passed before the aroma of cooking roots perfumed the clearing. The gloss of moonlight brightened, then disappeared, replaced by broken patterns of sunlight through the branches. Invigorated by the warmth and brightness, Colbey combined sword work with play. He sliced branches, using the same stroke to twirl them into patterns, then lay them gently as artwork on the forest floor. He swung among the branches by his free hand, sweeping from tree to tree like a squirrel. He knew a pang of guilt for draining some of the seriousness from that to which his life had riveted since birth. But he also saw the need to spend the energy that accompanied happiness. New ideas for combat came from unpredictable places, and life often hinged on befuddling enemies with bizarre techniques so long as they did not simply waste strokes or shackle one's own attention.

Reluctantly, Colbey drew his practice to a close. From experience, he knew that he could work his arm and sword for days if other matters did not interfere. For now, he could not spare such time, even for the necessary. Frost Reaver awaited him, and only he could stop whatever rot the magics had inflicted upon the stallion. The staff had assured him that its power would hold Shadimar's spell in stasis, but it seemed cruel to leave it there in any shape or form.

Though she let him keep his own schedule, Khitajrah had

reason for hurrying as well. Colbey sensed smothered urgency about her, mingled with the curiosity and cautious attraction she felt toward him. For understandable reasons, she held doubts about him. From what he could sense, caution warred with a belief that was not quite certainty. It seemed that they belonged together, yet she would not be rushed.

After a dinner of fresh roots, bread, and salted meat, Colbey and Khitajrah continued toward Béarn. Though he believed he passed the Fields of Wrath that had become the home of the other Renshai, Colbey made no attempt to cast about and find it. He knew the terrain only well enough to get them both fully lost. Past experience told him he would most likely find Arduwyn in the king's city. He could think of no one who would prove more vigilant in the woods.

Each day passed much the same as the one before. Every morning, Colbey practiced. They broke camp before midday, riding along woodland roads, occasionally meeting other travelers heading in either direction. Most of these avoided the oddly matched couple of foreigners, and many glared at the sword Colbey carried. When the rare caravan passed, guards inserted themselves between the Renshai and the goods they carried. Most of the time, Colbey and Khitajrah found themselves alone except for the company of horses and *aristiri*. They talked of many subjects, past and present, as heavy as the philosophy of law, chaos, and balance and as light as the weather.

On the third day following Thor's attack, Colbey and Khitajrah arrived at the king's city of Béarn. Colbey's horse kept its head low, red-brown forelock falling into its eyes, apparently tired from the long ride. Khitajrah's bay seemed a study in opposites. Where its companion drooped, it pranced, making tiny skipping bucks designed to display excitement rather than to unseat its rider. He had not asked her where she had gotten the beast, yet it gave him answer without need for words. Clearly, this horse had stabled in Béarn long enough to consider it home.

Colbey paid little attention to the cobbled roadways, the exquisite masonry, and the massive citizens that lumbered through the streets, though his mind registered every detail from long habit. Without the need to consciously think, his mind sifted mundane from potential threat, and he found the latter lacking. Nothing he saw suggested hostility from the Béarnides, either visually or by sensing the emotions around him. Curiosity did radiate from many of them, presumably due to the sight of a Northman riding at the side of one who, by size and coloring, could have passed for a Béarnian child.

Smoothly cobbled pathways brought Colbey and Khitajrah swiftly to the castle gates, the sights bringing back urgent memories. More than a year had passed since Colbey had ridden to Béarn to talk Arduwyn into accompanying them to rescue the Renshai from Valr Kirin and his Northmen. Then, known enemies of Sterrane, specifically the force of his bastard cousin, Rathelon, had kept security tight. Since Rathelon's death at the hand of Mitrian's husband, Garn, there seemed little need for rigid defenses or hostility.

Nevertheless, Colbey expected to find the armed guards who met them at the gate. A half-dozen men perched on the curtain wall, each with a sword and a crossbow. This time, at least, they did not nock or aim. Two others stood just inside the gate, on the castle grounds, their halberds crossed to further block the entrance. Despite the obvious weaponry, Colbey sensed no specific menace. The guards' stalwart presences seemed more formality than threat.

"Greetings." Colbey pulled up his horse, recognizing none of the Béarnides. Khitajrah also halted the bay, though it pranced a half circle before stopping. She, too, scanned the faces. Her expression told him she found no one familiar either.

"Greetings," one of the guards on the ground returned. His response seemed more dutiful reply than welcome. "Did you come for an audience with the king?"

Colbey dismounted, believing it impolite to hold a conversation at different levels. Passing the gelding's reins to Khitajrah, he approached the guard, halting at a polite speaking distance. "Actually, we came to see Arduwyn the Hunter. Is he at the castle?"

Khitajrah startled visibly, though she gave no explanation.

"I'm not certain, sir." The guard looked to his companion, who shrugged. "If you'd like to visit someone at the castle, I'll need to know your name and which town, city, or village you represent." He pulled out a pad and stylus.

Colbey smiled. "I represent Béarn."

The man frowned, lowering his stylus and meeting Colbey's gaze directly for the first time. "How is that so, sir?"

Colbey made a grandly flourished bow, of the type he usually despised, and recited the title he had had only one previous occasion to use. "Colbey Calistinsson, Knight of the Erythanian and Béarnian kings: King Orlis and his majesty King Sterrane." He doubted he had gotten the protocol exactly right, but it should suffice for introduction.

The guard's lips wilted into a frown, though Colbey felt uncertain which of his words displeased the man. Since the knights had loyally and honorably served Béarn, in shifts, for centuries, he found it difficult to believe his title bothered the sentry. More likely, he had recognized the elder Renshai's name. Colbey traced both guards' gazes to the chestnut gelding he had ridden to the gates, now in Khitajrah's control; and another possibility for their discomfort occurred to him. As a Knight of Erythane, he should have arrived on one of the famed white chargers, its mane ceremonially braided. The simplest tunics the knights wore would have put Colbey's traveling garb to shame, and he had yet to see an Erythanian Knight not wearing the colors of both kingdoms.

The sentries exchanged a few words in Béarnese, a language Colbey did not understand, though it bore some similarity to the Western tongue which he did. The guards on the ramparts remained in place. The sentry at the gate who had not spoken leaned his halberd against the wall near the gate, turned, and headed into the courtyard toward the castle. The speaker explained. "Pardon the delay, please. We just need to verify that. Standard routine."

A nervousness wafting from the guard suggested otherwise, though his stance betrayed none of the discomfort Colbey's mind powers forced him to sense. Still, he worked to place the other at ease rather than to challenge him. As much as he despised formality, he found it difficult to condemn caution when it came to the safety of a friend who was also a king. As urgent as his mission to rescue Frost Reaver was, he had no right to expect caution and convention to crumble before his eagerness. It only made sense for the guards to question a man claiming to be both a Knight of Erythane, without the customary trappings, and the Golden Prince of Demons, especially now that lies and deceit had appeared in the world.

Khitajrah's gelding trumpeted a shrill whinny, distantly answered from the stables in the courtyard. Colbey reclaimed his reins, not wanting to burden her with two horses when hers was misbehaving. Khitajrah slid to the ground, clipping on the lead and removing the bridle. The bay quieted somewhat, dropping its head to graze on wisps of growth between the road and the curtain wall. Colbey dressed down his own mount in the same manner, also loosening the saddle slightly. By the time he finished, the sentry returned, his superior in tow.

Colbey recognized the newcomer at once. Sterrane's captain of the guards, Baran, sported the usual huge, Béarnian frame, though in his case there was far more muscle than fat. A youthful face peered out from between the customary black beard and the officer's dress issue cap with its blue plume. Unlike the heavy cloaks over mail worn by the sentries, Baran sported the lighter fabric of the inner court. They did wear matching tabards, Baran's proudly displayed, the guards' partially lost beneath their cloaks. This showed a tan bear rearing against a blue background, Béarn's royal symbol.

The sentry retrieved his halberd and took his position wordlessly. Both guards fell into attentive stances at either side of the gate, leaving only the metal bars and distance separating Colbey and Baran. The captain approached, his aura one of curiosity and caution. Colbey sensed no fear and developed an instant respect for the captain. His friends had already assured him of Baran's competence, but he had had no chance to assess the captain's skill during their single brief previous meeting. Then, he had received little from the Béarnide but suspicion.

Colbey spoke first. "Greetings, Captain Baran."

"Greetings, Sir Colbey." Baran studied Colbey through the bars, clearly having more difficulty identifying the old Renshai than Colbey had had recognizing him.

"I didn't realize Béarn's 'routine' included summoning the king's highest officer to examine visitors."

"Usually it doesn't." Baran spoke the truth, despite the insult it might imply. "Only when the visitor claims to be someone other than his appearance would suggest." He continued to look Colbey over, brow furrowed in thought. Obviously, he did not feel comfortable confirming or denying Colbey's claim by looks alone. Then his gaze shifted to Khitajrah, and the creases deepened. "Found him, did you?"

Khitajrah nodded, looking distinctly uncomfortable herself.

Khitajrah's uneasiness seemed logical to Colbey. Surely, when she had inquired about him, as Baran's question suggested she had, she had intended to kill him. He doubted she had mentioned her true purpose to anyone in Béarn.

Baran did not await a verbal reply but returned to examining Colbey almost immediately.

Tiring of the scrutiny, Colbey widened his eyes in question. "Well? Do I pass inspection?"

Baran scratched at his beard, the casual gesture hiding a host of strong emotions. Colbey sensed uncertainty, a need to temper security with respect for an honored guest. Obviously, he did not feel at all sure of Colbey's identity. Yet, if Colbey had spoken truth, the delay could quickly become offensive. "You've changed," the captain said at length, opening the way for Colbey to volunteer the information that troubled him.

More interested in haste than dignity, Colbey rescued Baran from his dilemma. "My hair's lost its white, and I broke a sword en route." He ran a hand through the short, gold locks, then indicated the drooping sheath at his left hip. "There are ways to change the color of a man's hair, Captain. Believe me, had I meant to impersonate myself, I would have made it white."

Baran seemed a bit more comfortable, though his silence indicated he had not been totally convinced.

Colbey honed in on incidents that would prove his identity. The need made him smile, and it took self-control not to laugh. In the past, his name had inspired everything from terror to mass attack. Remaining unnamed had usually proved the wisest course. Surely, no one would claim his identity along with the scorn, enmity, and fear that it inspired. Yet, as King Sterrane's friend, he would be given access to the monarch and his kingdom. He understood the demand for caution. "My first and last time here, my friends and I had a private banquet with the king, Mar Lon, you, and Arduwyn. We requested the hunter's help; and, when he agreed, his wife stormed out, enraged. Nevertheless, Arduwyn assisted us in freeing hostages from Northmen. One of ours, Garn, stayed to assist you in moving a prisoner for trial from Erythane to Béarn. The prisoner never made it here."

Colbey paused, assessing Baran's expression. Though he knew the details of the incident, he saw no need to question the captain's methods in front of his charges. The prisoner had been Rathelon, Sterrane's cousin, who had terrorized the kingdom for longer than a decade, intending to assassinate the king and take his place on the throne. Familiar with Sterrane's methods of punishment, merciful to the edge of näiveté, Baran guessed Sterrane would imprison Rathelon, at worst. As the previous captain of the guard, Rathelon knew the dungeons well enough to escape them, and Baran feared the king's cousin would restart his spree of murder. In truth, Baran had requested Garn's assistance knowing that the hot-tempered ex-gladiator would challenge Rathelon to a battle before they made it back to Béarn. As a representative of the kingdom, Baran was forbidden from such a challenge, but the law did not cover Garn. Baran's plan had worked without a hitch. Garn had joyfully seized the opportunity to battle and kill an old enemy, and Colbey doubted Garn ever really understood the politics involved.

Colbey added carefully, "And Sterrane's reign will be long and beautiful." It was a joke only Baran and Sterrane shared. As children, they had misunderstood the much bandied phrase: "May your reign be long and fruitful." Baran and Garn had turned it into a private quip guaranteed to set one another into fits of laughter. Colbey worried about revealing such a deeply personal secret. He had obtained the information only accidentally, a stray thought unmasked while trying to rescue Garn's mind from poison at the time of his death.

"I have one more question," Baran said softly. "In advance, I apologize for the need to ask it." He avoided Colbey's sharp, blue-gray gaze. "What are your intentions at the castle of Béarn?"

Baran's discomfort clued Colbey that the captain wanted something other than the specifics of his mission. He was essentially asking if Colbey intended harm to the king or members of his court. Though offended by the query, he swallowed his pride to answer. "We came to talk to Arduwyn and, of course, in peace. I mean no harm to my friend the king, or to any of his people. If it would make you feel better, you can bring Arduwyn here to me." The sequence brought back home the impending *Ragnarok*. A day would come, soon it seemed, when every man at every cas-

tle gate was met with the same grueling suspicion. Though
it saddened Colbey, it still seemed far preferable to the
world's destruction, reinforcing his commitment to seeing
the *Ragnarok* stopped, if possible, or, at least, the rescue of
mankind when the gods fell upon one another in war. Betrayal and deception were only the worst of chaos' presents
to the world of law; it brought new ideas and freedom as
well.

Colbey sensed increasing agitation from Khitajrah that
seemed related to each mention of the red-haired hunter by
name. Although he had told her he needed to find a woodsman living in Béarn, he had not specified whom until they
waited before the castle gates. He would have to question
her later about how she knew Arduwyn. It seemed hard to
imagine the little hunter making anyone uncomfortable.

"Thank you, Colbey; but no. If His Majesty knew you
were here and we didn't send you directly to him, he'd have
my head." Baran loosed a single laugh that sounded strained
almost to the point of hysteria. "Well, not my head, of
course. That's not his way. But I can't stand to see him disappointed. Besides, he's the only one Arduwyn ever tells
about his comings and goings." Baran took a step back and
gestured to the guards. "Let them in."

The sentries pulled open the gates, then took posts on either side, the butts of their halberds planted on the ground
and the shafts vertical.

Colbey waited until they seemed settled in their new positions, not wanting to abandon propriety for eagerness.
Calm deliberateness would place Baran more at ease. Then,
having left the appropriate pause, Colbey led his gelding
through the gate. Khitajrah followed him.

While one sentry closed the panels, the other approached
Colbey. "Sir, the horses can stay here. Your gear will be
safe. You'll have to leave your weapons."

"No," Baran contradicted immediately. "You can keep
your weapons with you." The look he gave the sentry promised a later explanation, but Colbey believed he understood.
He could disarm an enemy and use the blade as swiftly and
competently as his own. If any man in the courtroom carried
a sword, as undoubtedly the guards did, any need for hostility would find that weapon in Colbey's hands. It made far
more sense to garner the Renshai's trust than to chance such
a thing.

"Colbey, Kayt, come with me."

Leaving the horses, the *aristiri,* and the gear, Colbey and Khitajrah followed Baran through the courtyard, across the moat bridge, and into the interior of Béarn's castle. He brought only the staff, clasped in one hand. It looked conspicuously out of place, a walking stick onto which he placed none of his weight.

Little had changed since Colbey last traversed these corridors. The blue and tan brocade swinging from the animal-shaped torch brackets had gathered no dust. Once, Mitrian had told him, precious gems had swung in gaudy, wealth-flaunting strings. But Sterrane had channeled the castle's unnecessary decoration back into gold for its citizenry. Still, no one could mistake the high king for a pauper. Murals swept over every inch of the walls. The artists had skillfully worked interrupting doors into the scenery, either by meticulously changing the perspective until they became invisible or by working the teak panels and archways into the picture.

Baran and his followers passed a few guardsmen in the corridors, and the captain exchanged soft and brief conversation with each. As they neared the courtroom, Colbey watched Khitajrah study a war scene in fascination. It depicted Renshai storming a Western city, the barricades weakening and the blond reavers engaged in sword battles, one Renshai against many. The scene brought back memories of Colbey's youth during the Renshai's hundred year exile from the North. Then, they had wandered from the Eastlands through the West learning skills—from monks, barbarians, and the world's finest sword masters—that formed the basis for the Renshai maneuvers. Sword training and war. His life had consisted of nothing else, nor had he missed those other aspects of existence that so many took for granted. Sword training and war. He had needed nothing more since birth. Now, in his seventies, it seemed strange to consider commitment to something new. And yet, he had.

Baran motioned Colbey and Khitajrah around a silk-clad merchant with a six man entourage. Coffers and chests filled the hallways, and the mixed aroma of spices perfumed the corridor. Clearly, the merchant had brought gifts or barter for his meeting with the king, or perhaps he chose to pay his tax in goods. He frowned as Colbey and Khitajrah threaded around his entourage, but he said nothing about the unfairness of their audience out of sequence.

Baran flicked a hand to indicate that Colbey and Khitajrah
should wait against the wall, across from the courtroom's
double doors and the pair of sentries before it. Then he
slipped over to talk with the guards.

Shortly, the Béarnides pushed open the panels. Two
guards exited, escorting an aging Béarnide between them.
The grin on the man's face indicated that things had gone
well with his request or trial, which did not surprise Colbey.
He knew Sterrane's gentle manner well, and his mercy had
become legendary.

"Come with me." Baran headed into the courtroom immediately after the guards and their charge had left. Colbey indicated that Khitajrah should go first, then followed her
through the portals. The doors swung shut behind them.

The oddity of Béarn's guard captain serving as escort
must have struck guards and courtiers immediately because
the room settled into a hush as the three traversed the long
gold carpet that ran between rows of benches. Only a few
members of the nobility sat, scattered along the seats.
Colbey suspected Sterrane's policies had become predictable
routine to them. Yet, as simple as the king's judgments and
dealings seemed, Colbey knew Sterrane was capable of
clever thought when the situation demanded it. His methods
and morality were as guileless as they appeared most of the
time. Few would believe or understand the stability that
Sterrane, as the West's high king, truly represented. Only
Colbey's scant Wizard's training and power to read emotion
as well as words told him that Sterrane served as the fulcrum
of neutrality, a balancing axis for the world of man.

Khitajrah's apprehension had become a constant, but it in-
creased sharply as they entered the courtroom. She caught
his hand suddenly, her grip warm and damp. "I didn't know
we'd come before the king. There's something I should have
told you . . ." She trailed off, her whisper nearly audible to
everyone in the otherwise silent room.

Colbey frowned, shaking his head to indicate the problem
would have to wait. Already, he could sense the bowstring
tautness of the guards stationed behind and on every side of
the throne. Passing private messages now would only arouse
false suspicions and risk misunderstanding.

Baran trotted ahead to announce the pair. "Majesty, forgive the interruption. I thought you'd want to see Sir Colbey
Calistinsson and the Eastern woman, Kayt."

Another step, and Colbey came close enough to recognize features. Sterrane appeared as always: robust and happy, his beard well-tended and his features friendly. Attentive at his right hand, Mar Lon went rigid. Apparently taking their cues as much from the king's personal bodyguard as their captain, the guards shifted uneasily, hands slipping hiltward.

Sterrane's smile seemed to encompass his entire face as Colbey moved closer. His dark eyes revealed unabashed joy as well as excitement. "You find each other! That wonderful. Really wonderful." He started to rise, but Mar Lon's hand on his forearm kept him in place.

Colbey supposed it was an essential precaution, not necessarily aimed against him. Sterrane's habit of expressing his joy with hugs and concern with touch might pose a danger to the childlike monarch in many situations. Colbey doubted the guards cared much for their king's tendency to place himself in perils nearly impossible to avert.

"Thank you, Sire," Colbey replied, no other response seeming appropriate or necessary. He wondered what Khitajrah might have said that made their coming together seem significant to King Sterrane.

The king studied the pair closely, puppy eyes flitting from one to the other repeatedly. "Not see . . . not see match." He struggled for the last word, and the one he chose made little sense to Colbey. "Who mother? Look like mother?"

The words seemed nonsensical to Colbey. Sterrane's broken speech made understanding impossible. "Excuse me, Sire?"

Khitajrah fielded the question. Still grasping Colbey's hand, she squeezed to indicate that he should play along with her. "Majesty, it was my mistake, and I apologize for involving you in it. It turns out Colbey's not my father after all."

Though shocked, Colbey suppressed the urge to glance at Khitajrah. Instead, he gave her hand a warning gouge meant to indicate a lengthy discussion to occur later.

"Oh." Sterrane's mouth clamped closed, his lower lip suddenly appearing huge. He seemed vastly disappointed as well as surprised. "Oh," he repeated.

Colbey changed the subject to the matter about which he had come to Béarn. He had no intention of having truly important issues become lost beneath a chaos-inspired lie. "Sire, it's good to see things well here. I came to speak with Arduwyn. Is he here?"

Sterrane turned his leonine head back to Colbey. "Was here. Left for woods days ago."

Now it was Colbey's turn to frown. Arduwyn had grown up in the forests near Béarn and his home city of Erythane. If he wanted privacy, no man could find him there. "Maybe you can help me, then. I sent my horse to Arduwyn. That's what I came for."

All sorrow disappeared from Sterrane's demeanor, replaced by eager thoughtfulness. "White horse? Knight horse?"

"Frost Reaver, yes." A spark of hope flashed through Colbey. "You saw him?"

The king nodded vigorously. "Brought here with Ardy. Traded for his horse." He turned a brief glance to Khitajrah, who looked away. "We send message to Erythane. See who lose horse."

"Reaver's here?"

Sterrane shook his head. "When Ardy leave, horse throw fit. Kick down stall. Follow."

"I'm sorry," Colbey said, only partially so. It bothered him that, under other circumstances, he would have found Frost Reaver here. However, it did please him to find the strength of the horse's loyalty to his command. That seemed to bode well for reclaiming an animal that had become as much companion as mount. "Could you spare a guide? With one, it'll prove hard enough finding Arduwyn. Without one, it'd be impossible."

"Me find one," Sterrane promised. "You two stay dinner? Sleep night?"

Though tempted to push on as soon as possible, Colbey considered. He knew Sterrane missed adventuring and his old companions from before he had become king. He sensed a desperate loneliness about the monarch that needed satisfying, a loss of the weighty responsibilities that came with rulership, if only for a moment. Though Colbey had never shared the closeness of a real friend the way Garn, Mitrian, and Arduwyn had, it would do the Béarnian well to have some visitors; and he and Khitajrah could use fresh food and rest. "Sire, your hospitality is appreciated."

Sterrane fairly beamed.

The feast brought back distant memories of Colbey's last visit to Béarn, including the need to tend to business that

nad assailed him both times. Now, Sterrane entertained far
fewer guests. He chose a seat at one side of the table, directly across from Khitajrah and Colbey, with Baran and
Mar Lon at either hand. The chairs at either end were vacant. Colbey let Sterrane make most of the conversation, answering questions as briefly as politeness would allow. Mar
Lon said nothing, silently assessing every word Colbey
spoke as if to analyze the effects of chaos on the Western
Wizard. Baran seemed far the more human of the two.
Though attentive to his king, he added his piece to the conversation at intervals, responding appropriately to jokes and
comments, no matter their source.

Apparently sensing or understanding Colbey's interest,
Sterrane dwelt longest on the goings on among the Renshai.
Colbey discovered that they believed him dead, which did
not surprise him. He had last seen them at a time when his
age hung heavily on him. The death in glory he always
sought had become a moment to moment obsession. He had
left them for the forests, cradling the body of Episte, the last
of the last. Loki's pronouncement finally seemed to gain
meaning with the image. Always, Colbey had believed himself the last of the full-blooded Renshai. But it was Episte's
father, Rache Kallmirsson, who now claimed that sad honor.
The means of Episte's death seemed even more appropriate
now, his suffering ended by the final symbol of the Renshai:
the last *nådenal,* the priest-blessed mercy dagger of Sif.

Colbey also discovered that Rache Garnsson had married
Arduwyn's daughter, Sylva. The Renshai tribe would live
on, its bloodline even farther removed from its Northern or-
igins. Neither of the youngsters had a significant amount of
Renshai blood, though Colbey felt certain both had Renshai
ancestors. Of all the Western cities, only Béarn and its sister
city of Erythane had thought to befriend the marauding
Renshai during their time of exile. The Erythanian women
had taken to the Renshai's few redheads, and Arduwyn
surely descended from at least one such union. Rache's
grandfather had been as blond as any Northman, probably
due to an ancestor's coupling with Renshai. Though a member of any of the other seventeen Northern tribes could also
account for such a feature, the Northmen's xenophobia made
this unlikely.

Colbey found his mind wandering to such matters long after Sterrane switched the discussion to his own wives and

children. A fresh variety of food left Colbey in a comfortable state that bordered on torpid. As pleased as he felt with the continuous improvement in the West since the War, here things always seemed right. Through the millennia, the line of Eastern Wizards had worked to find the perfect balancing forces for the West's high kingdom. They had convinced Odin to make the bards loyal bodyguards to the kings in addition to their other duties. One by one, they had set the stage for Sterrane's rulership. Yet now that the massive, childlike Béarnide had finally hit his stride, now that the shattered Renshai had nearly become a tribe again, now that common men and women had learned to use the first trickles of chaos to enhance themselves, the world perched on the brink of *Ragnarok*.

It all seemed grievously wrongful, a violation of a deep, eternal fairness. Colbey understood Loki's explanation in a way no other could. To a point, he had sanctioned the same beliefs. He had loosed chaos because of the need to avert the stagnation that had come with law too long unopposed. Loki had even convinced him that some of the gods must die, that the rise of chaos made them unnecessary at best and an anachronism at worst. Still, Colbey felt certain that, with Sterrane and his descendants as its central point, mankind could flourish with a shifting balance of law and chaos. Already, he had seen the changes they had made to adjust to its coming: dedication and inventiveness as well as suspicion, caution, and doubt.

Yet the matter seemed moot. The lord of all fire giants, Surtr, was destined to destroy Frey and the elves he represented, then to set man's world aflame. Colbey found some solace in the knowledge that mankind was destined to repopulate, from a single man and woman hidden in the trunk of the World Tree. The elves and any other faerie folk who might exist would be utterly destroyed.

A knock on the chamber door jarred Colbey from thoughts that had made him oblivious to the conversations still in progress around him. The door edged open cautiously, and a guard's head poked through the crack. "Sire?"

Sterrane responded in the Béarnian tongue, his obvious fluency an eerie contrast to the choppy incompetence of the language he had used throughout the feast.

The guard continued to use the common trading language, apparently in order to gauge the reactions of Sterrane's guests to his words. "Sire, a hawk flew into the castle, and we can't seem to catch it. Sire, it looks—"

An echoing call from farther down the outer hallway cut him off. The guard pulled the panel shut. Something thunked against the wood, followed by a dry rustle of feathers and an angered squawk.

Colbey tried to clear up the mystery. "I'm sorry, Sterrane. It's probably mine. There's an *aristiri* hawk that travels with me."

Mar Lon spoke his first words of the dinner. "An *aristiri?* Are you certain?"

Colbey shrugged, taking no insult. He hardly considered himself a competent bird identifier. "It's a rather large hawk, though it weighs less than a sword and sings like a *richi* bird."

A timid knock again sounded from the opposite side of the door.

"Let bird in." Sterrane's voice thundered, inappropriately loud for an enclosed space; but the volume was necessary for the guards to hear him through the door.

The door swung open. A red falcon careened around the corner, making a right angle turn in midair then diving into the room. It was not Formynder, yet Colbey recognized it. *Swiftwing.* The first stirrings of dread rose within him, and he touched the staff leaning against his chair to ascertain its continued presence.

The falcon circled the table, alighting on Colbey's arm. Though smaller than the *aristiri,* it sank its talons through cloth, toenails scratching but not embedding in the flesh beneath. His gaze went naturally to the parchment bound to one scaly leg.

Mar Lon smiled, though his eyes revealed no mirth. "I hate to contradict the great Knight-mage, but that's not an *aristiri.*"

"I know." Colbey ignored the bard, believing his answer enough to imply this was not the bird to which he had referred either. He stripped the message from its leg, unrolling it with a caution that bordered on delay. He remembered the years he had spent in Santagithi's court and how the great general/strategist had met every situation, good and bad, with the same stalwart courage and not a second of hesitation. Still, every fiber of his being told him that the Cardinal Wizards had done something massive and ugly this time.

They had left him alone too long for anything else to be the case.

The message read:

> "We have the Renshai. Don't bother to look; you can't find them. Leave the staff by the Renshai cottages and no harm will come to them or you. Any other action will ensure their deaths."

The signature was an illegible single rune, but Colbey did not need it to know who had sent the note. "No reply, thank you," he told the falcon, uncertain whether it understood words or intentions. He turned his attention to the guards still in the doorway. "Free the hawk, please."

As if on cue, the bird flapped from Colbey's forearm, headed for the opening. The guards stepped aside to let it leave the room, then closed the door behind them.

"What say?" Sterrane asked, sounding concerned.

Colbey shook his head, his first thought to keep the problem to himself, at least for now. Oddly, despite a myriad of worries, responsibilities, and uncertainties, the wisdom that came to him had been spoken by an enemy turned friend in a Pudarian tavern: "If you don't learn to share what you are, Colbey Calistinsson, you'll know only loneliness and those who care most for you will suffer." *There's more at stake here than the preservation of a Northern tribe. I can't handle three Wizards and their apprentices alone.* Colbey wrestled with the thought. *If I bring an army, we may or may not stop the Wizards, but the Renshai will surely die.* He considered Mitrian, the dedication, proficiency, and strength of character that had made her Rache Kallmirsson's logical choice to continue the line. His own years of training her had confirmed the rightness of that decision. Tannin, Tarah, and Modrey carried the Renshai blood and the natural dexterity trained into the line. Rache had inherited everything good from his mother and grandfather, and the strength his ex-gladiator father had given him would add new dimensions to a tribe that had always relied solely on quickness and skill.

Ideas continued to tumble through Colbey's mind in an instant. Experience told him the Cardinal Wizards would prove oblivious to any but magical weapons; he had no means of knowing that the shattering of the Pica Stone had made the Wizards vulnerable. He also understood that the apprentices, by virtue of surviving the Tasks of Wizardry, might also have gained that protection. That seemed less certain, however. The Tasks had been supposed to grant him the same security; yet they had not. Whether that came as an effect of the world appearance of the Staff of Chaos or as a result of his success with the Eighth Task, he did not know. Much, he could learn only by doing battle with the Cardinal Wizards; but that, in and of itself, might prove a death sentence for the Renshai.

Colbey closed his hand around the staff. The time had come for some guidance from a finer, older strategist than himself. For all his decades of war, Renshai had dedicated themselves to individual skill in combat. He knew little of tactics.

Ah. For all the times you've dismissed my contributions, now you come to me for advice?

Don't sound so surprised. It was the deal we made from the start, remember? You advise, and I choose what to do with your opinion.

Knowledge, the staff corrected.

Knowledge, then. Colbey had no intention of arguing semantics. Besides, he had to concede that the staff's reliance on established fact rather than intuition might prove as much its strength as its major weakness. *What do you suggest?*

First, I don't know exactly the effect bringing me and my opposite into the world might have caused. I can't predict whether the Tasks still provide invulnerability. That decision lies in Odin's hands.

Though he knew Sterrane and the others around the feasting table patiently awaited an answer, Colbey continued listening raptly.

You're my champion. You can't turn me over to the others, nor even go through the motions of such an action. Somehow, you'll have to get the Renshai back.

Basic stuff. Colbey grew impatient. *The question is, should I enlist aid?*

You can't fight all of the other Wizards alone.

The challenge immediately raised Colbey's battle instincts.

The staff interrupted. *Spare me your warrior's pride. The Cardinal Wizards have suppressed all but their most basic magics for years. As the world gains chaos, that's no longer *the case. I still believe no single Wizard has one spell that could kill you. However, with two or three of their minds linked, I think they could muster the power. Certainly, no mortal could stand before such an association. To your advantage, the Cardinal Wizards have little direct experience with major magics, and they know that they risk the Ragnarok the more power they call forth in one place. Given the situation, though, that may not deter them much.*

The staff hesitated a moment, as if to regain the proper train of its thoughts. *In answer to your question, yes. Without some companions, you're doomed to failure. If you bring too many, the Wizards will either flee with the Renshai or murder them. But consider those companions carefully. No doubt, some or all of them will die. If the Wizards remain invulnerable, your companions can help only to a degree.*

Who do you suggest?

A strange sensation flitted through Colbey's mind and staff hand at once. *I'm afraid, my champion, that your instincts there will undoubtedly prove better than my knowledge.*

Colbey glanced around the table at his dinner mates. Although it seemed to him as if a long time had passed, the moments of mental conversation and thought had not lasted long enough for anyone to prompt him to speak again. He came to an immediate decision. Without a word, he passed the parchment to Sterrane.

The king perused the message for some time. Apparently, he had learned the Cardinal Wizards' personal runes during his time with Shadimar, for he recognized the signature at once. "Carcophan?"

"Along with Trilless and Shadimar. They're working together now."

Sterrane looked hurt. "Can give staff?"

"No, Sterrane, I can't. The cost would be incalculable."

Baran and Khitajrah looked confused. Only Mar Lon followed the course of the conversation between king and Renshai. "May I see it, too?"

"Sure. Show it to anyone here, with the understanding that its contents don't leave this room." Colbey grinned briefly, able to raise a modicum of satisfaction despite the gravity of the situation. "Might give you a different look at the Cardinal Wizards."

Mar Lon read, his expression unchanging until the blank

look seemed locked on his face and he no longer moved except to breathe.

Baran had to gently pry the parchment from beneath the bard's fingers. Then the message made its rounds, ending back in Colbey's hands. Khitajrah gave his knee a meaningful squeeze beneath the table that he guessed she would explain later.

Despite his usual gentle innocence, Sterrane addressed the matter with uncharacteristic seriousness. "Shadimar like father to me," he admitted, referring to the Eastern Wizard having raised him from age eight to young adulthood. "But not stand for kidnap from anyone." His soft eyes met Colbey's. "Me help any way can. Just tell how."

"Thank you," Colbey said. "Your support means everything and may make all the difference between success and many blameless deaths." He did not add the *Ragnarok,* not wanting to have to explain unnecessary details that would have no bearing on the actions of Sterrane's men.

"I want to go," Mar Lon said. As if awakening from a trance, he slowly raised his attention to Colbey. "I want to go with you."

Colbey frowned, his feelings on the matter mixed. Although Mar Lon seemed to have fallen prey to the same conclusions about Colbey as the other Wizards, the Renshai knew a major difference existed here. Despite his misconceptions, Mar Lon was obligated to support complete neutrality. He did so with a thoughtfulness that could and had sent him to unfitting methods. Still, though he lacked Sterrane's natural, instinctive bent for balance, he did tend to find the proper path once his mind sorted the facts. And it was the bard's right to attend all functions of the Cardinal Wizards impartially. Colbey nudged the bard toward the proper formality, lost in need and befuddlement. "That's not my decision, Mar Lon." He inclined his head to indicate Sterrane.

Mar Lon flushed, obviously mortified. The loss of protocol snapped his daze as nothing else could have. He glanced quickly to the king. "That is, Sire, if you're willing to spare me."

Sterrane replied so slowly that every eye switched to him before the words emerged. "Not need spare. Me go."

The announcement seemed senseless.

"You go," Mar Lon repeated, lapsing into Sterrane's broken common in order to understand it. "You go? Go? You, Sire?" Then, the realization struck Mar Lon, and his long-held pall evaporated. "Oh, no. No, Sire. It's far too dangerous."

"My decision," Sterrane said, his voice holding more authority than Colbey could imagine from the childlike monarch. "Me go."

Mar Lon's fist crashed onto the tabletop, sending his wine glass tumbling. "No! I won't let you put yourself in peril!"

Wine splashed a purple arc across white linen, and Colbey caught the glass as it toppled over the edge of the table.

Sterrane glared at his bodyguard. "Me king. Me decide. Me go."

Colbey replaced the glass with a casual movement. "Actually, Sterrane, it's my decision. Mar Lon's right. It's too dangerous."

Sterrane rose, towering over the others at the table, his gigantic frame suddenly very obvious. *"Me KING, damn it. If me say go, me go!"*

Colbey had never heard Sterrane swear before. The shocking strangeness of the expletive magnified its significance a thousandfold. "Don't you understand? I don't want you there."

Sterrane leaned toward Colbey until the edges of his beard prickled the Renshai's cheek. "You insult my fight skill?"

"Certainly not." Colbey withdrew. It seemed insane to confront any man this adamant, and he had never seen Sterrane unrelenting about anything. "I just don't know how to tell you how important your life is to every man on our world. It would take too long, and I'm not sure even I completely understand it. You can't be placed at risk without better cause."

"Wizards crazy. Mitrian, Rache, Sylva in trouble. No cause better." Sterrane stepped back, but he did not sit. "We leave tomorrow. You, me, Mar Lon. Who else?"

"Me, Majesty, of course." Baran broke in before Khitajrah could speak.

Sterrane whipped his head to the speaker, his expression still outraged though it was no longer necessary or appropriate. "Not you. You stay. Regent to Xanranis."

"What? Me?" In his horror, Baran dropped the amenities Colbey had already forsaken from friendship. "Xanranis is only ten years old. I don't know anything about running a kingdom." Finally, he regained enough control to continue with the customary respect. "Please, Sire. You stay. I'll go as your representative."

"You." Sterrane jabbed a finger at Baran. "You stay regent. You . . ." He indicated Mar Lon. "You come with me, if want. Me." He stabbed the same finger at his own chest. "Me go. Next one gainsay me, thrown in dungeon."

"That's—" Colbey started.

King Sterrane interrupted immediately. "That include you, Renshai."

Khitajrah glanced from face to face, clearly bewildered by much of the exchange. Baran and Mar Lon tensed, ready for action if it became necessary.

Colbey raised his brows, widening his frosty eyes. There was no need for warning or challenge. Sterrane knew an attempt to arrest the Golden Prince of Demons would result in the wasted lives of most of his guard force. Nevertheless, he doubted Sterrane would threaten idly. "I don't understand your insistence, but I respect it. Come then, if you must, but I hope you change your mind. There's only two others I want along. Khitajrah, of course." He patted her thigh beneath the table. "And Arduwyn. To bring more would only increase the danger. And it's possible once we get there that I'll find it better to deal with the Wizards myself."

Baran's frown made it clear he doubted the possibility, though he did not challenge it aloud. Clearly, he had his own concerns to grapple.

A smile covered Sterrane's face nearly from ear to ear, and he, once again, became the docile giant Colbey had come to know. "Leave tomorrow. We find Arduwyn. Everything get fixed. You see."

Though he lacked the king's childlike faith in happy endings, Colbey could not help but smile back.

CHAPTER 26

From Nowhere to Nowhere

Moonlight trickled between the slats of a decorative shade on the guest room window, throwing white stripes of light across an imported carpet. Colbey perched on a pallet set the perfect height for use as a seat as well as a sleeping place. Silk sheets enwrapped the straw ticking, the thicker cloth beneath it protecting him from stabbing pieces of hay. An ornate teak dresser stood in a far corner of the room, one of its four drawers holding all of Colbey's gear, with room to spare. A matching desk filled the opposite corner, a pitcher and a basin of warm water on its top. Colbey had just stripped off his clothes, washed, and settled the staff and sword within reach, when a timid knock sounded on the door.

Colbey donned the light linen sleeping gown the Béarnides had left for him on the pallet. He had always felt it rude and cruelly intrusive to enter others' minds unless they had proved themselves enemies or needed his aid. He relied on the strongest of emotions, those so intense they radiated from people without any need for him to search. This visitor must have considered something long and hard; even through the door, Colbey could perceive a sense of purpose, the kind that comes after a well-pondered decision. He also discovered affection. Nothing about the other seemed deceitful or dangerous. "Come in."

The door slid open, and Khitajrah stepped through the crack. She closed the panel behind her. She also wore a Béarnian sleeping gown, of a feminine cut and trimmed with ermine. Her small frame was lost in the folds, the garments fashioned for women twice her size. Despite the bulkiness, Colbey could not miss the slender arch of hips and thighs. Crossing the room, she took a seat beside him on the bed.

"What can I do for you?" Colbey asked, banishing the facetiously lewd replies that came to his own mind. He had

sacrificed sexual pleasure for so long, he dismissed it easily.
Sterrane had granted Khitajrah a similar guest room of her
own, so she surely had a purpose for coming to his now.

"What's going on?"

Colbey squinted, uncertain of the question. Again, he
sensed no hostility or accusation, but the specifics of her
query defied him. "What do you mean?"

"I mean, what is it the king and his bodyguard are joining
us to do? Besides finding Arduwyn."

Mention of the red-haired hunter's name reminded Colbey
to ask about Khitajrah's earlier discomfort. For now, though,
it seemed polite to address her concerns first. "You read the
note."

Now Khitajrah's state of mind revealed that he had hit the
root of the problem. He sensed a thread of frustration, and
the feelings of desire had strengthened as the nearness of
their position translated to a tangible warmth. "Most Eastland women can't read at all. My husband taught me our native language, but I never had reason to learn the Western
tongues."

Of course. Colbey felt like a fool for not recognizing the
problem at once. Her poking him beneath the table while she
glanced at the parchment should have cued him well enough,
but concern about the Renshai had usurped lesser matters.
"The other Wizards captured the Renshai and are holding
them hostage."

"Ah," Khitajrah said, the smallness of reaction hiding a
deeper understanding.

"And we have to rescue them."

"Ah," Khitajrah repeated.

Now Colbey found her less easily read. "You don't have
to help if you feel the risk is too great. Or for any reason."

Khitajrah tilted her head and looked up at Colbey. A band
of moonlight lit her brown eyes into a sparkle that could
have made an aging beggar look beautiful. "I have reason to
despise some of your people."

"Not really."

"Two of them killed my husband. I loved him with all my
heart, you know."

Colbey pinned her gaze with his own. "One of the two is
already dead, but that's not really the issue." He placed a
comforting arm around her. "Khitajrah, you're not a warrior,
but you should have known your husband well enough to

understand. Warriors fight for causes. They don't hold personal grudges against enemies who serve the opposite side. On the battlefield, it's only important to die at the hand of a more competent warrior. To do otherwise becomes a man's own shame." He moved from general to specific. "Your husband would have respected Mitrian, not wanted you to avenge him."

Khitajrah considered for some time. "I know you're right, but I have to work things through on my own."

Colbey granted her that need. "I have two questions for you, as long as you're here."

Khitajrah nodded to indicate she would grant him the same courtesy.

"First, I understand your dislike for Mitrian, but what's between you and Arduwyn?"

Khitajrah winced. "How did you know?"

"I read people." Colbey did not go into detail, letting Khitajrah draw the natural conclusion that he did so by watching attitude and movement. "You get nervous every time someone mentions his name."

"I didn't know it was that obvious." Khitajrah shifted, balancing part of her weight in the hollow between Colbey's body and the arm he had used to comfort her. The touch thrilled them both. "I took something from him when chaos was with me. He got it back, but I wouldn't blame him for holding a grudge. Mar Lon knows all about it."

"It's Mar Lon's curse to thrust his ears and opinions into everyone's business."

"What's the other question?"

Colbey smiled, this one far more personal. "Do you remember when we first met? In the tavern in Pudar?"

Khitajrah winced. "When I tried to get close enough to kill you? Hard to forget."

Colbey made a gesture with his free hand to dismiss those particular details. "You said something that stayed with me, something I've twice since used to help make important decisions. You said:" He tried to recapture the phrase exactly. " 'If you don't learn to share what you are, you'll know only loneliness; and those who care most for you will suffer.' What did you mean by that?"

Khitajrah flushed. "I'm not usually that eloquent. Mostly I was mad . . . and frustrated. I saw the way you handled those Pudarian guardsmen. If you did half the things legends credit you with in the war, you were those men's hero. Yet you found your own solitude more important than their flattery or their need to glorify their champion. That's a sure sign of someone who spends way too much time alone. I guessed that you dedicated yourself to personal causes so deeply, you tended to ignore everyone around you. But a man with your abilities gains followers, whether he likes it or not. Your aloofness has to hurt those people."

Khitajrah's cheeks reddened further. "And when's the last time you let someone get close enough to do this?" Without further warning, she wrapped both arms around his shoulders and kissed him, lips and tongue exploring timidly.

Despite his long abstinence, Colbey found himself as excited as a youth. But, before he could respond, she pulled away, glancing hurriedly around the room.

Cued by her sudden alarm, Colbey jerked out of her grip. "What's wrong?"

"The last time I did that, your hawk tried to rip my scalp off."

"The *aristiri* chose to stay outside. You know that too, you little squirrel." Colbey drew her into an embrace of his own, forcing a kiss that made her catch her breath. A jerk on her gown sprawled her to the pallet, and the fabric fell open to reveal just enough to stir an unstoppable need. He entered her, living her pleasure along with his own. Yet, through it all, he knew a strange wrongness, as if he was a stripling attacking his first girlfriend in her parent's home long before he had the wherewithal to pay for the consequences. It did not distract him enough that he could not finish.

Tannin Randilsson awakened to the prickle of grass beneath him, the cold touch of wind, and the contrasting wash of warmth from a campfire near his head. Disoriented, he lay still, searching his memory for explanation. None came. He last recalled settling into his bed for the night after two grueling sword practices, one given by Mitrian and the other inflicted by himself. Since the day she had caught him in bed with the farm girl from Erythane, she'd treated him with an icy, withering hostility that pained him to his core. He had never slept with another woman since, had not had more than a vague, undirected urge to do so. And no matter how long or hard he practiced, his sword maneuvers never again pleased his relentless *torke*.

Concerned by the oddity of surroundings his mind still could not place, Tannin cautiously opened his eyes to slits. Firelight revealed several figures in a clearing he recognized as the Fields of Wrath, his home since birth. Mitrian lay beside him, and he caught a glimpse of others sprawled out in a line beyond her. The fire flickered and roared near the head of the central figure, a man he guessed to be Rache. Past the campfire, the flames creating a partial wall between them, several others slept. These, Tannin did not know at a glance, and he would have to twist his head to see more, revealing his awakening. Instead, he turned his attention to the periphery of vision.

Toward the feet of the sleeping Renshai, a single man crouched at guard. Blond hair revealed his Northern heritage, and mail links imprinted a covering, well-tailored cloak. A sword girded his hip, the first weapon Tannin had noticed, though his prone position and squinted eyes did not allow him to see to the extent of his vision. The man seemed vaguely familiar, but Tannin dared not risk the movement or full opening of his lids required to identify the other. More so, something seemed terribly out of place about the scene, though it took several moments of directed staring to find the anomaly. If he lay in the familiar place he knew, he should have been able to catch a glimpse of Mitrian's cottage. Instead, the field seemed to end at a line of forest.

Tannin shivered, unnerved by the many oddities. Usually, he slept light as a cat. It made no sense that someone had moved him from his bed without awakening him. Clearly, they had not awakened the other Renshai either, or he would certainly have heard the sounds of battle. The missing cottage only added to the mystery, and the natural feeling of dread its absence raised. It seemed plain that he and the others had become prisoners. The means for escape appeared obvious.

Slowly, Tannin reached over and touched Mitrian's arm, trying to make the motion seem random, related to his sleep. The Renshai had perfected many forms of communication designed for wariness. He prodded her with a message: *lay still until signaled.* And he added, *pass that to the others.*

A tensing of Mitrian's arm cued him that she had awakened, either before him or in response to his touch. Tannin waited while she informed Rache, and the message continued down the line of "sleeping" Renshai. He knew it could get only as far as whoever had not yet awakened or the baby, if it lay among them; yet he hoped that would prove far enough. No matter his course of action, it would only gain a temporary reprieve. Weaponless, the Renshai became comparatively crippled, more knowledgeable than most warriors about martial skills yet never so able as with a sword in hand.

Tannin groped around him, hoping darkness and the flickering shadows cast by the flames would hide the movement. His searching fingers found cool sprigs of grass, tree-shed leaves, and occasional small stones; nothing that could serve as a weapon. Then his hand brushed a slender limb. He explored it in silent blackness, unwilling to turn his head to cue the guard to the direction of his gaze. It seemed long enough to serve his purposes, devoid of jutting twigs that might rustle as he drew it toward him. Once he began his movement, it would have to lead quickly to committed action. His plan, small as it was, required that the guard use instinct, rather than vision, to identify the weapon in Tannin's hand.

Tannin clamped his fingers around the limb. Once started, he could not turn back. His own life seemed a necessary sacrifice, but the others might still live if he handled the matter well enough. Still, though he knew he would have the chance to die in combat, he could not help hesitating before paying such a heavy toll. The glorious end should have been all that mattered, yet he could not help thinking of the things he had left undone. Although he had slept with a woman, he had never known one's love. He had never fathered a child. And he had never earned his *torke*'s respect. That last, somehow, seemed the worst tragedy of all.

Tannin shoved aside considerations of his losses to free his mind for warfare. He would need all of his concentration to see to it that some of the Renshai did not die and that none died needlessly or in other ways than combat. Ignorance of his enemies made it only slightly more difficult in his mind. The guard, at least, wielded a sword. What the others carried mattered little. Though trained only with swords themselves and disdainful of all but natural defenses, the Renshai were trained to cut past or through armor, shields, and parry of every type.

One, two, three . . . Tannin sprang to his feet and charged the swordsman in silence. He used his body to shield the

stick from the guard's view, then slashed with a bold commitment. Dancing flickers of flame and the sureness of Tannin's strike must have convinced the Northman he had
somehow acquired a sword. The other met his "attack" with
a swift draw-block. The limb shattered against steel. The
guard shouted a warning, and Tannin continued his motion.
Seizing the guard's wrist, he applied rolling pressure against
the tendons. As the sword fell from the Northman's hand,
Tannin snatched it in midair. *Tvinfri.* The name of the
Renshai maneuver came naturally to mind as he performed
it, with sloppy success. Even as he caught the hilt, he
whipped the blade about in a directed cut that bit into the
guard's shoulder, slashed a shallow line across his cloak, and
jangled against mail. On the backswing, Tannin slammed the
hilt into the man's face. The Northman staggered, nearly
falling.

Only then, Tannin recognized his opponent: Olvaerr, son
of Valr Kirin. The youngster had grown into a man in the
two years since Tannin had seen him, but there was no mistaking the angry blue eyes and features so like his father's.
Tannin realized other things, too. Mitrian, Rache, and Modrey had risen, the latter clutching the irritable toddler just
awakening from sleep. Tarah had climbed to her knees, still
groggy. The four enemies beyond the fire also sprang to
their feet, and Tannin saw Shadimar and his wolf among
three strangers.

"Run!" Tannin shouted to his companions. The last he
knew, Shadimar had been a friend of the Renshai. But nothing about their current situation suggested he meant them
any goodwill. Without weapons, the Renshai seemed destined to die at the hands of an enraged Wizard, deaths without battle or honor, without chance for Valhalla. "Run!" he
screamed again. "Just run!"

Tannin's own battle reclaimed his attention. Recovered,
Olvaerr ducked beneath the guard Tannin had opened to
glance at his companions. The Northman made a wild sweep
for Tannin's shin with his foot, and a knife blade flashed red
in the firelight.

Tannin back-stepped, saving his balance and thrusting simultaneously. The Renshai maneuvers focused on attack, the
best defense a dead opponent. Again, the blade rattled on
mail, the complicated Renshai triple twist an instant too late.

Olvaerr's knife cut a fiery track across Tannin's sword forearm.

For an instant, Tannin lost his timing. The wound made
his muscles spasm, and he lost his grip on the sword. A
blade touching ground was dishonored. Trained to snatch
swords from air in spar, he switched hands with a grace that
bordered on instinct. He countercut left-handed, the abrupt
change catching Olvaerr fully off-balance. The blade slid beneath mail, tearing a hole in the Northman's thigh that bled
in a sudden geyser.

Olvaerr collapsed, soundless, into a spreading puddle of
blood. Only then did Tannin's attention broaden to include
more than his own battle. A curse rattled harshly in his ears.
His first glance revealed no sign of the Renshai, but all four
of the enemy remained in position near the fire. The wolf
had disappeared.

Even as Tannin's quick glance registered those details,
something unseen struck him with a blow so hard it hurled
him forward. Unable to defend, he twisted as he fell, head
striking the ground with enough force to make it ring. He
landed on Olvaerr's corpse, blood smearing his face and
hands. He gasped for breath, trying to roll free of the dead
man and face the unseen enemy as well. Then his muscles
locked into painful contraction, and he screamed without intention, back arched to its limit, arms and legs rigid and un-
responsive.

Tannin choked down another scream, not wanting the
Renshai to come back for him and place themselves at risk.
His mind told him that the unnatural attack had to come of
magic, and he had no idea how to fight against it. As his
muscles remained at the height of contraction, the agony
swiftly rose in a frenzied crescendo. Pain shattered composure, and all rational thought fled with it. Soon there was
only the pain, and the screams ripped forth repeatedly in a
mindless agony that left no place for understanding, even of
identity.

Then, abruptly, Tannin's muscles went lax. The suddenness of the change lanced a pain through him that made the
previous one seem meager. Then, slowly, sense started seeping back to him, though all he could do was remain unmoving, unanticipated tears coursing down cheeks sticky with
Olvaerr's blood. Ropes bit into his wrists and ankles, the
ɔices around him hazy and only partially comprehensible,

their speech liberally sprinkled with curses. The oblivion
that overtook him felt like mercy.

Shadimar growled a string of curses that seemed endless.
He kicked Tannin's unconscious body until Carcophan
wrested it away, using the ropes to dangle the Renshai upside down from the limb of a tree on the Fields of Wrath.
Even then, Shadimar did not feel vindicated; and the staff's
anger pulsed through his mind, feeding his already rabid
outrage. He snatched up the sword he had pried from Tannin's failing grip, slick from tip to hilt with Olvaerr's blood.
"Die, you god-cursed, savage bastard!" Brandishing the
sword, he swung with all his strength for the Renshai's
throat.

A hand's breadth from his target, Shadimar met abrupt resistance. The sword slammed into a magical barrier, the
foiled blow vibrating through Shadimar's fist. He shouted in
fury, whirling around with a suddenness that sent
Dh'arlo'mé skittering from the path of the blow. Ancient,
gray eyes locked on Trilless. "You stopped me, you witch.
Why did you stop me?"

Trilless met him, stare for stare. "Because you're letting
anger drive you too far. Because the chaos Colbey loosed
has addled even you. Pain and torture are tools of evil. If
that's not reason enough, remember that we have to have
them alive and unharmed for Colbey to bargain."

Shadimar glowered, but he did lower the sword. "A bargain with chaos is no bargain at all. He'll lie like the force
he champions, and we should be no more bound by a promise broken."

Trilless and Carcophan exchanged meaningful glances
that Shadimar could not read. "The weakest of the Wizards,"
Carcophan reminded. "The second to fall to chaos."

The words only further fueled the Eastern Wizard's rage.

Trilless glared at her opposite, her own anger eclipsed by
obvious concern. "Resist, Shadimar. Look to the Staff of
Law, and let it give you its strength. No matter Colbey's
bent, we must follow the tenets of law."

The gentleness of her words dispersed some of the crazed
anger that made deep consideration impossible. He sensed a
morality to her points, yet the staff he consulted reassured
him that chaos could only be defeated by a lesser dose of it-

self. At times, besting an enemy meant using its own tactics against it. The unexpected had won many battles.

Carcophan sneered. "When I tried to avenge the death of my apprentice, you accused me of sleeping with her." His catlike eyes glittered. "Now I see why you couldn't understand the natural relationship between a beautiful woman and a man." He directed his gaze to Olvaerr's corpse.

The accusation was ludicrous. In his day, Shadimar had loved women as much as most men did; responsibilities had swept thoughts of sexuality and relationships from his mind decades past. He and Olvaerr had shared nothing but a student/teacher association, yet the loss still addled and enraged him. It had taken long consideration and effort to find one capable of replacing him as Eastern Wizard who also vehemently hated Colbey. Now, the two Northmen would never stand opposed. Shadimar whirled on Carcophan. "We could have recaptured all the Renshai if you'd worked with me. Why did you let them run?"

Carcophan smiled. "I saw no reason to do otherwise. Where will they run to? Our displacement spell only took a small piece of man's world with us, and there's no way to return without some knowledge of magic."

The realization that Carcophan spoke truth further annoyed Shadimar. Had he focused his attention on rescuing Olvaerr sooner, rather than on the fleeing Renshai, he might have saved his apprentice. The lapse turned rage into irritation, and he cursed his costly mistake. Perhaps Trilless had a point about the chaos Colbey had loosed miring Shadimar's sense of judgment. He would need his wits about him, and it only made sense to ground his reason on the staff.

Carcophan picked up Olvaerr's sword, wiped it clean on Tannin's cloak, then handed it to Dh'arlo'mé. "I presume you know how to use it." Without awaiting a response, he gestured at Olvaerr's sword belt, blood-splattered and still around the corpse.

The elf glanced at Shadimar, as if to ascertain that the Eastern Wizard would not find taking the sheath and belt a personal insult to his apprentice. When Shadimar said nothing, he set to work freeing the necessary gear. While the elf worked, Carcophan patted the sword at his own hip that had once belonged to Chezrith. Though he knew how to use it, his magic would serve him so much better it seemed needless to carry it. Still, it was safer in Carcophan's hands than placed where any Renshai might steal it.

Carcophan addressed Shadimar again. "I presume you have some contact with the wolf."

Shadimar nodded absently, touching the animal the only way possible, through emotion. He discovered that Secodon still tailed his quarry, though his superior speed could have caught them had Shadimar not given explicit instructions to remain safely behind the Renshai. Soon enough, the escapees would circumnavigate the world the Cardinal Wizards had created and find themselves back where they had started. Yet for all their movement, it seemed as if this should already have happened. Shadimar went wary, and he felt his concern echoed in Secodon's manner.

"Where is he?" Carcophan prodded.

"Can't tell location," Shadimar shot back. "But they don't seem to have stopped fleeing since the escape."

The Cardinal Wizards turned, as one. Running for this long, the Renshai should have come full circle. Yet, apparently, they had not.

Suddenly, a wave of shock and pain buffeted Shadimar, driving him to his knees. An instant later, an animal yelp of pain split the air. *Secodon!* Shadimar rose, forcing away agony that was not his own, unable to locate cause or circumstance any more than he could directly pinpoint the wolf itself. A different pain plagued him then, the realization that he might lose a long-time companion whom he loved. The wolf had been a part of his life for nearly two decades, its devotion and loyalty a constant that never needed questioning.

A mournful howl cleaved the air, full of ancient pain and followed by a series of whimpers.

"He's hurt," Shadimar explained unnecessarily. "We have to help him." Despite the significance of saving a companion, Shadimar did not lose sight of the situation. Even swordless, the Renshai were dangerous. It made little sense to rush to the aid of a friend, only to fall into an enemy ambush. And the danger had become more awesome and obvious since the shattering of the Pica Stone had destroyed their natural imperviousness to anything other than magic.

The last though, at least, had a solution that came partially from the staff and partially from the memories of the previous Eastern Wizards. "We need to find and help Secodon,"

Shadimar said carefully. "We need to recapture the Renshai. But first we need to protect ourselves."

Carcophan plotted strategy. "Trilless, I suggest you and your apprentice stay here and guard this one." He indicated Tannin. The Renshai stirred in his bonds, the movement making his body sway. "The others will probably come back for him. Shadimar and I will tend the wolf."

A pitiful series of whines pierced the air, making it seem to drop in temperature. Each sound cut Shadimar, but he forced himself to tend self before companion. "I think I can come up with a spell that protects us the way surviving the Tasks of Wizardry once did."

Carcophan and Trilless gave their companion their full attention.

Shadimar followed the guidance of the staff as he spoke. "It's temporary, of course, but it ought to last through the day, at least. We can cast it again tomorrow."

"Let's do it," Carcophan said. "Show us how, and we'll cast our own. No need for you to take all the risk."

Carcophan left much unsaid beneath an offer that seemed otherwise appropriate and generous. It made sense that he would want to understand the casting details so he could protect himself without needing to depend on Shadimar. It also seemed logical to share the exposure to chaos. Already, the lords of good and evil seemed certain that Shadimar had suffered too much of it.

For an instant, Shadimar was seized by a selfish desire to keep the staff's knowledge to himself. Once the Staff of Chaos had been wrested from Colbey and destroyed, the three forces of law would again operate in opposition: good, evil, and neutrality. Spells unshared would serve him alone. Still, he also realized that this particular ward would give him little advantage. If he found the need to battle the other Wizards, it seemed unlikely to be with nonmagical weapons. Argument would only delay the care Secodon desperately needed. Already, he could no longer hear the wolf's cries, though he still felt its agony as his own. "Very well. Join me." He blanked his mind, except for the direction of the staff.

A moment later, Shadimar felt the other Cardinal Wizards fuse into his thoughts. Not wanting them to drift to his personal affairs, even peripherally and accidentally, he started right in on the spell.

As was often the case, the magic had at least one unexpected side effect. Tannin moaned, the chaos of the summoned magic awakening him in an instant. Light snapped
into focus, outlining first Shadimar, then Carcophan and
Trilless as they imitated the signals and sounds of the spell.
Gradually, the white glow muted to gray silhouette, then disappeared from sight. Still, Shadimar could feel a faint tingle
of presence, as if tiny insects crawled beneath his skin. He
hated this effect, but it seemed worth the protection.
"Ready?"

"Ready," Carcophan replied, scratching absently at his
arm. Trilless nodded to indicate she would remain behind.
They had not traced Dh'arlo'mé with a similar spell. The release of chaos on a tiny world seemed too dangerous when
other confining and defensive spells might become necessary. Trilless would have to shield her apprentice as the others had not managed to do for their own.

So far, things had not gone at all as Shadimar intended. A
nearly endless life without need to fear anything he did not
call down upon himself had made him reckless. From this
moment on, caution would have to usurp overconfidence.
Shadimar felt certain there would be no more mistakes.
"Let's go."

Though Shadimar could not determine precise location,
the wolf's pain drew him like a beacon. They walked into
the forests north of the Fields of Wrath without fear,
Shadimar using his staff as a walking stick. Neither the
Renshai nor any force of nature could harm them now. Still,
they tried to move in relative silence.

The walk took longer than Shadimar anticipated. The
woodlands should only have lasted a few steps before re-
joining the opposite side of the clearing they had left, yet
they continued far past the Wizards' expectations. Shortly,
Shadimar became alarmed. "You don't think our spell failed
and we're still on man's world, do you?"

Carcophan shook his head briskly, face scored by a frown.
"I felt the magic pop, and we spent all that time sealing off
the gate. Besides, I could tell from the camp that we'd left
the Renshai's cottages behind." His yellow-green eyes slit-
ted, making them look even more feline than usual. "You
still haven't got the feel for that staff. You're making your
spells too powerful. That's why we called a *kraell,* too, instead of the lesser demon we tried to summon on the

Meeting Isle. It's a good thing it's law you carry, so it can balance out at least some of your overaction."

Shadimar hated accusations. Yet his first instinct, to defend himself, passed quickly. It did make sense that the staff amplified his incantations. So far, he had expended the standard amount of magical energy for spells. It might serve him better to tone down his work. "You may be right. I'll keep it in mind."

As usual, Carcophan took the matter one step too far. "I know the idea bothers you, friend; but it might prove safer to let someone stronger wield the staff."

All camaraderie vanished in an instant. "I should have known that's all you wanted from the start. I can't seem to make you understand. The difference between your abilities and mine, no matter how significant you feel it to be, pales to nothing once you view the chasm between the staff and either of us." Shadimar's fingers tightened around the polished wood. "I've told you before, I'm its intended champion. The staff would not have you."

Carcophan raised his hands to indicate that he had no intention of pressing the matter further, at least for now. They continued along the woodland roadway, the most logical route for Renshai more interested in placing distance between themselves and their captors than in creating any kind of diversion. The wolf's pain strengthened as they drew closer. Shortly, Shadimar caught a glimpse of a shaggy figure lying still near the roadway. A human leaned over the creature, doing something Shadimar could not distinguish at a distance. The wolf's pain had disappeared with its loss of consciousness, yet Shadimar's contact told him Secodon still lived. For the moment that surprised him. The presence of another suggested at least one Renshai had remained behind to finish it off. Even without a steel weapon, any of the tribe knew enough about killing to have already completed the job.

Confident of his magical protection, Shadimar headed toward Secodon at a dignified trot.

The other looked up at his approach, now recognizably Mitrian. A broken arrow shaft jutted from Secodon's neck, caked with blood and partially freed from its rest. As the Eastern Wizard approached, Mitrian raised a sharpened stick as thick as her wrist. "Stay back, or I'll use it."

Although he feared nothing from her himself, Shadimar

stopped to spare his four-legged companion. Rage flared. "You won't last long against my magic. You're already going to pay for harming Secodon. If you compound that mistake by killing him, you'll pay that much more dearly."

"Harm Secodon? Me?" Although incredulous, Mitrian did not sacrifice her position, and her eyes sought and found Carcophan. The Southern Wizard remained in place, scanning the woodlands for other Renshai. "I'd no more hurt him than you would. I heard his cry and came to help."

Mitrian's assertion seemed impossible. "Then who injured him?"

"Whoever shot this." Mitrian tossed the broken shaft of an arrow, crudely fletched with unmatched feathers.

Shadimar watched the piece arch from Mitrian's hand to the dirt pathway, skidding beneath a pile of shed needles. He frowned. It made no sense for Renshai to turn to arrows as a means of defense. Although Mitrian could shoot, Renshai honor forbade her from doing so except when hunting food, and she had not left the presence of the Wizards long enough to have crafted such a weapon. But no one except the Renshai could have injured Secodon. The Cardinal Wizards had only moved a small portion of man's world here, a portion that should have contained only the Renshai, Wizards, and apprentices. Realization struck. *But we brought more of man's world than intended.*

Carcophan answered the logical question by casting a spell of his own. "There are eleven living human presences on the world." He released his spell. "Six Renshai, four of us. That leaves one stranger."

Mitrian relaxed visibly at the pronouncement of six living Renshai. Apparently, she had worried about Tannin. Almost immediately, her expression changed from one of relief to anger. "Shadimar, what's going on? I thought we were friends. Why would you take us with magic? Why does the trail end when it used to continue? And why does the forest look the same and different at once?"

Shadimar glanced at Carcophan for assistance, then followed his own judgment instead. Mitrian had a clear head and was intelligent enough to understand the need for maintaining law whatever the cost. "I'm sorry for the surprise welcome. We didn't think you'd come without a fight."

That seeming self-evident, Mitrian waited for Shadimar to continue.

"I'm not sure how to make you understand, but I'll do my best. Colbey's fallen under the influence of powerful chaos magic—"

Mitrian interrupted, face alight with obvious joy. "He's alive?"

Carcophan cleared his throat. "Whoever is trying to slip around behind me had best freeze before I kill him with magic."

Shadimar left the tending of the other Renshai to Carcophan. No weapons could harm them, and he trusted Trilless to guard Tannin well. "Unfortunately for us and the world, yes. He's alive, and committed to causing the *Ragnarok.*"

Mitrian squinted, obviously doubtful.

Shadimar sighed, with no intention of explaining his motives in detail. "Remember, Cardinal Wizards can't lie. Colbey wound up with a singular powerful object, the pure representation of chaos. And it's eating away at his judgment and his mind. If we don't get it away from him soon, he'll destroy himself and the world with him."

Mitrian lowered the stake, stroking the still wolf gently. "You're certain?"

"Never more of anything in my rather lengthy existence."

"And you figured you could trade us for the magical . . . thing?"

"Staff, yes." Shadimar planted his own staff to identify the offending object. "I'm sorry I had to use you and the others for bait, but it's the only thing to which Colbey's rapidly warping mind still holds an attachment. Soon, even that loyalty will fail, and chaos will make him selfish beyond salvation: ours or the gods."

Mitrian pursed her lips in obvious consideration.

Shadimar drove his point home. "I know you have ties to Colbey stronger than those to me. But even though we forced you here, I promise we have the best interests of you, the world, and even Colbey in mind. If we fail, the price will be the world itself and every man in it, us, and nearly all of the gods as well. Do you understand?"

"I understand," Mitrian said, at length. "If we cooperate, do you guarantee the safety of every Renshai?"

"To the best of my ability."

Mitrian glanced at Carcophan.

"With one qualification," the Evil One said. "I promise

Colbey's security only after he gives up the staff and only for as long as he keeps the peace as well."

"All right," Mitrian agreed. She made a brisk gesture toward the woods, and Rache slipped up behind her, swiftly followed by Tarah and Modrey, clutching his child. Mitrian stepped aside to let Shadimar tend the wolf.

As the Renshai moved beyond reach of crude weapons, Shadimar examined the damage. The wolf would take some tending, but not here where the stranger could fire upon him or any of the Renshai. He cradled the limp animal into his arms, cheered by its warmth and the breath stirring from its muzzle.

They headed back toward the camp.

CHAPTER 27

Hunting the Hunter

Colbey, Khitajrah, Sterrane, and Mar Lon left the castle before sunup. Béarn's king chose the shortest course through his city and a time that would minimize the number of citizens who saw him go. Apparently, his simplicity made him leery of fanfare, though he surely could not keep his departure secret for long. At the least, the nobility would notice his absence at the court, and the courtroom sentries would find themselves guarding the young heir and his warden rather than their monarch. Still, Colbey felt a comfortable mixture of relief and pleasure at Sterrane's decision. Citizens in ignorance would not try to question or follow. The fewer people who knew of his mission, the more chance at success it had.

As it stood, Colbey had no idea how to locate the Cardinal Wizards' hiding place for the Renshai and no clue who to ask for help. The only logical possibilities included tracking signs of passage from the Fields of Wrath or luring the Wizards to him with the hope of securing his staff. Either course meant going to the Renshai's cottages once Arduwyn had been found.

Sterrane had supplied the finest of his horses, exchanging the bay and the chestnut for well-rested steeds of equal or better quality. He rode a massive buckskin that clearly served as the royal mount, its golden coat so dark it blended as well into the brush as Colbey's chestnut mare, Khitajrah's dark brown gelding, and Mar Lon's bay.

The *aristiri* joined them at the stables. It ranged ahead, flying in wide circles over the forest, returning at intervals to alight on Colbey's shoulder or the horn of his saddle. Somehow, its course seemed always to take it between Colbey and Khitajrah, though it did not peck or poke at her as it had once previously. Colbey took little notice of the singing hawk's choice of route, though Khitajrah became more annoyed as the sun's tip appeared over the line of trees, slanting light across the woodland pathway.

"If I didn't know better, I'd say that bird was jealous of me," Khitajrah grumbled.

Colbey wisely held his tongue. Khitajrah's reaction revealed a jealousy of her own, and it made far less sense for a woman to feel rivalry with a bird. Still, Formynder seemed like no normal *aristiri*. Its every look and action appeared uncharacteristic for a hawk, and much about it felt more human than animal.

Mar Lon chose the route he believed most likely to reveal Arduwyn. The escape from the castle set the stage for hushed secrecy, though it seemed counterproductive as well as unnecessary. Colbey believed Arduwyn would find them if he realized he was being sought by friends. Yet, though the shifting of deer and other animals might warn the little hunter of humans nearby, it would not reveal their identity or purpose.

They camped as the sun dropped below the tops of the trees, bathing the forest in gray. Colbey practiced sword forms while Mar Lon prepared a meal from the generous pack of supplies and Khitajrah confined the horses with ropes strung between the trunks. She left them a space of ground tangled with underbrush, the weeds and sheltering vines without brambles, palatable to the animals. Then, Mar Lon fetched water for humans and horses alike from a nearby stream, his bard-inherited curiosity forcing him to catch as many glimpses as possible of a Renshai in training. Though aware of Mar Lon's occasional presence, Colbey paid him no heed. The bard could learn little or nothing from the capering of a Renshai sword master honing himself in silence. Without knowledge of Colbey's choices or the training to follow them, the bard could not even imitate the strokes.

At length, Colbey reluctantly pronounced himself finished for the evening. He returned to camp, settling in to eat with the others, tossing an occasional meat scrap to the *aristiri*.

Khitajrah waited only until everyone had finished eating and spread blankets for the night before broaching a matter that had, apparently, plagued her for some time. "Mar Lon, would you call us 'together in a cause'?"

Mar Lon glanced at Colbey before answering. Clearly, he trusted the old Renshai's judgment about such matters before his own. On the surface, Colbey did not see how anyone could believe otherwise. Clearly, they all came for the same purpose, but he sensed something more significant underlying the question. From Khitajrah, he perceived an innocent desire for information only Mar Lon could give her. From Mar Lon, he got dwindling distrust and a faint concern that Khitajrah might be feigning her loyalty and might pose a threat to any or all of them. The specifics did not accompany the radiating emotions.

Still, Colbey believed he understood enough. He felt certain Khitajrah could not have faked the depth of joy and excitement she had shared with him the previous night, though he had detected an accompanying uncertainty. Then, he had attributed it to the many things that made them an unlikely couple: vastly different cultural and religious backgrounds, a thirty-five year gap in age, and the knowledge that Colbey and Khitajrah's family served on opposite sides of a war. Now Colbey felt less sure of the cause of Khitajrah's vague discomfort that night, but he did know for certain that it had nothing to do with treason.

Colbey responded to Mar Lon's unasked question to the best of his ability. "I've trusted her at my sleeping back. And I'd do so again."

The information did not seem to fully appease Mar Lon.

Sterrane watched the exchange without judgment, though he did seem disturbed by the rudeness of his bodyguard.

Khitajrah addressed the problem directly. "Chaos was ousted," she said cryptically. "And it won't return."

Colbey nodded agreement, though it surprised him that Mar Lon had known about Khitajrah's loathsome visitor. Nothing he had seen or heard indicated the bard read minds. In fact, Shadimar had taught him otherwise, that only the Cardinal Wizards could share mental communications of any kind. Apparently, he had caught her in a lie and his vast knowledge allowed him to make the obvious assumption.

Sterrane tipped his head, clearly confused by the exchange, though he did not interrupt it. Apparently, whatever Khitajrah had told Mar Lon had not gotten passed to the king.

Again, Mar Lon turned a casual glance to Colbey. It seemed strange for the bard to trust him just one day after he had studied the aging Renshai as if he expected some sudden, horrible mutation into demon form.

"First, she's quite correct. We banished chaos, and I think she's strong enough to keep it at bay from this time on." Colbey sighed, launching into the same explanation he had tried to impart so many times without success. "Second, I don't know how to get you, or anyone else, to understand. Yes, I brought chaos to man's world. Someone had to do it eventually, and I was as much chosen as given the decision. I did what I believed right. I loosed the forces together, in struggle, rather than barring either from our world. I would rather have bonded them in balance, but I wasn't given that choice. Though I once dared to doubt the wisdom of the gods, I believe they knew best this time. A constant, perfect balance might prove as overly simplistic and predictable as law alone, limiting in its own sense." He glanced quickly at Sterrane. Though listening raptly, the king either did not recognize his own description or denied the comparison. "I still believe in ultimate balance, but I think slight shifts might prove necessary for the world to continue."

Mar Lon freed his mandolin from his gear, though he did not play. With a Cardinal Wizard there, he could speak openly, without the musical constraints placed on him when he taught mortals. "It took thought and consideration, but your 'balance' argument made sense to me long ago. You may not know, but I refused Shadimar's offer to become his apprentice for that reason. Because of my position . . ." Mar Lon did not define what he meant, but he did glance at Sterrane to confirm his dedication to the king's cause of utter neutrality. ". . . I can't support the extremes that are every Cardinal Wizard's cause. *Every* Wizard, Colbey. For all your talk, you have no choice but to champion your force, like the others."

Colbey smiled slightly, careful to keep condescension or mockery from his expression. There were still things Mar Lon had not surmised and Colbey did not feel ready to reveal. "There is always a choice, Mar Lon. Remember that."

Mar Lon seemed skeptical. "Are you telling me you don't believe Odin always intended each of the Cardinal Wizards to champion one of the four forces: good or evil, law or chaos?"

Colbey's grin remained, fixed in place. "I belive that was Odin's intention, yes."

Khitajrah and Sterrane watched intently, obviously seeing

an importance to the discussion that they could only partially understand.

Though Colbey's title freed Mar Lon from the need to make his points in song, he apparently realized he had some duty to educate the mortals as well. He sang at the volume of his speaking voice, without musical accompaniment, the tune an obvious variation on an old Northern ballad:

"Image this scene, all who would understand:
A mother horse with a hoof caught in a band,
A capering foal, at her side it does wait.
Comes a dog craving blood, though no hunger to sate.

"The dog wants the foal for the joy of the kill.
The mare protects though struggle does her leg ill.
Let's call the horse good, for her great sacrifice;
And call the dog evil for his bloodthirsty vice.

"To represent law: a man, product of culture;
And above it all hovers a chaos-warped vulture.
The man would tame dog, take it home for a pet;
Horse and colt plow his fields, their lot in life met.

"The vulture would rather the other three fight:
Man stabs dog, horse stomps man then dies of dog's bite.
Then feast on the flesh of all three as a treat,
The rampant destruction of chaos complete.

"One Wizard per force, Odin keeps our world stable.
Each spreads and serves his cause as he is able.
The Four in opposition should result in balance,
Unless one should choose to dilute his vast talents."

His obligation met, Mar Lon returned to his more personal conversation as if he had never interrupted. "You admit it's your god-granted destiny to champion chaos. And yet, you claim to sanction neutrality instead."

Colbey easily returned to his place in the discussion, only slightly put off by song in the middle of discourse. "There is no law, at least not one Odin enforces, that says a man always has to act by gods' intentions."

"What are you saying?" Mar Lon's expression and tone revealed the incredulity that also floated to Colbey in waves.

"I'm saying Odin sees all, except into the future. His vast and lofty wisdom allows him to make reasonable predictions, of course, but he can't know everything that is to come. By stories, that's the one thing he strives for most and knows he can't have." Colbey's smile vanished, and he twisted the gold ring on his finger absently. He understood he was treading the fine boundary of blasphemy, but past experience and knowledge of his parentage made him bold. "Surely, he set up the system of Cardinal Wizards to account for and cover all of the most likely futures. But he had no way to foresee me." He delivered the final stroke. "In my opinion, mankind's guardians, at least those who propose law and chaos, would serve their charges far better by working in concert to keep balance rather than struggling in opposition."

Mar Lon's thoughts became so powerful, Colbey could not avoid them, even if he tried. He braced, preparing for the wrath of gods, even as he considered Colbey's words. For millennia, the Cardinal Wizards had believed two guardians of neutrality existed only to work together to oppose good and evil. Now, it seemed clear that Odin had selected two so that they could eventually champion law and chaos. Then, he had created the Eighth Task, its specifics such that one who completed it proved himself suitable to handle his charge. *But there was no corresponding task to demonstrate the worth of the other Wizard to handle the opposite force.* The thought froze in place, unable to be banished, and its intensity wafting from Mar Lon's mind pained Colbey.

It was an idea Colbey had not considered in that manner, though he had always trusted his judgment more than that of Shadimar. The thought reminded him that Shadimar had called himself, and the previous Eastern Wizards, the least powerful of the Four. Given that knowledge, it occurred to Colbey that Odin might have intended an Eastern Wizard to succeed at the Eighth Task, knowing the Western Wizard would prove more competent. Yet that seemed no more likely than for Odin to expect a Western Wizard to succeed, with the knowledge that the strongest of Wizards would use and distribute the forces best. Perhaps, Odin saw more than even Colbey had credited.

Mar Lon managed to free himself from his thought-lock. "Colbey, Shadimar and the others seem heavily influenced by chaos. Do you think it's possible your attempt to champion balance instead of chaos might have sent the chaos you're supposed to bear to them instead?"

Colbey sorted his thoughts, surprised to find he felt more comfortable with generalities than the truth Mar Lon sought but should find for himself. "That's one explanation. But I believe they could resist chaos if they wished it. We all make our own choices." He changed the subject, believing he finally had Mar Lon on the right tack but not wanting to say so much that the bard could not come to the conclusions himself. To say too much would leave Mar Lon wondering whether the Western Wizard had planted lies in his mind. He addressed Khitajrah. "Why did you want to know if you and Mar Lon served the same cause?"

Khitajrah hesitated, drawn suddenly back into a conversation that she had started, and then become a distanced spectator to rather than a participant. "Once our causes came together, he promised me a song I very much want to hear."

"Ellbaric's song." Mar Lon confirmed. Obviously, he had known what she wanted from the start. Finally, he turned the request to Sterrane. "I can't do it justice without chords. Do you think the noise might draw unwelcome visitors?"

The king shook his head. "Might bring *welcome* visitor. Might bring Ardy."

Colbey nodded. "Of course, he's right. And we'd all love to hear you play."

Khitajrah smiled nervously, clearly glad to have won the battle, though still discomfited, either by the possible details of the song she had requested or by the suggestion that Arduwyn might come.

Mar Lon sat, cradling the mandolin in his lap, then naturally settling his hands to the strings. Without further encouragement, he began to play, the minor chords of the introduction bringing tears to Khitajrah's eyes long before the words began:

"Torn from childhood,
Thrust into war.
Taken from farm fields
To slog through the gore.

"But Glory is myth
Honor simply death

*On cold foreign fields
He would gasp his last breath.*

*"His family would say
That their son died in vain
They would first see just death
Overlooking the gain.*

*"He went 'cause they told him
There was no other way;
The enemy's day . . .*
                       must end.
*He went without fanfare
Only friends knew his name;
He'd return without fame . . .*
                       In a box.

*"Yet if it meant one more man
Would remember lost brothers
Then chose peace over war
It would save all the others.*

*"Death should not be mourned
Rather used as a lesson
If he taught just one soldier
Then his end was a blessing.*

*"And if his demise brought
Justice to any
Celebrate his death
For the good of the many.*

*"He went 'cause they told him
They needed his sword;
In the name of our lord . . .*
                       Sheriva.
*He went without fanfare
Hoping only to show
That a man cannot grow . . .*
                       With war's fever.

*"Yet for all his war loathing
He would once only die*

Some might live their lives better
If they contemplate why.

"Long after he's gone
And his sword's turned to rust.
Those who cared will remember
A child rotted to dust.

"But live heroes' lots fade
As youth turns to age
Their survival glorifies
The wars that they wage.

"He went 'cause they told him
He went far from home
Leaving only a poem . . .
                    as a plea.
He went without fanfare
Nothing won only lost
Too high, the cost . . .
                    Of victory."

As the final notes rang from the mandolin strings, unaccompanied by Mar Lon's mellow voice, even Colbey found his eyes moist. The actual words seemed unpolished and unprofessional compared to those the bards had written through the millennia, yet Mar Lon's voice did them justice and the simple, happy tune gave the message a contrasting deep significance. Colbey recognized the obvious intention of the writer. Many would have considered him incapable of understanding the sentiment, yet he felt as sorry for the plight of nonwarriors forced to war as any.

Colbey remembered riding across the beach at the end of the Great War, the excitement of his own wild war passion and glorious battles dwarfed by the misery of farmers who had seen and done more than their consciences could bear, who had survived when their friends and neighbors had died and knew as much guilt as relief. The Western peasants and craftsmen had mostly come of their own free will, brandishing the tools of their trade more often than the weapons needed by the warriors of their towns. Even lacking the forced command, they had known the terror of joining a war they could not hope to survive, praying that, at least, they would not die in vain. Only the childish naïveté of the poet differed from the soldiers Colbey had known, for the boy who had written Mar Lon's song truly believed mankind might place sentiment and sorrowful memories before ongoing greed.

Colbey drifted off to sleep recalling his plans for the last of the Renshai, that they would become soldiers for hire to fight the battles men like Ellbaric should not. Khitajrah's crying did not disturb his rest.

Khitajrah dreamed of shattered families, blood, and graveyards, windswept and solitary to the point of epitomizing loneliness. She awakened with a start, night cold prickling her skin into gooseflesh and a dream-discomfort that bordered on fear sending shivers the length of her body. She forced herself to come fully awake, concerned about drifting back into the same nightmare. When her thoughts kept returning to the pictures her mind had drawn in sleep, she rose. Performing some routine action, coupled with a short, invigorating walk, might drive her thoughts on another tangent.

As Khitajrah stood, Colbey stirred. Then, apparently recognizing the movement as harmless, he curled an arm protectively about the staff, patted his sword without opening an eye, and went back to sleep. The *aristiri* perched on a branch over the Renshai's head, feathers ruffled and head sunk to its chest.

Khitajrah headed into the woods, seeking a place to empty her bladder where neither her companions nor passersby could observe. She found a place within a few steps, shielded from the camp by a screen of briers and from the road by a line of trunks. Raising her dress, she squatted, the urine steaming slightly as it touched the cold ground.

Khitajrah had finished when a man's impassive voice threatened her from the foliage. "Speak me one good reason why I shouldn't kill you."

Startled, Khitajrah rose, instinctively straightening her skirts. An arrowhead peeked through a gap in the undergrowth lined directly at her on a drawn bow. She caught a glimpse of red hair through the greenery.

Khitajrah's skin washed clammy. "I—" she started, then stopped, considering her reply more carefully. Her life depended on it.

"Be quick about it," Arduwyn said. "The string is digging into my fingers, and I might have to let it go."

Gradually, Khitajrah's scattered thoughts came together. One thing seemed certain: bold sarcasm would keep her alive longer than desperate begging. Time would bring Colbey to her rescue. "I can give you three good reasons. First, you got your horse back. I made certain of that."

The bow did not move. The string remained fully drawn.

"Second, I'm truly, deeply sorry and willing to make the matter up to you in any way I can."

Still, the bow and arrow did not move, although Khitajrah thought she saw a strange expression taking shape on Arduwyn's half-hidden features.

"Third," Khitajrah added the most salient point, "I came with good friends of yours to find you. Colbey and the king of Béarn need your help, and they believe I can help as well. We have a cause to handle, that of our friends. Our own feud, if you insist on carrying it on, can wait."

"Sterrane is here?"

"Yes."

The arrow withdrew hesitantly. "A thief would also lie."

"Yes." Khitajrah relaxed as the threat lessened. "But I'm neither anymore. I wasn't in my right mind at the time. Again, I'm sorry."

Arduwyn remained in place.

"The camp's just back that way. Look for yourself."

"I know where the camp is." Arduwyn dismissed Khitajrah's offer. "I recognized Colbey, Mar Lon, you, and a Béarnide buried to his hair beneath the blankets. I just can't believe it's the king himself."

Khitajrah played her card. "He insisted on coming. The mission is so important."

Arduwyn studied Khitajrah in the shadow-dappled moonlight. She thought she saw interest as well as distrust in his expression, and the combination gave her chills. Surely, she misunderstood his intentions, and that made him fully unpredictable. "Go on, back to the camp." He shook the bow at her. "If you're lying, I'll shoot you. Don't think I won't do it to spare my friends the sight. If I don't trust you, I certainly don't trust you in their presence."

Khitajrah could not suppress a shiver, though so many she knew said positive things about Arduwyn. She suspected he would prove the good and fair man the others believed him to be—eventually. She led him back to the campsite.

This time, Colbey came fully awake, hand wrapped around his sword hilt from the instant Arduwyn set foot in the clearing. Mar Lon, too, came swiftly awake; and even Sterrane stirred, his shaggy scalp and one eye appearing from beneath the covers.

Khitajrah considered jokingly claiming that she had found Arduwyn, but abandoned the quip. In his current mental state, the hunter might consider it a falsehood rather than a jest.

As they recognized Arduwyn, all three of Khitajrah's companions rose and smiled. Sterrane caught his friend into a welcoming embrace, and Colbey politely waited for the greeting to finish. The instant the two men parted, he caught Arduwyn's shoulder. "My horse?"

Arduwyn nodded sagely. "Frost Reaver. I thought so. Didn't have any of those swishy ribbons the regular knights always wind through the manes. He's at my camp. Tied if he hasn't already broken the lead. He can't stand me leaving him anywhere. Why is that?"

Colbey dismissed the question. "Too complicated to explain. It involves magic and such, and I'll take care of it right away. Just tell me where to find him."

Arduwyn's single eye rolled past Colbey, riveting on the *aristiri* where it perched overhead. "There she is!"

"What?" Colbey whirled, the others also searching for the focus of Arduwyn's gaze.

Without a direct answer, Arduwyn moved to the oak whose branches supported the hawk. "Beautiful." He explained, without taking his attention from the bird for a moment. "I saw her flying and followed. Then I heard Mar Lon's singing. That's how I found you. I haven't seen an *aristiri* in years. They've become so timid." His eye narrowed, and he tore his gaze free with obvious reluctance to look briefly at Colbey. "Usually." The single word requested explanation.

Though concerned for Frost Reaver, Colbey obliged. He would need Arduwyn's cooperation to find his horse. "First, I hate to question your knowledge of wild animals, but the hawk's a he. He's stayed with me quite some time now. I'm not sure why, but his company is welcome. He's a great guardian." He smiled, referring to the bird's silent acceptance of Arduwyn's presence in the camp. "Usually."

"She." Arduwyn corrected the correction. "I admit I haven't seen many *aristiri* in my life, but I haven't forgotten how to tell gender." He demonstrated with a finger, tracing patterns in the air before the hawk. "The breast stripes go this way." He made a vertical motion to indicate the dark bars that lined the underside of the *aristiri* from neck to feet. "On the males, they're horizontal. Also, the black trim on the males' necks forms a larger patch."

Colbey suffered the details quietly, knowing from what seemed like a more reliable feature that he, not Arduwyn, was right. "It sings."

Arduwyn squinted. "Are you sure?"

Khitajrah nodded vigorously to confirm Colbey's observation.

"More beautifully than Mar Lon."

Now Khitajrah shook her head doubtfully. For all of the *aristiri*'s trills and melodies, it lacked the harmonies Mar Lon's mandolin sounded in accompaniment; and words always added depth to a song. She did not contradict, however. Opinion was a personal thing she could not challenge or deny.

Even faced with this evidence, Arduwyn chose to believe in rare exception rather than doubt his own knowledge. "Than you have an unusual companion indeed. A singing *aristiri* female. Never heard of such—"

An animal scream of rage cut over Arduwyn's words. A massive, white stallion thundered into the clearing, its pale eyes rolling and its nostrils flared red as blood. Its gaze went first to Arduwyn, and it took a hesitant step toward him. Then its nostrils widened further and it snuffled scents from the air. Suddenly, it whirled to face Colbey, hooves chewing divots from the mud. Another wild challenge trumpeted from its throat. Its ears pinned flat, it charged the Renshai.

CHAPTER 28

Willing Prisoners

When Mitrian looked northward, the Fields of Wrath appeared as they as always did. In every other direction, however, it seemed the same and strange at once. Just a glimpse toward the south, where an unfamiliar horizon filled the area where the cottages should stand, made her dizzy to the edge of nausea. The Cardinal Wizards' magic bothered her, in practice and in theory. She understood why they had felt they had to capture first and explain later, though she did not see the necessity. Clearly, the Wizards had had no intention of releasing the Renshai, even if Mitrian and the others chose not to go along with the plan. That seemed odd for the Eastern Wizard who had so long acted as a guardian to Mitrian and her father's people.

The Cardinal Wizards and Dh'arlo'mé sat in conference near the forest's edge, apparently no longer feeling a need to guard their prisoners closely. The Renshai kept to a huddle of their own, trading opinions and suggestions. It seemed wrong to sit idle while others kept the world's greatest swordsmen weaponless and prisoner, even willingly. Yet for now Mitrian saw no wiser course. She believed Carcophan's assertion that they had created another world, consisting of a small section of the old one rolled into a ball. When she considered it in this manner, she believed she recognized portions of the forest, misplaced but otherwise the same.

Vashi, the toddler, roamed about the clearing that defined a portion of the Fields of Wrath, avoiding the stabbing branches that jutted from the forest. Tannin lay in restless sleep, an involuntary moan occasionally escaping with an exhalation. Mitrian winced in sympathy, hating herself for caring. At intervals, her gaze fell to the least respectful of her students, marking the hair still partially held into randomly loosened braids or that spilled in golden waves to the grass. The blue-white eyes rolled open at intervals, childlike in their pain. For the thousandth time, she damned the youthful masculinity that made him act like an idiot, cursed the love that might have been.

"Renshai willing prisoners." Rache's voice startled Mitrian's attention back to where he, Modrey, and Tarah sat, watching Vashi's every movement. "I don't care what they say. I won't stand against Colbey."

Mitrian shuffled to her son's side and took a seat beside him. "It's not a matter of standing against him. Shadimar's going to help him."

Rache made a wordless sound that expressed his doubt clearly enough. "Trusting Wizards before one of our own."

Mitrian sighed. She did not appreciate the possible need to work against Colbey any more than Rache did, but she knew things he could not. "Shadimar has protected us since long before you were born. Without him, I, and therefore you, would never have become Renshai. King Sterrane would have died with his brothers and sisters. I wouldn't have had the courage to run away with your father, and you wouldn't exist. Without the Eastern Wizard convincing me to go, and later doing the same for my father, the West would have lost the Great War. Sterrane would never have tried to reclaim his throne. Without Shadimar's sanctuary during our own war, all of us would have died at the hands of the Northmen's armies." She turned to face Rache directly. "Surely you remember when Colbey came to Shadimar so near death I would have finished the job to end his suffering. Without the Wizard's help, he would already be dead. Shadimar cares for Colbey, and I believe he'll do what's right for him. And for us."

Rache went sullenly silent, not wholly convinced.

Oddly, Mitrian did not feel quite right about the situation either, despite her attempt to remain just in a volatile situation. The Shadimar she knew had done all the things she mentioned and many more. Yet he had also once wrongly accused Colbey of becoming a demon. The Eastern Wizard had always seemed eternal and serious, as hard as the ancient mountains his gray eyes invariably brought to her mind, yet never had he seemed so cold or determined. Always before, he had faced life's problems with proper sobriety, but the rabid desperation and intensity she noticed about his person now seemed out of place. When the time came, she would let her own judgment determine her course of action.

"Did you ask about Sylva?" Rache's question seemed more like a plea.

Mitrian nodded. She had chatted minimally with Shadimar on the walk back to the fields, but she had asked about her daughter-in-law. "He said she wasn't with us when they cast the spell that made us sleep. She must have gone for an early morning hunt."

Rache nodded thoughtfully. Sylva often rose before the sun to catch the last of the night animals or to find a suitable position to wait for those who awakened at dawn.

Mitrian did not tell Rache about the strange glances Shadimar and Carcophan had exchanged, as if her mention of the huntsman's daughter had answered an important question. Long consideration made her wonder if they believed Sylva responsible for the arrow that had injured Secodon. It made little sense to her. If Sylva were here, she would have joined the Renshai, not just fired at an animal she presumed an enemy. And Mitrian knew something Shadimar did not. The archer had shot at her prior to hitting the wolf. A wild tangle of brush, a tree trunk, and a sudden stop had rescued her from the attack. Secodon had not proved as lucky.

Tannin rolled in his sleep. Pain caused him to tighten reflexively, which only seemed to make it worse. He gasped, pale eyes falling open.

Rache sighed, wincing in sympathy. He started to rise.

Mitrian caught his arm. "I'll take care of him this time."

Rache's eyes widened slightly in surprise. Although none but Tannin and Mitrian knew the details, the other Renshai could not help but notice the strained coldness between their *torke* and Tannin. Without explanation, Mitrian headed over to tend the ailing Renshai.

Shadimar had gathered a variety of herbs for his wolf, giving the Renshai as many of the leftovers as they could use. Colbey's training had included healing, history, and philosophy as well as sword technique. To die in any manner but heated combat doomed a Northman's soul to Hel, the worst of tragedies. When the *Ragnarok* came, the hordes of Hel would war against the gods while the souls of heroes in Valhalla fought bravely by the Divine Ones' sides. Therefore, the treatment of disease and wounds following nonlethal battles held strong precedent in Renshai society. Mitrian tended Tannin's injuries as muscle strains, with warmed compresses of herbs mixed with berries that opened skin pores to allow sinew to absorb the cure. She tugged his tunic up, noticing the bruises for the first time. Someone had pounded on Tannin with fist, boot, or weapon.

Tannin kept his eyes open, submitting to Mitrian's ministrations without a word or sound. He trembled beneath her touch, though whether from pain or something else, she could not tell. Though she despised herself for it, she enjoyed examining the naked flesh of his chest, muscles honed and defined by her training. Dried herbs matted the hair, and the smooth bulges felt comfortable beneath her hands. She knew guilt for the pleasure the sight and feel of him gave her. His beauty hid a core as rotten as any enemy's. No foe had scarred her as deeply.

Tannin seemed to grow more agitated by her attempts to soothe and heal. Finally, she pulled his tunic back into place, massaging the poultice onto a neck knotted as hard as a boulder.

"Why did you do it?" Mitrian spoke softly enough so the others could not overhear, though she still sounded loud after the previous lengthy silence.

Tannin blinked, long lashes hiding and revealing the seafoam blue eyes. "*Torke,* I hoped the rest of you would escape while I fought."

Mitrian redirected Tannin. "That's not what I meant."

"Oh." Tannin blinked again, with cautious deliberateness. "What *did* you mean, *torke?*"

Mitrian saw no need to recall the situation in detail. It would only raise rage again. "You know what I meant."

Tannin laced his fingers, stalling. "You mean—"

"Yes."

"Back at home."

"Yes."

"The late lesson."

"No. I mean the reason for the late lesson."

Tannin squirmed, ignoring the pain movement must have caused him. The emotional discomfort seemed worse. "Men have needs."

"Women have needs, too."

Tannin finally met Mitrian's gaze.

Mitrian drove the point home. "Why would you choose some brainless, unwashed whore over another Renshai?"

Tannin stared, eyes locking with Mitrian's, though the flush that tinged his cheeks made it clear he would rather look away. "You, *torke?* You would have . . ." Unable to find a suitably respectful euphemism, he skipped the concept altogether. ". . . with me. You and me?"

Now that she had bared her soul, Mitrian went defensive. "Why not?"

"You and me." Tannin smiled despite the pain. "I can't think of anything I've ever wanted more."

Now, it was Mitrian's turn to blink in stunned wonder. "Then why did you do . . ." The same words failed her. ". . . what you did?"

Tannin craned his neck as well as he could. Unable to find the location of the others, he sat up stiffly, making certain no one else had come within range of his voice. "Need, I guess. I don't know. Maybe I just wanted to get your attention."

"My attention." Mitrian snorted. "You got it, all right. Was it worth it?"

"No," Tannin admitted. "I destroyed everything, didn't I? There's no chance anymore."

"Why didn't you just ask me?"

"I invited you over lots of times. We just talked about sword strokes." Tannin sighed, seeking an explanation Mitrian could understand. "You're my *torke.* If you didn't feel the way I did, it might have ruined my chance to become the best swordsman I can. I didn't want to lose my lessons for boldness."

"So, instead, you nearly lost them for stupidity."

Tannin bit his lip, clearly torn between his need to defend his actions and to appease his *torke.*

Mitrian shook her head, still attracted to her only unmarried student, yet wondering if she dared start something with a man whose judgment she did not trust. She tried to place herself in his position; and, strangely, the comparison fit. She had had a crush on her father's sword master, her first teacher, from the day she started liking members of the opposite sex. Yet she had always considered him leagues above her, even ignoring the ten years of age between them. The feelings she had known for Colbey could have defined respect, and she would never have considered romance with the Golden Prince of Demons. First, he seemed incapable of the depth of emotion necessary to sustain a relationship. Her awe for him placed him above the level of manhood, and the idea of considering him performing the same functions as other men seemed the nearest thing to blasphemy.

Suddenly, Mitrian felt sorry for Tannin. He had battled his own fears and surrendered to respect. In order to protect her status, he had chosen a foolish way to gain her attention. Yet, in the end, the maneuver had come full circle. In a warped, difficult way, he had finally learned the knowledge that could have come with a simple question. Now, Mitrian believed, he had learned his lesson. If and when they returned home, things would change significantly, and the prospect excited her.

Now that he had defined the situation, all of Tannin's hesitation disappeared. Seizing Mitrian's arms, he pulled her down on top of him, kissing her with a depth and passion she had never known. The rest of the world seemed to disappear around them.

The woman had no understanding of self or location, only the unshakable certainty that she owned the woodlands and the "others" did not belong. She perched on a boulder, slender frame lost amid vines and sheltering brush, red hair falling in a wild and tangled wash around her face. She could identify every bird in the treetops by a few notes of song, yet her own name defied her.

She picked one limb from the pile she had gathered, sighting along it to ascertain its straightness. Making a slit in the front, she added the last triangular stone head. Soon she would need to resort to whittled wood, her dagger barely sharp enough to aid nature when it came to shaping stone. She bound the tip in place with rabbit gut dried to leather, then started working on the feathers, placing and tying with practiced precision. She added one more arrow to the ten in her quiver, among them the more capably made ones with feathers dyed pink and green. Those, she had found with her upon awakening, their source a mystery. No bird in this forest bore wings of either color.

The woman set to work carving a chunk of wood with the utility dagger she carried in her pocket. Someone, she could not recall who, had hurt her badly. Someone had, apparently, struck her head hard enough to steal consciousness, identity, and all semblance of memory, except for long-ingrained knowledge that had become like instinct. The force had sent her tumbling across sticks and rocks that had torn bloody furrows from her arms, legs, and torso, stamping bruises across hips and shoulders. That someone would die, as would all who dared set foot in her forest.

She continued, shaving wood to partially bevel the edges to deadly sharpness. A breeze riffled the branches overhead, dropping a single green leaf that spiraled to the ground at the woman's feet.

Caught by surprise by Frost Reaver's murderous frenzy, Mar Lon and Khitajrah skittered from the stallion's path, inadvertently leaving Colbey to face the monster alone. Colbey held his ground, not even bothering to draw a sword. By choice, he would battle his friend with one weapon only, and it had no edge. Ignoring his companions, he thrust his consciousness into the stallion's mind.

The probe crashed through the same hovering fog of chaos it had met before, frozen in place and no larger than when he had last faced it. Time had softened it, and natural horse instincts impinged on every corner: hunger, thirst, desperate need to protect the hooves, a catalog of odors, and the danger of things thrashing suddenly into peripheral vision. It still reeked of the need to kill, directed at Colbey's scent alone.

Distantly, Colbey heard the slam of approaching hoofbeats and the crash of gear scattered in the stallion's frenzied charge. The magic could be easily destroyed now, but he might not find the time before massive hooves pounded him to oblivion. Desperately, he swiped at magic locked in place and shape. It gave like cobwebs wherever he touched, effortlessly dispelled, yet not fast enough. Colbey gave up this course of action, mind leaping for the site of Frost Reaver's spirit and loyalty.

It lay crushed and haggard beneath the heavy brunt of Shadimar's now-failing magic. Colbey directed the flow of his energy there, lending his own strength where Frost Reaver's had become damaged. Methodically, he added life and power to the bond that had once existed between them. He heard a warning scream that sounded leagues distant. Afraid for Mar Lon's sword or Arduwyn's bow, Colbey pulled back from his task just long enough to shout a message. "Don't hurt him! No matter what, don't hurt Reaver!"

The lapse nearly proved fatal. The stallion's chest slammed into Colbey hard enough to send him rolling, and a hoof scraped hair from his scalp, missing the skull by a whisper. *Rescue or defense.* Colbey made the decision instantly, as always. He had only the time it took the stallion to rear and to smash speeding hooves, backed by three-quarters of a ton of muscle, against his head.

Once he made the choice, Colbey committed fully to it. He seized the growing strand of loyalty, channeling all the power he could muster to it. The tendril glowed red, like a sword first drawn from the forge. Then, Shadimar's magic collapsed to colored powder around him, taking the horse's killing rage with it.

But momentum proved Frost Reaver's undoing, rechanneling a mass of moving force nearly impossible in mid-stroke. The stallion whinnied in terror.

Colbey found strength where he thought he had given all, scissoring awkwardly aside as the hooves crashed to ground, gouging turf. Dust filled his nose and mouth, the last vestiges of Shadimar's spell grating between his teeth and driving him to a sneeze he could not muster.

A soft, pink nose whuffled in Colbey's face, lipping at his shoulder until greenish slobber glazed his tunic. Around Frost Reaver's head, he could see that Mar Lon and Sterrane crouched, the bard with sword and the king with ax in hand. Beyond them, Arduwyn stood with bow drawn, sweat spangling his spiky hair. He had wrestled hard with the decision of whether to let the arrow fly.

Colbey allowed his lids to fall back in place, sick with the strain. He sank peacefully into unconsciousness, his last thought to wonder whether Frost Reaver's apology might drown him in snot before he awakened.

Colbey awakened later in the day, strength returned and companions hovering. Apparently, Khitajrah noticed the similarity between Colbey's current state and that after he had helped her repel chaos, because no one asked Colbey how he came to lie unconscious without a mark of injury on him.

"You all right?" Arduwyn asked cautiously.

Colbey glanced about until his gaze fell on Frost Reaver, grazing with the other horses. A newcomer had joined the animals, a blotchy paint as well-conformed as its neighbors, apparently Arduwyn's mount. "I'm fine now." To demon-

strate, he sprang to his feet, bounding to Frost Reaver's un-
saddled back.

The stallion stiffened, then trumpeted a joyous whinny as
he recognized his rider. Colbey whipped his sword free,
lashing into a wild practice that tuned mind as well as body.
The remainder of his pressured fatigue disappeared, replaced by a clarity that made life a joy, despite the threat to
the other Renshai. Nothing seemed impossible. Somehow, he
would free his loved ones, and the staff would remain in the
proper possession of the Western Wizard and his successors.

Arduwyn followed the crisp sweeps and lunges as swiftly
as his single eye could move. "A simple crawl would have
sufficed."

Colbey laughed, passing the hilt from hand to hand, never
allowing it to fly long enough that an enemy might capture
it in the instant he had no control. "I've got my sword, my
horse, and my trusted friends. What more could I need?"

As if in answer, the *aristiri* dove from its perch and
dodged through the perilous flurry of attack, banking and
maneuvering like a bird a third its size. Arduwyn watched
in awe as the creature challenged the world's quickest and
most skillful sword master. No normal animal would have
dared such a feat; survival instinct would have prevented
even consideration of such a thing. Colbey suspected that
Arduwyn's interest stemmed as much from seeing his own
audacity reflected in its actions as from its unnatural risk. In
the last several decades, few men but the little hunter had
dared to confront the elder Renshai in any manner.

Colbey continued his swordplay while Sterrane, Khitajrah,
Arduwyn, and Mar Lon packed up the camp. No one pro-
tested the king assisting in the labor. They knew too well
that protestations would prove useless. In his simple way,
Sterrane would help. To ask him to sit aside while work
needed doing would prove more insulting than granting him
the regal leisure his position accorded him. Colbey, con-
versely, found no cause worth abandoning his swordwork.
No matter the job, it could wait until his blades had been
honored and tended.

They traveled throughout the day, camped the night, and
started again the following morning. Arduwyn ranged ahead,
with or without his horse, returning to steer the group
around new deadfalls or past copses entering their season for
thorns or burrs. Sterrane conversed happily with his com-

panions about any topic he or they cared to raise, humming tunelessly whenever conversation lapsed to silence. Apparently bothered by the discordant lack of melody, Khitajrah found excuses to keep the monarch talking. In turn, Mar Lon kept a close watch on the proceedings, vigilantly guarding his king as much from her as from potential outside threats.

Colbey's excitement waned as the party drew closer to the Fields of Wrath, and he found himself suffused with the familiar inner calm that accompanied the knowledge of forthcoming battle. He knew uncertainty as well. More than a year had passed since he had last seen his people, leaving them in the care of a student he had trained, he believed, to competence. That the Cardinal Wizards had captured the Renshai alive seemed to prove them still invulnerable to the cut of normal weapons. No others could have taken Renshai without casualties, no matter their abilities or numbers; and the Renshai would have fought to their own last warrior.

The rattle and crunch of hooves on leaves from ahead seized Colbey's attention. His hand went naturally to his sword hilt, gaze probing the brush for some glimpse of the approaching figure. He recognized the horse first, the black and white splotched figure of Arduwyn's mount unmistakable. It crashed recklessly through the brush, willowy weeds and small trees bending, then snapping taut, from beneath its belly. Colbey rode to the lead to meet the hunter first, the uncharacteristically noisy and careless approach warning him of something amiss.

Colbey waited only until Arduwyn reined up beside him. "What's wrong?"

"The forest." Arduwyn loosened his hold on the reins, and the paint pranced, snorting, its excitement cued by its rider. It displayed none of the panicked need to flee that would have stemmed from something it personally considered a threat. "It's ... well ... it's changed."

Colbey's hand fell from his hilt. He could not fight this enemy with a weapon. "What do you mean 'changed'?"

Mar Lon, Sterrane, and Khitajrah pulled up, as eager to hear the explanation as Colbey.

"At first, I noticed that the landmarks seemed to have shifted. Slightly, at first, so things just felt wrong." Arduwyn fingered stray patches of mane over to the right side of his horse's neck. "Then I found trees down, sturdy ones, too many for nature to have done it alone. I got down and stud-

ied the breaks: jagged and splintery. No man or animal cut
through those trunks, yet none of the brush seemed singed.
No sign of fire or lightning." Arduwyn glanced from face to
face. Clearly, he had finished, yet no one seemed even half
as bothered by the things he had seen as he was.

Colbey waited patiently. The description hardly seemed
significant enough to agitate the red-haired hunter so severely. Still, he would not underestimate the importance of
the matter. If Arduwyn noticed something awry or inexplica-
ble in the woodlands, it surely held consequence. Anything
that the hunter could not justify with knowledge or logic
might hold magic as its explanation.

Arduwyn frowned, apparently disappointed by the lack of
response.

Colbey took control, trying to give Arduwyn's concern
appropriate consideration without alarming the others unnecessarily. "Arduwyn, you lead. Everyone stay quiet. We'll
need to use caution." He turned his full attention to the
hunter. "Did you see the Fields of Wrath?" Though he questioned casually, he held his breath while awaiting the answer. No matter the enemy, the Renshai would fight, and he
wondered whose blood or corpse he might find smeared
across the meadows and cottages.

"No. I didn't get that far." Arduwyn addressed the question directly, ignorant of the underlying significance. "I saw
the changes and the trees and . . ." He trailed off, embarrassed. Obviously, he had expected his news to strike his
companions as painfully as himself.

Colbey did not press further. It made sense for them all to
come upon the danger and the possible horrors together.
"Let's go."

Arduwyn headed back the way he had come, the others
following two abreast: Colbey and Khitajrah followed by
Sterrane and Mar Lon, the bard riding slightly behind his
king to protect him from dangers at the rear. Apparently, he
found Colbey an effective shield from enemies that might
strike from ahead. The *aristiri* rode Colbey's saddle, balanced on the cantle.

Colbey watched Arduwyn's back as they rode the path
toward the Fields of Wrath, but he did not need to look
for visual clues. The hunter's uneasiness became tangible,
growing toward alarm the farther they traveled. Long after
Arduwyn become noticeably agitated, Colbey saw nothing

that would concern him had he journeyed alone. Finally, however, a sense of foreboding touched even him, though he felt uncertain whether it came from inside himself or as a consequence of too long exposure to Arduwyn's nervousness. The staff also seemed discomfited, finding traces of its opposite fouling the air.

As the group moved forward, the vague wrongness finally gathered a source. Just as Arduwyn had described, trees littered the ground or leaned horribly, caught in neighboring crotches of branching limbs. Beneath them, the ground appeared crumbled, the soil bunched, dark and damp, as if rooted up from layers deeper. Shattered limbs littered the earth, jutting from piles of displaced leaves and needles. The trail zigzagged strangely, its long-standing diversions around rubble lost amid the more recent destruction.

Frost Reaver waited docilely. Although the stallion did not paw, Colbey sensed the animal's uneasiness. His triangular ears jutted forward, attentive to the road and dangers ahead. He kept all four hooves firmly in place on the dirt roadway, prepared for necessary movement in any direction. The other mounts remained calm as well, though whether because they had as much training or just lacked the sense to notice the changes, Colbey did not try to guess. Whatever had toppled trees and piled earth bore no relation to anything he had ever seen or known. If Arduwyn also could not identify them, Colbey doubted the source could be anything but magic. It brought their dilemma into vivid and frightening detail. If Colbey could barely recognize the aftereffects of the Cardinal Wizards' sorcery, he could scarcely hope to rescue and protect friends from it.

Doubts descended on Colbey, and they seemed trebled for their strangeness. Never before had he questioned his ability to handle enemies. Always, he had shattered his foes on the battlefield, and even vast numbers had not daunted him. He would challenge armies single-handedly, knowing he might slay them all or gladly die in the attempt and find Valhalla. Now, so many vast and unfamiliar concepts lay at stake. He had to fight an enemy he could scarcely hope to predict, even with the help of the Power Staff. Although his sword could score strikes against the enemy, those of his friends might not. And maintaining the balance complicated the matter further. If he killed one of the Cardinal Wizards, he would have to deal with the consequences that loss might inflict on the shifts of causes and the world. And if he died, it might leave no one to see that mankind survived the *Ragnarok*.

As if I really might have the knowledge and focus to save them myself. The doubts spread insidiously, and Colbey banished them with his usual confident will. Either he could keep the world safe or not. The possibility of failure would not prevent him from trying, now or in the future.

Arduwyn cried out, his voice full of surprise and terror. Concerned for the destruction he might find, Colbey spurred ahead. Frost Reaver slammed through lines and clumps of shrubbery his rider did not try to identify. The stained pink hooves chewed rents in a ridge of earth that seemed as unnatural as the crumbled trees. Then, as they topped the rise, the Renshai cottages came clearly into view. Arduwyn stood before them, mouth sagging open to expose a straight row of yellowed teeth.

Colbey had seen the Fields of Wrath only once a year ago, yet even he could tell they now appeared little like they had in the past. He saw no fields, only towering, asymmetrical forest smashed together at the corners, ending abruptly at the cottage lawns. Jagged, wooden wreckage stood as mute testimony to what must have once served as a pen holding horses or livestock. A garden lay, torn in half, remnants of its neatly tended rows swallowed beneath the earth. The cottages seemed untouched.

By the time Colbey finished surveying the oddity, the others had pulled up. Aside from Khitajrah, they wore the same lost, incredulous look as Arduwyn. Clearly, it took a recent knowledge of the area to fully understand the destruction.

"Ruaidhri's eternal mercy." Mar Lon evoked the highest of the Western gods.

Sterrane stared, brown eyes wide. "Gone. *Ground* gone."

It seemed impossible, yet the evidence looked clear even to Colbey. Someone had hacked off a chunk of ground like a surgeon removing a massive tumor, then spliced the edges together into an ugly seam. Luck alone had saved the cottages from tumbling into the craters and ridges left by the process.

Colbey dismounted amid a flurry of questions that he ignored until they faded into insignificant background noise. Gesturing Frost Reaver to remain in place, he took the staff in hand and headed for the first of the cottages. The door opened easily to his touch, revealing a jumble of overturned crates that had once served as furniture. A box in the corner held notched swords and daggers of varying lengths, used but lovingly saved instead of discarded. He saw no blood.

Quickly, Colbey searched the remainder of the dwelling, kitchen and bedroom. The rumpled blankets and indented pillow revealed a hasty departure that left an oiled and polished longsword uncovered on the pallet. The sheath hung from one of the bedposts. Colbey confiscated the weapon, placing it into his own empty sheath, a perfect fit. Apparently, the tribe still modeled their weapons to Colbey's taste. Surely someone had seized the owner of this home asleep. No waking Renshai would have left a sword behind. Despite the folds and wrinkles in the bedding, Colbey saw no sign of a true struggle nor any dark stains that might indicate a battle. Whoever had taken this Renshai had done so without awakening him. *Magic,* Colbey guessed.

Magic. The staff confirmed.

What kind of magic?

The staff offered nothing useful. *I couldn't begin to guess. The possibilities are limitless ... almost. I do know the Cardinal Wizards can't enter the minds of individual mortals to influence them. It's not Odin's Laws that hold them back, either. It's just not an ability they have.* The staff paused, erasing its own assurances. *At least they couldn't last I knew. Unlike you, my opposite's champion probably bound himself to his cause. The strength and abilities of the other staff, I can't begin to guess.*

Colbey drew away from the staff, seeing no purpose in further conversation. In this matter, it seemed to know and understand little more than he. Colbey left the cottage.

Once outside, Colbey discovered that his companions had taken the liberty of searching the other homes as he had done. Unlike him, they had entered these buildings many times in the past. Knowledge of which belonged to whom and the proper positioning of belongings made it easier for them to search; so they had finished more quickly than Colbey. They, too, had gathered weapons, including Mitrian's familiar wolf-hilted sword.

Colbey studied the weapons at his feet, cringing at the inadvertent dishonor. Renshai would never allow their swords, nor those of honored opponents, to touch ground. Still, he chose to say nothing, certain his friends had meant no harm or disrespect. He scooped Mitrian's blade from the pile, then glanced from face to face. "Any sign of a fight? Any people? Animals? Notes?"

Every one of Colbey's companions shook his or her head. "It's as if something snatched them from sleep," Arduwyn added unnecessarily. "Sylva's bow and quiver are missing." He glanced between the trees, as if he might catch some glimpse of her through forest that stretched over most of the country. "I can't fathom why they'd let her take her weapons and not the others. Unless they left her behind."

Colbey frowned, many possibilities coming to his mind at once, though he did not voice them. Arduwyn's only child meant as much to the little hunter as the Renshai tribe did to Colbey. To speculate would only raise the ugliest possibilities in Arduwyn's mind, hampering his effectiveness when it came to guile or battle. Already, the elder could read Arduwyn's confusion. The redhead considered remaining behind to stalk his daughter through leagues of brush and foliage.

Colbey considered talking Arduwyn away from his considerations, but he chose silence instead. Although he would miss Arduwyn's support as an archer and his quick, clever strategies, he might prove of little use against Wizards. And if Sylva had, in fact, remained behind, it only made sense for Arduwyn to try to find her. Instead, Colbey nudged Mar Lon with the hilt of Mitrian's sword. "Here, take this."

Mar Lon's fingers closed over the crafted pommel, but the look he gave Colbey revealed uncertainty. "I have a sword."

"This one has some magic to it. We may need that to fight Wizards."

Still, Mar Lon hesitated, apparently assessing the appropriateness of Colbey's choice for wielder of what might prove their only useful weapon other than Harval.

Catching the drift of Mar Lon's concern, Colbey replied without waiting for verbalization of the question. He kept his voice low, so that only Mar Lon could hear. "At all costs, we must protect Sterrane. Anchored by his simplicity and justice, man's world has a chance. Without him, I may as well let the Cardinal Wizards destroy the Staff of Power and all mankind." He tapped the polished wood pole thrust through his belt, still wishing for a more comfortable and less inhibiting means of carrying it. In his hand, it hampered his sword strokes; and he could not risk dropping it in battle. Tucked in his belt, it impaired the freedom of movement necessary to perform the precise Renshai maneuvers that made his people superior sword masters. "Of everyone, including Sterrane, you're in the best position to defend the king; and I know you claim that responsibility gladly and with total dedication."

Now Mar Lon accepted the weapon proudly, fastening the second sword belt around his waist atop the first. He angled both hilts so that he could draw either as it became necessary.

Colbey passed around the remainder of the swords, knowing the Renshai would want to rearm as soon as it became possible. The need to approach each companion revealed Arduwyn's absence, though Colby had not seen the hunter leave. *Searching for Sylva.* He shook his head. Since the Cardinal Wizards had, apparently, taken land as well as prisoners, it seemed possible that Sylva had gone with them, intentionally or not. Or she might have been sucked down into one of the many cracks or crevices that scarred the earth as the end result of the Wizards' magic, forever trapped and smashed beneath masses of earth and stone. Colbey dismissed the concern. Though he knew sorrow for Arduwyn and Rache, Sylva's fate meant little in the face of the impending annihilation of all mankind. Colbey knew he had discovered a situation in which the cost of the battle might prove worse than losing face and honor to surrender. Soon he might have to choose between the members of the Renshai tribe and the fate of all mankind, might have to sacrifice all those he loved in order to allow all others to live. *But are those others worth it?* He thought of the budding guardsmen in Pudar, their dedication typifying the welcome change the world had undergone since the Great War. He considered the farmer who had tended Frost Reaver, his innovations a symbol of the beneficial shift chaos might affect along with its trickery. Guilt squeezed Colbey's chest, yet he could not dispel the need to ponder: the value of Renshai against all of humankind.

"Where go?" Sterrane asked, the simple directness of the question crumbling the complicated intricacies of Colbey's thoughts. "Here not find Renshai."

Colbey frowned, recalling the message they had received in Béarn's castle. The Cardinal Wizards had asserted they had hidden the Renshai too well for him to find them. "We stay here. It's the only common ground they gave me to work from." *Leave the staff here, they told me. And I have. I chose to stay with it, and so did my friends.*

Khitajrah accepted Colbey's decision easily, but added the detail to Sterrane's basic question. "Should we lie in wait for them? Hidden, perhaps?"

Colbey trusted his instincts, shaking his head to indicate such tactics would prove unnecessary. "They'll use caution, I'm certain. By magic, they'll know we're here. Better a direct confrontation. With them, I think we'll get more by open talk than surprise attack. They're too smart to bring the Renshai with them."

Without questioning Colbey's decision, Sterrane sat cross-legged before the door to Mitrian's cottage, waiting. Mar Lon stood sentinel in front of his king, fingers draped casually across the wolf's head that formed Mitrian's hilt. Colbey could sense need wafting from the bard. To unsling and play the mandolin he carried would break the tension, but it would fill his hands and hamper his ability to guard his king.

Again, Colbey did not interfere. His concern for Sterrane's life outweighed that for Mar Lon's peace. If it cost the bard his comfort to keep Sterrane safe, it seemed a price well worth paying.

Khitajrah expended nervous energy by climbing to the roofs and windows of the Renshai cottages to scout.

Colbey leaned against the mortared stone of Mitrian's home, senses naturally attuned for enemies, though he made no conscious effort to look. The horses nipped at the crazed array of grass remaining in the ruins of Renshai pastures. The *aristiri* flew broad circles overhead, disappearing and reappearing at irregular intervals, occasionally stooping through the green thickness of upper growth. Colbey's stillness left a dense hush through which he heard the rustle of foliage as rabbits and *wisules* scurried in their daily search for food and safety. Other hawks came, gliding silhouettes against the sky, while songbirds and squirrels sent seed pods and berries tumbling from branches to click against the fallen wash of leaves.

As day wore into night, Colbey found no sign of the Cardinal Wizards. The natural music of the shattered forest became a lullaby, so unlike the violence his mother had described to soothe him to sleep as a baby. Mar Lon, Colbey, and Khitajrah slept in shifts, without need to discuss a formal watch. And the night slipped past without sight or sound of any Wizard but the guardian of the West.

CHAPTER 29

Gateway

Colbey awakened to the sensation of a new presence. He had heard no sound that did not belong in forest night, and the chilling breeze felt no different than it had moments before. His eyes snapped open, and his ears naturally sifted the air for other noises than the normal orchestrated shrill of insects, the courting squeal of nocturnal *meirtrins,* and the whirring call of foxes. His hearing still found nothing amiss, but his mental gift told him otherwise. Someone had approached so quietly he had not disturbed Mar Lon on watch.

Colbey probed the area with his mind as well as his eyes, though he knew the effort would cost him vitality. His consciousness touched another fraught with concerns nearly as weighty as his own. He discovered a oneness with the forest, an understanding of nature that could only come from a single source. Recognizing the other as a friend, Colbey instantly withdrew. He would never invade the thoughts of one he trusted. "Arduwyn," he whispered.

As the hunter responded to his call, Colbey carved movement from darkness. He rose, meeting Arduwyn halfway. "Did you find anything?" He hoped Arduwyn had searched for signs of the Wizards' and Renshai's trails as well as for his daughter.

"No." Arduwyn seemed troubled by his finding, a disappointment that went beyond his missing daughter. His failure encompassed much more. "Not a footprint. Not a single sign of recent passage but our own." He sighed. "Sylva's good in the forest, but even I leave enough trail for me to follow."

Colbey believed the answer obvious, but he put a name to it anyway. "Magic."

"Do you think they erased their passage?"

"I think they may have left no place from which their passage needed erasing."

Arduwyn fidgeted. "Do you think they destroyed . . ." He

trailed off, motioning toward the missing space that had once defined the Fields of Wrath and much of the surrounding forest.

Colbey guessed the hunter's concern at once. Whether by intention or accident, the Cardinal Wizards might have murdered Sylva in their efforts to prevent pursuit. He could feel the rising heat of Arduwyn's anger, intermingled with a hovering grief no vengeance could displace. "I can only guess at what they might have done. There's no use in that. Until we have evidence otherwise, best to assume the Wizards took Sylva with the others. If she's alive, we'll rescue her, too. If she's dead, there's nothing we can do for her."

Arduwyn nodded once, but he seemed unsatisfied. A vast chasm existed between the awareness that worrying served no purpose and suppressing that concern.

Colbey tried to redirect his thoughts. "So you found nothing useful?"

Startled, Arduwyn jerked. Apparently, his mind had far outstripped the conversation. "Only what we saw the night before. A massive piece of ground is missing, and the earth seems to have seamed itself back together."

Colbey pursed his lips. He had suspected such a thing, though his ignorance of landmarks had made him uncertain of the details. Of all the people he knew, he trusted only Arduwyn to recognize specific pieces of forest and their rightful places on the map.

"And one other thing."

Colbey came to immediate attention. "What's that?"

"It's probably nothing."

"Right now, we have no place to look. Anything is something."

Khitajrah slipped up beside Colbey, drawn by the conversation and Arduwyn's return. Through the darkness, Colbey could see Mar Lon sitting in Mitrian's doorway, watching. Sterrane's snores revealed that he still slept, oblivious to his friend's return.

"When I was a child ..." Arduwyn lost a sob he had clearly held back for some time. The lapse widened instantly to a wild floodgate of tears. "... my father taught me that nature never forms sharp angles or patterns. It's true, too. In all my years in the forests, I've never found so much as a stone with a straight ..." He choked off the last word, his pain obvious, even without the explanation of thoughts that

Colbey alone could read. Arduwyn's mind seemed unable to shift from his own lessons with Sylva in the woodlands. "There's a broken tree among the others. Apparently, it cracked at exactly the level of a fork in a tree some distance away, and its higher trunk fell precisely so as to land in that fork. And nothing else got in the way."

Colbey tried to picture the scene Arduwyn described.

Arduwyn demonstrated by placing both arms rigidly in front of him, then bending them at the elbows so his hands pointed skyward. "Think of these as the two trees." He indicated his forearms by shaking them once. He spread his left thumb and forefinger to make a fork, then bent the fingers of his right hand only at the last knuckles where they joined the hand. He rested the fingertips into the cleft he had made. "Like this." The pattern formed a rectangle, with the two long sides representing the tree trunks.

Colbey shrugged, understanding the image yet seeing little significance to it. "I'd think that happens all the time. One tree falling on another."

"The falling part." Arduwyn let his arms drop back to his sides. "Trees fall all the time. It's part of nature's normal cycle. Just not in parallel lines and perfect, straight angles."

Colbey took a deep breath, releasing the air slowly through pursed lips. Logic told him this phenomenon bore no relation to the Cardinal Wizards and their kidnapping of the Renshai, yet they had no other leads to follow. As small as the oddity sounded, Arduwyn had noticed it so it required exploration. Besides, the hunter had come back to camp without his horse. Surely, he had left the animal there to mark the place, with the intention of returning soon.

"It's probably nothing," Arduwyn reiterated.

"Probably," Colbey admitted. "But we can't take that chance. Why don't you examine this thing more thoroughly? And take someone with you."

Arduwyn glanced at Khitajrah, and Colbey felt a brief spark of emotion from the hunter that time did not allow him to define. He did catch a flash of anger, tempered by something he touched too fleetingly to name. Arduwyn's gaze swept to Mar Lon and Sterrane, then back to Colbey. "Who?"

Colbey hesitated, knowing he should go, yet loath to leave the king of Béarn in the path of enemies. The Cardinal Wizards were his problem. He could not afford to have them arrive in his absence, while he stared at tree trunks in the forest.

"Me," Khitajrah said.

Again, Colbey sensed rising anger from Arduwyn. This time, he also found discomfort as Arduwyn grappled to master other emotions evoked by Khitajrah's presence. The Renshai kept his response geared toward what he heard, not underlying thoughts and unintentionally radiated feelings. "That makes the most sense. Sterrane can't go, and I don't think you'll pry Mar Lon away from his king now. I should stay in case the Wizards come."

The sensations wafting from Arduwyn changed drastically. For an instant Colbey caught a full blast of desire. Then, self-hatred rose to squash the seeds of interest. Memories surfaced, of a chaos-influenced Khitajrah offered hospitality and returning only theft, lies, and betrayal. The whole became swallowed in a blanketing mass of bitterness directed against her. Arduwyn gave no sign of the upheaval progressing inside him. Clearly, he saw the wisdom in Colbey's choice. "Come on, then." Without further encouragement, Arduwyn faded into the woodlands.

Khitajrah paused to give Colbey's hand a reassuring squeeze, then she followed the hunter, her thoughts too mild to waft to Colbey's senses. Clearly, she shared none of Arduwyn's outrage. By outward appearances, she seemed to relish the opportunity to spend some time with him alone, presumably to right the wrongs she had committed against him.

Colbey considered the situation a few moments longer, glad to forget the dilemma of Renshai and mankind for a time. He sat, back pressed to the mortared stonework of a cottage, seeking signs of Arduwyn's and Khitajrah's passage. But he saw nothing. Each moved silently and unseen. Though Khitajrah had learned this skill in the overpopulated cities of the Eastlands, she seemed to have adapted to woodlands during her short stay in the West. Given some time alone together, Arduwyn and Khitajrah might find much in common, if the hunter could forgive the crimes chaos had driven her to commit. Once Arduwyn dropped the barrier that malice had built between them, his attraction to Khitajrah would surely slip through.

Colbey smiled at the irony. Once again, it seemed, the scrawny archer might challenge the wolf. Not since seven-

teen tribes of Northmen had banded together to annihilate
the Renshai had Colbey met anyone so persistently willing
to oppose him. Arduwyn's courage had become apparent
from their first meeting, when the hunter had found Colbey's
heritage reason enough to rouse strangers against him. Gradually, they had made their peace, learning to respect one another, though they had never become friends. Repeatedly,
Arduwyn had traded gibes with a Renshai toward whom others feared even to glance. He had stolen Colbey's kill in the
Great War and had, through audacity alone, stopped Colbey
from mercy-slaying a friend wracked by poison-generated
hallucinations.

That last battle, Colbey knew, he should never have surrendered. Arduwyn's concern had forced Garn to die in
withering agony, in the gladiator pit he had long ago escaped. Yet, this time, Colbey wondered if he might not give
in again. Despite Freya's apparent sanctioning of his relationship with Khitajrah and the pleasure of their lovemaking
several nights past, something seemed to be missing. In his
youth, when he still imagined himself becoming half of a
couple, he had never considered a relationship with any
woman who could not give him a real challenge in mock
combat. Arduwyn and Khitajrah seemed far better suited to
one another: close in size and build, far nearer in age, and
both as attentive to scenery as to people.

The *aristiri* settled on a ledge directly over Colbey's head,
whistling trills that played soft harmony beneath the rhythmical constant of Sterrane's snores.

Colbey leaned back and closed his eyes, trusting wariness
to take over where his senses failed. The whole train of
thought seemed unnecessary, an abstraction; yet it was not
like his mind to consider the trivial. Whatever happened between Arduwyn and Khitajrah, the fates would sanction. Ultimately, the decision rested with Khitajrah. Leaving Mar
Lon in charge, Colbey allowed himself to drift back into
sleep.

Arduwyn padded silently through freshly piled leaves and
over soil erupted into ridges by the Cardinal Wizards'
magic. Though he did not turn back, he remained aware of
Khitajrah's every movement through the brush. To his surprise, she followed with a grace and caution that made her
passage scarcely louder than his own. If she ever became

fully acclimated to forest, he grudgingly realized, she might become the quieter of them.

The need to listen for the positioning of another brought back vivid memories of Arduwyn's excursions with Sylva. His mind threw him back to days when her overzealous attempts to move quietly made her noisier than a racing herd of deer. It had taken months to teach the basics that seemed natural to Arduwyn: the routine process of selecting each footstep to go around or over any object rather than stepping on it, adjusting pace to ground and cover in a way that balanced speed and equilibrium, avoiding or flitting through the most open or densest spaces where showing self or making noise became inevitable, and keeping the eye, ear, and mind attuned to every detail.

Arduwyn's eye stung. He rubbed at it, and his fingers came away moist. Once the tears became realized, they quickened, and Arduwyn's thoughts anchored on his daughter's gentle voice and her calm understanding of the woodlands and their call. Sylva's mother had always condemned Arduwyn's escape to nature when life became too difficult for his heart to handle. Her reasons were sound, he knew. Running from problems no more solved them than drinking oneself into oblivion, and it left loved ones to handle their grief alone. Yet, even as a child, Sylva had understood. He envied her ability to face adversity, to assist others through it, and to reserve judgment when others could not manage it as well. Like any child, she had had her moments of deviltry. But, whether in looks, temperament, or behavior, she seemed to have inherited the best both parents had to offer. *From me, that wasn't much.*

An image of Sylva formed in Arduwyn's mind. He pictured her hair, red and silky, the color of his own but with the length and superior texture of Bel's. He saw her in a moment of joy, her dark eyes alight, cheeks scarlet, and a smile making her entire face seem alive with magic. The vision proved too much. Arduwyn's control snapped, and he dropped to a crouch on the forest floor. Directed thought abandoned him, leaving only a limp sorrow, and his mind flashed images of his daughter, his wife, and the three children who had become his by marriage until disease had taken two of them.

Khitajrah touched a shoulder tentatively. "Arduwyn?" She

shuffled around him, seeking his face, incapable of reading his huddled misery from behind.

Arduwyn buried his face in his hands, unable to control his emotions yet feeling foolish for his lapse. He would not let her see him crying. In some cultures, a man's tears made him weak and soft, unfit to lead his family. Though Erythanians did not condemn masculine sorrow in that fashion, he still chose to hide his frailty from a woman who had already betrayed him once.

Even without direct visualization of expression, Khitajrah pieced the clues together. She sat beside him, saying nothing.

Arduwyn struggled for control, glad Khitajrah had chosen silence. Any words would have snapped the delicate strands of his growing mastery and embarrassed him as well. The sympathy of a thief and liar would only have rung hollow.

Still quiet, Khitajrah placed an arm around Arduwyn's shoulders.

The touch jolted Arduwyn. He froze, rigid, the stream of tears halting in an instant. The proper response would not come to him, mentally or physically. He dredged for revulsion, but his heart belittled the attempt, delving instead for the attraction he had buried. It seemed foolish, certain anguish to allow himself to fall for a woman who had and would betray him. Yet the passion existed, beyond his control. Her beauty drew him in, her grace and manner hooked him, and he did not know how long he could battle the stronger, natural instincts that made him want to have her right here in the forest.

Where Arduwyn's rational mind failed, grief took over. Another wave of images battered him, and the tears began again.

Khitajrah caressed Arduwyn's shoulder, expressing just enough warmth and caring to ease the pain. Surely, she had had long practice at soothing the bereaved. "Can I help?"

Arduwyn took a cautious breath, wanting his reply to emerge strong, still trying to hide the tears though it had become fruitless. "No," he managed. "You wouldn't understand."

"I might."

"You wouldn't." It was unfair, and Arduwyn knew it. As a widow, she would, at least, have needed to deal with the loss of her husband. As an Easterner, she might well have lost family and friends. He swallowed hard, guilty for his insistence. "My daughter, barely fifteen, is the wife of one of the Renshai. I have reason to believe the Wizards left her. She may have gotten caught in this." Without looking up, he gestured to the woodland ruins, the trees uprooted and jutting at angles, the ground puckered into unnatural mounds. Verbalization of the problem opened the dam, and the rest came tumbling out. "I lost two of my wife's three children, whom I loved as my own. Then my wife. And now our only daughter, the last remaining symbol of our love. Sylva means everything to me."

"I'm sorry," Khitajrah said, the words trite but her inflection speaking volumes in sympathy. Her voice revealed tears of her own. "I lost two sons and a husband to the war. My last son was killed in a courtroom, defending me from injustice. I do know how you feel. And I know there's nothing I can say or do to make it easier." Her touch disappeared, and Arduwyn heard the rustle of her moving closer. "I also know that you're giving up too soon. You don't know for sure Sylva's dead. We may find her yet, and she'll need you at your best. Sometimes, the world and its forces tempt people with strange things."

Arduwyn did not understand the last of Khitajrah's statements, but it seemed to have great meaning for her so he let it rest without questioning. He raised his head, sacrificing dignity to let her join in the sorrow she understood only too well. It was, perhaps, not the worst in the world, and certainly not the only, though it seemed so to Arduwyn. And, for the first time in his life, Arduwyn did not run. He allowed Khitajrah to share his pain.

The sound of hoofbeats awakened Colbey in an instant, and he scrambled to his feet before the animal topped the rise. Mar Lon rose an instant slower, and even Sterrane's snoring broke cadence for a moment. Arduwyn's paint floundered over the ridge; apparently he had, in fact, left it at the landmark he and Khitajrah had gone to examine. Colbey noticed at once that the hunter returned alone. He tensed, concern coursing through him with a suddenness that made him naturally seek a target.

"She's gone!" Arduwyn shouted, loud enough that even Sterrane sat up sleepily, blinking his eyes against the moonlight.

"What do you mean 'gone?' " Colbey grabbed up the staff in a stiff hand, realizing that he had kept his fingers curled around its wood throughout the night.

"She walked under that fallen branch I told you about and disappeared."

"Disappeared? Khitajrah?"

Arduwyn nodded. Catching its master's nervousness, the paint shuffled sideways, its neck in constant motion. Apparently mistaking Colbey's concern over Khitajrah's welfare for mistrust, he added, "I did everything but follow. The indentations on the leaves end right at the opening, and they don't start again on the other side. She didn't climb or run. I watched her. She just went in, like through a doorway, and never came out on the other side."

Doorway. Colbey's mind went instantly to his voyage on Captain's ship and the hazy ocean gate they had passed through to get to the Wizards' Isle. He recalled the elf saying something about the need to pass through gates to go to other worlds. *Another world!* Abruptly, much became clear. *No wonder the Wizards thought I'd never find the Renshai.* "You didn't follow her."

"No." Arduwyn flushed. "I almost did, but it seemed foolish to repeat the same action in ignorance." His expression told Colbey the hunter sought some support for a decision that might seem like cowardice and abandonment.

"You did the right thing," Colbey replied mechanically, knowing Arduwyn too well to condemn, his mind already leagues ahead. "She should be fine, although she may have to face our enemies first." He did not explain further, keeping the details and their implications to himself. Likely, the Cardinal Wizards would not kill Khitajrah. However, if they recognized her as having significance to Colbey, they might hold her along with the Renshai, one more beloved life he might have to sacrifice for mankind to survive. Now he locked the thought away even from his own considerations. Until he spoke to the Wizards, he could not dismiss the possibility of compromise.

Mar Lon and Sterrane joined the conversation, having heard most of it as they approached. The king spoke first. "Magic? Kayt gone? Maybe dead?"

Sterrane's ignorance of gates seemed strange to Colbey given that the Béarnide had spent the majority of his childhood life under Shadimar's care. The oddity emphasized how Odin's Laws had tightly curbed the Cardinal Wizards' use of enchantments and how the drawing of chaos onto man's world had sundered those restraints. Magic had gone from scarce to common almost overnight. "Moved to another place, I think." Colbey stated his theory, though he had no way of knowing for certain whether Khitajrah had blundered into a gate or a trap. He glanced around the cottages. "Leave the horses here. I don't know where this archway leads, if anywhere, but the terrain may not suit them." He wondered if it might leave them in ocean, like the Meeting Isle gate. It seemed unlikely, but a possibility he could not wholly dismiss. "If it takes us to the Wizards, we'll want to stay as quiet as we can."

Colbey's mind embraced every theory, from the possibility that the gateway would lead to a random location to the instant death of anyone who entered it. His ignorance of magic frustrated him, forcing him to make decisions for others' lives with far too little explanation. The staff's claim that the Wizards would need to band together for slaying spells made the latter seem less likely. *It would fit the spirit of the chaos-touched Shadimar, though, to leave such a trap. If I entered, carrying the staff, it would accomplish exactly what he wanted from the start.* "Let's go."

Arduwyn led the way, the others following in a somber quiet that made their every movement seem loud enough to echo. Colbey conversed with his staff as they went, mind occupied but senses attuned for unfamiliar noises. *What do you think?*

Finally, you ask.

Colbey ignored the sarcasm. *And do you answer?*

The staff avoided the facetious question to make a point instead. *I believe that if the Wizards had intended for you to find this natural doorway, they would have made it more obvious. Had you not brought a woodsman, had he not wandered off to find his daughter, seeing every minute detail out of place, you would never have found the way.*

Colbey considered. If the Cardinal Wizards had not intended for him to discover the archway, it seemed unlikely they had created it to kill. Pieces of the explanation still jarred, however, and he hoped the staff might shed some insight. *But if they didn't want me to find it, why didn't they hide it better? And why no guard?* He continued following Arduwyn through the foliage, winding between tree trunks.

We still don't know for certain this archway comes of magic.

Will you be able to tell when we come to it?

The staff trickled amusement into Colbey's mind. *I'll recognize the presence of chaos, yes. There're traces all around here, but they ought to concentrate around something as powerful as a gate. I might even be able to differentiate between offensive magic and incidental.*

Incidental. What do you mean by that?

Unintentional side effects. Magic is as unpredictable as its chaos.

You ought to know that. Colbey tried to hold the thought to himself, but some of the accompanying annoyance and bitterness must have crept through because the staff seemed amused.

Despite their knowledge and ability, the Wizards have little practical experience with magic, especially in large quantities. Most likely, they intended to leave no gate passable by anything short of magic. The quantity of chaos freed here had to cause some unexpected problems. As random as it seems, magic requires law to direct the chaos, and the unanticipated side effects of spells usually have a logic to them. Even as an unthinking part of a whole force, chaos despises being manipulated, so those side effects more frequently than not work against the caster in some fashion.

Colbey put the information together in a practical manner. *So this thing is most likely a gate. The Wizards probably don't know of its existence. And it almost certainly leads to the world where they currently are.*

Yes, yes, and yes.

Convenient.

Not really. Given the ability of the Cardinal Wizards to form magical protections and fortresses, it's always more dangerous to attack a Wizard on his "home ground" than to draw him, angered beyond thought and consequence, to you.

There's no choice in that matter. Khitajrah's already gone.

There's always a choice.

I won't abandon a companion, especially a lover sanctioned by the goddess of lovers herself.

Then you've made the choice already. Don't mistake that for having no choice at all.

"Here it is." With a broad gesture, Arduwyn interrupted Colbey's nonverbal conversation.

The landmark appeared precisely as he had described it, the trunks and fallen branch forming a perfect rectangle with the ground serving as one of the shorter sides. Colbey motioned to his companions to stay back while he examined the natural structure from every side, careful not to pass beneath the frame. He opened his mind to the staff's assessment.

No mistaking it. It's magic. May I show you?

Please do.

An image took shape in Colbey's mind, a sudden explosion of light and color that sent him instinctively into a defensive crouch. Strands twined around the trunks and branches like thready, multihued snakes. The colors shifted without pattern, glimmers sparking and boiling from various locations in a random fashion Colbey could not hope to follow. Awestruck by the beauty, he stared until his vision blurred the whole into a spinning wheel of pigment, each of a thousand colors strangely pure and primary despite their need for mixture. *Bind fully to me,* the staff whispered, its mind-voice sensual amid the whirling vortex of color that paraded through Colbey's dry eyes. *Only I can give you the power to stand against Shadimar.*

No! The need for freedom pulled Colbey fully from the enthralling beauty of chaos' magic. *Whatever the other Cardinal Wizards believe, I won't wage war using enemy tactics. Honor comes only of sticking to my own vows and dignity after lesser foemen have abandoned their own.*

I'm not asking you to abandon honor, only to embrace a larger one. You're my champion, and I'm your destiny. Without me, you and every friend you have in the world could not stand against Shadimar.

Colbey's cheeks felt awash in flame, and the urge seized him to bash the staff repeatedly against the tree trunks until it broke. *I believe in who and what I am. No cause is worth abandoning my honor. You may stand beside me as a friend, but you can't have me as your slave. Now it's your turn to choose: obey the wishes of your champion or fight me now mind against mind.*

The splashes of color faded back to the dull wood of the trunks, though the scene would never quite look the same to Colbey. *You know I can't break a vow to my champion. I said I would not oppose you, and I won't. But I will still let* *you know when I believe your reasoning has become clouded.**

Colbey nodded grudgingly. The compromise fell in his favor. As little as he appreciated a subordinate questioning his actions, at least this one could not speak aloud. *And the magic?* Colbey tried to place the conversation back on track.

*Standard. No malice I can detect. The almost total lack of structure, aside from the framework, makes it likely chaos rather than the Wizards built the thing. I don't think it's a trap, but it may not prove a regular gate either.**

*What does that mean? Practically.**

*The way to move from world to world is through gates. Most places, like the Meeting Isle, have permanent openings. That is, they can be entered and exited from the same place at any time. The gods' world, Asgard, is like that. There's a gate on the Bifrost Bridge that links it with man's world. Other places, like Alfheim, where the elves live, don't have permanent gates. To get there or to leave requires a spell to open and close a temporary portal. That's why you almost never see elves here. From the amount of free chaos scattered about, I believe the Cardinal Wizards created a new world using ground from man's world. They intended for it to require temporary gates, but this artifact formed as a result of the magic.**

Colbey felt a twitching in his mind that he took to be a mental gesturing toward the "doorway." *You mean "side effect," don't you?**

*I'm not so certain anymore. I can sense some tampering by the Wizards, an attempt to bend the excess chaos. Probably, the creation of a new world naturally causes the simultaneous creation of a permanent gate to it. Apparently, the Wizards tried to shut down that gate, with only partial success. Their decision not to guard the opening suggests that they believe they disabled it completely.**

Colbey did not like the sound of the staff's explanation. *Partial success? You mean we might get halfway through the gate and end up stuck in some magical void? Or we might get sent to an unrelated world?**

*All possibilities, plus more others than I can count. I can, at least, reassure you that the Wizards did not intend this to be a trap. I believe they intended it not to exist at all.**

Colbey sucked air through his teeth, then released it in a long sigh. The staff had given him more information than its earlier protestations suggested it could, yet the knowledge raised as many questions as it answered. The intent of the Wizards mattered little if the end result was the same. *So it's still possible that walking through that doorway will kill us all.*

Possible, but unlikely. If the Wizards blocked it, you should wind up where you started. If it sends you to another world, you should be able to just turn around and walk back through the other side of the gate.

Those odds sounded better to Colbey. *What do you suggest?*

I still suggest you make the Wizards come to you.

Colbey discarded the advice. He would not desert Khitajrah to an unknown fate. He glanced back at his companions, trusting his own instincts more than the knowledge of the staff. "I'm going through. If it's as I believe, I should be able to come right back. If I don't, anything might have happened. Sterrane, you and Mar Lon go home. We can't risk you." Colbey studied the Béarnides. Mar Lon nodded curtly, but Sterrane avoided his gaze. "Arduwyn . . ." Colbey paused, wanting to send the hunter home as well but knowing Arduwyn had as much at stake as himself. ". . . do as you want. You usually do anyway."

Without awaiting a reply, Colbey walked through the magical portal.

CHAPTER 30

The Green and the Pink

Remembering his last transport between worlds, Colbey closed his eyes, preferring to face danger momentarily, rather than persistently, blinded. White light pulsed against his lids, brilliant enough to seep into his retinas even without sight. He opened his eyes, blinking away spidery afterimages, the subsequent darkness of his surroundings a pleasure. He stood in woodlands much like those he had left. If not for the missing companions and archway, and the jagged lines and blotches etched across his vision, he might have believed nothing had changed. The night insects kept up the same clicking, trilling chorus; and a throaty fox call rolled through the stillness. The clean aroma of damp spring greenery seemed unchanged. The wind carried a faint, intermittent odor of musk. The *aristiri* balanced on his shoulder, its feathers fluffed, apparently unaffected by the blinding lights and magic.

Colbey did not move, concerned about losing the location of the gate. He twisted his neck, finding the area behind him as unrecognizably wooded as that in front. He saw no sign of the natural archway or the gate. He took a shuffling backward step. His boot heel kicked up a divot of mulched leaves. Otherwise, nothing happened. He shifted back again, this time certain he had cleared the gateway. Still he remained in unfamiliar forest, without sight or sound of his companions. Colbey strode forward, regaining the position he had found himself in on his arrival. He turned, taking a long stride through the remembered location of the gate.

Colbey collided with Arduwyn, who had apparently followed him through the gate. The force jarred them both to the ground. The *aristiri* squawked, taking to the air with wild, awkward wing flaps. Colbey rolled to his feet, and Arduwyn rose a moment later.

Colbey scowled, embarrassed by his clumsiness. "I see you considered your decision a long time."

Arduwyn shrugged. "There was nothing to consider. If Sylva's here and well, I had to come. If she's dead, then my fate didn't matter."

"Sterrane and Mar Lon?"

"I told them to stay."

"So did I. Do you think they'll listen?"

Arduwyn shrugged again. "Mar Lon will, I think. It mostly depends on how determined Sterrane is. And how fully he trusts your instincts. You chose going through as the best means to free Renshai. Sterrane may see that as reason enough to follow."

Colbey let the matter rest. Now that he knew the consequence of entering was not death, Sterrane's decision lost some of its significance. Still, he would rather face Wizards without the king's safety at stake.

The *aristiri* perched in a tree overhead.

Ah. * The staff's partial communication intrigued Colbey. *Ah?*

The Wizards did manage to erase the gate from this side, apparently thinking they got the whole thing. * It anticipated Colbey's call for practical details. *We can travel from there to here but not back.*

So we're stuck here?

It would seem so.

How do we get back?

Magic. No other way.

Can you work this magic?

I'm the device. You're the Western Wizard.

Colbey ended the communication. If returning home relied on his knowledge of sorcery, they would remain trapped on this Wizard-made world for eternity.

Arduwyn studied the forest, gaze rolling from the ground to the uppermost branches. He wandered a few paces in each direction. "Amazing." He looked directly at Colbey. "I know where we are."

It seemed unlikely. "Where?"

"The woods outside the Fields of Wrath. This is the missing piece of forest."

The last remnants of the Wizards' plan fell together for Colbey. One section of trees, deadfalls, and brush looked the same as any other to him. Colbey could no more doubt

Arduwyn's claim to identify a specific part of the forest then he could a man recognizing the town that raised him. "Don't ask me how, and I think the 'why' is obvious. Apparently, the Wizards moved the Fields of Wrath and the Renshai together, creating a whole new world in the process."

"Amazing," Arduwyn repeated, not questioning Colbey's knowledge either. He pointed to the ground, swinging his arm to indicate a direction Colbey could not hope to fathom without the sun's position to guide him. "Someone went this way. The tracks begin right where you're standing. Kayt probably."

Colbey moved up beside the hunter, but no farther. In the incomplete darkness, he could see few of the signs of passage Arduwyn indicated, and he did not want to make Arduwyn's job more difficult. "Let's go, then. You'll have to lead." He glanced backward as he spoke, hoping Sterrane and Mar Lon had returned to Béarn, yet skeptical. Sterrane had fussed too strongly about coming along to surrender this close to their goal. Still, it seemed pointless to wait long. Colbey would rather surprise the Wizards than give them more of an upper hand. Time would only obscure Khitajrah's trail, and she might need their help.

Arduwyn headed in the indicated direction. Colbey waved the *aristiri* to him. "Formynder."

The hawk arced down from the tree to land on the Renshai's wrist, apparently understanding the gesture as easily as it had his intention to carry it when it had grown weary of travel.

Colbey felt foolish talking to a bird, but he saw the need to try. He hoped the tales of the Western Wizards' supposed natural rapport with feathered creatures would aid him now. "Watch for Sterrane. Help him find us if he follows."

Though the *aristiri* made no sound, it flew back to its perch on the tree, remaining there as Colbey trailed Arduwyn through the brush.

The winding night air carried the intermingled odors of animals, sap, and pollen; and it washed away the humidity locked beneath the forest canopy. Sticky, yellow seed pods clung to Arduwyn's jerkin and the thin fabric of Colbey's shirt. The high-pitched cadence of insects seemed to rise and fall like tide, masking the minimal noises of Colbey's and Arduwyn's progress.

A premonition of peril hammered Colbey suddenly and

without warning. He grasped Arduwyn's belt, jerking the hunter backward into a clumsy dodge. An arrow whizzed past Arduwyn's shoulder, its tip plowing through leaves. Momentum sent it tumbling end over end.

Colbey jerked his attention to the direction from which the missile had come. He saw no movement, and his eyes failed him. He crouched, sacrificing defense for the moment it took to sweep the area with his mind. A quick and superficial search revealed two strangers, separated by a significant distance. Such tactics did not fit the Cardinal Wizards.

Arduwyn went low, too, keeping thick trunks and tangled copses between himself and the archer. He slipped his own bow free, clamping an arrow to its rest. Soundlessly, moving with a slow steady motion, he slunk to a better position. A sudden, horrified intake of breath revealed his location to Colbey, if not to their attacker. Apparently, the hunter had found something as unnerving as an unseen enemy shooting to kill.

The forest went still, aside from the music of the insects and a light breeze still twining between the branches. The patience of the enemy archer made Colbey cautious. He hoped it stemmed from limited ammunition rather than competence. He freed Harval from its sheath. Confident of his ability to cut and dodge, he attempted to divert the archer or archers while Arduwyn found the best place from which to return fire. "Hold your attack. We're here in peace."

Another arrow sliced through the brush. Colbey sprang aside, sword slashing the shaft with a brisk motion that snapped the thin wood. The crude arrowhead spun in one direction, the feathered end in the opposite. A second arrow followed instantly, cut from the air by Colbey's sword. The third clipped skin from his forearm as he severed it. The loss of timing irritated him. He considered charging the archer, but he knew the other could shoot him dead before he came within sword range. To die in a blind rush of anger would foul his honor and prove pointless as well.

Colbey dropped to his belly, knowing he needed to elicit the position of the second presence his mind had touched. Unseen, it proved far more dangerous than the archer. He could not afford to concentrate for too long; the price in fatigue and lost defense would prove too great. Quickly, he channeled power to his thoughts, extending them to touch the second stranger. His probe met pain and a conscious attempt to feign death. Most likely, he had located a victim rather than a companion of the archer. The enemy, it seemed, worked alone.

Colbey withdrew at once to tend to his own defense, believing he had found the thing that had shocked Arduwyn moments before. Again, he tried to draw the enemy archer's attention, leaving Arduwyn free to attack. Colbey rose. "I can break as many arrows as you can shoot. If you insist on testing that, I'll kill you when you empty your quiver. If you stop now, we can talk. Neither of us has to die."

Silence followed, but at least no arrows came. Abruptly, something bumped Colbey's elbow. He spun, recognizing Arduwyn in time to pull the strike, then whirled back to keep the other archer from catching him off-guard. He spoke in a hushed growl. "Never startle an old Renshai. You may find your head beside your feet."

"I found Kayt." Arduwyn waved toward the direction in which he had disappeared. "She's hurt. Needs your help."

"I know," Colbey whispered in reply, though he had not yet made the obvious connection between the injured party his mind had located and Khitajrah. "Parlay first. We can't help her if we're dead."

The voice of a young woman floated eerily through the darkened forest in song:

> *"I am the queen*
> *Queen I am*
> *Queen of the forest am I.*
> *The night wind blows*
> *The wolf howls drift*
> *On wings of a bird I will fly ...*

Arduwyn stiffened, limbs rigid nearly to the point of seizure. "Firfan."

Colbey caught his arm.

"That's Sylva." Arduwyn stood suddenly. "Sylva!"

Colbey tightened his grip, jerking the hunter safely back behind the copse. A rattle behind them revealed that the archer had shot another arrow.

"That's Sylva." Arduwyn struggled, cuffing Colbey with a wild sweep of his arm. "Let me go, damn it!"

"Are you sure that's her?"

"I know that voice. I wrote that song."

> Queen of all
> All that I see
> Queen of the sky and the trees
> With the deer I shall walk
> With the sly foxes stalk.
> As a hawk I shall glide on the breeze.

"Be still. There's something wrong."

"It's you, holding me down when my daughter needs me." Arduwyn shouted, "Sylva! Don't shoot. It's your father."

An arrow carved through the foliage between the two men, plowing beneath a layer of leaf mold. A second followed an instant later, the tip gouging Arduwyn's thigh.

Arduwyn gasped in pain, hands falling naturally to the pink and green feathered shaft jutting from his leg. A curl of blood welled around the wound, a small sample of what he would find when he removed the arrow and its wood no longer pinched the damaged flesh in place. Arduwyn shifted, spoiling Sylva's targeting, gritting his teeth against an agony he could blame on no one but himself. "She's running low on arrows."

"How can you tell?" Colbey rose to a crouch. His honor would not let him lie still behind a coward's shield of brush. He would fare better, mentally and physically, avoiding and parrying the attacks.

"She's using the better ones now. Colbey, what's going on? Why would my daughter try to kill me?"

"I don't know, but I'm going to find out." Colbey began shifting energy from body to mind. "Give me some covering fire, or talk to her, or something. I'm going in."

"In? In where?"

"Her mind." Colbey did not wait for the natural string of questions to follow. He concentrated his thoughts and nudged them toward Sylva, oblivious to Arduwyn's voice or movements.

The destruction became obvious at once. Sylva's thoughts formed no logical sequence Colbey could decipher. Unlike Episte and Frost Reaver, where the chaos had charged Colbey like a she-bear protecting cubs, nothing remained here to bother him. The magics had come and gone, hammering thought and reason into a tangled, incoherent jumble. He withdrew, catching part of Sylva's response to whatever Arduwyn might have said to goad her.

". . . not belong must die. I am the forest, and the forest is me. I am the queen."

Arduwyn remained low, protecting Colbey's still form with his body. The Renshai stood, prepared to dodge arrows again, though his mind felt fuzzy and his movements slow and thick.

"What did you find?" Arduwyn pressed at once, his hands clenched and his tone desperate.

Colbey shook his head. "It's not good."

Arduwyn's features faded to a chalky white.

"Always before, I've had a battle to fight. This time, the enemy did its damage and left." Colbey took his attention from Sylva momentarily to glance at Arduwyn. He looked back in time to slash another arrow from the air with a single, deft stroke. The routine need for defense did not break his chain of thought. "I'd guess the magic hit her hard and fast. No specific tampering to fix." Colbey grasped for a concept a person who had never entered another's mind could understand. "It's like a tempest ripped through, then moved on. Just wreckage."

"Wreckage?" Arduwyn kept his eye open so long, Colbey could see it drying. "Wreckage can be fixed."

"Rebuilt. I don't know how to do that." A movement overhead seized Colbey's attention. He studied the object from peripheral vision. The *aristiri* circled. *Damn, we don't need Sterrane brought into this.* Colbey hoped, but doubted, the hawk had gotten his instructions wrong.

"What *can* we do?"

"First, we have to stop her from shooting at us."

"I'm not killing my daughter."

"I didn't ask you to kill her."

Arduwyn dove for the loophole. "You're not killing her either."

Colbey addressed the staff. *Can you do anything?*
I'm the device—

Colbey cut it off. *I know. I'm the Wizard.* He broke contact before the next thought. *Useless.* Without taking his eyes from Sylva, he addressed Arduwyn again. "What do you want me to do?"

Still on the ground, Arduwyn seized the fabric of Colbey's britches. "Get back in her mind. Do whatever you do. She's my daughter, damn it. You have to try."

Colbey knelt, freeing himself from Arduwyn's grip to

keep it from inhibiting his lightning dodges. Fatigue and the staff hampered him more than enough. Visions of Episte came to mind, and he knew his best try might not prove enough. Exerting effort on a lost cause seemed madness now, leaving him to face the Wizards with mind clouded, body exhausted, and so much at stake. "Talk to her."

"What?"

"Talk to her. Distract her. While I'm working, I leave myself defenseless." The idea rankled nearly as much as the one before. To die at the hands of a superior enemy would please him. To let a young archer turn him into a pincushion while he lay helpless in the dirt would, deservedly, damn his soul to Hel. He let the concept go. For now, he had work to do.

Colbey gathered the energy of body, mind, and soul, probing delicately for the details of Sylva's magic-wracked brain. He found her easily as he glided into a cavern of instincts and basic emotions. A red glow filled most of the space, a warm and discomforting prickle against his searching consciousness. It seemed to consist of equal parts of desperate rage and fear, spurred by a strangely unmotivated certainly that if she did not kill first, she would become the victim.

The idea strengthened abruptly. Colbey caught an image of threat. Then he felt Sylva lurch, fitting arrow to string and drawing.

For an instant, Colbey hesitated, caught between returning to self to shout a warning, thereby wasting the energy he had spent so far, and letting Arduwyn handle the danger alone. He chose the latter course. The hunter understood the situation; Colbey had little choice but to trust Arduwyn's ability. Instead, the Renshai set to work, stepping away from Sylva's current abstraction to take in a full picture of the damage. He discovered more squashing than tearing. The magic had flayed some thoughts, but most remained intact, only their patterns lost, not necessarily their content. Pain had caused her consciousness to retreat to the distant past: to childhood then beyond into animal suspicion and basic instinct.

Now that he had taken in the whole picture, Colbey dared to steal a moment peeking at the world through Sylva's eyes. Arduwyn stood before her, fully unprotected. He had tossed aside sword, bow, and quiver to speak with her in innocent defenselessness. Sylva had nocked an arrow and drawn, the point flickering toward Arduwyn's throat as she aimed.

Without time for strategy, Colbey scrambled to communicate with the staff in concepts rather than wasting precious moments for words. He managed to make clear the importance of holding her rage and her elemental need to destroy at bay in the same way the staff had frozen Shadimar's spell in Frost Reaver's mind.

For once, the staff obeyed without question. It drew a circle around the prominent killing concept, driving it to the center of the bank of instinct in which Sylva's inner being had become trapped. The bow remained aimed and drawn in threat, but she showed no sign of releasing at the moment. He could catch little of Arduwyn's words, but he could tell the skinny hunter was talking. He only hoped Sylva would listen.

Even as the staff drew borders, it made its limitations known. *Work fast and carefully. It's not chaos or magic I'm holding, but human thought. My power is scant here.*

Colbey dove for the area the staff had cleared, swimming through a natural tangle of normal, but primal, function: thirst, hunger, survival, and cravings. The Wizard's magic had ripped past this area, severing the pathways to the next higher portion of Sylva's mind, the area that, apparently, held her memories of childhood. A flicker of Sylva's consciousness danced around the confines, occasionally thudding against the staff's conjured boundary as it quested for the rage that had driven her actions until that moment.

Colbey tried to bridge the gap between instinct and memory, but his probe proved useless when it came to creation. He could look, but he could not build. His own ability to skip unhindered from place to place frustrated him. Somehow, he had to get Sylva from instinct to function, from emotion to thought; but the spell seemed to have slashed the ties between them. He dropped back, touching the staff's rage-confining ring. It thrummed against his probe, weakening. The instant it fell, Colbey knew, Arduwyn would die.

The thought goaded him, lending him a second wind that he needed. His own energy dwindled; the need to plot, to stretch his mind to Sylva, and to work within her was draining stamina faster than the most grueling sword practice. Once again, he tried to fashion a temporary route across the gap, and once again he failed. His own consciousness became faded, a winking gray spot in the shadow of the spark that revealed Sylva's vibrant presence. He noticed that she had ceased to hammer at the staff's barrier, though it continued steadily to wane. Instead, she seemed to spend more time at the frayed edges of her prison, as if to help Colbey with his bridge.

Catching his breath, Colbey watched as Sylva repeatedly soared up passageways that started wide, then narrowed into nothingness. He could see the jagged edges the magic had left after tearing the connections, and the glimpse showed him one thing more. One pathway remained intact, back-lit in the splash of white Sylva's presence revealed to him. It seemed thread-thin and friable, but it fully bridged the gap. Somehow, he had to guide her to it.

Yet the method evaded him. In order to guide, he would need to understand the bridging thought; but to touch a thought that appeared no thicker than a hair seemed folly. If he broke it, he damned her to eternity as an unthinking animal, driven only by the understanding of kill or be killed. Better she found the way on her own, yet that seemed nearly as impossible. She had not discovered it so far. If she did not soon, the staff's barrier would fail; and her slaying frenzy would come back in a wild wave that would cost Arduwyn, Khitajrah, and himself their lives.

Colbey fell back, oblivion pounding at him. Exhaustion had stolen his dexterity for finer technique, and he felt certain he could do nothing to escort Sylva down the last remnant of ascent from madness. For a moment, he let all thought slip from his own mind, the nothingness a comfortable and restful reprieve. Then, he noticed Sylva's presence dancing about near the bridge, missing it by a hair's breath.

Colbey lurched to Sylva's senses, trying to find the incident that had sparked the change in direction of her thoughts. She continued to stare at Arduwyn, the arrow still nocked but the bow lowered; and the words that seeped through her hearing gave Colbey enough information, he hoped, to cue Arduwyn.

Colbey pulled out of Sylva's mind, ignoring the buzzing in his head and the desperate need for sleep that pinned his limbs in place. "Deer," he whispered. "Remember something about deer. Hurry!"

With Colbey's departure, the staff had no choice but to leave as well. Sylva's bow jerked upward, targeting Arduwyn's throat.

Arduwyn slipped naturally from shared memories of crafting arrows to deer. ". . . green and pink. Pink not white. *Because I realized that white, from a distance, looked like the warning flash of a deer's tail."*

Colbey winced, trying to gather strength to rescue Arduwyn, but he scarcely managed to straggle awkwardly to his hands and knees.

Sylva jerked as she released the string. The arrow flew in a harmless arc, missing Arduwyn by a full arm's length. "Papa?" Her voice sounded infantile. She dropped the bow, expression twisted into a hideous mask of confusion. "Papa?"

"Sylva." Arduwyn rushed forward, clasping her in a desperate embrace. "Firfan's eternal charity. Sylva."

Colbey's head sank to his chest, but he forced himself to crawl onward. There was still Khitajrah to tend.

By the time Colbey awakened, sunlight streamed through the branches, turning the skeletal foreboding of the ancient trees a welcoming brown and emerald. He had managed to remain alert long enough to tend Khitajrah's and Arduwyn's wounds, both significant yet neither fatal so long as infection did not take hold. Colbey hoped his ministrations with herb and salve would see to that. While he worked, he had heard the arrival of Sterrane and Mar Lon, paying them no heed. To split his concentration then, while fatigue had crushed his vision to a tunnel, would have spiraled him into unconsciousness. Better to choose sleep on purpose than to allow the darkness to overtake him.

Colbey sat up, and Mar Lon spun at the motion. He crouched between Sterrane and Khitajrah, attentive to the edge of paranoia. Nevertheless, he managed a smile for the Renshai.

Colbey glanced at each of his companions in turn. Sylva slept, her red hair sweeping around her like a cape, snarled with nettles and burrs. Arduwyn kept one arm looped protectively about her shoulders, his injured thigh twisted at an awkward angle that would leave it as stiff as the wound itself did. Khitajrah's V-necked dress revealed the bandage wrapping her chest. No blood had seeped through as she slept, attesting to Colbey's timing of the pressure needed to clot. At first, the arrow had appeared to be lodged in her chest cavity, a guaranteed death. Fortuitously, however, a rib had diverted the arrow beneath lung and heart; and Khitajrah had escaped with nothing worse than a pain that Colbey's herbs had dulled. Sterrane lay in his usual placid pose, his snores more gentle than usual. "I told you to stay behind."

The corners of Mar Lon's mouth slid downward. "And I did. For as long as I could keep the king waiting. When my duty to guard clashes with my duty to obey . . ." He shrugged, not bothering to finish the thought.

Colbey grinned cruelly. "Personal honor has its place. Servitude is grim."

"Oh? And how would you know, *Sir* Colbey Calistinsson, Knight of the Béarnian and Erythanian kings . . ." Mar Lon returned a gibe equally malicious. ". . . in name only. With all of the benefits but no real obligations or ties to either king."

Colbey glanced at Sterrane, as always amazed by the way one so childlike and naive awake could seem still more innocent asleep. "That's not completely fair. I understand the importance of Sterrane at least as clearly as you do."

"Then why did you let him come at all?"

Colbey shook his head. "I didn't let him come. You were there. He wouldn't let me, you, or anyone stand in his way."

"You could have stopped him."

"How?"

"You're Renshai. And from what I've see and heard, a damned fine swordsman."

"Yes, I suppose killing Sterrane would have stopped him. But wouldn't that have defeated the original purpose?"

Mar Lon crouched, exasperated. "You could have *convinced* him to stay. In a very *convincing* manner."

"Ah." Colbey finally caught a clear grasp of Mar Lon's point. "I could have *convinced* him, but I would have become renegade, with every army of the Westlands at my heels." He rose. "The Renshai have enough enemies without turning friends against us, too. I worked long and hard to turn prejudice into friendship, to start to build a new life and meaning for the Renshai. Don't expect me to sacrifice my people to save one king's bodyguard some of the trouble of performing his duties."

Mar Lon pursed his lips, silent for some time. "I'm sorry. You're right. I'm just worried. If Shadimar's really gone renegade, there's no telling what we're up against. And you know how trusting the king is. Shadimar raised him. He's like Sterrane's father."

Colbey took some encouragement from Mar Lon's comment. "So now you believe Shadimar's the villain instead of me?"

Mar Lon met Colbey's gaze directly, with clear hazel eyes. "I still think it's your handling of chaos that's at fault. But Shadimar does seem to have become most affected by it."

"Neutral to the core." Colbey smiled. "As it should be." He glanced through the huddled branches. The conversation finished, at least to his mind, he shifted to more pressing matters. "Get some food together. I'll wake the others. The longer we sit, the more likely the Wizards will find us at a disadvantage."

Mar Lon set to work.

CHAPTER 31

Parlay on the Fields of Wrath

Impatient, Shadimar paced, smashing a brown slash through the otherwise grassy meadow. Back supported by the oak from which they had suspended Tannin, Carcophan watched his colleague fidget, gaze tracking the Eastern Wizard's to and fro course. Shadimar kept the staff clenched in his right hand, and its constant poke and retreat had left a periphery of rat-sized holes surrounding the pathway his repetitive tread had worn. Dh'arlo'mé stood with his weight balanced, clasping his hands into various positions, fingers flicking red-blond hair from his face or readjusting his collar at intervals, though neither needed tending. Clearly, his mistress' absence unnerved him.

The Renshai stood or sat as the mood pleased them, exchanging whispered conversation that Shadimar had no interest in hearing. Should the Renshai try to attack or to run, they would find themselves stopped short by the magical barrier the Cardinal Wizards had bonded to build. Even if the prisoners charged the wall of sorcery in a moment of weakness, before the Wizards thought to reinforce it, even should they somehow find a hole in the chaos of the spell, they would kick and bite until they fell dead of exhaustion. The Wizards' personal protection spells would thwart their attacks, even if they somehow managed to capture a sword from Carcophan or Dh'arlo'mé.

A crack appeared in the fabric of the world, its edges shimmering through the rainbow's spectrum. Shadimar stopped, watching the display in fascination, though its power seemed small compared with the combined forces that had raged through many of their recent spells. Returned from the world of men, Trilless stepped through. The rift sealed shut behind her, chaos-colors fading into normal background, fuzzy, gray vibration lingering long after the obvious magic had disappeared.

Dh'arlo'mé walked to her side, the speed of his movement mocking the dignity of his previous stance. Carcophan studied her with mild curiosity. Shadimar stretched with feigned nonchalance, placing both hands on top of his staff and meeting her gaze directly.

"People came to the Renshai cottages," she said.

"Colbey?" Shadimar asked hopefully.

"Maybe. I don't know. I found five horses and more than one type of footprint. If he came, he did not do so alone. And he did not leave the staff."

Shadimar tightened his grip on his own staff, uncertain what to make of Trilless' findings. Until now, their occasional forays to the cottages had revealed no sign of visitors. It made sense for Colbey to come, yet not to leave without some message for the Wizards: cooperative or otherwise. "What type of horses?"

Trilless made a stiff-fingered gesture to indicate limited knowledge in this area. "Good ones. Of the type rich men might own or breeders might use to show potential buyers the best of their stock."

Shadimar made a thoughtful noise, annoyed that the horses appeared during Trilless' time to check for Colbey's compliance.

Trilless continued, "I found a white horse among them, pretty enough to belong to the Knights of Erythane, though it carried none of the braids, symbols, and trappings."

"Frost Reaver?" Shadimar scowled. "Impossible. Then Colbey can't be among them."

"Or it's another white horse." Carcophan supplied his first words of the conversation, his composure mocking Shadimar's distress.

Keeping his hands high on the staff, Shadimar drew to his full height. "I have to go. I might be able to talk to the horses."

"Too dangerous." Trilless' lower lip went thin and blanched. "We've cast too much magic in that area already. What good to find Colbey there if we can't use spells against him? What use to take the Staff of Chaos from him when we've drawn so much into the world that the *Ragnarok* occurs anyway? Soon enough, we'll have to replenish our own protections and their bindings." She gestured toward the Renshai. "The more chaos we call, the stronger Colbey becomes."

Carcophan sighed, obviously annoyed by the need to take his opposite's side. "Horses don't understand abstractions and strategy. What could they tell you besides useless information about their riders?" He simulated an animal voice; but, more accustomed to addressing reptiles and their kith it sound higher-pitched, sibilant, and more sloshy than any beast Shadimar knew. "The *heavy* two-legs. The loud one who doesn't share his apples."

Shadimar grew insistent, scarcely daring to believe his companions could not see the usefulness of discussing the matter with the horses. "They could tell us if Colbey's come."

Carcophan returned to his normal tone. "What difference if he has or hasn't? Did you expect Colbey simply to bring the staff and leave? He'll look for the Renshai first. When he can't find them, he'll have no choice but to bargain. We may have to confront him once, but it won't last long. He's playing chess, a single pawn against three queens and a pile of captured pieces. If he harms one of us, he loses his tribe; but we can kill him with impunity." Carcophan smiled, his emotions well-hidden. "Now, Shadimar, get some rest before your pacing turns these fields into a canyon."

Shadimar sat, though his mind still worried the problem. And the staff that he knew contained the knowledge of the universe supported his ideas.

Colbey slipped silently through the second growth trees and underbrush, guided toward the Fields of Wrath by Arduwyn's occasional touch. The archer's injured leg slowed their progress to a crawl, and Khitajrah kept several paces behind, her stumbling gait a result of the pain-masking herbs. Under other circumstances, Colbey would have left both of his wounded companions behind for the much-needed sleep their healing bodies craved. Yet here, it seemed folly to break into couples or leave anyone alone. Together, they stood a chance against the Cardinal Wizards. Separated, they would fall prey, one by one, to magic.

Colbey halted for what felt like the thousandth time to give Arduwyn a chance to catch up. At the camp, it had seemed natural to split their party in half; it made spying and searching more complete. In trios, they could stand more united against the Wizards, at least until the others arrived. He had selected Arduwyn and Khitajrah as his companions, keeping the next strongest warrior and the hardiest of the archers with the king at the expense of weakening his own forces. He hoped that dividing forces would not work against them.

The *aristiri* circled far overhead, and Colbey saw only occasional glimpses of it between the branches.

As if on cue, Arduwyn pulled up beside Colbey, gaze tracing a flash of scarlet in the sky. "I think she's trying to tell us we're nearing the clearing. And the Wizards are there."

Colbey followed the hunter's stare, but the *aristiri* had flown from sight. He saw only patches of blue sky, striped with boughs and wind-swaying leaves. "How can you tell that?"

"Her spirals have tightened. She's narrowing in on prey."

Colbey accepted the description without comment, uncertain whether to consider the Wizards the predator or the quarry. He suspected some of the hawk's antics were meant to reveal their approach and positioning to Mar Lon Sterrane, and Sylva; and he hoped the girl could read the flight patterns as well as her father.

"Do you want me to scout ahead?" Arduwyn whispered.

"No." Colbey listened for the sounds of Khitajrah's approach, but she had gone still as well, keeping her distance so that her lumbering would not give them away. "We're all quiet. We stay together. Will you be all right?"

Arduwyn nodded vigorously, though his pain reached Colbey in aching waves set off by every movement. Khitajrah's muffled agony drifted to him as well, masked by the herbs to a deep, dull throb. If it came to war, Colbey knew he could rely only on his own skill; and that thought made him frown. Back in Béarn when the message had come, he had first considered facing the Cardinal Wizards alone. Now, with friends' lives at stake and dragging the injured to a meeting that might prove fatal, Colbey doubted the decision he had made in the king's feasting room. It might have been better for all if he had left the others behind.

Even as the thought arose, Colbey recognized the fallacy. Without Arduwyn, he would never have discovered the gate. Had Khitajrah not chosen to walk through it, Colbey might have dismissed Arduwyn's finding; or he might have entered himself and fallen victim to Sylva's bow. Colbey suspected the appearance of Arduwyn and himself had interrupted the completion of Sylva's attack. If they had come later, Arduwyn's daughter probably would have finished Khitajrah. Sterrane's simple insight kept him approaching problems at the practical level, and the king might find the words to convince Shadimar where Colbey failed. If it came to war, Colbey felt certain he would appreciate Mar Lon's sword.

"Let's go." Colbey crept forward, Arduwyn keeping pace at his side. The favoring of one leg made the hunter's movements unnatural, and he instinctively slowed them to smooth his gait. Even injured, he moved in silence.

Shortly, the trees gave way to a grassy meadow sprinkled with wildflowers and trampled in patches where Renshai habitually practiced swordplay. Colbey's eyes registered these details, even as his gaze riveted on the figures in the clearing. Shadimar and Carcophan stood face to face in opposition. Their voices came to Colbey as rumbles, punctuated by brisk gestures of arms, heads, and hands. Occasionally, a shouted word pierced the air, its meaning lost to the obscurity of their discussion. Seemingly oblivious, Trilless sat with her back propped against a tree, chatting more softly with a figure Colbey did not recognize. Loose, red-blond hair draped the stranger's back, the locks speckled with red highlights from the sun. He wore a flaccid-fitting robe and cloak that could not quite hide the odd musculature and willowiness that Colbey now associated with elves. Beyond the Cardinal Wizards, the Renshai milled without obvious concern or threat. Apparently, they knew no strong thoughts, pain, or pressure because not a single emotion wafted from any of them.

Before Colbey could consider his next course of action, Carcophan whirled to stare into the opposite side of the forest. "Who's here? Show yourselves!"

Shadimar spun, suddenly alert. Trilless rose cautiously, and Colbey caught a glimpse of her companion's face. The high, sharp cheekbones and canted eyes clinched his race. The Renshai tribe, too, abruptly became interested, their eyes scanning the clearing.

Colbey touched Arduwyn's arm to indicate he should remain in place. For now, Carcophan seemed more interested in their companions at the other end of the clearing. The Wizards held no grudge against Sterrane, and Colbey doubted the king, Sylva, and Mar Lon faced much danger. However, the Wizards' concentration on those three would leave Colbey free to do whatever the situation demanded. He studied the other Renshai, divining their emotional state from movement only. The child seemed irritable, bored with remaining in one place too long. Tannin moved with a stiffness that indicated injury. Tarah, too, lacked her usual grace, though her walk did not betray pain as Tannin's did. Modrey, Mitrian, and Rache seemed normal, aside from a tendency to pick at a nonexistent sheath or sword belt.

Carcophan's voice rang out. "I said show yourselves! You have until I count to four, then I'll burn down the forest and you with it."

Another moment passed in silence, except for a sudden surge of mental activity. Colbey could tell that the Wizards were sending messages furiously, but he did not waste energy trying to read them. In a moment, he might need each modicum of physical strength, every lethal trick at his disposal.

"Not hurt." As Colbey watched, Sterrane stepped from the forest, Sylva behind and Mar Lon a step in front of him.

The Wizards' surprise seemed to blend into one massive shock. Colbey felt the surge, though the Cardinal Wizards feigned composure with ease. Shadimar edged toward the king and his entourage, obviously intending to question their presence. Before he could speak, Carcophan whirled, gaze tracing the forest edge. "There're three more out there. Show yourselves or I carry out my threat."

Arduwyn gripped Colbey's sleeve.

"And I won't spare your companions," Carcophan added with deliberate cruelty.

Colbey shook off Arduwyn's hold and strode into the clearing. "Let them go. All of them. It's me you want."

As one, the Cardinal Wizards and the elf spun toward Colbey. The mental communication became a roar, ideas rebounding among the three Wizards. They spoke in a raucous chorus, devoid of harmony, their audible words as incalculable as their shared considerations. White streamers filled the clearing, tangled like webs about the Wizards and the captured Renshai.

Colbey's fists gripped his sword hilts, and he tensed to attack. Yet, despite the activity in the air around him, he sensed no malice or directed threat. Even as the strands gained color, flashing through a wild, patternless spectrum that encompassed every hue, he sensed concern in their magic rather than menace.

The staff confirmed the thought with one of its own. *Defensive magics. Shields and barricades, I'd guess.*

Shields and barricades. Colbey could not hide his scorn. He remained in place, maintaining the somber fearlessness that once characterized all of the Cardinal Wizards. An odor like sulfur and the crisp electric aftereffect of lightning burned Colbey's nostrils. Khitajrah had slipped up beside him. His friends seemed uncertain but interested, completely unaware of the grandeur of the magic that Colbey experienced. Clearly, only he and the other Wizards could see the color and crackling glory in the workings of magic, the agony of its stench, and the tingle that built in its wake, vibrations that prickled Colbey's skin like tiny bee stings.

Colbey remained in place, unperturbed, hoping to rattle the Wizards with his composure alone. "One more spell, and Harval dances through your throats." He patted the hilt to remind them he carried one of the few weapons that could cause their downfall.

Shadimar's nostrils flared. Otherwise, the Wizards showed no sign of the boil of emotions Colbey sensed within them. Their binding to create spells had made them nearly inseparable to his mind gift.

Shadimar looked at Sterrane. "Sterrane, my fair child. Good to see you again. I hope Béarn is well. How did you come here?"

Colbey drew breath, knowing his covering response would come to late. In his guileless way, Sterrane would surely tell all to his mentor.

Sterrane pouted. Even across the clearing, Colbey could see the king's lower lip jut and swell. "Béarn *not* well. You take friends capture."

Shadimar's lips pursed, and his eyes narrowed like a father about to lecture a disobedient child. "Sterrane, you know me well enough to trust me. Have you ever seen me do anything outside the best interests of the Westlands? Do these look like prisoners to you?" He inclined his head toward the Renshai, all of whom now stood in a row watching the proceedings. The pattern of their chosen stances told Colbey that some unseen barrier blocked their path; and, though their lips moved in conversational patterns, he could not hear even a dull murmur of their exchanges.

"You always work *for* West," Sterrane admitted. His mouth remained in its downward bow, lower lip bulging. "Before. Why take Renshai?"

Shadimar rolled a careful look at the Renshai tribe before answering. He measured his words, a sure sign that they could hear him. "It was the only way, Sterrane. Colbey's dangerous, a pawn of chaos. Whatever he told you, beware. He plans to destroy the world. I did only what I felt I had to do to stop him. You understand."

Colbey kept his mouth shut. Protestation now would only make Shadimar's point seem valid. The other Wizards remained silent also, content to let Shadimar represent them, at least until their purposes clashed.

Sterrane's pout dissolved, his lip tightening back to normal size. His dark eyes went wide; but he assumed no expression Colbey could read, torn between his mentor and a companion he trusted implicitly. "Colbey not chaos. Not." Sterrane struggled to put the concept into words he could scarcely manipulate for normal conversation. "If was chaos, not loyal to Renshai. Not come save them."

"Ah." Shadimar smiled, apparently glad for the point Sterrane had chosen. "Whether he has come to rescue or damn them remains to be seen." He swung about to face Colbey. "You need only give us the staff you carry. The Renshai, your friends, and even you will leave here free and unharmed."

A sudden flurry of conversation among the Renshai reinforced the realization that they could hear the exchanges around them, though the barrier prevented Colbey from reading their thoughts or listening to their discussions. Their attention shifted to him. Tarah and Modrey studied him with nervous interest. Rache and Tannin stared with a fierce criticalness befitting Renshai. Mitrian looked stricken, her eyes crinkled and her mouth twisted.

Colbey said the only thing he believed he could. "You know I can't give you the staff."

"Because you would place ownership of a polished stick before ones you claim to love."

Colbey kept his gaze on Shadimar, bombarded by the emotions of the myriad around him. He sensed uncertainty among his friends, a wavering rather than a break in their loyalty. Trilless seemed smug. A bitterness colored Carcophan's amusement, a sour rancor whose source seemed other than Colbey. Colbey addressed the Renshai directly. "Because this so-called 'polished stick' contains a force that makes the Cardinal Wizards seem little more than fettered slaves." He turned his attention back to the Wizard. "I don't bow to terrorism. My honor, and that of those involved, does not allow it. If I gave you the staff, it would make a mockery of the exchange. We would all die within the day."

Colbey sensed anger and scorn beneath Shadimar's sullen mask. Nevertheless, the Wizard pitched his voice to soothe. "Colbey, beneath what the staff has made you into, I know there's a fair and honest man. Do you think, for a moment, that the world is safer in your hands than in those of the world's guardians chosen by Odin?" He unfolded his arms broadly to indicate Carcophan, Trilless, and himself. "Give us the staff. We'll destroy chaos, and the world will fall back into harmony."

Colbey sighed, his mind forming arguments his tongue would never speak, not even to remind the Wizards that he, too, had been selected by Odin. He had rehashed the same ground with Shadimar too many times to believe he could convince the Wizard now. "I can't give you the staff, and I won't. Surely, you'll take something else in trade for the Renshai."

Before Shadimar could reply, Carcophan cut in. "There is one other thing we will take." Though he addressed Colbey, his glare fell fully on the trio at the opposite side of the clearing. "We'll take the life of this murdering little witch . . ." He jabbed a steady finger at Sylva. ". . . along with the staff."

Stop it! Shadimar's mental reprimand struck so hard Trilless recoiled, and even Colbey felt it ring clearly through his mind. *Keep your grudges private. Better yet, Wizards hold no grudges at all.*

Arduwyn crouched into a hollow between a standing tree and a deadfall, arrow to string in an instant.

Though he made the movement appear casual, Colbey deliberately stepped between Arduwyn and his target. He doubted the shot could do anything more than further enrage the Southern Wizard. "Surely, we can find a compromise." Colbey spoke to Shadimar, ignoring Carcophan's outburst. To the best of her ability to remember, Sylva had already explained how she came to wander the woodlands in madness, her memory ending just after she had slain the woman threatening Rache.

"No compromise," Shadimar returned. "The world can't afford it. The staff or the Renshai. Your choice."

Colbey traced the knurling on Harval's hilt. "I need time to think."

"Take time." Shadimar wriggled his fingers toward the Renshai, murmuring something Colbey could not decipher. Spots and random squiggles defined the wall caging the tribe, appearing as red-hot images then fading back into obscurity. Colbey could not know for certain; but he guessed Shadimar, about to say something the Renshai would not approve of, had stolen their hearing as well as their freedom. "But not too much time; we've waited long enough. For every half day you delay, one Renshai dies."

Outrage sputtered like a fuse through Colbey, but he squelched it before it became an all-consuming explosion. Without a word, he turned to leave, trusting his own instincts to guard his back. Should any Wizard start a spell for the purpose of attack, he would meet a Sword of Power in the hands of a berserk Renshai.

"One last thing," Shadimar called.

Colbey froze, but he did not turn. He hoped the stiffness of his demeanor cued the Cardinal Wizards how close he had come to violence.

"We have a right to know how you got here."

Colbey hesitated longer than propriety demanded, but the Wizards seemed not to notice. Centuries of existence had made them maddeningly patient. Colbey recalled how his own ignorance of the Wizards' repertoire made him cautious. Had the lives of so many not fallen into his hands, Colbey and Harval would long ago have resorted to physical combat. The unpredictability of the Wizards and their spells had become the key to their danger. Now, he hoped, misconception about his powers would beleaguer them at least as much. "Magic," he replied. "I used magic."

"What kind of magic?" Shadimar demanded.

Colbey chose not to answer.

Back at camp, Colbey let rage overtake him until the world seemed to blur behind a burning, red curtain. Coherent thought receded, lost in the boil of Colbey's fury.

"What now?" Arduwyn asked, pillowing Khitajrah's head
on his uninjured thigh. She breathed in erratic patterns to
avoid the pain, and the need for her body to heal apparently
made her sleepy. Sterrane slumped on a log, his meaty hands
cupping his face and black hair jutting from every hole and
crevice of his grip. Mar Lon strummed his mandolin softly,
apparently willing to sacrifice Sterrane's safety to draw him
from melancholy. Sylva stroked the crests of her last few arrows in mindless repetition, head low.

Guilty for Khitajrah's pain, though he had not caused it,
Colbey knelt beside her. He stroked the Eastern-dark hair,
pulling sweat-dampened strands free of her forehead. She
caught his hand, smiling sweetly through her pain.

Arduwyn's jealousy pulsed against Colbey, and he could
feel the hunter wrestling the emotion down with guilt.

"Do you see the sword Mar Lon has there?" Colbey nodded toward Mar Lon's hip.

"I see them both," Khitajrah replied.

"The one with the hilt shaped like a wolf's head. It belongs to the Renshai woman. The dark-haired one, not the
blond."

Khitajrah grunted, saying nothing.

"Do you see the yellow gems of the eyes?"

Khitajrah squinted. "Not from here."

"They're there. One's broken."

Khitajrah considered the significance for a moment.
"That's the magic?"

"Yes." Colbey squeezed Khitajrah's hand, then freed his
own from her grip. "The item you've been seeking."

Khitajrah smiled, lids sagging closed, features becoming
peaceful.

"I don't know what the next day holds, so I thought it
best to tell you now in case I can't later. The sword belongs to the Renshai. It has to stay with them, you understand."

"You'll tell them to let me use it? Just once?"

"I'll ask them." Colbey glanced from Arduwyn to
Khitajrah. Each grimace from the woman sent a wave of
concern and sympathy grinding through the hunter. "If I die,
ask them yourself. Arduwyn will stand behind you, I believe."

Arduwyn nodded vigorously, though he had no way to understand the significance of the request.

Khitajrah groped for Colbey's hand, caught it, and clasped it with affection. Then her fingers fell away. Every wrinkle fled her features, and her breathing became regular and rhythmic.

Arduwyn stared at Colbey, desperation and sadness as clearly in his gaze as radiating from his person. "You and her . . .?" He left the question unfinished, prodding Colbey for an answer the Renshai felt too confused to understand himself.

"I don't know," Colbey admitted. Untangling relationships seemed of little importance in the wake of other matters. "But I never shied from healthy competition, and you never hesitated to stand against me before." He smiled. "Let the battle begin."

Shocked, Arduwyn found no reply.

Colbey stole the reprieve to rise. Before he could cross the clearing, Mar Lon turned the conversation back to its original question.

"What do we do now?"

"I think." Colbey strode from the campsite and deeper into the forest. The *aristiri* wheeled from a distant treetop and zigzagged after the Renshai. Within the space of a short jog, he found a suitable place and launched into a practice more energy consuming and brutal than even most of his own, while the hawk studied him and his maneuvers from a nearby limb.

The world disappeared, along with its problems and paradoxes, as Colbey gave himself fully to his sword and his goddess. Though he always gave his all to every practice, this one put his previous work to shame. He became a silver flicker of flame, whirling and reversing with a speed that seemed impossible. A sword in each hand, he cleaved a thousand imagined enemies and faced a million more. Despite the beauty of his speed and grace, the lethality of his movements could never be mistaken for dance.

Colbey lost all concept of time. At intervals, he knew, his companions came to talk to him. He heard none of their proclamations or entreaties. His soul escaped through an opening he made, seeking Sif to beseech or demand a solution. His flurry of offense never lost its dimensions of prayer. He performed for his goddess and to sharpen his skill, for no other reason, though rage added power to each skillfully executed stroke. Yet Sif did not answer. And

Colbey continued his sword work, oblivious to constraints of time or place.

Arduwyn paced, intentionally inflicting the pain that came with movement to take his mind from the worry he could displace no other way. His throat seemed to pinch closed, throttling him with responsibility that even the agony of his wound could not erase. The Renshai needed tending. And the one man who could help them had retreated so far into violence that no mortal could draw him back to reality.

Mar Lon sang to the cadence of Arduwyn's pacing, slowing the beat gradually, as if to draw the hunter to a stop. Despite the grandeur of the music, its intention failed. Arduwyn's conscience bucked against the peace, finding him undeserving of the solace it promised. He waited only until the last notes pealed from the instrument before turning his discomfort on the bard. "We have to do something." Arduwyn glanced through the branches. The morning had aged enough to make the midday deadline loom.

Apparently surrendering to Arduwyn's mood, Mar Lon replaced his mandolin, kneading away nervous energy against his sword hilt instead. "What can we do? None of us can budge Colbey. We have to wait for him."

"Why?" Arduwyn returned. His gaze jerked from Khitajrah's sleeping form, to Sylva who watched him intently, to Sterrane who had not raised head from palms all morning.

"Because it's his situation. We're along to help him."

"It's our situation, too." Arduwyn held out a hand to his daughter, and she came to his side. "Her husband and some of my closest friends' lives hinge on settling this matter swiftly. We can't wait for Colbey to indulge himself slaughtering shadows. We have real enemies to face."

Sterrane finally looked up. "Shadimar *not* enemy."

Arduwyn did not relent. "He is if he kills Renshai to get what he wants from Colbey."

Sterrane narrowed his eyes, but he said nothing.

Arduwyn released some of his own pent-up anger to soften his words. "Fine. Maybe Shadimar's right, and Colbey's the enemy. Or maybe they both believe what they're saying and each has a legitimate point. Let's go and find out."

"What are you suggesting?" Mar Lon's tone revealed his incredulity. "We promised Colbey our support."

Arduwyn had no intention of betraying anyone. "Colbey's used to handling problems with violence. He's no diplomat. Now he's faced with a problem and, instead of considering it, he's out finding himself an enemy he can best with a sword instead of his wit. Maybe we can negotiate where he failed."

Sterrane's face bunched in serious consideration. "Talk Shadimar? That maybe work."

"Of course it maybe work." Arduwyn adopted the king's speech pattern routinely, the thought of doing something, anything, relieving some of his restless need. He gathered his belongings, stacking the longer term items and hefting personal gear.

Mar Lon shifted his mandolin to his back, out of the way of free movement. "What about her?" He waved his fingers at Khitajrah.

"She'll be safe here. Clearly, the Wizards aren't planning to hunt us down." Arduwyn strapped his quiver in place. He had every intention of negotiating peacefully, but it made no sense to face a potential threat completely defenseless. "Let's go."

CHAPTER 32

In Ruin and Confusion Hurled

Though the clearing and his companions had faded in a blur of savage sword technique, Colbey gained an explicit clarity of mind that he knew only in battle and with the grandest of practices. The world slowed to a crawl, granting him more than enough time to map out each split-second maneuver, to consider and act faster than others could think to watch the motion. For hours that passed like an instant, he thrust, slashed, and spun, battling mock enemies by the thousand, offering earnest prayers to his goddess so she might steer him to the proper course that would allow her chosen, the Renshai, to live.

But Sif gave Colbey no signs, no guidance that he could fathom. Once before, when he had needed to decide the fate and direction of the Renshai tribe, she had come to him in a triple image, battling him three swords to two and three bodies to one. Without words, she had directed his thoughts, Colbey believed, to a future he had tried to turn into reality: the Renshai as hired soldiers following their morality and honor. Another time, she had told him to have faith in himself after the Wizards and powers condemned him. Yet this time, when the life of every person and every Renshai lay at stake, it seemed as if Thor's wife had abandoned him.

Colbey spun, quicker than a cornered stag, sword whipping through two vision of enemies to meet four more at his back. Harval and the rescued Renshai sword jabbed, curled back in opposite loops, then licked out again. Assuming failure, Colbey blocked the ripostes, then drove in again for another attack.

The *aristiri* glided down from its perch to land on the grass in front of Colbey.

The Renshai did not slow for an instant. He hacked and stabbed at the same enemies, imagining them dodging strokes no man had ever escaped, seeing return slashes as quick as the ones he delivered.

Long, human legs sprouted from the hawk body, as muscled as any warrior's, their slender proportions perfectly female. As Colbey stared, locked into a deadly crouch, feathers gave way to linen and mail locked to full hips, a delicate waist, and breasts that held his gaze far beyond politeness. Then, all signs of the *aristiri* disappeared, and Freya stood in its place. A shield girded her left arm, and a sword graced her other fist.

Colbey remained in position, uncertain of his next words or actions.

Freya studied him in the full light that wove through the branches announcing the coming midday. "I'll have that spar you promised now."

Colbey smiled. Before he could reply, Freya charged him. Her sword sped for his chest.

Colbey sprang aside, returning the attack with a lightning quick one of his own. Harval rang against the shield. The other blade slid harmlessly from cloth-covered mail, creasing a wrinkle through the fabric that made its threads glitter and wink in the sunlight. Freya returned a thrust that Colbey's right-hand sword battered aside. Harval leapt for her gut.

Blue fire seemed to caper through Freya's eyes, enhancing a beauty that already seemed impossible. He recognized battle joy, a perfect echo of his own magnificent excitement. The swords stabbed and sliced with lethal grace in imponderable patterns and at a speed Colbey's pounding heart could never match. Happiness swept him from head to heel, and his heart cried out for a daily partner with the skill of this one. Decades had passed since he had capered with a woman who could match him stroke for stroke, and that at a time when his own ability had been far less. His night with Khitajrah seemed to fade to insignificance. The sensuality of giving his all to a woman, of fending as many sword cuts as he gave, brought a euphoria that usurped even that of sex itself.

No longer simply slowed, the universe seemed to jerk to a halt, half an hour of combat fleeing in an eye blink. Then, Colbey swirled his blade driving in with a sudden charge that brought him under and through Freya's guard. Harval stabbed through mail, guided to sweep harmlessly across

Freya's side. Colbey's shoulder hammered into her chest. She fell, breathless and sprawling, this time unable to roll quickly enough to avoid the cross of steel he pressed to her throat.

Freya's breasts rose and fell in a heavy pattern, and sweat added a sheen to her ivory skin. The necklace glimmered and twitched with every breath, and the metallic threads sewn through her garments hurt his eyes. Her golden hair spread in a wave around a face blindingly beautiful. Winded, she spoke in spurts of gathered air. "As skilled . . . as your name . . . Kyndig."

"Colbey," he corrected, finding himself equally breathless. He could not remember the last time any single spar had tired him.

"Kyndig," Freya repeated. "The children of Thor . . . are named . . . for warcraft." Her voice became more fluent with time. "Magni, might. Modi, wrath. Thrudr, his daughter, power." Her steady, sapphire gaze met his. "Kyndig, skill."

Colbey removed the threat, sheathing his swords. He had won the battle, yet no sense of triumph accompanied the victory. The glory and excitement had come and gone with the battle itself, its end leaving him only with a different, deep and only partially familiar longing. His loins burned, and the fire seemed to spread throughout his being. He wanted to correct Freya again, to insist that she use the name given to him by the mortal parents he'd loved rather than the god who had chosen to abandon him. But the point seemed unimportant. His gaze traced her figure in a cycle he could not seem to stop, memorizing the perfection of arcs, curves, and bulges. "You're the *aristiri?*"

"Yes."

"Why?"

Though the question implied interest in the transformation, Freya's explanation addressed the real question. "I needed to watch you. Had I come in my true form, I would have caused no end of problems and changes to man's world."

Colbey did not probe for details. The gods' avoidance of mankind seemed to confirm Freya's comment well enough. "Why did you need to watch me?"

Freya raised an arm, a silent request for help with rising.

Absently, Colbey leaned over and gave her his hand, a hundred more questions pressing into his mind at once.

Freya wrapped callused fingers around Colbey's palm, her grip seeming soft and delicate despite the hoary buttons worn by the hilt of her sword. Without warning, her hand tightened painfully, and she jerked with an unexpected suddenness that overbalanced Colbey.

Colbey scrabbled for equilibrium, failed, and fell. Only an instinctive twist kept him from landing fully upon the goddess. "Why . . . ?" he started, his next words suffocated beneath Freya's lips.

The kiss rallied Colbey's senses like nothing ever had. In an instant, the world and its every problem disappeared, replaced by an inferno of need that threatened to consume reason. He jabbed his tongue into her mouth, sucking in the sweetness of her saliva and breath. One hand slipped through the collar of dress and mail, desperately seeking breast and nipple. The other tugged at the skirts, hunting entrance beneath garments constructed for war, never for passion. He slithered on top of her, mind emptied of all thought except a vital desire.

Freya returned the kiss with an eagerness that encouraged Colbey. Her passionate caresses nearly sent him over the edge too soon. Still, she disengaged her lips from his mouth before he had found the necessary gaps in her clothing. She whispered in his ear, warm breath stirring something animal before the words registered. "Careful, Kyndig. Don't smash anything, or I'll never carry your baby."

The words seemed nonsensical, but concentration on her voice brought reality back into focus. Horrified realization replaced desire in an instant, and Colbey's lust died to a painful throb. "Gods!" He sprang to his feet, straightening his clothing, averting his eyes so that Freya could do the same. His hand slipped to his hilts, prepared to fight a divine retribution that never came. Surely, the goddess could forgive no man or god what he had done. Even the AllFather himself did not dare lay a finger on Freya. If the goddess did not inflict her revenge, the many gods who wanted and could not have her surely would.

Nothing answered Colbey's transgression. No gods slammed him with killing spells. No massive weapons soared from the sky.

Cautiously, Colbey glanced back at Freya.

The goddess lay, propped on one elbow, a smile of amusement touching her lips.

Colbey's mind replayed as much of the last few moments as he could, ripping through the shroud that desire had drawn over his wits. Freya had pulled him down on her. She had initiated the kiss. He had taken things much further, but she had not resisted nor made any attempt to stop him. For reasons he did not dare to fathom, Freya wanted him. And he wanted her more than anything he could remember. The fire in his loins sparked to life again, and he overcame need with will. "You said something about a baby?"

Freya rubbed a hand across her lower abdomen. "Some day."

Confusion replaced the wild craving that still compelled him to finish what he had started with the most beautiful of all beings. "With me?" Colbey frowned, wishing it could be true. Desire drove him to lie, to hide his inability to sire children for the chance to spend his days trying. He had lost one wife and many potential others for their knowledge of his limitation. But the thought flashed through his mind only briefly, without need for consideration. He would not tolerate deceit, especially to a goddess he respected. "I'd like nothing more. But it's just not possible."

Freya continued to smile, saying nothing.

Colbey explained. "My seed is sterile."

"Are you sure?"

"I'm not a virgin. I'm also not a father. Women I've slept with have had children with other men."

Freya swept to a sitting position. "Maybe you just didn't find the right woman before."

Freya's words seemed meaningless; Colbey shook his head. His marriage had lasted years, and his wife had borne her second husband three children. Images rose, of her warrior limbs guiding sword strokes in spar, her short locks a golden frame about features his love for her made beautiful. That love had become driven to his core, smothered by the tasks of daily living. It now rose to the surface for the first time in decades. When he compared it with the excitement he had known during his spar with Freya, they blended together in a silken match. Since the goddess had appeared in his dreams, he had come to love her. His admiration had grown, without his knowledge. Though he had not known about the hawk-guise she was wearing, the bond had thrived; and he had mistaken it for many things: attraction to a bird, compassion for Khitajrah, a directionless need for companionship.

Yet, clearly, love alone was not the answer. "I loved my wife."

"I'm sure you did. But she was mortal." Freya swept her legs in a graceful arc. "Gods' seed doesn't sprout easily; if it did, we would pack the heavens with babies. Odin has sired offspring from giants and goddesses, but never mortals. Thor has impregnated giantesses and at least one mortal; yet his own wife, who bore a son before their marriage, remains barren for him. In fact, no goddess has carried Thor's child. Several of the gods have no children, though married for centuries. It'll take time, but it can happen. And I believe it will."

Colbey considered the implications of being a god's son, thrilled as much by the prospect of fatherhood as the chance to earn Freya's love. Yet it seemed unlikely that impending *Ragnarok* would grant them the years or decades needed to conceive. Even if it did, there seemed no purpose to creating an infant only to see the child die.

"Come here." Freya gestured Colbey to her.

Every fiber of Colbey's being goaded him to do as she bid, not from any irresistible divine or magical urging, but from his own yearning for her. He resisted. Physical distance had given him perspective. "No."

"Why not?"

"If I come too close, I'll ravish you."

"Ravish me?" Freya laughed. "What makes you think you could take me against my will?"

Colbey ran a hand along Harval's hilt. "This. Do you need another demonstration?"

"Yes. Hundreds of thousands of spars. I'll win more than one."

The challenge intrigued Colbey, a daily battle with a goddess nearly his equal with a sword.

"You don't need to worry about ravishing. I'm as eager as you."

Hunger blazed, and the fire returned. Again, Colbey resisted. For the first time, the position of the sun overhead registered, and guilt hammered back desire. "First I have to handle the Wizards."

Freya rose, brushing skirts and armor back into place.

"You'll help me, I presume. The *Ragnarok* affects the gods as much as men."

"That's why I can't assist. Not even to advise." Freya looked sincerely sad. Her eyes lost their glow, and the smile vanished. "The balance is tenuous enough. If a god interfered now, I believe it would immediately set the final battle in motion."

The implications struck hard. "I'm half-divine."

"But raised a mortal. You're already in this too deep to extract. Good luck, Kyndig." Red feathers flashed in a sudden arch, then Freya disappeared. The *aristiri* winged a spiral toward the clouds.

The sword practice had brought Colbey no answers, divine or otherwise, yet exhilaration lent him a second wind that gave him a new clarity of thought. Freya's promises refreshed his reasons for living, equally reinforcing the need to help the rest of mankind survive as well. As he hurried through the brush and toward camp, his course seemed no less difficult but infinitely clearer. He had little choice but to give the Cardinal Wizards one last chance to barter. Should they refuse, he and his followers would regroup for attack, arming the other Renshai as swiftly as time allowed. At least some of the Renshai would survive. And if the Wizards died, he would have to hope the system Odin had created would find its own solution.

A curled mass of brush parted stiffly before Colbey, limbs jabbing through his lightweight tunic. Shadimar had claimed he would kill a Renshai every half day Colbey dallied. He had not specified times. Midday seemed an obvious choice for the first sacrifice, but Colbey felt certain the Cardinal Wizards had not yet carried through on their threat. Surely, they would warn him before they took a life, using the imminent murder to strong-arm Colbey into a hasty decision. It went against Trilless' championed tenets to slaughter innocents, and he believed even Shadimar held the Renshai in enough regard not to kill them out of hand for personal gain. Still, it made little sense to dawdle. The sword practice had proved necessary to stimulate mind and body. Anything more was only delay.

Colbey pressed through the last copse, emerging into the encampment. Khitajrah sat, sagging body supported by a deadfall. Packs and blankets lay in rumpled piles strewn

over the leaf-cushioned stretch of ground. His other companions and their weapons seemed to have disappeared.

Colbey froze, train of thought interrupted by sudden, all-
encompassing wariness. He measured the pertinent in an
instant: no blood, no evidence of a struggle, and Khitajrah
appeared no worse than when he had last seen her. She
stared back, a welcoming half-smile on her face tempered by
concern. He sensed mild discomfort, but none of the desperate terror that would have accompanied an attack and the violent loss of friends.

Khitajrah anticipated his question. "They went to talk to
the Wizards one more time."

Alarm stabbed through Colbey, and he stiffened. "Without
me?"

The answer seemed obvious, but Khitajrah understood the
need for explanation as well as confirmation. "They tried to
get your attention, but you seemed beyond reach. They were
worried about Wizards' deadlines and Renshai lives."

Colbey took the last step into the clearing, gaze tracing
the route his companions must have taken, need driving him
to follow as swiftly as possible. "When?"

"Moments ago. Not long." Khitajrah staggered to her feet.

Colbey strode to Khitajrah's side, steadying her. "Come
on. Let's go. Quickly."

Khitajrah allowed Colbey to support much of her weight.
"If time's that important, you'd better leave me."

"No." Colbey headed from the clearing, prodding
Khitajrah forward with an arm around her back. "It's not
safe to leave anyone alone. Especially trapped on another
world and with magic about." They headed into the brush,
seeking the pathway the Renshai tribe had carved through
forest from the Fields of Wrath.

Once on the roadway, Colbey and Khitajrah moved reasonably swiftly, hindered only by the woman's inability to
take deep breaths and the long, awkward staff the Renshai
was forced to carry. Khitajrah questioned, though whether
from a need to soothe or to force an issue, Colbey could not
guess. "Is it possible they might bargain better without you?
Emotional distance makes for clearer heads and opener
minds. And the Wizards might handle the problem differently when not dealing with one they see as an enemy."

Colbey denied the possibility. "Distance was why I
needed the practice. And why I became so entrenched in it

they couldn't rouse me.. My mind couldn't be clearer." He rushed Khitajrah past rows of brambles. "Remember, the others have friends and relatives at stake, too; and running off without the warrior who has a sword that can strike the enemy doesn't seem like clear judgment to me. I'm also the only one who knows enough of what's going on to make a fair exchange."

Khitajrah gave him no reply. They continued on in silence, the road to the Fields of Wrath seeming endless, far longer than Colbey remembered from their first parlay. With time, Khitajrah's gasping breaths elicited more impatience than sympathy. Finally, the woodlands seemed to thin, the trees becoming sparser, younger, and smaller in height and breadth. Human voices wound between the trunks.

Colbey slowed, keeping Khitajrah slightly behind him, shielding her with his body. He edged forward until the exchange became ungarbled. He recognized the speaker as Arduwyn. From his voice, he stood ahead and slightly to the right of them; and his tone betrayed exasperation.

". . . must be something else you can take in trade."

Shadimar replied. "There can be no compromise. Man's world is law, and chaos will destroy it. Why press *me? Colbey* holds the doom of gods and mankind in his hands."

Arduwyn's frustration rose to tangible levels, and his tone betrayed it. "I press you because you're the one threatening the lives of people you once considered friends."

"Just bring us the staff," Shadimar said, his calm emphasized in the wake of Arduwyn's desperation. "No one has to die."

"No one," Trilless added softly. "No one or everyone. The choice seems simple to me. If you get the staff from Colbey, the Renshai and the world will live on."

Arduwyn shouted, control lost. "Get the staff from Colbey? Three Wizards together can't do that. What makes you think any of us could?"

Colbey frowned, but he passed no judgments. Arduwyn's question did not necessarily imply that he agreed with or would attempt such a thing.

"You can try," Shadimar said.

"The world depends on it," Trilless added, her voice soothing and goading in its gentleness. The claim had become trite, at least to Colbey.

Mar Lon joined in then, speaking his mind freely in the

presence of Wizards. "So you say. Colbey's carried the Staff of Chaos for months now. That seems like more than enough time to send our world crashing down."

Shadimar fairly crowed. "Lies, theft, deceit. You can see his influence already. Our work to restore order has kept the world on keel so far, but it's teetering. Time's running short. We need the staff. We can't afford to compromise, and neither can you."

Arduwyn made a noise that sounded like a choked back scream. "We're getting nowhere. One thing's certain. Your feud is with Colbey, not with us. And not with the Renshai. You're butchering the horse because the mule won't plow. *What could serve chaos more than slaughtering innocent people for another's offense?*"

A blast of sudden rage slammed Colbey. Carcophan answered, his voice a shout. "Look who's talking about killing innocents. The father of a vicious murderer."

A raw mixture of emotion followed the pronouncement. From Shadimar, Trilless, Arduwyn, Dh'arlo'mé, and Mar Lon, Colbey sensed impatient irritation, a need to bull past what must have become a tedious issue. From Sterrane, he received only a steady wash of sorrow and hope.

Sylva's fury nearly matched Carcophan's own. She shouted. "I'm sick to death of your accusation! Your apprentice was about to kill or mutilate my husband for no reason but jealousy! I'm not sorry I killed her. She and all like her deserve to die. She wanted Rache, and she couldn't have him. Maybe she got tired of sleeping with a *shriveled up, old* goat!"

The mood changed at once. Before Colbey bothered to assess it, the staff pulsed against his mind in warning. Impressed by its frenzy, he let it in, immediately deluged by its anticipation of a massive gathering of power. Conserving time by using concept instead of words, the staff let him know someone prepared a huge and aggressive spell.

Colbey did not waste breath for warning. Releasing Khitajrah, he charged. He had barely raced into view when a jagged flash of light speared from the clearing. His staff-sight added the chaos slashes and colors the others could not see: patternless movement writhed within the directed confines of the magic.

Colbey's mind collected details in an instant. Clearly, the spell had come from Carcophan, and Colbey's mind gift told him the Southern Wizard had borrowed some power from a link with Shadimar as well. The deadly sorcery sped for Sylva where she stood, feet braced, in the forest. Arduwyn sprinted to protect her. More familiar with magic, Sterrane sprang first, before Mar Lon could think to anticipate the action. Sterrane and Arduwyn crashed together in midair. Smaller, the hunter bounced and rolled from the impact, and the spell slashed through Béarn's king. A flashing corona engulfed Sterrane, flipping through the spectrum more quickly than Colbey could think to name the colors.

Sterrane bellowed in surprise and agony. His limbs went rigid, then loosened. He spasmed a second time and a third, lapsing into a wild convulsion while Mar Lon grabbed and clutched, furiously trying to stabilize his king. Then, as suddenly, Sterrane went still. The last vestiges of magic sizzled into oblivion, visually gone, though Colbey could still feel a dangerous tingle that made the air seem vibrant and watchful.

The staff's nonverbal warning came faster than any physical action could. *Too much chaos here. Another large spell, and the End will have begun. Once in motion, the* Ragnarok *cannot be stopped by anyone.*

Colbey skidded to a halt at the clearing's edge, treading the fine line between preventing a spell and forcing one in defense against his attack. The three Cardinal Wizards stood, crouched and ready for battle. Their mental exchanges trickled to him in snatches, warped and only partially intelligible. The shock of missing his target had claimed most of Carcophan's anger. Shadimar and Trilless chastised their impulsive colleague with rage at least as strong. Whether or not they understood the danger of more magic, Colbey had no intention of testing their linked forces again. Beneath the combined consciousness, he sensed a restless power as awesome as that of his staff.

"No!" Mar Lon screamed. "No! No! No!"

Colbey left Sterrane's tending to his companions, not daring to look away. Between his sword and the other Cardinal Wizards, the destiny of mankind and gods rested. Even the Béarnide's injuries could not take precedence at the moment. Yet, though he deafened himself to Mar Lon's self-degrading tirade, Arduwyn's soft words came clearly to him. "He's dead. Gods! Sterrane is dead."

Mar Lon screamed with an anguish so basic that Secodon

looked up from his sickbed and managed a feeble howl. The Renshai stood, all accounted for, hands pressed to the invisible wall, faces etched with horror. Colbey could not separate the dread wafting around him from his own. Without the king and his simple mercy, he could not help wondering if rescuing mankind held significance any longer. Stripped of balance, the positive changes would become unstable and lose all meaning. He jerked the staff from his belt.

At that instant, with the staff precariously balanced, Arduwyn stepped up from behind Colbey and snatched it from his hand. The whole had an unreal quality. Never had anyone taken anything Colbey did not want them to have, and he could not believe the events of the last few moments had made him so unwary. He watched in fascinated alarm as Arduwyn raised the staff.

"Here, may the gods damn you all! Nothing is worth this!" Arduwyn jabbed the staff toward Sterrane's corpse and Mar Lon, hunched defensively before his charge. "Nothing." His bold words degenerated into sobs, and tears leaked from his eyes in a steady stream.

"Wait." Colbey had not yet played his last card. He contacted the staff *Can you stop him?*

Not forcefully. I'll do the best I can, but the Wizards may try magic against me. We can't afford that. Hurry.

The Cardinal Wizards said nothing, although a smile slipped onto Carcophan's lips. Shadimar stood, impassive, his own staff sturdy as a tree trunk in his grip. Trilless stared at Arduwyn, tensely expectant.

"It's a mistake." Colbey remained in place, gaze locked on the Wizards, cued to any movement that might indicate preparation for a spell. He could hear the echoes of the staff's appeals to Arduwyn, catching the gist of its need to remain in its champion's hands without hearing its every word. He could also feel the rising of chaos in the form of gentle magic, a dying breath compared with the previous holocaust triggered by Carcophan, a tug and whisper to draw Arduwyn to Shadimar.

Concerned for the balance, Colbey addressed the Cardinal Wizards. "No more magic, please, or it's over." He could feel Carcophan and Trilless stirring in reluctant agreement and Shadimar's irrational denial of what they all knew was truth. Even receiving only radiating emotions, Colbey recognized little of the Shadimar he had once known. The consciousness of the Eastern Wizard's staff enfolded him, as swollen as a feasted tick. "I promise, I won't interfere so long as you don't use magic." Colbey hated the need to cripple himself, but he saw no other way. The deepest portion of his mind, the part that ran on instinct and emotion, showed him reality from a different perspective. With Sterrane dead and the Renshai's fate hanging in the balance, the exchange of hostages for staff seemed to lose its vast significance. *Let them champion chaos* and *law.*

They'll destroy me, the staff reminded.

Not once they realize what you are.

Arduwyn shuffled a step toward the Wizards, jealously guarding the staff from Colbey, clearly watching for the slightest tensing that might indicate an attempt by the Renshai to reclaim his property.

Colbey remained in place, silent and true to his word. The cacophony of emotions bombarding him seemed suffocating. For the first time, he wasted energy holding some of these others' thoughts at bay. Mar Lon's grief and self-loathing all but upended reason.

You leave me no choice. The staff gave Colbey no more warning before opening itself to Arduwyn, revealing its inner core with a rawness that struck Colbey, an inadvertent spectator, as hard as a physical blow. Arduwyn reeled, a scream wrenched from his throat. Realization made him gasp, and the staff retreated. The whole had lasted less than an instant; yet, a moment later, Arduwyn returned the staff to Colbey's hand without explanation.

"Liar!" Shadimar shouted. "You tricked him." Even without the staff's direct assistance, Colbey sensed the drawing of chaos for magics that, whatever else their purpose, would fling the world into an endless spiral of madness called the *Ragnarok.*

"Hold your magic." Colbey thumped the base of the staff on the ground, keeping his left hand free for Harval. "Just hold it, and I'll give you whatever you want."

For an instant, Shadimar hesitated. Something monstrous and ugly rose inside him, a power so vast it threatened to overwhelm the universe. Trilless and Carcophan rallied to Shadimar's defense, their fused being whittling the creature only slightly. The imminent sorcery disappeared, leaving the Wizards' unanswered mental questions about it in its wake.

Shadimar managed to speak, his voice uncharacteristically

shaky. "We want only one thing. Give me the Staff of Chaos."

"I can't give you that."

A wave of frustrated rage slammed Colbey. Shadimar's face reddened. "You just said you would."

"I can't give you that," Colbey repeated, "because it's already in your keeping. Shadimar, if it's the Staff of Chaos you seek, look to your own hands."

"I have only the Staff of Law." Shadimar shook his staff, drilling its base into the dirt.

Colbey could feel the Cardinal Wizards' consciousness braiding tighter, weaving a net against a force to which Shadimar had submitted willingly, holding it at bay until the Western Wizard could explain.

Colbey kept his gaze unwavering, dropping his protections against the external sorrow that hammered him. He dared not waste more physical energy holding others' thoughts aside. His own emotions seemed ragged and insignificant, reined by clear and present danger. "Remember on the Meeting Isle when I gave you that staff? I told you I offered the one thing that could oppose me, the single object that could prevent my loosing chaos on the world."

Shadimar interrupted, "The Staff of Law." All color had drained from his face, and Colbey could read nothing from the Wizard who had once been his blood brother. Trilless' and Carcophan's presences burned so much brighter, as if Shadimar had become crushed by the force he championed and only a brittle skeleton of his former self remained.

"I gave you the Staff of Chaos," Colbey corrected. "Even with the Staff of Law, you didn't have the power to stop me. Giving chaos to you was the only way to keep me from freeing it."

"You arrogant bastard!" Carcophan seemed impressed despite his horror.

Realization sparked through Shadimar, strongly enough that Colbey could now sense the Eastern Wizard's presence through the others. Understanding came in a vast procession: explanations for spells far more massive than intended, the summoning of a *kraell* instead of a minor demon, the decision of chaos to attack Colbey instead of Shadimar, personality changes he had not noticed until Trilless and Carcophan helped to hold the bonded staff-force at bay. *Chaos. Gods, chaos! I inflicted it on the world.* His anger flared stronger, now directed inward.

Colbey felt the Staff of Chaos straining at its bonds, trying to force the Wizards to expend more magic to hold it, thereby strengthening its cause. Soon, whether through the use of too much magic, or the use of none at all, chaos would smash through the barriers and tumble man's world into the *Ragnarok.* All other worlds would follow in a great chain reaction.

I can help, Colbey's staff said.

Colbey needed to hear nothing more. Gently, he added his mind to the Wizards' link, one of the Cardinal Four again. The power of the staves rushed free, contained only by the consciousness of their champions. Energy pumped through Colbey in a wash that seemed ceaseless. He let the staves clash inside him, locking his thoughts on self and morality, clinging to personal honor and beliefs that seemed puny in the shadow of pure law. The other Wizards seemed to wither, swimmers lost in the vast ocean of power from both sides. The battle raged, chaos and law twining into a vast and violent blur, tendrils of raw, basic power cuffing Colbey's mind at intervals. He clung to self, tearing Carcophan from the interlocking web, hurling him from their fused minds and the battle. The Southern Wizard could do nothing here but die.

Having freed Carcophan, Colbey turned his attention to Trilless. He had chosen evil first, since Trilless had a ready apprentice should he fail. The swirl of the combat around him made thought difficult, but the balance must always come first. Keeping to the edge of the battle, he discovered the champion of goodness, grabbed her, and shoved her mind from the contact. Only then, he tried to find order in the mass of motion around him.

Colbey found no evidence of Shadimar. He had discovered the Champions of Good and Evil driven to the periphery of the mind link, their cause unrelated to the frenzy of current battle. Apparently, Shadimar had become trapped in the center or battered to death beneath the onslaught.

The law-force pulled enough concentration from its enemy to inform its champion. *Center and alive. Dead, he could no longer maintain contact with mind link. Chaos would become trapped in its staff once more.* It gave no

more hint or direction, concentration returning to its opposite.

Though the staff had remained true to its word, resisting
the urge to goad Colbey to action, the Renshai understood its
desire. It wanted him to slay Shadimar, to commit chaos
back into its container while law remained free to rule the
worlds once more. The suggestion carried a desperation and
a common sense that the Wizards had tried to convey from
the start. The worlds had prospered under law's rule. Chaos
promised destruction. Only Colbey's convulsive grip on self
allowed him to keep perspective. *And knowledge. With
chaos also comes growth and inspiration.*

Yet the means for balance now defied Colbey. The battle
swirled and raged about him, smearing the boundaries between thought and emotion, external and internal. He
clutched to his morality tighter, tapping both chaos and law
for direction and wisdom. *Balance.* He dared not allow them
to fight until one became the victor.

Law slammed Colbey's mind with a message. **Damn it,
I'm protecting you! Don't open gaps for chaos. It'll kill
you.**

The words brought Colbey the final answers he sought.
Obediently, he plugged the holes he had created to his innermost thoughts, trapping out law as well as chaos. The
staves' strategy seemed clear: kill its opposite's champion
and trap the other force back inside the staff-container,
thereby opening the world to the winner's influence alone.
Most of the battle had become defensive, a swirling, formless fight geared to protect each force's own champion from
the enemy.

Colbey focused on his mind gift, seeking the seams where
offensive intent met defensive, separating law from chaos by
touch. He wove toward the middle, keeping self in the for-
tified portions of his cause, dodging chaos attacks with the
same skill and agility he used against sword strokes. He
would always face rather than hide from an enemy, but he
discarded the swerve from Renshai honor inherent in using
anything as a shield. His battles came before and after; this
current war was not his.

As Colbey fought toward the center, law displayed its displeasure and concern with raw emotion. Colbey did not need
the warning. His mind carved chaos from law without ex-
pending energy; the vastness of their power made them easy

to read. The deeper Colbey penetrated, the thicker chaos became until he found himself avoiding constant attacks, battle joy rising even without the possibility of returning physical offensives. He sent a mental call ahead to Shadimar. *Brother, come to me.*

Shadimar gave no answer.

Again, Colbey mind-called, hoping he radiated sincerity and worry, still keeping inner calm. *Brother, come. Else one of us will die, and his force will stand unopposed.*

The return sounded like a dying whisper. *You're no brother of mine.*

Colbey ignored the statement, sensing none of the hostility it implied. *Come. I can't force them back into the staves alone.* Colbey guessed he would have to do so one power at a time, and he could not control the free force while he worked with the other.*Once they're contained, we can think clearly. We'll find a compromise. We'll find a way to ask Odin himself, if we must.*

Insight sparked momentarily from Shadimar, too swift for Colbey to read in detail. He received only a glimpse of a possible means to contact Odin that bore some relationship to a pair of blue gems in other hands than Shadimar's own. The Eastern Wizard remained silent a long time in contemplation.

The battle grew to whirlwind intensity. Colbey dodged, time making him breathless. Soon, he would have to retreat and rest or succumb to chaos.

At length, Shadimar spoke, *I'll come to you. But only if you give me Harval.*

My sword? The idea of handing away a weapon struck something primal. *You know I can't do that.*

Harval is my creation.

And I wield it.

At my insistence. Give me Harval, or I will not come.

Fatigue weighted Colbey's limbs, alarming him. Once he finished with Shadimar, he had no way of knowing whether the battle would end or if the three Cardinal Wizards would continue to oppose him. Without Harval, he stood naked against Wizards and creatures of chaos. Yet without Shadimar's assistance, either law or chaos would be utterly destroyed. One way or the other, the Ragnarok would follow. *Agreed, then. Come to me now.*

Shadimar's form emerged from the gray swirl of combat,

ringed by defensive chaos. His consciousness came first, questing blindly. His mind gift more directed, Colbey sent his thoughts to Shadimar as a guide, and a part of their fused minds linked into a single entity shielded from law and chaos alike. The contact allowed Shadimar to draw close enough to reach out a hand for the sword.

True to his word, Colbey removed the weapon from his sheath and handed it, hilt first, to Shadimar. Though he showed no outward signs, he despised the need that made him sacrifice his weapon, even to its creater. His concern about Shadimar's intentions with that weapon sent his right hand creeping toward his opposite hilt. It might not cut the Cardinal Wizards, but it could still hinder them.

Shadimar accepted the hilt.

Colbey tensed for a rush of attack that never came. The emotions wafting from the Wizard mixed confusion, self-loathing, and strength of purpose. Shadimar back-stepped to the limits of their protecting bond. He created a slit in their joint defense, drawing a wisp of chaos to him. The sword floated in front of Shadimar, and he finally met Colbey's fierce blue gaze. Without a wielder, Harval plunged toward Shadimar, effortlessly finding a track between his ribs.

Caught off-guard by the suicide, Colbey sprang for the hilt too late. His hand grasped the familiar pommel, and he fought the magics that drove the point toward Shadimar's heart. As the Eastern Wizard's strength failed, Colbey managed to tear the steel free, but the damage had already been done.

Shadimar sank to the ground, blood trickling from chest and lips. *It was the only way,* he said, then death stole all movement.

A wolf howl cut above the trailing silence, a deep-throated song that seemed to define agony.

Then, as suddenly as it had arisen, the storm of powers disappeared. Colbey found himself surrounded by the familiar, eternal hugeness of law alone. *We won!* it told him, sharing all the joy of the ages.

Tears sprang to Colbey's eyes, and the innocence of his sorrow rebuffed law's pleasure. Though exhausted from his need to evade chaos' attacks, he did not let his defenses down for an instant. *You promised never to force yourself on me.*

Surprised tainted law throughout. *You still don't see the

need to destroy chaos? Your friend ... your brother *killed himself for me.*

From habit, Colbey cleaned and sheathed the sword. He knelt at Shadimar's side, clasping a clammy hand in sympathy. He saw no reason to defend his loyalty to balance once more. He gathered no words to explain how Shadimar's dedication to his cause, in ignorance, had driven him crazy; or that Colbey giving himself to law would only bring about the same results. He managed to speak, though his words seemed to have nothing to do with the matter at hand. *He wasn't my brother. Now go back to the staff.*

Law made an echoing sound of strangled rage. *But we won.*

You won. The rest of us lost. Go back to your staff.

But ...

Colbey threw law's words back at it. *I'm the Wizard, you're the tool.*

Reluctantly, law retreated, and Colbey finally escaped from the mind link he had had no hand in creating. Clouds obscured the sky, though no rain fell. The Renshai tribe remained in place, apparently still trapped by their barrier. Secodon sat near the edge of the woods, his muzzle pointing skyward. Another howl traced a mournful path through the cosmos, stirring deep knowledge. Regardless of the magics of the Cardinal Wizards or the interference of gods, it had become too late to stop the *Ragnarok* anymore. The Wolf Age, Colbey knew, had begun with the song of a Cardinal Wizard's pet.

Trilless and Carcophan stood over Shadimar and Colbey, their uncertainty tangible. Each held a round blue sapphire, Trilless rolling hers from hand to hand and Carcophan's crammed into a muscled fist. Dh'arlo'mé remained aloof and behind the others, his hands clenched and long fingers balanced. The Staff of Chaos lay near Shadimar's hand. Though still and masterless, it seemed alive, a dull wooden sheath hiding a force that could cut souls like paper. Its call pulsed through air that had become stifling with humidity, the staff's promise of knowledge and power drawing those few who could wield it like a siren's song. Colbey placed a hand on his hilt in warning. Any Cardinal Wizard who reached for chaos would face Harval.

Colbey's companions surrounded Sterrane's body, the archers crying uncontrollably, the bard pacing and muttering, and Khitajrah trying to soothe Arduwyn and Sylva. The Freya/*aristiri* spiraled down from the sky to land on a branch overlooking the clearing.

Though Colbey knew he could defend himself, and that little mattered but the coming destruction, he wanted the truth known. "He killed *himself*."

"We saw," Trilless said softly. Wafting thoughts told Colbey that the movements and actions they had undergone in the mind link had actually occurred in plain sight while the thoughts, battles, and mental conversations had remained private. "*We* loosed chaos on the world?" Trilless indicated herself, Carcophan, and Shadimar's body."

Colbey rose, feeling obligated to reply. "Yes."

"You championed law?"

"Balance," Colbey corrected, wiping away tears. "But you knew that from the start."

Carcophan and Trilless exchanged knowing glances. For an instant, their minds touched, and Colbey clearly read the words they shared:

> *Man now or elf*
> *If hate turns to self*
> *And the need to atone should arise:*
> *Break this stone*
> *Call justice home*
> *And follow the path of the wise.*

Without context, Colbey could not understand the significance of their words; but he placed them together with Shadimar's momentary consideration of the blue stones and the sapphire each Wizard clutched in his or her hand.

"Now," Carcophan said softly, and Trilless nodded. Their agreement, though quiet and friendly, seemed as horrible to Colbey as the coming War. As one, they clenched their fingers closed upon the gems; and these shattered, crumbling into azure dust. The wind swirled the glittering fragments, sprinkling them through the air until they became lost against the background of darkening sky. The first droplets struck Colbey, though whether they came from above or from the powdered magic, he could not tell.

For a moment, time stopped. Then, a rumble ground through Colbey's hearing, and the earth quaked in rhythm with the Chaos Staff's beckoning hum. The sky cracked open, with an explosion of thunder. Rain spilled through the clouds, and lightning etched blinding forks against the dismal expanse of horizon.

The shaking stopped, but the storm continued. Grayness bunched, as if forming clouds on the ground, and from the center of that drab configuration stepped the Guardian of the Eighth Task. He stood in a silence that seemed to usurp the crack of thunder and the steady wash of rain, broad-brimmed hat drawn low over his single eye. In each hand, he held a familiar sword. The right looped about Ristoril, the Sword of Tranquillity that Colbey had faced in the hands of Olvaerr's father. The other held the Black Sword of Power, the one that had completed the triangle of ruin, bringing the promise of *Ragnarok* and Episte's madness at once. He tossed the blades, the first landing neatly at Trilless' feet, point stabbing into the ground. Carcophan caught evil's creation by the hilt.

Secodon howled a third time, his voice mellow yet grating as a scream. The sound brought images of hopelessness and agony, driving Colbey to contemplate the crumbling of mankind into oblivion. The world would go on in the same primordial nothingness that it had known before Odin split the forces of law and chaos. But all beings of law, all men, elves, most gods, and their creations would disappear, swallowed by the Destruction.

You could have prevented it, the staff tried to convince Colbey, truly believing its claim.

Colbey knew better. *No. Odin himself could not avert this fate.* Yet even understanding that the End was imminent, and realizing that Odin seemed to have come to destroy his many creations, perhaps before chaos could do it for him, Colbey could not surrender to despair. He had only one charge: mankind. The focus might give him a means where even gods had failed.

Odin's voice, though soft, carried over the thunder. He addressed Carcophan and Trilless. "Do as you must."

Carcophan raised the sword, but his chin sank to his chest. He spoke words Colbey could never hope to understand, the same spell that had ended Shadimar's life. Trilless, too, began an invocation.

"Stop," Colbey said.

The air seemed to chill in an instant. Trilless and Carcophan obeyed, though whether from curiosity or shocked surprise at the Renshai's temerity, he did not know.

The rain drummed on branches and deadfalls. Colbey kept his gaze fixed on the One-Eyed One, ignoring the stares of every creature around him. "Carcophan and Trilless are innocent. They needn't die for my decision or for Shadimar's ignorance." He stepped around the Cardinal Wizards, approaching the AllFather, and every stare followed him. "It was my destiny to wield chaos. How can you blame these two for my decision to switch to law instead?"

Odin's head swiveled to Colbey until the single eye seemed to pierce him with all the sharpness of the spear in his hand. "Destiny?" He laughed. "What do you know of destiny, Kyndig? *I* created the system of the Cardinal Wizards. *I* determined that the Western and Eastern Wizards would, one day, champion law and chaos. And *I* chose to make Western stronger than Eastern precisely because he would wield the more important of the powers." A smile curled from the edges of the god's cheeks, forming so gradually it seemed as if it had been there all along. "It was your *destiny* to wield the Staff of Law, exactly as you did."

Annoyance prickled through Colbey from a nameless source. Something about the gray god's smug talk of destiny and fate irritated the Renshai. He would and had served the gods gladly when the choice had been his own; but no deity, Wizard, or man could turn him into an unwitting pawn.

The rain quickened, lightning striping the clouds in irregular pulses. Odin continued, gaze still locked on Colbey. "The system of the Cardinal Wizards has grown obsolete. You know that. And it has to end before I can set the new order in motion." He made a disdainful gesture of dismissal at Carcophan and Trilless, not bothering to glance toward them. "Carry on."

Colbey pinned the god's fiery stare with his own, two eyes to one giving him the advantage. He could meet Odin's gaze squarely, without need to flicker from eye to eye. "Why bother with a new system? Mankind is doomed, as well as most of the gods; and your own destiny won't spare you. How can a dead god oversee the balance?"

The grin seemed permanently lodged on the gray god's face. "First, Kyndig, the new balance will hinge on a son of Thor. And they, as you know, will survive the *Ragnarok.*"

Colbey knew Odin expected him to keep that balance, and

the realization that he had already dedicated himself to that
cause enraged him. Once again, his actions would fall neatly
into Odin's design.

"Second, unlike the other gods, I have managed to avert
my fate."

The *aristiri* shrieked, fluttering to the ground. The feathers fell away in folds, gracefully revealing Freya's natural
form. Golden bracelets, necklace, and threads from throat to
heel squirmed and glittered with every angry breath. "You
traitor! You pretended not to care. You sat in silence while
the others tried to stop the Destruction, stating only that
gods *would* die. You made us believe our fates could not be
avoided."

All mortal eyes jerked to the goddess in wonder. The Wizards lowered their weapons, for the moment reprieved.

Thunder crashed in Colbey's ears, accompanied by a jagged slash of lightning that spidered between both horizons.
Odin shrugged, the smile still in place. "My nonchalance
was not an act. I knew from the start that some of us had to
die, and since Kyndig's birth that I would cheat the Fates.
What others chose to make of my silence was their own
misperception."

"Bastard!" Freya hissed, the vehemence of her curse making even Colbey cringe.

Odin's massive shoulders rose and fell again. "What matter to you, Lady? You'll survive and your lover with you,
your future bratling one of the few to repopulate the heavens. With Kyndig on my side, I'll defeat the Fenris Wolf;
and I'll live on. If the others wish to survive the *Ragnarok,*
they can find their own Kyndig." The matter finished in his
mind, Odin once more returned his attention to Carcophan
and Trilless, quoting the first prophecy created for the Cardinal Wizards:

"A Sword of Gray,
A Sword of White,
A Sword of Black and chill as night.
Each one forged,
Its craftsman a Mage;
The three Blades together shall close the age.

"When their oath of peace
The Wizards forsake,

Their own destruction they undertake.
Only these Swords
Their craftsmen can slay.
Each Sword shall be blooded the same rueful day.

"When that fateful day comes
The Wolf's Age has begun.
Hati swallows the moon, and Sköll tears up the sun."

Odin finished, "You brought your weird upon yourselves. The time for payment has come."

Colbey did not turn to see the reaction of Odin's command, nor did he attempt to defend the Wizards again. Since the start of the system, each Cardinal Wizard had chosen his or her time of passing. Their lot did not concern him. They would have to champion their own fates now.

Yet for whatever reason, each chose not to try. Magic prickled at Colbey's back, tainted with threat aimed only at themselves. The Wizards' presences winked out of Colbey's mind-sense, and two more corpses joined Shadimar's on the ground.

The transparent barrier that segregated the Renshai tribe disappeared. Cautiously, Mitrian, Rache, Tannin, Modrey, and Tarah approached their friends, the latter carrying the sleeping toddler in her arms.

Colbey watched them walk, their movements crisp, agile, and wary. He reveled in their martial knowledge, finding their potential staggering. The idea of losing them rankled, and a new anger swept him that went far beyond becoming Odin's chosen toy. Whatever hand the AllFather had played in Colbey's development from birth to Wizardhood had ended. Whatever else happened, Colbey would find a way to preserve mankind. Loki had convinced him gods' deaths were an inevitable necessity. That mankind would die, even with the understanding that it would start again from a first man and woman, seemed a travesty he pledged himself and his sword to prevent.

Having spoken his piece and seen to the necessary, Odin turned his attention to what remained. His gaze fell first on Dh'arlo'mé. The elf stood apart from the conflict, attention on the sodden bodies of the Cardinal Wizards he had chosen to join. To Colbey's surprise, Dh'arlo'mé met the god's eye and his fate bravely.

Yet here, Odin tempered his judgment with mercy. He raised his arms, and the two Swords of Power flew back into his hands:

> *"Wizard only in name,*
> *Your Mistress to blame*
> *Her bones rightfully soon entombed.*
> *Go back to the one*
> *Who calls you her son*
> *Alfheim is already doomed."*

As Odin spoke the final word, a slit appeared behind him, a glimmer of light that only brought emphasis to the gloom. Colbey caught a momentary glimpse of bulbous trees and aqua sky before it seemed to swallow Dh'arlo'mé, returning him to his rightful place on the world of elves. As the rent closed, restoring the continuity of ground and sky, Odin clapped the swords together. They seemed to melt, turning liquid before Colbey's startled gaze. Then they came together again into a single, larger blade entity. That, too, lasted moments. The conglomeration disappeared leaving the gray god's hands empty.

Something stirred at Colbey's hip as a presence winked to life in the sheath that had once held the soulless, steel servant that had represented neutrality. Harval seemed to take on a life of its own that fused all the forces of the universe. Yet the image Colbey gained without tapping his mind gift told him it would remain only a tool, a container for powers that had no skill but that given by their wielder, serving the new entity that Odin had selected to guard the balance. Trapped into a role he had already taken willingly, Colbey felt his annoyance flare to rage. Still, he remained silent, ideas swirling through his mind while Odin worked.

Odin chanted again:

> *"Send mankind home*
> *Where they may roam*
> *Until their fate destroys them."*

Another hole appeared in the fabric of place and time, tearing at those remaining on the Fields of Wrath. The force grew stronger, sucking grass, downpour, and sky through the rift, as if to consume them. Colbey held back, letting the

others precede him, fighting the whirlwind of god-created
magic for as long as possible. At length, when no others remained and even the edge of forest had been tugged into the
void, Colbey calmly entered the gate, eyes shut tight against
the flash of light he knew would come. Odin's smug assessment trailed him through:

> *"Always the last*
> *Even your die is cast*
> *Your skill at my side in the War."*

EPILOGUE

Harval felt strange in Colbey's hands. The hilt seemed to vibrate as the worlds' powers settled into a wary compromise, and a high-pitched ringing hammered Colbey's ears until pain knifed through his head. He scanned his mind gift, finding a level at which the resonance of the sword matched that of his thoughts; and the noise faded to silence. The world seemed to gain new focus. As he glanced about the Fields of Wrath, he found color in air and rain. Trees, sky, and people gained a spectrum he had never known existed; and tints he had always believed solitary and solid separated into an assortment whose scope he would never have thought to imagine. The forces of the world had become his to command, the world's balance a burden he had willingly accepted.

The staves lay abandoned on the Fields of Wrath, their menace a ceaseless prickle against Colbey's skin. Rain continued to pound from the sky, though the thunder faded to a distant rumble and the lightning etched its patterns only intermittently against the gray backdrop of sky. The horses left by the magical gate had returned to the fields to graze. After a friendly reuniting with his master, even Frost Reaver had left to join their quiet meal.

Sterrane's body sprawled across gingerly placed stones, Mar Lon guarding him now in death as he had in life. Arduwyn, Sylva, and Rache gathered and shaped wood for a box. They would need to carry the king back to his city for a proper and fitting send-off. Having been introduced, Khitajrah and Mitrian chatted, too far away for Colbey to overhear their discussion. Although Freya seemed to have disappeared, Colbey could feel her presence nearby. Even with the *Ragnarok* inevitable and her brother's and colleagues' lives soon to be forfeit, she had not abandoned Colbey.

Tannin approached Colbey boldly, his gait still stiffened

from Wizard-inflicted injuries. "*Torke,* I can think of nothing I would appreciate more than a spar and lesson from you. Would you grant me that honor?"

Colbey lowered Harval, now fully in tune with its grip and balance. He relished the chance to assess Mitrian's teachings, and he would never deny the Renshai what might become their last spar. Soon, the Great Destruction would begin, if it had not already; and Surtr's fire would scour heaven and earth in a conflagration that would leave no man alive.

Tannin proved only the first of many spars, as every Renshai clamored for one more chance to pit his or her sword against the master swordsman, to get one more teaching session from an unmatchable *torke.* Colbey liked what he saw. Every one of the Renshai had improved, their boldness giving him matches that would have sent him into a crescendo of excitement if not for the responsibilities thrust upon him, the understanding that they would all soon die, and the tantalizing promise of myriad mock battles with Freya. Still, the ceaseless action cleared his mind, twisting reality into new perspectives. By the time Arduwyn's box was completed, Colbey had discovered the answer he sought. And in every way but one, it pleased him.

Respectfully, Colbey joined the gathering around the piled stones. Mar Lon, Arduwyn, Tannin, and Rache had hefted the king's body into the box, using the stones as a dais for the coffin. For several seconds, no one spoke. Nine adults studied the corpse, the face as childlike as the simple wisdom he had embraced and the judgments he had rendered. The royal crest gleamed in branching flashes of lightning, and rain drummed varied pitches on wood, stone, and metal. Every eye added its moisture to the rain-soaked figures huddled around the Westlands' king. Even Colbey could not hold back the tears.

Mar Lon unslung his mandolin, sliding it into playing position. Chords pealed forth, as sorrowful as the gathering yet strong as the ceaseless cascade of rain. Notes slurred into one another, the bard's usual crisp style lost to grief. Clearly, he created the words as he went, the rhyme scheme, intentionally or purposefully, emulating Odin's chants. The trip back to Béarn would give Mar Lon a chance to perfect his talent before playing at the king's final rest. But the Renshai and their friends shared the bard's grief in its raw innocence, undulled by consideration or time:

"All bow your head
The king is dead
No peace left for the world.
His bodyguard
The only bard
In shame his failure hurled.

"He died for naught
No solace bought
The Destruction still a-brewin'
His life could make
Great peace awake.
But now there's only ruin.

"Good-bye Sterrane
All loss, no gain
We wish our king the best
The king is dead
The king is dead
No hope left for the West."

Obediently, all heads dipped low in a silent moment of respect. Colbey felt Khitajrah's approach, and it bothered him. Though she had far less at stake here, in friendship or patriotism, he had expected her not to shatter the tribute.

"I need your help," Khitajrah whispered in his ear.

Without raising his head for a glance, Colbey waved her silent.

"I need your help," Khitajrah repeated softly. She touched his hand with cold steel.

Colbey glanced downward. The flat of Mitrian's sword lay against his fingers, the wolf hilt in Khitajrah's grip.

Colbey inclined his head away from the gathered mourners to indicate they should talk elsewhere. The two moved to the edge of the woods where their conversation would not disturb the others. "She let you borrow it?" Although Colbey had suggested as much to Mitrian during her lesson, he had not expected the Renshai's *torke* to hand her weapon away.

"I want to use it now."

"What?" Hope rose within Colbey, but he kept it guarded. The inadvertent life-restoring property of the sword's magic had seemed insignificant in the face of the wholesale slaughter of mankind, but he had known it would make Khitajrah happy until Surtr's flames took her and her newly restored son. Now he saw an opportunity to plug the last gap in his plan. He shook rain-soaked strands of yellow hair from his eyes.

"I want to use it on the king. Chaos didn't say how it works, though. I thought maybe the last of the Wizards might know."

Though he knew nothing of magic, Colbey stuck with the practicalities. "Are you sure you want to do this?" He tried to hide his excitement, needing to ascertain that Khitajrah had not given up her prize under duress.

"And if his demise brought Justice to any, Celebrate his death For the good of the many."

Colbey recognized the stanza as one her youngest son had written, from the song Mar Lon had performed while they searched for Arduwyn. "I don't understand."

"I'm not sure I do either," Khitajrah admitted. She took Colbey's hand, meeting his gaze with an urgency readable in her eyes even without his gift. He sensed that she wanted him to understand without words and knew she expected him to enter her mind for answers.

Invited, Colbey made the excursion. He explored the frenzied conflict of need, desire, and responsibility that jumbled inseparably in the superficial reaches of her mind. His explanations of the need for balance mingled with myriad other thoughts. She understood the significance of King Sterrane, simplicity incarnate, yet the epitome of equilibrium between the powers. She knew that Cardinal Wizards had made world changing sacrifices for his life, that many people had died to pave the way for his reign. In a world soon fully beset by a ruinous force it little comprehended, Sterrane would have become the wielder of both staves, the pivotal point on which all balance might have rested. Without him, there seemed little need for Colbey to try to salvage the world. Soon enough, it would crumble beneath the eternal struggles of its separate causes.

Khitajrah's insight amazed Colbey. He had not realized just how much he had let her know, nor how much more she would surmise. The woman's love for her now-dead children seemed to occupy at least an equal portion of her thoughts. Yet the poetry of her youngest had made the final decision for her. Ellbaric had reveled in his death even before it had come, finding benefit in the lesson it taught those who came after him. Somehow, Khitajrah would find the victory beneath defeat.

Colbey sensed the last thought as justification. The pain the decision caused Khitajrah battered him in a way the concept could not. She had considered long and hard. Even Ellbaric's insistence that he had not died in vain could not stay the certainty that he had. It could not soften Khitajrah's loss. Yet, even through a mother's grief, Colbey sensed that she knew she had made the right decision.

"Thank you," Colbey said. "And if the world could understand your sacrifice, they'd thank you as well." He made himself a mental promise to see to it that Khitajrah and all of her sons became immortalized in the bards' songs. He accepted the sword.

Understanding did not accompany it, however. It felt like normal steel in his hands, though finely balanced and impossibly sharp. Only one nearby could help fathom its magic. "Freya?" he called tentatively.

The goddess emerged from the forest, yellow hair rainplastered to head and shoulders, her golden form a replacement for the missing sun.

Colbey explained the situation briefly. "Chaos believes the gems in this sword can restore life to a man. We'd like to use it now, but we can't guess how it works. Would you help us?"

Freya sighed. The movement, though slight, sent her clothing into a shimmering dance. "The *Ragnarok* is already started. No action of mine on man's world matters anymore. I'll do what I can." She stared at the huddled and miserable group surrounding Sterrane's body. "But why? Why bring him back only to have him bake in Surtr's fires with the rest of these? It seems more cruelty than kindness."

Colbey smiled. He took Freya's hand, though he sensed their closeness pained Khitajrah, adding fuel to an agony that already raged like a bonfire. Yet Colbey knew it could be no other way. His love and loyalty truly lay with the goddess; it always had. His decision to rescue mankind and the Renshai had already doomed him to follow the other half of his birth heritage. Odin had seen to it that he would take his place among the gods, willingly or otherwise; and Colbey had no intention of doing so without first accomplishing the single goal he had come to place even above his lifelong dream of dying in valiant combat. He and Khitajrah belonged on different worlds. His involved a wife who could challenge him daily, honing his sword skill in a way even his usual practices could not. His involved the responsibilities inherent in a balance so vast and fragile even Odin had not fully trusted himself to moderate its minuscule irregularities and temporary asymmetries. Though she did not know it yet, Khitajrah had a place, too, in Béarn, with an archer who already cared for her, a bard who could eternalize the courage of herself and her sons, and the simplistic king whose life they hoped to restore.

A long and thoughtful pause filled the gap between Freya's question and Colbey's answer. "The system of the Cardinal Wizards failed with time, as Odin knew it would. He wants to put the balance in one being's hands now, and I understand that. But it can't work that way for the same reason Odin couldn't modulate the balance himself. Just as you said, every small action of gods on man's world has massive consequences." He glanced at Khitajrah, knowing she had the facts to comprehend only part of his explanation. "As lifetimes pass, I'll have to become more like my father and less mortal. I can balance law and chaos on the grand scale, but it'll take a mortal to make the fine adjustments on man's world. I can't think of anyone more suited to that than Sterrane. His justice and simple mercy come of raw instinct, nothing more; yet that's the one thing that can't be swayed by the staves he'll keep or by any being. We'll only have to see to it at least one heir carries on his or her father's basic neutrality."

Here, Colbey realized, the Renshai also had a new role toward which he and their goddess would guide them. The tribe would become guardians to the high kingdom and its heirs, a force to assure that the crown passed always to one as guileless as Sterrane.

Freya returned her gaze to Colbey, her hand callused but gentle in his grip. "Kyndig, that's all well and good for the moment. But the *Ragnarok* will bring an end to all mankind, including Sterrane. Why bother?"

"Because . . ." Colbey kept his voice low. All of the stories he had ever read or heard stated that Odin could see all from his high seat, but he could hear no better than a man. Colbey's mind gift told him no one nearby spied on the conversation. Still, he saw no reason to let the knowledge fall on any ears but Khitajrah's and Freya's. ". . . apparently, I'm the force that can alter the course of the *Ragnarok*. Odin believes I must fight at his side, aiding his battle against the Fenris Wolf. Surely, that would rescue the largest number of gods' lives and the strongest as well. But that's never been my goal. I believed Loki when he said several of the gods must die to rescue balance."

Khitajrah stared, lips parted and silent. Clearly, she understood just enough to realize that the level of conversation far exceeded her knowledge.

Freya's hold on Colbey's hand tightened. "Odin's wisdom is unmatchable. He's always right."

"Yes," Colbey admitted. "And that infuriated me."

Freya shrugged. "You get used to it."

"I won't have to. He's going to die." Colbey considered the many actions Odin had called destiny. "So far, nothing he claimed I *had* to do was anything I wouldn't have done anyway. It's easy to say what's already happened is fate. Just because he puts facts together well doesn't mean he can predict the future." In truth, Colbey had often heard this to be Odin's only weakness, a need to understand the future and a failing that seemed inevitable. "And I don't believe in destiny. If there was such a thing, why did Odin need a system of Wizards just to see to it that standard prophecies were fulfilled?"

Khitajrah remained quiet. Freya tried to anticipate Colbey's point. "So you won't help at the *Ragnarok?* Are you saying Odin's mistake is believing you would?"

Colbey released Freya's hand, amused to the edge of laughter. "I'll be there. There's not a Northman in existence who hasn't lived and died for that opportunity. But I won't help Odin." He passed Mitrian's sword back to Khitajrah, freeing his hands to seize both of Freya's and meet her gaze squarely. "According to the legends, your brother Frey will give Surtr a close fight before succumbing to the fire giant's skill. With my help, I believe Frey can kill Surtr. No fires will wash the worlds of man or elf. Mankind, and your brother, will survive while the rest of the events of *Ragnarok* will come to pass." In tune with the balance, Colbey knew Frey's survival would have little effect on it.

Freya considered the words for some time. Colbey could feel her joy buoyed, instantly suppressed by some thought, then allowed to rise again. "That could work," she finally admitted.

"That will work." Colbey harbored no doubts. Since his meeting with Loki, he had realized that mankind's destruction or continuance meant little in the wake of a war between gods. The Cardinal Wizards had taught him that fate was not a constant. For once, Odin would lose; when he placed personal gain over wisdom, his predictions must fail him. This time, Colbey had the upper hand. And, though it felt strange, he saw the necessity. Odin had to die. And mankind would live on in exchange.

The conversation seemed to have come to an end, so Khitajrah directed it back to the matter currently closer at hand. "The sword? Can we save him?" She inclined her head toward Sterrane. The Renshai and their companions had wandered from the coffin, breaking into smaller groups to mourn and console one another. Mitrian and Tannin clung together. Arduwyn talked softly with Mar Lon, who still clutched his mandolin, gaze locked on his king. Modrey and Tarah tended their daughter. Sylva and Rache crouched near the edge of the woods, the redhead stroking Secodon's fur while the wolf licked her face. More dog than wolf now, Shadimar's pet could never return to the wild; and it gladdened Colbey to see that even the animal had found its place with a person who would care for it as least as well as its former master. On Asgard or man's world, Frost Reaver would always have a place at Colbey's side as well.

Freya responded to Khitajrah's question by addressing Colbey. "You're the one with the power to mind link. Look at the magic. See what you find. If you bring her ..." She indicated Khitajrah with a nod. "... you may find traces of chaos' thoughts on the matter. Bring me, and I can interpret."

The concept sounded intriguing, the specifics still vague. "Bring you where?" Colbey asked.

"Into the magic of the gems."

The idea sounded insane. Colbey had never attempted to enter an inanimate object before; experience gave him no reason to believe he would find anything there. Yet an item instilled with magic might prove different. Cautiously, he entered Khitajrah's consciousness, careful to avoid the many private and intimate contemplations. He added Freya to the mix, unable to fully block the vast output of love and knowledge that seemed to merge with his own. He felt a twinge of understanding emerge from Khitajrah, a brief realization that she had never cared for Colbey with the intensity of the goddess. Then, the idea disappeared as larger concerns usurped it. Colbey thrust their combined consciousnesses toward the gem eyes of the hilt.

A web of magic met his gaze, seeming endless and patternless in its scope. Stray bits of chaos, still in Khitajrah's keeping, directed him to a hole in the matrix. The winking colors and twisted netting bore no particular meaning for him, but he divined understand from Freya. Once, the magics had contained the soul of a man, a Renshai slain by illness and thus damned to the cold depths of Hel. A Wizard had held the soul in stasis, unable to restore life, yet keeping it forever entombed in stone. With Freya's help, he traced the darkened areas where Mitrian's shattering of a gem had released the Renshai to his miserable, but appropriate, doom. He located the frayed edges, where chaos' backlash had sparked an unpredicted side effect, the ability of the gems to return life to another.

It seemed the perfect definition of chaos. It could not restore life to the one who sought it, but it would revitalize another at random. The ancient, Hel-locked Renshai had sought reprieve and lost, had paid for the resurrection of a stranger decades or centuries later. Still, though Colbey could define the location of the spell, he had no knowledge of how to trigger it. The holding of three mind links wore on him, and fatigue closed rapidly toward darkness. Defeated, he started to retreat.

Hold! Freya shouted in his head. Light arched from her fingertips in a strand, highlighting the iridescent chaos in a random outline. *Show me the proper place.*

Colbey directed, helping Freya find the precise silhouette of the various areas of magic. Her perception told him that parts had become defunct. Others held the blade polished and sharp. All of these, he avoided, driving full concentration to the matter at hand, the space that had once confined a human soul.

As the last glimmering line fell into place, Colbey withdrew in triumph. *That's it.*

Freya triggered the spell. The area within her pattern

glowed, faintly at first. Then it flashed in a wild explosion, the brightness more a feeling than a sight. The strength of sudden power blasted Colbey, shattering his mental attachment to the sword; and the human/goddess mind link ruptured as well. Flung back into his own body, Colbey found himself on his knees. He glanced first to Freya and Khitajrah, both of whom had managed to remain standing, their gazes fixed on the coffin.

The "corpse" sat up, rubbing black hair and rainwater from his eyes. His voice emerged weak and shaky compared to its usual booming bass. "Me hungry. When eat?" He blinked and squinted, the light obviously painful. Then, apparently recalling his last moment of consciousness, his pale face lapsed into worried creases. "Sylva well?"

Renshai, archers, and bard swung toward the sound. An instant later, they converged on Sterrane, pulling him and one another into frenzied hugs. Their joy defied need for explanation. Surely, they simply believed Arduwyn had pronounced the death too early.

Khitajrah caught Colbey into a final embrace that expressed regret and grief, joy and hope. Familiar with his gift, she saw no need for words. Good-byes seemed unnecessary. Likely, in one way or another, they would meet again.

Colbey returned the hug with sincere affection. Finally, Khitajrah pulled free. Turning, she headed toward the frenzied hubbub of shouting, cheering, and tears without a backward glance.

The staves remained on the ground, Sterrane's problem and property now. The rain continued to fall steadily, though the lightning and thunder had died away. Colbey took Freya's arm. "And now for a battle and, if you'll have me, a wedding."

"A battle? Leave it to Kyndig to make the *Ragnarok* sound like a border skirmish." Freya laughed, the sound as lyrical as Mar Lon's lightest ballad. Colbey had given her a certainty of hope where before had lain only destruction. "And as to marriage . . ." She caught at the gold ring on his finger that she had given him months ago. "I already own you."

"Own me?" Colbey tossed Freya's hand away. "More powerful gods than you have tried to run my life."

"Yes," Freya admitted, blue eyes alight with pleasure. "But I've succeeded."

"Have you?" Colbey scooped the goddess into his arms, the warmth of her closeness exciting beyond any battle joy. He carried her into the woods, hoping that, in the moments or hours before the *Ragnarok* started, he would have time to prove her right.

APPENDIX

People

Northmen

Årvåkir (AWR-vaw-keer)—NORDMIRIAN. Odin's name for Olvaerr Kirinsson. Literally: "Vigilant One."

Asnete (Ahss-NETT-eh)—RENSHAI. A valiant, female warrior who had a tryst with Thor.

Calistin the Bold (Ka-LEES-tin)—RENSHAI. Colbey's father.

Colbey Calistinsson (KULL-bay)—RENSHAI. The leader of the Renshai and the Western Wizard, a.k.a. The Death-seeker, a.k.a. The Golden Prince of Demons.

Episte Rachesson (Ep-PISS-teh)—RENSHAI. Rache Kallmirsson's son, an orphan raised by Colbey. Killed by Colbey after being driven mad by chaos.

Himinthrasir (HIM-in-thrah-seer)—RENSHAI. Colbey's wife, long dead.

Kyndig (KAWN-dee)—Colbey Calistinsson. Lit: "Skilled One."

Menglir (MEN-gleer)—RENSHAI. One of the two founders of the Western Renshai. See also Sjare.

Olvaerr Kirinsson—(OHL-eh-vair) NORDMIRIAN. Valr Kirin's son.

Peusen Raskogsson (Pyoo-SEN Rass-KOG-son)—NORDMIRIAN. One-handed general of Iaplege. Brother of Valr Kirin.

Rache Kallmirsson—(RACK-ee)—RENSHAI. Santagithi's guard captain, now dead. Episte Rachesson's father.

Ranilda Battlemad (Ran-HEEL-da)—RENSHAI. Colbey's mother.

Sivard (See-VARD)—ASGARDBYRIAN. King of Asgardbyr.

Sjare (See-YAR-eh)—RENSHAI. Founded the Western Renshai with Menglir.

Tenja (TEN-ya)—VIKERIAN. King of Vikerin.

Valr Kirin (Vawl-KEER-in)—NORDMIRIAN. Lieutenant to the high king in Nordmir and Trilless' champion. Peusen's brother. Killed in single combat with Colbey.

Westerners

Arduwyn (AR-dwin)—ERYTHANIAN. A one-eyed hunter.

Avenelle (AV-eh-nell)—AHKTARIAN. Elderly woman on Ahktar's tribunal.

Bacshas (BOCK-shahz)—PUDARIAN. Nephew to deceased King Gasir. Oldest of four nephews.

Baran (BAYR-in)—BÉARNIDE. The guard captain of Béarn.

Barder (BARR-der)—BÉARNIDE. Baran's father. A loyal court guard of usurped King Valar. Killed in the coup.

Bel (BELL)—PUDARIAN. Arduwyn's wife.

Clywid (CLIGH-wid)—AHKTARIAN. A man on Ahktar's tribunal.

Davrin (DAV-vrin)—MIXED WESTERN. A previous bard. Mar Lon's father.

Fyn (FINN)—PUDARIAN. A horse merchant. Proprietor of Crossroad Fyn's.

Garn—An escaped gladiator from Santagithi's town. Mitrian's husband and father of Rache Garnsson.

Gasir (GAH-zeer)—PUDARIAN. The previous king of Pudar. Killed in the Great War.

Gertrina (Ger-TREE-na)—AHKTARIAN. The tailor's wife.

Haim (Haym)—PUDARIAN. Tokar's apprentice, now dead.

Jahiran (Jah-HEER-in)—PUDARIAN. The first bard.

Lirtensa (Leer-TEN-sa)—PUDARIAN. A dishonest guard.

Lonriya (Lon-REE-ya)—Mar Lon's great-grandmother. Creator of the *lonriset.*

Mar Lon (MAR-LONN)—PUDARIAN. Davrin's son. The current bard.

Martinel (MAR-tin-ell)—an ancestor of Mar Lon.

Mitrian (MIH-tree-in)—Santagithi's daughter, Garn's wife, and mother of Rache Garnsson.

Modrey (MOE-dray)—WESTERN RENSHAI. Tarah's husband.

Orlis (OR-liss)—ERYTHANIAN. The king of Erythane.

Oswald (OZ-wald)—AHKTARIAN. The prince of Ahktar.

Rache Garnsson (RACK-ee)—son of Mitrian and Garn.

Randil (Ran-DEEL)—WESTERN RENSHAI. Leader of the Western Renshai. Tannin's father.

Rathelon (RATH-eh-lon)—BÉARNIDE. Sterrane's cousin. Killed by Garn because of attempts to usurp the throne.

Santagithi (San-TAG-ih-thigh)—the Westland's best strategist, now dead. Mitrian's father.

Sharya (SHAR-yah)—ERYTHANIAN. A young, loose woman.

Sterrane (Stir-RAIN)—BÉARNIDE. Valar's only surviving child. The king of Béarn.

Sylva (SILL-va)—MIXED WESTERN. Arduwyn's and Bel's daughter.

Tannin Randilsson (TAN-in)—WESTERN RENSHAI. Randil's son and Menglir's great-grandson.

Tarah Randilsdatter (TAIR-a)—WESTERN RENSHAI. Randil's daughter. Tannin's sister. Modrey's wife and mother to Vashi.

Unamer (YOO-na-mer)—AHKTARIAN. The judge.

Valar (VAY-lar)—BÉARNIDE. Previous king of Béarn murdered by his twin brother for the throne. Sterrane's father.

Vashi (VASH-ee)—WESTERN RENSHAI. Tarah's and Modrey's daughter.

Verrall (VAIR-al)—PUDARIAN. The king of Pudar.

Viridis (VEER-ih-diss)—BÉARNIDE. A lieutenant of the guards.

Whidishar (WID-ih-shar)—AHKTARIAN. A hunter.

Xanranis (Zan-RAN-ihs)—BÉARNIDE. Sterrane's son. Heir to the Béarnian throne.

Xylain (ZIGH-layn)—AHKTARIAN. A member of Ahktar's tribunal.

Easterners

Bahmyr (BIGH-meer)—STALMIZEAN. Khitajrah's and Harrsha's middle son.

Chezrith (CHAZ-rayth)—PROHOTHRAN. A swordmistress. Carcophan's apprentice.

Diarmad (Dee-AR-mid)—STALMIZEAN. A veteran of the Great War with the West.

Ellbaric (Al-BAIR-ik)—STALMIZEAN. Khitajrah's and Harrsha's youngest son. Killed in the Great War.

Fentraprim (FAN-trih-prim)—PROHOTHRAN. Chezrith's father.

Harrsha (HAR-sha)—STALMIZEAN. One of Siderin's two first lieutenants. Killed in the Great War by Mitrian and Rache Kallmirsson.

Khitajrah (Kay-TAZH-ra)—STALMIZEAN. Harrsha's widow. Shortened form: Khita (KAY-ta).

Narisen (NAIR-eh-son)—STALMIZEAN. One of Siderin's two first lieutenants. Killed in the Great War by Colbey Calistinsson.

Nichus (NEEK-is)—STALMIZEAN. Khitajrah's and Harrsha's oldest son. Killed in the Great War.

Siderin (SID-er-in)—STALMIZEAN. Previous general/king of the Eastlands and Carcophan's previous champion. Killed in the Great War.

Waleis (Wah-LAY-us)—STALMIZEAN. A veteran of the Great War. Friend of Diarmad.

Outworlders

The Captain—ALFHEIM. An elf who captains the ship that takes the Cardinal Wizards to their Meeting Island.

Dh'arlo'mé (ZHAR-loh-may)—ALFHEIM. Trilless' apprentice.

quaracks (QUAR-aks)—man-eating humanoid creatures with animal intelligence.

Animals

Formynder (for-MEWN-derr)—an *aristiri* hawk.

Frost Reaver—Colbey's white stallion.

Precious Prince of Gold—a young buckskin stallion for sale at Crossroad Fyn's.

Secodon (SEK-o-don)—Shadimar's wolf companion.

Swiftwing—a red falcon. The Cardinal Wizards' messenger.

Gods & Wizards

Northern

Aegir (AJ-eer)—Northern god of the sea.

Alfheim (ALF-highm)—The world of elves. Frey's home.

Asgard (AHSS-gard)—The world of the gods.

Baldur (BALL-der)—Northern god of beauty and gentleness who will rise from the dead after the *Ragnarok.*

Beyla (BEY-lah)—Frey's human servant. Wife of Byggvir.

The Bifrost Bridge (BEE-frost)—The bridge between Asgard and man's world.

Bragi (BRAH-gee)—Northern god of poetry.

Byggvir (BEWGG-veer)—Frey's human servant. Husband of Beyla.

Colbey Calistinsson (KULL-bay)—The Current Western Wizard.

The Fenris Wolf (FEN-ris)—the Great Wolf. The evil son of Loki. Also called Fenrir (FEN-reer).

Frey (FRAY)—Northern god of rain, sunshine, and fortune.

Freya (FRAY-a)—Frey's sister. Northern goddess of battle.

Frigg (FRIGG)—Odin's wife. Northern goddess of fate.

Gladsheim (GLAD-shighm)—"Place of Joy." Sanctuary of the gods.

Hati (HAH-tee)—the wolf who swallows the moon at the Ragnarok.

Hel—(HEHL) Northern goddess of the cold underrealm for those who do not die in valorous combat.

Hel—(HEHL) The underrealm ruled by the goddess, Hel.

Heimdall (HIGHM-dahl)—Northern god of vigilance and father of mankind.

Hlidskjalf (HLID-skyalf)—Odin's high seat from which he can survey the worlds.

Hod (HODD)—Blind god, a son of Odin. Currently dead, he is fated to return with Baldur after the *Ragnarok.*

Honir (HON-eer)—An indecisive god who will survive the *Ragnarok.*

Idun (EE-dun)—Bragi's wife. Keeper of the golden apples of youth.

Kvasir (KWAH-seer)—A wise god, murdered by dwarves, whose blood was brewed into the mead of poetry.

Loki (LOH-kee)—Northern god of fire and guile.

Magni (MAG-nee)—Thor's son. Northern god of might.

Mana-garmr (MAH-nah Garm)—Northern wolf destined to extinguish the sun with the blood of men at the *Ragnarok.*

The Midgard Serpent—A massive, poisonous serpent destined to kill and be killed by Thor at the *Ragnarok.* Loki's son.

Mimir (MIM-eer)—Wise god who was killed by gods. Odin preserved his head and uses it as an adviser.

Modi (MOE-dee)—Thor's son. Northern god of blood wrath.

Njord (NYORR)—Frey's and Freya's father.

Norns—The keepers of past, present, and future.

Odin (OH-din)—Northern leader of the pantheon. Father of the gods a.k.a The AllFather.

Odrorir (OD-dror-eer)—The cauldron containing the mead of poetry brewed from Kvasir's blood.

Ran (RAHN)—Wife of Aegir.

Sif (SIFF)—Thor's wife. Northern goddess of fertility and fidelity.

Skoll (SKOEWL)—Northern wolf who will swallow the sun at the Ragnarok.

Syn (SIN)—Northern goddess of justice and innocence.

Surtr (SURT)—The king of fire giants. Destined to kill Frey and destroy the worlds of elves and men with fire at the *Ragnarok.*

Thor—Northern god of storms, farmers, and law.

Thrudr (THRUDD)—Thor's daughter. Goddess of power.

Trilless (Trill-ESS)—Northern Wizard. Champion of goodness and the Northlands.

Tyr (TEER)—Northern one-handed god of war and faith.

Valhalla (VAWL-holl-a)—The heaven for the souls of dead warriors killed in valiant combat. At the *Ragnarok,* these souls will assist the gods in battle.

Vali (VAHL-ee)—Odin's son. Destined to survive the *Ragnarok.*

The Valkyries (VAWL-ker-ees)—The Choosers of the Slain. Warrior women who choose which souls go to Valhalla on the battlefield.

Vidar (VEE-dar)—Son of Odin. He is destined to avenge his father's death at the *Ragnarok* by slaying the Fenris wolf, and he will survive the *Ragnarok.*

The Wolf Age—The sequence of events immediately preceding the *Ragnarok* during which Sköll swallows the sun, Hati mangles the moon, and the Fenris Wolf runs free.

Western

Aphrikelle (Ah-fri-KELL)—Western goddess of spring.

Ascof (AZ-kov)—The eighteenth Eastern Wizard. Obsessed with demon summonings. Was finally killed by a self-summoned demon in year 9083.

Cathan (KAY-than)—Western goddess of war, specifically hand to hand combat. Twin to Kadrak.

Dakoi (Dah-KOY)—Western god of death.

Drero (DREY-roh)—The twenty-second Eastern Wizard. The builder of the hidden escape route from Béarn's castle.

The Faceless god—Western god of winter.

Firfan (FEER-fan)—Western god of archers and hunters.

Gherhan (GUR-han)—The sixth Eastern Wizard. Killed by a demon in 3319.

Itu (EE-too)—Western goddess of knowledge and truth.

Jalona (Ja-LOHN-a)—The twentieth Eastern Wizard. Talked Odin into making the bards also the personal bodyguards of the Béarnian kings.

Kadrak (KAD-drak)—Western god of war. Twin to Cathan.

Niejal the Mad (Nee-EJ-al)—The ninth Western Wizard. Paranoid and suicidal.

Ruaidhri (Roo-AY-dree)—Western leader of the pantheon.

Shadimar (SHAD-ih-mar)—Eastern Wizard. Champion of neutrality and the Westlands.

Sudyar (SOO-dee-yar)—The fourteenth Western Wizard. Paranoid and agoraphobic.

Suman (SOO-man)—Western god of farmers and peasants.

Tokar (TOE-kar)—Western Wizard. Champion of neutrality and the Westlands.

Weese (WEESSS)—Western god of winds.

Yvesen (IV-e-sen)—Western god of steel and women.

Zera'im (ZAIR-a-eem)—Western god of honor.

Eastern

Carcophan (KAR-ka-fan)—Southern Wizard. Champion of evil and the Eastlands.

God—the only name for the bird/man god of the Leukenyans. Created by Siderin.

Havlar (HEV-ih-lar)—The first Southern Wizard.

Sheriva (Sha-REE-vah)—Omnipotent, only god of the Eastlands.

Outworld Gods

Ciacera (See-a-SAIR-a)—The goddess of life on the sea
floor who takes the form of an octopus.
Mahaj (Ma-HAJ)—The god of dolphins.
Morista (Moor-EES-tah)—The god of swimming creatures
who takes the form of a seahorse.

Foreign words

a (ah)—EASTERN. "From."
ailar (IGH-lar)—EASTERN. "To bring."
al (AIL)—EASTERN. The first person singular pronoun.
anem (ON-um)—BARBARIAN. "Enemy"; Usually used in
reference to a specific race or tribe with whom the barbarian's tribe is at war.
aristiri (ah-riss-TEER-ee)—TRADING. A breed of singing
hawks.
årvåkir (AWR-vaw-keer)—NORTHERN. "Vigilant one."
baronshei (ba-RON-shigh)—TRADING. "Bald."
bein (bayn)—NORTHERN. "Legs."
bleffy (BLEFF-ee)—WESTERN/TRADING. A child's euphemism for nauseating.
bolboda (bawl-BOE-da)—NORTHERN. "Evilbringer."
brishigsa weed (brih-SHIG-sah)—WESTERN. A specific
leafy weed with a translucent, red stem. A universal antidote to several common poisons.
brorin (BROAR-in)—RENSHAI. "Brother."
brunstil (BRUNN-steel)—NORTHERN. A stealth maneuver
learned from barbarians by the Renshai. Literally: "brown
and still."
chroams (krohms)—WESTERN. Specific coinage of copper,
silver, or gold.
corpa (KOR-pa)—WESTERN. "Brotherhood, town." Literally: "Body."
demon (DEE-mun)—ANCIENT TONGUE. A creature of
magic.
djem (dee-YEM)—NORTHERN. "Demon."
Einherjar (IGHN-herr-yar)—NORTHERN. The dead warriors in Valhalla.

eksil (EHK-seel)—NORTHERN. "Exile."

fafra (FAH-fra)—TRADING. "To eat."

feflin (FEF-linn)—TRADING. "To hunt."

formynder (for-MEWN-derr)—NORTHERN. "Guardian, teacher."

Forsvarir (Fours-var-EER)—RENSHAI. A specific disarming maneuver.

frichen-karboh (FRATCH-in kayr-BOH) EASTERN. Widow. Literally: "manless woman, past usefulness."

frilka (FRAIL-kah)—EASTERN. The most formal title for a woman, elevating her nearly to the level of a man.

galn (gahln)—NORTHERN. "Ferociously crazy."

garlet (GAR-let)—WESTERN. A type of wildflower believed to have healing properties.

garn (garn)—NORTHERN. "Yarn."

Gerlinr (Gerr-LEEN)—RENSHAI. A specific aesthetic and difficult sword maneuver.

granshy (GRANN-shigh)—WESTERN. "Plump."

gullin (GULL-in)—NORTHERN. "Golden."

hadongo (hah-DONG-oh)—WESTERN. A twisted, hard-wood tree.

Harval (Harr-VALL)—ANCIENT TONGUE. "The gray blade."

hastivillr (has-tih-VEEL)—RENSHAI. A sword maneuver.

kadlach (KOD-lok; the ch has a guttural sound)—TRADING. A vulgar term for a disobedient child; akin to brat.

kenya (KEN-ya)—WESTERN. "Bird."

kjaelnabnir (kyahl-NAHB-neer)—RENSHAI. Temporary name for a child until a hero's name becomes available.

kinesthe (Kin-ESS-teh)—NORTHERN. "Strength."

kolbladnir (kol-BLAW-neer)—NORTHERN. "The cold-bladed."

kraell (kray-ELL)—ANCIENT TONGUE. A type of demon dwelling in the deepest region of chaos' realm.

kyndig (KAWN-dee)—NORTHERN. "Skilled one."

lessakit (LAYS-eh-kight)—EASTERN. A message.

leuk (LUKE)—WESTERN. "White."

loki (LOH-kee)—NORTHERN. "Fire."

lonriset (LON-ri-set)—WESTERN. A ten-stringed musical instrument.

lynstreik (LEEN-strayk)—RENSHAI. A sword maneuver.

magni (MAG-nee)—NORTHERN. "Might."

meirtrin (MAYR-trinn)—TRADING. A specific breed of nocturnal rodent.

mirack (merr-AK)—WESTERN. A specific type of hardwood tree with white bark.

mjollnir (MYOLL-neer)—NORTHERN. Mullicrusher.

modi (MOE-dee)—NORTHERN. "Wrath."

Morshoch (MORE-shock)—ANCIENT TONGUE. "Sword of darkness."

mynten (MIN-tin)—NORTHERN. A specific type of coin.

nådenal (naw-deh-NAHL)—RENSHAI. Literally: "needle of mercy." A silver, guardless, needle-shaped dagger constructed during a meticulous religious ceremony and used to end the life of an honored, suffering ally or enemy, then melted in the victim's pyre.

noca (NOE-ka)—BÉARNIDE. "Grandfather."

odelhurtig (OD-ehl-HEWT-ih)—RENSHAI. A sword maneuver.

oopey (OO-pey)—WESTERN/TRADING. A child's euphemism for an injury.

orlorner (oor-LEERN-ar)—EASTERN. "To deliver to."

pike (PIKE)—NORTHERN. "Mountain."

prins (PRINS)—NORTHERN. "Prince."

ranweed—WESTERN. A specific type of wild plant.

raynshee (RAYN-shee)—TRADING. "Elder."

rexin (RAYKS-inn)—EASTERN. "King."

rhinsheh (ran-SHAY)—EASTERN. "Morning."

richi (REE-chee)—WESTERN. A specific breed of songbird.

rintsha (RINT-shah)—WESTERN. "Cat."

Ristoril (RISS-tor-ril)—ANCIENT TONGUE. "Sword of tranquillity."

sangrit (SAN-grit)—BARBARIAN. To form a blood bond.

skjald (SKYAWLD)—NORTHERN. Musician chronicler.

svergelse (sverr-GELL-seh)—RENSHAI. "Sword figures practiced alone; katas."

talvus (TAL-vus)—WESTERN. "Midday."

thrudr (THRUDD)—NORTHERN. "Power, might."

torke (TOR-keh)—RENSHAI. "Teacher, sword instructor."

Tvinfri (TWINN-free)—RENSHAI. A disarming maneuver.

ulvstikk (EWLV-steek)—RENSHAI. A sword maneuver.

uvakt (oo-VAKT)—RENSHAI. "The unguarded." A term for children whose *kjaelnabnir* becomes a permanent name.

Valhalla (VAWL-holl-a)—NORTHERN. "Hall of the Slain."
  The walled "heaven" for brave warriors slain in battle.
Valkyrie (VAWL-kerr-ee)—NORTHERN. "Chooser of the
  Slain."
valr (VAWL)—NORTHERN. "Slayer."
Vestan (VAYST-in)—EASTERN. "The Westlands."
waterroot—TRADING. An edible sea plant.
wisule (WISS-ool)—TRADING. A foul-smelling, disease-
  carrying breed of rodents which has many offspring because the adults will abandon them when threatened.

Places

Northlands

The area north of the Weathered Mountains and west of the
  Great Frenum Range. The Northmen live in eighteen
  tribes, each with its own town surrounded by forest and
  farmland. The boundaries change, and the map is correct
  for the year 11,240:
Asci (ASS-kee)—Home to the Ascai. Patron: Aegir.
Blathe (BLAYTH-eh)—Home to the Blathe. Patron: Aegir.
Drymir (DRY-meer)—Home to the Drymirians. Patron:
  Frey.
Devil's Island—an island in the Amirannak. A home to the
  Renshai after their exile.
Dvaulir (Dwah-LEER)—home to the Dvaulirians. Patron:
  Thor.
Erd (URD)—Home to the Erdai. Patron: Freya.
Farbutiri (Far-byu-TEER-ee)—Home to the Farbui. Patron:
  Aegir.
Gilshnir (GEELSH-neer)—Home to the Gilshni. Patron: Tyr.
Gjar (GYAR)—Home to the Gjar. Patron: Heimdall.
Kor N'rual (KOR en-ROOL)—Sacred crypts near Nord-
  mir.
Nordmir (NORD-meer)—The Northland's high kingdom.
  Home to the Nordmirians. Patron: Odin.
Othkin (OTH-keen)—Home to the Othi. Patron: Aegir &
  Frigg.
Renshi (Ren-SHEE)—Original home of the Renshai, now a
  part of Thortire. Patron: Sif & Modi.

Shamir (Sha-MEER)—Home of the Shamirins. Patron: Freya.

Skrytil (SKRY-teel)—Home of the Skrytila. Patron: Thor.

Svelbni (SWELL-nee)—home of the Svelbnai. Patron: Baldur.

Talmir (TAHL-meer)—Home of the Talmirians. Patron: Frey.

Thortire (Thor-TEER-eh)—Home of the Thortirians. Patron: Thor.

Ti (Tee)—The original name for Devil's Island.

Varli (VAR-lee)—Home of the Varlians. Patron: Frey & Freya.

Vikerin (Vee-KAIR-in)—Home of the Vikerians. Patron: Thor.

Westlands

The Westlands are bounded by the Great Frenum mountains to the east, the Weathered Mountains to the north, and the sea to the west and south. In general, the cities become larger and more civilized as the land sweeps westward. The central area is packed with tiny farm towns dwarfed by lush farm fields that, over time, have nearly coalesced. The easternmost portions of the Westlands are forested, with sparse towns and rare barbarian tribes. To the south lies an uninhabited tidal plain.

Ahktar (AHK-tar)—One of the largest central farm towns.

Auer (OUR)—A small town in the eastern section.

Béarn (Bay-ARN)—The high kingdom. A mountain city.

Bellenet Fields (Bell-e-NAY)—A tourney field in Erythane.

Bruen (Broo-EN)—A medium-sized city near Pudar.

Corpa Bickat (KORE-pa Bi-KAY)—A large city.

Corpa Leukenya (KORE-pa Loo-KEN-ya)—Home of the cult of the white bird, created by Siderin.

Corpa Schaull (KORE-pa Shawl)—A medium-sized city; one of the "Twin Cities" (see Frist).

The Dun Stag—A Pudarian tavern famous for its ale and frequented by travelers and merchants.

Erythane (AIR-eh-thane)—A large city closely allied with Béarn. Famous for its knights.

The Fields of Wrath—Plains near Erythane. Home to the Western Renshai.

Frist (FRIST)—A medium-sized city; one of the "Twin Cities" (see Corpa Schaull).

Granite Hills—A small, low range of mountains.

Great Frenum Mountains (FREN-um)—Towering, impassable mountains that divide the Eastlands from the Westlands and Northlands.

Greentree—A tiny farmtown.

The Hungry Lion—a Pudarian tavern frequented by locals.

Iaplege (EE-a-pleej)—A secret gathering of cripples, criminals, and outcasts.

The Knight's Rest—An inn in Erythane.

Loven (Low-VENN)—A medium-sized city.

The Merchant's Haven—The inn in Wynix.

Myrcidë (Meer-si-DAY)—A town of legendary wizards, now in ruins.

Porvada (Poor-VAH-da)—A medium-sized city.

Pudar (Poo-DAR)—The largest city of the West; the great trade center.

The Road of Kings—The legendary route by which the Eastern Wizard is believed to have rescued the high king's heir after a bloody coup.

Town of Santagithi—A medium-sized town, relatively young.

Shidrin (SHIH-drin)—A farmtown.

Sholton-Or (SHOLE-tin OR)—A Western farm town.

Strinia (STRINN-ee-a)—A small, barbarian settlement.

The Western Plains—A barren salt flat.

Wolf Point—a rock formation in the forest surrounding Erythane.

Wynix (Why-NIX)—A farmtown.

Eastlands

The area east of the Great Frenum Mountains. It is a vast, overpopulated wasteland filled with crowded cities and eroded fields. Little forest remains.

LaZar the Decadent (LA-zar)—A poor, dirty city.

Prohothra (Pree-HATH-ra)—A large city.

Rock of Peace—A stone near the road from Rozmath to Stalmize where the bard, Mar Lon, preached peace.

Rozmath (ROZZ-mith)—A medium-sized city.

Stalmize (STAHL-meez)—The Eastern high kingdom.

Tower of Night—A single, black tower originally built by Carcophan's magic, then rebuilt with normal materials.

Bodies of Water

Amirannak Sea (A-MEER-an-nak)—The northernmost ocean.

Brunn River (BRUN)—A muddy river in the Northlands.

Conus River (KONE-uss)—A shared river of the Eastlands and Westlands.

Icy River—A cold, Northern river.

Jewel River—One of the rivers that flows to Trader's Lake.

Perionyx River (Peh-ree-ON-ix)—A Western river.

Southern Sea—The southernmost ocean.

Trader's Lake—A harbor for trading boats in Pudar.

Trader's River—The main route for overwater trade.

Objects/Systems/Events

The Bards—A familial curse passed to the oldest child, male or female, of a specific family. The curse specifically condemns the current bard to obsessive curiosity but allows him to impart his learning only in song. A condition added by the Eastern Wizards compels each to serve as the personal bodyguard to the current king of Béarn as well.

Cardinal Wizards—A system of balance created by Odin in the beginning of time consisting of four, near immortal opposing guardians of evil, neutrality, and goodness who are tightly constrained by Odin's Laws.

The Great War—A massive war fought between the Eastland army and the combined forces of the Westlands.

Harval—"The Gray Blade." The neutral Sword of Power (see Swords of Power).

The Knights of Erythane—An elite guardian unit for the king of Erythane that also serves the higher king in Béarn in shifts. Steeped in rigid codes of dress, manner, conduct, and chivalry they are famed throughout the world.

Kolbladnir—"The Cold-bladed." A magic sword commissioned by Frey to combat Surtr at the *Ragnarok*.

Mjollnir—"Mullicrusher." Thor's gold, short-handled hammer so heavy that only he can lift it.

Morshoch—"The Sword of Darkness." The evil Sword of Power (see Swords of Power).

The Necklace of the Brisings—A necklace worn by the goddess Freya and forged by dwarves from "living gold."

The Pica Stone—A clairsentient sapphire. One of the rare items with magical power.

Ragnarok (ROW-na-rok)—"The Destruction of the Powers." The prophesied time when men, elves, and nearly all of the gods will die.

Ristoril—"The Sword of Tranquillity." The good Sword of Power (see Swords of Power).

The Sea Seraph—The ship owned by an elf known only as the Captain that sails the northern seas.

The Seven Tasks of Wizardry—A series of tasks designed by the gods to test the power and worth of the Cardinal Wizards' chosen successors.

Swords of Power—Three magical swords crafted by the Cardinal Wizards and kept on the plane of magic except when in the hands of a Wizard's champion. It is prophesied that the world will end if all three are brought into the world at once. This event has occurred. (See Ristoril, Morshoch, and Harval).

The Trobok—"The Book of the Faithful." A scripture that guides the lives of Northmen. It is believed that daily reading from the book assists Odin in holding chaos at bay from the world of law.

Lines of the Cardinal Wizards

Western

Reign	Name	Sex	Apprenticeship	Notes
0–747	Rudiger	male	– – –	
747–1167	Montroy	male	695–747	
1167–1498	Jaela	female	1122–1167	
1498–2013	Melandry	female	1460–1498	
2013–2632	Dorn	male	1977–2013	
2632–2933	Tellyn	male	2599–2632	
2933–3759	Dane	male	2880–2933	
3759–4741	Annika	female	3705–3759	
4741–5085	Niejal	male	4691–4741	*
5085–5633	Bael	male	5020–5085	
5633–6236	Renata	female	5602–5633	
6236–6535	Caulin	male	6178–6236	
6535–7455	Sonjia	female	6500–6535	
7455–7926	Sudyar	male	7406–7455	**
7926–8426	Shelvyan	male	7878–7926	
8426–8814	Natalia	female	8380–8426	
8814–9522	Rebah	female	8771–8814	
9522–10,194	Muir	female	9476–9522	
10,194–10,556	Vikeltrin	male	10,146–10,194	
10,556–11,225	Tokar	male	10,500–10,556	***
11,225–	Colbey	male	none	

*Insane
**No contact with other Wizards
***Passed title to a visiting Renshai rather than his trained successor to
  purge insanity from line

Eastern

Reign	Name	Sex	Apprenticeship	Notes
0–636	Kadira	female	– – –	
636–934	Rhynnel	female	601–636	
934–1299	Raf	male	897–934	
1299–2086	Aklir	male	1258–1299	
2086–2988	Trinn	female	2057–2086	
2988–3319	Gherhan	male	2940–2988	*
3319–3768	Benghta	female	3317–3319	
3768–4278	Shorfin	male	3742–3768	
4278–4937	Annber	female	4246–4278	
4937–5439	MiKay	male	4900–4937	
5439–5818	Takian	male	5400–5439	
5818–6298	Seguin	male	5788–5818	
6298–6657	Resa	female	6265–6298	
6657–7221	Elcott	male	6612–6657	
7221–7665	L'effrich	female	7180–7221	
7665–7971	Dandriny	female	7640–7665	
7971–8289	Mylynn	male	7941–7971	
8289–9083	Ascof	male	8243–8289	**
9098–9426	Pinahar	male	– – –	
9426–9734	Jalona	female	9389–9426	***
9734–10,221	Zibetha	female	9700–9734	
10,221–10,737	Drero	male	10,187–10,221	****
10,737–11,126	Donnell	male	10,700–10,737	
11,126–	Shadimar	male	11,000–11,126	

*killed by a demon
**killed by a demon
***Built the escape route from Béarn's castle
****established the bards as the Béarnian kings' personal bodyguards

Northern

Reign	Name	Sex	Apprenticeship	Notes
0–790	Tertrilla	female	– – –	
790–1276	Mendir	male	743–790	
1276–1897	Reeguar	male	1217–1276	
1897–2739	Ranulf	male	1848–1897	
2739–3138	Chane	male	2688–2739	
3138–3614	Sigrid	female	3087–3138	
3614–4128	Quisiria	female	3570–3614	
4128–4792	Brill	male	4083–4128	
4792–5289	Xansiki	female	4751–4792	
5289–5854	Johirild	male	5254–5289	
5854–6531	Disa	female	5813–5854	
6531–7249	Tagrin	male	6492–6531	
7249–7747	Elthor	male	7202–7249	
7747–8369	Frina	female	7700–7747	
8369–8954	Yllen	female	8312–8369	
8954–9628	Alengrid	female	8922–8954	
9628–10,244	Sval	male	9590–9628	
10,244–10,803	Giddrin	male	10,210–10,244	
10,803–	Trilless	female	10,762–10,803	

Southern

Reign	Name	Sex	Apprenticeship	Notes
0–810	Havlar	male	– – –	
810–1306	Kaffrint	male	767–810	
1306–1821	Pelchrin	male	1270–1306	
1821–2798	Schatza	female	1762–1821	
2798–3510	Ocrell	male	2750–2798	
3510–4012	Laurn	male	3461–3510	
4012–4690	Quart	male	3954–4012	*
4690–5189	Ufi	male	4687–4690	
5189–5925	Achorfin	female	5130–5189	
5925–6617	Mir	female	5872–5925	
6617–7217	Nalexia	male	6574–6617	
7217–7793	Buchellin	male	7177–7217	
7793–8508	Amta	male	7747–7793	
8508–8991	Kaleira	female	8450–8508	
8991–9614	Zittich	male	8940–8991	
9614–10,284	Pladnor	male	9565–9614	
10,284–11,002	Bontu	male	10,220–10,284	
11,002–	Carcophan	male	10,968–11,002	

*killed by Ristoril

Mickey Zucker Reichert

THE RENSHAI CHRONICLES

☐ BEYOND RAGNAROK   UE2701—$6.99
☐ PRINCE OF DEMONS   UE2759—$6.99
☐ THE CHILDREN OF WRATH   UE2860—$6.99

THE RENSHAI TRILOGY

☐ THE LAST OF THE RENSHAI: Book 1   UE2503—$6.99
☐ THE WESTERN WIZARD: Book 2   UE2520—$6.99
☐ CHILD OF THUNDER: Book 3   UE2549—$6.99

THE BIFROST GUARDIANS

☐ GODSLAYER: Book 1   UE2372—$4.99
☐ SHADOW CLIMBER: Book 2   UE2284—$3.99
☐ DRAGONRANK MASTER: Book 3   UE2366—$4.99
☐ SHADOW'S REALM: Book 4   UE2419—$4.99
☐ BY CHAOS CURSED: Book 5   UE2474—$4.50

☐ THE LEGEND OF NIGHTFALL   UE2587—$5.99

☐ SPIRIT FOX* (hardcover)   UE2806—$23.95
  *with Jennifer Wingert

Prices slightly higher in Canada   **DAW:195**

Jennifer Roberson

THE NOVELS OF TIGER AND DEL

OTHERLAND
TAD WILLIAMS

Otherland. A perilous and seductive realm of the imagination where any fantasy—whether cherished dream or dreaded nightmare—can be made shockingly real. Incredible amounts of money have been lavished on it. The best minds of two generations have labored to build it. And, somehow, bit by bit, it is claiming Earth's most valuable resource—its children. It is up to a small band of adventures to take up the challenge of Otherland in order to reveal the truth to the people of Earth. But they are split by mistrust, thrown into different worlds, and stalked at every turn by the sociopathic killer Dread and the mysterious Nemesis. . . .